JOE THE NEANDERTHAL

A NOVEL BY

DINO BLYER

Order this book online at www.trafford.com
or email orders@trafford.com

Most Trafford titles are also available at major online book retailers.

Print information available on the last page.

ISBN: 978-1-4907-5384-3 (sc)
ISBN: 978-1-4907-5386-7 (hc)
ISBN: 978-1-4907-5385-0 (e)

Library of Congress Control Number: 2015900742

Cover image by Jessica Guerra

Trafford rev. 01/07/2016

www.trafford.com

North America & international
toll-free: 1 888 232 4444 (USA & Canada)
fax: 812 355 4082

CONTENTS

Three Flash Drives in a Bottle

ACKNOWLEDGMENTS xi

Flash Drive Number One
Joe Begins his Narrative Summer 2016

When Will the Background Become the Foreground? 3
She Smiled Like a Piano 12
Babies in Bars 27
Man and his Cymbals 42
An Emotional Situation 56
Get This Show on the Road 75
Gobs of Makeup from the Gorgeous Gopi Gal 97
A Happy Confusion 113
Kali Danced in the No Mo Zone 132
The Cat and the Wife Too 146
Does It Taste as It Sounds? 161
The Full Business Carry 180
The King of Oomph 202
¿Cuándo Sale El Próximo Ferrocarril? 222

Flash Drive Number Two
The Continuing Narrative of Joe the Neanderthal

A Ton of Botox 233
Ted the Gorilla 255
A Cure for Asthma 269
Girl with a Vision on Course of Collision 286
Lourdes Tests Her Mother Out 297
When the Cheap Go Pits 305
The Problem with Noise 322
A Girl Goes Shopping 329
Slash and Burn 345
Field Trip to the Human Female Community 367
Thyoneus the Thirst Bopper 376
Rott Weiller and the Rhythm Retreivers 389
The Donnah Parfrey Show 403
Sunita's Housewarming 414
A Look into the Factory 422

Flash Drive Number Three
Ziga's Report to Interstellar Command

Assisted Editing 435
A Pair of Gray Metal Eyes 455
Via the Blabbermouth 479
Club Crème de la Crème 484
Visiting Mom 495
Battle of the Men Machines 506
The Maharajah's Funhouse 514
Get Out and Get Out Now 529
Eve Once 538

Letter to Edwin Jenkins from Alfred Riaz 542

To Julia

In every crowd, there is an enemy of the crowd.

--- Elias Canetti

ACKNOWLEDGMENTS

I am deeply indebted to my good friend Duncan Idontknow (the guitarist formerly known as George Leutz) who is, at the time of this writing, the World Champion Record Holder for longest Q-Bert game ever played. Duncan's heroic achievement, which took place over a four day period in February of 2013, concluded at a few minutes shy of eighty-five hours. His achievement was an inspiration to me because it represented and fostered the notion of all things epic, and made me want to attempt something epic too, namely the book you are about to read. Duncan's knowledge and expertise of that arcade sport, as well as of other video games from the 1980's, were invaluable to me when writing this story. For that, I am forever grateful. In addition, Duncan is one heck of a good guitar player.

Also, I would like to say that the characters in this novel bear no resemblance to actual people. This is especially true with regard to the main character's less-than-benign prejudice towards bass players. Quite the contrary --- in real life, my bass player Dave Lorenz is truly a remarkable and inventive player as well as being a wonderful human being.

Three Flash Drives in a Bottle

(Letter from Edwin Jenkins Ph.D. to Dr. Alfred Riaz asking for funding)

May 10, 2520

Dear Dr. Riaz:

Although this is a preliminary plea for funding, I hope you won't mind its informal character. If it is a cursory note, it is simply because time is of the essence if we are to discover more. The shelf life of these things is indeed limited --- I don't have to tell you that archaeologists have had a long history of having to cope with the problem of looters whose actions constantly compromise the provenance of artifacts, thereby making our jobs three times more difficult. With that thought foremost in my mind, I enclose with this letter copies of three ancient accounts which were found in the forms of three pen drives discovered in the course of the 2520 season on our archaeological dig located in the vicinity of Ikaria, the area known previously by its ancient name of Wildwood, New Jersey. Our carbon dating tech tells me that the artifacts are from the Early Archaic Period, which places their age at just over 500 years ago in the common era.

Although, we as archaeologists, are of course never averse from gaining the opportunity to study treasure troves of the spectacular variety such as art, grave goods, jewelry, gold and silver work, as well as all manner of precious and semi-precious artifacts and the like, including remnants gleaned from massive architecture, we are, in recent years, primarily concerned with documenting human behavior. The fact that these artifacts were recovered from a trash heap speaks volumes, perhaps more than if they were discovered among the ruins of corporate edifices from that long ago era. We think by now it nearly goes without saying that artifacts which are out-and-out trash tell us far more about the way in which ordinary people---the so-called "salt of the earth"---lived their lives. And my sarcastic colleague Dr. Barlow is quick to remind me that these discoveries are certainly nothing if not that. He never gets tired of saying, "Congratulations, Dr. Jenkins. I think you've found yourself a real goldmine there." But both he and I think you will agree that the following accounts, piecemeal though they may be, fall into the category of the latter. They constitute the mess of someone's, and more likely, some persons' lives.

Accordingly, we, as excavators of said slag heap, fully expect to learn much. While the conclusions from this study are of course months if not years down the line, our initial hypothesis is that these finds may constitute some of the earliest, if not the absolute earliest, evidences of cultural contact between species from widely disparate galaxies. As if this were not enough, these discoveries are also promising on quite another level, which is that at least one of the writers of the two accounts presented herein seems to have himself been a throwback to a much earlier form of "human life." I say this in quotes because as you know, that term really doesn't mean much these days if in fact it ever did.

Perhaps our research will shed light on this. In short, as you are well aware, the spectacular finds garner major attention, but the more humble discoveries, such as this one, give us greater insight. Accordingly, I hope you will give that aspect of our operations its full weight as you consider whether or not to fund our project. It is suffice to say that I will give you a more in-depth analysis of the project at a later date. However, as funding for these matters is so tenuous and nebulous these days, I decided to take the liberty of sending you an incomplete report sooner rather than later.

As with so many excavations of this kind, we are sure to encounter many instances in which the archaeological record will present more questions than it answers. However, my colleague and I believe, and you no doubt believe also, that being inundated with the data from such anomalies should never prevent us from the zest for future discovery. Moreover, I hope you will see from the accounts presented herein that the spirit of discovery never seemed to impede those beings who lived so very long ago. Indeed the spirit of discovery seems to have infused every aspect of their existence.

Perhaps we should follow their example? Yes, I do believe that we should. Therefore, I would ask that you send us the appropriate monies, so that my colleague and I might accomplish that task. As always, I thank you for your time and kind consideration in this matter as well as for your good efforts in my and Dr. Barlow's behalf.

Respectfully,

Dr. Edwin Jenkins
Director of Operations for the Wildwood Project

FLASH DRIVE NUMBER ONE

Joe Begins his Narrative Summer 2016

WHEN WILL THE BACKGROUND BECOME THE FOREGROUND?

The bare hint of a night breeze made its way from the dark flatness of the ocean and straggled westward, wafting across the boardwalk. In the early summer heat, a Neanderthal finds this welcoming. I breathed it in, savoring it with wild greedy gulps. I was starved, and the salty air was sustenance --- sort of like airline food --- pretty ordinary fare just on its own, but when mingled with the prospect of travel and something else, such as the blare of the "Free Bird" cover song coming from an amusement boutique loudspeaker, it nearly had the promise of adventure. Earlier, the carnival barkers had conned me into throwing a few baseballs into a bin, and I'd won myself a "*fabuloso* prize." Those kinds of things are usually of little or no use to Neanderthals, so I gave it to a passing Cro-Magnon couple with a noisy two-year-old. The bawling baby suddenly clammed up and looked at the prize with a curious unblinking eye. The parents thanked me profusely. I long ago learned that there are good and bad Cro-Magnons. Pondering this for a moment, I continued my stroll before pausing to listen to another barker go through his speech about the wonders of saltwater taffy. Apparently, it's real healthy stuff.

Three piers jutted out into the placid water more sluggish lake than churning sea. I scanned in vain for the occasional breaker crashing into the pilings, but the beach was too long for that. Only languid ripples lapped the coarse gray sand. That was the best the Atlantic Ocean could conjure up on this particular evening. I yawned a big Neanderthal yawn and walked on to where I happened upon two twenty-something girls who were having a drunken argument. They bobbed and weaved in that curious arms-and-legs akimbo grace that blotto Cro-Magnons acquire just before they violate each other's personal space and then fall down in a big babbling heap. A guy in a wheelchair, who looked exactly like an A-list celebrity named Brad, but with Popeye forearms, was acting as a referee. I had to give him credit. The way he maneuvered that chair was real darned impressive. Damned if he wasn't an artist, getting to do intricate turnarounds, tricky backwards-and-forwards wheelies, funky pirouettes, and all. What a graceful fellow! A regular gymnast in his own fashion. Probably good at basketball too. But I could see that Brad had his hands full. Those girls were hell bent on God only knows what. Perhaps it was better to give them a wide berth. I kept walking.

I was a Neanderthal on the run and doing a decent job of it. The Cro-Magnons that my evil sister had hired hadn't bumped me off yet! That scuffle with them back in Seaside Heights had been unintentionally ecstatic. I'd smashed them gently and dumped them in the rose bushes. Don't get me wrong. I'm not gloating. I've got no martial arts fantasies. I didn't want to make them mad, but I had to survive.

It's hard being a Neanderthal --- someone in danger of becoming an obsolete mammalian creature. The Cro-Magnons were after me with their sharpened spears. And they know how to handle weapons so much better than me. And as if my virulent sibling were not enough, I also had to contend with running away from that doctor --- the one who was so profoundly challenged when it came to the subject of empathy. Jeez, that guy liked to experiment till he was blue in the face. No doubt he was still salivating about exploring what happens when you incubate HEKn cells with polystyrene latex beads. How do the the phagocytic dynamics react in that combination? His preliminary results were that it can lead to death, especially if there is a heavy concentration of latex beads and melanin that enters into the mix. Well, damn. I could've told him that! And I could've saved him a lot of test tubes. What the guy really needed was someone else to practice on. He was a mastiff who wouldn't let go. But I needed to banish him ... and the psychotic sister from my mind.

Resuming my walk, I came upon a funhouse. I hadn't been to one of those since my dad brought me to one up north when I was six years old. That had been such a great time. Afterwards, he'd taken me on the rollercoaster, and then later on, an airplane ride. What a thrill! I figured I was overdue for a visit. The mirrors of the funhouse had been my favorite then. Why would there be any reason to expect that they would not be my favorite section now? Their overblown distortions offered the union of entertainment, together with the bonus points of allusion to another reality. Can't beat that!

So, I purchased a ticket from the attendant and made a beeline for the mirrors. I stared into the most ridiculous one I could find and observed my inquisitive face staring back. For a Neanderthal, it was an ostensibly handsome face, but on the near horizon of going to seed. It had been a good life, yet also an unfulfilled one. Some ill-defined aspect was missing. To be brutally frank, it had always been missing. This was the face of an outsider --- someone who had always been in the background and never the foreground. When would the background become the foreground?

I immediately noticed that my brow ridge was the most susceptible to the distortions of the mirror. The natural furrows on my forehead had been amplified, not really beyond recognition but rather, to their true recognition. This was not a function of the shiny glass itself. No way! I was a true Neanderthal. No doubt about it. With a growing sense of pride, I felt my brow ridge. The bone protruded outward more than normal. You see, it's some sort of "adaptation to the natural environment." That was why, in an earlier time, I had never been able to find a suitable football helmet. But all things evolve towards extinction. I started to sing a tune to myself. It was something I been thinking about for a quite a while.

> "I am a Neanderthal; my head is not so small
> Been around a long long time and now I'm getting tossed
> Got a bony brow and an even bigger heart

> But that don't mean nothing from the ones who think they're smart
> I am a Neanderthal; I don't know how to throw
> Stabbing beasts from up real close is the only way I know
> It's very very dangerous, I put myself in harm
> Many times the mastodons have gone and broke my arm"

Yes, it had really been quite a long run. However, up until now it had been a life of entirely too much feeling and not enough thinking. That was the consequence of "following your heart." Now the party was over. From here on in, it would be a rough ride.

> "I'd been a good boy with walls undefended
> Should've been a bastard like Nature intended"

My life had been fraught with all manner of failure. Breathing had led to nowhere. My most recent grand ambition was to become a stranger to my own life. That would make all the difference. Yes, how wonderful it would be to surprise myself.

My mind raced and changed gears, making my Neanderthal imagination go haywire. Oh my sister, my sister Meghan! How could she have done such an awful thing? She'd sicced her Cro-Magnons on me. Thinking about that, my pulse quickened. The danger of the situation had made me exuberant. I knew it! The survival instinct was kicking in. I found myself in a giddy mood, cozy and safe, as if I'd captured a small hopping animal...an insect or a frog that I had right there in my cupped hands where I could peek at it any time and whisper to it too if the muses moved me. So, having the urge to run, I impulsively broke into a full ecstatic sprint, stopping abruptly right behind an old man who turned suddenly.

"What the hell ya doing, pal?" he snarled.

"Nothin'. I'm just feeling happy all of a sudden."

"What you gotta go and be so happy about?"

"I don't know. I just felt like it."

"Don't you know better than to be happy? What are you, crazy? Never sneak up on someone like that. People'll think you're some kind of mugger. You undertan', son?"

He patted me on the shoulder. I slouched my head and shoulders and looked down at a long gray crack in the weathered boardwalk. In another year or so, that board would need to be replaced.

"Sorry. I apologize. I - I - I wasn't thinking. Don't know what came over me."

Jeez, that was close! For a second there, I thought that might've been one of my sister's goons and my good fortune had run out.

I was the six year old who'd taken his wet bathing suit off too soon. Shame on me. Why is it that Cro-Magnons are always on such a long leash? They can make one money-losing movie after another, and they still get another chance to make more money-losing movies. Curiously, we Neanderthals can have just one less-than-stellar afternoon, and we get chased off the property.

I decided it was time to go back to the hotel. Retracing my path, I came upon the arguing girls and dear celebrity Brad. Cro-Magnon kids have a long and sorry-ass history of not being able to handle their liquor. How would they ever master the fine art of driving drunk if they couldn't stagger down the wharf in some semblance of a straight line? More practice at the calisthenics of leaning back and touching the tips of noses would be required. Talking slower works like a charm. That's the key to faking them out and pulling the wool over their eyes. They could've bet on it if they wanted, but I knew they wouldn't. This is why the world is going to hell in a hand basket. I pointed my finger and offered some sage advice to one of the girls.

"Girl, always pay attention to the signs your body is giving you."

The Cro-Magnon female didn't pay me any attention. She was too busy taking care of the rigorous business of beating the tar out of her opponent. What a waste of perfectly good glutamate molecules! From her pretty top to her pretty painted toes, they were all in danger of being repossessed.

The tow-headed one had landed a serious right cross and had gotten the upper hand. Wide-mouthed and surging upward, she was the shark out in the ocean, thrashing away, struggling to devour a stark and scary music.

"Girl," I said, "You fight like a guy."

Dear Brad was beside himself. He looked at me imploringly just as Blondie nailed Big Red spot on with a curve-fisted upper cut that stunned her enough for Blondie to get a hold of Red's ponytail. Blondie yanked it viciously back and forth. After that, what with her head going round and round like some sort of freakin' lasso, things went way downhill for Red. In a second, she was lying listlessly on her right shoulder while Blondie smacked her head up and down on the rough splintery surface of the boardwalk. She was starting to bleed, which was mildly amusing for a dark inkling spiraling deep within me. It made me dizzy. Sometimes I hate that. Sometimes I love it, the ice cream sundae place that's cold and hot. Where in the world did that byzantine shadiness come from? Probably from where adenine plus guanine plus a shuddering neural event equals euphoria, but this Neanderthal never asked for *that*. Never. Honest. Scout's honor ...

... Somewhere a voluptuous goddess was emerging from her bath. The water cascaded off her curving form in warm rivulets. She smiled at the boy, toweled herself off, and brought him lovingly towards her. She reassured him that everything would be alright. The boy thought to himself that this was perplexing, the most fun he'd had in six and a half years of life so far. He was supposed to do something, but he couldn't quite figure out what it was. The Goddess was the best next-door neighbor anyone could ever hope to have. The milk and cookies had been very good. She said there would be lots lots more where that came from and not to think about it too much. It was a very poignant moment, one that he would never forget. She dried herself again and went over to the radio. She turned it on, and it played the most beautiful music he had ever heard. He was transfixed at the stunning sounds that were enveloping his body. He looked up at Her body and asked Her to dance. The Goddess was a magical vision of blinding beauty, and the boy looked forward to worshipping at her feet for many years to come, so it was no small wonder that he was the most surprised person on the face of the earth when she

capriciously grabbed his face by the cheeks and slammed him backwards into the tiles of the shower stall. The Goddess looked him deep in the eye and said, "Don't say anything to anyone about this!" The boy struggled some, but managed to reply, "Don't worry, Mrs. H., I'll never tell. This is too pretty for any of them to know." She pinned him against the wall, laughed a chorus of echoing guffaws, and in a charmingly husky voice, she whispered, "Joe, I gave this to you because I knew you could handle it."...

... But like most Neanderthals, I'm a terrible archaeologist --- all those stratigraphic units to sift through are so time-consuming. I know their motto is "Dig faster and deeper," but there's no guarantee of finding anything. So, why should I bother? Better to let the Goddess go on her merry way.

Besides, I couldn't think about ancient history for very long because a crowd was forming. Some were cheering for their hometown girl. I figured at this point I'd better do something fast, so I stepped in. I waded through the flurry of fists and dragged Blondie off from her. I was amazed at how light she felt! Yanking her, I expected a Great Dane and instead, got a Chihuahua! Pound for pound though, the *Chihuahuena* put up quite a full blown tussle, swinging around like an effin' lunatic. I was in the process of making a discovery: this was kind of fun and I couldn't for the life of me figure out why. The milling crowd surged forward for a better view. They seemed to know Blondie and her *compadre.* Maybe they did this act all the time, and it was staged happy horseshit, and I was interfering in their fun and games. She was huffing and puffing, a dervish of negative energy, and every word that flew out of her mouth was total trash. She kicked and screamed. I was more excited --- worried that people would notice.

"Listen, girl" I said, "You're not allowed to kill her."

I was congratulating myself on a point well made, when someone from the crowd managed to corral Big Red at least temporarily.

"Dammit! Where the hell are the cops?"

This spot of sumo wrestling went on for a while. The guy holding Red kept staring at me with a desperate look in his eye. Dear celebrity

Brad, the focus of all the consternation, was wheeling himself back and forth frantically shouting for the girls to calm down.

"C'mon Brad," I said. "You're the movie star. You're supposed to be able to handle these difficult social situations."

Maybe someday if I studied real hard, I could be as cool as him. But Brad wasn't buyin' it, and there wasn't an approaching endgame to this because the cops were nowhere in sight. Finally, I said what the hell. The police were taking their sweet time. So, I let Blondie go like a fish back into the stream. No sooner did I do that, than she lashed out and gave me a mean slash across the forehead. ACHH!! And I'll be damned if they didn't do it all over again, going right back into the mash up. Well, that was it. Fun and games were over. I was outta there. I'd done my gig. You go girl, like a lamb to the slaughter. Be beat up from the feet up. Follow the lead and dance like a dead woman and find your foundations of a boyfriend. You shoulda been a jungle plant 'cause the flora change, but the fauna can't.

Hearing sirens, I ran down the boardwalk in the general direction of the hotel thinking, wow, dear celebrity Brad must have some stupendous tongue. He'd done his gig --- perhaps too well --- and I'd done mine. The cops would be there soon. Glutamate molecules are only for those who can handle them.

I peered back into the murky blackness of the early summer sky --- somewhere out there in the placid waves. There She was, hovering ghost-like over the surf. The Siren was calling me again. She looked as stunning as ever --- a body sculpted for a million fantasies.

I addressed Her formally: "Dear Goddess, You know that You're the only one I've ever loved. Can't You give me some kind of sign? I take this music thing so seriously. And I do it for You and for You alone. I only want to make people happy. You showed me what to do when you played the radio. I thought that was supposed to be my mission in life. Yet you shatter my expectations at every turn. I follow your lead and I get a spasm in my sixth rib. That makes me feel I'm doing something right, but then you pull the rug out from under me again and again."

"Try to be patient, Joe. Just be patient."

I wandered further inland. The restaurants got less expensive. The blare of live music emanating from a nightclub drew me in, and I wandered toward it. The sound was impressive, and I made a note that I would have to check out the band that was responsible. But that would be in due course because there was minor business that required my immediate attention. Searching for temporary respite, I retreated into a side alley of the club. Safely ensconced behind a row of garbage cans, I was out of every line of vision and so, could go ahead with the procedure.

It was necessary to let the dragons out in order to stave off another Neanderthal moment. You see, my brow ridge and lower jaw were actin' up again, so I had to do something to keep things on an even keel; otherwise, my whole being would swerve into total chaos, and powers of concentration would be in danger of being seriously compromised. I mean, if I didn't attend to this urgency, how in the world could I fully appreciate the beauty of the band? And the beauty of the band was especially enchanting since the murmuring surf seemed to be melting into the song and taking the chorus into a direction that had never been intended.

I quickly found a vein and used the bazooka. The dragons were ecstatic. They'd been chompin' at the bit and were glad to be let out for a walk. As always, I was pleased to meet them. Someday, I would be able to get rid of them. But that would be someday. For now, I could put that off. There was no hurry. Like the Goddess said, I would have to be patient.

SHE SMILED LIKE A PIANO

Oh to hell with the patience thing. The archaeologists have the right idea: faster and deeper is the way to go.

"Good evening my fellow Americans! I cannot impress upon you enough the importance of doing one's gig. It's what made America great! That's what I want our President to say sometime soon."

The bar crowd broke into rowdy applause. Bowing deeply like a Japanese *yakuza,* I punched my hand into my fist presidentially, and paused to take a shot of *Absolut.* You see, by then, I'd licked my wounds and retreated to the hotel bar. I'd had more than a few, lots more than a few. That was my reward for being Mr. Johnny-on-the-spot. The sting on my scratched forehead was receding fast, but I knew it would return in the morning with even greater ferocity.

However, the new focus of my attention was the house band which consisted of a short nervous-looking bass player, a spindly hot babe singer, a butch girl guitarist who cranked out searing riffs *a la* Jimmy Page on her fire engine red Gibson Les Paul, and... and...and that was it. There was no drummer, just a rhythm box --- a programmable beat box whom I'll call Ziggy. I guess it's force of habit, but I give every beat box the name "Ziggy." I loved it that the threat to Ziggy's continued existence was a drum kit tucked neatly away in the corner. If Ziggy had even a megabyte of artificial intelligence at all, at that moment he was, like a sparrow cringing from a hawk, mindful of the kit --- leery and somberly respectful of its devastating power. It was too bad that, for whatever preposterous reasons, the otherwise talented band here had decided on enlisting the services of lame little Ziggy. This depressing situation pissed me off to no end. I wanted to smash him into a million pieces.

But wait! I looked back into the crowd just to the center of the room and a few feet from the end of the bar. If I wasn't mistaken, there was a camera crew in the house, and they were filming the whole gig. At first, I thought this evening's little soiree was something destined for a youtube or facebook page. No, no, I could tell this was different. A director, who had a wraparound headset, was gesturing silently to her crew, and there were lighting screens placed strategically around the room. The more I looked at what was going on, the more this had the look and feel of a *major Hollywood production.*

And the other odd thing about this club was the lighting behind the stage. It was unusual. Of course, there were the usual spotlights and rotating strobes, some of which harkened back to the disco era, but this battery of lights was supplemented by an enormous fish tank positioned just in back of the stage. In the tank were several floating cuttlefish. The graceful creatures would drift in time to the music that was being played, and they also seemed to change color depending on the mood of the tunes. I recalled reading somewhere about these kinds of fish. If my memory was accurate, it seems those strange fish, who were relatives of the octopus, literally wore their emotions on their bodies. That was a wonderful thought. How fortuitous of them to be so direct in telling the huge crowd exactly what was on their minds even if the people out there would never learn their language! No doubt they could act like Etruscans --- they had so much to say, but no one to understand them. I had to say that looking at them was real darned relaxin' and that was something I never expected. I chalked this one up in my category for the bizarre. Back and forth they went as if following the currents of some unknown tide within the tank. I quickly noticed that it was very easy to fall under their pleasant spell, so I purposely looked away and concentrated again on the band.

On some songs, the bass player would put aside that instrument to twiddle buttons, buzzers, and bells on the beat box. He'd loaded Ziggy up with all kinds of sampled crap --- wood blocks, whistles, cowbells, castanets, maracas, claves, and congas --- a grand buffet of umpachumpa music. What a clever fellow! Such a posh and polished program! He was covering his tracks well. Never give a real drummer any space left to play in. Better to be safe than sorry. Paint him into a corner. And the bass player hadn't forgotten the cheesy, tick-tock cymbals either. Tick-tick-tick. Clicky-clacky. I hate those the most. People gush and breathlessly say, "They're so accurate!" Yeah, so ask me if I care. They have all the soul of bad cartoons.

Once between songs I yelled, "Bongos may also be used."

I made a jazzy cymbal sound with my voice. The babe singer's eyes fluttered. The bass player looked more nervous. He saw me stare at her wagging butt. No doubt, the guy with steady-cam number three was preserving all the nuance of the situation for posterity.

"Hey, this doesn't sound like Miles Davis to me. This ain't no Johnny Cash."

She fiddled with her microphone, but she wasn't annoyed. Why was that? Even the butch girl was laughing herself silly as she made her axe cry and moan. I love lezzies. Love their work ethic. Then the bass player, just to show us all that he was getting so down with his crew, turned to his laptop and started doing some rock star windmill moves with his right arm over the keys. Since when did a laptop become a musical instrument? This was utter blasphemy. Heresy. He should be burned at the stake. He was starting to irritate me even more than Ziggy. Under my breath, I prayed that he'd get a rotary cuff injury. To you O' Lord, hear my prayer! Alas, my silent pleas went unanswered, so I turned to the bartender.

"Hey, this bass player's not so good."

"Are you some kind of expert?"

I pondered that for a second. "Yeah, you could say I am. Remind me to ask him, 'Who's your teacher, bro? I'll give him a lesson.'"

"No kidding. He's that bad?" He paused, dug a PBR out of the ice, and gave it to a hipster. I reached into my wallet, brought out a dollar, and contributed more to the tip pile.

"What's your name?"

"Joe. And you are?"

"Jim."

"The pleasure is Joe's and what Joe needs is another beer." I drunkenly slapped myself on the wrist. "Bite your tongue, Joe. There you go again, talkin' nonsense in the third person."

The bartender laughed at this admonition. "Only famous people are allowed to do that. Who do you think you are, James Brown or somethin'?" He did a Soul Man move from behind the bar. I gestured at the bass player who had a super serious look on his face complete with furrowed brow.

"He looks like a devo, Jim."

"What's a devo?"

"It's masculine for diva."

I pointed to the cuttlefish that were swimming in the aquarium in back of the stage. "Say, Jim. I rather like this cuttlefish idea."

"Oh you like that one. I've gotta take credit for it. I thought it would be kind of unusual. Not every bar has its very own cuttlefish."

At just that moment, the jellyfish-like creatures both changed color from red to blue. Jim laughed. "Hey Joe, I think they both like you!"

I moved closer to the tank and stared one of them in the eye. And his eye blinked and pulsated on various shades of blue.

Jim chuckled again. He was good at his job, better than most. He understood the difference between public and private. Most Cro-Magnons don't. They think a bar is simply an extension of their cushy apartments. Savor the lush upholstery, boys and girls! Well dammit; it's not that at all. I'm telling you these things are important to keep straight and ship shape, so there's no confusion. You mix categories and you're only asking for trouble. You'll get your ass in a sling. But the things I think are important most people think are worthless.

You never know about these dives. The customer is always wrong. Every thin-skinned overgrown Cro-Magnon hipster baby boy takes offense at the whim of a thought. Life itself offends him. You could get thrown out for routing for the Minnesota Twins for cryin' out loud, or you could get bounced for saying that Princess Di might've been offed. Mind you, I was never any big fan of hers, but remember, there are editors in these places, and they're worse than the ones in the Coliseum. Real bean counters. Under their strict tutelage in these bastions of small-mindedness, you'll stumble through life on tenterhooks and become practiced at the genteel art of talking about nothing. Hang your head in bashfulness, boy. God forbid you should ever feel passionate about something. Yo bro no! Go to the penalty box now for a five minute major...

> "What can I say? It's how you feel
> When you talk about life surreal
> In those times, you'll offend someone
> Piss off everyone under the sun" ...

... Sorry, I'm off the topic. The tyranny of the topic. My main point is this: you could blindfold me, put a bass in my hands, turn me around ten times, and give me a month's worth of pointers, and I could still do better than this guy onstage. And bass is not even my gig! I've heard it before. How do they describe a devo's style? Impressionistic? Painterly? Well, I'm as avant-garde as the next Neanderthal, but that's the tip off.

Not that I had some kind of murky crystal ball or anything, but I could tell just by looking at this alleged musician that he could be a huge problem. There always is a problem. Sadness insists on having equal billing. The trick is sussing it out from the get go. It's a skuzzy little gnome that needs to be put in its place. Oh, how I love to hear its squealing as it beats a hasty retreat after I've knocked it ten feet across the room!

What was this pretend bass player there for? Certainly not to play music. Nothing as complicated as all that! Damn, he was the kind of guy who, if he couldn't figure something out in twelve seconds, then he'd think it wasn't worth going to all the trouble. Lazy bastard with his dumb ass beat box. That's always been *my* problem. I'm not good at being someone's slave. I could never quite get the hang of it. They tell me I'm "difficult." It's code for saying I don't want to be kicked in the teeth. Uh, excuse me sir, but your shoe is in my face. However, I *always* do my music gig, no matter what. Some things are sacred in this bleak world of ours. And it would have upset me to the end of time to see that spindly babe singer's voice going to waste for *no good reason*. That would be a crime against Nature! So what was a good drummer to do? Well, audition for them of course. That suddenly became my plan.

The set was drawing to a close. A kind of natural cadenza was taking place when the babe singer switched gears and went into a lush contralto before the final bloodless tick tock of Ziggy's cymbal pattern sputtered out. I chugged on my beer, leaned back on the rounded rail of the bar, and appreciated whatever bliss this mood had to offer.

"We'll be right back in fifteen. Be sure to tip those bartenders and waitresses." The bartender's iPod came on with a booming house beat. The cuttlefish at the back of the stage expressed their wholehearted approval by changing from green to yellow. They flapped their florid skin and seemed to boogie. I saw my opportunity and swooped down. The butch guitarist was the most vulnerable. She would be my victim. Somewhere in the synapses of that cerebellum of hers was a surly voice that screamed for something Dionysian. Or was it Venusian? No matter. Music shouts louder than religion. She sat down at the bar and was about to order a cold one when I stepped forward.

"Don't worry, Jim. I've got this one. I'm buyin' for the lady version of Jimmy Page."

"Oh, why thank you so much." She looked genuinely flattered. No doubt Mr. Page was her guitar god even if she was inclined to worship goddesses. I had the newfound courage to think that this cockamamie scheme might just work out.

"Say, that is one nasty looking cut you got there" she ventured.

"Yeah, well it serves me right for trying to break up a girl fight on the boardwalk."

"Let that be a lesson to you." She grinned girlishly. "All I can say is thank God I've never been in any kind of a fight like that before."

"Ha, you old schoolmarm. And all I can say is ladies can be so effed up."

"I know." This time she nodded mannishly. She could go back and forth. How malleable was that?

"You know you've been a very bad boy."

"And I need to be punished. Please let me bow down to you."

"OK boy, feel free to go bow wow wowing."

"Do I have your permission?"

"Yes. Show me that you're worthy!"

I bent down and touched her feet. The left toe was especially alluring. On rising, I noticed that her mouth had dropped a half inch. This caused me, and her, to retreat a half step like two surprised tango dancers.

"Just a little respect custom I picked up in India. I rather wish that it would catch on here."

"Don't bet on it." She took a hefty swallow from the pint.

"Let me make amends by doing you a good turn."

"And what might that be?"

"Let me be your drummer. You desperately need one."

I introduced myself, and she told me her name was Kathy. After I did that, I looked over and noticed from the corner of my eye that steady-cam number three from the TV crew had just filmed this entire exchange. Perhaps I was going to be a movie star after all, not that it had ever truly crossed my mind in a remotely considered way. But there he was squinting through the lens making sure that the focus was right and checking the depth of field. Not only that, but the TV director lady was lurking behind him, pacing back and forth. I figured that I should act natural --- as if I weren't on some kind of a set.

"Seriously," I said. "Let me cut to the chase. I like your playing, but you guys need a real drummer. Little Ziggy the beat box doesn't quite cut it."

"How did you know his name?"

"Just psychic I guess."

"Yeah, I know. Ziggy's not my idea of fun either. You're preachin' to the choir when you talk about that subject. I've been trying hard to get them to see the error of their ways, and I'm not havin' much luck."

"Maybe I could be of some service."

"You play?"

"Oh, yes. Since the sixth grade. Your band is a bright red Ferrari that I could easily rev up to a hundred and eighty-five on the straightaways." I sighed in mock disdain, milking the pause for all it was worth. "But of course, if you want, you can just use that sleek beautiful creature to go pick up groceries from around the corner. Sort of like what you're doing right now. How sad."

Well, the muses of flattery must have been looking down favorably on me because one thing led to another and in no time at all, the rest of the band was involved in a *deep* discussion. I tactfully waited, staring at my shoe tops letting them duke it out before stating my case. I could tell that the operator of steady-cam number three was getting real excited. I love it when Cro-Magnons take pride in their work because all too often they could care less as long as they get a payday. Bloody mercenaries.

"You see guys, I'm not against machines. They have their place when you don't want an actual bank teller. Let me explain. Playing music is a little like sex. You can have it with a person, or... or you can have it with a machine."

The singer moved uncomfortably on her bar stool. She started to smile, then thought better of it. Kathy was grinning. I could tell she liked to get off on both --- the acoustic and the electric.

"So I'm here if you want me... and... and...Ziggy the machine is there if you want *him*."

Well, Kathy called a huddle. One of those dreadful conferences called a "band meeting." Usually, nothing ever good comes out of them. They invariably degenerate into piss-and-moan sessions of the lowest order.

Kathy pressed her point. "Let's at least give him a chance. Look Ben, we've got a drum kit right here. We don't even have to go rent a studio."

Then the babe singer put in her two cents' worth. "Ben, the worst that can happen is that he sucks. How complicated is that? For us it's a win-win situation."

At this point the director of the camera crew decided that she had seen and heard enough and that it was time to register her opinion because, when you stopped and actually thought about it, hers was the only one that mattered. She said that this impromptu drummer walking in from the boardwalk with a nasty scratch on his face was exactly what the doctor ordered --- the stuff of great documentary.

"You can't make this shit up. I am the director and I say, 'Do it!' Better yet --- I command it."

Well, well, well. In light of that edict from Hollywood on High, what could they do? The kids had to do as they were told, or lose their chance to be on TV. Accordingly, some of what people uttered from here on in was pure pretending and some was totally real. The things that were a reasonable facsimile of reality were whatever happened to straggle across my brain or whatever raw emotions happened to seep through all the scripted nonsense that the TV director lady foisted on us. Thankfully, as it turned out more than half of it was genuine, but the only sure-fire *cantus firmus* was the thrill of the music itself. With that in mind, I continue my tale...

... Ben was miffed. He was bummin' and bummin' bad. Things were not going according to plan. His beloved Ziggy was slippin' away. He had that indignant flustered look that TV actors sometimes get. You've seen it before --- the forehead gets all crinkly, so you wanna take a rake and pull it down. Stammering at me he said, "Just so you'll know, Joe. I've got a degree in jazz studies."

"And I give you high marks. Straight A's. My hat is off to you," I replied. I wanted to tell him that I had a black belt in Indian *tabla* and that I was fully capable of playing Lester Young half notes, but I bit my tongue and played dumb.

Jim registered his opinion. That might have been the tipping point right there. "Ben, my intuition's good on this one. Give him a chance."

Way to go Jim! I owe you one. They put it to a referendum, and Ben was outvoted. I'd been given the green light. Strange as it would seem, when I glanced over at the cuttlefish, they were pulsating on various shades of green. I took a moment to adjust the kit and located a pair of almost pristine hickory sticks, courtesy of Jim the bartender. So it came down to the wire. Showtime! My moment to be a spark plug.

"CUT", the TV director lady yelled. "Give Tommy a second to reload!"

So, we waited around for four or five till Tommy, the operator of camera one, got back in business.

While he was reloading, I'll tell you what was going through my mind...

...What never ceases to amaze me about auditions is that the situation always seems like a bunch of dogs sniffing each other out. A lady singer thinks she's checking me out, but don't be fooled! I'm checking her out! I'm thinking, "She knows this, this and this, but she can't do that." And she's quite aware that I'm checking her out. Sing for me, dear lady, and drum for me, dear ruffian! In this way, we lounge away to our hearts' content in a blissful transgression, and the rest of the world is none the wiser. We both know the language, and the rest of the world doesn't. Sometimes if it's good, we fall in love for three minutes. After that, she can go back to her boyfriend...or girlfriend as the case may be. And then she can look in her mirror, touch up her preening lips with a quick gloss, and say to herself, "Whew! Safe again!"

I figured since this was my first audition in quite some time that I should probably take it easy and play something really simple on the first verse. I would be playing for my life. I *had* to pass muster with these guys. There was not much choice in the matter. Yeah, I know, we talked about that earlier. You remember them --- the gangsters who were after me? Well, those golly woggles were real, so this plan of mine was a matter of life or death! And the crazy doc was real too. No, no, I knew that I mustn't forget him because he always needed someone to practice on, and I knew he should go and find someone else.

But back to the music that was about to be played --- understand that the deal is to get right under the skin of the song. You have to listen real hard and ask yourself, "What realm is this tune in?" Next, you have to guess and make some split second choices. When your guesses are good, your heart and your hands will grab a shiny world...for you and for others. And listen up! Make no mistake about it. These trivialities matter! They matter big-time. They shape and frame the soundtrack of our lives. I get rather teary-eyed just thinking about them because drums are the gateway drug to other things. But those things are not more profound. When you think about it, you easily come to the realization that the contest is not even close...

...OK Tommy, are you back? Not quite yet? Alright, just a second? Well, speed it right up! What d' ya think this is? Some kind of amateur hour? Don't let it happen again. That's the problem with reality: you have to stand around until the technical staff gets it right. Yeah, good. You got it solved. You sure now? So we can continue...

The whole band got back on the bandstand. Tommy and the lighting director had gotten their acts together by then. Even the cuttlefish lurking in the tank in back of the stage seemed to be waiting in colorful expectation. The singer cradled an older model vocal mike that went directly into the board. No cordless remote in her pretty, lacquered nails. That was a good sign --- her umbilical to the band, the potential to keep her an honest woman. That's another thing --- Beware of a lady singer who doesn't play an instrument! She'll think she's better than you, and of course she's not. She's not even close. She'll warble and belt out a line as if to say, "Behold! Look at my fluffy trilling bird that I keep in a satin-lined box and bring out on special occasions for everyone to clap to. Tra-la-la-la-lah! Tra-la-la-la-lah!" She'll dote on her spoiled pet, not knowing quite what to do with it until one day it gets bored and flies away.

But I didn't worry too much 'cause I knew *all* her cheap tricks. In this moment, I felt incredibly strong --- strong enough to overcome even *that* horrible bullshit because, let's face it, they're *always* gonna pull a fast one! It's only a question of time. Enjoy it while it lasts. Even those things may come to nullify it. That was a bridge I would dream myself over when I came to it. In the meantime, I could hope and pray that this Gwen girl wouldn't be the type of singer who had pitch protectors bristling in from every direction so that no matter where the errant voice happened to take her, there would be some piece of technical wizardry that would be more than glad to protect the tonality. But I had to banish that thought to the back of my mind since there was urgent business to attend to, the business of doing this here gig.

Kathy plugged into her amp and looked at the singer who suddenly blurted out, "Treat me gentle, Kathy. Or you'll never see my titties again."

She had an impish soulful look on her face. A roar of laughter came from the crowd. She let out a banshee wail over the blaring PA., and a wall of ethereal noise screamed from the cabinet to my left.

"Don't worry, Gwen baby. You cannot paint the Eskimo cat with that sound. I don't ask for much in life. I only want to explode once in a while."

Kathy grinned and unleashed a thunderous stream of jagged feedback on her red Les Paul. I did a quick pummel on the toms and a press roll triplet combo on the snare before underscoring the whole thing with a brash wallop on the cymbals. Tommy and steady-cam number three were digging this. So was the TV director lady who nodded her approval.

"Jangly string jives a backwards strum. Buzzing quake licks the curving hum!" Gwen replied.

Overkill. I love it. Do it again! Do it again! She was an expert; she didn't care what eighth note she hurt. It would definitely be fun watching her run roughshod over 'em.

She turned to her public. Her public adored her, but the camera loved her.

"What would we ever do without 4/4 time?" she said. "It's a good thing no one ever copyrighted it 'cause we'd all be in deep trouble."

Kathy chimed in and, addressing the crowd as if this were some sort of medieval jousting tournament, she introduced me: "Gentlefolk, let the vulgarities begin. Musician, steer your balancing hand to bring us lucky equilibrium. You are the sailor to our lost and found island, a restful oasis to slake the thirst of our sagging amusements and brimming passions."

Some drunk in the crowd yelled, "YEEEAH."

Camera two was able to catch that. Then Kathy counted off the tune, and I laid down a thick groove --- a basic 4/4 except that it had a filigree arabesque rumba *rasa* going on between the ride cymbal and the rack tom. Gwen went into her vocal:

> "Nomads glide through a sea of space
> Search for magic chance explore..."

I watched her every move looking for cues. She was doing a Beyoncé high steppin' move with the mike, like a surreal workout at the gym. Already she was sweating under the soft focus stare of the blue spotlight. The only thing missing was the obligatory wind machine to make her hair do a swirly goddess dance. The crowd ate it up and spurred her on. So did the sparkling cuttlefish behind the stage who seemed to take on the role of the Greek chorus. Glancing back at them, I could see that they were having a blast as they commented on the action. I did a light splash on the high hat, then an accent on the bell of the ride. The lead singer lady leaned forward to the lip of the stage and wailed urgently:

> "Time curled brightly, a blue green place
> Saucer dipping to shout for more..."

Ah, a song about aliens! Little grey men with strangely-shaped heads. Hey, I can relate. Why can't they hurry up and take over?

I could feel the verse chompin' at the bit, itching to morph into a chorus. Keep it simple, Joe. Keep it simple....NO, NO, NO!! That's enough of that! Stop this coy business of treading water! I *had* to go hog-wild. And I did.

> "Crystal blip sparked towering dome
> And scattered night like seeds to sow
> Peeking games through desperate zones
> A human blinked in afterglow..."

Oh sweet breath of shining possibility, your twang of string mirrors twinge of soul, and hearts glisten in dews of novelty. A gong makes us dizzy and we don't know why. The drum played itself. Honest, it wasn't me! A scattershot roll nudged a miracle of breath and punctuation, blasting a sculpture of throbbing sound. The cuttlefish drifted in their salt water tank, beaming from yellow to green, making me wonder about what that would mean. Kathy took the bait and cranked out a doubly demented ninth chord --- her salute to fluid asymmetry. I turned to the singer. She smiled like a piano, then howled a bent note like a stray dog in the dead of night. Wide-eyed in wonder, she stared at new topography. Camera one zoomed in for her close up, getting the whole thing. Yes, it was true. What the drum wants, the Goddess wants too. I could feel my way into her heart. Wild blood crashed through her soul, careening through the ventricles.

The gig was mine. Ziggy would die, and I would live. At least for now.

After the final cymbal crash had died down and the last chord had crunched to a halt, I ducked outside the club for a breather. It was a gorgeous night --- certainly one that would go down in my own personal history book. The ocean murmured in the distance and a bird tweeted in a nearby tree. Overcome with glee and wanting to share it, I whistled and chirped in imitation to the bird's song, and it answered right back with an unmistakable note of confusion in its warble, as if asking for clarification. But the very fact that he'd asked was cause for celebration. This spot of improvisation with the pick-up band had made me feel that anything was possible --- including interspecies communication.

My blood was racing too, and no doubt would have outrun that of the lead singer. I knew it would take me a while to come down, perhaps even hours, if the past was any indication of the future. Gimlet-eyed, yet wide awake, I gave the heavenly bodies a prolonged and rigorous stare, and after a few seconds, one of the celestial things appeared to *move*. It went on like that for another minute or so before spinning off into more than one star. However, at some point they all came back together as one and only one, but not before putting on quite a wild and wooly show of sweetness and light. Was there something out there that was "from away"? No, not at all. Lots of things may have been made possible by this late evening musical mash-up, but that outer space thing --- *that* wouldn't be among them. That couldn't be possible.

"Joe," I said. "You've been drumming too much." I went back in search of the diminishing crowd, looking for perpetual space.

I thought about the people who were after me, namely my sister and that other lunatic --- the researcher who just wouldn't take no for an answer. For the sake of this golden opportunity, I had to make believe that they didn't exist. Even as they adamantly insisted that they did.

BABIES IN BARS

"Washin' the weeds in the amigdala
Goin' down the river in my gondola
Gushin' and a geyserin' in the hypothalamus
Sloshin' my blues away"

Oh cherubs would be up all night, carving such beautiful shapes. I was crooning the lyrics, wrapping myself around the syllables for my audience of one --- a girl at the bar with a spritely Bangladeshi accent who was egging me on. Here was a swooning cheerleader in a stupor, acting as if I was her very own personal trained seal, but I didn't mind. The young stunner sported a full-length plaster leg cast and when she wasn't perched precariously on the barstool, she hobbled around on crutches. She hoisted a cone-shaped glass, some pink yellowy concoction with a thick wedge of lemon impaled on the rim that Jim had thrown together on the fly. He had dubbed it a "Pan's Pant" in honor of the occasion.

"Go Joe, go!" she exclaimed excitedly. "Great singing. Not bad at all for a drummer. Maybe you should do the lead vocals."

She stole a glance over at Gwen the singer who gave her a stink eye. The stunner had the look of a woman who'd just had sex, but of course she hadn't. She was following me around, now and then taking a swallow off the Pan's Pant, and quite frankly I was enjoying the view. The situation was not all that different from those times just afterwards from, you know --- doing it --- when the lady in question spoons up behind you and says sweet and silly stuff like, "Oh please let me hold it. I wanna know what it's like to be a guy." Aw shucks, this was too good to be true. Somewhere in this dwindling crowd was a hubby or boyfriend who was about to introduce himself and piss all over the fantasy. Until then, I could chat up this lovely casualty of the music whose enchanting balcony seemed to be spilling out of its corral.

But in the meantime, Kathy and Gwen had made it official, or rather, the reality show director made it official: I was the new drummer for the band. What a relief! For the first time in months, escape seemed possible. I could reach out and grab it. The Cro-Magnon thugs were somewhere on the back burner for the time being. I could go out on the road and basically hide in plain sight while I figured out how to handle my evil sister. And what a way to keep my sister Meghan's hired killers at bay! I mean, what were they gonna do? Shoot me on TV for crying out loud?

What was also great about this triumph of mine was that it represented one more gain in the my ongoing battle to have the background become the foreground. If and when that became an accomplished fact, then I could go about the serious business of saving the world from itself. I mean, Dad had always told me to set high goals for myself, and what could be higher than that?

But those ambitions would have to wait it out for a bit longer because, even though I was savoring my latest achievement, Jillian, the reality show director, was laying down the law. She was busy with her flunkies who were hurriedly taking notes and making script changes. I got the distinct impression that I'd made a bit of a splash. Her new directive was the following: whenever we were on camera, Kathy and I were supposed to hate each other, and Ben and I were supposed to be best buddies. Naturally, most of that was total bullshit. If anything, Jillian had it completely wrong: I couldn't stand Ben, and I rather liked Kathy and Gwen. But I had to go along with this preposterous charade or otherwise, the Cro-Magnon thugs would whack me, and worse yet, nobody would get to be on TV.

Jillian laid down the law with me too 'cause it seems she had a problem with my outfit, which in her opinion was less than the high watermark of sartorial splendor. "If you think you can drop in here," she lectured, "lookin' like a raggedy muffin all the while thinkin' that you'll still get the gig, then you've got quite another thing comin'. Yes, I'm well aware that you're a drummer, so you work in the furnace room, so to speak, but the next time I see you I want to see you decked out in something a little more up to speed for this reality show."

"OK, OK… I'll do the best that I can," I offered.

"I'll set you up with one of my stylists, and we'll have you lookin' like a rock star in no time flat." Then she was off to bark a few more orders, leaving me to ponder my triumph.

Whew! I'd passed the audition. And to top it off no one had asked to see my bloody resume. Frankly, I'm both amused and amazed at all the great music that never ever gets made because of resumes. Sometimes late into a long night's sleep I can almost hear that unmade music trying to break through into this side of reality. In the dream, the resumes are stacked high into a huge thick wall, and the Goddess of Music is lying around right behind it on a plush divan. Her body is a sumptuous banquet for anyone who would care to partake. Only trouble is, she looks lonely as hell, and she wants everyone to know about all the good things you're missing out on. She wants you to know that good can spring forth from out of nothing. Fortunately for all of us, there's nothing quite like that in any other areas of life.

"By the way, what do you guys call yourselves?" I inquired.

"We're going by the name '*Babies in Bars*.' It's a working title. We might even use it as a title for the show. Actually, it was Jim's idea because he hates the soccer moms who come in at four in the afternoon to get all soused before pushing around their strollers."

"Not bad. Alright, I get it. You're going for the irony thing. That's cool."

"The concept of this reality show is that *Babies in Bars* is a bar band that plays watering holes in and around the Jersey shore. Each week the band gets stuck in some sort of sticky wicket that they have to extricate themselves from --- you know, the usual rock and roll predicaments like drunken audiences, hecklers, bad drugs, and rip off club owners. Why it was just last week that Gwen poured a banana daiquiri into a concert grand piano after a club owner stiffed the band on the door money."

"Ha! I guess that was timed release disaster."

"From an audience share point of view, that episode will probably be our highest rated show. For now, it's the one everyone in the biz seems to be talking about."

"I would've loved to have seen his face on that one. She sounds like a wild woman. Hope the band has a bouncer."

"Oh, we do. Absolutely. It's part of the budget for the show."

"Does the budget include trashing hotel rooms?"

"I think that's where they draw the line in the sand."

"I'll make a note of that."

"Yeah, I know you're a drummer, but ease off on the Keith Moon mayhem. We can't foot the bill for that high level of insanity."

"No problem. Just remember though, that if you want good drumming, you might expect some level of wackiness. I mean, this drumming business is not exactly playing cards. It's a tough job, and someone's gotta tear the playhouse down. But hey man, I wanna thank you ahead of time for letting me know what the budget is, and where I stand."

I ordered a stiff drink from Jim and drifted across the room to mingle with my new band mates. From the conversation, I could get a feel for where they were at. Gradually, I was able to figure out everyone's relationship to one another. The broken-legged Bangladeshi had some connection to Ben. What was it? Girlfriend, manager, wifey, barfly, groupie? I'd sort it out in due course. It was quite fortuitous that Jillian had sent the camera men home for the night, so that everyone could let down their guard. Thank God for unions. Ben ordered a beer and left it on the bar, sipping it bent over, with his hands clasped tightly behind his back. That looked very, very odd. What was his problem?

The Bangladeshi girl hobbled up and rubbed him on the nape of his neck.

"You see, Joe, Ben's so darned over-civilized that he long ago forgot how to use his hands. To tell you the truth, I don't understand why on earth he bothers keeping them around anymore. He might as well lop 'em off."

Ben stopped in mid-slurp. "Sunita! Behave yourself!"

"Gee baby, I'm doin' the best I can," she replied with a trace of sarcasm.

"Just remember, Sunita. You only have a high school education."

The sarcasm drained from her face and was replaced by a quivering lip. Yeah, I thought --- that would be the wife. But ouch, that was the kind of chat that would get your ass shot off with some girls.

Sunita, ever the cheerleader, took another big sip from her Pan's Pant. "With music, I never cease to be amazed at what the cat drags in. And it just dragged in Joe Myers, drummer extraordinaire. Now Ben, maybe your music will get the fuck off the ground and soar high up into the wild blue yonder."

Ben took another slurp and scowled. I gave him a quick smile to put him at ease, and turned my attention to Kathy and Gwen who were necking and kissing passionately in the corner. Gwen especially had a beautiful flushed look, no doubt from the lingering residue of the performance. Slightly embarrassed, they stopped kissing and suddenly turned to stare at me. They had the look of two school girls who were trying to be good, but weren't having much luck.

"Don't stop on my account," I offered.

They broke into a unison giggle, and I marveled at the skewed ratio if yin to yang. It was good that they were together. It was good for the imagination of the culture. At that moment, seemingly joined at the hip and shoulder, they were almost the same person. No, I thought. Don't stop. In the beaming afterglow of a performance, it's really too much effort to stop. They wanted this feeling to never end because the real world paled in comparison. Anyway, who in the hell would want to go *there*? The real world, I mean. Not going there --- that was something a drummer could understand. That was something a Neanderthal could understand. Maybe it was something they could understand too. Let us pray.

"Great gig," said Kathy.

"Thanks to you," Gwen added quickly. "While I was up on stage, I kept saying to myself, 'Sweet Jesus, who loaded this thing?'"

"I did, and that's quite the compliment."

Kathy moved closer. "Joe. Let me introduce you to my guitar. I call her Roxy."

"Hey, B. B. King has Lucille, and you have Roxy."

"And all is right with the world," added Gwen.

"I like it that she's fire engine red."

"That's her personality. Joe, I'm a woman with grandiose plans. I hope you understand that."

"Oh, I get it absolutely. If people don't have grandiose plans, then they really have no business playing in rock bands and wasting everyone's precious time. We're talking sheer outrageous atavistic fantasies here, and if they don't have them, then they don't follow their hearts. And if they don't do that, they should be selling shoes in some peasant town like East Dover Foxcroft."

The woman with grandiose plans pondered that for a second and replied, "Maybe I shouldn't have followed my heart. Mine's very dark --- a scary place indeed. A goddess once said it in a song I wrote."

She nodded to Gwen, and they both broke into a spritely *accapella*:

> "Kali laughed and she danced
> Shiva saved the world
> She said follow your heart
> So she looked and it was dark"

"Uh huh," I said, "Who can really trust the heart? It's biased towards the present, mired in the mundane. Besides, the Ted Bundys of the world should never ever follow their hearts. Lord help us if they do."

Gwen added her inebriated thoughts on the subject, "Your Honor, having eight dead women under the bed doesn't make a boy all bad."

She was well on the way to becoming more than a little blasted, and I worried for her. After all, drummers have to *protect* their singers, to rescue them from the vicissitudes of the world. Her darting eyes were moving more slowly now and were starting to look like they belonged to some sort of woozy grasshopper because Jim the good time Doctor Feelgood was serving up free shots of rotgut tequila. Damn, that stuff went down hard.

"Yeah right," added Kathy. "Perhaps it's better to do a hundred eighty degrees in the opposite direction. Be an actor and do something that's not the least bit you. Take up accounting or paralegal studies, and you'll find true happiness. You'll learn to like it, but it won't be you. No never. Never in a million years."

"Sort of the way people do with arranged marriages in other countries."

Yes, I was thinking. Love never happens at first sight. Then Gwen gave me a drunken history lesson about the origins of the band. This latest chapter --- the one that I had helped to write that night --- was typical of the way these things frequently unfold: the drummer was the last person to complete the sound.

"What would happen, Gwen, if everything started with the drummer first?"

"Oh, that's a fun question, the kind of thing that Kathy would think about, but I don't believe it would ever cross Jillian's mind."

Suddenly, Gwen went into a raspy cough, and she wheezed uncontrollably. Kathy struggled with her gig bag and after fumbling around for a few seconds, she produced an inhaler which she gave to Gwen who desperately inhaled its contents. Kathy turned to me.

"It's nothing, Joe. Gwen's an asthmatic. She gets these attacks every now and then, so I have to be ready for them."

"Yes, you have to be ready for them."

Sunita slithered back into the room on her wobbling crutches and drunkenly butted into the conversation: "Gwen's attacks usually happen when there's too much excitement. And one thing you provided tonight from behind the drums was lots of excitement. From your perch in the back, you're in charge of pleasure. If you control the endorphins, you kinda sorta have 'em by the balls. That would be the slave controlling the master. And we can't have that, can we, Ben?"

I glanced to my left to see Ben scowling again. "Gosh," he replied. "I don't think I've ever heard it put like that, but perhaps there's some truth to that I guess."

I could understand that this was a touchy subject for them. So I tried to be diplomatic: "Well, for someone who's short of breath, Gwen can certainly bellow pretty damned loud. I'm sure she doesn't need to be controlled by anybody, least of all by me."

But Sunita wouldn't let up: "When something new comes into the world, it competes with something old. It refers to something very old, which in turn, summons up an ancient moment that bites the present in the ass."

Ben was getting very nervous. "Look baby, I think you may have had too much to drink." He directed his remarks to Jim the bartender and said, "Jim, no more for her tonight. She's had last call."

"No problem, Ben."

I looked at Gwen. She was getting better already, and she flashed me a reassuring smile.

"My asthma's not as bad as it was when I worked for a law firm. All the stress made it worse. Nowadays, the attacks aren't quite as often, but somehow there're a lot scarier."

"I'm sure you'll get better," I replied. "Music will make it happen. And I look forward to that day."

One the most striking features of Kathy's appearance was the tattoo on her neck. It featured big and brash curly lettering boldly stating her soul mate's name over a background consisting of a heart with an arrow gliding through it. It started at the top ridge of her collarbone, proceeded northward and followed the line of her lower jaw before skirting the edge of her earlobe. On a scale of big impression, I gave it about a nine, and I strongly approved. Drummers like to see commitment, and that sure as hell was a lasting connection 'cause it was something hard to erase. And no doubt a lot of pain went into that. That would be the kind of pain that would matter. Curiously, Gwen's swan-like neck was devoid of any ink. If she could do that to Kathy, would she do that to me, her hired help? But such petty thoughts could be easily dismissed. Surely, Gwen would come around to getting a reciprocating tat sometime soon. I could just picture what it would be --- perhaps something with a heavy metal biker theme? Yes, that would do rather nicely.

Meanwhile, Ben had managed to come to terms with being outvoted, and it looked as though he was coping magnificently.

He even went so far as to offer a toast. "But it wasn't until *Babies in Bars* added drummer Joe Meyers to the lineup that their careers really took off. Bottoms up."

"Cheers."

"Here here!" Kathy and Gwen chimed in.

"And," Ben continued, "If a drummer can't play in ten and a half, then what the hell good is he?"

"A fuckin' loser."

"You're absolutely right. Every musician should be able to play music you can lurch to," I replied.

"Joe, I can't believe it took us seventy-eight auditions to find you. Why would I want a beat box when I can have you backing us up?"

"Gee, I guess I don't know why. It doesn't matter though. Music's the main thing, right?" I gave myself a pat on the back for being so professional although I had the nagging feeling that being professional wasn't worth the trouble.

"Joe, I wanted to talk to you about something else."

"And what's that?"

"Sunita and I are married."

"Well, good for you. Congratulations!" So that was the connection. I should have known better.

"But not to worry, Joe. Sunita's got something she wants to tell you."

"Yes, do I wanna know?" I inquired.

Sunita crutched forward with a bashful look on her face. "Joe --- Ben and I have an open relationship."

"Congratulations. That's very modern of you. Ben doesn't play traditional music, so why should both of you be traditional people?"

"Right, Joe. What she means to say is that she and I go with whoever catches our fancies ..."

Sunita sipped on her drink, wavered on her crutches a bit, and then finished Ben's sentence for him. "And Joe, you really catch my fantasy...err, I mean fancy."

She polished off the dregs of the Pat's Pant and with a flourish put the empty glass on the bar.

"Goodness gwacious! What should I do? I've barely been in the band for ten minutes. I don't want to upset any apple carts."

"You're not upsetting any apple carts," Ben replied. "Besides, maybe I can talk to Jillian about it, and she can write it into the plot."

This was getting very baroque even for me. I loved the guy 'cause he was pimpin' his own wife for Christ's sake. Despite that bizarre karmic fact of life, I looked over at Sunita and thought, yeah; I could do her the favor if she insisted. Only if she insisted.

At this point, Ben and I adjourned to the men's room where he offered me up a line of coke to sweeten the deal. I knew I'd purchased something very exotic. It was a wonderful male-bonding kind of moment. A few moments later, Sunita barged through the door as if she owned the place. The guy at the side urinal near the door zipped up hurriedly and skedaddled out of there.

"Ben's trying to get addicted, but he keeps spinning his wheels."

"Sunita! Behave yourself!" Ben commanded imperiously.

"I wish he would get addicted. Then maybe something interesting would happen."

"Sunita! I thought I said behave yourself."

"No, I don't wanna behave myself. I wanna be bad."

"I said behave. Behave and behave now!"

"Wait'll you hear what Ben does for a living in his day job," Sunita countered.

"He has a day job?" I replied. "I thought playing bass for *Babies in Bars* was his day job."

"I'm hoping that he'll be able to kick it as soon as the band takes off, which should be pretty darned soon now that you're the drummer," Sunita said excitedly while she lit a cigarette.

She ran her hand lightly along my arm. "So lemme see 'em right up close. These are the arms that are attached to the hands that made every blast of that divine ruckus for the ears of all those people out there tonight. Well, I think I wanna kiss 'em." And she did.

Ignoring this, Ben continued. "Joe, come on by tomorrow. I'll invite you to my place of employment."

"So what do you do?"

"Oh, just come on by and let it be a surprise. Now let's have another toot, and I'll give you the address."

Hmm...this was real darned fascinatin' and in some ways, a bit of a dilemma. You see, my motto has been to be skittish of things that are fascinating. They have a strong tendency to be things that'll never qualify for a payday --- could be damned dangerous too. Either way, fascination has the full blown potential to blossom into a complete dead end.

But at that moment, I decided not to think about this too much because the reality show known as *Babies in Bars* was a payday. Or was it? What more would I need for proof of safe fascination --- a letter of employment? Hell no, this was a rock and roll band, not some slip-and-fall shyster outfit. Now, if I could only stay alive for a while longer, I might actually get to accomplish something. Yo bro, you can't hold down a job if you don't have no blood pressure.

Yes, it was definitely a payday for sure. Still, I thought I'd better make absolutely sure 'cause you never know about these things. So, I knew I should talk with Jillian to nail that one down.

I managed to get her attention just as the last of the crew were packing up the gear. "Umm, Jillian, we haven't discussed the matter of my pay."

"What? You can't be serious!"

"Hey, I beg to differ."

"Differ all you like. Differ till the cows come home. We're not payin'."

"Stop and think about what you'll be getting."

"OK. I'm stoppin'. I'm thinkin'. I ain't payin'."

I heard what she said, but I charged straight forward full steam ahead anyway. "You'll be getting' lots for your money. Let me give you a partial inventory. I can play beats that make the mountains shudder and shake. There's the funky four-four. That one sets the ecstasy in motion. That should be worth about at least $600.00 per week, minimum. Then there's the punk rock speed freak boogie with a double kick drum ramble. That'll set ya back another $700.00 right there. On top of that, there's the blues shuffle for $1,200.00 to say nothing of the asymmetrical seven-four. That'll cost ya a pretty penny because it's rather rare and exotic, and you don't see it so much around these parts 'cause it's an endangered species. And I'm only just now starting to tally things up. When all is said and done, with expenses and everything, you owe me $5,000.00 a week minimum. So, will ya pay, cash, credit card or Pay Pal?"

"Excuse me, I don't believe I'm hearing this. Are you completely quantified by now?"

"Maybe not yet, but I'm close to it."

"Sorry baby, Hollywood trumps everything. We can get everything for free 'cause we deal in images. You traffic in sound, so we shut you down."

"I object."

"Take it or leave it, buddy."

"Maybe I'll have to think about it."

"Think about it all you want."

"Yes, and I think I'll take my business elsewhere. I think I'll go and get another drink."

"No, you can't. The bar's closed. Jim just now did last call."

"Why'd he have to go and do that? I was only getting started."

"Joe, I thought you loved to play drums, so why pollute it with filthy lucre? You seem to think that every sound you play has to be the Ker chink of some distant, imaginary cash register in the sky. Well, I gotta say, that's so short-sighted of you! Another thing to consider is that by being on the show, you'll be getting lots of free publicity and name recognition. People will know you in Valencia, Spain and Helsinki, Finland and Christ's Church, New Zealand and maybe even in some boondocks place like Papua, New Guinea or Emperor Franz Joseph's Land. Don't you know that counts for something --- something that you can't easily put a dollar value on? Joe, when you really start to think about it, there are things in this world of ours that are invaluable and incalculable. Anyway, music is one of them. It's all about freedom. Freedom! Freedom!"

Jillian may have been a director, but in her heart of hearts, she was truly an actress. She gave this thought about an eight beat rest to let the line drag out and have its full effect, and I scanned the knots on my shoe laces while I formulated a rejoinder. From the tone of her voice, I half-expected to hear the PA system chime in with "America the Beautiful." Then she went on with her patriotic speech: "It's one way of making people feel free and happy. So get out there and make people happy. And understand that freedom has to start from someplace, so it might as well be you, if and only if, you decide to make it for free! So, you better wise up and wise up soon, or you're outta here! Understand?"

"But ... but ..."

"But you gotta eat? Don't worry. You can eat from the company food truck. Consider that one to be on the house. And you can also have unlimited refills of all the coffee you can drink." She gave me a big paw on the back of my shoulder and acted as if she were an old friend who hadn't seen me in eons. I breathed in the phony camaraderie.

"Aw c'mon!" I said. "That's not the least bit fair! I wanna contribute to the gross national product."

She shrugged her shoulders. "Take it or leave it. We can always go back to having the beat box do the back beat. How would you feel about that?"

Knowing I would feel badly, I ground my teeth, one bicuspid to another, to imitate a backbeat and stared at the floor. I thought of that devo, Mr. Ben, and how much I hated his silly beat box. I pondered all of the things I would have liked to have done to it --- like throwing it from a 10th story window or putting it under a semi's left rear wheel. Right then, I knew that it was a zero-sum game --- Ziggy's gain was my loss. Nothing he could do would ever lead to my advantage. I relished the idea of breaking him to bits. I did another three or four backbeats with the two bicuspids. I was slowly coming to understand that if I elected not to comply with Jillian's oppressive contract, then I wouldn't have had the chance to do that. That would create a sadness beyond my endurance.

The big mystery to me was: how in the world did this lady suss that one out? She had gotten a bird's eye view of my brain. She knew that beat boxes made my blood boil. I didn't answer her question, but no doubt she could see from my expression exactly what my thoughts were on that particular subject.

So she continued on in the same vein. Part of me was listening to what she had to say and the other part was simply paying attention to the hills and valleys of her voice, and the more I listened, the more it seemed to be an abrasive music that my ear would someday get used to, and once I got used to it, it would sound as though it made absolute sense for every second of the day. She gave me a big speech about commitment and how important that is in the world today because it's the thing that holds relationships together. She told me that if people can't make a simple leap of faith, then nothing would ever get done. The world would grind to a halt. How sad --- to go through life with such a profound and abiding mistrust for one another! But not to fret --- there is an antidote because commitment's the thing that holds any business arrangement together. Yeah, and it probably holds society together, and isn't that a comforting thought? And when she said that, I had to kind of laugh to myself 'cause I'm a pretty loyal sort of fellow. I'm such a loyal sun of a gun. I throw my loyalty around like it's goin' outta style. But the trouble is when I do that to the lead singers, to the lead whatever, I'm loyal because they're the ones who're supposed to know how to lead. I reckon that's why they're called *lead* singers and all. That's how they get they're names. And it's a division of labor I suppose. They're good at what they do, so I guess they're worthy of loyalty, right? I mean, why not do stuff that you're good at, instead of stuff that you suck at? Well, as you can see, the answer is clear as day. So after I'd told myself that it was true, then I knew I was on the right track, and I could start to worry about other, more important things than loyalty.

As I mulled this one over in my head, Jillian went on with her speech: "Look, let's be realistic. We'll have you try out for the part. Perhaps you'll be good enough. But then again, maybe you won't. It's just like life. There are no guarantees. We can't take the chance on paying you right away because the budget for the show is so tight. And only time'll tell to see if you work out. In the meantime, we'll sit back and see how it goes. We can call it an internship. And like all internships, this one will provide you with an educational experience, one that you can put to beneficial use at a later date in your career. We can't rush these things. Hell, there's absolutely no sense in throwing good money after bad. We have to apply market forces. I'm sure you'll understand. You do understand, don't you, Joe?"

I wavered and walked away to lick my wounds, then glanced back to see that she was looking very proud of herself.

And that was how I became an indentured servant. But that didn't matter much 'cause no matter how hard she tried to trivialize what I did, I would be loyal and make it more important than she ever imagined.

MAN AND HIS CYMBALS

In the future, everyone will be in a state of perpetual training, so they'll never be deemed worthy of pay. The boss boss will always want to take a wait-and-see attitude to be sure that you'll "work out." All tasks will be conducted in the spirit of pursuing an "educational experience." However, as some small consolation, it might not be without its perks. One of the perks of being in the band known as *Babies in Bars* was that Jillian, my new kinda sorta, almost boss, gave me a company car. Since she was being real generous, I figured that now was as good a time as any to go on a joyride. I was at an intersection waiting for the light to change. It seemed to take forever. Finally, I put my arm out the window and said, "Change!" and magically, I got a green. Needless to say, I was feeling rather full of myself, which was good for a spot of euphoria. The whole audition thing had made me feel as if I'd just gotten out if church, which put me in a devout mood. All I've ever wanted was something worthy of my hunger for reverence. I'll be delirious with the world's pain if that's what it takes in this big complicated nothing that surrounds us. Pain is important. It gives us depth perception.

So I went to the address that Ben gave me. It was a place of pain decorated to look beautiful. Ben was working intently on the eyebrows of a face that would never burst out laughing again, nor for that matter, would she ever cry. He had to highlight the arches of the eyebrows to give her the right expression: not too solemn, not too exuberant --- a model of moderation. Despite this, the lady didn't give a damn about anything --- you name it. But she wasn't going anywhere for at least a couple of days. Ben could fuss around for as long as he wanted. And I could be reverent for as long as I wanted.

He stepped back to get a view from a different angle; at that moment he reminded me of a golfer who was plumb-lining a putt. "There, there...not bad. She looks pretty good."

Yeah, I thought --- sort of imitation good. She was a beautiful thing that did not move.

"Hey man, I liked jammin' with you. I liked your playing, especially the way you make the cymbals dance. You're the whole package --- a man and his cymbals."

"So let me get this straight about your wife Sunita. I mean, what you said about her the other night. You're giving me a free pass?"

"Hell yeah, I'm giving you multiple free passes --- as many as you want. You climb up. You are validated."

I loved the man's cavalier attitude. What was he covering up?

"Of course, she has quite a colorful history," he continued. His voice had all the blasé charm of a man who'd just sold a used car.

"And what do you mean by that?" I inquired.

"What I mean is that she's a bit haunted."

"Oh yeah?"

"Yeah, she used to delaminate rather easily. But I always say that's part of the price of admission. Every now and then after an amorous interlude, she would get a crazed look in her eye, and she would remind me that three of her lovers had died. Then her stare would become even more riveted, and she would ask me, 'Ben, do you think you'll be next anytime soon?' After that, her face would get a deathly pallor, and she'd laugh herself silly like a young witch. Then I'd get a shiver and a fright which wouldn't last long 'cause the next thing I knew, we'd be back at it again. It was a bit unnerving though. But the crisis has passed. If not, I'm sure you'll get used to it."

"So three of her boys have met with untimely deaths?" I asked.

"Uh huh, really. One in a car accident. Wrapped himself around a tree. Another one succumbed to some weird illness that no one could quite figure out. It stumped even the best doctors. And the last one ...umm... well let's just say that his heart gave out."

"I see. Somethin' sounds embarassin'. The little death led to the big one."

"Also, to make matters worse, her parents were terrible --- a loose woman and a fascist father. It's hard to bail yourself out of that double-whammy."

"Well, thank you, Ben, for passing that little bit of information on to me."

"But not to worry," he continued, "Last month we both went to a shaman and had whatever it was that was bothering her exorcised. Well, the guy did a great job, some kind of heap-big-magic, pow wow ceremony, and since then, she's totally like new. All the ghosts have flown the coop. Before that, she went off at the drop of a hat. The glazier did a boffo business in my house. I was constantly having to summon his services at ungodly hours. I honestly thought that her melancholy would fund the man's golden years. But now she's making decent progress."

"Say, that's great news. Mental health --- I'll root for that!"

Ben turned his attention back to the silent lady and made an adjustment to the rose-colored lighting, which sure made her a lot rosier looking.

"The family will be here pretty soon. I hope they don't make a big deal about the way she looks."

"Yes, I'll bet they can be damned difficult."

"Oh, can they ever be that way!"

"Lemme make a wild guess. They'll criticize you, saying that she looks fake."

"Yeah, you're right. How did you know? What they apparently don't realize is that she's pretending to be alive. Their expectations are way out of control. I don't work miracles. Resuscitation is beyond the pale."

"So if they're gonna be that way, why not hand 'em the real deal and don't even bother to gussy her up?"

"No, no, no. I'd never do that because they could never cope. Real demise is too hard to take. Better to make it as artificial as possible."

I thought of Ziggy the Beat Box and *his* cymbals. He was as artificial as possible. Then I thought of Sunita, Ben's wonderful gift to me. I hoped she wasn't pretending to be alive.

"What the average man or woman doesn't comprehend, Joe, is the need for pageantry. Hell, if given a chance, they'd act as if expiration didn't quite happen. They act like it's a fart in an elevator, something damned embarrassing, and if you take away the pageantry, death can kind of sneak out of there, and nobody will ever quite notice it. Into every life --- and extinction, there should be a modicum of pageantry. That's the way I feel about it."

"And that's why we need artifice --- so that people won't act artificial?"

"Exactly. But to change the subject just for a second. I have to leave to check my e-mail. Hold on for a bit, and I'll be right back." And with that, Ben left the room. I suddenly found myself in a very quiet room. I mean, here I was alone except for the company of the cool and silent lady sleeping in the box. I looked at the pictures on the wall and decided to think about other things.

I thought about the 1956 World Series, but not for long. I was glad to see that Ben and I could relate on some level. That made this Neanderthal feel cautiously optimistic because based on the previous night's performance, it was clear to me that he was a pretty so-so bass player, which might not spell absolute disaster if he could simply be a decent guy. Could he be a decent guy? Could he make a big effort to not be in the way? Only time would tell. The problem is that limitations in cahoots with a wildly distorted Ego usually conspire to make Cro-Magnons complete dicks --- or bitches as the case may be.

This could be one of those special situations. What kind am I talking about? OK, I'll tell you. There are those situations --- usually in newspapers --- when you see the pic of the man who's killed the supposedly squeaky clean and lovable boss. Right there next to that pic of the killer is another of the squeaky clean boss. You read the story and the people who knew the victim all paint a rosy picture of the dear and unfairly departed. Then you stare long and hard at both pictures, and something doesn't add up. Something doesn't quite jibe. It seems the squeaky clean fellow has an evil glint in his eye; at least that's what the grainy picture in the pulpy paper tells you. The Hollywood people know this, and they love to gloat. They never get bored of tellin' us that the *camera doesn't lie.* But after looking at that picture of the dead boss, you wanna say the homicide was absolutely justified. You root for the killer and say "right on" for doing such wonderful work for good riddance. In those ostensibly sad situations, you know in your heart that a contribution for a higher purpose and a greater good to society has been made. Of course the police don't quite see it that way. But that's neither here nor there because Ben had that look, that grainy newspaper look. Was he one of the squeaky clean bosses? Only time would tell. The camera may not lie, but the makeup does.

I thought about a possible future. Yes, it was possible, but not probable. I was a magician, so I wouldn't allow it. I tried the future on for size, and it felt rather devilish: we were going over a new tune and he was saying, "Hey man, I'm not very thrilled with that drum idea of yours. Can you play something else?" and so I played something else, and then he said, "No, I don't think I like that beat either. How about something else?" and so I played something else and he said that one was no good either and this went on and on and on until just to make the sick game stop, I went back to the first idea that he didn't like only to have him tell me how much he loved it and why didn't I play this one for him sooner? In fact, he chided me a bit for holding out on him. At that moment, he felt so creative. I could see the joy in his eyes. I mean, I wanted to push his face right into a puddle of mud. I was thinking that he couldn't sing, and he couldn't dance, so what kind of a man was he? Not much, so I smiled to myself 'cause this old trick of going back to the first choice works like a charm. But really that horrible future won't happen! Like I said --- I won't allow it. Dear crystal ball, please put a cork in it. I beg you.

And Dear Joe, stop being such a cynical bastard. Can't you trust Cro-Magnons? I looked over at the silent lady again. She was pretty in her box. She might not be there to lend a helping hand, but at least she wouldn't be the kind of person who would set up a thousand and one road blocks. She could be counted on for that. The average bass player can't be counted on for anything. They want you to listen to them, but they rarely can listen to you. They're either mercenaries or insufferable petty artistes. This one might be a combination of both. True, he would probably lecture me about how sensitive he was and how insensitive I was, but that would be a clever ruse. If anything, he was the one who had it all wrong. A Cro-Magnon shouldn't automatically get a real brain. It's an entitlement he may not necessarily deserve. Perhaps he should get something second rate, a ganglia instead. Yes, that might be what he really needed --- an extra-sensitive, spangled nerve, so that similar to a lobster, he could live to a ripe old age if left unmolested. A nerve might teach him to feel. That would be as sensitive as he would ever need to be. Anything more would be purely overcompensation. Still, the question remained: can a creature that is only equipped with a ganglia play music? Time will tell. I would do the best I could to keep an open mind.

But stop it, Joe! Have some manners. Don't you know that manners are the nature of society, and you do not want to lose any anticipations, so responsibility and respectability are the first considerations when you start to work? Damn! Knock it off, Joe!

For a second there, I was almost talking to myself in the third person again, just the way that James Brown or Abe Lincoln, the *Uber* Soul Men, used to do.

I moved closer and reverently looked one more time at the silent lady in the box. The Goddess may take many forms, but this was the Goddess at rest. Ahh, the Goddess --- She demands a capital, and She gets one --- even Her pronouns --- especially Her pronouns. And more often than not, contrary to other self-centered icons, She actually deserves it. Yes, She was worthy of something. What was it? She was sleepy and wanted to swoon on up to heaven. Perhaps she would become an angel if she was a good girl. I would make her a good girl. I reached out my hand over her and said, "Change!" and She suddenly rose up from the embroidered satin pillow! Hey, what was it with me? I could make anything happen. That's what drummers do: they make people feel more alive. She sat upright and moved awkwardly, trying very hard to burst out laughing or to burst out crying. The marionette movement was somewhere between a tango and a Balboa swing dance, only clunkier. She tried to open

Her eyes, but to no avail. And then just as suddenly, She flopped back down to the satin lined interior, looking even more permanently passed away than She had before. Nice try, I thought to myself. I would chalk this up to my hallucination and Her defunct intuition. Still, didn't this prove to anyone who happened to notice that I'm a very sensitive creature? Hell, I'm so sensitive I catch a cold twenty times a year. Top that, Mr. So-So Bass Player!

While I gazed at the silent lady, I began to make my plans for the afternoon. It would definitely be necessary to go back to the bar early on, before Jim started his shift. That way I could sit down at the drums and make some gorgeous noise that would inch the world forward on the path towards saving itself. The background was making decent progress in its quest to become the foreground. And as a bonus, I thought, "Who knows? Maybe a good mess of racket would keep Ben's devilish future from happening." I knew I could do it because I'm very good. Very, very good. Omnipotence is a fun feeling. And a twenty-five minute drum solo might be just what the doctor ordered. Don't you think it's so much more civil to take out your rage on a drum kit than to take it out on a human being? Well I do. Uh huh, these habits die hard for a Neanderthal. I honestly can't figure out why I never got to become leader of the free world, but go figure.

So, you might have guessed by now, I'm not so good with social media. There are tons of keys to hit and too many pics to parade, peruse and parallel. Rejoice Hallelujah greatly! Oh social media, social media! Most likely, there will be another photo of a "Christian woman" looking for a nice Christian man. In the picture, she'll be beaming brightly, and her legs will be wide open. Clear to China. Only problem is I'm an Orthodox Druid, not a conservative or reform. We believe in sacrifice; the others don't. So much for religion. Sorry Ma'm, I don't think I can help you out of that one. Maybe my medulla will make that limping perspective walk in a straight line because ramblin' gamblin' giddiness really might smack those spinning trickster ladies into happiness and give the girls some gravitas.

Maybe or maybe not, but in the meantime, my fingers would wander to my brow ridge to see if my supra-orbital ridge was bursting outward again. It was still there as thick as ever. I was living in total humongousness. Everything I do is a monstrosity, something that tugs at the seams, which is fairly common among us Neanderthals. You Cro-Magnons don't get stressed out about this the way I do 'cause your chins support your faces. I, on the other hand, don't have that lucky option. My skull needs support, and the big brow is the support it gets from all the wear and tear put on it from the lower mandible. Oh how I wish I could make it go away so I could become a Cro-Magnon like the rest of you. It must be wonderful to go through life with the certain knowledge that you are an "improvement" over what came before. I love all of you. No matter how hard I study, you're so much more sophisticated than me. You're my role models 'cause I'm a monster of all trades and a master of none. You show me how I'm supposed to live! I only want to stumble through life without hurtin' anyone. Is that do-able? I'll have to think about it. People are always making a big deal about how they are reinventing themselves. Jeez, I'm a Neanderthal. Each and every day of my existence is spent making frantic efforts just to stay one step away from extinction. I can never make myself new. I just do one thing well. But whatever will be will be. Trying to be happy is not a part time job. Every moment of my existence is plagued by some sort of infraction. Feeling rather bi-polar, I was wondering now about how I was losing ground:

I am a Neanderthal;
I lose my way of life
The tides are getting higher;
The game is getting few
Blowing on my flute of bone,
I get a curvy tone
For all those times I sit and stare,
I feel I'm getting blue
I am a Neanderthal;
They suck out all my life blood
My way of life is getting old;
I'm sinking into mud
Cro-Magnons on the mountain tops

Have got a way with words
They got a better view
Of the mammoths in their herds

Whew! Good going --- for now my latest werewolf moment was over. I could concentrate on more practical concerns.

"OK Ben, so I'll see you tonight for the gig. I'll be there early for the sound check."

"Great! I look forward to it."

And for the second night in a row, the show was spectacular. At first, I thought Kathy was going to hog all those sixteenth notes for herself, but she backed off and let me have some of 'em. And that worked out just fine, so that when the music burrowed deeper and deeper into the heart and soul of the night, those same notes got bluer and bluer. The crowd let us know that was alright. We killed 'em. I was learning fast. I always do. And what was even better was that Kathy's guitar playing was absolutely scorching. As a matter of fact, for a second there, I almost thought she'd burst into flames. There you go again girl, playin' with matches. I'll just hang around and do some aiding and abetting.

The next day Ben and I were having dinner at an Italian restaurant not far from the boardwalk. Of course we weren't completely alone. The camera crew was there to accompany us, but after a few sips of red wine, we forgot they were there. Actually, I was getting so spoiled I was startin' to act as though they were my support staff. Ben was seemingly in a good mood, and evidence of that was the round of drinks, supplemented with shots of bourbon, that he'd purchased for us.

"Here's to the band, Joe, and also, to music in general."

We raised our glasses.

"Yes, to both of those things! Cheers!"

"Gee thanks so much, Ben. This is above and beyond the call."

I chugged down the shot and chased it with some beer. We got to talking about playing music, and he told me about how easily he got stage fright. "Joe, sometimes when I'm on stage, a scare creeps up and comes over me. I get so afraid of makin' a mistake, and then of course when that happens, I usually do make a mistake and then I feel absolutely awful. I just can't get over it. I can't get it out of my mind. And the mistake or, much worse, the mere thought of a mistake, haunts everything I do."

I gulped on the beer. "But what if a mistake made you find something new? How would that one feel for you?"

"You're so lucky. You don't get afraid."

"Sure I do." I pointed to the cameras. "I'm afraid of them. And that's funny 'cause I really thought I'd forgotten them. But now I remember them, and I'm afraid." One of the camera men gave us both a sheepish smile and then ducked for cover behind his machine.

"Look at him," Ben replied. "I think he's afraid of us."

"So c'mon. Relax. He's havin' fun with us. We can forget all about him."

"Once there was a gig about a year ago when Kathy, Gwen, and I were on stage and we hadn't rehearsed at all. Kathy looked at me and said, 'Ben, I have no idea what we're gonna play. I don't know what key, what tempo, what rhythm; I don't have a clue what we're proposin' to do.' She was bein' really mean to me --- makin' me feel as though I was about to walk on a rope without benefit of a net. I got so scared I almost walked out. I was totally freezin' up."

"Sounds like a lotta fun to me, not knowing what you're gonna play, that is. Sounds like it was total freedom --- the great escape."

"Well, I not so sure about that." He sadly gazed across the room. I gazed around too and thought about how some people can't handle freedom. I got sad. Then the food arrived, and he cheered up and soon we were tucking into the lasagna and eggplant parmagiannia when Ben noticed that two beautiful women and a rather nerdy looking guy were seated at a nearby booth. The three of them looked preppy. I surmised that they were on a long weekend from Yale or Princeton. Suddenly, Ben began to pay close attention to them. He was obviously annoyed at something, but I couldn't figure out what it was. The Ivy Leaguers seemed pretty innocuous. They could have walked straight out of a Ralph Lauren ad --- nothing very threatening about that. The ladies were gorgeous in a tedious sort of way, and they weren't wearing shoes that sparked any flamboyant interest of mine, so I hadn't given them much notice. To my mind, each of them could have been a bowl of vanilla ice cream. Ho ho hum.

Suddenly, Ben looked at me with a conspiratorial eye. "Joe, this guy is ruining my mood."

"Awh Ben. What's wrong? He's not doing anyone any harm. Least of all to us."

"Yes, he is. He really is." There was a touch of urgency in his voice.

"Naw! No way. Leave him alone. He's totally benign. Maybe you don't admire his fashion, but that's no big deal."

"He's ruining my fantasy! He doesn't deserve either one of those beautiful babes. I do!" Now there was a touch of infancy in his voice.

"C'mon, man. What are you talkin' about? Look man, we gotta mind our own business. Wouldn't that be a good idea? I think it would be, don't you?"

"No, he's messin' up my fantasy. Those cuties are being wasted on him."

"So let him have 'em. They're not even very hot. As a matter of fact, the one on the left has a guy's ass. Leave 'em alone."

"No way! He's got to pay for his crimes."

"The crime of stepping on your fantasy? It's a misdemeanor at best, and that would be stretchin' it. C'mon man. Get real."

The baby boy reached over to a plant pot that separated our booth from theirs and picked out a piece of bark that was nestled around the stalks of a fake rhododendron. He put the bark on the table and placed his thumb and middle finger together right behind the bark. He squinted as he aimed, lookin' like a nefarious scientist pouring chemicals.

"Hey, Ben," I whispered, "I see what you wanna do, but please. Don't do it. I'm beggin' ya. Please don't do it."

He gave me a huge goofy grin and then shot a glance at the guy and his two lady friends before flicking the bark with his middle finger. Like a field goal place kick, the bark flew upwards at about a forty-five degree angle, gently hitting the man's aquiline nose and dropping square in the middle of his veal scampi. Good God, what had this wanker of a bass player gotten me into? I never signed on for this. I made a mental note to never beg again. I had to improvise. The only thing I could think about was to laugh and get myself ready for the punch up. Under the table, my fists were flexing.

The preppie didn't know what fleck of dust had hit him, but to his gentlemanly credit, he collected himself rather quickly. He got up, picked the bark out of his food, and marched over to the front of our table and indignantly announced, "The next time this bark comes over to my table, I'll knock your lights out!"

Of course that man didn't have the strength to back up his threat. Some things are best left idle. Out of self-defense, I laughed as loudly as I could. That was my way of punching him out so he wouldn't get near. Ben chimed in too. I got the feeling that the volume protected us. The guy chickened out. A spasm of exhilaration and a streak of guilt shot through me, each competing to take center stage. The spasm won. May the gods forgive me. Please remind them to tell me to never beg again. The camera man smirked. That devil! He knew that we hadn't forgotten him.

After the totally predictable war of words, we stumbled drunk and disorderly into the early evening. I felt like a man who'd escaped from a multi-vehicle pile-up on the BQE. The sun was just then beginning to set, and streams of orange and red slinked across the sky. To my surprise, I could see that animated blink in the middle of the firmament again. This time it was bolstered by more light in the background, but nonetheless there it was: stroboscopic and cartoonish, right beside the full and foggy moon. Perhaps it was getting bolder? And of course, it showed off, giving us a herky-jerky display of sweetness and light.

Later, I found a secluded spot and shot up. That made me feel a whole lot better. I caught a glimpse of myself in the mirror --- I was dancing in total slow motion. If I hadn't known better, I would have thought I was doin' tai-chi.

The next day Jillian invited me into her editing room where she was looking over the rushes for the restaurant scene. I could see the flickering images go by, which made me relive both the embarrassment and the moment of triumph when the yuppie boy backed down.

Jillian especially loved the part about the nub of tree bark hitting the preppy's nose. "Joe, this is gonna be a match made in heaven. Already I can see how it's gonna work. I'm getting' big plans, and it's all because of you that I'm getting' them." She had that excited look that people get right before they get to do the thing that will no doubt become the high point of their lives.

"And who's being matched and who's going to heaven?" I asked.

"Why that would be you and Ben, of course. You see, Joe, what audiences really like the most, aside from car chases and lovey-dovey girls, are examples of male bonding. So, no matter what happens, you and he have to be best buddies. Both of you will stay together through thick and thin. And consider that an executive order. It's one of the carved-in-stone premises of this show. I want the entire audience to see how loyal you are."

I gave her a disconsolate look, and Ben gave me a morose peek right back. He knew that I knew that he was a complete scaredy cat."

"Remember, Joe. I am the director. What I say goes."

"Hey, you've got no argument from me," I told her. "All I do is play drums 'cause I know it's a division of labor around here."

"Friendship is a wonderful thing, isn't it?"

I looked over at Ben and could see that he was doin' a weasely expression in the corner.

Ben's behavior had led to nothing. It had opened me up onto the wide vista of a dead end. I had given him the benefit of the doubt because he was supposed to be the expert. And experts are supposed to be well informed. They've got all their credentials together. I'm so happy for them.

He had pulled this act with a person, so that was on the periphery of forgiveness. But if he pulled this act with a song, I would afford him precious few chances to try this cheap trick again. Going down dead ends for the sake of going down dead ends would be taboo 'cause songs are sacred. They're more important than people. If he didn't make something work, I would have to pick up the pieces and make it work and then take my very own up-close-and-personal executive action. When I do that, people are sure to get pissed. They'll tell me I need to be put in my place. But good luck if you can get me there 'cause I'll only be too happy to slam you into your place first. As far as I could tell, Ben was walkin' into worthlessness.

I thought back to what he did for his day job --- he seemed to like beautiful things that did not move. That explained a lot.

Still, the thing about this that noshed on my soul was that I liked it when he annoyed someone. That way, I could annoy someone by one degree of separation. Doing it that way would somehow make the whole thing not really count. Yes, Jillian was right --- friendship was a wonderful thing.

AN EMOTIONAL SITUATION

Sunita had said that Ben was great at creating music that never was, nor would ever be. Her observation confirmed my initial gut reaction, but I would soon begin to comprehend the depth of her remarks. Even so, I was fully prepared to consider that my judgment might have been too hasty. I'd been thinkin' if this, this, and this were true, then that, that, and that would always be the result. But there never is an always. Something about Ben told me that he wasn't just another crappy bass player with a penchant for anti-social behavior. Maybe I had been too abrupt in my critique?

I say that because there in the corner of the room, I could see Ben playin' beside a saxophone player of the tenor variety. The tenor was groovin' along, his fingers flickering up and down the thick brass buttons of the horn, though I had to say that his playing was a bit stiff. Something was off. The way the tenor man hit the sonorous notes in the lower register mimicked the funky sounds of a certain late, great, and very famous jazz/fusion player. The guy had each and every signature move of the dearly departed musician, but those sounds would be an imitation of the famous reed man when he was having an off night. All of the moves were there, only the feelin' wasn't spot on. Perhaps that was what gave the jam session a certain bizarre charm, what some would call "amiably quirky." I couldn't quite put my finger on exactly what it was. A veneer of perfection had been presumed, but it wasn't completely convincing, especially since it had been juxtaposed against Ben's dilettantism. The tenor man would play melodiously and then would go gritty on the ear before capriciously swerving into a honking squawk that reminded me of certain predatory birds.

After a while, it dawned on me that this was not a real human being at all. This saxophonist --- this thing --- was some sort of cut-and-stitch robot. Could it be that Ben had created this machine by means of a high range technology that wasn't available to the general scientific public? Somehow Ben had taken a little bit of this and mixed it together with a little bit of that and in the grand scheme of things, he had come up with a fair to middlin' approximation of the late great tenor man's playing. But was that really real? No, no way could Ben have done it. The possibilities were whizzin' through my head faster than the saxophone runs that the tenor man was playing. If Ben had in fact pulled off such an extraordinary feat of engineering, then clearly, this robot, this virtual musician, was actually going full throttle into the business of making music that never was, but now had the distinct possibility of actually becoming. The Goddess of Music would be pleased. Somewhere she was applauding.

"Joe, let me introduce you to Gulf. He's the robot that I've been workin' on for the last three years."

Ben put down his bass and unplugged from his amp. He lit a cigarette and blew some smoke into the stuffy air of the windowless room. Gulf got in one last yelp on the tenor and stopped playing. He hung onto his sax and looked as if he was about to say hello to me. He had the comportment of a former frat boy who'd previously been obsessed with sports and craft beer, but after discovering drugs, had now gone head over heels into the spin and sway of music. And that conversion had made him truly blossom. The evidence was that his face was bemused, yet peaceful, similar in many ways to the visage of a sadhu whom I'd once befriended in India. I was waitin' for a gem of wisdom or flippant comment to come out of his mouth. So I waited... and I waited...and it never came. Despite this minor shortcoming, everything about Gulf's countenance suggested that this was a true music man, someone who wouldn't be suckered into the vortex of low echelon dramas and assorted hijinks that often comprise the public personalities of so many pop stars. No, Gulf was different than that.

Right away I could tell he was of a higher order. Even if he was a machine.

Ben took another blasé drag on the cigarette. "C'mon Joe. Lemme show you how he works."

Ben put his index finger on a place near to Gulf's left shoulder and pressed some sort of toggle switch gizmo, at which point Gulf proceeded to slump forward. I thought that Gulf was about to fall on his face, so I rushed to my right in an effort to break his fall, but I soon understood that that wouldn't be necessary. Gulf simply slumped, and he did not deign to fall.

"Ben, what's going on? What's Gulf doing? Who is he?"

"Gulf is not a human, Joe. He's a robot. In fact, he's the latest most up-to-date kind of robot that ever existed. But he's still in the R and D stage. Just now, before you came in, I was running him through his paces."

Ben was justifiably proud of his creation and was quick to open up a panel in Gulf's back which revealed some of the machine's inner workings. There under the lid were the innards of the innovation. It was especially enchanting the way in which the organic and inorganic seemed to flawlessly coexist. Everything about the arrangement of working parts hinted at a matter-of-fact quality imbued with total tranquility. Or did it? Maybe there was a war going on. The cellular skin splayed out like the tendrils and fangs of a pernicious reptile, flowing over the edges and synthetic grooves of the cold metallic circuit boards, giving the impression that cells were about to feast and then gorge on the components of the machine. Or was it the other way around, and the gelatinous plasma was being wolfed down by the man-made parts?

The scene kept me second-guessing at exactly who was eating whom. I gazed in aghast wonder at Gulf's machinery as Ben offered up an explanation of his complicated yet spectacular gadget. No doubt he so wanted to talk shop to someone who would have understood what he was talking about, but I could see in his eyes how he was forcing himself to simplify. "You see, Joe, I had to make an end run around that snooty-nosed intelligent design crowd. They weren't as smarty pants as they thought they were, and they were so totally barkin' up the wrong tree. While they were busy congratulating themselves for nothing, I laughed out loud at their 1960's way of thinking. I knew right from the start that all their sacred cows were wrong. At first, I tried to work with them. I wanted to work with them in the spirit of true collaboration, only it soured fast. Basically, they let me know in no uncertain terms that I had to agree with them, or they would drum me out of the profession. But the problem was that the facts and the data, which were starin' me in the face, were leading me to conclusions that were diametrically opposed to everything they believed. So, I disagreed --- I disagreed long and loudly. And they were only too happy to dismiss me from their ranks. I lost my job. Well, I took a deep breath, stepped back, and tried a different tack. With my new approach, I was successful because I did my research by having one system breed with another system. You see, I kind of let evolution do the heavy lifting for me. It was a gargantuan task, utilizing complex algorithms in the context of frequency filtering. After that, it involved rigorous evaluation of offspring from billions of combinations. In order to comprehend aural information, the process mimics natural selection. I figured if it worked in Nature, then what the hell, why not try it again? Why fight it? I kinda consider myself to be a natural sort of guy."

I looked him in the eye --- he would never be a natural sort of guy. He took a last puff on the cigarette and then stubbed it out.

"Great," I replied. "Don't fight the feelin'. I guess it was a case of computers having massive orgies."

"I suppose that's one way of thinking about it. And if you said that, you would be pretty accurate. You see, evolution takes millions of years, sometimes more. But I don't have that kind of time to wait around twiddlin' my thumbs, nor does anyone else. So, your comparison to orgies is not that far off because, when doing this research, you need to have very promiscuous machines so you can get the maximum amount of progeny, which in turn means you can get the biggest bang for the buck with the results. I tell ya it was polygyny and polyandry on a massive scale. Inputs were paired up with outputs. Each machine had his or her very own hot and heavy stable of stars. Porno for machines. No puny librarian libidos were allowed. The more results I have, the more I can hone in on the best choices. So, you see, the machines need to have free rein to gorge themselves silly on all the delights the cyborg garden has to offer. Then I get to be God, so I can edit all the choices. Now the only trouble is that I've got to find suitable partners for Gulf. To do that, I'm gonna have to find viable candidates from the human female community. So I need to merge the hard circuitry with the wetware of the brain. And I've had decent but not perfect results. I guess you could say it's a work in progress. Another huge improvement is that Gulf operates by synthetic touch. He can feel in the sense of touch, but he doesn't stop there. He has synthetic emotion as well. That's why he's going to be such a great musician. He'll be able to put feeling into his playing by pretending to be happy or making believe that he's sad. And he'll be capable of imitating any nuance or gradation on the wide spectrum of that continuum. And nobody'll ever know the difference between that and the real thing. To me, that's kinda sorta the *piece de la resistance.* Singin' the blues will never be quite the same. As you can see, Gulf is pretty darned impressive. Don't you think?"

I gave him the short super-polite applause that one hears at certain salons, the kind where the tips of the fingers go light on the palms of the hand. "Bravo! That's what we need in this world of ours --- another actor. But I can see he's going to be the consummate thespian because he'll be so in touch with his emotions. He'll be able to inhabit them and detach from them at will. And emotions are the wild frontier."

"Yes, emotions. That's the category where I really upped the ante. And for Gulf, emotions are brand new. They haven't lost their sheen. He hasn't gotten bored with them the way so many humans have. But he's still trying to gauge them and to know where their limits are. Lucky for him, his virgin memory gets to interact with emotions that have none of those lingering stains from a troubled past which require so much psychological elbow grease and rigorous scouring just to facilitate the minimal semblance of a happy existence. Nonetheless, sometimes the novelty of his feelings swells up from below to overwhelm him, and at other times they barely register. At this juncture of his development, he has a distinct tendency to over and under-compensate. His level of socialization is a little wonky. Moderation is not his strong point. So, for him, the music thing is a kind of therapy to bring his emotions into the proper perspective."

"Aha, music as checks and balances! The forefathers would have been proud."

Ben rubbed the surface of his creation and took on a new thought: "Do you remember those big aquarium tanks that were in back of us when we played together at the club the other night?"

"How could I forget. Glowin' and flashin' and brimmin' with light like that, those fish were downright kaleidoscopic. I thought I was looking into a camera obscura with fireworks."

"They put on a good light show, didn't they?"

"Wow! I'll say they did!"

"Well, I was the one who convinced the club owner Jim to use that for a light show instead of the usual stroboscopic globular effects. That enigmatic species of fish --- the cuttlefish --- communicates by means of color. You might say they wear their emotions on their sleeves. Their reality is devoid of words. Their colors do all the talking for them, so they get right to the point."

"I guess they have no use for privacy. Their fantasies are on constant display, and they don't have an embarrassed bone in their entire bodies. They cut through all the bullshit and let it all hang out. Their most embarrassing feelings have it the worst 'cause they have absolutely no place to hide. It's sorta like havin' a glass bathroom in the middle of the living room."

"Not exactly. You see, they have been known to blush. They like to blend in, and I suppose there would be a good case to be made that they're the ultimate bullshit artists. But what I did, which was where others fell short, was to identify their pure emotions. I cut through their three main points of obfuscation. There were only three, and the scientific experts like to call 'em 'uniform, mottled, and disruptive.' So, once I'd figured out how to be uniform, mottled, and disruptive right back, I could fool them. When that happened, they were vulnerable, and I could zero in on their pure emotions. But you're correct. After you see right through their camouflage, it's a eureka moment." Ben paused to let this sink in. He kept me waiting.

"Aw, c'mon man," I replied. "Now you're actin' like a cuttlefish."

"How true! So, while we were playing music at the club the other night, the cuttlefish were reacting to the sounds that we created up there on the stage. You see, right about when I was beginning my experiments with robotics, I was also going into an extended study of those slippery creatures. Here, let me show you. Follow me."

Ben led me into a side room off from his main laboratory. There in the center of the room was a large tank which housed two of the fish that he had just described. I watched as the creatures languidly floated through the salt water in the tank, looping their jelly-like flaps over one another like ethereal lovers. As they did this, their colors changed, sometimes gradually and at other times suddenly, from green to red to blue and then right back again. Then their tentacles did a slow motion, tai chi, sugar-push dance motion with the billowing skirts of their primitive fins. I got the eerie vibe that they were reacting to my presence and were trying to make a good impression, which made their unconventional forms downright puzzling because at first I didn't think they were capable of such a performance, but in no time at all, they won me over, and I didn't know whether to clap my hands or shake the primitive fins. I quickly opted in honor of applause.

"Joe, let me introduce you to Vim and Vod. They have varieties of intelligence that neither you nor I can ever begin to conceive of, let alone fathom. However, they have a very practical function. Most of the time, they reside behind the stage at Jim's Bar. In that setting, their job is to create liquid mobiles for drunks to contemplate. You see, looking at them often becomes a deeply meditative experience. The boozers really get off on it. But today Jim gave them the afternoon off, so they're payin' me a visit. I brought them over for some quality time. They love each other, and as you can see, their having a grand old get-together today. They're giving Gulf something to contemplate. You'll notice that they're equipped with the full complement of emotions. What I did was to incorporate certain aspects of their emotional palate into my research with robotics. And

I've had stunning success. Previous experimenters with robotics had the mistaken notion that emotions and machines didn't mix. Although I believe those people were partly correct, I figured I'd better cover every base. If you're gonna have artificial intelligence, you should probably go all the way. And cuttlefish seemed as though they would be as good a place to start as any other."

He clearly wanted me to have several seconds to register and then to savor the depths of his achievements, so he didn't say anything while I gazed at the strangely colored creatures as they drifted around the aquarium, all the while melting from one emotion into another. Occasionally, I could see what he'd meant by the uniform, mottled, and disruptive thing, which made me feel a deep desire to change the color of my skin too. In fact, I almost wished that I could snap my fingers and become a rainbow myself just so I could keep up with them.

At length, he interrupted the show of light, saying, "Come with me. I'd like to show you something else."

He led me back to Gulf and flipped another toggle switch, this one near the back of the machine's neck. The switch activated some sort of sprocket mechanism, and the top of Gulf's head popped open. "Let me show you his brain. Don't be shy. Have a look."

I moved forward and peered into the thing's brain. So this was where all the action was. I was surprised to see that the lobes and creases in the machine man's cerebrum, cortex, and cerebellum pulsated with the same intensity as the floating cuttlefish. Gulf's brain was a vibrant rainbow racked with blinking slivers of pinpointed light: turquoise, burgundy, vermilion, orange, lustrous purple, yellow and pink topaz, crystalline shades of jade, and rich oscillations of shining ebony, the total effect being not unlike the iridescent flash that one sees upon suddenly opening a jewelry box. It was such a scene of spiritual beauty! Just lookin' at it, I was practically slain in the spirit. And whether these opalescent points comprised a fake or real intelligence was rendered into being a moot issue. The thing looked real. It certainly had the appearance of harboring and fostering an authentic intelligence. That was close enough.

"Yes, Joe. Gulf's having emotions too. And in a way not so very different from our cuttlefish friends. Let me show you something else." Ben pressed the toggle lever in different directions and Gulf's face, depending on the way in which Ben manipulated the gradations of the switch, changed from giddiness, to buoyancy, to exhilaration, to pathos, to anguish, and finally to melancholia. That was the big one. Tears began to stream down the machine's cheeks and the lips curled in response to some unknown torment.

Ben continued with his demonstration. "I almost get teary-eyed watching the show. And don't you see, it all starts with touch. I suppose it's sorta like what you as a drummer are doin'. You have a certain gift for touch, for slammin' the sticks on the heads of the kit, and from that, you're able to take the audience to an ecstatic moment." Ben flipped the lever back in the other direction, and the machine responded accordingly. "You see, we're gonna go back to basics, to an emotion that always a favorite. Right about now, Gulf is having a frenzied moment."

I could see that Gulf was indisposed: he was in the midst of some sort of epiphany. His cheeks and forehead were wrinkled into the contortions of laughter. His brain continued to blink, sparkle, and twitch, and his face nodded in appreciation for whatever it was that he was thinking.

"Joe, I believe you and Gulf and the cuttlefish have more in common than you think."

I was thinking but not saying, yeah, that would be because I was a man and his cymbals. But that was of secondary importance. I was having a hard time keeping my own emotions in check, let alone pondering the possibilities of the fake emotions that were soon to be felt by Gulf and then foisted upon the world at large. Right away, the competitive urges were beginning to seethe and rally within me because my instincts knew a threat when they could behold it. And since Gulf was going to be fake, I figured I might as well be that way too, so I decided to put on a pretty good show of disingenuous amazement. "Ben, you've really outdone yourself. It's all pretty darned amazin'. Gulf is definitely an improvement over Ziggy the Beat Box."

"Oh God. Don't remind me. Ziggy was child's play. I'd still like to get Ziggy back into active rotation, maybe for a song or two. I'm currently in talks with Jillian about doing that, and she keeps givin' me a big fat no. But my long range plan is to get Gulf into the band. You see, Joe, Gulf's gone way beyond image analysis, speech recognition, and adaptive control. By now, he's feeding forward into the neural networks. When tasks are repeated, the bonds between the neurons get more muscular. They wanna burst out and get to doin' something. And if they're gonna do that, then it might as well be somethin' new instead of somethin' old."

"Yeah, sorta like practice. Which is somethin' I thought you weren't too keen on."

"You're right. I hate practice. That's why I want to delegate it to Gulf. He's almost at the stage where he can improvise. That's the ultimate goal. None of that reading specks on lines of staff paper for my baby. This ain't no symphony sophomoric philharmonic!" He waved his arms laterally and vertically in the manner of an intense classical conductor before continuing on his rant. "Nosiree! I want him to be able to make it up on the spot --- every damned bit of it!"

I drew closer at the maze of circuitry that inhabited Gulf's very realistic looking back. In fact, the surface of his back was so realistic that he looked as if he could use a quick trip to the spa to have some pretty Asian lady rip out the hair with a strip of sticky tape. But no big deal. From the vantage point of an imaginary audience, he had the look of being an almost person. Maybe at some point, he could become an almost musician. I could almost picture him standing up there on stage eager to jump into the next chorus of whatever song Gwen and Kathy had conjured up.

Ben went into an explanatory mode: "I wanna be able to manipulate the sound of this virtual saxophone machine, so my laptop can spit out notes in the same way that the legendary Lex Pattin would play them. That's the guy whose playing I programed and patterned him on."

"I'll bet that might cause a few problems with the estate of late great tenor saxophonist Lex Pattin."

"Not to worry. Lex was a musician for cryin' out loud, so how powerful could the estate be? Answer --- not very! The internet has seen to that. His estate can whistle for their money. Ha, ha, ha! My lawyers are more bad-ass than his lawyers."

His voice trailed off, and he took on a more serious tone. "But all joking aside, you have to understand that it wouldn't be as if we were havin' Lex right there on stage with us. No, no. Absolutely no way. I mean, what are people out there in the audience all the way back in Row Double Z gonna say? Are they gonna tell us, 'Yo Ben my man, isn't that Lex jammin' with you?' And I'll tell 'em no. 'If you think it's Lex, then go ahead and prove it. Prove it to me right here and now. I freakin' double-dare ya!'"

I laughed an uneasy laugh. Not only was Ben a crappy bass player, but he was also a creepy bass player. Then I stared at Gulf again. I wanted to say, "Gulf, you're such an underachiever!" I studied his fake face and then glanced at Ben. I was appreciating the fact that I could most likely come to like Gulf far sooner than that would ever happen with Ben. Perhaps I could help his fledgling emotions along as a kind of mentor because maybe even synthetic emotions might become worthy of empathy. In the history of lots of things, this hadn't really come up before. But then a humorous thought entered my mind: yes, of course Gulf would qualify for empathy. Having such a jerk of a dad would be more than enough for him to make the grade. And Ben was nothing if not that.

"I suppose you're right," I replied. "I mean, what kind of accusations could they come up with --- that you stole Lex's persona? How can you steal his persona? Lex is dead, and Gulf isn't even a real person, so how can he have a persona, let alone steal a persona from someone else? But you'd be surprised at how far the law goes when it comes to persona stealin'. They get more crazy on that score than they do with theft of services. Ask any person infected with that Hollywood bullshit. I'd almost be willin' to bet that bein' a machine would be a big issue as far as that's concerned."

"He'll be able to beat the pants off of anything that the late great Lex Pattin might have played. He'll be able to do all the stuff Lex never got around to doing. I guarantee it. Gulf will be able to see the full palette of notes that are at his beck and call, and he'll be fully capable of summoning them at will. He'll have the capacity to cherry pick the best note for the right moment. Think of what that'll do for the so-called spirituality of music. The world will become a better place, and best of all, Gulf will be totally devoid of ego."

"I suppose his ego will be in the service of your ego?"

"You're darned right it will. And I'll make him toe the line! Under my tutelage, he'll act like he's in some sorta Marine boot camp. But the other thing that'll be great about having Gulf in the band is that I'll never again have to worry about making a mistake because Gulf's playing will be like so totally spot on. Mistakes will only be a dim memory."

Yes, I shuddered to think, but did not say. I recalled how just the other day Ben had said what a scaredy cat he was about making mistakes. Poor boy! It must have been such a huge relief for him to look forward to that ideal prospect. "So," I replied, "What we have here is the latest in artificial intelligence?"

"Absolutely. Gulf can emote. And I wanna take my time and gloat. Artificial intelligence once had a bright and sunny future only to run into some awful disappointments. Don't get me started on how many dead ends there have been. However, I've done a more-than-decent job of ironing out the kinks in the process. But that's not enough. Anyone can cobble together some sort of perfect recording. It's so commonplace that people don't pay attention to it anymore. They yawn their faces off. Audiences want something new. And that's what I wanna give 'em. What I wanna do is to be able to make it so the new virtual side man can actually look as though he's playin' right there on stage with you and Kathy and Gwen and me. Wouldn't that be semi-spectacular?"

"Yes, I suppose it would." I paused to scratch my chin 'cause I knew I was lyin' through my teeth.

Ben touched the toggle switch on Gulf's shoulder again, and this time the machine responded abruptly by walking a few feet to a closet which he entered. Turning around to face me, Gulf waved goodbye before shutting the door. His sax still lay on the table. Ben said, "So that's it for today. Show-and-tell is over for now. But sometime soon, I wanna get Gulf into the band. I think it'll do wonders for the overall sound. That would have ripe possibilities for interaction. I've got some big plans --- I wanna make Gulf as a prototype for others of his kind. As I see it, there should be lots more. One Gulf is not enough. He screams out for more. As far as the near horizon is concerned, we could probably get some amazin' video footage that Jillian could use for the show. And the thing is, nobody in the audience will have a clue that Gulf isn't a real person."

"Well, it might be fun to keep 'em guessing."

"Oh, you mean like the way they're guessing now about you?"

"What do you mean by that?"

"I mean you're sorta like Gulf. You're not all human either."

Damn! How did Ben figure that one out? He had wandered full force into a touchy subject. I looked at my watch. Yes, it was time to be going. I had to practice drums. I had to do Neanderthal things. And Gulf had to do cuttlefish things. I told Ben that I looked forward to jamming with Gulf sometime soon. And it would be great to have a sax player in the band. Perhaps Gulf could be a novelty item? I mean, there probably weren't a hell of a lot of groups with a robot on staff. I said goodbye and thanked him for showing me where he worked. Then I went back in the direction of the front entrance.

I walked through the parlor where the young lady from two days ago had been laid out in her fancy box. To my surprise, she was still there. She hadn't changed much. She was still looking like a bigger version of a Barbie doll, and she was still sound asleep. Like totally conked out. Life had flown the coop. Kaput! And that was rather odd because how long did Ben plan on keeping her around? Didn't she have someplace where she had to be goin'? Like the graveyard maybe? Then in a flash it occurred to me! She wasn't really dead. She had simply been put on hold. Would it be possible that she was just another one of Ben's robots and the funeral thing was all a bunch of smoke and mirrors? I looked at the flowers that surrounded her motionless form. They were beginning to wilt.

Ben entered the room and went up to the girl in the coffin. "Oh, I suppose you're wondering about her. I don't believe I introduced you. Joe, meet Gina. She's one of the cyborg females that I tried to mate with Gulf. You see, she didn't quite work out. She wasn't entirely viable, so I couldn't adequately mingle the wetware with the circuitry. She turned out to be just another routine cyborg hybridization. How boring! The whole experience made it increasingly clear to me that if I want a good match, I'll most likely have to get a real human female for Gulf. I mean, the DNA from both parties will be so surprised it won't know what hit it."

"Yes, when they go skinny-dipping in the genetic pool, they won't have to worry about diving in and bumping their heads on the bottom."

He leaned over the seemingly dead body that was cushioned and cradled in the folds of the elaborate satin bower. He adjusted the upper shoulder of Gina's dress to reveal another toggle switch which he activated, immediately causing her to sit up in the casket. She opened her eyes in the same way she'd tried but failed to open her eyes two days before, only this time she was successful. She stared directly into mine. Needless to say, I was seriously spooked. I turned to look at Ben, and he was laughing uncontrollably. I nearly turned again to run, but Ben flicked the toggle switch one more time and the young lady went back into her state of perpetual repose.

"Jeez, Ben. When I saw her two days ago, I thought I was hallucinatin', but I guess she really is a machine."

"No, she's a mixed bag. Half and half."

Ben let out a dismissive sigh and continued. "But no problem. Sometimes ya win, and sometimes ya lose. You hafta be patient and hang in there. I wanna see how the neurons in the brain get and stay connected. Decoding the cells in the early visual cortex is not a walk in the park. That one takes a lot of time to tune and tinker. But I'm a very confident fellow. There are days when I take Gulf out, and he and I go girl-watching. I do that because I want to get a feel for what turns him on. Then I take him back to the lab and make the necessary adjustments. I let him know that someday soon he'll find the woman of his dreams. And I'll be the one to find her for him." Ben pointed to the primped and packaged Barbie doll. "This one just wasn't his type of girl. I think he really likes women with a bit more of a Mediterranean complexion. None of that wispy Waspy femininity for him! Anyway, that's what he keeps tellin' me. I like it that he's getting real particular and fussy about the girls he finds desirable. I mean, he's almost like a rock star in that regard. No doubt that will serve him well when it comes to the sax-playing thing."

"Watch it with that. If you don't nip the rock star bullshit in the bud, soon he'll want you to spend all of your time taking green M&M's out of the buffet spread. If that happens, it would be hard to wean him from his pain-in-the-ass ways."

"Good point. I'll be sure to keep that in mind. But, as I was saying, I tell him to be patient. I'll get him exactly what he wants. When we accomplish that, then we can look forward to a good mating and the next Gulf will be even better. I'll call him Son of Gulf, and he'll be a fully functional improviser. I tell ya, this whole experience has got me to think and feel as though I'm some kind of first-time dad. I mean, who would've thunk it?

Well, I for one woulda never have thunk it. Ben woulda made an absolutely horrible parent.

But Ben continued: "Yes, I'm a proud parent, and Gulf is my boy. And I want only the best for him."

"Yeah man, I suppose that being a parent has its rewards. Only thing is, why limit yourself to teaching him how to play saxophone? You could teach him how to throw a baseball too. But then again, maybe not 'cause he looks too old for Little League."

Then I turned my attention back to the cool and silent girl in the ornate jewel box. "So what are ya goin' to be doin' with her?"

"Gina's one of my failures. I mean, look at her. She's insufficiently Mediterranean. Gulf was just not that into her. But she wasn't all for naught. Hell no, I learned a lot from her, but now it's time for her to go. Tomorrow she's going to her final rest out at Happy Valley. I like to line up all my failures and then when the time comes, I can take care of them all in one fell swoop. It's more economical that way."

Ben nodded to me, indicating that the show-and-tell had concluded for the second time. Then he lowered the lid over the sleeping Barbie doll.

But the show-and-tell really wasn't completely over. No, no, no --- not by a long shot. Ben had one more false exit still in him. With an upwardly pointing finger, he turned around like an old school TV detective and blurted out another bit of his expensive food for thought: "Joe, you see, it's like this --- before I got involved in this robotics stuff, I'd been doin' lots of thinking, and I came to a rather strange conclusion about life in general."

Hell, everything about Ben was rather strange. Why should this revelation be any different? He lingered on this statement as if to prompt my reply. I let him linger, but the pause got to be too long, so I figured I might as well ask him what his strange conclusion was since he was damned if he would volunteer it. That was another thing I was slowly discovering about Ben, which was that he liked to test people out by having them endure lots of dead air, so he could see how they reacted.

"OK," I finally said. "What was it? What further profound and cryptic thoughts did you come up with about this life-in-general business?"

He could sense the annoyance in my voice, which no doubt in his mind, lent credence to the point he was about to make. "Joe, I've decided that I really don't like people very much. In fact, I'll go one step further and say that I'm pretty sure I hate 'em. I hate 'em all. I feel it with a passion. There's not one redeeming feature."

"Oh, I get it now. That's rather bold of you. The reason for all of this robotics research is that you think you can do better. You believe you can produce a superior prototype than simple old garden variety Homo Sapiens."

"Exactly. You nailed it. That's how I feel about the whole thing."

"It's so nice to know how you really feel. Too many people hide their emotions, and when that happens, it usually leads to some sort of unhappiness or misunderstanding. But gosh, Ben. With this overabundance of candidness, you've got me wondering now. You put me in a quandary."

"How so?"

"If you hate human beings, then where the hell does that leave me?"

"Oh, I know what you're thinkin'. But don't you worry about a thing 'cause believe me --- even the cuttlefish know what you're thinkin'. You're safe because both you and I know that you're not completely human yourself. You're not one of *them*."

"Yes, Ben. I was afraid of that. You would have to figure it out, wouldn't you?"

"Don't you fret. Your secret is safe. It's the reason that I picked you."

"Picked me for what?"

"Oh you think I invited you over here today as some sort of happenstance. No, no way! I've got it all thought out. I selected you because I thought that crude quality in you would make you an ideal companion for Gulf. What I mean is, you could kind of be his life coach. You could help steer him in the right direction. In that way, you could be very useful to me and to Gulf."

"Gee, Ben. That's great. The blind leading the blind. I've always wanted to be that kind of a friend. He and I will stumble along together, bumblin' into whatever hardships life has to offer. But look, I really have to go. I've got lots of things to do today."

"So go. Go ahead and do what you gotta do. And here, have a drink on me." He reached into his wallet and produced a ten dollar bill which he stuffed into my shirt pocket. "Ha! That's another thing I figured out about you right from the start!"

"What's that?"

"That you're a drunk."

I was getting the impression that Ben could look into my skull in much the same way as he was able to look into Gulf's.

But before I could say anything, he said, "We'll talk later. And I'll see ya at practice. Oh, and enjoy that drink, you hear?"

Yes, I heard and only too loudly. It was good that the three of us could be so open about our feelings.

I fished around for my car keys and went on my way wondering if he hated people so much, then why did he bother to go to so much trouble to give Gulf feelings? He should have made him out to be a cold heartless bastard just like dear old dad. But no, that was too simple an explanation. He had to give him a simulated heart and a pretend soul just for the sake of the challenge. For Ben, the situation was like looking up at steep mountains that needed to be climbed --- he would always want to scale them just because they were there and he needed to see over the top of them. He might not have believed in feelings: however, that didn't mean he couldn't put them to some purpose of his own devising.

But as I put the key in the ignition, I couldn't help thinking about what would happen if I outlived my usefulness. Would I be relegated to becoming another disposable mishmash of a creature like Gina had been? Hadn't she simply outlived her usefulness? Clearly, I had to do something for my own protection. And since I was apparently being groomed to be Gulf's mentor, and since Gulf was supposedly going to be an alleged musician, then perhaps the time was quickly drawing near when I would have to investigate the possibility of seeing how well Gulf would handle drugs.

So, I went and had that drink that Ben had bought me. And then I had some more. And then I had some more after that. That was right about when my ideas got brighter and brighter until they positively sparkled and lit up my head. It didn't last long though. Without any warning, it disappeared. Then the sadness was overwhelming, as if a giant wave had slurped itself from out of the nearby sea, only to jump over the dunes and the boardwalk and drench me to the bone. I got to thinking, indeed I got to obsessing, about that creature of Ben's creation. Something about the situation wasn't quite fair. It wasn't right that Gina should be thrown away like that --- to be chucked out like so much trash. I resolved that something had to be done and done soon. After draining the last of the Wild Turkey, I left the bar and quickly drove back to Ben's place of business, being extra careful what with the drinkin' and drivin' and all.

By now he had closed up for the evening, although I have to say there was no problem breaking in. I've learned a few things from my days as an addict. Certain tricks work like a charm. I mean, they never get old. And that one was sure as hell no different. I was hoping and hoping. I was hoping it wasn't too late. Yes, the coffin was still closed. No doubt the disposition would not be until tomorrow. The only problem might be the lock. Surprisingly, the lock didn't present much of a problem either. Clearly, my life skills were being put to productive use. After opening the ornate box, the next obstacle would be to start up the gizmo. And there it was right under the fold in the neckline of her dress! I quickly flicked the switch, and right on cue, she sat up yet again within the delicate case of rose satin velvet. Honey, we have to stop meeting like this! This time her eyes were wide open. I knew that nothing would shut them now. This time she'd be wide awake forever. However, she still didn't talk. Hell, something told me she'd figure that one out in due course. You can't rush this stuff. Something about her face told me she'd been waiting for me. So I helped her out of box, and at first she was unsteady on her legs, staggering back and forth like a colt that had just been born. But then she found her stride. I glanced at her outfit --- she was wearing the classic little black dress, and she was rockin' it. No doubt she would survive and survive well in a hostile climate. She could live by her wits, her body, and then some. I gave serious thought to what Ben had said about her bein' what was it --- half and half? What did fortune have in store for her in this precarious existence? I wished her well with whatever it was that she had to work with deep inside her rag and bone of a brain. I let her out the front door and watched her carefully as she lurched down the street on her high heels. Not to worry. She would get the hang of it. I thought about those mean and inconsiderate things that Ben had said about her and how Gulf wouldn't like her because she wasn't the apple of his eye, about how she had a "wispy Waspy" beauty that some wouldn't appreciate. But as I watched her stumbling down the street on her newfound legs and stiletto heels, I muttered to myself, "Don't worry, sweetheart. Someday some boy will love you with your wispy Waspy-ness and all."

GET THIS SHOW ON THE ROAD

Most mornings I fight with my clothes, and this one was no different. For Neanderthals, pockets are especially oppositional --- they just won't cooperate when I'm getting ready to greet the day, so I usually wind up saying something like, "Pocket, you're going down!" Well, after I'd subdued the unruly offender who was passive/aggressively holding my spare change, I looked in the mirror, gave my hair a quick tousle, joodged my collar, and left the hotel room. It was late morning on the day after the most recent auspicious gig. I mean, there were so many that I'd sorta lost count. I thought about the new lead singer. She could be dangerous. If given half a chance, clamoring tom toms could make her that way. I muttered to myself, "Don't worry, girl. I've got a vivid imagination. It can take you to the stratosphere. I could drop you off there, or I could take you home." That made me feel like a million dollars --- semi-divine, as if I would be conquering the world in very short order. The only thing delaying me from making that an accomplished fact were a few trivial details that needed to be put in order. Until then, I had time to kill.

I knew at some point that I would have to think more deeply about whatever demented hellhole Ben had tunneled into. It seemed that Ben was quite the innovator. Under his stewardship, the gap between dead and alive had been foreshortened or maybe eclipsed. The lovely Gina, the one that I'd just released out into the wild --- she was Exhibit A for that. What in God's name was that girl --- cyborg, robot, clone, or just plain old reanimated corpse, or worse yet, a Frankenstein monster? Ben had hinted that Gina was a small taste of what might be multiplied into larger things to come. While surveying the flatness of the ocean, I was thinking about what would happen if there were whole battalions of her kind, upgraded of course and refined into beings of increasingly higher order, since Ben had been so forthcoming in spelling out his grand intentions to me.

But these speculations were far too much to ponder right then and there. Later, later --- I would deal with that further on down the road. This dilemma was depraved, but it wasn't about me. I didn't create it, so it would have to be put on hold. The band---that was so much more important.

The bright morning sky got me to thinkin' about the demographic I belong to. You and me, we're Neanderthals. Our natural inclination is to put our handprints on the walls of caves, so we'll have better luck shooting the mammoths, but we live in civilization and that's not an option. As a next best thing, we have to think about it. Our hands give us power, enabling us to control the days and win by default. We have to keep the win streak goin'. That's why we blacken up our hands with soot and print them on the cavern wall right between the stalagmites and stalactites. And when that happens, the next day is a sunny dream of complete bounty beyond any earlier expectation. And late at night on the day before the chase, we play some music on our flutes and wooden drums. Chuka-chuka-chuka. La-di-dah, la-di-dah. That way we'll have plenty of luck to tide us through. But enough of this stuff. You know what I'm talkin' about. It's neither here nor there 'cause there are other fish to fry, and you are also well aware that we're ambivalent about hand/eye coordination. It's the reason we have to get in so darned close to the wooly beasts in order to close the deal. Throwing a spear is such an issue. It's too damned obvious --- sort of like Mayans knowing about the wheel, but reserving it only as toys for their children. I wanna tell 'em, "It's okay. I can dig where you're comin' from!" You see, to us, throwing is synonymous with cheating. There's something darned dishonest about it. It offends the spirit, and more importantly, our sense of violence. We love to pay lip service to the notion that the best violence keeps the tricks to a bare minimum --- what you see is what you get in the mouth. Just because our imagination tells us what to do doesn't mean we have to obey. In dreams, Neanderthals and Cro-Mags do any number of crimes on a nightly basis. We're both guilty. That much we have in common, yet our stubborn refusal to obey means that in the long run we leave ourselves open to those who would comply. I keep telling them we shouldn't be demure so easily. That's our fatal flaw.

A great interest sidled up to me: I had the urge to be high up in the sky first looking down upon this petty ridiculous world of ours and then staring out to sea. The sea made me think about Ben's cuttlefish and how they liked to change color. Sometimes I wished I could change color. The cuttlefish seemed to be fond of blue. It worked for them. But I wondered what green and purple had in store. No matter. Like I said, I would think about it later. I went to the boardwalk to see if there were any rides operating yet. Perhaps the Ferris wheel or one of the roller coasters had started, or better yet, that back-and-forth swinging pirate ship ride that I always enjoyed so much? No such luck. It was too early for any of those. For the next best thing, I settled for a miniature golf range. What I liked most about this place was that each hole had a theme of sorts --- dinosaurs on the par three fifth, mermaids on the par five tenth, and sea serpents on the par four thirteenth. The best part was the third hole where you had to shoot under a red windmill, banking the ball off from the green monster in the middle, then through a squiggly section and finally into the hole. I was beyond confident, but nonetheless, a bit concerned; lately these bouts of megalomania were occurring with increasing frequency. Most likely the drum was responsible. "He" was the culprit!

I assessed the first hole. The club selection was rather limited, but no big deal.

Lining up the ball and doing my best Tiger Woods impersonation, I muttered to myself: "If Myers sinks this putt, he wins the British Open."

I moved the putter back and made a smooth stroke. The ball went through the whole obstacle course and lipped the cup before coming to rest on the blue bumpers in the corner. So much for omnipotence.

"Aw no. Myers gets another chance 'cause he wasn't really trying."

Golf is bar none the hardest game ever --- the perfect combination of mind and body, but hell, this wasn't golf. This was closer to Donkey Kong, Q-Bert, or Lady Bug. Where was Coily the Purple Snake? Where were Ugg and Wrong-Way? Or the hordes of dragons waiting to eat up my ball before it got to the hole? They must be around there somewhere, I thought. I went to retrieve the ball and to see what contraptions, booby traps, and predicaments the next hole held in store, but stopped short when I saw a familiar unpleasant face --- there was Ugg! It was the thin ugly one I'd had the dust up with back in Seaside Heights. He had my ball, and he and his fat friend Wrong-Way were coming toward me. The thin one threw the ball at me, and it caught me squarely in the shoulder. Wincing in pain, I turned and ran, knowing full well that one of them would be shooting at me in a split second. I slipped behind the orange stucco pterodactyl whose enormous bat wings graced the seventh hole and took a sharp dive and somersault down the embankment. Sure enough, I heard a shot ringing out and caroming off the stucco as I landed on my feet. A sliver of shrapnel winged me on the elbow. Seeing the thugs out of the corner of my eye, I darted into the crowd and sprinted toward the end of the pier where it was pretty easy to blend in with the crowd. Still, I kept up a furious trot before cutting through a cotton candy stand, bumping into a balloon blowing clown, and then tiptoeing along the lip of pier on the other side of the water park near a row of coin-operated telescopes. I didn't have a lot of leeway. The distance from the wall to the drop off into the water was about six inches. I gingerly sidestepped along the narrow strip and doubled back by going around the wall surrounding the water park. The ocean looked inviting --- swirling, turbulent, and more than a little primordial soup-like. I considered myself lulled --- the Goddess was beckoning me. I was half-tempted to jump in, but I thought better of it and fought off the impulse until I came to the end of the wall where I peered around the corner. There they were --- Ugg and Wrong-Way --- peeking over the edge looking for me.

"Bill, you had him and you let him get away. What the hell's wrong with you?" He slammed his fist on the railing to make his point.

"Andy, it wasn't such an easy shot, and besides, in case you didn't notice, we're not exactly in a remote unpopulated area right now."

Andy was pissed off at his partner. "You were playing with him."

"So what if I was. It was fun."

"Fun! What the hell is that? Explain to me where fun even enters into the picture. Listen man, we've got a job to do, which is to shoot this guy and shoot him fast. You know Bill, maybe you're not cut out for this line of work. Maybe you could do with less improvisation and a bit more structure. Also, far be it for me to tell you what to do, but could I see a little more subtlety, a little more finesse from you?"

"I *am* being subtle. Hell, I'm an artist for God's sake. I'm only doing this hit man stuff on the side. You knew that when you took me on."

"I knew it! I should never have taken on a dilettante. I only did it as a favor to Alex."

"Sorry, tough luck. What's done is done. Besides, killing him outright is so damned ... obvious. Why not do something a bit more indirect?"

"My friend, there are few things more direct than a bullet slamming into someone's skull. I'm *telling* you to be direct. Leave your palette and brushes at home."

"Andy, I'll see what I can do. But for the record, we hardly ever use a palette and brushes anymore. Most of the time it's whatever objects we find on the street."

"Yeah, well fix it, and fix it now!" He smacked him on the back. "Listen pal, if you don't shape up and shape up soon, I might have to be whacking you instead of this Joe the loser guy. Do you understand?"

They both laughed uneasily.

"Yeah, I get it."

"Good. Well sear it into your brain!" Just to drive home his point, he slapped his left hand with his right before continuing with the thought. "I love that moment when people understand each other. It's an epiphany of sorts. Since you're an *artiste,* I'm sure you would appreciate that."

"OK, OK. Like I said, I get it, Andy"

I edged back on my precarious position, but could still hear the rest of their conversation clearly.

"Bill, it looks like our quarry got away this time, but don't worry --- he can't go far. We'll catch up. In the meantime, let me talk to you about my very own incentive program. I told Alex that I might have some doubts about your talents. I let him know that I have faith in you. You may be a beginner, but you show potential. And potential should be rewarded. That's why I want you to know that if this hit goes down alright, and I have every reason to believe that it will, then there's gonna be more in it for you. The reason I say that is because our client has a little old lady stashed away in some nursing home. And this little old lady is worth millions. So, if we do this right, the gravy train might never stop. We just might get the chance to off the little old lady. Of course, that one might be a bit tricky. It might mean that we have to be even more on top of things in the finesse department --- if ya know what I mean."

"Hey man, I never signed on to hit some little old lady! That might be right about where I draw the line."

"Aw c'mon, Bill. Don't be so high and mighty for God sake! Is that what I get for havin' faith in you? Right now, you make me wanna rethink the whole deal."

From my perch, I could hear the sound of Andy giving Bill a smack. Then one smack was followed by another and another until I could hear Bill's voice starting to sound contrite.

"What do I have to do, Bill, to get you to freakin' behave?"

There was still another smack --- this one bigger than the others. "Yeah man, how's that one for a bit more incentive?"

I peeked around the corner to get a side view of their faces. Yes, right then, the guy named Bill was lookin' submissive, like some kind of wolf exposin' his neck to another of his kind.

"OK, Bill. I'm so glad we got all of that straightened out. That's so important, doncha think?" He whacked him again.

"Yes, I do believe that's a great idea. Now where the hell is this rat bastard? Let's get him."

They stared out to sea again and then looked down. That was their big mistake. They were leaning out looking into the churning water that crashed into the pilings at the base of the pier. It warmed the cockles of my heart to see that the Atlantic Ocean had amped up the surf from what it had been the previous night. Today it was downright hypnotic --- a true siren who demanded a sacrifice. And that was what I would give her. I had my chance, and I took it. We Neanderthals might have our hang-ups about throwing, but we have no misgivings about pushing. It didn't take much for me to shove both of them headfirst over the railing. Their momentum followed the path of least resistance and in they went, going ass over teakettle. I didn't stop to see them hit the water. Glug, glug, glug! There ya go ya great big Ugg. In that split second, I turned tail and raced back to the main part of the boardwalk. A change in venue would be required. Returning breathlessly to the hotel room, I hurriedly threw my belongings in a bag, and ran down to the front desk to pay my bill, before heading in the direction of the bus terminal.

Under these rapidly changing circumstances, I thought it best to make some quick phone calls. The first was to touch base with my elderly senile mom, the same elderly senile mum that the thug named Andy had just now referred to. After all, the whole reason for the thugs being on my tail in the first place was my horrible sister. Maybe Mom might be able to convince the horrible sister to act reasonably, so I gave her a call.

"Hi Mom, it's me Joe."

"Joe, it's so good to hear your voice. How...how...you doing?"

"Not so good, Mom. Meghan's thugs are still on my tail. But on the bright side, I gave 'em the slip back in Seaside Heights, and about twenty minutes ago I pushed 'em off the pier. Got to keep the unfriendlies at bay. I'm about to go on the road again. Just hooked up with a new band."

"You be careful now! Those band things never seem to work out well! Don't let them treat you bad. You hear? They always disrespect you, and it pains me so to hear them disrespect you."

"Mom, the girl singer's good. She's real real good."

"Yeah, where have I heard you say that before? The true test is whether she can sing well when she's shitfaced. Can she jump through that hoop, Joe?"

"I'll have to get back to you on that. But Ma, are they treating you well there at the home? Sorry I mean, assisted care facility. How's the food?"

"Aw Joe, I can't complain. I'm not exactly sure, but I might be back in school, and there are lots of teachers telling me what to do. I half expect them to send the old lady next door down to detention. Or maybe they'll go and have her pick dandelions. The priests do that sometimes for punishment make-work projects. They make the kids rip 'em out by the roots without bending their knees. They love to watch. Go figure."

"Yeah Mom, that's great. How's Meghan doing?"

"I don't know 'cause she's hard to find."

"Mom, you know that Meghan and I don't talk to each other anymore. She said something about me that was very bad."

"Yes, I know. I know what she said. I just think it's so sad that my own daughter turned out to be such an asshole."

"It's not your fault, Mom."

"Whatever happened to the little girl I once knew?

"She left home and went straight to hell."

"Yes, what a disappointment she's been. My very own flesh and blood --- she's rotten to the core. That gnaws at me every day --- makes me wanna burst into tears. But I'll try to do better. Really, I will..." Her voice drifted off. I could hear her sniffling.

"Ma, you've got to talk into the receiver."

"Oh yes, you're absolutely right. I'll talk into the receiver. In this life I've had so far, I'll try and remember the good times --- like when you and I used to go for a soda at Phelps Drugstore on James Street, and then you'd take me to the park and we'd make out in the big black shiny Buick with the rumble seat. I'll never forget that. It'll be with me to the end of days..."

"Mom...Mom...Listen to me..."

"And you put it inside me..."

"Mom, that wasn't me! That was Dad! And all of that took place long before Meghan and I were ever born."

"...Oh...you're right. That did happen first, and you came along much much later. Sorry, Joe. It's just that as you get older, you look and sound just like him, and it gets confusing."

"Anyone could make that mistake. It's all right, Ma. Really it is. But don't get me wrong, Mom. I love it that you say exactly what's on your mind."

"I think the reason why Meghan is acting like such a bitch is that she never had any male children. That was where she went wrong. If she'd had a big strong strapping boy like you, all this unpleasantness wouldn't be happening. Hell, every mom wants that."

"Look Mom, I can't believe I'm hearin' what I'm hearin'. But don't second guess yourself. You did the best you could."

"Joe, I want you to know I still hold out hope that you and Meghan will get back together, so we can become one as a family again."

"Mom, I have to be honest with you. That's not going to happen. Please don't get your hopes up on that one."

"Don't worry. It's going to happen someday. Joe, the trouble with you is that you don't think positive."

"I take the world as I find it, Ma."

"You should take it as you wish it. In the meantime, what I wish is to get this show on the road."

"What do you mean by that, Mom? What show? What road?"

"I mean that I feel I'm just waiting around. I'm bored. I wanna get going."

"Get going and do what?"

"And die. It's really about time. I wanna get on the road. I'm tired of waitin' around."

"Please don't say that, Mom"

"And please don't fault me for being a curious person, Joe. I have tons and tons of curiosity about what's gonna happen next. I wanna see if the Afterlife is everything it's cracked up to be. Or maybe there isn't any. Maybe it's gonna just be nothin'--- a great big blank with lots of static. That's okay. I could float around through tides of nothin'. I suppose I could get used to that with a little bit of practice. I could tread water. Or maybe it's gonna be the reincarnation thing.

That's okay too. I could groove to that 'cause I'm real flexible, and just like you, Joe, I can improvise. I can go with the flow. Maybe I'll get to be a cat. Yes, being a cat would nice. I could yowl in the morning and wake up the humans to let 'em know it's time for my brekky, and after that, I could cozy up real cuddly-like in someone's warm lap. And after they go to work, I could spend the entire afternoon holed up on a quilted blanket that they've stuffed into the closet. And when I know they're comin' home --- and I'll always know when they're comin' home 'cause I'd be able to sense them from at least three blocks away --- then I could wait for 'em at the door, or…or…or not. I could just as easily choose to slumber away right there on the cushy couch."

"Yes, a life of ease and pleasure."

"I'm real curious about what it's going to be like."

"And there's little doubt that you passed some of that curiosity on to me."

"Meghan sure as hell didn't get any of it!"

I could hear her laughing on the other end of the connection. That was good. The tears had melted away.

"Joe, it's almost time for my excursion. They've got everything planned out here right down to the minute. The planning is so good that people almost don't have time in their busy schedules to get Alzheimer's. We're forgetful to begin with. But the staff here goes one step further and makes us forget that we have the forgetful disease."

"I know. How crafty of them. Those sly devils! Look, we'll talk about it more real soon, and Mom, I don't want to hear any more talk about 'getting on the road.' You hear?"

"Okay, Joe."

"You promise."

"I promise."

"Good, Mom. It's a deal. If you were Dad, we'd both go down to the tavern and have an ice cold beer in a big frosted mug to seal the deal. But you're not, so all I have is your word. And I know you, Ma. Your word is as good as gold."

"I know what your Dad would do. I know 'cause he was a crazy old drunk!"

"C'mon Ma. He wasn't that bad. Yeah, he had some faults. But don't we all."

I paused a second, thinking about what to say. I couldn't linger too long what with the unfriendlies back there fishing themselves out of the water. I figured I'd better wind it up.

"So bye for now. Talk to you soon."

"Love ya, Joe."

"And I love you back.... One more thing, Ma, do me a huge favor. Please don't tell Meghan where I am."

"Oh Joe, you don't have to say that. You know I'd never do that. You're my young prince and always will be. I'm so proud of you. You're my crowning achievement. You made it all worthwhile. I remember when I had to take you to the emergency room for ten stitches after you ran into that big oak tree when you were playing touch football. I marveled at you! Any ball that was thrown to you within ten feet was a ball that you could catch. Most of the time, you could make something out of nothing even if the quarterback couldn't hit the broad side of a barn door. What a wizard you were!"

"I still feel that way, Ma, when I'm playing drums. No matter how bad the melody and harmony are, I can still make something out of nothing."

"That's the spirit, Joe. No matter how much they beat the shit out of it and screw it up, I'm sure you'll think of something that sounds nice. Go out there and make some magic. Make something out of nothing. Make something out of whatever the entire world has crunched and crinkled. And one more thing --- as you wade through this here life, understand that you're a metaphor for things you might not have volunteered for."

"That's a good one, Ma. I'll try to remember it."

I could hear her starting to get misty again on the other end of the line. She made some vocalizations and tried to summon up a sentence, but then her voice trailed off again into incoherence. After a pause, she suddenly got back on the path of sense, telling me with a newfound confidence, "Joe, I'm so glad we've had this talk."

"Yes, and me too. Ma, I'm kind of worried about you now. I get the feeling things aren't going so well. So, I'm gonna call you three or four times a week from now on."

"Aw Joe, you don't need to do it that much. That's too often. Just make it one and a half."

Yes, Ma. One and a half. One and a half from now on."

I checked my cell to see about the charge. Yes, there was just enough juice left. My next call would be an unpleasant one. But it had to be done. I rang up my sister Meghan.

"Hi, Meghan, it's me Joe."

"Oh no, it's you."

"Uh huh, you're not my favorite person either, but we've got to talk."

"Why couldn't you have done something more constructive like selling used cars?"

"What can I say? I followed my heart. I tried to be Genghis Khan, but I didn't have the knack for it, so I became a drummer."

Well BONG BONG BAM BOOM Whup-dee-doo and boogaloo! You're gettin' better every five minutes. Have you been out there passin' auditions again? Well good for you. Maybe someday they'll dress you in a tux, tails, and bow tie and award you with a tympani, so you can be the slave of the community college symphony philharmonic! They'll say, 'Jolly good show, boy!' You fucking loser! You're a Neanderthal and always will be. You'll forever be a knuckle dragger. You know Joe, I think I hate music, and the reason I hate it is because *you* play it. Who needs something that constantly misrepresents itself? Either it's some pseudo-quasi-spiritual gobbledygook, or it's smarmy Vegas style razzmatazz --- sounds to lose your shirt to. I prefer to think of you musicians as cockroaches. You're everywhere, invading the crannies of every district, and each of you makes the most overblown claims about music's healing power. You're a herd of megalomaniacs, selling hokum and quackery at every step."

"Yeah, yeah, yeah, I'm not so good with the lugubrious thing. You, on the other hand..."

"Look, I've a half mind to hang up right now."

"Music is the great escape, Meghan. I'm forever doing a reality check to know how lucky I am. All the people out there --- they don't have what I have."

"Yeah, this is your thing. They're outsiders. They don't belong in your exclusive club! So, you can sit back, play music, and laugh at them 'cause they're not part of your in-joke. Trouble is, the real joke's on you! Ha, ha, ha!"

"You sure know how to hurt someone."

"So what do you want?"

"First of all, I want to ask you if you're recording this call."

"No, don't worry about that."

"On second thought, you're absolutely right. You wouldn't be able to do that. You want to be high tech, but you haven't got the chops."

"Shut up!"

"Look Meghan, do you suppose you could call off those goddamned thugs? I'm getting awful tired of running."

"You wish. Get this straight! I'm *never* callin' 'em off. Never. So you might as well get used to it. Sooner or later they're gonna kill ya. Mark my words. So if I were you I'd be very afraid."

"I know we once occupied the same womb, but at different times...so I had always hoped that established fact might make you feel sentimental enough to act decently towards me, but apparently that doesn't cut much ice with you."

"Oh YAWN YAWN YAWN. And after that, to top it off, an even bigger yawn. I can't help it. I'm just one greedy bitch. I want it all! Deal with it."

"So sending hit men after me is going to solve that?"

"Quite frankly, yes."

"The deal breaker was the lie about me raping you."

"Mom almost believed it. She almost changed her will to keep you out. Nothing ventured, nothing gained. And besides, with Mom's money and everything, I've gotta be practical and look out for my family. Gotta think about what's best for my children. Try to see it my way --- I have to be a good mother and bring home the bacon. Don't ya think?"

"Yeah, a case of simple home economics. I'll bet you learned that in high school. Bogus accusations of rape are just another pragmatic business decision."

"I have to provide for my family. Family is a sacred subject. It's what keeps this nation strong and on an even keel."

"Hey, you got no argument from me. Who could hate the notion of family? I sure as hell couldn't because right now I really don't have one. You kinda sorta took it away from me. So, speaking of family, how are the kids doin'? I'm always interested in what my nieces are up to."

I could feel her start to growl at the other end of the call. "You leave my daughters out of this! Do you hear?"

"Aw, c'mon. I'm only interested in how they're doin'. What's so awful about that?"

"I don't want you near them. And if you do come near, they'll be hell to pay!"

"Oh, I get it. If I did come near them, if I happened to have a nice normal half an hour with one of them over say, a cup of coffee, then that would mean that all those lies you told them about me might come crashing down. And you wouldn't want that one to happen now, would you?"

"Everything I've told them about you is the absolute gospel truth! I've got nothing to worry about on that score."

Her voice had a certain lilt to it that made my ears hurt. Each sentence competed with its predecessor, trying to outdo the other on which one could appall me even more.

"You're wrong...You're wrong," I continued. "You're wrong; you're wrong; you're wrong!"

"What? Are you working on another one of your silly songs? Catchy chorus you got going there, Bub."

"Look Meghan, the rape story was beyond outrageous. The act itself is just not my style 'cause Dad never stopped telling me to be a gentleman. If he had been alive to hear that, he would have said that kind of forcin'-yourself-on-a-woman thing just ain't masculine. So, after I heard the horrendous lie for the very first time, I sat around enraged for about forty-five minutes, stifling the urge to upchuck my granola bars and go punch a wall. Then after that bit of agitation was over, I said to myself: 'Meghan, you're not even my type. If I'm gonna rape someone, then the female in question might as well be my type and be semi-gorgeous. You miss by a mile on both counts, so why should I go to all the trouble?'"

"It doesn't matter. So what if I struck out on that one! I'm fully confident I'll hit paydirt with the hit men."

Ha! That one gave me a giggle. I thought to myself --- far be it for me to break the news about the two goons walkin' the plank and going overboard. But not to worry. She would learn about that setback soon enough. Still, it took a great effort not to gloat.

"Joe, consider your goose cooked. I'm a very patient lady. But I do wish Mom would hurry up and die. That would simplify matters immensely. Her lust for life is getting rather tiresome. In fact, this long and protracted good-bye of hers is borin' me to tears."

"You make it very difficult to say, 'I love you.'"

"Yeah, but you have to 'cause I'm your sister, and sisters need lovin', so live up to expectations and love me! Do what the rest of the world tells you to do."

She made a kissing sound with her voice, and I cringed. "Fla-la-la-la-la! Love, love, love, Joe. It's such a wonderful thing! Don't you think so?

"Not after what you've done to it."

"No? Really, you don't? Well I know so. I guess in my true self I'm a hopeless romantic, trippin' over my own girlish heart that goes pit-a-pat. Remember Joe, you can't have love unless you have hate too. There's no long without short, no big without small, no slim without fat. You get the picture, don't you?"

"Meghan, I think I've lost track about how many times the world has told me I have to feel a certain way, only to feel exactly the opposite."

"Joe the contrarian. Joe the barbarian. Joe the Neanderthal. Let me give you the inside dope on this whole hate thing. You have to see my point of view. Then you might have some smidgeon of empathy.

I was at a cocktail party years ago and was in the process of tying one on, getting drunk as a lord. I figured I'd tell a story, you know, to liven up the party. So, I started talking about you. I don't know when it first entered my mind, but like a bolt from the blue, there it was, resplendent in all its shining skuzziness: I told 'em you banged me. I thought that would be a real crowd pleaser. Suddenly, everyone was oohing and ahhing, and they were paying me lots more attention than they ever had before. Well, in no time at all, I was the life of the party! No more Miss Wallflower. A wave of happiness crashed over me. I was a superstar! So what if it wasn't the least bit true. The subject of sister-boffing is quite the show stopper! Always a classic no matter what the season of man or woman. What was I supposed to do then? Tell them it was all one great big horrendous lie? I would've been the laughingstock of the party. No Joe, it's like you used to tell me about playing music: you can play any note as long as you play it with '*a-thor-ity*.' I always appreciated the German accent that you put on it, as if you were talking to the big man Thor himself. Some people are better at *a-thor-ity* than others. And I'm damned good at it."

Well, you get the basic idea. Her monologue droned on --- wending, weaving, and doubling back on itself. Nothing would ever change her. The evil was deep down in the DNA, marinating in the mitochondria and meandering up the chains of adenine and guanine. I held the phone off to the side as the imperious blather spewed forth like an insane volcano. And every now and then, she'd punctuate the whole screed with a laugh that would creep me out right down to my bone marrow. After a while, there wasn't much a fellow could do except to press the end button.

For a minute or two, I thought about what she's said about love and how important it is in this world that each of us inhabits. What a hideous monstrosity she had created! For her, love was a safe shell. She could find refuge there and nurse old wounds and when the crazed lady got good and ready, she could go out into that very world to exact warped revenge for whatever perceived slights that had been inflicted upon her person. This was the hideous distortion that was being pawned off as love. Under the imposition of such bankrupt conditions, could any decent man be faulted for not wishing to participate?

I took quick stock of my situation. So...this was what it was like to be a villain, or should I say to be vilified. This was the feeling of wearing a pair of shoes that were two sizes too small. With great difficulty, I might still be able to walk around in them simply because I was a human --- correction, hominid individual --- just as a villain is arguably a hominid individual too, but there the similarity ended. It was funny because I didn't feel like a bad guy. I ran my fingers up my arms and shoulders and then my face and neck just to do a double check on that. The skin tingled to the touch, letting me know in no uncertain terms that, although the average epidermis enjoyed more than a fair share of transgressions, even it had some semblance of standards to uphold. I had gotten confirmation: none of this body belonged to a bad man. While that may have been true, I realized there were people out there who thought I must have been a monster. Just as there were sister-bangers, so too were there sister-believers. Bangers and believers make the world go round! Protesting her accusation would only make me appear even guiltier than I already wasn't, a fact not lost on Meghan which she had purposely incorporated into the design of her grand manipulations. No doubt the hit men I'd shoved off the pier had been fed a steady stream of lies by her. They'd probably used those to psyche themselves up to get into the appropriate murderous frame of mind so necessary for being an in-demand top notch murder-for-hire. Hey! Artists need to get into the mood. They do serious work. I could imagine Mr. Wrong Way talking to his young apprentice, saying, "Look Bill, it's not as if we're going to be killin' some choirboy or anything. This Joe guy deserves whatever misfortune can fall his way." Yeah, Billy Boy, I hope that one worked for you. And what's more, you schmuck, I hope you can swim. This time you got burned. Sizzle, sizzle, pop, bang!

What a sick joke! Why in the world didn't I ever see this coming? From about the fourth grade I had known Meghan was unequivocally horrible. That was when she gave me a stick of juicy fruit, bursting-with-flavor gum for my birthday. Oh, thank you very very much! But I'd talked myself into thinking, "No Joe, you have to give her the benefit of the doubt." Well, it was too late to second guess now.

And Mom ... what was the deal with her? As she edged closer and closer to death, I was having weird feelings. And these feelings felt real bad. Mom, in your life I've always tried to be a fixture. But I'm afraid to say it's not a pretty picture. I remembered a faded photo from the family album. Sunlight had played havoc with the colors. Blues ran into grays, reds into yellows. Mom was nineteen years old, and she was lying on a beach. I could see a breaker swelling in the background with a crown of foam outlining its crest. Mom had a gardenia in her hair, and she had a Betty Page face staring wonder-eyed into the camera. Jesus, she was beautiful. The gardenia was such a nice touch. I'll bet Dad really appreciated that. A fellow could get dizzy looking at it and then fall into the flower. I looked at her face again. It was the face of a smart, decent, and curious female being. How could she spawn such a vile creature as Meghan? I knew for sure that the recessive gene was to blame. There's no escape. Mom was good, only trouble was, good can skip a generation.

But that was such a long time ago! I'd never known myself to be a mama's boy. Joe, you're such a wuss! Suck it up and get over it. Fight it off like a real man! The rest of the world plays by all that sentimental love bullshit. But you're different. You don't need that laughable distraction, that rapscallion faun that hops around creating such a heap of jealousy and provincial malevolence in the universe. You're better. You're way up in the sky, and you get to look down. It's the reason you decided to play drums in the first place --- so you could have it both ways: you could be out on the periphery where no one would bother you, but you could still have an effect on the center. There's an excellent chance you could be the most subversive man on the planet. It's your way of pouring sugar in the gas tank when sugar screams to be poured in the bloody gas tank. Get a hold of yourself, boy.

> And you were, yes you were a saboteur
> Slashing tires, poisoning wells and sinking ships
> Pouring sugar in the gas tank
> Drilling holes in the bottom of the boat
> Spiking drinks in the restaurant

Enough! Enough! You've got work to do. Quite possibly, the whole world is depending on you, and they don't even know it. That's OK. Let them be as oblivious as they wanna be. I can suffer fools.

This life of mine had once had such enormous promise. I had talents, but I'd been content to say, "Not to worry. Talents are always there. They're a larder that you can raid at will. Joe, use them at your convenience. There's no great hurry! Take your time. Their shelf life is beyond even your comprehension." Well, the talents had waited around long enough. They're the ultimate "girls." If you keep 'em waiting too long, they'll think you've got no interest in them or that you're not worth the trouble. Either way, you won't be a prize catch of the day. Eventually, Nature herself gets pissed. You think you can test her out till she's blue in the face; well you got another thing comin', boy! Listen, pal! You respect Her! You respect Her, and you respect Her now!

But I knew that I could turn it around. It wasn't too late to save myself from a squandered life. I remembered what the Goddess had told me when I first spoke to her as a little boy. The Goddess reserves a special contempt for those who choose not to participate. She doesn't like it when you don't appreciate Her gifts. From now on, I would be a participant. But first, there was so much to unlearn. My talents had been in hibernation, languid and drowsy with sleep, but now they were going to wake up.

I pondered my next move. Part of me wanted to board the next bus and get the hell out of Dodge, but that would have been too easy. The prospect of being in another cool band was tantalizing to say the least. After mulling this over for a grand total of about three minutes, I decided to take my chances with the band. It nearly went without saying, though, that the Muses didn't have to exactly twist my arm. After all, a true musician might as well be a junkie. He doesn't have much say in the matter because he's willing to die for it or worse yet, do it for free. And besides, these Jersey shore towns with their straight-as-a ruler beaches that didn't know the meaning of the past tense were a godsend --- a perennial favorite with criminals looking for the perfect swamp to get lost in. And I sure as hell needed to get lost. Of course, contrary to what my horrible sister would lead people to believe, I wasn't a criminal or anything, but even so, you get the drift. A swamp is a swamp. And as swamps go, this version was damned good --- a plush zone if ever there was one. Not caring whether my pursuers had or had not swum back to the pleasures of the boardwalk, I ran back down to the beach, knowing full well that vast feelings of omnipotence would look over me.

The long stretches of sand were starting to fill up with the weekend sunbathers and a golden-haired kite flyer in a red bikini steered her glossy, green, plastic bird across the shimmering noon sky. Transfixed by its dovetail dance, I watched the slender bird as it dipped, swooped, and shimmied far out over the angry surf. The red bikini dipped, swooped, and shimmied too. The effect was meditative, and a tune suddenly darted through my mind.

"Like a faraway castle
In interesting times
Less thrill for the belly
More joy for the climb
We'll learn a new language
And talk so funny
A mutant plumage
Will paint the sky sunny
Oh, we'll drink oceans of alcohol
In the land of the blind
We'll chase arrows where they fall
And feel what they find"

Yes, love would have to wait. Exhilaration on the other hand --- that was quite another matter. Another drink might be required. In taverns along the boardwalk, bottles were gleaming like jewels in darkened rooms, and bartenders were beckoning. Antique arcade games --- wanting to be noticed --- would growl, bark, and yap in the corner. I needed to salute and report for duty. In the distance, someone was cranking up the Ferris wheel, and I could hear females screaming blissfully on the rollercoaster. Those were the voices of heavenly creatures, sirens who seemed to say, "STOP, STOP...

Don't stop." Excitable girls! An old recording of a homegrown Vegas performer was blaring in steady rotation as a reassuring mantra. The gathering crowd looked very happy. And I was happy for them. Each sun worshiper hurried along eager to stake out a piece of prime turf. Lifeguards were climbing ladders to take their places. They slowly perked to attention, surveying the water, and looking for signs of distress. I kept walking, knowing that I would never feel so completely alone in all my life. That felt downright refreshing, so much so that I turned to the sea and addressed one of the waves as it curled and barreled up towards the slanted shore. "Come on world. Come and get me."

Swimming would be fun. Even if I had to watch out for the undertow.

But as I was getting ready to find a bathhouse to change into trunks and head on into the beauty of the Atlantic Ocean, my smartphone rang. I didn't recognize the number. I hemmed and hawed about whether to answer it or not, figuring someone would be trying to sell me something. It rang and rang, but after a few seconds I was feeling lucky. Maybe it was something I'd want to buy? So I took the call.

"Hi Joe, it's me, your friendly research coordinator. I just called to let you know that the entire staff here at the research facility are missin' ya."

Immediately, I recognized the voice. My heart sank. It was Doc McIntyre --- the not-so-good medical man who wanted someone to practice on. I didn't talk right away because I was too busy kickin' myself for taking the call.

The voice continued on in an explanatory tone --- "Joe, you escaped just when I was about to see how you'd react to fibroblast growth factor 2."

"No, I didn't wanna participate 'cause quite frankly, that growth factor business really doesn't interest me, so I never volunteered."

"You didn't have to. We saw an opportunity. We had to go for it. A living Neanderthal is too much of an anomaly to pass up. You were kinda like a fossil that I could bring back to life."

"No, no, you can't make me go back. And besides, now I'm about to go on TV."

"No matter. Consider that one to be a short detour in our plans. We're pretty patient over here. We'll simply wait until the damned show gets cancelled. And that shouldn't be so very long. I mean, who in his right mind would want to see a show about a living Neanderthal? The premise is too farfetched."

"You won't get me --- even after it's cancelled. I'll hide so you'll never find me."

"Yes, Joe. Don't you know it's necessary to suffer if you are to contribute to the progress of science? Don't worry. I'll be watching. And remember --- you can't really escape. C'mon back. Like I said, we're missin' ya." He lapsed into a callous laugh. "Ha, ha, ha! I'd almost be willin' to bet that you're still havin' a werewolf moment now and then. Ah, but I'm not a bettin' man. But seriously, Joe. We're really still in the dark about the relationship between skull size and right parietal lobe carrying capacity. How did Nature accomplish that? We were hoping that with a bit more data, provided by you of course, we could solve that one. C'mon! Don't be a spoil sport and bow out on us now! There's true knowledge that's lying around just anticipatin'. Please be a champ and help us out."

Then I could hear the callous laugh continue, which caused me to go on the offensive. "Doc, I'm not a champ because I sure as hell am not a chump."

The laugh guffawed onward for a few more seconds. Then the connection went dead.

GOBS OF MAKEUP FROM THE GORGEOUS GOPI GAL

Where was the hungry hyena with the beautiful concertina? I needed to have an elixir for later on, so I had to see Sunita and see her right away. I was out of breath from my dust up with the thugs, and she was long overdue for a visit. After all, Ben had pretty much handed her to me on a gold platter. As a matter of fact, I half-expected to see her with a bright red apple stuck in her mouth. That was so sporting of him. What a peach of a guy! I rang the buzzer and was answered by her cheery Bangladeshi accent.

"Hi, this is Joe, and I've come to claim my prize."

I could hear her laughing over the intercom.

"Where have you been? I've been waitin' forever. Come on up, Joe. Your prize is behind Door Number 11E."

She buzzed me in, and I took the elevator to the eleventh floor. I stared at the lit up numbers of the floors as the compartment ascended, absent-mindedly thinking about how musical the female voice is when it's put in the practice of seduction. Every hypnotic sound and syllable has some impossible shape or throbbing color. The elevator went up. I was plunging into bliss.

Apartment 11E was the second door on the right. I pressed the doorbell, and Sunita opened the door. There she was in all her spritely beauty, clad in a silken yellow and blue sari. Her smile was so attractive --- the promise of a deluge of beauty to come --- and she looked pleasingly vulnerable as she greeted me. In short, she was someone I could save, but I wasn't sure from what. It didn't matter.

For now, it was better to keep it vague on that score. I could fill in the blanks later. Of course she stood with the aid of crutches, her left leg swathed in a pink plaster cast. Her lovely toes peeked out tentatively from their thick fuchsia prison --- pouting --- as if they'd been punished and sent to their room for doing something bad. And most likely, they'd done exactly that.

She patted the plaster with her lacquered fingers, clicking the tips of her tapered nails on the unyielding rigidity of the cast. "Yes, Joe. It was a very bad break. The technicians call it a 'spiral plateau fracture'--- whatever the hell that means. I'll be in this cocoon for about three or four months, maybe longer. They even put some special metal screws in my leg to hold the bones together. Those'll be there for the rest of my life. I can just imagine going through metal detectors when I'm seventy-five. Think about it --- Homeland Security will have to give me some sort of special pass."

She smiled in a flirty way. I noted that Roman emperors must have felt the way I was feeling right then. Let the games begin. I glanced at her pretty toes again. The brightly painted nails reminded me of sapphires and rubies. It felt great to be in a jewelry store.

"Is the cast heavy?" I asked.

"Sure is. I'm carrying around a bit of baggage. I wish I could bend my knee, but I can't because it goes all the way up my thigh. My doctor says if I'm a good girl and drink lots of milk for the bones to heal, then I'll get something smaller and lighter than this hunk of lead. Until then, he's got me on pain management. I guess you could say that I backed up the truck until I heard an expensive sound... CRUNCH!"

She took two pills out of her purse, tossed them one at a time into the air, and caught them in her mouth before swallowing and chasing them down with a gulp of orange juice straight from the carton that was on the kitchen counter.

"You do that like a Golden Retriever catching a Frisbee."

"Yeah, well I've been getting lots of practice lately."

I pointed to her unwieldly leg.

"Race you around the block?"

She giggled. "So rude!"

"Let me see how far it goes up."

She laughed and gave me a playful light slap on my hand. I love it when girls do that. Is there something in that gesture which they can replay later? We'll see.

"Oh you want to see where it goes?"

"Let me see" I replied.

Of course she did a perfunctory and not very convincing show of resistance just to keep the time-honored ritual interesting, but then she lifted her sari to reveal the rest of her long leg cast.

"It seems to go on forever," I told her.

"Just like Draupadi's sari in *The Mahabharata*."

Yes, in all the excitement, I had completely forgotten that Sunita was from the Indian subcontinent. Right about then, my mind was off to the races thinking about various combinations.

"I'm sure Krishna would be proud," I ventured. "I'd be willing to bet that he's never had a hippity hop lady as one of his Gopi gals." I put my hands around her hips, and she gave them a wiggle.

"There's always a first time, even for gods as popular as that handsome fellow. You know, I've always been a big fan of the blue-faced trickster. Can you imagine me hobbling along in his parade of Gopis, while a flock of colorful peacocks linger on the riverbank?

Yes, I could. I sure as hell could. That would be such a scene of romantic beauty. But I deliberately ignored her question, concentrating instead on the faint trace of blue just below her black eye shadow and marveling at the way it flawlessly blended into the natural contours of her brow and nose. I also concentrated on her lacquered lips. Her lips said stuff --- they curved around phrases so sounds came out of her mouth. How cool was that?

"You're a trickster yourself, pretty lady," I replied.

"C'mon, Joe. I got a great idea. It's one of my sudden brainstorms. C'mon and follow me." She crutched into the bathroom, and I dutifully followed her. "Joe, you got me to thinkin'. You've inspired me. That's what a good lover is supposed to do. You got me goin', and now I can't stop. Now I wanna play some make-up make-believe."

"So what do you wanna pretend?"

"I wanna make believe that you're my very own up close and personal Krishna! But maybe we'll have to make do with purple." Now she was rummaging around in the medicine cabinet, making quite a small racket as she knocked over tooth brushes, shaving cream, tweezers, and expired pill bottles. Finally, she located the object of her search --- a small make-up kit which she triumphantly held up for me to see. "Yes, I do believe that purple would be better 'cause there's something rather royal about it." She uttered this with all the nonchalant charm of a fashion consultant or an interior decorator, and before I could register any objections, the gorgeous Gopi gal was applying gobs of make-up to my face. She was layin' it on thick, almost as if she were wielding a spatula like some sorta madcap Impressionist painter on a bender, but I guess you have to do that if you wanna make someone look purple-faced. No doubt for her, make-up was a kind of medicine.

"Hey, Miss Gopi, this is what a dog encounters when he's being put in a costume."

She giggled at that one, wavered a bit on her crutches, and replied, "Oh yeah? So hold still for a second, you great big doggy-woggy! I've got to get this right!" She was gesturing with an eye pencil and then buffing my cheeks with a tapered fine-haired brush. I winced a bit when she came at me with the brush a second time. The soft hairs did a tickle to my face, and now and then the powder smarted my eyes.

"I wanna see clearly about who I'm gonna be playin' with!" she continued. "It's only fair." Girls often talk about being fair. It usually means they're about to do something unfair. But I didn't care, so I held still until she finished the masquerade. At length, she leaned back on her crutches and studied me carefully with a critical eye. "There, there now. I think you will do. Yes, you will do quite handsomely. You're a reasonable facsimile of the purple-faced trickster!"

She put down the make-up kit with a gleeful flourish and then standing on her good leg, she put her arms around me. I love it when Halloween and amorous activities get mixed, especially at this early juncture in the relationship. Experimentation usually doesn't start until later.

"This will do for now, Joe. But next time I think I'll want you to be Hanuman, Ganesh, or maybe Shiva."

"Shiva saved the world with his *linga*."

"Yeah, and it'll be your gig to save my world!"

"So you save mine first. One hand washes the other!"

"It's a deal!"

"Even though we live in the Age of No, you let me live in the affirmative."

"Maybe...or maybe I just like to say yes."

"You silly thing!"

Pondering and wondering, I got down on my knees to get a close up of her toes. She smiled and wriggled them. The big one and its neighboring digit were absolutely breathtaking. I kissed them tenderly and ran my lips up the cast, the firm hardness of plaster beckoning me northward. Never had damaged goods seemed so enticing.

"It's almost like my leg has turned to stone for a while, isn't it?"

I didn't answer quite yet. I was too busy taking in the stunning view. "It's a piece of sculpture, some sort of modern art."

She wriggled her toes again. This time even more playfully.

"That's for my delectation?"

"Get me to the Museum of Art real soon, baby."

"Dangerous bird of the wild savannah, you'll look good in my diorama."

For a person with a rather serious injury, she looked happy, having a certain flushed glow, as though she would shortly be giving birth to something, but whatever it was, it sure as hell wouldn't be a child. And what I liked about this giant pod where her leg had recently taken up residence was that this encumbrance now kept the limb excessively protected --- in this capsule, nothing could possibly happen to it, and what was good about the excess of safety was that it might lead to a certain equilibrium, so everything would even out in the end.

Then I switched gears and lied a bit. After all, I had to get in practice for whatever script Jillian was cooking up. "You look so sad."

"I am. I hurt myself really bad. Please come and help me now."

She was suitably helpless, so I grabbed her by the hair and kissed her insolently. It suddenly occurred to me that, if any "saving" were to take place, perhaps it would be to save her from me, but that thought ran away quickly when she said: "Joe, I think your drumming may entertain me."

"Yes," I replied. "I will entertain you and then I'll go ahead and *retrain* you, but if you're bad, I may have to send you back to the factory for re-grooving."

"Uh oh," she answered in an affected forlorn voice. "You're saying I may have to be recalled?"

"Yes, I'm afraid so. You see, there's an imperfection." I pointed to her injured leg.

"Oh gee, we can't have that. Guess I'll have to be wrapped up and sent back like a faulty piece of furniture. Delivery not accepted." The corners of her mouth did a pirouette, and an inner light lit up her right eye. Then the jet black lashes fell down over it like a curtain at a theater only to flutter open again for a new performance.

"Yes, I'm afraid so, baby, 'cause you're such a bad actress."

I gave a hank of her hair a light tug. She giggled back at me and flopped into the creamy white pillows on the couch, a mass of lovey-dovey curves and tousled black hair, swooping and drooping into the deep crevices of the upholstery, giving her the appearance of a suspicious package of ribbons and bows ready to be opened.

"When does your husband come back?"

"Oh, don't worry your pretty little purply face about him. He won't be back until tomorrow. I told you he lets me go with whomever I please. You have his blessing. I wouldn't have it any other way. And besides, I'm the one with the money. Rank has its privilege! He's got to kowtow to me! He's out with God only knows who, so it's only right that I can be rumpa pum pumming with my paradiddle boy. I don't know if you've noticed this yet, but Ben writes great songs. Trouble is, he never gives anyone a listen. He keeps everything locked up in an ivory tower, so only he can enjoy them."

"No kidding? What a hog!" I made a squonking piggish sound with my voice and nose. "I'll bet his ivory tower is really a basement, so his audience is a bunch of hot water heaters."

"You're not far off the mark when you say that. He's not much of a rock and roller. I'll let you in on that dirty little secret. I can't tell you how many times I've watched the band's rehearsals, and he harps on everyone to play softer and softer. After that, he orders them to play slower and slower until the whole tune crawls to a standstill. It gets all wiggly waggly, melting into a tumbly weed of tangled noise. And Gwen and Kathy look completely confused. In that way, he sucks all the life blood out of the songs. What a vampire!"

"Or a Frankenstein monster," I offered.

"Well, he's really in the business of creating Frankenstein monsters."

"How's that?"

"He's a bit of a scientist. And for all I know, he might be good at it. But he keeps it pretty hush hush. And when I really stop to think about it, that probably works out OK for me 'cause I almost don't wanna know about what in the world he's doing. I'm sure he's cookin' up something that's out and out plain nasty, so I would prefer to remain as ignorant as possible. I play the dumb blonde on a daily basis."

I looked at her hair. She wasn't blonde, and she wasn't dumb. But I had to reassure her. "Sounds great to me," I said. I thought about Ben's experiments with Gulf and all of that robotics and artificial intelligence business, which was actually rather frightening. Did Sunita know anything about that? I sure hoped not.

"He really is in the wrong line of work," she replied. "He should be sawing away on a cello somewhere, playing string quartets, or maybe yodeling Buddhist sutras."

"Buddhist sutras don't make it," I said.

"Maybe he should be pursuing something more practical."

"Yeah, going to welding school would be a good idea."

"That's his true calling. Oh yes, and I nearly forgot. He writes good lyrics too. Quite possibly that's what makes him tolerable to Jillian. For this talent, she allows him to remain in the band. My only problem with his arcane ability is that it harkens back to when I was in English 101. At some of *Babies in Bars'* recent gigs, his stage persona gave me the distinct impression he was some sort of tutor doin' a good turn for an audience that was developmentally deprived, and it was his function to help 'em get ready for a big and scary test, but no one could remember what the test was supposed to be about."

"I get the feeling that *you* might be developmentally deprived. But Uncle Joe'll make you remember."

"I bet you will, my purply one. You see, I don't know if you know this or not, but I'm in need of extensive remediation." She gave me a knowing smile. Her theatrical streak knew no bounds.

"I know. I can tell by that look in your Little-Miss-School-Girl eyes. I guess I'll have to see what I can do."

Sunita's observation about Ben was a deep cause for concern. It was that damned words-versus-music business. It keeps rearin' its ugly head. I mulled this over as I stared at the bare light bulb hanging from the center of the ceiling. I hated it when music got ground under the boot heel of adjectives, adverbs, and pronouns, to say nothing of the utter tyranny of verbs. It was all very diabolical! Yes, I thought --- I would definitely have to do something about that problem. Sooner or later, I would have to piss all over his lovely words. Already I was realizing this might be the greatest challenge for me as a band member.

"The huge gap between Ben and you is you give value to a song by playing it, and he's under the mistaken notion that he can give value to a song by thinking it. He believes his way is supposedly *open* to all possibilities. Ha! He fancies himself as some sort of Mr. High and Mighty Concept Creator. What bullshit! It's why he can't bring himself to such mundane things as practicing. I love to see him fail."

I took careful notice of the cruelty in her voice.

"But still, you've gotta give him credit for being so gentlemanly," I replied. "I mean, think about it. He kinda sorta gave you to me. He's...what can I say, a contributor."

"So, come on. You're the beneficiary. Pay your tribute and kiss the contribution, Joe."

She fluttered her eyelashes again and offered up her lips. I turned away, and in the slowest voice that I could possibly muster, replied, "Let...me...set...the...pace... honey."

I kissed her leg --- the healthy one this time. It was hyperactive and rarin' to go somewhere and to gallop quite fast, only trouble was, something was holding it back. This beautiful body, this delectable organism, lying before me was pinned and anchored like a wild animal caught in a trap. Then I looked to my right --- somehow the jaunty, yellow and blue sari had managed to find its way across the room where it now lay in a rumpled heap on an ottoman. It didn't look quite so jaunty anymore. Clearly, the lady was too sexy for her sari. I thought of India again. Was I too sexy for my lungi?

"Am I still pretty, Joe? I've only broken some bones, right? My beauty hasn't gone away, has it? It's still here, isn't it?"

"No, not at all. It hasn't gone anywhere. Instead, part of you has gone into hibernation."

"And when it comes out, what will happen?"

"You and it will be prettier than ever."

"Come closer, Joe. What's that scratch on your head?

"It's nothing. Something that happened the other night on the boardwalk. It was a misunderstanding of sorts."

"The boardwalk is a place where a lot of misunderstanding happens."

She touched my forehead tenderly near the scratch. Then she kissed it, and I closed my eyes.

"Joe, you should really put something on this, so it doesn't get infected."

"One of these days."

I opened my eyes. From close up, the enchanting musk of every female neck, cheek, and lip whispered, gathered momentum, and propagated. No doubt she would be sure to tell me what was up while her boobs were hiding out and biding their time in her pesky bra. How annoying! But only a temporary setback 'cause she was impressed by my drumming --- as if to say, 'Hey boy, you've got musical ability. I give you five gold stars and the Good Housekeeping Seal of Approval.'

Yes, my dear, I suppose that meant I would be suitable for mating.

"You know, Joe, did anyone ever tell you that you have a rather bumpy head?"

"Many times."

"It's a cave man's head."

"I've known that since I was six years old."

Then she moved back a few inches, and her face took on a more serious tone. "You're a junkie, aren't you?"

The shock of the question knocked me backwards. It took me a few seconds to regroup. "How...how did you know?'

"Oh, I have my ways."

"I thought I kept it very secret."

"You're right. You're very good at that --- slick even. I love it when you pretend to have your program so together even though you're miles and miles away from attaining it. You think you've got everyone fooled, but you don't fool me. Not even for one second."

Why did she have to be so gosh-darned perceptive? Why couldn't she let me pull the wool over her eyes just like all the others?

"Thank you for being so forgiving."

"As I said, Ben has this really weird ability to never get addicted to anything. I tell ya, it spooks the hell outta me."

"He must have some sorta weird biorhythms."

"You probably sussed that one out when he treated you to a line the other night, which was rather generous of him. And generosity is not his forte." She looked away from me, but kept the smile on her face. "That was so funny. Right then, I was imagining you in all sorts of situations and predicaments."

"Oh yeah, like what?"

"You were a customs officer for a funky backwater country, and nothing he was bringin' in was anything that you didn't have already in massive supply, so you figured you'd better wave him through with no questions asked. Yeah, wave him through."

"Look Sunita, I'm a traditionalist. When it comes to drugs, I don't want any of that teenager bullshit --- none of that stuff that plays with perspective. With the Big H, whenever someone says,

'Would ya like another?' the answer will forever and for all time be a resounding 'YES.'"

"Remind me to talk to Jillian to see if she can get your daily fix written into the budget for the show."

"You could do that?"

"Yes, I could definitely do that."

"That would be so so wonderful if you could do that for me. It would be one less thing to worry about."

"Yes, my dear, I'm a powerful woman. I can make that happen. And what could you do for me?"

She took my fingers and ran them along her skinny arm. Then she flexed it like a circus muscle man and made a crooked face.

"Hey baby, you make the music go buzzin' through the bicep."

Her voice was taking me to a special world. She caressed my hands and then ravenously kissed them, desperately rubbing the palms to her face. Suddenly, I felt hot tears on my hands, and her body shuddered convulsive sobs.

"Joe, I think our hands are our most human feature, the smartest organs."

She continued caressing them before suddenly stopping and looking into my face with a penetrating stare. The tears were still welling from her eyes.

She rapped her knuckles on her head. "No, Joe, the smartest stuff is not what's in here."

Then she touched her chest where the heart was, before patting my chest too. Her fingers flexed and searched for the heart. It felt kinda good. "And certainly not what's in here."

"You may have a point there."

I patted the cast, and made a small cave against the creamy white pillow with my upper arm and shoulder. She put her head in the cave and snuggled up. "Your leg is the beginning of you and the end of you," I observed.

"Yes, and it's a man's job to find the beginning and the end. Hey, didn't you say something about doing one's gig?"

"As a matter of fact I did."

"Well, I do believe you'd better get crackin'. C'mon Joe. My petals are pushin'. You're the wanderin' bee. Come and find the flower. Be the brawny blues singer I've always dreamed about."

"I think..."

"No, Joe, you weren't invited up here to think. You were invited up here to feel and to make me feel. I'm sorry, but thinking is simply not allowed on the premises. Do you wanna get banned?"

"Absolutely not."

"I didn't think so."

"Ha! I caught ya, you little hypocrite! Look who's thinkin' now!" I lightly smacked her butt for emphasis.

She giggled again, undulated her frisky shoulders, moved closer and nuzzled up --- entering my gravitational pull, reaching out like a captured moon to give me a touch. Then she went over to the radio on the nightstand beside the bed. She turned it on and made some adjustments. While she was doing that, I made a brief inventory of all the lovely girly-girl things that made this room so much fun. Chief among these were the lace curtains which were parted ever so minutely in order to let in only the most discreet shafts of light. Then there was the fine-dripped candle that gave off a jasmine scent. A man can tell when he's movin' up in life --- he gets to have his very own fine-dripped jasmine candle. That means he gets enough light to make the love deal interesting --- none of that pitch dark nonsense that's strictly for her convoluted imagination.

As she was making her adjustments to the FM dial, she slightly hopped about on her good leg causing my heart to hop too. The radio responded with a swirly mix of static, white noise, and snippets of salsa and classical music, and in her own strange way, she seemed to be unconsciously dancing to this mishmash.

"You know, Joe, I believe this radio plays very good music, only the reception's not so great. The static's goin' ziggin' and zaggin'. What you need is a bit more tuning, so we can get to the right station."

"Uh ah! You're the one who needs the tuning!"

"So c'mon and tune me, baby."

The reception wasn't exactly spot on, so I figured it was my turn to try and get it right. But after messing with it for about fifteen seconds, the sound came in clear as a bell.

"There, there!" she said, sniffling a bit between a new round of tears, this one not quite as intense as before. "I think that's so much better. Don't you?"

"Yes, it sounds good now."

"You know, when I was a little girl, I was fascinated by the radio. I listened to it as soon as I got up and then again right after I got back from school. And when I was in school, I'd be daydreaming about the songs that would come out of the AM dial. For the longest time, I thought that when the announcer introduced a song, I truly believed there was a band right there in the studio of the radio station, and the band would play the song right away on demand. He could snap his fingers, and boom boom right away, they would knock it out and beautiful sounds would suddenly vibrate right on through the airwaves right across town, through the front door, down the hall, and into my ears. I could picture the musicians looking at the announcer 'cause you see, they had to be razor sharp. And they would play it perfectly again and again whenever the announcer, or better yet, someone from the radio audience, saw fit to make a request. Those musicians were so good, so talented, that they *never* made any mistakes, and the song always sounded *exactly* the same every time. And that was so different from me because in my own life, I made super-clumsy mistakes all the time, especially in arithmetic when I had to go to the blackboard. When I did that, I'd make a fool of myself up there in front of everyone. I felt completely humiliated. But those people inside the radio --- they were amazing! They were battin' a thousand every time. How did they manage to pull it off? It was so magical. My enchantment knew no bounds. To me, they were a bit like gods. And it wasn't limited to just men. When a woman sang, I would feel the same way. She was in the same glittering realm. And for the longest time, that was the way I thought about the radio. I stayed awake at night, waiting in anticipation for the morning when I would religiously tune in. That was the way I thought about music. And Mom never said anything to lead me away from this point of view. In fact, she kind of encouraged it. So imagine my deep disillusionment when my father told me that no, there wasn't a real live band in the radio station studio. Instead, there was a vinyl record right there on a turntable in the studio, and the announcer was queuing it up, and the record had been recorded earlier and this was the reason it sounded the same every time. That was the source of all this perfection that I could never hope to emulate. And to add insult to injury, my father said that someday that piece of vinyl would get scratched up and wear out and would have to be tossed in the trash. Well, I could hardly believe my ears. I did my best to fathom it, and when I coped, and it had finally sunk in, I couldn't begin to describe the depths of my sorrow. So, I confronted Mom about this. She laughed it off and told me that she had been keeping up the charade simply to encourage my vivid imagination."

"Wow! No kiddin'. You felt like that?"

"Yeah, I'm embarrassed to say I did. Somehow, I wish you could be like one of the little men inside the radio. Could you be like that for me?" She hopped around again. It was obvious she could understand the notion of cause and effect, or was it affect? I wasn't completely sure.

"Well, I'll be damned. I'll give it my best shot."

"Ah Joe, you're the best."

Now she was getting weepy again. Summoning up my best Bela Lugosi/Count Dracula voice, I said: "You've got bats in your belfry, my dear. But I think you're doin' fine."

And as suddenly as they had appeared, the tears receded without a hint they'd ever been there before. The young lady had more moves than an octopus, and I was definitely getting suspicious as she adjusted herself on the pillow. I could see she was going to tell me some *deep dark truth*. No doubt she'd expect the same from me. I felt I was in bed with the Great Maker ---- here a make, there a Make, everywhere a Maker Shaker. Part of me was talking to itself 'cause the Self had stumbled onto another planet. It was yelling, "Silence, boy! You make my ears sting. You've got to detach yourself. Space has more curves in this land. Even the drifting clouds are voluptuous and spilling into the blueness of the sky. If I drew a picture to show

Mother back home, she would laugh and chide me for my overheated imagination." This had been a banner day for the imagination --- both the Gopi Girl's and mine.

I drew her nearer, and my mouth touched hers. The lipstick tasted of bubblegum and apricots. Then I wondered about whether or not the young lady still harbored any strong allegiances to Ben. I hoped those feelings of hers were tenuous at best, or better yet, had flown the coop entirely, thereby leaving her completely mine and mine alone. This new shade of emotion was an anachronism 'cause it was the first flowering of a need to possess. Up until this moment in life, I could confidently say to myself, "Yeah, plenty more where that came from."

However, on this go-round, the stakes might be higher. I thought about it some more --- bubblegum and apricots might actually work for me. Then I thought about the other girl that Ben had been tinkerin' on and tweakin' back at his workshop. Had she been a person or had she been a machine? Perhaps she'd been a little of both. And Ben had made her that way. But this spectacular lady right there in front of me --- she was the acoustic version. I certainly wouldn't want Ben to be doin' to Sunita what he'd been doin' to the young electric version back at the workshop. Even a machine wouldn't deserve that. Thinking about it sent a spasm of a shiver through my brain.

I glanced at her one more time before the festivities would begin --- the Great Maker was a beached creature --- exotic, immobile and held down.

Fortunately, the Great Maker was not privy to these thoughts. "Oh God," she blurted out. "My life is a total shambles. I really want to be happy, but I'm chased and haunted by demons of every size and shape."

Yes, those devil demons can run the gamut. Indeed they do. What surprised me about this was that she said it coquettishly without a trace of real sadness. I wanted to say, "Liar, liar" 'cause her pants were truly in flames.

"Please help me," she went on. "I am completely lost."

"Aw baby, I don't think you can afford it."

"Oh yes I can."

The pills were kicking in. Soon the Great Maker Shaker would be falling in love with the whole world. It was slowly dawning on me that she was a lost soul. That could be good or that could be very very bad.

But in the meantime, Krishna was a happy boy. He was thinking about the hips that would soon be engulfing him.

A HAPPY CONFUSION

In her was better than honor. But where was she dragging me? She was a lethal weapon. I needed to aim her someplace. The girl was very musical. I adored the way she bent the notes. She went on and on and on. Each and every sound became an arabesque. I was so jealous. I wanted to do that too.

When slumber overtook me, I found myself flying high above the town puzzled why others could not flap their wings. I acknowledged that this was a dream, so I gave myself permission not to be scared. Then I saw that they had no wings to flap though they tried and tried again. Only I had them. The panorama from above was breathtaking. Try as they might, the rabble below couldn't propel themselves into the air. I watched this failing of theirs as my mood grew jollier until I decided to dive bomb at them furiously. Making them fall flat, I laughed until my sides split. But then they laughed back. Nothing could prepare me for that. A veritable roar it was, the racket so loud it knocked me out of the sky and jolted me awake. The next thing I knew I was wide-eyed and rumpled, ready to face the glare of the morning sun.

The fun-to-look-at anchorwoman stared into the camera, batted her eyelashes, and read me the news.

"Tell it to me, doll face," I said to the high def plasma.

"And this just in...Wildwood Police are looking into a bizarre incident that took place yesterday, in which two men fell off the pier. One of the men drowned, and the other survived, but one witness claimed to have seen a third man push the men over the railing and into the water. However, the survivor insists that the two of them fell. Police are continuing to investigate."

She turned to her co-anchor who shook his head in disbelief. "What a strange story, Beth."

"Well, we'll keep you posted on this one."

Beth shuffled her papers and then started to talk about weather and sports. I looked around Sunita's room. Such a scene of domestic beauty! Too bad I needed to cut it short. I could hear Sunita rummaging around in the kitchen, most likely making Spanish omelets or waffles. The news was a problem, so I hurriedly grabbed the remote clicker and switched to another station.

A pang of guilt crept over me. Where were my manners? What with her disability and all, the gentlemanly thing to do would be to give her a hand with the breakfast tray. I shouldn't be the one who was lollygagging. She should have been the horizontal one on her bed of pain while I got to play nurse, cook, and concierge. I could hear her now saying, "Joe, it's not fair!" Better to beat her to the punch. I rubbed my eyes, put on my pants, and wandered into the kitchen.

"And how is my purple-faced one doing this morning?"

"I'm fine." I did a double take and stared into a nearby mirror. There it was. The purple make-up was still on my face. For the time being, Krishna was still Krishna.

"Don't worry. You can wash it off later. For now, I want you to still be in character, and maybe we can talk to Jillian and she can write it in to the plot of the show." Then she gave me a wide grin, flicked a wisp of hair out of her face and said, "Joe, last night was so so great. I sorta stopped counting at nineteen."

I recalled the pleasant memory: she made lots of noise --- neighbors would wonder if I was helpin' or hurtin'. "I wasn't keeping score, but maybe I should have."

"Always keep score, baby. Everyone else does."

"I suppose someone's got to. But I thought it might get in the way of the fun."

"No way. Perish the thought."

I thought the thought, but decided not to perish it because Cro-Magnon ladies are so accomplished at keeping a running tally.

"I was never very good at keeping score. Say, I never got around to asking you before, and most likely by now you've only answered this about twenty-five times already, but how did you get hurt?"

"Oh that. I was changing a light bulb and fell off the stool while I was trying to reach it. Well, my leg went one way, and I went the other. I could actually hear it snap, and then when I looked at it, there was no great mystery about what had happened because it was at a preposterous angle. Both bones --- the tib and the fib took it on the chin."

"Sorry to bring up a sore subject."

"It's not sore at all, even if my bones are. It might have been the best thing that ever happened to me. In fact, each day I look forward to savoring all the second, third, and fourth random glances I'm certain to get. Crutching through mall parking lots, I know that everyone is looking at me. Suddenly the whole landscape is overflowing and crawling with anonymous watchers. They come out of every nook and cranny --- practically falling all over themselves --- acting so absolutely ridiculous that I almost feel embarrassed for them. Each person I encounter is stumbling upon some new and glossy enigma. When they see me, they've found a room in their houses that they'd never noticed before. They're swallowed up in a happy confusion because they don't for the life of them know how it escaped them until now. They can't quite put their finger on it. And with plaster it's totally socially acceptable --- none of that stigma that goes with being peeping toms. Lots of men, and women too, start offering to help me with groceries, shopping carts, and revolving doors. You see, the advantage of this is that everything can be reasonably explained as being under the socially acceptable guise of, how do you say --- 'helping her out'? Why just the other day I was surprised when a dog blinked at me with the most inquiring look on his face. He seemed as befuddled and hoodwinked as the rest of them. It just goes to show --- even other mammals don't know themselves."

"Yeah, reptiles, self-replicating viruses, and amoebas know everything there is to know in that department," I replied. "Their program is so together. They know what they want, and they go after it. Ambivalence never enters their minds."

"Joe, I think when this leg of mine is healed, I may still keep this albatross on for quite a while longer."

She patted the pink plaster, clicking her fingernails on the hard unyielding surface. I noticed that she liked to do that a lot.

"It might be difficult to go back to normal. I'm toying with the idea that I may never go back to business as usual. A healthy second leg might as well be a luxury that I can ill afford."

She started noshing on a bagel and then took a sip of coffee, before looking me straight in the eye. That was darned impertinent. No, I thought. You're not the Goddess! And don't pretend to be! I looked away and stared out the window. A flock of gulls was roosting in a tree. Out of the corner of my other eye I could see her waving at me. "Hey, Earth to Joe. Paging Joe Myers, I'm over here."

With her right hand, she grabbed me by the chin. I flinched and darted back into the bedroom. She hobbled after me in hot pursuit.

"Please don't ever do that again!" I said.

"Did anyone ever tell you that you have trouble looking people in the eye?"

Yes, it's just too personal. Besides, my dad looked at people in the eye, and he was a crazy man. Who in the world wants to be like him? I sure don't."

"You know what I think?"

"No, what do you think?"

"I think that dog that stared at me the day before yesterday was better at looking people in the eye than you are."

"He's a dog, and I'm not."

She was futzing around with the TV remote, which was driving me nuts. I hoped against hope that she wouldn't get some local news channel that would be repeating the story about my misadventures with the two thugs out on the pier.

"Some people might see that as a sign of not being on the up and up," she continued.

She flicked through the channels before deciding on an old rerun of *Magnum P.I.* For a second or so, she watched Magnum give a cute lady a lesson in snorkeling, but then she quickly lost interest. Whew! That was a close call.

"Well, let them think that I'm not on the up and up," I replied. "It's not true."

I ran back into the kitchen, and she followed. The Spanish omelet looked good.

"You're on the run from something, aren't you?" She leaned forward, and I could see she had that look of wanting to know everything about me. Well dammit! She doesn't get to know that. Some things are off limits.

"What makes you think I'm on the run from something?"

"I can see it in the eyes that refuse to look into mine."

"Yeah, well you're wrong. So much for your mind-reading abilities. Contrary to what you've been led to believe, the ears and not the eyes are the lens into the soul."

I pointed to my ears, and she drew close to them and peered inside, stroking my ear lobe with a painted finger. Then she took another bite out of the bagel and sprinkled some pepper on the scrambled eggs. I could tell she was making some kind of course correction and assessing all possible contingencies. How crafty of her! At length, she seemed to have figured it all out, so she sealed the deal with another sip of black coffee. I turned my head and gave another look at the seagulls out on the telephone wire. They hadn't gone anywhere. In fact, some terns had joined them.

"That's alright. It doesn't matter if you're not on the up and up. I might even get used to it. Think of it --- Joe Myers, international man of mystery. Yes, on second thought, I think I like that even better. I don't want you to go stale in my imagination. The up and up thing is vastly overrated. And besides, you can make a band rock. That's another happy confusion."

"You care about that?"

She reached over and kissed me. No, I thought. You're not supposed to be the Goddess.

"You care about that?" I repeated.

"Damned right I care about that. People can't live without happy confusions."

She was the first one who'd ever said that to me. Maybe she *was* the Goddess?

"What about that little habit of yours, Joe?"

"Oh yeah, that! After breakfast I'll have to adjourn to a secluded spot."

"To go shoot up?"

"Right you are. When I do that, it feels so bloody important. And in a little while, I know it won't be important at all."

"But I'll bet that in another twenty-four hours, it'll start to feel important all over again."

"Most likely drumming is even more important than that. Damned right it is! What are you, a mind reader or somethin'?"

She giggled and wolfed down the rest of her Mediterranean omelet. Yes, this lady knew me through an through.

If the purpose of drumming is to create a happy confusion, then the problem with the human voice is that it's so bloody fragile. Like a boxer, it can get smacked all over the ring for round after round, showing the crowd how tough it is, putting out its chin for all to crash, almost double-daring its opponent to shut out the lights, and then out of the blue, it gets left-jabbed in one fell swoop. And when that goes down, it doesn't even have to be a very big fell swoop. Every song has a glass jaw somewhere in its verse or chorus. A love tap could throw the whole rave up into a black hole. It's true --- a voice, male or female's, is an altogether different breed of animal. So, so delicate. You've gotta hold back, or you'll crush it. Something a Neanderthal finds hard to do. But as I wander through this Cro-Magnon world, I'm getting better at toning it down.

On the other hand, when you're backing up just a guitar, you're dealing with a very thick-skinned beast. It's a rough beast *vindaloo*. You're competing decibel for decibel with big ass amps, so each strum has the bite of a muscular symphony philharmonic. For all intents and purposes, you might as well be a mastodon in a china shop, clanking on the crockery. You can get away with murder. You can noodle away, bludgeon in the background, bash to your heart's content, spiking up whiplash moments and assorted detonations, and still be assured that ninety percent of the time, whatever you do, as long as you play in time, it will pretty much work and that there won't be a strident mix-and-match clash to worry about --- no rude car doors slamming in the middle of the pretty lady's lines. Ha! That queen of time will ride her golden barge. Watch your step 'cause her mind's unfurled. She's the boss, and she's in charge. It's a puzzle of reality. Approach it this way and you'll stay out of trouble. And you'll also make her look and sound pretty, which ain't half bad. And when you do that, you might find yourself worshiping her. She'll have gorgeous feet.

But I'm getting way ahead of myself. With a voice, you have to be sure that nothing you do cancels out what she's doing. Despite this, you never know completely where she's going to go. And that's her fickle prerogative. This is a full dance card of stuff to worry about, to say nothing of that other nagging doubt, which is that she may turn into a complete swollen-headed prima donna. Hey, don't for a moment laugh that off and think it's a remote possibility! Do so at your peril. I won't bore you with how many times it's happened before, but when it does, right before your very eyes and ears she'll metastasize into that spoiled child you may one day overhear in a department store casually saying, "But Mother, fur is the only thing that keeps me warm."

Another problem with being a timekeeper for hire is that you have to be a mind reader. It would be so nice if she had a chart you could read, so that you could get an inkling of what she wants. But trouble is, that's a nicety. She doesn't really know what in the hell she wants. She mystifies herself on a daily basis. All she wants is that it should be "awesome." What an overused word. I wanna say, "Excuse me, M'am. Can you define awesome? Please write it out for me. I want each and every half note, rest, and dotted eighth. Can you do that for me? Put it on the chart, and I'll give you any background that you want or require. That way, we're both on the same page of what in the hell you effin' want. I'm not convinced. Show me, pretty lady. Show me, or write it down to every dot. Otherwise, don't complain.

But that's the way they are. They can't feel, so they're paying you to feel for them, and you'd best deliver.

The only thing that gets you by is being ambidextrous.

That old evil bastard Dr. McIntyre, the not-so-friendly researcher of living Neanderthals, once told me on his good authority that Neanderthals occupy a crucial point on the evolution of human beings. He told me that our kind were all set and on their way to becoming human except for one key component, and that component was handedness. He said handedness, the preference of using one hand more than the other, was the first step toward being human. He explained that these proto-humans favored the right more than the left. It sorta began when hominids had to specialize 'cause when you bash a fellow being in the head, you have to hone in. Sharpenin' your manual manipulation really matters if you want a happy result. The crazy doctor went on to explain that in that bydone era, if you decided to be ambidextrous, you'd be equally bad with both hands --- a total klutz if ever there was one. Which is not so good for bringin' home the bacon. And so, after several million years, folks learned to specialize. But nowadays, there are some among us who long to register their complete disapproval for this glut of over-civilization. Doc McIntyre had lots of speculations on that subject too. He theorized that some rare individuals in this day and age yearn to go back and touch base. So they do --- they return only to discover that something has changed. On this go-round, they've become equally good at using both hands! That's what drumming is mostly about. They can whack a cymbal with either hand and from any angle. Or if they can't, then they pick up stakes and go somewhere else.

If you wanna know what's up now, you'll never find it in the present. You hafta look back. Despite having a heart as hard as anthracite, Doc was probably right on that score. Still, I prayed that his phone had messed up and somehow deleted my number, but I knew that probably would happen because it's so difficult to make yourself scarce these days.

It was bop-pa-dee-bop-in-the-sense-surround-breathin'-life-to-a-brand-new-song time. Every tempo was a new panorama. The

Goddess' bedroom voice deep within me sang seductively: "Come on, Joe. Come on up and check out the view." Gwen, Kathy, Ben, and I were working up a new tune. It was the latest in a batch of about twelve or thirteen rockers and ballads. With one notable exception, the band was pulling these songs together at an effortlessly rapid clip, and even I was semi-amazed at how quickly the work in the recording sessions was going. Gwen sucked on a brew and then played around with the words, trying to ferret out their hidden surprises and where they would take her...

> "Songs in the dungeon under dust again
> Where gold shadows sift in a muttering mind
> In this place we halt to hear strings bend
> Marveling at, marveling at the artifacts we find"...

... An open C hovered over the tonality. It sat around, ready to see what direction Gwen would go in. And what was Ben doing through this? Well, he was the notable exception --- the weakest link. He was messing up all over the place, making the whole ball of wax a slithering maze of twaddle and babble. One clam after another was emanating from his bass. Congratulations, Ben. You just earned yourself a C minus. I always knew you had it in you. You only needed a little more confidence. What I meant to say was, dude, you gotta believe. Alright, well hurry up and believe 'cause I got serious business to attend to. My function is to highlight the natural dashes and commas of the music.

He made my eardrums wanna run and hide. It was especially rough on the Eustachian tubes. To be perfectly blunt, the guy would have had trouble pushing a doorbell. Every move was too tentative. Touch a timid toe in the tepid tide, boy, with trust and trepidation. E-flat nuzzles C into a new constellation. Why couldn't he just do nothing? Then the new constellation might have had a snowball's chance in hell of exploding brightly. Nothing would have been better. Nothin' would have left me free to do somethin'. And Jillian, good old TV director lady, was the one who was able to figure that one out. I first noticed this after an especially piss-poor take by Ben.

I was resigning myself to doing another one when she intervened to say, "Relax, guys. Don't even think about doing it again. The engineer will fix the whole thing in the mix." Gee, where would Ben ever be without a computer to save his ass? The wonders of Pro Tools! Some guys have all the luck.

She reached over and yanked the jack plug out of Ben's bass amp. Wow! That was great. Maybe now she would give him a tambourine. I had to give Jillian grudging credit. As a result, I was starting to change my opinion of her. So many Cro-Magnons are self-proclaimed experts who think that they're able to play music simply because they're good at whacking away on water glasses in restaurants, but she was an inspired amateur. Three cheers for intuition.

"C'mon," she announced. "Gather round. I've got something to tell you. As you are all aware by now, the addition of Joe our newest member has improved things considerably. Joe is a very accomplished player, but more importantly, having him on board only adds to ever more innovative plot possibilities. On that very subject, the writers for *Babies in Bars* have decided to film an episode in which the whole band goes to see Joe perform in a drum solo contest ..."

I could hear a collective silent groan. And so could she, but she continued.

"... Now I know that drum solos may not exactly be everyone's cup of tea --- particularly the three minute variety --- but we're not really talking total music here. Instead, it's all about the drama and ego. And what's more egotistical than a drum solo?"

"Not much," Ben replied disconsolately.

"So with that in mind, Camera Two, you start rolling now!" yelled Jillian.

The camera man did as he was told, and soon none of us paid him the least bit of attention. For all we cared, he was a fly on the wall.

"Dig it, Gwen," said Kathy, "Think about it --- music stripped down to the barest of stark essentials. No pesky melody to fuss over. No clunky chords to contemplate. No timbre to tinker with. No annoying lyrics trying to get a word in edgewise. Just pure sound --- something you can wallow in."

"Distillation. I suppose I could get used to it," Gwen added.

Ben chimed in, "The first music was probably from Neanderthals beating on rocks and blowing on whistle flutes made out of animal bones."

He was glaring at me, and he'd just now used the word "Neanderthal." Had I been found out by the person who was the most suspicious of my secret? I felt compelled to act in self-defense. "I promise you, Ben, I'll do my best impersonation of being a Neanderthal."

I made a funny face for him. "Do I look apish enough?"

I made an apish noise and did an ape thing with my arms.

"Somehow, Joe, I don't think being a primate would be much of a stretch for you."

"So you think I'd be playin' myself?"

"Pretty much. Joe, the Cro-Magnons are comin'. Extinction can't be faraway."

I was thinking --- "Watch it with the catty remarks, Ben. Don't you remember? You and I are supposed to be friends. It's part of the script. Don't fuck with the script." Of course I couldn't say a thing. On the sidelines, Jillian was making signals, telling him to back off. It was great to finally have some small measure of control. Jillian had done a smash up job of neutralizing him. I wanted to say, "Ben, practice your losing face!" but I held off.

Feeling reassured, I continued. "Ben, isn't acting about finding that other creature deep within you?"

"That's the party line."

"I can hear us now," Gwen interjected. "We'll be saying, 'With this last album we all tried to regress as much as possible.'" "Like back to seventy-five thousand years ago."

"So, we did an entire album of pounding rocks together."

"But Gwen, we shouldn't be so judgemental. Who knows? Maybe a good drum solo could save the world."

"Save the world? You wish!"

"Yes, I'm wishing and hoping."

The thing about Kathy and Gwen that I soon discovered was that every now and then they would go into some routine of their own invention. This was one of those times, a moment that had the hint of being well-rehearsed. It was their ritual dance, and they both knew the cues that would lead to a proscribed set of answers. They seldom seemed to tire of it. How could they? Any fool could see that they were in the early stages of love, and although they might lay off goofing around in some repetitive direction for a while, a good spot of ridiculousness was a spritely song familiar to both lovers, so they didn't mind touching base with it as a way of making their bond even stronger than it already was.

"You know, Gwen, it used to be that you could have a good song with four chords and maybe eight beats."

"Really, is that so? I guess it's true if you say so. But who needs all that baggage? Why not pare it down?"

"Yeah, pare it down to three chords and four beats."

"Hell Kathy, why stop there? Why not whittle it down to two chords and two beats?"

"Hey lady, we're on a roll! Let's go whole hog and make it one chord and one beat."

"You said it, girl. It's the key of one."

"How do you count that tune, lady?"

"It goes ONE, ONE, ONE, ONE."

"And the lyrics go, 'We've had our brains removed. We've had our brains removed.'"

"If one can't be found, two or three will be lost in action. And they'll be lost in action forever. Watch 'em waggle to keep up."

Jillian took careful note of this exchange and added some new directions: "Don't demur from bein' cheesy. Let the cheese flow and go. Let it go into burgers. It's the way of the world. Bring on the surf music, the punk tunes, the um-pah-pah polka songs, the Farfisa organs, and spaghetti Western soundtracks. I like to think of it as the mozzarella of existence."

Gwen collapsed in gales of laughter. Kathy followed suit.

Off on the periphery, I could see a look of amusement creep across Jillian's face.

"CUT."

Right about then I was summoned by my smartphone. The damned thing goes off at the most inopportune times. I retreated to a neutral corner and took the call.

"Hello, who is this?"

"It's your good friend, Doc McIntyre. I tell ya all of us here at the facility are missin' ya. Why don't ya come on back?"

"Doc, I'm not the institutionalized type. Look, I gave it the old college try only after you forced me into it, but I'm simply not cut out for all the wear and tear that you wanna submit me to, so why in the hell don't you leave me alone? You can try out the fibroblast whatever-it-is on someone else."

"We'll never leave you alone."

"And why the hell not?"

"Because you're a blast from the past that we can't part with."

I tried to register a rebuttal and found myself stabbing the air as I made my points But I soon realized that I was talking to dead air.

The drum solo competition was the promotional brainchild of a very popular chain music store. The winner of this round would go to the winner-take-all twenty-five grand competition in LA, but by that time a few months down the line *Babies in Bars* would assuredly have bigger fish to fry, so if I happened to win this one, the chances of my showing up to that big bash-off would be slim indeed. All the more reason to make a good showing.

We got to the store early because the organizers said we had to. Otherwise, I would have risked not making a deadline that I soon learned apparently didn't really exist. No big deal. I didn't mind signing up an hour beforehand even if we wound up standing around looking bored. Besides, the delay gave me the opportunity to ogle a raft of expensive drum gear and sonic/electronic toys. The holdup also allowed the crew to set up, so it all worked out. The MC gave me an inordinately big handshake, and then proceeded to jump around like some sort of bunny rabbit on meth.

"Jesus man, can't you calm down for a second?" I asked.

"Joe," he explained excitedly, "in this contest everyone wins." In a twinkling, the rabbit morphed into a game show host, but he still seemed high on meth.

"I'm not too keen on those contests where everyone wins," I replied.

"Look, even if you only go up onstage and give the snare a single solitary whack and walk away, we'd still give you a pair of maracas or one of our rain sticks."

"Man, I don't accept Miss Congeniality prizes. What's more, I bet the other contestants feel the same way. Think of all the extra merchandise you'll save. That'll impress the suits at the home office."

He led me to the kit that every contestant would be playing. It was your basic monster octopus kit with a few layers of tom toms and an array of thick and thin cymbals sprouting front, left, and center. In short, no matter which direction you poked your head in, there was something loud to smack. Just staring at it under the lights made me wish I could grow a few more arms and legs to play this humongous rhododendron even better than I knew I was already more than capable of doing.

The contestants had arrived by now, and the MC had us all draw lots for the order of appearances. I had the good fortune of drawing number ten, so I would get to listen to the better part of the competition. Ha! Fate was saving the best to last. I don't practice false modesty. That would be a note not found in this particular tune.

Naturally, members of *Babies in Bars* were there as my fan club. I would really need them because there was safety in numbers. I could see that one particular contestant had brought along virtually his entire extended family plus half his hometown neighborhood. That did not bode well for me because, as any bar band knows, crowds matter. You've got to get out the vote.

One thing was certain: I would need to get into what I call the "plush zone." The plush zone is a place where the regular rules no longer apply. It's a place where sound and fury conspire to make up something new and completely different, with no apparent precedent. It's where every beat and shard of rhythm I venture to try works perfectly. Getting there --- that would be a piece of cake. I've cruised into it on countless occasions. Unfortunately, there would be no guarantees once I got there. So many times I've been in a gig situation, and I've managed to get into the plush zone. I'm groovin' along, and the musical path has an incandescent glow. Everything seems possible. The sheen is so brilliant that even world peace seems to make perfect sense. There it is --- right within easy reach. You wonder why it's taken so long for people not to get it. I mean, it's as though I've found THE ANSWER, and I'm pointing to it, so all they have to do is take notes or write it down. Then I look at the audience --- and darn, I'm getting it, but they're not getting it. In fact, they're making no effort at all. Shame on them. If people would only listen for a second, then all that happy confusion would become an accomplished fact. I mean, I'm a drummer and I really feel this stuff. No joke.

However, disappointment sets in. They're not comin' along for the ride. In fact, they're chatting away on their cell phones or eating their chicken curry. No world peace for you guys! I could be playin' to lava lamps for all they care. A groove is a terrible thing to waste. Melody and harmony have gained their full inattention and the mix has become sonic wallpaper. How sad! The people out there look content in a bovine slow-mo sort of way. But I don't get too discouraged. I know it's not going to work every time. That's part of the deal, and you might as well get used to it. You can't even trust the plush zone.

On other nights, I discover that I can't do anything right. I wanna pack up my gear and go home, and maybe slit my wrists. Then a tourist comes up and says, "Hey man, I may be just visiting from Albuquerque, but I know great music when I hear it, and you guys are awesome." Gee, the guy clearly doesn't know anything, but I can't go and break the news to him. I can't let the air out of his delusion. That would be unhealthy for him and for me. So I lie, and we both go home feeling better. Nowadays, I never know completely what "good" really is.

And then the gig would be over. From my point of view, that might happen before I would hit my stride. But the audience didn't think that way. For me, what was gone forever was something each one of them would remember affectionately until he or she was put in the ground or rendered into cinders. Yet I was stuck with it for eternity. I had to live with it on a daily basis. It's what a Neanderthal does.

There was no way of knowing the arch of the competition and which extreme it would follow, but my instinct told me that this battle was shaping up to be a case of young versus old and style versus substance. The MC explained the rules. The way the drum off worked was that each player got three minutes to strut his stuff. At the end of three, the MC would strike a large gong to indicate that time was up.

Well, the brief explanation of the rules having been completed, they got down to business, and soon the cacophony was in full swing. And of course the *Babies in Bars* crew was filming the whole deal. With the gong tolling away at three minute intervals, this felt like show time at the Apollo because some players were just so completely awful, you wanted the gong to sound way before three minutes were up and hope that someone with a large hooked staff would slither onto the stage and sweep them off. They were sheep without a shepherd. In fact, when one of them was doing his star turn, he stopped playing on the top kit for a few seconds and reverted to a monotonous stream of quarter notes on the kick drum. Talk about dumbing it down! Kathy and Gwen looked over at me and started to mouth the words, "ONE, ONE, ONE, ONE." Yes, the key of one --- it should be avoided at all costs, unless of course that was what the judges wanted. Who knew what in the world they wanted? But the key of one should be banned.

One after another the competitors took the stage to play the oversize kit, and one after another I became further convinced of my own superiority. I would shut them down, provided I could squeak by the kid and the vast constituency he had brought along. The kid was the drummer who played immediately before me. As if finding out that he'd brought along his own personal cheering section were not enough, Jillian told me that he was deaf in one ear. That was horrible news. What were the judges going to do? Vote against the handicapped? There was no way not to be upstaged.

Finally, it was the kid's turn. He led off with some mid-tempo funk clichés, things that I'd known since I was fourteen years old.

Wow, the kid was ever the show off. He was like a yappy lap dog who didn't want to be ignored. Accordingly, I lapsed into sarcastic thoughts: "I honestly don't know if I can do that, but I'll give it the old college try. Yeah, right." The kid did a triplet roll and wound up on a thin rivet cymbal which he choked to a stop, before pointing a stick at the judges, and giving them a big squinty-eyed wink. For a second, he looked like Long John Silver. Yo! That was a totally cheap shot. Exactly what did that have to do with the price of eggs?

Kathy nudged closer to me. "Hey Joe, I think for these guys that this isn't music so much as it's therapy."

"I promise not to be therapeutic once I'm up there."

She moved to the front of the crowd and clutched her leg pretending to be lame.

Momentarily distracted in her direction, the crowd gave a collective laugh, myself included, but I stopped short when I felt something metallic sticking in my ribs. A familiar man's voice whispered and proclaimed, "My friend, I assure you that this is not a drum stick. Your sister gives you her best regards."

I sweated quickly, quicker than I'd ever sweated before.

"Is that what I think it is?"

"You got it right, man. It's a gun."

"So, what do you do for a living?"

"Me? Oh, funny you should ask. I deprive people of life. I'm in the deprivation business."

I gulped and tried to figure out how to escape.

"Joe, you'd best look straight ahead at the kid."

I did as I was told. "Hey, I guess I'm in no position to disobey."

"No, most certainly not."

The voice let out an exasperated sigh. "Man, will you look at this punk? He's huffin' and puffin'. He doesn't make it look easy. He's working up quite a slather. God, I hope he doesn't get a heart attack, but he looks like he's headed that way."

The voice jabbed the barrel of the gun tighter into my ribs. Panicking, I glanced over at the MC. He had his mallet at the ready to clobber the gong. He hadn't let up much with the hyperactive attention deficit disorder act. He still was hopped up on something.

The voice smacked his lips and purred again into my ear. "The boy's insufficiently ecstatic, don't you think?"

"I ... I ... guess you could say that," I replied nervously.

The voice continued in a low whisper. "Don't move, and don't look back. Keep your eyes on the stage."

"Uh, what, may I ask, do you want?"

"I want a good drum solo. Do you think you could provide me with that?"

"I'll ... I'll ... I'll try very hard."

The voice did another gun jab and purred on. "This kid continues to hammer away. Clearly, he's familiar with the conventional wisdom. Ah, but he seems to be having trouble finding 'one." If 'one' can't be found, two or three will be lost in action. And they'll be lost in action forever. Watch him waddle to keep up. That might be good because then you might get a chance to rip him to shreds. But I'll tell you something right now --- I don't appreciate conventional wisdom. I want something different. Do you think you could do something unconventional?"

"Maybe. I'll, I'll see what I can do."

"Can you please tell me a story when you get up there?" replied the voice.

"I'll see what I can do," I repeated. My own voice had suddenly become so dry that I could barely get the words out.

"He's a man with no vision on a course of collision. Do you think you could beat him into oblivion?"

"I'll give it a shot."

The only escape was to tell a story. I was feeling alone in the world again. I had to keep that misery at arm's length. In my mind I was already up there playing. Words and sounds were floating through my head again as the hit man's gun played cozy with my ribs.

> I'm a free electron swimmin' in a sea of quarks
> Lookin' for a proton and a place to park
> Don't ya know I'm bummin', bummin' and bummin'
> bad?
> Lost the best atom that I ever had."

Out of the corner of my eye, I could see the meth head MC was getting into position with his mallet.

GONG! The kid's constituency let out a loud cheer, and he got up from the super-sized kit. He raised his arms upward in a V for victory sign, looking something like a South American politician who'd just finished a speech. The applause scoured my ears and hurt. This was when a part of my being came over me and got the upper hand. For better or worse, it always comes over me when I'm performing. And today was no different. Suddenly, it hit me hard. I viewed *him* and *them* as the competition. I wanted to outperform *him* so completely that he'd wish he'd never taken up a pair of drumsticks in his entire life. The nerve of him thinking that he could actually play the drum, the first instrument that man ever conjured up! A fleeting image of spear-wielding Neanderthals chanting solemnly over a chorus of drums flashed before my eyes as my blood ratcheted up to a fine boil. I wanted to totally humiliate him. And the gong only served to up the ante.

"Time's up," said the voice. "The Duke of Flash's solo's over. Thank God! He was pissin' out the joint. I would give him a half-hearted handclap, but as you may have observed, I've got my hands full at the moment. My good friend, I will not mince words. It's your turn to play the membranophones. Your moment to tell a story. And it better be good. I'll also have you know that I'm a very harsh critic. And one more thing, my friend, the purpose of drum solos is to save the world from itself. So get on out there and save the world. If you're a real drummer, then show me some drama!"

I turned to face my would-be executioner. He was young, probably about half my age, but even at a quick glance, I could see he possessed a face that was good at suddenly going blank.

"I'll tell you a story of a long ago and faraway place."

KALI DANCED IN THE NO MO ZONE

If you have only one *chapatti* a day, you will not have a fluffy stomach. You see, the travel thing is really not a walk in the park like it is in Europe. That place, with its stone-faced Beefeaters, charming waiters, and garrulous gondoliers, might as well be some quaint Disney Land. But here it's not easy, especially if you're a babe in the woods. First, you have to go to the Tourists Only Railway Ticket Office. It's in the Writers' Building in the old part of Calcutta. They haven't done a stick of repairs there since maybe about 1848. Large falcons survey the city from its ramshackle pinnacles, now and then swooping down on hapless crows and sparrows. Once inside, you see the bureaucrats reading their newspapers and taking their time. Like the *alaap* section of an Indian *raga*, they're in no big hurry to get through this tune. Things will happen when they want them to happen. You will soon discover that the word for "tip" and the word for "bribe" are one and the same. At that point, the rats start coming out of the holes in the walls. They strut around like they own the place and they kinda sorta do. You half expect them to say, "Hey buddy, how're ya doing?" in a low raspy voice. But they don't, so you sign the required forms, the bureaucrats slump to attention, and suddenly there are lots of the critters scampering around. Your wife begins to get pissed because the tail of one of them has slithered across her bare foot. Well, you get the drift. So, having gotten your tickets, you use the city as your home base and set off for side trips around the country. You zigzag across the land.

The trip back to Calcutta started uneventfully except for the occasional passed out peasant lying face down in the middle of the steep winding road. We were descending from the foothills of the Himalayas. The driver would come around a sharp turn and there the peasant was --- dead drunk on the worn median strip.

"Shouldn't we stop and help him out?" I inquired. The driver smiled and hunched over his wheel deep in concentration. I pondered the bald tires I'd seen earlier and figured, what the hell, this guy looked like a great driver. After all, he was still alive.

Mrs. Dhutt, a plump Brahmin matron from West Bengal, burst out laughing, slapping her pink-saried thigh.

"What? You must be joking. No, no, no. It's just one of those country people. He's tied one on. Too much toddy. He's lucky not to go blind. Let him sleep it off. That's if he's really drunk, but he probably isn't."

"What do you mean by that?" I replied.

"Most likely, he's stone cold sober and if we get out to help, his friends will come out of the woods and rob us."

I was incredulous. Sachiko was incredulous too, blurting out a loud "*Mo.*" It's Japanese for "For shame." --- short in her native tongue for "*Mo-eeh-yo.*"

"Stop it, Sachiko," I ordered. "Don't you know this is a no mo zone?"

She burst into tears.

In India, weed is totally legal, if and only if, you buy it in a government store. So we went down the road to the government store. There was a wild boar trotting down the main street of the village. People gave him a very wide berth until he ducked into the woods. What a relief! Let him go wherever he wants. We went into the government store and made our purchase. It had psychedelic posters on the wall, and guy was high. But hold onto that receipt he said, or you could find your ass very much arrested.

The British tourists didn't seem to care about their valuables. I told them they needed to buy a lock and chain in the railroad station; otherwise, the peasants would come in at some remote stop in the countryside and steal their valuables. They wouldn't listen. So they got to be very sorry. We call this comeuppance.

Manipur was definitely the dangerous place we'd expected. Everywhere there were all sorts of security personnel, roadblocks, and checkpoint Charlies. Understand that the place was trying to secede and had been trying for a long time. The authorities had put a curfew in place for six o'clock because the week before some kid waiting for a bus had been shot by the trigger happy soldiers. Tall opium poppies adorned the hotel's front lawn.

"It's a problem here!" exclaimed the lady at the check-in desk as she gestured to the addictive plants.

This particular establishment had been a big deal at one time, but since you needed to get special permission to even get into Manipur these days, it had kind of gone to seed. Our hosts were constantly arguing over which of them would have the honor of squiring us around their fair city.

The strangest part of this side trip was when our Hindu host Dr. Singh took us to a "VIP" party in the old section of Imphal. Suddenly, it became quite clear that Sachiko and I were the guests of honor. There were so few Westerners who ever managed to gain entry that when they did, it was an excuse to throw a party for their benefit. And what a party it was. The men were dressed in tuxedos and their wives wore what looked like 1950's prom dresses. They were indeed the VIP's that Dr. Singh had promised. The gang was all present and accounted for: these doctors, lawyers, politicians, police captains, and even a general or two, were the people who pulled the strings in this town. One of the generals drunkenly informed me that no Manipuri party would be complete without a round of songs. I glanced anxiously at Sachiko. She looked nervous. She was out of her realm. That was not good.

"Ev'y one mustht thing a thong of hith choosing," announced the general. "You thee Joe. We haf Jack Daniels here too."

I watched as each of the elegantly dressed inebriated couples got up and performed beautiful songs I would probably hear once, and only once, in my entire life. Sometimes the revelers even looked a bit like Fred and Ginger as they cavorted around the room. The burly Chief of Police and I each took turns accompanying the show. We traded off playing *tabla,* a folk drum used in a variety of Indian music. Soon it was my turn to sing. I chose to sing the Beatles' "Within You, Without You" and got quite a reception. They had never heard it before.

Then it was the Police Chief's turn to play *tabla.* He glanced at his hands, held them up for all to see and exclaimed, "These hands beat prisoners all the livelong day. Now they need another place to come out again to play."

I looked again for Sachiko in the drunken crowd. She looked alone and crestfallen in the corner of the room. Someone was trying to feel her up. I gently removed the groping hand and reached out to her, but she pushed me away.

"It's okay, Sachiko. We don't want to get in trouble here. Sometimes, I even get felt up."

The next day was weird too. We made a short trip to a lake a few miles outside of Imphal. It was the best kept secret in all of Asia. To get there, Doctor Singh and the driver had us on a road that wandered into a narrow valley. The good doctor explained that this was where one of the later battles of World War Two had been fought. It seems that the Brits were on one side of the valley and the Japanese were on the opposite hill. Dr. Singh explained that the Japanese Imperial High Command back in Tokyo had given their commander in the field a strict directive not to advance. Of course, the guy had to go and disobey it. Apparently, the Brits and Japanese teed off on each other with the heavy artillery. Way to go, Mr. Field Marshall! You're doin' a heck of a job, Mutaguchi!

The carnage was beyond belief, one reminder of it being a lone tree that had been shot up so badly that its limbs and trunk appeared to still be recovering from its wounds many decades later. Even its leaves seemed to be shell-shocked. Some timidly sprouted on the tips of a twig. Near the tree, we could see a war memorial on the left side which was where aged survivors of the Imperial Army would come every year or so to lay wreaths. My wife's uncle, the one whom she had never had the pleasure of knowing, was one of the dead. In fact, that was how we both managed to finagle the trip to this area of India in the first place because what with Manipur trying hard to secede and all, as well as local terrorists blowing up the reservoir every now and then, special permission was required. So back in New York, the rough and tough six foot five turbaned diplomat at the embassy had demanded to know why we desired to go to this forbidden area, which in the present was the place of so much violent strife. Sachiko had explained to him that we wanted very much to make a pilgrimage to honor the memory of her long dead uncle. We fully expected that the diplomat's answer would be no, but we had nothing to lose, so we asked anyway. To our utter surprise, the hulking Sikh man emerged from his office in a flood of tears, saying, "Oh this is such a lovely reason! Your permission is granted. But please be careful." Yes, we would be careful. We would be extra careful. The blubbering diplomat gained control of himself and went back into his office.

When we got to the lake, we looked down upon it from a high ridge. The bright blue water had tiny islands that appeared to float on the enchanting ethereal surface. Fishermen paddled in gondola-like boats, and every so often, would casually spear an island with long bamboo poles. It took me a while to figure out that they were spearing them so that they wouldn't drift away. Then they would collect the fish from traps that had been set near the shores of these islands. Suddenly, the fisherman could be heard having a conversation. Of course, I didn't understand a word, but strangely, I could hear it as if it were in the very next room despite the fact that the fishermen were over a hundred yards away. Doctor Singh explained that the lake had bizarre acoustical properties and that the light breeze interacted with the water in some mysterious way so as to refract the sound upward onto the surrounding ridge.

That was perhaps my first inkling that she and I had entered a place where the accustomed rules no longer completely applied. The challenge would be to see if she and I could adapt. Not long after that, we were on an all-night bus ride that was taking us through small but densely populated villages. I was awakened by a distinctive thump and asked the tourist in the next seat what had happened.

"It's nothing," he replied matter-of-factly. "The driver's goin' barrel ass tryin' to make up for lost time, and he just hit somebody. Probably ran right over him. Only trouble is --- if the driver stops to get out and help, he's sure to be stoned to death."

"So what does he do?" I asked.

"He just keeps on driving. A man's gotta do what a man's gotta do."

Conked out with her head up against the window, Sachiko still managed to utter a half-hearted "Mo!"

Fast forward to a week later: we were back in Calcutta taking *sitar* music lessons from one of the great pundits. I was playing *tabla* again, this time for the great pundit's class. I loved playing the drum and looking up to see the entire class playing the same *sitar* melodies over and over until they got the hang of it. James, an American from the Midwest, was one of the students. He was by far the best pupil, and the pundit was very happy with him. Often, the pundit would hold James up as a shining example of the ideal sitar player, comparing him to his son who was, quite frankly, a bit of a disappointment for Panditji. You see, pundits are always looking for reliable students to whom they can pass on a lifetime's worth of musical treasures, and Panditji's son was more interested in computer hacking and cricket matches. James milked it up, and he also hit it off really well with Sachiko. Sometimes, back at the apartment in Lake Gardens, she would even say, "Joe, why can't you be more like James?" James, James I thought. I'd only met him a few times and didn't get much of an impression except that he seemed like the type who wrote the most beautiful songs that no one would ever hear. I recalled going over to James' house. The man's cat had made more of an impression on me. Then there were a few times when I'd come back to the apartment and fall asleep under the fan, and Sachiko would come back two hours later from an errand in the city. She would definitely be in a better mood.

I stepped out into the heat of the day. Varanasi was like that, a labyrinth of ancient narrow streets where the stray dogs and the monkeys were in a state of perpetual war, and goggle-eyed young

Turks chewed *pan,* shoving their way through the crowds, all the while revving the engines of their shining motor scooters. I was alone this time, and Sachiko was back in the hotel trying to get a hold of herself. I wished I could've slapped her silly, but naah, I wasn't the type. That sort of thing was a note that just wasn't in this *raga.* But I was slowly discovering that that was really what she wanted. True, unpleasant things had happened. The train had been hijacked, which was about par for the course, and we'd been held hostage from about eleven at night until seven in the morning. We'd been forced to listen to political speeches in Hindi the whole time, and I'd asked an old man what the hijackers were talking about and the guy sorta shrugged his shoulders. Eventually, the local warlord, satisfied that had made his show of strength, let the train proceed on its way. He was so darned gentlemanly about it that he even bowed to my wife. Sachiko, however, was unimpressed. "It's all your fault! It's all your fault!" she yelled. Things were starting to take a turn for the worse.

I decided to go to the burning *ghats.* I was having a cup of tea from an indoor stall near the great sacred river when a loud crashing sound had interrupted my daydreams. I didn't give it much thought until the crash happened again, reverberating every ten seconds or so, through the walls of the tiny restaurant. I rushed outside to see an enormous dead cow being pushed down the steps of the burning *ghat.* A French tourist off to the side informed me that the farmers were pushing the carcass towards the river. The crashing continued until at last the straining farmers managed to get the beast into the water and the tourist and I watched it get carried away in the slow current, its stiffened legs peeking out from the ripples. I took a deep breath and invited the tourist to join me for tea. The tourist introduced himself as one Claude Ferrier from Paris. Soon Claude was ranting to me about how India wasn't living up to his expectations. Claude seemed like the type of person who never let a very skimpy command of a language other than his own ever get in the way of having a deep discussion. He would make his point like some sort of bulldozer, which I found to be very endearing. In fact, I found myself egging him on, urging him to describe indiscretions that I would never dream of doing myself. In my mind's eye, I kept saying, "Do it! Do it!" "No," I thought, but didn't say, "It's better to let other people do your acting out for you." Claude's favorite words were "arriving" and "transforming." Everything about India could be assessed with those two words. Basically, Claude was bummin' and bummin' bad. Apparently, he had expected some sort of old Vedic culture and what he got instead was this dog-eat-dog, smash-and-grab, hocus pocus shuck and jive, or something akin to crashing cows.

I reassured him: "No pain no gain. Take me, for example. I'm going through lots of pain right now. My wife is acting like a spoiled child. This country brings out the best and the worst."

Claude nodded and looked into the bottom of his tea cup. He was unpleasantly surprised to see several strands of mated human hair. He was deeply alarmed. I reminded the tourist that this was Varanasi, city of death, city of grossness ---the place where dyed-in-the-wool Hindus go to die --- the place that will never host the next Olympics. The tourist smiled nervously.

"It's okay" I said. "This water has been boiled to the right temperature. You won't get sick."

"You tourists," I continued. "You're so worried about getting sick. Don't you know you'll get sick? You must get sick. It's only a matter of time. One of the tourists that Sachiko and I met is this guy named James. He's a rich kid from Ohio who's determined not to get sick. Tells me that the only way to accomplish this is to eat strictly at expensive tourist traps like the Taj Bengal. I, on the other hand, continue to dine and tempt fate at all the funky *chapatti* and *masala dosa* stands in Dalhousie Square. I tell this guy I'm building up my immune system and then I flex a bicep. So, James decides to take a two week side trip to Bangkok, the capital of sin on this planet. After that, James is back in Calcutta regaling me with stories about his adventures in an endless succession of cat houses in Sin City. And this was the guy who was so worried about getting sick?"

Claude nodded and laughed.

"Joe, *mon ami*. You are arriving and transforming."

"Claude, my friend, I think she's having an affair with him."

"*Mon dieu*! Say it isn't so. How do you know?"

"I just know it. To tell you the truth, I'm at my wit's end. She's the one who teased for this trip, and she's got the sourest attitude you could ever imagine. Talk about arriving and transforming. Except for a few things, she hates it here. I think she can't wait to get back. Me, on the other hand --- I could just as easily stay here for the rest of my life. I rather like all the chaos. Everything from purchasing bottled water to a recording device is a protracted negotiation. Just the other day, I said to a storekeeper, 'I'm leaving the store with the merchandise now. There are fifty rupees on the counter. If there's a problem, please stop me before I get to the door.' Well, I just kept walking, and he didn't come after me."

"If she's really having an affair with him, why don't you take the wind out of his sails? Why don't you trade her for something?"

"You can't be serious!"

Now Claude was the one who was doing the egging on. I felt an uneasy sense of camaraderie, a feeling that we could be partners in crime.

"Joe, trade her and trade her soon. It'll only get worse."

I'd always liked people who would volunteer for someone else.

I left the teahouse and started back to the hotel. The sun beat down relentlessly. It was the hammer and the street was the anvil. A small procession was coming, no doubt heading for the burning *ghats*. There was a young woman laid out on a hand-pulled rickshaw. She was surrounded by relatives who were sprinkling rose petals on her motionless form clad in a white winding sheet. Already her serene face was changing color. Now there was a lady on her last rickshaw ride, going to the same place as the crashing cow, but with a stop at the *ghat* first! I suddenly felt an impossible sadness, a sadness without end. I desperately wished I could rescue her --- tap her on the shoulder, so she would wake up and go down to the bazaar to buy herself a pretty new *sari* and some bangles.

You see, in Calcutta it's like this: when you rent a house, the servants come with it. Mrs. Bhattacharyya, who would be our landlady for all those times when we weren't on the road, had explained this to us, but it really didn't sink in until the kids of the servants would show up at the window sill in the morning. Sachiko was quite taken by the two year old named Kuti. What a charmer! He was always doing some cute little dance or asking me to take him by his tiny hands and give him a twirl. He would get dizzy from that and fall in a heap on the floor only to get up again and say, "Joe, *abai, abai* (again, again)." He loved to be twirled.

Sachiko was so in love with the little tyke that she wanted to kidnap him. Sometimes, usually when the heat of Calcutta got too oppressive, she would sleep out in the outer room where there was a bigger fan. When I awoke in the morning, I'd go to that room and there would be Sachiko and Kuti curled up together, still deep in sleep. In those moments, I wanted to rescue someone again. She would wake up and say, "C'mon, Joe. Let's take him back to New York with us."

"Don't you think his parents might object to that?" I asked.

"Joe, I'm joking of course."

But I knew that she wasn't. I could imagine what it would be like if we took Kuti back to New York. In no time at all, he'd be wearing backwards baseball caps and surfing the web. Maybe, as an alternative, I should just stay there in Calcutta and Sachiko and James could go back to Ohio or wherever. I began to ponder Claude's proposal, the one about trading her for something. Oh, how I wished I could wake her up. It was the same feeling I'd had about the dead lady on the rickshaw. But that one was gone. Nothing could bring her back. Lesson to be learned: she must be worthy of rescue. Yeah, something in Sachiko was dead. Something irrevocable, something irretrievable. Ha! That was weird because in light of this new revelation, she had managed to redeem, in my eyes, some small measure of desirability. Yeah, but she was really gone. Gone forever. That was the allure. And like the rickshaw lady, being gone didn't necessarily mean that she would be out of mind. Rickshaw Girl, like the crashing cow, may have become a part of the great sacred river, but she would always have a certain power over me. No doubt Rickshaw Girl was acutely aware of this as, yawning seductively in some nebulous afterlife, she found herself laughing coquettishly at me. "Hey guy, put that in your pipe and smoke it!" she giggled. But perhaps I should exchange this feeling for something new? Claude was right. An exchange must take place. *Quid pro quo.* It was as it should be.

But another development was happening. I was acquiring a fondness for *tabla,* that musical instrument I'd been playing at Panditji's *sitar* class. I loved the voluptuousness of it, how you could bend notes on the larger of the two drums. And once you knew the rules, you could solo on it. Musically, it was like an enormous labyrinth, in which you could wander around at will, checking out what each side room had to offer. And what surprises they were! This was quite different from the usual rock and roll stuff that I was used to. Also, unlike that world, there was surprisingly little arguing. The beats all had names, and if someone didn't like them, well tough. Here they were never trying to force a drum to be something else --- as if it should be ashamed of itself for making such a glorious racket.

At first Sachiko and I liked the idea that the servants came with the bed and breakfast/ paying guest accommodations. It was an unexpected perk, but we soon discovered that it had one disadvantage: we had to be back by 11:00 PM, or Mrs. Bhattacharyya would be very upset about our waking up the household. Twice we were admonished of this rule, and we both made a concerted effort to be back on time. This worked out well for a time.

However, the problem all came to head when my *tabla* teacher, Kishan, invited us to one of his concerts at a Hindu temple about an hour's drive outside of Calcutta. We went in Kishan's car and got a bit of a late start, being that there was traffic on the Hoogly Bridge. There was always a traffic jam on the Hoogly Bridge. Kishan informed us that there would be a very fine girl *tabla* player named Vidya playing before him, and perhaps if we hurried, we might even get to see part of her performance.

"Take my word, Joe" said Kishan, "She's one of the best. She can really make the mountains move with her playing."

But soon it became clear that they were probably not going to catch the beginning of Vidya's set. We were almost at our destination when the weather became an added factor. Suddenly, the rain came out of the sky in torrents, and the thunderclaps started in. Sachiko and I looked out over a ridge to the right and could see power lines snapping, lighting up the night sky like writhing incandescent snakes. The wind became ferocious, buffeting the car back and forth. I was genuinely afraid.

Sachiko looked anxious. She whispered in my ear, "Why did we have to come? Now we probably won't be able to get back in time, and Mrs. Bhattacharya will be very angry."

Kishan reassured us, "It's only a little squall coming in from the Bay of Bengal. Not to worry. The goddess Kali is doing her thing. But it looks as though we may miss Vidya's part of the concert. However, I'll put on a good show. So, you have that to look forward to."

The storm subsided as quickly as it began, and we pulled into the parking lot of the Hindu temple. But when we got to the site of the small outdoor stage, we found the place in a shambles. The stage had been trashed, and the rest of the show had been cancelled. The promoter, who was a close friend of Kishan, was in tears. He had been planning this concert for months and now it had been destroyed by the weather. It seemed that as Vidya had reached the high point of her *tabla* performance, someone in the audience had spotted a mini-tornado, so everyone had to leave and run for cover. When they got back after the storm had abated, it was clear that the show could not go on.

"It's okay, my friend." Kishan was consoling the promoter. "We'll reschedule. All is not in vain." Kishan turned to Vidya who was dressed in a red sari with pink highlights. Despite the disappointment of the storm, she was beaming. "And they tell me you played quite a program. Yes, you almost made the mountains move, but you certainly made the stage move. Hey Joe, I think you should study with her too. She would make a great teacher, in addition to me of course."

I was thunderstruck. Vidya was a spitting image of Rickshaw Girl. I thought I was looking at a ghost. That sweet little Kali, Miss Goddess of Who-Knows-What?, had come back to me. And she had a look on her face as if to say she knew something I didn't. Obviously, Vidya and the ghost of Rickshaw Girl were new and ever-expanding versions of the Goddess of Music who had visited and would continue to haunt me from time to time solely for the purpose of checking up on me. My only wish was that She would stop doing this just to tease me and to get my hopes up. Why couldn't she stop throwing me bones and gristle? Why couldn't she give me something useful? She'd just then given a dazzling performance only to tear the whole playhouse down. Apparently, my job in life was to monitor her capacity for destruction. There was not much to look forward to except for years of haunting.

We all adjourned to the promoter's nearby house and discussed when to reschedule. The talks went deep into the evening. Sachiko got more and more angry. It was all my fault that we wouldn't get back to the house in time for the curfew just as it had all been my fault that the train had been hijacked two weeks ago. And furthermore, it had all been my fault that the taxi driver had driven too fast the other day, and it had been my fault that etcetera, etcetera, etcetera. Yes, it had been absolutely terrible. Nothing was right and nothing ever would be.

Finally, we piled back into Kishan's car and he drove us back to Calcutta. "I'll drop you in Jadavpur and you can get a hand-pulled rickshaw from there" he explained.

Sure enough, as he pulled into Jadavpur, I could see the long line of rickshaw drivers fast asleep on their rigs. Sachiko and I said goodbye to Kishan and got out of the car. We got into the first rickshaw in the queue and I gave the man directions in Bengali. Immediately, I had to endure a constant barrage of verbal assault from Sachiko.

"*Mo* Joe, what's the matter with you? You bastard! You knew this concert would go late. Now Mrs. Bhattacharyya will be so angry 'cause we'll wake up all the servants."

"Baby, how did I know it would go over? I'm doing the best I can. Besides, I thought I told you this is a no mo zone."

Her tirade went on and on until she topped it off with a round of vicious slugs to my back and shoulders. I just braced myself and turned away. I didn't do anything to protect myself. As the assault grew worse, the rickshaw driver suddenly laughed. He burst out first in a stifled guffaw which heightened in intensity causing the rickshaw to wobble. This only made Sachiko angrier, and she started yelling at him.

I blurted out, "It's okay my good fellow! Your driving is impeccable. A very good *baksheesh* is in store for you! Carry on, my man!"

Yes, my life was clearer now. Tomorrow I would have to make the trade that Claude had spoken of. Perhaps I could get James' cat. In the meantime, I would have to give this driver say 300 rupees and take him out for a toddy.

THE CAT AND THE WIFE TOO

Some cities'll treat ya like an adult
No automated teller to bail you out
Stars are blinkin' glintin' throught the gloom
They're adding alpha not a moment too soon

We were listening to the playback of the latest *Babies in Bars* song through Kathy's iPod, which she'd been kind enough to let me borrow so I could get the tune down snug in my memory muscle.

"Hey Joe, the interaction between voice, guitar, and drums is darned impressive. That Gwen --- what a set of lungs she has. Who would ever suspect that the lady has asthma 'cause she can let out a hell of a yell? Just one thing to remember, Joe --- make sure she's well-stocked with inhalers. Of course, the bass player ... well, that's another story. You may have to give serious thought to having him replaced."

"Bill, I think you should know that I have a long history of bad blood with bass players."

"I can't imagine why."

Bill paused to look at the high tide as its latest entry crashed and rippled up the wet sand. Then he ogled two thong bikini girls as they frolicked in the foam. The way they minced and scurried in the advancing surf was real satisfying.

"They were made for breeding, but they're not my type, Joe. However, if they were ..."

Bill didn't quite finish what he wanted to say. He had a wistful look. The hit man charged with overseeing to my imminent demise was one of those few Cro-Magnons who appreciated a good drum solo, even the extended variety. What a traitor to his class! By now, I'd let him in on all my pet theories about how it's a great big Cro-Magnon world that we live in, and he was mildly amused. I could see that he was a man who liked to engage in long discourses of gooey philosophy, so I explained to him that Neanderthals work hard, but it's hard for that work to mean anything, so what better reason to bag it all and go straight to the beach. By this time, I'd told him two stories: one at the drum solo contest and the second one out here on the surf and sand. The results had been auspicious: I'd managed to talk him out of killing me. For once in my life, I'd had the power of persuasion, but somehow I think his mind had already been made up.

"I guess I'm not much of a Cro-Magnon, Joe."

"Perhaps I should make you an honorary Neanderthal."

"Oh thank you very much."

"And I thank you for not making me dead. The trouble with being dead is that everything you've learned in life is all for naught. You're back to square one."

He raised a thermos and gave me a toast. "Here's to hardheadedness. We'll walk down the street, and we'll get busted. I say hey baby baby we're maladjusted."

"Definitely. As you stagger through this Neanderthal life, you will discover that people will unjustly accuse you of being a party animal. Nothing could be more off base. I'm telling you this for your own good. In fact, we like work. It's simply that ours has no value. So, we look elsewhere to someplace where our efforts might be better appreciated."

"You guys are such underachievers. One second you can make the world a better place and in the next, you might be walkin' on the cusp of worthlessness."

"But I won the drum contest, Bill."

"You won by a mile. And as an extra bonus, you got to save the world from itself --- at least for the time being."

"I guess you could say that's a work in progress."

“One that requires religious fervor! But seriously, you flat out left ’em in the dust, and you won because you made the drum tell the best story. And just now you told me another good story.”

“Yeah, but I had a little help from Jillian.”

“I was surprised at the low level of velocity among the contestants, excluding you of course.

“We live in slow motion times.”

“You’re right on both counts. Jillian did help you out a lot.”

“Wow! The kid and his crowd were righteously pissed, weren’t they?”

“Well, they apparently didn’t know the rules of television.”

“And please tell me the rules of television.”

“The kid failed to take into consideration that he was a guest star. Joe, it was *your* show. *Babies in Bars* rules! So you *had* to win even if it was a bloody reality show.”

“But I really told a better story than he did?”

“Damned right.”

“You sorta made it sound as though it was rigged.”

“It was rigged. It was scripted right down to the tee by Jillian’s writers.”

“God, that takes all the fun out of it.”

“No it doesn’t. Look, you were the *best,* but the only way you could possibly win was to have the clout of television. The kid didn’t get it. He thought being young made the whole thing a slam dunk. Well, he had another thing comin’. I loved to see the disappointment on his face.”

We were lounging under a massive rented beach umbrella drinking Side Cars out of a thermos that Bill had mixed up back at the hotel bar. It suddenly occurred to me that we were the only people there who weren’t in bathing suits. In fact, Bill was wearing a suit with a fedora. No matter. The fedora came in handy what with the sun and all. Soon we would be donning trunks and diving into the surf.

“You see, Joe. I fully understand where you’re comin’ from, but I don’t think you do. If you haven’t guessed it by now, Joe, I’m from the other persuasion. Therefore, I can be a bit more, how do you say it, objective? Let me give you some free advice. I'll give it to you straight up. No pun intended. For most people, success is a pretty clear cut deal. You want to get ahead, so you hit the books and get your certificate. We're a nation of certificate holders. Having accomplished that little feather in your cap, you suck up to the boss and, with even a half-assed effort or a paltry dose of luck you'll find yourself in a nice office with a good salary. After that, you're home free. You can sleepwalk your way through life. You can even screw up on a weekly, if not daily basis, and you'll get another chance. Yeah, it's true. But there are exceptions. For example, there was one guy that I whacked a few weeks back who, when he was looking down the barrel of my gun actually had the nerve to say, 'C'mon man, where's my second chance? Everyone gets a second chance.' The poor bastard expected it. He thought that wishing makes it so. I truly believe my bullet was the first time he hadn't gotten his second chance. You should have seen the look of astonishment on the man's face. No doubt the undertaker had his work cut out for him trying to get him to look less astonished for his final audience. But truth be told --- excluding the late and not-so-great target of my honest-as-a-Russian-made bullet, most people get umpteen chances. However, as you may have observed, it doesn't work that way with drumming. One screw up and you're out of there."

He poured himself another Side Car and continued in the same vein.

"Being good at that has nothing to do with success or failure. Why? Because you could get sucker punched from out of the blue. You're always going to be a part of someone else's project. Till the end of time it'll be a master/slave situation."

"I've learned how to suffer fools gladly. Melody and harmony, and their kissin' cousin timbre, will trump rhythm every time."

"Exactly. Look, man, a few hours ago I could have done much more than sucker punch you. I could have shut out your lights forever. I only stopped out of the goodness of my heart. And while we're on the subject of sucker punches, I'll let the cat out of the bag."

"What do you mean?"

"If you hadn't beaten me to the punch, I would have shot my partner Andy."

"Why?"

"He was starting to really get on my nerves."

"So much for loyalty among crooks!"

"What a whiner! Every day he filled my head with boo boo hoo. But in other areas, the guy was about as sensitive as an ox."

"So you need to be sensitive to be a hit man?"

"Yeah, in fact you do if you wanna know the truth."

"That sorta makes me feel uneasy, Bill. You got bored being around Andy. How soon before you get bored being around me?"

"Not to worry. I won't get bored 'cause you can make the drums talk. Also, I'm not easily bored and Andy was definitely pushing his luck from the get-go."

"You're the kind of a person who probably would like to put hallucinogens in the drinking water."

"You guessed it. That's me. Get used to it --- you're just the hired help, and you always will be. You know something?"

"What?"

"You may in fact be an artist. Ha! What a pretentious word! But people will forever call you a craftsman and steal your soul. Then you'll have to chase after 'em, knock 'em down, beat the crap out of 'em, and steal it right back. By the way, what happened to the wife in your story and that artist that she shacked up with?"

His question hit hard. The sadness welled up and flooded over me. God, that was a hurt that would never go away! One of a long line of devastating failures. Why couldn't I have one success, just a single project that would bloom into fruition? I had tried so hard to make it work. What self-deception. I'd fooled myself into believing that "love" was all that would be required. Love was what people with good intentions fell into. And surely, I was a man with good intentions because I wanted people to be happy in the world. And since I was a creature in this world, why shouldn't I be allowed to have that luxury? What better thing could someone bring to the table? If you brought it, everything was supposed to be fine from there on in. Well, I had brought it, but it had grown into a grotesque failure, an annihilation of everything good in my spirit and also of hers. And her spirit was probably more important than my spirit. You see, I was attempting to be completely selfless. I mean, it's so important to keep an open mind on these things, and selfishness is the opposite of having an open mind. That's what a Cro-Magnon practices every instant of his existence. I wanted to show them that selflessness would lead to real love. I wanted to be a good example. But the problem was that being inconsiderate was really the path that would have been best for all concerned. In short, I should have behaved like a complete hog. Then she might have loved me back. Selfishness would have shown her that I felt wonderful about me with a capital M and everything that my great big engorged Self came into contact with in the world. And that would have made her feel that I was the cat's meow and accordingly, that I was quite the catch for me, and more importantly for her. I tell you I should have been a freakin' fascist. That would have led to absolute love.

Bill interrupted my languid daydream, bringing me back to the present. "So, Joe, what happened to the wife? Tell me, is that too touchy a subject?"

"Oh...oh...her? Oh, I traded her to James, and they moved away to Vermont."

"And you got the cat?"

"Yeah, for a time. But then I foolishly lent the cat back to James and the beautiful critter got eaten by a wolverine."

"That's not fair. James can't have the wife and the cat too!"

"So I discovered."

"You can't have a cat in Vermont. It'll get eaten by the *uber* weasels. The whole woods are infested with 'em. They're the hit men of the wilderness. I'm from California, Joe. And we do some mighty weird stuff out there, but I don't think I've ever heard of anyone who's traded his wife for a cat."

"But Shasta was a very good cat!'"

"And you too are a very good cat. But you may get eaten up by the world if you don't get eaten up by a crazy wife first."

"The problem with me and her was that we didn't quite fit. Literally. It's true --- the angle was all wrong. Decent people don't like to talk about this. But if that seriously sad fact was the foundation for the dissolution of the relationship, then why in the hell can't we talk about it?"

"The problem is that there are so few things you can talk about without someone getting mad. It's easy to believe, but so hard to behave. Many people might object. But a reality show is quite different. There you have a license to be as rude as you wanna be 'cause there's no filter."

"My ex would've loved it because in the life she'd led so far, she'd never had a chance to be rude. They wouldn't let her. In Japan, being rude is the ultimate sin."

"Yup, very astute observation, my friend. I think you may be learning. That was most likely the reason why she found your buddy James so enticing. But listen up! This reality show is going to be your big chance, which brings me to more germane subjects. There's something you and I have to discuss right now. Joe, you realize, or I hope you realize that your sister will be very upset that first Andy and now yours truly didn't exactly do what we were paid to do."

"She wants me dead."

"You get the picture."

"So, she's going to be sending someone after us to complete the job, or rather to fix the job that I messed up on purpose."

"I know her well. She wants her money's worth."

"Well, my friend, you may have to beat her to the punch," he continued.

"Bill, what in the hell are you talking about?

"I'm talking about whacking her. What in the world do you think I'm talking about?"

"But, aside from…from…from moral considerations and all that, it's not practical."

"Sure it's practical. I can make it practical for you."

"Look, she's my sister. I can't just go and have her bumped off. That wouldn't be right."

"And try to tell me that what she's doing is right for you. Joe, Joe, listen to me. It's either you or her. You know where she's coming from. Don't you?"

Uneasily, I nodded in agreement.

"I got a plan, Joe."

"Good lord. Plan or no plan, I can't sit by and let this happen. It wouldn't be right."

"You wanna live to play drums again, or at least I hope you do. I wouldn't have spared you if you thought otherwise."

"No, no way. I'm not going to be party to knockin' off my sister."

"I'm afraid you don't have much choice in the matter, Joe."

"What d'ya mean by that?"

"I mean that if you don't say yes, I'll fulfill her end of the contract and kill you."

"You can't do that."

His voice seemed to descend an octave, which was a very unnerving effect. "Oh yes, I can. Watch me now."

He suddenly pulled my left arm and got me in a vice-like judo hold before yanking my shoulder one way and the arm bone in another direction, stopping just at the pain threshold, which was when and where the tendon screamed for mercy.

"ACCH!!"

I could tell Bill was a man of some experience in the thug game. The reason for this was that he was good at making it seem as though he and I were simply two guys horsing around on the beach. To any of the folks in the general vicinity, none of this arm-twisting business would have raised a shadow of suspicion. Then he let up and gave the tendon what it wanted.

"That's not fair."

"Few things are, Joe."

Already the tendon was feeling better as it silently yelled at me to get a move on.

"Bill, that's my arm. It's a perfectly good arm. Not one to be wasted. And I need my arm to play drums."

"Good point. You're right again. It must be fun being right so often."

He released his grip, and I massaged my shoulder.

"Thank you, Bill. From the bottom of my heart, I thank you."

"Do you think I go around sparing people for no good reason?"

"Oh yeah. I remember now. You're a hit man. There's got to be something in it for you."

"I know. It's so easy to lose sight of that. I'll grant you. It's easy to lose track of. As easy as fallin' off a log."

"When you went up there at the contest and played your heart out, you made it worth my while to spare you. So now you've got to return the favor. Think about it. Do you think for a second that your sister will be in a sparing mood once she finds out about Andy taking a header off the pier and once she hears about my double-cross? How do you think she's gonna feel about me? I've got me to worry about."

"I suppose you're right. But I never thought of it that way."

"So consider it time to think about it that way. And let's be perfectly clear --- disappoint me and I will surely diss you, if you get my drift. Do we understand each other?"

"Yes, I think we understand each other."

"Remember dude. The artist is always alone. I don't think that little tramp Sunita fully comprehends that."

"How did you know...?"

"How did I know about her? Simple. While Andy was out being incompetent, I was watching you the whole time. I even saw you in that song and dance that you had with the two tough ladies on the boardwalk."

"No?"

"Yes, really. That blonde girl had a wicked right cross. She could kick ass. Watching that was like watching a very good double play. It made me wanna sit back and applaud. I could've put a bullet in your brain right then and there, but hell, that would've been no fun at all. You see, Joe, I'm an awful lot like you. I think what you need is to become an awful lot like me."

"I don't know if I'm up to the task."

"Sure you are. I have a lot more confidence in you than you do. Here's what we'll do. Before Andy recruited me for the hit, he'd made all the arrangements and the contract with your sister. She never got to meet me, so she doesn't know who I am. You know about those side businesses that she has, don't you?"

"No, don't believe I do."

"Well, she deals meth on the side and she also has a pistol license business that's really lucrative. Andy told me all about it."

"She deals meth?"

"Oh yeah. And maybe a little coke too. Anything to make extra money. But with her everything is completely about appearances. She does this extra stuff so she can get money to fund hubby's political campaigns. The pistol license biz is her main racket, but the drug thing is a moneymaker too. Of course, that's where she's really vulnerable because once the boys in organized crime get wind of what's happening, then she's in for a real ride. The pistol biz could also get her ass in a sling if it ever got out. It could hurt Hubby's political ambitions."

"A pistol license business --- what's that."

"It's like this --- if someone wants to get a gun, legally of course, then they have to go to the local police station and fill out a whole bunch of paperwork. And if you fill it out and pass muster with them, then you can get a permit to carry a weapon."

"Really?"

"Yeah, I know. It's weird, but that's the way it works. Only most of the time the cops don't want you to have a gun 'cause, you know, it would be just one more nut who would have the potential to shoot at one of their own. So what they do is they find problems with your paperwork. And they do it again and again until after a while you just give up. So, for them, when that happens, problem's solved. Most people simply get frustrated and quit. But what your sister does is to waltz the applicant through the bureaucracy of the paperwork. Hell, what's fucked up is that she and others like her could give a damn who winds up with a gun permit to legally carry a weapon. All she cares about is her money. She doesn't care if the gun eventually finds its way into the wrong hands. For all she knows, a gun could wind up in the hands of a terrorist."

"No kidding?"

"Right. All she cares about is money. She's forever worried that she's going to run out. It's her obsession --- that, and right wing politics. So lemme get to the deal here. A minute ago I was tellin' you you had to get serious about killin' her before she kills you, and if I hear ya right, you don't have quite the stomach for that kind of dirty business. So alright, I get it. I can understand how that might make ya feel kinda icky. So let's compromise. I'll meet ya halfway. Instead of bein' that dastardly, we get the goods on her so you can get the goods on her husband, and that'll sink his political career, which in turn will scare the hell out of her so she'll back the hell off. How's that one sound to ya?"

"I could get used to that scenario. It's seems more palatable on this end."

"Good. I'm happy that ya feel that way. So it's a deal. What we should do is go to her and have a little fun with her. I'll pose as someone who wants to get a gun permit. I'll give you a full report on what happens. Is that OK with you, Joe."

"Amen to that. We'll talk about it some more, but right now I gotta go."

"Sure, ya gotta go. I understand. I'll see ya later. But can I ask you one favor before you leave?"

"OK, what's that?"

"Can you and I have a little toast."

"Gee, I don't see why not. Yeah, fine. Let's do it."

He futzed around with the thermos again as he had trouble opening it. After a few seconds he managed to remove the top. Then he poured more of its contents into two small glasses, one of which he presented to me.

"Most toasts are for success, Joe. But I want to make this one to be in honor of failure."

"For failure? It doesn't sound very traditional to me."

"Well, it's not meant to be. Let me explain. This one will be for the complete failure of her mission."

"Oh now I get it. Yes, to the failure!"

We raised our glasses.

"To the failure."

Each of us chugged it down. And with that, he got up to leave, and I got up to leave too. But for Bill, this proved to be a false exit.

"Another thing, Joe --- I can tell just by looking at you that you have a problem with smack."

"What is it with you people? Am I so obvious?"

"Yeah, Joe. In fact, you kinda wear it on your sleeve. And I can tell by the way you fidgeted after the gig that your connection may be messin' up and not comin' through for you."

"It's true, Bill. There are moments when he's a bit slow with getting me what I need."

"But not to worry, Joe. I've got my connections, and I can keep you in good supply. Is that a deal too?"

"Yes, that would be so wonderful."

"I'm certain that we can come to some sort of arrangement, don't you?"

"Yes, I'm certain too. It would be one less thing to worry about."

"So cheer up, my friend. Things are lookin' up in general. The world is goin' well for you right now. Stand up and enjoy yourself. Everything's gonna be alright." He turned away and started to walk across the long expanse of white sand in the direction of the boardwalk, but then he glanced back at the ocean. "Joe, is it high tide or low? It's something to do with the planets, and I can never quite understand which one it is."

One of the bikini girls passing by answered his question before I could. "Can't ya tell? It's gonna be high tide and the surf'll get bigger," she gushed, before running by the sandcastle that was about to be flooded by the surging water.

That was Bill's cue to get on out of the sun. He told me he had arcade games on his mind and after that, he had to mosey on back to the boardwalk to get on the roller coaster. I watched him as he slowly walked across the wide expanse of sand. He sure looked rather out of place what with that silly fedora hat of his. I had the dicey feeling that he was in all likelihood a hipster of sorts, but maybe that wasn't such a bad idea because it might make him less suspicious if I had to enlist him as a roadie. And that was a very big thing to think about right about then because *Babies in Bars* would soon be going out on the road. Bill could be useful if he were handled correctly. But if I made a mistake, a bad decision could blow up in my face. I turned my back and looked out to the sea again, relishing the meditative drone of the waves.

Just then, I heard a voice from behind me. "Joe, Joe, it's me, Gulf. You remember me. I'm the robot that Ben's been working on."

"Wow! It's you. I didn't expect to see you out unsupervised."

"Yeah, it's true. Dad keeps me on a tight tether. But today I managed to sneak out while he wasn't looking."

I could sense a hint of rebellion in the robot's voice. That made me feel great. Anything that could make Ben feel uneasy was totally OK by me.

"Gulf, when I met you the other day, we never got the chance to talk."

"What with me being a robot and all, I'll bet you never thought I could talk."

That was true. When Ben had been showing him off to me, he'd been more concerned with demonstrating Gulf's saxophone playing capabilities instead of his conversational skills. Consequently, I had been of the opinion that Ben couldn't talk. I thought that the fellow was a mute who clearly was not deaf. I mean, how could he be deaf if he played saxophone?

"Joe, I wanted to talk to you about the band."

"Well, I'm so glad to see that you have something to say. When we first met, I got the vibe that you were under the control of your master."

"Yes, Ben wants me to become a full-fledged member of *Babies in Bars*. You see, he wants me to audition as soon as possible. And I'm really having to woodshed on sax. Ben's downloading tons of information into my data banks, and I'm trying to make some sense of it. Frankly, I'm feeling a bit overwhelmed."

"Yeah, so chin up, my friend. Jolly good show and chop-chop cheerio! I'm sure you'll work out 'cause I hafta say that your sax playing is pretty good for a beginner. In fact, it's gone from being pretty good to being pretty god-like. Perhaps you and I could get together and make some noise sometime soon?"

"Why thank you. That's very nice to hear. I'm doing the best I can, but I can't help feeling that I'm a cog in a project not of my choosing. I'm trapped in the falsity of Ben's project. Joe, I'm tryin' so hard to break out of it, but something's holding me back. I want to have an authentic experience."

"You're a robot for cryin' out loud. You can't have an authentic experience if they paid you because your feelings are all make-believe."

Gulf broke up and tumbled down. How could he trust happiness if his version of sadness was so patently pretend? His circuitry couldn't handle the dimensions of the project. I had to remind myself that Gulf was a work in progress and this was expected --- it was par for the course. The young fellow was prone to regression simply because he was a young fellow. Gulf was teasing and anticipating, trying to bloom into becoming a full-fledged member of the human race. I told him, "Yo bro, I wish you luck, but I'm frankly skeptical. But that doesn't mean that we couldn't jam someday."

I somehow found it easier to look into Gulf's face, which was rather odd since 99% of the time, I have such a hard time looking anyone in the eye. But with Gulf it was so much easier because his eyes, nose, and mouth weren't real. If they weren't real, then they couldn't stare back at me and put me on the spot. What a relief! I might as well have been looking at a bronze statue in a museum.

The more I looked into Gulf's face the more I came to remember the other night when I'd talked with Ben. I recalled that he had told me about how he'd hated all people, each and every one of them, no matter how cruel or nice they might have been. Gulf had been created as Ben's retort to humanity. Gulf's very creation had been Ben's megalomaniacal fuck-you to the entire world. It was an uneasy thought to process. I made a mental note to someday ask Gulf how he felt about that, which got me to thinking then about what precarious predicament I might find myself in since I was theoretically part of humanity too. I knew then that getting Gulf messed up on drugs might be my way out of that predicament. Well, I was looking at the ideal moment --- the opportunity was standing right in front of me.

"Gulf, are you happy?"

"Sure, relatively speaking, I'm feeling great despite all the crazy stuff my dad is tryin' to do to me. I suppose I can't complain. The happiest part will be when the downloads are completely finished and I can concentrate full time on playin' my sax and, oh yeah, I wanna get a girl too."

"Yes, of course. I can understand how that might be a priority, but what I wanted to ask you was whether you'd like to try something that would make you feel even happier than you are right now?"

"Why, yes of course. I'm happy right now, but you can never have too much happiness, can you?"

"No, you can't. But if you should manage to get any extra, you might have more than you need at any given moment, so that means you can save it up for later just in case you run out. And I know what with you bein' new to the ways of the world and all, that you probably think whatever minor inconveniences, setbacks, and disappointments that you may have experienced so far pretty much tell you the whole story of the way life really is. You're most likely thinkin' gee, this is as complicated as if gets. Well, understand Gulf, there is so much more. Life can wear you down. It can grind you to a pulp and spit you out. And you might wanna save up some happiness for a rainy day."

"Oh, I sure as hell don't wanna run out."

"No, we can't have that. If that happened, then maybe you and I wouldn't be able to jam together, and that wouldn't be any fun, now would it?

"That would be no fun."

"I think you need to take precautions."

I stared into his eyes. I couldn't believe it because for some bizarre reason, I seemed to have him under my power. This was new power, like I'd never felt before. And I decided I wouldn't stop there. No, I had to go forward.

"Look Gulf, let's you and I go someplace and shoot up. I think you'll like it. In fact, I know you'll like it. Come on, let's go. Let's go someplace where there aren't so many people around. I think your Dad would like a place where there aren't many people around. In honor of him, let's go someplace that's sparsely populated."

And so we went there, and Gulf became very happy.

DOES IT TASTE AS IT SOUNDS?

After my chat with Gulf, I elected to go for a swim. The sun had ducked behind a row of spindly clouds, thereby rendering the saltwater in a different light. Now the currents vaguely reminded me of a mass of swirling, sudsy beer, one of those brews from way out West where the selling point is the sanctity of the pristine mountain water. In my confused state of mind, I wondered how it was that this devil ocean of ours managed to avoid seeping between the grains of the porous sand and drying up completely. The ripples, both big and small, chanted and seemed to say, "Hurry up, Joe, we've been a very patient lot here." And I answered back, "Yep, I know. I'm a patient. I'll be right with you." I was thinking about Bill and Gulf and was having mixed feelings. It had been great to make new friends. However, I had some reservations. But with Bill, there wasn't much of an alternative. I had to give him credit because he'd gone against the grain by not shooting me dead. In that way, he was an outcast among outlaws. Naturally, I would have to be very careful. If I didn't do as the man asked, he'd call in all the chips, and my evil sister's magical thinking would not-so-magically come true. Still, I had this nagging uneasy thought that he could turn on me at any time without much provocation.

And Gulf was an enigma --- part person and part machine and with cuttlefish brains to top it off. I had to hand it to him. He was a freak of Nature who was doing his best to cope. He seemed to have a good heart, only the difficult part was that he was controlled by a crazy man.

The ocean was lurin' me again. I was set to go diving into those talkative waves when I noticed a chunky mustachioed guy in a sport coat with a white monogrammed golf shirt. He was having a tough time with Jillian's camera crew. You see, following her directive, they really did shoot practically everything because she had told us, "I never know what I'll use for the show and what will wind up on the cutting room floor." Yes, this is the modern world, and we don't have cutting room floors anymore, but Jillian was from another era. Perhaps she was a Neanderthal too?

The guy looked really annoyed, and if I'd been in his shoes, I would've been too. He was running a gauntlet. Everywhere he turned, the freakin' cameras were staring him in the face. Finally, the guy managed to get through them all, at which point he flashed me a badge and Wildwood Police ID. The expression on his face seemed to say, "Joe, this is going to be the fourth degree."

"Jeez Louise! What in God's name is going on?" he inquired.

"They're filming, Officer," I replied.

"Don't they ever let up?"

"After a while, they'll give me a break. After a while, they might even give *us* a break. They have to go to lunch sometime."

"Doesn't it bother you?" he continued.

"Not yet. But I know it will sometime. I'm still intrigued by the novelty. All this attention is the cat's meow. Right now, I'm kind of used to it. I'd forgotten they were there until you showed up. What can I do for you, Officer?"

"Fielding. Officer Robert Fielding."

I always like to be on the safe side and call the policeman an "officer" even though so much of the time they're rude, and probably don't deserve it. You see, I have no problems with authority.

"Mr. Myers --- that's your name, isn't it?" he asked.

"Why? Yes, of course. Joe Myers. That's me. What would you like to know?"

"I understand that you just the other day passed some reality show audition. Is that right, Mr. Myers?"

"That's what the camera crew is all about. I completely blew 'em away. Passed the audition with flying colors. I'm rather proud of it, if

I do say so. The band is going to go on the road real soon. It's great. I mean, everyone wants to be on TV, so here's my big chance. My career is definitely on the up and up."

"Congratulations, Joe, that's something to be proud of. I know I'd love to be on a reality show too. Back at Headquarters, we've got some real characters, and we've got some great guests too. Most of them are in lock up though. I'm sure it would be good for a few laughs. But I wanted to inquire about something."

"What could that be?"

"Well, you may have heard about the drowning that we had out here the other day."

"Oh yeah, I think I heard something about that. Yes, I heard about it on the news. They said it was in broad daylight."

"Funny thing about that guy --- he went off the pier. That in itself was rather unusual. There's this old guy we have on the force. He's about to go into retirement. We've got him doing desk duty and whatnot. About the only thing he's good for is trivia, especially trivia about the Wildwood Police. Well, he told me that falling off the pier and drowning like that is so rare that the last time it happened was 1949."

"Thank goodness that it doesn't happen very often, Officer. I mean, it's pretty darned tragic. Who wants that stuff to happen?"

"I sure don't. But when it does, I've got to investigate. And you know what we found on him when we pulled that unlucky guy out of the water?"

"I have no idea at all. Tell me."

"We found a piece of paper in one of his pockets, and that piece of paper had your name on it, Mr. Myers."

"No kidding? Why would he have that? I don't even know the guy. I had to hear about him on the news."

"It is rather odd, don't you think?"

"Yes, very strange."

"So you must have known him?"

"Known him? Why would I know him? Please tell me his name."

"Okay, I will. His name, as far as we can determine, was Andrew Collins."

"Never heard of the guy."

"Really, are you sure?"

"Damned right."

I scratched my chin and picked up a flattened pebble which I threw side-armed across the water so that it skipped three times.

"But wait a second. I'll bet I can explain why he would have a piece of paper with my name on it. He's a stalker. Yes, that's it. Jeez, I'm not even completely on the show yet, and suddenly I've got stalkers. They're the walkin' talkin' disease of our time. That's Hollywood for you. You're a star even before you're a star."

"Here a star. There a star. Everywhere a star star," replied the good Officer.

Sergeant Fielding picked up another pebble and threw it on the water. This one skipped four times. I gave him short applause which he acknowledged.

"That explains it," I continued. "He was a stalker. He must've seen me pass the audition and then, for whatever reason, decided to follow me. I mean, think about it, Officer Fielding. There are a lot of wacko people out there. It's sad to see this one take a header though."

"Maybe. I suppose that it's possible, perhaps even probable. Still, something's not right. You know, Joe, before I was on the force, I was in the merchant marine, and I often got to go to Nigeria. They have a wonderful saying there that kind of fits this situation."

"And what's that?"

"They like to say that it doesn't quite taste as it sounds."

"Hey man, being a drummer, I like the turn of phrase even if it really doesn't fit what we're talking about. It sounds --- err, I mean, tastes as though you've got your work cut out for you. I wish you success. As a matter of fact, I've got a better euphemism for you. It's one that I picked up in India while I was living there years ago."

"So tell me all about it."

"When you accomplish a difficult tack and you do it with flying colors, they say that the snake is dead, and the stick is unbroken."

"Wow! I'll bet they've got a lot of snakes over there."

"They sure do. And we've got a lot of snakes over here too. And it's so satisfying when you get them."

"Yeah, you can say that again. I can appreciate that proverb of yours. It's even better than mine. I'll tell it to the boys back at the station house. But the other funny thing about this whole drowning craziness was that there was someone else with the victim when he was either pushed or fell in."

And at that moment, I knew Fielding was playin' games with me. 'Pushed or fell in' --- what total bullshit! The guy was tryin' to put words in my mouth, but I wasn't gonna take the bait.

Mindful that he was tryin' to pull a fast one, I answered him with a question. "And you think he was pushed in? I thought they said that he fell in?"

"I dunno, my friend. I'm beginning to think that he was pushed in."

"Really! If that's true, then maybe this other person that you just now referred to is your man. What do you think about that?"

"Hmm...you may be right. Only problem is the man's disappeared. He's flown the coop."

"All the more reason to suspect that the guy's guilty as sin, that he caused the victim to drown."

I pinched myself. What was I doing? Bill was my savior and a newfound friend. Why was I casting aspersions on him? I didn't know why. Perhaps it was simply my survival instinct that was kicking in again. That damned self-centered device works on automatic pilot for crissake! OK, maybe that was good. But a new thought entered my head to reassure me, which was that this Keystone Kop that I was talking to didn't have the slightest clue as to who Bill was. Officer Fielding didn't know Bill from Adam. Ha! No clue about Bill, so your case is nil.

"Okay, that could be."

"The other thing that could be is that the drowned man was simply a fellow who lost his footing, and he also had the misfortune of not knowing how to swim. Quite frankly, I'm amazed at all the things that people don't know. It's a wonder that anything ever gets done because of the ignorance of the world."

"Yes, you're right. I could be making a mountain out of a molehill. This could be taken solely at face value. There might be nothing nefarious about it. A drowning is a drowning, and there's not a helluva lot to say about it."

He picked up another pebble and skimmed it on the water. This one went five times.

"Hey, Officer. That's pretty good."

"OK, Mr. Myers. For the time being, I think that will be all. But I will ask you to keep me posted if you should happen to come upon a few revelations about this unfortunate little incident. And bear in mind that you'll be the very first person on my mind if we have any further discoveries or inquiries."

"Really?"

"Yeah, really. You can bet on it."

With that, Sergeant Fielding smacked his lips to indicate that this particular interview was over, at least for the time being.

"Good. I can go now?"

"Yes, you can go now. But I caution you! Don't go very far."

"You'll know where to find me, Sergeant."

"Yes, I certainly do. You'll be right there somewhere on the high end of the cable dial. My remote will find you."

"Are you sure you don't want to keep better track of me? How about one of the ankle bracelet global positioning devices? Shouldn't I wear one of those?"

"Mr. Myers, I don't think that will be necessary. We only do that for guilty people and another thing --- you need to think that one through completely. Wouldn't it interfere with your drumming? We wouldn't want that to happen now, would we?"

I smacked my palm against my forehead.

"You know, Sergeant, that thought never even crossed my mind, but you are absolutely right. It would mess up the songs of *Babies in Bars.*"

"It would mess up your time. I don't think the band would like that at all."

"Not at all."

He turned and started back to the boardwalk. The phalanx of cameras were still there. One of them zeroed in for a close-up.

"OK, here I go again. Wish me luck."

"Hey Officer, I consider them my security blanket."

"Yeah, well they're a pain in the ass."

"Damned right."

"Do you believe in God, Joe?"

"Jeez, what the hell kind of police detective question is that?"

"I'm not an ordinary police detective. And besides, there's no such thing as an ordinary police detective question anymore. Television, the medium you're about to be working in, changed all that. Thought you might wanna know that in your new gig."

I struggled to think of what to say next.

"Well Joe, do you?"

"Not only do I believe in God, Officer Fielding. I really think there's more than one. In fact, I think there's thousands of 'em, and not one of 'em has a clue. The Great Makers keep making up the story as they go along. Here a make, there a make, everywhere a Maker Shaker."

"I like that, Joe. I think you're making up the story as you go along."

"Oh Officer, words are so cheap. I could give a damn. I'll place my bet with sound any day."

"Yeah, who can tell where life will take us? The story can get so bizarre sometimes."

"Speaking of bizarre --- *Babies in Bars* is soon to be auditioning some weird kind of robot half-breed. If that comes to pass, I'd be almost willing to bet that it'll be a big boost to our ratings."

"Yeah right! He's not a real robot. He only plays one on TV! This show of yours gets more and more ridiculous every hour. But the robot thing takes the cake for sheer lack of believability."

"Don't be so certain of that. I saw how he works. He's not an actor and for that matter, neither am I. I think that might be the ticket to real success. Mind you, I've been trying to find success for years now. And I keep striking out. This one's different though. I can feel it in my bones."

"It's too bad we didn't meet before now. I'll see ya later. And good luck with your internship."

"Damn! He would have to give me a last second jab like that. Why is it that everyone seems to know where a Neanderthal's weak spots are?"

He gingerly sidestepped a series of tidal pools filled with lots of barnacles and periwinkles. Then, as a crab scurried out of his way, he made a slight slip which caused his patent leather shoes to get wet. The sergeant turned to look back at me. I waved as he looked down at his now dampened oxblood cordovans. Hey! It served him right for that wisecrack about my internship. I could see him smiling and cursing beneath that thick moustache of his. The crew kept filming away to their hearts' content.

But enough of these interruptions! I had to get back to the Atlantic Ocean. I paused for a second, raced into the water, splashing through the wavelets and then diving head first into a large breaker that was on the verge of crashing. The feeling was cold and blue. That was to be expected. But I knew full well that very soon I would feel completely numb. That would be good because from then on, it would be easy to stay in for a long time.

Since it was now written into the official format for the show, I figured I'd might as well have some new and more frightening interaction with Ben. Jillian was tellin' me that a frightening interaction with Ben was pretty much becoming part of the show's formula. People would certainly be looking forward to it. And we had better not disappoint.

This time we were drinking at a road house in South Jersey, somewhere near to the wilds of Freehold. Wherever it was, it had a sizeable biker contingent. Ben and I were tossin' down the local brew which each of us noticed left something to be desired; however, it's always been my feeling that you have to be patient with these things. I mean, what did he think this was --- some sort of Parisian bistro or something? And what did the patrons of that establishment think Ben was --- some sort of social critic or something? Well, as one might come to expect, things got a little out of control when Ben started flirting with the lady friend of one of the bikers. I gotta say the biker guy was kinda sorta almost gentlemanly. For a guy with a

"Here Comes Trouble" T-shirt, a "Born to Kill" tattoo, and a Viking headdress, he was being downright reasonable. I mean, the guy was positively a vision of enlightenment for cryin' out loud. He went over to Ben and politely told him to knock it off. But of course that was like telling the cat not to eat the canary. After about a five minute stretch, Ben was back to his old tricks. And the girl was falling for him and shootin' him preposterous come hither glances. She was totally taken in by the fact that Ben was on a reality show. Nothing like TV to get the girls goin'. No doubt she thought this was her big moment to be on the small screen. And she was workin' it for all it was worth. After a while, Ben put his right arm around her and began feeling her ass. Well, that one just about sealed the deal. The beefy biker came around from the side of the bar and gave him a single haymaker that knocked him out cold. That was all there was to it. The scene had everything --- high drama, bad behavior, pointless hijinks, and a black eye. Out went the lights. But afterwards, I could tell by her expression that this flirtation had only been a fleeting *divertissement*. For a second there, she might have wanted to get out of herself. But she didn't really want to get out. What she really wanted was to go back to the arms of that tattooed love lump. At the gig that night, Ben had the look of someone who'd been hit by a shovel.

Then I even got to play the part of the loyal friend 'cause the next day when Ben had sobered up, he asked, "Joe, how bad was it? How bad was I?" I purposely didn't answer, preferring to let him fill in the blanks by himself.

But he couldn't fill in any of the blanks, so I figured I'd better tell him what had happened. "You bit her on the ass, Ben."

"Awh, no. Tell me it's not true."

"Yes, Ben. It's very true. Truer than blue. We had to run and run fast. The proof is in the putting. Look in the mirror. Look at your face. I think it needs refurbishing, don't you?"

Right then, he got about as close as he would ever get to being embarrassed, but not really. I knew in my heart that he would never be embarrassed about anything.

"You know what's great about you, Joe?" he remarked. Again, I purposely didn't answer, but he rambled right ahead anyway. "What's great is you're my friend right through thick and thin. You're the best. You're the real deal! I can count of you forever."

One question burned clearly in my mind --- was Ben a masochist? Did he pick a fight with the tattooed love boy simply to get tagged on the chin only to love every second of the pain? Not long after this, we were arguing about something else, and he said, "Gee Joe, you wouldn't want to hurt me now, would you?"

Yeah, I really wanted to hurt him. I really wanted to hurt him so bad. And the nation's television audience knew it too. The nation's television audience would eat it up. Jillian's ratings would never be higher --- until the next frightening interaction of course.

It didn't take long. Ben sat down at the piano and played some random chords. A casual listener sitting at any bar might have come to the conclusion that he was more than a little drunk, but that would have been a big misperception. Members of the film crew too, might have been among those who would have come to that conclusion. They gathered together and pointed their lenses, waiting to capture a candid shot, understanding that Ben's fingers wanted to wish that he was over the top and profoundly inebriated. But that would have been far from the truth. No way! And no way absolutely. In fact, Ben was acutely sober. Too much so. His splayed fingers stumbled, and the chords clinked away, searching for a common denominator, each digit humbly trying to cooperate, doing the best it could to make the best of a bad situation. Limbs were doing their level best to accommodate, but it was a mixed deal. No effort was being wasted. Not in the least. Sometimes one of his thumbs hit a clunker or two and the fallout created an unintentional trill or *apogiatura.* From the chords' point of view, the problem was that the technique of the player didn't live up to the high expectations of the black and white keys being played. Despite this, after a while, a segment of a partial song seemed to float into being. An idea was being generated. But I knew we shouldn't celebrate too prematurely because the harmonies weren't too keen on what was being played. The harmonies were annoyed at this development. They weren't down. They really didn't like where this was going. But they had no say. They were under the yoke. That was what was odd. As the hands staggered on, causing one misstep after another, the chords began to object. The hands were part of a new language --- the language of music. And the words that were so much a part of that language were rebelling at what was being said.

Notwithstanding this, every arm, leg, finger, and foot was well aware that until now the repertoire of *Babies in Bars* was the result of collaborations between Kathy and Gwen. However, one day as we neared the end of a rather long practice, Ben announced that he would like to make a contribution of his own. He introduced us to his new creation. He was so proud of himself, and I have to say I was proud of him too. He played it through a few times, and I'll admit it was kinda sorta good --- not great, but it had potential. Not every song has to be a home run. Singles, doubles, and triples are good too. Gwen, especially, was getting off on the tune, and she was trying out this, that, and the other lyric idea to see which ones worked the best. Then something interesting happened. Ben said he had two different ways of arranging the chords of the song. He demonstrated both of them, calling one the "A version" and the other, the "B version."

After the short show-and-tell, he said, "Now which one of them do you guys like the best?"

We all looked at each other and Kathy spoke first. She said, "Ben, I think I like both of them. Good work, Ben. I'm impressed."

And Gwen said, "Yeah, each of 'em has its merits."

He looked at me for my opinion, and I indicated that I was pretty easy on the whole thing and could go either way.

"Okay," he replied. "But if you have to decide on just one, which version would it be --- version A or version B?"

"Gee, that's a hard one, but I do believe I'd have to go with B. What do you guys think?"

And all three of us concurred --- B was the better version. And the three of us all laughed and Kathy said, "Great! So I guess that does it. It's settled. And what's cool is that it'll be a nice new addition to the rest of the songs on the next album."

I said, "It's wonderful when agreement is so simple." Then I did a light press roll around the kit just so we could celebrate.

"Not so fast," Ben replied. "I wrote the song, so I get to pick which version I like the best."

Gwen and Kathy were taken aback by this development to say the least. And I was startled too. "Gosh, I suppose you're right," said Gwen. "The writer gets first dibs on the direction of the tune. Nothing should ever trump the primacy of the creator. Right?"

"Absolutely." Ben replied. "Supremacy --- I wouldn't have it any other way."

"Well, alright," Gwen ventured. "If you put it that way, I guess you are the main man. So which version do you like, Ben?"

"Uh huh, I've given it a lot of thought, and after running both versions by again and again, I have to say that I like Version A the best."

And then I found myself thinkin' but not sayin', "Well, that's great Ben! Why did you even fuckin' bother to ask us what we think, you prick?"

Another cheap trick he liked to play over and over was to deflate the momentum of a gig by claiming that someone was out of tune. It was no matter that technology had improved to the extent that a guitar could be tuned in a few seconds, and all one need do would be to look at a graph on a pitch finder. No, in this instance, technology did not serve to uphold his agenda. So, he had to go primitive analogue on us and look elsewhere for his delights. He would employ this strategy at the most inopportune moments just as the performance was coming into the full throttle of ecstasy. Consequently, Kathy and he would have to stop everything and go into the tiresome process of making sure we were absolutely pitch perfect. Twang, twing, bing went the guitar strings as they fished around for the proper note. For Ben, infinitesimal inaccuracies would not do. While this was going on, he would talk to the audience about how he had been blessed (or was it cursed?) with perfect pitch and how this was an unfortunate joke that Mother Nature had played on him, but it still was hard work that needed to be done and now they, the audience, would just have to grin and bear with it. He presented the problem as though it were some dilemma that they the audience could help out on, if and only if, they and we the band had the right attitude. This pronouncement almost would make me tumble off of my drum chair 'cause Ben hadn't been blessed with anything of the kind. In fact, I, the drummer, had more sense of pitch than he would ever have in his toenails, let alone in his ears.

This one note samba of his droned on and on, and after he was sufficiently satisfied on that score, he would proceed to say that that was not enough. Oh no, no. There was so much more in store for the band, who at this point had been robbed of their forward motion. In fact, Kathy and Gwen's faces would register chagrin as they watched the crowd starting to exit the premises. No, what would happen next was a sight to behold. Ben would pontificate, saying that it was not enough that the band be totally in tune, but more important than that was the necessity that the bass player actually *tune the audience.* Part and parcel of all this stuff and nonsense about tuning the band was to make sure the audience was in the correct frame of mind. I mean, how else could they come to appreciate the beautiful sounds that were emanating from Ben's bass guitar if they themselves had not been adequately tuned in advance? So, in order for this music appreciation class to take place, the crowd needed to be brought to the proper pitch. What a colossal waste of time! It was so disheartening to watch the people leave. My heart sank into my stomach as I watched the exits get crowded. But it wouldn't last for long, and I knew in my stomach that something needed to be done. As soon as we had finished with Ben's utterly pointless ritual, the people would start to come back, as if to say, "Well, we're glad you shit that stupidity out of your system. Now we can have a good time." The big question was: could the band have a good time because apparently there was someone in its midst who had a huge problem with the notion of fun.

And so another time, Jillian had the cameras follow us to a baseball game where we sat in the bleachers. For some reason, which I could never quite fathom, Ben's grandfather came with us.

And Diane, Ben's girlfriend of the moment, was there too. It was so much fun to listen to the old guy talk on and on about how proud he was of his dear, talented grandson. I could see the pride in his eyes. It was so intense that it nearly put a tear in mine. And the game went on and on just the way that the old man went on and on singin' the praises of his progeny's progeny, but he was much more fun to listen to than watchin' the game because his joy seemed to give me a kind of renewed faith in humanity. I mean, I say that because, it you haven't guessed it by now, I'm someone whose faith in humanity is rather tenuous at best, which is not to say that it's nonexistent, but let's just say it's in short supply, and it only wants to multiply. A well of happiness was percolatin' inside me as I basked in this golden moment. I was beginning to believe that I might have to reevaluate my world view.

Well, the game was pretty dull --- a total forgone conclusion, and Ben and gramps both duly noted that the seventh inning stretch was comin' up, and Ben said, "Yeah, isn't that great, and maybe Diane and I should do somethin' really outrageous," and Diane said, "Oh Ben, that would awesome! Let's do somethin' truly outrageous," and then when the seventh inning stretch came up, Ben and Diane both stepped out of their clothes and ran out onto the field, and wasn't that just so funny --- watchin' a couple of old retired cops chasin' these two nude people racin' around deep center field while the cameras captured it all? I mean, that was just so incredibly funny, funny, funny! I thought one of 'em was about to have a heart attack. After they were arrested and hauled off to the pokey with the cameras in hot pursuit, I looked over at the old guy and could see the sadness in his face. He looked like he'd been punched in the gut. It wasn't long after that that the old man died.

These incidents would get me to wondering about their effect on Ben's ultimate creation --- the robot boy named Gulf. Would he grow up to be exactly like his dear old demented, dastardly dad, or if he had any streak of rebelliousness in him, would he deliberately go off in the other direction to find his happiness, assuming of course that, with those cuttlefish brains of his, he could indeed find the emotion of happiness? But I suppose that was rapidly becoming an accomplished fact because I was discovering my own formidable ability to manipulate him. Lately, Gulf had become a preoccupation with me. Like I said before, the robot boy's happiness and mine were beginning to merge. Quite frankly, I was more than a bit bowled over by how quickly Gulf had become addicted to heroin. In no time at all, he was comin' to me earlier and earlier to get his fix. And he was beggin' for it. He had the look of a cat waiting for his food in the morning, beckoning outward, indicating the empty bowl and the need, the constant need, to have it filled to the brim. In fact, he was so much like a cat that I half-expected him to meow at me and to rub his face against my leg. I guess that was a function of how well Ben had made him. He'd endowed his creation with the same cravings that so-called normal people have. Ha! Ben had made him too human, which was of course another way of saying that he'd erred too much on the side of making him like an animal. I found it rather amusing since Ben as much as told me straight up that he was trying to get away from all things human and animal. If he'd been right there in front of me, I would have told him to be careful what he wished for.

Another indicator that Ben had done his job too well was Gulf's preference for listening to recorded music on old-fashioned stereo systems. Once I caught him spinning vinyl, and he assured me that he had become a rabid audiophile and insisted on listening exclusively to analogue instead of digital. In this way, he had become a traitor to his origins. Probably, this preference had something to do with his cuttlefish half --- cephalopods would never be caught dead listening to digital. It took a supreme act of will on my part to refrain from running to Ben and blabbing this info to him.

But getting back to the addiction thing. Naturally, Gulf's newfound addiction was not without a price --- it meant that I had to hit up Sunita and Jillian for more smack. But that wasn't such a big deal because I knew I could always give 'em some new bullshit excuse which I knew they'd be gullible enough to swallow. I reasoned it out and found a good rationale. I figured that since I was a junkie and they both knew I was a junkie, then they'd kinda sorta gotten what they'd bargained for. Hey, if they wanted good drumming, then they had to know that they'd somehow gotten a tiger by the tail. If they didn't understand this, well, that was their own tough luck. Hell, Jillian wasn't payin' me! She was still hung up on that bullshit notion that my internship with the band was supposed to be "an educational experience." That was one way to lookin' at it. Another was that I was the one who was educating them. Either way, sooner or later, they'd come to the conclusion that I wasn't to be fucked with. I would give them an educational experience.

The other potential disaster that I had to scope out was that the robot boy was, according to his creator, only the first of many more to come. Ben had hinted that if he had his way, there would be whole armies of Gulf and his kind. That was all the more reason why I had to nip this fleur du mal in the bud. My only self-defense was Gulf's total corruption.

And that was becoming more and more clear since Ben was directing his own songs. When he did that, he loved to give me cockamamie instructions. My favorite moment was when he said: "Joe, for this next song, I want you to pretend that it's early morning, and the dew is glistening on the grass of the forest. The birds are twittering in the summer air, and a fox is coming out of the woods to see if he can catch a rabbit. Also, there's a deer that's comin' out of the forest too. I almost forgot that part. And he's got gigantic antlers, and he's dreamin' of a beautiful lady deer. The rutting season has begun. Only thing is --- there's a hunter with a bow and arrow who's about to ruin his day, so he can step into another reality. For the deer, sudden death will be a truly psychedelic experience. I want you to play the drums just like that. Play 'em with those images in mind. And another thing --- and this is very important 'cause if ya miss this part, then the whole effect goes down the tubes --- play the drums as if they weren't drums at all. Play them as if they were a concert grand piano that you just happened to stumble upon while you were hiking in the woods. And you're not a drummer at all, but instead you're Frederic Chopin. Play the membranophones like Fred would play 'em. If ya can do that for me, the song will sound wonderful.

Remember, it all depends on you to make this a sure-fire hit. We got a lot ridin' on this, baby!"

"No problem, Ben. One Fred Chopin Mojo Special comin' right up."

Never underestimate the power of terrible music. You could get cancer of the ear drums or the sound waves could get carried to the auditory nerves and who knows where they'll lead to? The Eustachian tubes have to figure out what to make of it. I suppose that filter mechanisms serve a very important function. I often tried to evaluate Ben's tunes. I was trying so hard to keep an open mind because drummers have to give the benefit of the doubt even when the doubt leads to nowhere --- to a malnourished ghost. Our way of following is to lead, so others may pick up the slack, and beautiful sounds may bud into life. But seriously, that noble aim doesn't always get materialized, so when that happens, which is more often than not, what was the purpose of terrible music? Should it be the backdrop for dance? No, Ben's music didn't aim to collide with that rather high-minded option. On that subject, I did recall how Ben had, on the first night I had ever seen him, put his hands behind his back and sipped a glass of beer. This showed that there was no connection between hand and head. So how could there be a linkage between hand and ear? How could there be an elixir for later on? Did his music attempt to be the foil for movement between two human beings bobbing back and forth in a social setting? No, you couldn't give it that much credit since Ben couldn't dance his way out of a paper bag. He couldn't make a woman move from one corner of the room to another by any lead of his body. Hell no, his body was incapable to hinting at that. Hips and hands were on a different wave length. Perhaps his songs could accompany baseball games? I came up with that one while I was watching a twilight double header in a bar. At about the sixth inning, I tuned into one of Ben's songs on my iPod. After a few balls and strikes, I decided that the answer to that question was no, because there really was far too much physicality there --- in baseball that is. But Ben's music had nothing to do with the wind up and the pitch. It had nothing to do with sliding into third base. Did it have pretensions to large lush chords? When you're thinking about this stuff, you usually have to entertain that possibility. And when you ponder that, you have to touch base with the notion that the sprawling harmonies automatically justify themselves, so that thick blocks of notes in and of themselves automatically cluster into an ambient menu of tinted spirituality. When you hit that mark, people will assume you're talkin' profundity. What utter pomposity! Or, in Ben's case --- pompissity. However, if you were looking for fake spirituality in Ben's music, you'd be bound to be disappointed. Well OK, if that wasn't the case, then how about melody? Maybe that was what his music was all about? No, you couldn't say that either since the were no twists and turns in the top note, nor were there undulations and pivots in the bottom. So much for counterpoint. That was a deep dead end too. Having said all this, in the big picture, there was precious little to give him credit for. I was thinking he was 0 for 5. But on all of these themes, I was deeply skeptical. Still, as a perpetual session man, I would have to withhold my judgment. So, as long as we're giving the benefit of the doubt, we have to think about terrible music as a means of social interaction. In that context, it's the jingle for our lives. If that's the case, then the mundane aspect constituted the best answer to this dilemma of discovering the true worth of Ben's music. It's something that everyone can talk about, so that explanation in and of itself would justify its existence. Way to go, Ben! I had finally zeroed in on what was going on. Seen in this new light, perhaps I could surprise him and really make a deer come out of the woods. Phew! What a load offa my mind! Now that that was settled, I decided I'd have an elixir for later on.

But Ben's antics were the least of my worries. I say that because not long after this incident, I got a text message from Doc McIntyre. The guy just wouldn't let up. There was no end to his pain-in-the-ass ways. Now he was harassing me with a different mode of communication. One that went like this:

> Hi Joe
>
> How ru? 4got 1 thing when we talked. U R my intellectual property.

IP from now on. U got to understand. U R chance of lifetime 4 me. Get it?

Took out a patent and U don't belong to Nature anymore. 4 fibroblast Xperiment to work I needed that & now I have it. Got my six month provisional on the patent & then I'll go for the big enchilada --- the big patent.

Then nobody'll be able to have U cept 4 me. The idea of your protruding brow ridge will be something I can get a royalty from & don't U 4get it. Buy 4 now. See U soon.

Your good friend
Doc McIntyre

I quickly erased the message before kicking some sand on the beach. This guy would never let up. I felt more and more trapped because I knew I was running not just from my sister, but from this crazy man too. In the meantime, I had to get busy with sending my confidant Bill on his mission to infiltrate my sister's organization. That had to be done and done fast if I was to have any continued chance for survival. I needed a full report.

THE FULL BUSINESS CARRY

Well, well, well, Joe, I suppose I'd better give you a full report. My mission to Meghan's place of business was downright weird --- real hobgoblin creepy crawl free- for-all folderol. That racket of hers is one sleazy operation. While I was waiting my turn, I could hear her going through her sales pitch on the phone. I'll tell my frightening interaction to you, Joe. It went something like this:

"You want my advice, Jeannette? Dump him as a friend. Better yet. Shoot the bastard...yeah...Then you can feel happy. It's the way you feel when you total your car and your mom buys you a new one."

Meghan laughed and slapped her knee to congratulate her own joke. It was a boiler room operation, the kind that might someday be farmed out to Third World countries. But Meghan is always a bit behind the times. For now, the rows of cubicles would stay in the good old U.S. of A. No out-sourcing for her. How patriotic! She made me wanna give her a twenty-one gun salute. Meghan was flipping through her desk calendar and making notes. Then she was on to the next customer, a walk-in, who'd been fidgety and was waiting rather impatiently. It seems that the guy had some sort of a rap sheet which may or may not have been problematic.

"Easy easy, Mr. Gilson," Meghan said matter-of-factly. "Having an arrest record needn't preclude your getting a gun permit. Don't get discouraged. Don't beat up on yourself! You're hyperventilatin'. You got too much oxygen in your brain. Take a deep breath and calm down. Relax. Why it was only the other day that I had a customer phone in who said he had a record, and I asked for what, and he said, 'Meghan, lemme fax ya my rap sheet' and here I was expecting a single piece of paper with one or two lines on it to come slidin' outta the machine. I mean, over the phone, the guy sounded like a goddamned choir boy Eagle Scout. Clean as a whistle. Well, I swear the freakin' paper started rollin' outta the machine like it was some sorta effin' dictionary or encyclopedia. I mean reams of the stuff, connected and doublin' back on itself. And what kinda stuff does he have on his rap sheet? Breakin' and entering, aggravated assault, forgery, mail fraud, grand theft auto, DWI and leavin' the scene. I tell ya he's a regular angel. When it was over, I found myself sayin' 'This guy shouldn't have a gun in a gazillion years.' Well, that was last Thursday, and today we're doin' his final paperwork. I tell ya, the man's gonna be one of my success stories --- a dark horse who's come from behind. So, what's the little problem that you have on your police record?"

"Aw nothing much. Just a drunk and disorderly conviction from when I was in high school."

"Oh hell, that was eons ago. Look, Mr. Gilson. Don't sweat it. That's small potatoes. If I were you, I wouldn't give it much of a thought. As far as the pistol license is concerned, you're in like Flynn."

Soon I managed to get an audience with her. She came out from behind her desk and offered me her hand. "Hi, I'm Meghan. How may I help you?"

"Hi, I'm Bill. Pleased to meet you. Saw your ad and I'd like to see about getting a pistol license, and a friend of mine keeps telling me that getting one is a real hassle."

"Yes, that's true if you opt for getting one all by yourself, which I don't recommend. That's why we're here in business to serve you. The problem is the cops don't want you to have a gun permit. So what do they do? They nickel and dime you to death."

"How do they do that?"

"They'll say, 'Sorry Bill, you filled out this box okay, but you put in one digit of the ZIP code wrong. Whatta bummer! You gotta do it all over again!' So you're back to square one. They treat all of us like we're a bunch of suckers. And they'll never tell you what you did wrong in one meeting. They'll drag it out to twenty-five meetings until you get exhausted with the whole process and give up. That's what they're bettin' on."

"Aw this sounds like the old country. But my brother back in Italy always told me things are different here in America. Here everyone pulls together."

She looked surprised, but continued anyway. "Well then, you do it over again, and they have a nice new line up of bullshit, lame ass excuses… anything to trip you up because they don't want you to have a gun."

"Yeah," I said, "but they're probably right. I mean, think about it. If you were a cop, would you want you to have a gun?"

She gave me a very pregnant pause and an uneasy laugh on that one. Hell, I knew as well as anyone that she shouldn't be granted that privilege.

And Meghan replied, "Ummm…"

"It's a mine field out there," I said.

"Jeezuz, you said it!"

"OK, so how do I get started?"

So she gave me a complete rundown of the whole process, which if you wanna know the truth is kinda boring. But then she tried to sell me on the various options, and the one that everyone and his brother wants is something called the "full business carry." Everything else is an exercise in sheer pointless limitation, a complete waste of time 'cause if you want to carry a gun, you might as well go all the way and carry it with you from the beach to the grocery store to the restaurant to the car wash to the you-name-it.

She explained: "Bill, the thing about the full business carry is that, let's say you get home late and for whatever reason, you wanna go take a few shots at the firing range. The full biz carry would allow you to do that. If the spirit moved you, you could go off to the range at any time, day or night. You never know when you might get the urge to shoot at something at 3:00 in the morning. And it's real relaxin', almost kinda Zen, like a deep meditation. When you're standin' there pumpin' bullets into the target, it's as though the floor is givin' a massage to your feet. Your mind is free to roam wherever it wants, and the thoughts just empty right on outside of your head."

"Wow! Pretty psychedelic stuff. I'll bet the little elves come out from the corners of your eyes and say, 'Yo, Meghan! What's happening?'"

"Well, maybe not that much." She shuffled some more papers on her desk and then continued. "Also, don't you think it would make for a great date? The girl would be so impressed! With the limited, you wouldn't have that capability. You see why it's a much better deal."

"Actually Meghan..." I began.

Meghan interrupted. She was clearly not really interested in listening to me because she was trying to snag another sale. She soldiered on: "Perhaps you carry a lot of money on a daily basis? The more money you're carrying, the more qualified you are to get a full business carry 'cause you've got to be prepared for anything. If you stop and think, there's a lot to be afraid of in this world. We live in a very unsafe time and place."

At this point, I did an interruption of my own. "Ummm, the thing is that..."

And I'll be damned if she didn't interrupt again with that relentless sales pitch of hers. "When I drive home after getting the groceries, just before I turn off the key in the ignition I say, 'Uh huh, I'm safe. I made it back one more time.' It's the same feeling I used to get when I was in the sixth grade, and I was playing dodge ball at the playground. You know that feeling you get when you've either escaped something or you've gotten away with something absolutely awful?"

"Yeah, I know exactly what you mean. You wanna hop, skip, and jump and go giddy-yup. It happens to me every day. It's like fallin' in love twenty-five times in twenty-four hours. Look Meghan, if I can get a word in edgewise for a second, I just want to say that I'm probably not your usual Pistol Licenses 'R Us customer..."

"Bill, the way it works is like this. The police department wants you to make mistakes on the paperwork, but we at Pistol Licenses Super Limited know all the sorry ass excuses that they use to trip you up. Why can I say that? Because I'm the Director of Operations. I know all their cheap tricks 'cause I used to work for them."

"Yep, you know all the happy horseshit. Look! Listen to me for a second, god dammit! I'm not your typical Pistol Licenses 'R Us customer. I'm sick. And I don't have any health insurance. I gotta get cancer treatment somehow, and I don't care how I do it. So you see Meghan, I really want a gun only. I could care less about the legality of the thing 'cause getting myself arrested is the whole point."

Meghan looked as though she'd been sucker punched. She rubbed her eyes for a second and sat way back in her leather-lined chair. Then she took a deep breath and leaned forward, putting the tips of her fingers together. "Lemme get this straight. You've got cancer an' you wanna rob a bank or do some other crime, so you can get the health insurance when you go to prison?"

"Exactly. As you're well aware, the healthcare thing never quite happened. The crazy politicians sabotaged the whole shebang. It was almost up and running, and then they pulled the plug. They liked it when it ALMOST happened. People in pain --- that was what they really wanted. None of that helpin' folks out for the good of the country bullshit. Hell, they hate the country. They wanna see it go down the tubes never to reappear again. Too bad! I guess I was misinformed 'cause my first grade teacher had told me that mattered. Now I know it doesn't matter one bit! But for me personally, I'd really gotten my hopes up and just as suddenly as they appeared, they'd gotten dashed. Basically, the way they saw it was that it was too much goodwill and decency in one package. It had to be destroyed. So, as a result, I'm back to square one. I have to think of innovative ways to stay alive. And I'm not the least bit well connected. So I've gotta rob a bank, so I can get convicted, so I can go to jail, so I can get my healthcare, so I can stay alive. You being in the biz an' all, you'd surely have a firearm lying around some place on the premises that I could maybe borrow for an afternoon."

"Yeah right. So you can rob a bank?"

"Hey, I've done my research. I promise you nobody'll get hurt. And I promise I'll give you your gun back."

"Uh huh. You travel to someplace like California where they have really cushy prisons, the kind where rich cons escape by callin' up a car service after they've gotten in their nine holes of golf for the afternoon."

"Damn right! I'm so lookin' forward to minimum security. I think I might take up a new hobby, and maybe get caught up on my reading. An' best of all, they'll have health insurance. Unlike some people in this crazy world of ours, I'd kinda sorta like to live. I suppose that's too much to ask. Their attitude is: 'So, Bill, you wanna live? Great. Well, we'll make sure that you don't! In fact, we'll go far out of our way and make a special point to see that you don't. We'll take you by the hand and help you go straight to hell. Wanting to live is just way too big an ambition for an ordinary man or woman to have. Someone has to knock 'em down to size. I mean, we have to draw the line someplace, and it might as well be there.'"

"Bill, there's no way I'm just gonna hand out a gun like it's some kinda popcorn or lollipops. I've got my professional reputation to think about."

I was thinking, gee, we'll see how professional this lady is, so I deliberately amped up the purr in my voice, playing it like a movie star. The only question in my mind was just how long it would take her to fall. I glanced at my watch to find the starting point. I figured another two minutes. "Yeah right! Your reputation!" I continued. "You work in such a fine upstanding line of work."

"Stop it! Stop it right now," she protested.

Now it was my turn to interrupt: "I look at you, and I see a girl who's in a bottomless pit. You are one sad sad honey. I'll bet some people who come through here call you the 'gunny honey.'"

"Look Bill, I'm a very busy woman. I don't have time for all this bullshit today. I mean, look at the long line of customers I have waiting after you. There's a tremendous demand for what I want to sell."

I turned around to look at the rest of the waiting area, and sure enough, it was a roomful of crazy people. No doubt it had been a banner day for day passes.

I continued my own interruption: "It must be so awful workin' here sellin' what? Sellin' the potential to kill? What a lonely job! If I had my druthers, I think I'd rather be some sorta undertaker. I mean, the corpses would make for more logical conversation."

She was unnerved for a second, but regained her composure very quickly. "It's a good job, a great business opportunity, a big contribution to the economy. And I… I… I…have great life."

"Uh huh. Sure ya do."

She got teary, and I continued. "Seems real darn great to me. Peachy keen. But I only wish you could see yourself."

Now the tears really started to flow. And they were doin' it right on schedule! Her two minutes were up! I reached across the desk and brusquely grabbed her by her hair. Her face changed. She registered surprise, to say nothing of pain, but then she smiled because she somehow enjoyed it. The sadness that had been there seconds before hadn't stuck around, so I trotted out my deepest and brawniest voice again. I released her hair. She brushed it with her hand.

"Meghan, you said something earlier about going on a date to the pistol firing range."

She was impressed by my baritone and replied, "I was only trying to get a good commission."

"So doncha want that big fat juicy commission?"

She smoothed out her dress. "Yes."

"Well, let's go on a date. Will you take me to the firing range? I've never been. It'll be the first time for me. I promise you I'll be real darned impressed."

She was caught off guard, but not for long. She shuffled some more papers. She adjusted the calendar on her desk.

She smiled. "Yes, I'll meet you there."

"Tonight at eight o'clock."

She looked happier.

So, we hooked up and went to the target practice firing range. What a date it was! I pulled her hair, and she pulled mine. We had a bang up time of it. The bullets kept ripping into the target. It was the old-fashioned police variety, the kind with a crude cartoon drawing of a big super bad boogie man criminal who had a gun pointed straight back at the shooter. That was so the person doing the practicing would feel this was the real deal. The only thing missing was some deep red blood. The bull's eye sustained more and more bullets. We used our imaginations to connect the dots. We were all smiles. Then we left the pistol firing range and went to her apartment. It was different from the place where she lived with her hubby. When she opened the door to her place, I was damned if I didn't see that the entire flat was tricked out like a dominatrix's dungeon. So we engaged in some recreational activities --- the usual whips, chains, and tie-up gadgets. Nothing terribly innovative. Despite that, her face got more and more excited. She pretended to be a horse. She had a bit in her mouth, and she whinnied. We made believe that this was the Kentucky Derby. So, I whacked her with a riding crop. After she'd won the race, she tied me onto a wheel and blindfolded me. Then she twirled the wheel, which spun dramatically. She let me go --- very slowly and only when she felt good and ready. She was very emphatic on that point. She explained that each and every second of life was made up of strict rules and rigid sanctions. We made love. And then there was the pillow talk. She took a drag off some weed and passed it to me.

"My plan is pretty darned simple," I said between puffs, "I'll hold up the bank. Then I'll walk calm as can be to the lobby, take out my cell phone and call the cops. No one gets hurt. What a piece of cake. I get sentenced to the big house and get my cancer treatment. I'll be a model prisoner and with any luck I'll be out in three years. The judge, citing 'extenuating circumstances,' might even give me a big reduction. Who knows? The whole sorry mess could wind up degenerating into some media circus, and I could get a payday. Everyone wins."

"For cryin' out loud, will ya stop talkin' such abject nonsense?" What surprised me was that she acted as if we'd been together for years instead of less than twenty-four hours. "Don't worry baby. I'll figure out how to get you some health insurance. Maybe I can spot you for the chemo bill. Ya don't have to go and rob some bank."

"Meghan, you don't understand. I have what's called a pre-existing condition. Nobody's gonna insure me with that. Armed robbery is the only option."

"Awh, Sweety, don't be so negative. C'mon, let's cuddle. I hope you're in a submissive mood."

"No, I'm not," I replied just before I slapped her vinyl clad bottom.

She smiled. "You're lookin' so peeked. Must be the illness."

"Yeah, it's the illness. What a sick fellow I am."

The next day was great. The early morning sun was coming through the window of Meghan's bedroom. I got out of bed being careful not to wake her. I quietly got dressed before reaching into her handbag and stealing her gun.

So that afternoon I went out and held up a few liquor stores. You know how it is, Joe. Trigger men like me get restless. We're like blues guitar players and child psychiatrists. We have to keep our chops up even when we have some down time. I scared the hell out of 'em. The cowering clerks behind the cash registers made me laugh! But just so Meghan wouldn't suspect anything, I put the gun back in her purse, and she never mentioned it again. In fact, I don't think she ever discovered that the thing had been missing.

And then something strange happened. She was so taken with me that she decided to do some play acting. She loved drama. I know! Who would have ever guessed? She said she wanted to see what it would be like if she were the customer and I was the gun permit agent. After she'd established that new set of parameters, she suggested a few trysts in a rundown hotel or two. I'm guessing that only added to the cachet as far as this nasty lady was concerned. There's nothing like a trashy motel parking lot and a throbbing neon vacancy sign to get a certain kind of girl in gear. To top it off, she decided to film much of the action with a hand held camera that she could also put on a tripod for the more horizontal shots, and there were lots of those as well as some vertical ones too. Later, she'd let me look over the footage 'cause she loved to be looked at from after the fact. Then she could be the control-freak revelator and make herself be born again. Of course, I had to oblige --- how could I say no to that? Looking over the rushes of this extravaganza, I couldn't help thinking that I was some sort of latter day freakin' Federico Fellini perusing my latest grand epic on the female of the species. Meghan was mugging for the camera which captured the entire scene. It was late morning before she had to get back to hubby. She could take her good ol' time. Through the viewfinder, I could see her upwardly pointing index finger with her blurred face in the background. You see, she had set it on soft focus. That made it more romantic for her. She spoke in a feigned distressed tone and giggled. I adored the sheer phoniness of it.

"I've got to have a gun! I've got to have a gun!"

"Yeah baby, and not so long ago, it was me who needed to get a gun."

I squinted through the viewfinder again. Now her finger blurred, and I could see her distressed face behind the finger. Meghan was seen more completely. She was in her bra and knickers. She got up from bed and cavorted seductively around the room. She was a bit drunk. Bottles, cans, and cigarette butts littered the room. Her bra went to half- mast. Behind the camera, I looked in wonder and saluted. I uttered the next line in a Bruce Willis tone of voice: "God bless America."

"I warn you. I've got a finger cam, and it's following you every step of the way." She moved her finger from right to left as if it were a camera. I turned my camera around, and I too had a seductive demeanor. Imagine that.

"So, in addition to making my try for the gun license permit," she blurted, "we're making a documentary film."

"Yeah baby, you're making a movie. Careful now! I'm the director. I'm framing the shot. You've got to have a gun! You've got to have a gun!"

"Yes, don't we all. Goin' for the big enchilada. Goin' for the whole nine. That's what I like to see. Ambition. Don't forget. We're doing this for each other --- going for the full biz carry together."

The camera zoomed and showed us together.

"Well, what'll it be, Meghan? The limited, or the full business carry?"

"I... I... want the full business carry, baby."

She put her finger to her lips like the muzzle of a gun and blew on it. She put her finger into an imaginary holster as if it were a gun. I turned the camera back. I could see my face.

"It's like I've always said --- the limited is for wussies. And I can tell just by lookin' at ya you sure as shootin' ain't that. You pack quite a wallop." She did a shaky dance. I touched her arm near the inner elbow. "Hmmm... Let's see what we can do for you, big big Bill. For starters, are you carrying any cash on a daily basis, Mr. Triano?"

"Oh, I've got plenty of that."

"And I have a lot too." She pointed to her purse. She giggled flirtatiously, her slippery slidey voice swooping into a lower register. She took her wallet out, and scattered bills around the room. Then she took out a hundred dollar bill and set it on fire with her cigarette lighter. She watched it closely until it burned out. She tossed the blackened bill onto the bathroom floor. Her bare foot with painted toenails was seen as she stepped on the ashes. Her face was seen. She took out two more one-hundreds and did the same.

She said the next lines in a baby doll sort of voice. She seemed forlorn and faraway. "No, big Bill. I don't carry lots of money. But you never know what could happen. People could come through the window and hurt me at any time."

"I know, I know. You don't have to convince me. You're preachin' to the converted. Our right to bear arms is under constant threat. Ya gotta protect yourself. The trouble with the government today is they don't want ya to protect yourself. They don't wanna make you feel safe."

"What am I gonna do if I can't get the full business carry? I know if I have a police record, I may not be able to get it."

The next second she was on the verge of tears. Later in the viewfinder, I could see myself patting her on the back and playing with her hair. Really, I was growing quite fond of her hair.

She stammered: "I... I... I changed... Three years ago I changed a price tag on a boot in a Thom McCann's over at Fulton Mall...and I got caught. A mall cop hauled me in and the store prosecuted. They never gave me a break. I had to go before a judge and everything. It was so humiliating. That imperious lady sat back there behind her wide track podium whackin' her wooden gavel. She never missed an opportunity to use it. The noise of that thing almost drove me crazy on the spot. I put my hands over my ears. I thought she was goin' for a world record or somethin'. Her black robe was slung high over her shoulder like a beach towel, and she lectured me like I was some sorta common criminal. She told me what to do and how to behave. Worst of all, she told me who to hang out with. What nerve! Right then and there, I wanted to lob a fragmentation grenade at that self-righteous cow and tell her where she could go, but I had to bite my tongue 'cause I was afraid she'd tack on real jail time instead of my just havin' to slink around Cadman Plaza pickin' up trash."

"And you think that misdemeanor might be a roadblock towards getting your pistol license?"

"Yeah, but you don't quite understand, Bill. I wanna take out my pistol and clean it with an oily cloth, look at the bullets, touch the bullets, twirl the magazine and hear it click. Bend it and pull it back. Bend it and pull it back. Make like I'm shooting. Get my cigarette in the corner of my mouth, squint, and pretend to aim."

"So that's why you want the full business carry?"

"No, that's why *we* want the full business carry."

I could see her in the viewfinder looking weird. "I need it. I need it. I wanna go bang bang."

"Uh huh. The usual cowboys and Indians stuff."

Her cell phone rang. She took the call. "Hello. Oh, hi Sweetie. How's Chicago? It was a long day with the venders, yes? Pretend, pretend, pretend.... Ha! Oh nothing much. Just one day like any other. Yeah, the city's still here even though we get amber alerts every other day from the government. It'll always be here no matter how many times we beat the shit out of it... Such a bad joke, darling... Seriously, it's here and it always will be here... I know, darling... Tell that to the Indians. They didn't have car bombs! Ha ha... Sounds like it was the same on your end... The kids are fine. Don't worry. Take your time. We'll do a movie or something when you get back. Talk to ya later. Kiss kiss."

She flipped her cell phone shut, and then smiled. I smiled too.

"Bravo, baby!"

She kissed me.

It suddenly crossed my mind that I was playing the part rather well. If I wanted to, I could be an actor in her blurb of a blab as long as I associated her words with my actions. Or was it the other way around? I had kinda lost track. "Alright," I continued. "Where was I? Yes, the full business carry. Glad to see that you're going for it. The Thom McCann thing ... Don't worry. I can fix that."

"What I want most of all, big Bill, is for you to help me on something."

"And what's that?"

"I have a brother that I want dead. Will you help me with that?"

My god, Joe, I thought she'd never get around to asking me that!

So, even though I didn't really have cancer, I didn't tell her that. I never let on. Hell no, I wanted to see if she'd take the bait just like you told me to. And I'll be damned if she didn't take the bait. She swallowed it hook line and sinker! My Camille act brought out whatever paltry residue of maternal instinct that was still lurking in her. She, being the pragmatist that she was, could put that to use in other ways.

"Bill," she said. "I've been studying hypnotism. Don't you wanna be hypnotized by me?"

I looked at her hesitantly and answered, "I'll have to get back to you on that. That has the look and feel of bein' kind of a sticky wicket."

As I stared into her sparkling eyes, it was becoming clear that she was about to make some sort of a course correction.

"Bill, the more I think about this bank robbery thing of yours, the more I'm getting into it. Maybe you should do it. I think it would be fun. Just the thought of it makes me wanna encourage you. You wouldn't mind if I helped you on it now, would you?"

"Hey baby, is there any rule that says funding cancer treatment shouldn't be fun?"

"Hell no, let's do it, Bill. I'll help you, but on one condition."

"What's that?"

"I want some of the money to go to another good cause."

"And what cause is that?"

"Why, my husband's political campaign of course. He's running for the United States Senate. I could use the extra money for that. That cash would definitely come in handy."

My head began spinnin' for a moment and then stopped. She wanted to use the money for politics? That was even stranger than using it to underwrite my supposed health expenses.

"Gee, I suppose you're right, Meghan. But the more I think about it, the more I think that maybe I won't rob that bank after all. Maybe I'll take you up on your offer."

"What offer is that?"

"Your offer to pay for my chemo."

"Oh that. I'd completely forgotten about it. Consider my offer retracted."

I looked at the floor for a second before glancing up at her. She wore a cold stare. She asked me again if I wanted to be hypnotized; only this time she was speaking in a sweet low seductive buoyant voice, and she was holding a silver pendant up above her shoulder. Her voice felt like slender fingers gently touching my forehead. She was letting the pendant swing back and forth. Back and forth. At first, I thought it was a joke, that she must be kidding, but slowly I got floppy-eyed and started to go along with it. Back and forth. This went on for quite a while before she asked me if I wanted to rob a bank. She said some other things too, but I forgot what they were. What I remember most was that she told me to forget what they were... she told me to forget... she told me to forget what they were ... My head got slouchy, and I got drowsy, and I scratched my head for a minute or two before saying yes to whatever it was she said.

Then barely half a day passed, and she showed up unexpectedly at the hotel where I was staying.

"Bill, I have very good news. And I decided it was so important that I should deliver it personally."

"Baby, what is it?"

"Your pistol license permit just got approved. The cops put it on the fast track. Ta da! Here it is."

"That's beautiful. Maybe I should have it framed and put on the living room wall when I decide to go back home."

"And as an extra special bonus, you will receive an amazing prize... a gift, a token of our love."

"I love it, Meghan. Finally, I'm a winner."

I took the present from her hand and opened the box. The gift was a revolver.

"Oh Sweety," she gushed, "I hope it's what you wanted." She rubbed the gun with her fingers. I admired her long sharp nails. They were painted in the same shade of red that the pistol target range should have had, but didn't.

"And the bullets are right here."

"Thank you sooo much, Meghan. You are the rainbow of my life."

"Glad you like it. And congratulations for getting your full business carry license. You'll never have to feel unsafe again. How does that feel?"

"Oh, what a huge relief! That's one great big load offa my mind!"

So, we did it. We went and robbed a bank. She even went so far as to scope out the place for a few days before we actually did the deed. Damned if she wasn't quasi-scientific about it. She gave me a full inventory of what surveillance cameras were in place as well as some intelligence reports on which ones were most likely to have grainy deteriorated images that would render them useless to the cops. How she got that I'll never know, but the lady certainly has got connections. Then she started to get creative about my disguise, acting as if it were some sort of funky Halloween costume. For a second, she toyed with the idea of making me up like "a scary assistant coach," but she decided that that would attract too much attention.

However, on the day in question, she agreed to wait outside in a parked car and chain-smoked cheap cigarettes while I did the deed. Well, I entered the bank. The formality of the Corinthian columns seemed to beckon and lure me on into a warm place that was filled with promise and potential. At first, I thought it was odd that I didn't have the least bit of nervousness about doing this. I was reposed and composed. I was clear and supposed. It seemed that all my experience in life had been leading me to this moment. And I got the feeling that she felt exactly the same way. I entered the bank, waited in line, and then passed a note to a lady teller who read its contents. My note indicated that I had a bomb and that I would blow the place up if she didn't comply. She reacted with the usual fear and then proceeded to put slim stacks of bills through the teller's window. Then I placed the stacks one at a time into a bag that I had brought along. When she was finished, I walked calmly towards the revolving door to make my escape. At that point, a bank security guard came rushing out into the lobby and confronted me. The guard nervously shook a service revolver at me, and the gun suddenly went off narrowly missing me. I jumped back, collected myself and fired back, shooting him dead. He crumpled to the floor. I mean, what could I do? The man made me feel so unsafe. What a heartless bastard! For a split second, I could see myself lyin' dead on the marble floor with my spirit flowing out of me. After that, I could fast forward, and the image stopped abruptly and without warning. Then I could see him bleeding profusely, but I didn't miss a beat. I ran away with the bag of cash and made my getaway in Meghan's waiting car. She loved it. She even gave me a big wet kiss as I was driving away.

Later, after the bank hold up, she and I were at a skuzzy dive bar counting money from our heist. Except for a caretaker who seemed to be one of Meghan's flunkies, there were no other customers around. Outside, the bar had a sign that said, "Closed for Renovations." The caretaker stepped up to the bar and told his story. He'd been in Afghanistan and Iraq, for two tours no less! Been trained to kill. I figured he was an attack dog.

Meghan said, "Young man, you can't figure out the difference between civilization and brutality. That could be useful. No matter. Soon you'll get clobbered with an answer or maybe you'll give one. But for now you're crazy. By the way, Tony, have you ever been hypnotized?"

"Can't say that I have."

"Well, if you ever decide that you want to, I'm very good. I'd love to practice on you."

The caretaker chuckled. His eyes, cheeks, and nose seemed to say, "What a presumptuous lady!" I think he knew better than anyone about who the crazy one was. My, my but the guy was good. Despite his youth, he'd been around the block one or two times, so he didn't miss a beat. Not for one instant. I had to hand it to him. He went on and on telling Meghan and me about how he had a girl who was freakin' out and testin' him. Apparently, his gal pal was the type who liked to find out just where the limits were and then cross ever-so-slightly over the line. Once over that line, she could smile at him and look so seductive, so she could double-dare him to cross. I thought to myself: what an idiot that girl was!

I told him, "You can't test out a soldier who'd been through what you've been through."

"She'll learn or she won't. If she doesn't, she'll get smacked. Go complain, girl, but don't come cryin' to me." He was pretty flippant about the whole thing. He made me wanna talk to the girl so I could set her straight, just for the sake of her own well-being.

He looked over at Meghan who was counting the money and sipping a cold one. She slid her tongue over her upper lip in a reptilian lick. The three of us toasted our glasses. I thought long and hard about how far this whack job of a woman named Meghan could wheedle me into doing almost anything. Just thinking some horrible thought was enough to make her want to act it out through me. Despite this, something in me made me feel as though neither the bank heist nor the other unfortunate occurrence had actually happened. That wasn't me who did that. That was someone else.

Meghan's hands were riffling through the stacks of cash. "This batch is done. Ready to go to the Chinese laundry."

"Or rather, the Grand Caymans' laundry," Tony replied.

Suddenly, from a side door two thugs barged in brandishing guns. One of them said, "Not so fast, big man."

His partner yelled, "Get your hands up now!"

"So you thought you'd go into business for yourselves."

"And on our territory no less."

"We'll show you what happens to enterprising boys and girls like you."

I turned to Meghan. She looked terrified.

"Please, we didn't mean any harm," she exclaimed.

"See boys," I said, "to show you our good faith, we'll let you have some of the money."

Then I threw a stack of bills into the faces of the two thugs. A gun went off, but missed. I threw the first punch at the first thug. The caretaker threw the second and then the third and fourth. The ecstasy was crawling through me. I knew the caretaker would come in handy! Something about them told me that I could take 'em. They were dumb crooks. The caretaker and I could smell their weakness. They weren't real men. How could they be real crooks? Then everything escalated, and the thugs got badly beaten up, courtesy of the caretaker and yours truly. At one point, Meghan helped me out by stabbing a fork into Thug #1's shoulder, and the guy screamed in pain. The caretaker gave him a vicious kick while he was lying on the floor. Then the caretaker, Meghan, and I gathered together the satchels full of money, at which point the caretaker and I noticed another bag that had been brought along by the two thugs. How could we have been so unobservant? That was a mystery to me.

Meghan picked it up and looked at the caretaker and me. "What's this?" she asked.

"Lemme give it a look-see," I said. I peered into the bag and saw that it was filled with cash and lots of it. The green gleamed in the interior light.

"It's the money that they've been collecting this afternoon from all of their shake-downs."

Meghan's eyes got predictably greedy. "Hell, we might as well relieve them of their heavy burden."

The caretaker got nervous. "I don't know if that's a very good idea 'cause knowing what these guys are capable of, they're probably gonna be itchin' to get it back if this here money decides to go and take a walk. I vote that we leave it here."

"And I vote that we take it," replied Meghan. "So Tony, you're outvoted." She snatched up the bag of money and shouted, "C'mon, let's get outta here!"

We bolted from the bar just as the thugs were starting to come to and piled into the Meghan's car. Immediately after she turned the key in the ignition, I glanced out the window to see the limping thugs in hot pursuit. There was a late night, high speed, tire-screeching chase through mostly deserted streets and then out along the sea road which bordered the lonely saltwater, razor grass marshes. As we were making our getaway, I got a little bit distracted by the sheer beauty of the place where land and sea made their connection. The sky was alive with stars and in some places seemed to merge with the ocean. It was hard not to think about simply forgetting the thugs and going down to the water's edge to take in the view of the bright moonlight that shimmered on the glassy waves. I thought about all the fish and crustaceans cruising around out in the deep end. It must be fun to chase each other along the ripples of the sandbar. Oh, I'll bet those fish can be flirtatious. They love to play tag! I wondered if they had a better deal out there than the deal that we have here on dry land. Yeah, it took quite an effort not to be suckered in by Mr. and Mrs. Fish, but I was able to tear myself away...

... Finally, we managed to lose the hapless thugs. Meghan looked back and told me that the gangsters' Lincoln Town Car appeared to have run out of gas. I could just picture them sitting there looking at the empty gas gauge and then getting out to push the car to the side of the road. As the Mafiosis' car receded into the distance, Meghan, the caretaker, and I turned down a side road and roared off into the night. She was very relieved.

Tony laughed in the back seat and then rolled down the window to look back. By now the gangsters were completely out of range, and I could revel in the sheer overblown dimensions of their incompetence.

And I wasn't alone in feeling that way. No, no, not in the least. Tony was of the same mind. "You know, Meghan. This spot of fun makes me almost wanna go out and get hypnotized."

"Yes Tony, that can be arranged. Let's do it tomorrow, first thing." She reminded me of the old-fashioned dentist who's only too eager to get out his pliers at the drop of a hat.

"Oh Mrs. Mastrianni, I can't wait. I'm so looking forward to it now." His eyes had a gleeful look.

"I promise that you won't be disappointed."

I looked over at Tony and could see him rubbing his palms together.

"So, Joe. That's it. That's my full report of what happened --- the whole story of the full business carry."

I smacked my lips and gave Bill a close stare from head to toe, before spitting my wad of gum into the gutter and watching the rainwater carry it away. It glided along randomly, bobbing like a floating corpse before joining up with some candy wrappers and torn Lotto tickets, and then disappearing into the culvert. "Bill," I said, "crime goes every which way --- over, under, and on its face. The beast knows no bounds. It wants to get the upper hand. In this chord, the triad will shove you to the side, bro, just like you're some sort of passin' tone." I paused for emphasis and then continued. "Don't you realize that you've been had? Don't you realize that you've been a complete sucker?"

"No, whaddya mean? I never get suckered in. I've never been had by anyone in my entire life."

"Bill, you're still under hypnosis! How many of those hypnosis sessions did she give you?"

"Oh, I dunno. Seven or eight. Maybe more. I wasn't really keeping score."

I tapped him lightly with the palms of my hands. "Come on, man! Snap out of it."

After about a minute, he seemed to be coming to his senses.

"You understand, Bill, that you actually offed someone, don't you? Has that fact carved itself into your brain? Well, I hope it has. Tell me if it isn't true."

He looked perplexed and as he came to, his face began to register the awful reality of what he had done. In that instant, he kinda burst into tears.

"Bill, one more thing I wanted to ask ..." I milked this one for all it was worth.

"What's that, Joe?

I let him wait.

"C'mon, Joe. What is it you wanted to ask me about?"

I let him wait some more.

"What is it, Joe?" I loved the impatience in his voice.

"Awh, it's nothing, Bill. I just wanted to ask you if you're feelin' safe. You <u>are</u> feelin' safe, aren't you?"

And it was clear that we were being watched again by the menacing eye in the sky that never was far removed from anything. Bill pointed up at it, and we watched right back at the dazzling ball of light that scurried across the heavens. For once, he seemed glad that there had been a distraction, something to take his mind off from the enormity of his moment of self-discovery. Bill's misfortunes were definitely cause for concern since in the long run they could easily become my misfortunes. Perhaps he was more in need of supervision than my sister? The man's adversities weighed heavily on my already troubled mind, but I was betting that my exhilaration from the music project known as Babies in Bars would pull him through.

The very next day, Doc McIntyre, the scourge of my prior existence, appeared to me again, this time in a dream. Harassing by text message and crank phone calls were not enough. Here was a fellow who was a genius for every mode of communication, so he had to ratchet it up a notch. I had been slumbering away probably not very far into the part where the snoring starts in earnest when damn, there he was yammerin' at me just the way he had previously yammered in my waking hours. This time he was looking me straight in the eye with the same bloodless eyes he'd used to stare at me before, and he was giving me a dissertation on the wonders of melanin and how he was planning to apply this cutting-edge technology to his long range goal which was to create a modern day Neanderthal with what was left of the old population. And the old population? That residue would of course be me.

"Joe, melanin can be used for so many functions. Right off hand, there's ion storage, coupled oxidation-reduction reactions, UV light absorption, and free radical scavenging. But there's so much more ..."

As he got more excited at the mere thought of these possibilities, his eyes bugged and bulged out of his head. For me, the eyes were a huge distraction, but my dream insisted that I listen to what he had to say: "We could do a simple swap from the melanocytes to the kertinacytes, and we could do that exchange directly over the nucleus of the keratcinocyte. This would lead to a number of fruitful possibilities --- there would be exocytosis melting off into extracellular space, dendrite cytophagocytosis, and nanotube transfer. And darn, I nearly forgot --- we could shed the malanocytes and do a phagocytization procedure. That possibility seems to me to be the most interesting paradigm at this point in my research. Naturally, none of this can really come to pass unless we have the most important component. And the most important component would be you Joe. So once again, I find myself in a pleading mode. Please come back. Please come back. We need you so much more than that ridiculous project known as *Babies in Bars*."

"Why do you need me so much? Am I that rare?"

"Yes, you surely are. Not only are you not quite human, but you're hellbent on finding your true self. That combo makes you an A-Number One Speciman."

"Really? If that's true, then why don't you follow *your* true self and come after me in person instead of resorting to text messages, crank calls, and now dreams?"

Then he started in on an answer which I've now forgotten. The only part I remember is that his words jolted me awake.

THE KING OF OOMPH

Dotted eighth notes --- how cool was that? What a wiggly lady Gwen was. Her belly was swimmin'. The navel was particularly pretty. Just like Billie Holiday, she was all over the beat, puttin' her whole body into it. Ben, if you were good, you might have noticed that. But you're lost and never will be found. First she was in front of the beat, then she was in back. At some point, she'd call a compromise and settle for bein' smack dab in the middle. I was helpin' out on every turn of the path, lettin' her know where the one was. If she couldn't make up her mind, I would do it for her. And I would do it by bein' rock steady 'cause only one can play that game. Ben, you were so out of it that Jillian turned off your amp completely. She did that 'cause you never have figured out when to go out of the chord. You're insufficiently dissonant.

Where would we be without dissonance? There would be no spice, nor would there be consonance. Inebriation would have no meaning. In New Orleans and Austin, audiences don't really believe in iPods. They hardly believe in juke boxes. The locales themselves have become celebrities --- ideas with a rough appreciation for the moment. There's nothing canned about it. In most places, frenzy is missing in action, but there Dionysus hasn't died out completely. No way. He's exiled, alive and well, and hiding out --- following a busy itinerary of crashing on dingy fourth floor landings and flopping in broken down trailer parks where the pillows have burst open and there are feathers flyin' around all over the kitchen. There, he can get totally blasted on cheap red wine while he makes "big plans."

He knows full well that it shouldn't be all Apollo all the time. A combustion must take place because the eye is faster than the hand, and the hand is quicker than the voice. Accordingly, he takes a trembling swig from the bottle and proceeds to make adjustments for this failing of Nature.

So my "internship" was going well despite the lack of pay. The educational experience was becoming more and more invaluable with every passing day. We had gone on the road, in search of crowds who loved to guzzle --- none of that two drink minimum New York City bullshit for hipsters who take an hour and a half to figure out if they like something or not. I laughed at the way they listened to old music again and again and called it new. No way would we do that 'cause everyone knew that we played maximal music for maximum people. I took solace in the notion that drumming --- at least my kind of drumming --- dealt in excess. If there was no overload, there was no meaning. In fact, some rock critic guy dubbed me as being "The King of Oomph," and the nickname took hold. I actually got to like it.

Life was sailin' right along with few obstacles. The tempo was chuggin', burstin' at the seams. I could see the world rush past me, framed by an open tour van window. Endless oversized tractor trailers gleamed in the summer sun, hogging the asphalt, lugging their payloads of merchandise purchased on eBay and Amazon. For me it was a spiritual experience to know that that cargo would be destined to support sedentary and second hand lifestyles everywhere. Someday, even their sex would be cut and paste. I knew it would be that way because then I could run in the opposite direction and follow the white line down the middle of the road. I love the road--- always have. No matter what dreary hotel we stayed in, the brimming day seemed to splash over the horizon. Every night was a new adventure, and from my catbird seat in the back, I could be the chief cook and bottle washer. That was my function. Bill came along too. He wanted to be my roadie, and I figured that I might as well let him 'cause after what had just happened, he really needed to hide out and make himself scarce as much I did. He was a fast learner. And he and Sunita kept me well-supplied with a seemingly endless supply of smack, so I could concentrate on what really mattered. Bill became my babysitter. He watched over me when I had too much and chauffeured me to and fro.

That was his major contribution, but not his only one. As a roadie, he knew his stuff. In no time at all, he understood the proper tilt of the ride cymbal and the exact angle of the medium thin crash. This was a good arrangement because that way I could keep an eye on him. Based on what he'd told me so far, as long as I played drums well, he would be my protector. That would be good considering what my scoundrel of a sister was up to. Bill was great. He always bought the best clothes. And when he got bored with them, he gave 'em to me! I tell ya, the guy was my taster. After a gig, women would come up and go gaga over my red shirt. Sunita was severely bummed. Tough luck, lady! This was my time. And the bartender girls usually had some overblown drama they they'd amplify to the max. That was a way to sex up the biz. They wanted the liquid to pour into welcoming gullets. And why not let it froth forth? I'd be watching the high def plasma, lookin' at cheap shots and adoring it. I was an actor. I wanted to kill for those lines.

And the gigs --- they were the gigs of the gods, and people would kill for them too. I could hear the roar, and I basked in it. I battered back on the floor tom with a thud and thunder combination. And the roar could hear me loud and clear. What a lucky boy I was! Night after night on the road I got to hear Gwen go through her paces, belting out some wild song she'd written about her favorite flat screen television set. I never got tired of hearing her delicious rant, nor of backing her up. She sang it this way:

"My TV will never die
It babbles on forever
Static wave against grey eye
Remote that spins bland pleasure"

You go girl, tell it to me! Tell it to them out there! Tell it all the way back to Row Triple Z. She was testifying, and I was right there with her every step of the way while she filled them in on everything they wanted to know about cop shows, police chases live from L.A., soap opera divas, infomercials, courtroom dramas, feel good doctors, manufactured consent, charismatic leaders, and blurbs for super burgers. She rambled on in the same vibe while I underscored the whole thing with a well-placed crash or two:

"... Menu lists our hearts' content
Pundit sticks like clever glue
Amplifies his blather spent
To melt events for you
Sky cam buzzes noon time chase
Buzzing copter egging on
Burning rubber robbers brace
Spike strip puncture drives upon
Plot that lathers sudsing soap
'Stop the wedding' starlet shouts
Catharsis cries a rope-a-dope
Falls again not finding out
Low rent begging cheap surreal
'Who's the father?' host man brays
Aw shucks forced fun feely feel
Dr Glee smiles sunny days
Tough talk gumshoe scrounging clues
Shadow haunts what really is,
Walks the perp on breaking news
And gathers life like honest biz"

Way to go, girl. Lady, you have just now entered the plush zone. You're out of iPod Land. You will notice that things are different here. I could see her looking back from the edge of the floodlights, incredulous as I bounced a stick off from a rack tom and caught it on the fly before comin' down hard on the high-hat. That was a sure fire way to get a crowd on their feet.

This song was built for speed, so her voice was no longer completely hers. A part of it was now mine, a prized possession I could reach out and caress. It was a source of great pride that my new acquisition could purr or dive bomb on two seconds notice. This kept the people guessing out there. Her public didn't know whether to expect a feathery whisper or an unhinged glissando, so they were going wild, grabbing to touch her after their accumulated hysteria had transformed her into a goddess. The new Kali had been unleashed and was running headfirst into the world. I wanted to show her off, to flaunt her to the end of time. Sometimes she'd get very drunk before a show, and she'd make lots of mistakes. But none of those fuckups seemed to matter. She barreled through whatever bloopers she happened to croon and made them new. Those notes started out as one thing, but spiraled out of her mouth as quite another. This drove her girlfriend Kathy crazy, but I didn't mind gussying up the background a bit as long as doing that managed to make the sagging foreground look amazing. Of course, afterwards, people would come up to Gwen telling her what a genius she was and how she was "pushin' the envelope" or "takin' it to the next level." What abject nonsense! Naturally, that would piss off Kathy more than a little bit, but nothing serious because the whole project was fast becoming a juggernaut that nobody could stop. What did worry me though was that Gwen might one day come to actually believe in all that trumped up adulation.

To my way of thinking, it was okay for me to be a megalomaniac, but she should never be granted that power and privilege because she hadn't a clue about how to use it. And what was my power? Answer: I could see a sizeable portion of her soul. I wanted to say, "Dear lady, your soul is showing!" Seriously, the compulsive hide-and-seek anticipation between song and drum magnifies that awareness. What's more, if a singer has a lover in the band, then the lover will know it too. I glanced at Kathy's eyes, and they flashed right back telling me that she recognized this quirky ability of mine. Good. We were kindred spirits. Another set of ground rules had been established, so there would be no misunderstandings. When the lover of the babe singer is a guy, he can be a total pain in the ass. He'll be constantly on red alert trying to keep an eye on his woman. He'll shoot down every good idea just on mean-spirited principle. Once he's sunk his hooks into the band, he'll play the part of the informed expert on the music biz who needs to be "consulted" on even the most trivial of details. He will wait, like all good Cro-Magnons, to ensure that nothing threatens the chance for his genes to get passed on, even if it means that fun gets killed in the process. And most of the time, his genes should *never* be passed on in a million years. But Kathy's face told me such dubious currency would not be valid here. No doubt that was because, in this configuration, genes wouldn't stand a chance in hell of ever getting passed on, so I returned her glance with one of my own to let her know that there would be nothing to worry about.

There were, however, other things to worry about, one of which was that every now and then I would come back to the hotel real late after partying hard, and there would be a strange couple sprawled out in my bed --- never the same grouping twice. How fucked up was that? Of course, I would congratulate her on what a nice pair of twins she had, to say nothing of her beautiful sparrow's nest, and she'd have the nerve to go into some half-baked indignant feminist routine, at which point, I would have to say, "Listen, dear Goddess, you're in my bed, and so I get to say anything I want to about your precious rack." So, even though I was being reverent as hell and wanted to bow down and touch her feet, she'd start to get ashamed and all, and hem and haw, and then they'd both skulk out of there like rats from a ferret so I could go to sleep, except that I might still have to pick the dirty used works out of the tub in the morning when I wanted to take a shower. I had to be careful not to stick myself 'cause you never know what you'll catch. The whole thing was a party that never seemed to fully come to a complete stop even when you wanted to call a halt to it and get your breath. But what could I do? The fun times sure outdistanced any trivial problems like these.

And what were some of the other drawbacks? Well, for one thing and much to my annoyance, Sergeant Fielding came along. He told me he wanted to keep an eye on me and that watching me on premium cable TV wasn't good enough. He let me know that I was a "person of interest" and that he wanted to get to the bottom of Andy's suspicious drowning. He kept hinting that I might actually have something to do with it. Bastard! I could see him there at every gig, usually off to the side, trying to look as if he were blending into the woodwork. At one point, I told him that he was nearly as ubiquitous as Jillian's camera crew. He even would have the audacity to show up wearing a *Babies in Bars* tour T-shirt.

"Don't worry, Joe. You'll get used to me breathin' down your neck just like I'm getting used to living on a TV production set. Now, maybe you'll know how I feel."

"Officer, you're a guy with entirely too much time on his hands. Where does that penny ante police department of yours ever get the money for your kind of extravagance?"

"Oh, I pulled some strings. And besides, I'm going into retirement soon, so I wanna have a last big go round, if ya know what I mean. I wanna do follow up studies on all the people I've arrested over the years to see how well they're doing --- a kind of where-are-they-now program. I wanna see who's a success story and who isn't. Who's been naughty and who's been nice. I figure it'll put my entire career in the proper perspective. And what's great is that, as far as I know, nobody else has ever conducted a study of this kind."

"Yeah, well why can't you do it at someone else's expense?"

"I'm afraid you don't get to decide that, Joe. I think you may be a person with too much creativity and not enough habit."

"There you go again, Officer. Last time we talked, it was comparative theology, and today it's life's inner meaning. What'll it be next?"

"The next thing will be to get this damned iPod of mine to work. Are you good at repairing things?"

"No, I'm terrible with anything mechanical. The trouble with iPods is that every song has to be a home run, or better yet, a grand slam."

"Yep, no singles, doubles, or triples allowed."

I looked at the iPod. "Hey man, lemme see it for a second."

He handed it to me. I gave it a cursory examination and decided that it was unfixable, so I handed it back.

"Look Officer, you don't need this piece of junk when you've got live music to listen to."

He looked away and muttered something else about solving the case of Andy's mysterious disappearance.

I said, "Don't keep reminding me!"

Then he went to order another drink. Everything the man said was a smokescreen --- something I had to be wary of. I wanted to tell him that he had more ink than a giant squid.

Sunita came along too, or rather, she gimped along. For some inexplicable but amusing reason, she remained obsessed with my hands, so there was even more kissing, sobbing, and slobbering than there had been before. She marveled about how wrinkled my fingers were and called me "the wrinkly man." Sunita also constantly compared me to previous lovers, saying that my predecessors had all been "fossils." The woman was checking her private inventory on a daily basis. She begged me: "Please don't become a fossil, Joe. I don't think I could ever handle that." I told her I didn't know what made me so special, but that I'd keep going on in the same vein if that was what she wanted. It felt good to be the ongoing instrument of someone's pleasure even if it meant that I was just a thing --- a lump of sweating flesh. Those pleasures were in the service of preserving my life and bolstering her illusions. I could become the pawn of her wild and wooly imagination. That might be a cheap thrill. I couldn't quite put my finger on it, but there was something creepy about her 'cause whenever I was kissing the young bacchante, I thought I was kissing Death itself. But I didn't care. Ladies and Gentlemen, may it be clear to all! I kiss the Greatest Unknown. What big fun. What a voluptuous shiver! Made me wanna jump for joy. She had the whiff of being a complete disaster. But, as disasters go, what a beautiful disaster she was. I mean, what the hell, why not have another one? I figured I should go for it because by now I knew enough about life to never second guess any of the strange stories that might be scampering through a woman's brain. Circulation is sufficient. Soon she might love me for being something I'd never dreamed of. Naturally, by then I'd have to dump her. That would make me feel sad because I knew she really did respect my hands. No one else in the world had ever respected my hands.

Of course, the other thing that I had to be mindful of with her was what Ben had told me. Namely, that three of her exes had met with untimely ends. With a normal girl that would have been something that would have put a damper on the festivities. But she was far from bein' a normal girl. And besides, from my point of view, it would be fun to tempt fate. And since I was enjoyin' what fate had dished out to me of late, I figured that Krishna was on my side.

But on the subject of her perpetually injured leg for just a moment or two --- I got the feeling that her leg was nearly healed, but that didn't matter very much because she was still encased in plaster. She was enjoying herself too much to have the thing taken off. No way in hell would she do that. She wanted to be a Superstar, and she needed her prop. Sometimes I would look over at her when she was sunning herself beside a hotel pool decked out in her orange string bikini, and it seemed that the plaster was swallowing her alive. The sweet lady was in the process of being gobbled up and scarfed down, but I couldn't figure out from what. The troubled actress crossing the stage of this reality show was on the verge of being eaten by the scenery.

I thought about her often, more often than of many whom I've come to know on an intimate basis. I pondered why she seemed so hesitant to have a healthy leg. So, I went and asked her why. And her response took me by surprise. "Joe," she said. "I'm trying to remake myself piece by piece, part by part. And I figure that my left leg is as good a place to start as anywhere else." Jeez, I thought. What a weird answer, but she was a weird girl. The only problem with that notion was that she seemed to be permanently stuck. Nothing ever seemed to get better. Nothing ever seemed to improve.

By contrast, Jillian proved to be quite the workhorse. She supervised the whole tour as well as the television crew, and together we cranked out lots of marketable material for a wide, albeit cultish, TV audience. Like so many reality shows, she ran a mighty tight ship, so if the supposedly off-the-cuff scene didn't do so well on the first go-round, she'd have us do another take, tellin' Ben, "Gee, can we do that one more time, and on this take can you be even more annoying than you were before?" And Ben would be only too happy to oblige.

In just a few months, we had fans everywhere from Patagonia to the Arctic Circle and in between.

Surprisingly, one from those millions of fans was my sister Meghan. Oh yes! Really! She still called up regularly to make more and more crank death threats, but I could tell that even she was captivated on some level, suckered in by the Hollywood horseshit. That world rivaled hers for its unbridled ability to manufacture fake outrage. No doubt she realized this and felt a competitive urge to up the ante since she was so accomplished in that department herself. To do that, she had to watch the show on a regular basis in order to come up with new and more innovative strategies of attaining counterfeit empathy. She became addicted to the characters, especially to Gwen, which was a little worrisome to me. So, I made a mental note to keep track of that because who can ever figure out completely what strange paths lead singers will follow and what lunatics will follow them? There she went, shimmying across the stage --- singing her little asthmatic lungs out:

> "I'll keep it simple
> I won't be bold
> My opinion's not
> Silver and gold
> Straight ahead
> Right on course
> My centaur shakes
> From the tumbled down horse"

Yeah baby, I thought to myself --- wouldn't I like to get onto your tumbled down horse. I mean, check it out --- she and I were actually hearing and making the same notes at the same time. How cool was that? I might as well have been in her. In my fantasies about her, which happened intensely on a nightly basis, she was a lady wandering *sadhu* mystic, who'd recently decided to live high up on the slope of a steep Himalayan mountain. The beautiful babe had been practicing austerities and hadn't eaten a bite in seven years. She'd saved a bundle on food, but now with me in the band, she was waiting to pig out. I'd make sure that the *Babies in Bars* band would be her banquet. In the fantasy, she would every so often wind up doing something vaguely agricultural --- picking rice, gathering millet, or husking corn. What a good strong peasant girl she was! She'd come in after a long day in the fields, and a bead of sweat would trickle from her brow. That drove me crazy, which of course only added to her cachet. I kept my fingers crossed that she wouldn't have an asthma attack onstage and decided that maintaining a positive mindset would be the best insurance against that ever happening. In the meantime, Gwen's lyrics were fast becoming the chorus of her life as well as mine, so it was anyone's guess how many other lives were dancing to that tune.

All this was not to say that my sister Meghan's captivation with Gwen would ever veer Meghan away from her ultimate goal in life, which was of course to do me in, but nonetheless, she now saw the changes in circumstance to be a challenge for her ever-expanding murderous intent. Since she would call up to heckle me, I thought it only sporting that I should give her a razz or two in return. In a pompous tone, I would declare: "And now a rebuttal by Joe Meyers." After that, she would hit me with a fresh barrage of insults, and I could hear her growling under her breath. Then she would hint at some even more creative malfeasance that she was cooking up, but just to keep me guessing, she would never get very specific, and then I would bait her some more and say, "Meghan, you and your friends are all witches, and the cauldron's in the basement, and don't you forget it; don't you forget it!" and that would shut her the fuck up for about three days. Something about the situation made me feel invisible. I could see her, but she couldn't see me. Clearly, I was on a roll and would not be stopped anytime soon. Still, she filled me with such white hot rage that I would often talk with her as though she were right there in whatever faceless hotel room I happened to be staying in while *Babies in Bars* was on tour, so much so that I frequently found myself ranting, or worse yet, singing to the walls, saying hey dear sister, this one's for you:

"It's a war that you wage all the time
Bombing bridges, lighting fuses to the dynamite
It's your mission to mess up things without contrition
To put some spite in someone's life
To put some blight in someone's life
Don't it burn ya to see me riding in a limousine
With a smiley face that's peachy keen
Yes, a smiley face that's peachy keen"

"Did you like that one, Meghan? Good. I knew you would." Then I'd do a drum roll on the chair and that would tide me over for a little while. A warm feeling would overcome me, and I would slump into a deep contented sleep. Under this backdrop, the months passed quickly. The cities blended into one another. I remembered looking at the tour itinerary, and it didn't feel like an itinerary at all, but instead, more of a schedule of fun. And then we were in New Orleans. The sign next to the front door of the club read: "Out-of-town bands --- remember where you are." When I got on stage, I was in back of the beat on the verses and way out in front on the choruses. The Goddess lectured me about the dance. Understand that I know what I'm talking about. "Make me feel very good, Joe, or I'll make you feel very bad," She said.

More often than not, I made Her feel damned great. The Goddess made me feel that the world was my oyster, and I made Her feel like She was in the spotlight. I guess you could say She was my publicist. As *Babies in Bars* got more popular, we attracted greater media attention. When that happened, other pop stars paid attention. They did that 'cause we were on the map. When you're on the bloody map, people pay attention. One of those people was a mega pop star lady. I won't describe her in detail. She wasn't worthy. She got enamored of me, and she was pleasant to look at. It became clear that the Goddess had thrown me yet another bone. The mega pop star lady and I had a good "intertwingling" --- that was the pop star lady's contribution to the English language. She told me she wanted to coin a new word and urged me to use that expression at every opportunity so that by some stroke of luck, it might go into general circulation.

I told her, "Good luck, but don't hold your breath." However, the big problem was she was mostly talk. She rarely put out. What a superfluous girl! Well, I wouldn't put up with that crap for five minutes. I was the King of Oomph, and I didn't give a damn how bloody famous she was. I said, "You have five minutes to put up or shut up! What's the matter? You think it's unbecoming to do it with a drummer? You hesitate to mingle with the slave class? You think I'm a disgrace to my livery? Well, get the eff out! You don't put out? Well, I'll put you out on your Sports-Illustrated-bathing-suit ass!" Naturally, in the aftermath, there were lots of catty blogs and news items about was a bastard I was supposed to be, only problem was --- those commentators forgot to mention what a withholding bitch she was. Give me some credit. I'm being generous, so I described her with the B-word. I could've been nasty and described her with the C-word, only it didn't matter 'cause the general public failed to buy her pain-in-the-ass story. In short, she wound up lookin' ridiculous. I mean, what did that lady think I was --- her help? Her implied response was 'yes.' But I wouldn't stand for it. Not for five seconds, let alone five minutes. I let her know in no uncertain terms that I and I alone would give the song permission about when to begin. I dumped her ass faster than one of my single/double paradiddle combinations. In hindsight, she was not much more than a passing eighth note in my existence. I watched as she bummed and bummed bad, and I felt glad.

Being on tour was the most fun that anyone could imagine. Sometimes we would have to compete with recorded music. It was such a complete blast to shut that genre down. There were few people that I hated more than DJ's. They don't contribute to anything. All they did was appropriate. They'd present a song, and then act as if they'd created it. The audience applauded. I felt the false clapping. They made beautiful things less expensive. But we were "live" and in the moment, so they would never approximate what we could do. In retrospect, it was so much fun to remember their disconsolate faces. They knew in their hearts that they couldn't come close.

That was about when bratty Ben started to change for the better. Perhaps the Goddess had something to do with it? Who knows? I'd love to give Her the benefit of the doubt.

The entire band was bathed in a reddish strobe light, which made the crowd look bizarre and surreal as they moved in a jittery meter to the sounds we were producing. Kathy, the high priestess of time and space, was anointing them in a rain of coiled distortion and suspended eleventh chords from her red Les Paul while I rattled off a time storm of machine gun snare fills over a grinding pulse of double-kick eighth notes. The melody, hanging on for dear life, bobbed and weaved on top of this turbulence. Watching the audience struggle to emerge from the blackness, I couldn't help but feel they were writhing their way out of some cold exquisite marble, trying to find a frantic ecstasy. And it was *Babies in Bars'* function to coax them out of the dead shine of the stone, to hoodwink them into life itself. From my perch in the back, I preferred to think of the whole lot as being a bunch of weird shut-ins who'd finally been let out. This was their opportunity --- the flood gates had been torn asunder. They were mastering the vocabulary of a foreign language, so their faces reflected surprise that these new exotic words actually had meaning.

The Chinese meth dealer who would invariably show up to our gigs there constantly waved his arms at me and made contorted faces as I flailed away on the kit. And peering bug-eyed over the cymbals between volleys of thunderous fills on the kit, I made scary faces right back. On those nights, we deliberately played in odd jarring meters, as if to say, "We dare you to dance to this!" But there were no objections that any of us could hear. The sound was lopsided --- a true reflection of the world that it lived in. The meth dealer was pleased.

Kathy was doing a scrambly riff, a root and a fifth up from that and ... a fifth up from that. Dakata-dakata-da. The lady was marauding over three frets stretching diagonally with her fingers staking out fresh terrain. Down up down. And a mirror of that. And then an echo of that. She was feeding off from Gwen's energy, lingering and goading her to commit herself, eagerly anticipating the second when those delicious lips would break into an arpeggio grin as C modulated to D minor. Gwen sang away, oblivious with her eyes closed:

> "The gaggling gulls roost on the rocks
> The clouds paint up the sky
> A dry wind scurries 'cross the path
> Her scent perfumes the land"

Gwen wheezed a bit on the last line, but not to worry. Her asthma seemed to be under control. Knock on wood. Her girl Kathy was playing the role of alchemist because, up until those gigs, Ben had grudgingly acknowledged that Ziggy the Beat Box was, not so much consigned to the trash heap as he was, for practical purposes, put on the back burner. Jillian had called Ben's bluff, which meant he could feel free to take his bat and ball and go home. This required an enormous effort on his part because onstage there would never be a computer hanging around that would "quantize" him. So, he had to comprehend that he didn't really matter. Whatever sounds he managed to produce were totally beside the point. Superfluous. He could have produced them, or he could not have produced them. Either way, it was of no consequence. In the immediate situation, other forces held sway. Not to brag, but the man had clearly entered my orbit: my scruffy god of rhythm had trumped his god of bad harmony. Mom was right. It was the primordial beginning; something had been made out of nothing. Life had hatched from out of death. In short, Ben had been tamed, and no one in the band was more aware of that than he. A precious quantity had been restored. What a cause for celebration! And the songs themselves had been begging for it. The good thing about this sweaty reality show was that it gave the songs as well as our meandering jams, the public seal of approval. You could almost hear their sighs of relief. A stiff yoke had been taken from their backs. Unfettered by such burdens, the songs could now go about the serious business of dispensing memory from sound. Now people were allowed to like us. Without TV, that would have never been possible.

Kathy's fingers, scurrying around the strings, knew that only a true transgression would do. Once Ben's overly sensitive personality reflected on this, it knew that all bets were off. The mangy Id and slicked up Super Ego had to shrug their shoulders, come to a compromise, and make the best of it and give Ben special permission to go crazy --- which was exactly what the conceited boy did. Accordingly, Ben's robot boy Gulf got put on hiatus for the time being 'cause Ben was suddenly having too much unexpected fun. He had nothing to lose and everything to gain. He had to git. So he got with my program. And what were the results? Well, they were beyond the wildest expectations. Under my hedonistic tutelage, the cornered boy came out of himself and became a new and slightly rawer creature. The tip off was when he started to take his bass back to the hotel room and actually practice. He was learning that it wasn't all about result. Sometimes process has to enter the picture. Of course, he did his routine of kicking and screaming. That I could have predicted all along. But in this latest round of gigs, he was nonetheless a sight to behold. His playing, even weighted with its obvious limitations, morphed into that of an over-the-top, swaggering, drunken sailor of a man, becoming something far, far afield from his own nature. And the cities themselves took part of this sea change in him. They gloated. Yes, they had to take their share of the credit. And how did Ben feel about this? Well, he was jubilating till he was blue in the face. The guy was a new person. Women especially were taken by this latest version of Ben. There had always been women who lurked on the periphery of the band. In the course of things, they had pretty much discovered what the essential Ben persona had to offer. Some could go with that, and some would search for wetter pastures, but this new Ben was quite a departure from the one that they had known. He was truly "new and improved." It went without saying that this did absolute wonders for his love life.

And this did wonders for the sound. The tunes became vehicles for each of us to fly. Gwen continued with her vocal:

"We're fishermen out on our rafts
We light out early, we light out fast

Tacking mast, billowing sail
Chart the course for whiskey grail
Four million years of evolution
You're its greatest contribution
A dream I plan each night to chase
And wake each morning to find erased"

Gwen played piano like an amputee --- yeah, one-handed, but it still worked out fine. The crowd went bonkers. The meth dealer led them on, falling on the floor with his arms and legs pedaling upwards, doing his cockroach dance. The reverb on the snare sputtered off into never land. Gwen and the rest of us slammed into the next song. The lyrics went:

"Savor the glimpse of new weather
Remember the fun it will be
Cloud house we'll storm together
Swallow the rain as it flees..."

But my so-called friendship with Ben was bringing out a dark side to my own personality. I say that because, right after he had begun to have such success with the ladies, he came to me and said, "Joe, I need your advice on something. I've been goin' with this cute young thing, and she has an equally cute sister. In fact, she's nine and a half on the Cutie Pie Scale. And one thing I've noticed about these sisters is that they're both very competitive with each other. One of 'em is always afraid that the other is gonna get something better. The girls keep a running tally. So, early on, I noticed this aspect of their personalities. Well OK, that's no big deal. I can live with that 'cause, hell, those sisters have lived with this weirdness all their lives. By now I'm sure they're totally used to it. Anyway, things are goin' just fine, but now I wanna make 'em finer still, so I think what I wanna do next is to take it to the next level. I wanna put the moves on the other sister. But I suppose if I did that, then the really competitive sister might have issues with that. Only the problem is I really wanna go ahead and do it anyway. My body is tellin' me that I should do it. Well, I've been wrestling with this dilemma for the better part of twenty-four hours now. One hour I feel one way about it, and in the next, I get diametrically opposed and go the other way. So what I wanna ask you is how you would weigh in on this thing. How do you feel about it? Do you think I should go ahead and fool around with the other sister?"

I thought of what my correct response would be. I thought about it for about a minute and a half. Then I looked him right in the eye and said, "Yes Ben, I think you should go ahead and do it. Absolutely. It's definitely the most prudent course of action. I mean, to tell the truth, I can't see any other way out of this dilemma. And you're right. It sure as hell is a dilemma. So yeah, do it ... or rather, do her. You have my blessing. If you body feels that way, then you really have to abide by what it wants. There is no other way."

And Ben went right ahead and followed my advice. Not long after that, Ben told me that one day right after the deed had been done, he'd just gotten back from doin' an errand when the first sister told him that she's found out that he'd been foolin' around with her sibling. Ben said that he'd nodded and told her what had happened, and at first, the young lady had pretty much indicated that it was alright, that she was totally fine with it. Ben said that had given him a renewed sense of happiness, and he went ahead and proceeded to fold the laundry as if nothing had ever happened. He told me he was feeling so much better because the cute young thing had confirmed that there was no problem. He was feelin' so good about himself that he practically went into some sort of meditation, and in a strange way, he nearly had an out-of-body-experience. Then, seemingly out of nowhere, she went crazy on him. One minute things were fine and the next minute, she was comin' at him with a knife. She was carvin' the air in front of him, which put the fear of God into him, so Ben hightailed is right on out of there and never went back. And I told him, yeah, he really did almost have an out-of-body experience.

But what did this adventure reveal about me? What had I unearthed about my own persona? I'd egged him on to do something that I would never have dreamed of doing myself. Then I remembered that I always liked people who volunteered for others.

Yes, but that was others, so it really was OK. That was not me, and it never would be, which was the reason it felt so safe and cozy. Thinking about this, I balled up in a fetal position just so I could feel safer and cozier, and that made me fall asleep. When I awoke, I didn't feel safe anymore.

However, safety could be sought in other areas. None of this was of any huge cause for concern because, compared to the sanctity of being in a great rock band, relationships didn't amount to much. Safety --- the real refuge, had to be found on a grandriose scale. What I mean is that the safety of the world is more important. And it was in this aspect of the band's collective persona that Kathy gave me the most encouragement. Early on she had been intrigued by something I'd said, which was that music could change the world. Well, she took it one step further and said that a drum solo, if it was great enough, could save the world too. I thought about this and said that I was deeply skeptical, but she egged me on and insisted that in the next series of gigs, I should be given a spot where I would do a full-fledged bombastic solo turn complete with crashing cymbal rave-ups. Needless to say, it didn't take much insistence on her part to get me to agree. And Jillian thought it was a great idea too, which gave the camera crew more stuff to do. But the real joy of this would come on the following day when Kathy would present me with a tabloid newspaper that would have a dramatic headline showing that some worldwide catastrophe had been averted at the eleventh hour. She would be all smiles and would say, "See Joe, you're the King of Omph. You're saving the world from itself. And you're doing it one gig at a time!" And I would reply by saying, "That's what a King of Omph is supposed to do."

It was about this time, that Ben was able to convince Jillian that adding his robot boy Gulf to the band as a saxophone player would do wonders for the ratings. At first, she was not so keen on this idea. However, when I put in a good word for him, she figured why not give him a try? The new premise for the show was to keep the audience guessing: was he or wasn't he a robot? The audience became so divided on this point that soon there were forums on the worldwide web devoting long and convoluted discussions on this very subject. On one of the episodes, there was an exchange between Kathy and me about Gulf's robotic status, and I temporarily rendered the whole thing a moot issue by saying, "Who cares if he is or isn't. All that matters is that he's a helluva sax player." The stiffness of his sax playing was quite the crowd pleaser, but since he was learning as he went along and was getting voluminous additions to his database on a daily basis, there would be instances when he would discover new territory. The new terrain was a much dirtier sound --- one that I helped to encourage with more than a few battering ram drum rolls. And by this time, Gulf had become totally addicted to heroin and for all intents and purposes, was now under my sway. I doled out his daily ration of heroin as if it were some solemn liturgical ritual and I was the High Priest. And afterwards, he would fill me in on Ben's latest experiments with robot research. Judging from what he told me, Ben's program was going full speed ahead because other robots of Gulf's kind were being produced. Gulf reiterated that the plan was to produce as many as possible so that Ben come eventually start a whole new species.

¿CUÁNDO SALE EL PRÓXIMO FERROCARRIL?

But like I said, I had pretty much given up talking to Meghan. Little Miss Deal Breaker needed strict supervision, and there was no one on the near horizon who could give it to her. Except for the usual agenda of insults, my conversations with her were closed. However, that didn't stop me from talking to her hubby. Why not call him up and shoot the breeze? Man to man. I had heard from a very reliable source that he was running for office --- the U.S. effin' Senate no less. Gee, we could chat about life, politics, and sociopathic women. Say, Allen, did I ever tell you about my misadventures in Mexico City? That was a fun escapade that could've ended badly, but the young lady's pimp was surprisingly understanding. That was a golden chalice of bareback intermingling. She turned me over and shoved me upside down enough to send me deep into the next century and a life or two beyond that. I often think about Her. The Goddess of the moment didn't know a word of English. I didn't know a word of Spanish with the exception of "*¿Cuándo* sale el *próximo ferrocarril?*" Yeah, I know that doesn't count, but it was the Adam and Eve thing. Between us, we could've created an entire world. Quite possibly, She may have been the best of all. Somewhere in the saxophones She's a blushing beauty. I can see Her now. She's grown up and long out of the business. Got a hacienda in Puerto Vallarta with a herd of servants falling over each other. You would know about that, Allen. Your wife's a travel agent, working in a dying industry and rippin' off little old ladies. Why can't you make her stick her head in a refrigerator, Allen? Then maybe she would wise up. Mom is extremely disappointed. Where do you get the money for that high and mighty lifestyle? Where do you get the money for that high and mighty campaign? That's what I wanna know. Running for Senate is not cheap. And you haven't worked in years. Alright, alright. Don't get all huffy. I'm just askin'. I get zoned in to this stuff.

That being said, my talks with Mom got even more strange and alarming. We'd start off touching all the usual bases --- how's the weather up there? Have you made any friends? And we'd talk about Dad and what a crazed piece of work he was, how he'd once driven a gang lawn mower straight into a peat bog and how we'd laughed our asses off on that one. But then I'd ask her about Meghan, and she'd say that my sister had called up the other day and said, "Mom, you have nothing. You have no money left. It's completely gone. The entire wad has gone to the nursing home. How do you feel about that?" And of course when I talked to Ma, I had to spend a good ten minutes with her trying to calm her down. Way to go Meghan!

Exactly what was my sister up to? More and more it sounded as though she wanted to induce good old Mom into having a good old fashioned fatal heart attack.

But to change the subject for a second --- during a brief break from the tour, Kathy and I were playing a low key gig. Those are the kinds that pay the most 'cause no loudness is permitted at a cocktail hour for movers and shakers. I mean, I was playing brushes for cryin' out loud. That's right. Betcha never thought I could stir the old soup, but I can. You'd be surprised at what I can do. Kathy was a big surprise too. She was playing Bach, Pachelbel, and Vivaldi and that other guy whose name escapes me --- the Water Music Man. Who in the world would have ever thought she could do that? Well, maybe I would've conjured it up 'cause I was starting to get *very* proud of her. In fact, prior to this, I would often find myself in the midst of vivid dreams where I would touch her hair and ponder how proud I was of her. Maybe that's what real love is --- being proud of someone. I knew that I would have to watch my step 'cause it's so easy for a

Neanderthal to get in over his head. Someone could get offended. It's so easy to run off the rails, so… so I guess I'd best get back on track…

I glanced at her again. Kathy was engulfed in something big. We were also doing swing jazz and the standard round of businessman shuffles. They really dug this stuff. Maybe a Hammond B-3 might've made it better, only who in the world can ever lift that thing? But the party was dwindling down. The rich people were getting their coats and heading for the exits. Drunks were collapsing on beds in the various side rooms and the scantily-dressed hostess who played around with a pink feather boa was busy figuring out how to get them the hell out. Ethanol was rapidly moving through nephrons, and the nephrons were getting nervous. Kathy and I had launched into our cover of "Song of India" by Tommy Dorsey, which was exactly the sort of understated aural wallpaper that this gathering demanded, when I noticed a certain rich, famous, and extremely powerful man coming up behind her. He nuzzled up, putting his hand on the nape of her neck. I could see her startled reaction and could also see her attempt to pretend that it wasn't happening. She kept playing the tune, perfectly capturing the Dorsey horn part, only doing it with the help of her tremolo whammy bar as I nonchalantly dragged the metal wire brushes across the calf skin head. The trick was to look as bored as possible even if I wasn't. This ancient tune was sure a lot of fun to play. Down through the ages, I could almost feel all the hands who'd touched it to keep it in working order. They'd done a great job, and now they were passing on the torch to Kathy and me. I knew from the start that we would live up to the task.

But the rich and powerful man was clearly over his limit. He had not been drinking responsibly, but hell, he was rich, powerful, and famous too; he didn't have to drink responsibly.

"Hey baby!" he whispered. "I've been at this party for two fucking hours, and I'm bored right out of my skull. The only reason I stuck around was 'cause of you."

The rich and powerful man kept running off at the mouth. From my place right behind the drums, I could hear everything.

"The only reason I stuck around was 'cause of you."

But he'd already said that. But he'd forgotten that he'd said that. He stuttered onward and downward, and as the fondling got more intense, the whole rap started to take on an onanistic vibe.

"Hey Baby! You're so beautiful. You're so beautiful."

I could picture him back in his cushy uptown mansion grocking at centerfolds. In a twinkling, he was moving from her neck to her boobs, which caused Kathy to muff her splendid rendition of the Dorsey horn part. Well, I'd had just about enough of that. The Dorsey horn part was semi-divine! She'd had just about enough of that too, but she kept playing. What a professional! I was so proud of her that I jumped over my kit and grabbed the sonovabitch by the collar of his worsted suit, ripping the fabric right down the back. Then I slammed him into the rack toms and medium thin crash cymbals, making him shake, rattle, and roll. It was probably the first time he'd ever played drums in his life, but I had to hand it to him: he had decent technique because on the way down to the plush wall to wall carpeting, his bald head did a rather nice double drag Swiss Army triplet on the edge of my snare drum. Bravo! Sir, as you continue your drum studies, you will gradually pick up on the art of leading and following at the same time. Right now, you have a big case of beginner's luck --- an acute case of the cutes. Remember always to practice, practice, practice.

However, the movers and shakers were not amused. I angrily stood over him, goading him to get up while the provocative hostess screamed bloody murder as she ripped her pink feather boa. I thought she wanted to strangle me with her pink feather boa. I mean, you'd have thought I was killing the guy. And he was a complete mess, a sight for sore eyes. He should have been embarrassed, but he was too rich to be embarrassed. Soon a security guard was summarily summoned, and I was handcuffed and taken into custody. I spent the night at Rikers until Jillian, Kathy, Gwen, and Bill bailed me out in the morning. Jillian loved it, lecturing me chapter and verse on why there's no such thing as bad publicity. And she was absolutely right. Even though the camera crew had not been around to shoot this "unfortunate incident," she said that was no problem. The next day she had us do the entire thing over again so she could film it.

Jillian assured me that this might very well be the best episode of *Babies in Bars* yet.

"Joe, the whole world loves someone who can stick it to the Man. That, so much more than drumming, is your true occupation."

Recalling the Dorsey horn part, I did a swing out dance:

"Kick, kick, kick across, double kick, and down."

Then I did a cuddle step with an imaginary female partner. Bill was there to egg me on. What a guy! I looked across the street. There was that bloody tosser Sergeant Fielding taking notes again. Why couldn't I shake him off?

He approached me and said, "Joe, after what happened last night, I'm surprised to see you up bright and early, and lookin' so chipper."

"Remember, Officer," I countered. "This is a reality show. I'm immune. You can't catch me. You can't catch me 'cause I can't even get myself arrested. It's what happens when you step out of iPod Land."

"Yeah, but you really pissed off someone high and mighty this time. No one messes with that guy!"

We were back at a restaurant about three hours before a show. This one was going to be at a civic center somewhere in Idaho. Spectacle seemed to follow us around like a loyal old dog 'cause that persistent flashing orb had just then put in another appearance in the sky. This time it didn't even bother to wait around until nightfall. That's what I loved about the thing --- its basic honesty. It was so sincere that it had no wish to suffer any foolish pretense. It figured why not let it all hang out? Naturally, it had to put on a huge display of technical ability just so we'd all know that it was indeed a serious character. It topped off the big demonstration by flashing a penetrating strobe directly into our faces. How we didn't get our retinas fried I'll never know. Kathy and Gwen were blown away and couldn't stop talking about it. Kathy managed to get some of it captured on her smartphone, and the quality was pretty good, that is, until the thing mysteriously went on the fritz. No jiggling camera from her! No way! Her hand was as steady as a rock, despite the fact that she'd had, by my count, about seven beers. Gwen even went so far as to propose that we somehow try to integrate the thing into the show. Catching it on camera would definitely be quite a trick though. We might have to just go with the smartphone video, despite the bothersome static that interfered at the most inopportune moments.

"I'll talk to Jillian about it. If that doesn't send the ratings through the roof, I don't know what will."

"Rock and roll and little grey men. What a concept!"

Then Kath lit up some weed and lost herself in a cloud of smoke. Turning to me she said, "Joe, last night both you and I had the swarming crowd in the palms of our hands. We made it that way. Liquid silver was swimming through their veins."

"Yes, they were truly spellbound 'cause we're in the spellbinding business."

I looked over at the ubiquitous camera men who were faithfully recording every second of the moment. Ah, it was so nice to be leading an edited life.

Most of the time I was beginning to feel pretty good about myself. I, the truest of true Neanderthals, was making decent progress in my goal of remaking my life. Successes were starting to pile up. Failures were slowly receding into the past. I was discovering that there was every good reason to gloat.

Of course, that was when Bill, the reader and screener of my fan mail, brought a letter to my attention. It seemed that Doc McIntyre, my old stalker friend, had decided to go back to older methods of communication:

> Dear Joe:
>
> I keep telling you how much we miss you here at the facility. And I know that my pleas keep falling on deaf ears. But in the name of research, something tells me to go on. Science demands answers. I've been following the work of other innovators who are as committed to basic research as I am. And the

guy I'm seriously impressed with is the bass player in your band. I actually think he's a bit of a visionary.

More about him in a minute. First, I want to fill you in on my latest project here at the institution --- the one that you seem to be so loath to go back to. What we've done is to come up with a way to bio-print. We didn't need much. The basic idea is not so very different from a Xerox machine. What we had to get was paper, printer, and ink. Just imagine those three items, only with the suffix 'bio' in front of them. Oh yes, and I almost forgot --- you need one more thing, and that's a bio-reactor. But hell, getting that's a piece of cake. So really, the process is kinda like going to Staples for office supplies. Think of the ink as a multi-cellular speck of dust, and from that we can get a spheroid. After we've gotten that act together, we'd have to decide whether we want to go single or multicolored. That's where I had a brilliant idea. It concerns those jelly-like friends of yours, the cuttlefish Vim and Vod. You see, we've honed the concepts down to a Tee. It's the refinement of the logistics that needs more work. The way I see it the cephalopods could be so invaluable. In their natural condition as the consummate glitter freaks, they could make it so easy to go for the wide spectrum. After we've accomplished the fine tuning, we could prepare the bio-cartilage and put it into hibernation, so it comes in handy for later on. But that's not the best part --- what's interesting from my point of view is the paper. Yeah, the bio-paper! It's a cross-linkable hydrogel that makes believe it's a cellular matrix, just what you'd find in Nature. Of course, I'm skippin' over a lot of stuff here, but you get the idea. The hydrogels help the cells to take on the character of regular multidimensional systems. Since the hydrogels are so damned fluid, their slipperiness would make the cell aggregates come together. We could upload them onto the printer heads, and very much like a Xerox machine, the printer spits out the ink, stamping down layer upon layer. The cells are then replicated in a climate controlled environment to maximize their numbers.

Well, Joe. You get the drift. I'm sure you can see where this is all leading. Yeah man, you guessed it --- I want to do a bio-print of you. Yes, you! I'm not content to have only one of you. No way! I want to make as many of you as I can. So let me get right to the point --- what I want you to do is to ask Ben if he and I can join forces and become a team. You'll do that for me, won't you? If not, I'll have to see about getting you back to the facility once the show gets cancelled. Give me your answer soon. Yeah, I know what you're probably thinking. But I really don't think you have very much choice.

Respectfully,
Your good friend, Doc McIntyre

I looked at the envelope and could see that it had come from my old address at the institution. Naturally, it didn't take much prompting for me to tear the whole thing up.

FLASH DRIVE NUMBER TWO

The Continuing Narrative of Joe the Neanderthal

A TON OF BOTOX

The lady wore a mink stole. She didn't give a damn where it came from. Dollars and style sucker punch each other on a daily basis. I remembered well those times when the predatory woman talked a blue streak about love --- how she'd never been adequately served (or was it serviced?) in that department of life, how she'd taken the whole project rather capriciously--- and then somehow, against huge odds, she'd transformed herself, or rather, her man had transformed *her,* and then everything had been an entirely new ballgame. She'd seen the light, and now she was a convert. Love --- she'd finally gotten it. She'd solved the delicate calculus. And when you really stopped to ponder it, love was the be all and end all. Well damn, when the lady was up to her old tricks of poisoning the well, nothing was further from the truth. The problem with some people who talk about love all the time is that they seldom are capable of giving it or receiving it. They yap a lot, but they can't put out. All they do is take. They're the ones who'll smack you when you least expect it. All the better to smack them back.

It was two weeks later during another break in the tour. Bill and I were watching from the far off perimeter of the crowd and except for the occasional placard emerging upwards like a periscope, our view was largely unimpeded. Meghan was basking in the moment; these festivals of public phoniness were her element. Hubby was announcing that he was running for a major political office, and there she was by his side. He went on and on about how this was the poorest state in all of this great land of ours, and how it deserved better... and...and...she had a ton of botox on her face.

"No new taxes!" he bellowed into the microphone. "This is our year; we've waited long enough. We're a state that's on the rise!"

"WE'RE ON THE RISE! WE'RE ON THE RISE!" The crowd was going bananas. I half-expected them to collectively drool all over the TV cameras.

I paid close attention to Meghan. She was practically having an orgasm while Hubby made his speech. Comprehend that she wanted the big payday. Well, if I had had a hat, I would've tipped it for the sheer obnoxiousness of this tribal ritual. Hubby was using every cheap trick in the playbook.

Just then Meghan piped in: "And Allen, my friends..."

APPLAUSE APPLAUSE, even dumber, wilder applause...

"Allen is my gift to this great state!"

I thought Yo Allen, love the way you're milkin' it. Are you effing serious? What would this clown say next? Maybe he would wrap himself in the flag and then go take a nap like an Egyptian mummy, or maybe he would tell 'em, "We're not from the right wing. We're not from the left wing. No, my friends, we're just the opposite." Then I could watch the crowd look to the right, then to the left, and then up and down like a bunch of dashboard bobble dolls. They might do that if they didn't break their necks first. Everywhere I looked, people were avoiding some gigantic issue or pretending not to understand some simple truth, and hubby was helping them to the max, talkin' in code, so they could get even better at playing the game of "We Don't Know."

But Allen went on and on and on again. There was so much more that Allen had to say. "Fellow citizens of this great State, we must not let big government push us around. Understand that government is the ultimate problem because it's forever telling you what to do and how to do it. It's always putting rules and regulations in your path that are designed to mess up your lives. Understand that every achievement that you have made is something that you have achieved solely through your own talents and abilities. You, and you alone, made that happen. You don't need them. You *are* your own boss, and you are in the driver's seat. You don't need their tax-and-spend nonsense. What you really need is someone who can go to Washington and put a stop to it. People of this great state realize that what this Senate race is ultimately about is autonomy. Let me say that again --- AUTONOMY! You are in charge. You're the ones who call the tune, not some bureaucrats in Washington who don't understand your problems. And the other big thing that we need to reassure ourselves of is the need to protect our sacred right to bear arms. Nothing should be allowed to threaten that great principle. And let me tell you this right now --- there are people out there who would deprive you of that right. They would take that right away from you in five seconds if they were given half a chance. Accordingly, I'd like to solemnly promise to each and every one of you today that if elected, I will do everything in my power to see that such a usurpation of your sacred rights will not happen. And what is the first thing that those folks in Washington will try to do? Answer --- they will try to regulate semi-automatic weapons. Yes, that's the first thing they'll try to do. And after that, lemme tell ya, it's all downhill from there on in. Absolutely and for sure!"

APPLAUSE!

I glanced back at the crowd as it exploded into a deranged applause that was even bigger than the roar that came out of a crowd at a *Babies in Bars* gig. Then I looked up to the platform where Allen was standing and spewing forth nonstop choplogic. There was my dear sister standing with him just to the right of him. I hated the supercilious smile on her face. It was a face that had had too much plastic surgery. Yes, it was true that on some shallow level it bore some resemblance to what some might call attractiveness, but if a casual observer stared at it more closely, he would discover a caricature, as though the surgeon had had an off day. And he'd had an off day not because of any lack of talent, but rather, because what he'd had to work with was so rotten to the core.

But for me, her face was not the main issue that caught my attention. No, no. There was something more pernicious. I looked into the eyes of various members of this mob. Each of them seemed to have the same vacant look that Bill had gotten just after his interaction with my sister. Surrounded by the milling crowd, I came to believe there was a subtext to this insanity because they all looked drugged --- drugged in the worst of all possible ways. Could it be that they had been sampling from a batch of the very same unholy cocktail that Meghan had served up to my best friend?

I felt a ferocious rage welling up from my heart. I wanted to get back at her. There was no way in hell that I wanted to practice what some people are fond of calling "Christian charity." No way on God's green Earth would I get bamboozled into that! Turning the other cheek was never a part of my being. I was far too competitive for that nonsense. I didn't have lots of wishes in this life, but one of them was that I wanted to see my sister in *jail*. In fact, I fantasized about going to visit her. For once in my life, going through security would be big fun. I would nod my appreciation to the burly guards as they patted me down. That's right. Frisk me now. Oops, I think you missed a spot. There, there, now you got it right. Then in the visitors' room, I would say, "Hi Meghan, I'm having big fun. I hope you're having big fun too, workin' in the license plate factory for chump change. One thing I've learned dear sister --- I must always operate from a position of strength! Cro-Mags like you never get tired of asking for mercy, but they seldom give it." I wondered about what she and hubby's sex lives must have been like. For all his showy political swagger, I bet that their reality was quite different. I could picture her flogging him to within an inch of his life. And he would be lovin' every blessed second of it. Yes, the predatory lady was right about finding love. That was the most truthful thought that had ever romped across her depraved brain.

Suddenly, and without warning, I thought of Mom. I was twenty years old, and I'd walked in on her as she was talking girl talk to one of her confidants. They were chatting each other up. It was about men. What a pair of absolute magpies the ladies were! Leave it to the girls to figure shit out. Mom said, "Well, if he can't get it up, then what the hell good is he?" Jesus, I couldn't believe my ears. That was my mom saying that? I'd never heard her utter such brazen purply stuff in my life. I never knew she was capable of that. Stunned by what she said, I retreated from the door and hurried back down to the beach where I settled in for about two hours. The gulls came up to greet me, made some random half-hearted squawks, and then flew away. They didn't want to get near me after what I'd seen and heard. I watched the tide bring up wave after wave. The rhythm made me mesmerized. Just like sex, Nature was repeating her secrets in ever more novel ways. In the meantime, I would have to save Mom.

Only trouble was --- there was so much more than Mom that needed to be saving. After watching the glazed eyes and wild expressions of the people at the Allen Mastrianni campaign rally, I realized that the entire world needed to be saved. It needed to be saved from itself. Lookin' at that herd of idiots who were sure as hell goin' to be voting for that vicious loser, I was certain that the only thing that would bring them back from the brink would be some vague spiritual mumbo jumbo. The best I had to offer was my drumming. Mom was absolutely right. But I hadn't seen it until now. Her words echoed: "Joe, go out there and make some magic. Go out there, and make something from nothing!" --- They echoed in my heart. Perhaps the drum solo competition had only been the beginning. Perhaps there was so much more to do.

As I saw it, the big issue was that Meghan had so many people fooled. Although it's true that much of life is about appearances, one can't say it's completely about that. Some of the time substance abounds. I was thinking that just as certain psychologists are wrong when they brazenly say all aspects of existence can in some convoluted way be related to sex, so too can normal folks be wrong in thinking that every iota of our lives is under the dominion of love or the wish for it. Surely, some genuine affect concerning life and its relationship to love must seep through now and then? It can't all be fake. Tell me it's true.

What was so disheartening was how absolutely fooled the people were. Why couldn't they figure out that my sister, and by extension her lunkhead husband, were dyed-in-the wool frauds. The heart of the matter was that they used love as a shield. No, I'll go further and say that they used it as a weapon! They *looked* like a loving couple. And he *looked* like an average guy, one whom another equally average guy could have a simple conversation with in a bar. Perhaps that was what the yardstick was for these kinds of things --- the ability to have a passing conversation between a fellow stranger in a bar about a subject that everyone can easily relate to. I mean, how easy is it to commune and empathize on the subject of love? It's as easy as falling off a log. It's the one thing that passing strangers can understand. It's what makes the world go round, so there's no reason to believe that any perfect stranger couldn't weigh in on the subject. Love is so much more easy to weigh in on than say, art or music or politics. And I quickly surmised that both my sister and Alan's handlers were thoroughly aware of what I'd just then been been thinking about. They knew this so much better than I knew about even one of my most complex drum beats, and that would be saying quite a lot. The ability to connect with total strangers is what politics is all about.

I looked back at my sister and saw how effortlessly she hobnobbed with the crowd. In this regard, she was actually more skillful than her beloved Alan. And as a team, the two of them were positively pillars of the community. Yes, it was then that I fully comprehended what I was up against.

"Listen to me you great big lug. I understand you're running for the Senate?"

Bill was laying some impressive intimidation on the wannabe Senator. We had slipped past security with some bogus ID's and barged into his office.

"Allen, don't mind us. We only wanted to give you a high five for your ambition. It's nice to see someone who sets his sights high 'cause it makes us wanna set our sights high too.'

Allen was righteously spooked. He shot up from out of his fine upholstered chair.

"Who...who let you in?" he stuttered.

"We let ourselves in, Allen," Bill exclaimed matter-of-factly. "Hi, I'm Bill. I don't believe we've met. But I can assure you that your wife Meghan and I *have* met. We actually did some business. She might've told you about it. Then again, from what little I know of her, she probably didn't."

"Are you part of the campaign?"

"Indirectly speaking, I suppose."

"Please tell me the nature of your business, Mister…Mister…"

"Bill Triano. And this here is Joe Myers. Oh, the nature of our business? Well, that would be connected to the nature of your wife's business. You see, Allen, she hired me to kill Joe."

"That's impossible. My wife would never hire anyone to kill anyone. She's a very gracious loving person. I'm insulted --- insulted to say the least. Get out! And get out now!"

Just then the door opened and in came Meghan. She was so startled that her mink stole almost fell to the floor, but she caught it as it started to topple from her shoulder.

As ever, Bill was in fine philosophical slash professorial form.

"Hegemony," Bill began, "breeds a pretty green money pile, Meghan. It's the kind of heap that affords mink stoles. We wouldn't have it in a funkier economy. Yes, this is conducive to fostering a self-satisfied belief that one's financial accomplishments are solely the fruit of a purported, yet specious genius. Of course, that brand of genius usually winds up being quite a pushover."

She took one look at both Bill and I and turned white as a sheet. I wanted to tell her that whatever accomplishments she had were totally secondhand.

"Hi Meghan. Remember me. I'm Bill. When we met first met, I was in disguise, and it was Andy Collins who did most of the talking. Unfortunately, since then he's had a tragic accident."

"Jesus, Meghan. You actually know him?"

"I've never seen this man Bill in my life. Of course, that's my terrible brother who's made my life an unending hell."

"How can you say that?" I replied. "I bless your happiness --- wherever it was dropped."

"He's lying, Allen," she countered. "But I do know Andy. He's a very nice man who works on the campaign."

"Yeah, well Andy's dead."

Her eyes darted left and right, then fluttered. She was fishing for an answer. "No… no, that's not possible. True, I haven't seen him for a while, but it was my understanding that he was doing some special polling project for the campaign staff."

"Meghan, I think his special project was to bump me off." I replied. "Instead, I pushed Andy in the water back in Wildwood. Apparently, swimming wasn't his forte."

Bill went over to a vacant desk, pulled out the chair and sat himself down before nonchalantly crossing his legs and putting them up on the desk. The candidate and his adoring wife were still too shocked to say much. I thought Allen's jaw would be dropping to the floor at any second.

The phone at the desk suddenly rang and Bill picked it up. "Hello, Allen Mastrianni Campaign, how may I help you? Oh just a minute. Hold on. I'll look that up right now." He opened the steel desk drawer and placed the phone inside, and turning back to face the still thunderstruck Meghan and Allen, he exclaimed, "She thinks she's on hold, but she's really in my desk drawer."

"Listen, Bob or Bill or whatever your name is, I don't know you. Now get out this instant, or I'll call security."

"Oh no you won't. If anything, I'll call security first."

Bill leaned forward and opened the drawer an inch or two. He picked up the receiver. "Caller, are you still there? I'll be right back." Then he leaned back in the chair and slammed the drawer shut with his foot. "Oh sorry, my foot must've fallen asleep," he yelled into the land line before slamming it down.

"Meghan," I said, Please get off my back. The only reason I'm here is to try to have some semblance of a normal life."

"You're a Neanderthal," she snarled. You'll never have a normal life."

"Look Meghan," Allen interjected. "I could care less about these scruffy people. What really concerns me is how this might affect the campaign if any of your Machiavellian stunts gets out."

"Allen, I haven't done anything of the sort. What are you accusing me of?" my sister countered.

Bill fished around in the side pocket of his suit coat and produced a crumpled bulging manila envelope which he offered up for Allen and Meghan to see. "Perhaps this will refresh your memory, Meghan?"

Allen moved closer to look at the envelope and then tried to grab it. Bill moved it away just out of Allen's reach. "Uh uh! You can see, but you cannot touch."

"Meghan, it's got your handwriting on it! How did that happen?"

She was taken off guard. But she was still good at improvising. "Simple," she countered. "He must've stolen it from somewhere in the campaign headquarters. Didn't I hear something about some money that had gone missing? Well, this must be it."

"Yes, but this envelope has your handwriting on it."

"I'm sure that can be explained. This thug Bill filched it. If he could get by security today, he could no doubt have gotten through it before."

"That is a bit of a stretch, Meghan," replied Allen.

I glanced at Meghan's face. Her eyes said that the jig was up.

"Look Allen, I did it for us. With the campaign and all, I didn't want people to think that our family was associated with some raggedly muffin, ne'er-do-well drummer. It just wouldn't look right. Also, Mom wrote him into the will, and I'm sorry, but that just won't do. He didn't deserve any of that. I, on the other hand, deserve it all. And I'll get it all. How did you think this campaign of yours got funded? Did you think that the money came in like a bolt from the blue?"

"Well…I…I…" Allen was at a loss for words.

"Allen, the money for this campaign is coming from that little old lady who's stashed out there in the nursing home. You can thank your lucky stars for her wad of cash. I've been tappin' the till. Without that rather handsome bundle, you'd be a total nobody. I hate nobodies!"

Bill butted in and put in his two cents worth. "Meghan, don't knock nobodies. They make up ninety-nine percent of your husband's constituency. It takes an awful lot of nobodies to make a somebody."

I glanced at Allen who had a crestfallen look on his face.

"What's the matter, Allen? You're look like you're goin' punk on me now. Did she hurt your feelings?"

"Oh Allen, I didn't mean it. You're not a nobody. You're my best somebody. Come to me now." She went and gave him a theatrical hug. I was starting to feel sick. But Meghan continued: "I was getting round to telling you this fact of life one of these days, but I kept putting it off. So, now you know. And now that you know that, you might as well know that sooner or later we've got to get rid of my brother."

"Meghan, I can't believe I'm hearing this. Why did you do it?"

"I just told you. Doesn't it make perfect sense? I think so."

I studied Allen's face. He was good at improvisation too. I could see that, like all candidates, he was kinda sorta nuts. He had the disease, and it had infected his every pore. I could tell that he wouldn't get all bent out of shape about some silly-ass moral compunctions. Hell no, he was going with the flow. And it didn't take him forever to figure out that the best thing for his campaign was to kill both Bill and me. Why in the hell did I follow Bill's advice to come here? If anyone should have known about sleaziness, it would have been him. I thought he was supposed to be an expert witness on these things.

"Meghan," I said, "how does it feel to just *lose* like that? To have a hit man just wimp out on you and make a defection to the other side --- that must be the mother of all bummers, no?"

Meghan's face rapidly changed from one of consternation to a look of exquisite calm. "Look Joe, I've got a great idea."

"Yeah, what's that?"

"I think we should bury the hatchet. We should let bygones be bygones. Don't you think that would be wonderful? Let's pretend that everything is like it was back when you and I drove to school in that old gas guzzler. That would be so wonderful."

"Are you kidding? After what you said about me. I don't know about you Bill, but calling someone a rapist is pretty much the worst thing that a woman can ever say about a man. It's kind of hard for me to go back to the way things used to be, not that they used to be any great shakes. No, no, far from it."

"What if I really said that I was truly sorry? Wouldn't that make a big difference with you?"

"And what proof would I have that you wouldn't go back on your word?"

"You'll just have to take the chance I guess. And don't forget, Mom still has some of her faculties. She's not a complete basket case at this point. I'm well aware that you've visited her, and I know what she's said about you."

"You do? How did you do that?"

"I have my spies at the assisted care facility. They keep me right up to date on everything. Also, one more thing --- what if Mom starts to get, you know, senile. Don't ya think you and I should come to an agreement about how to deal with that?"

"And pray tell me. How would you like to deal with that?"

"I think if she gets comatose, we should pull the plug. There's no use having her hangin' on for no good reason. I mean, think about her quality of life. She'd be in a pronounced vegetative state…"

"I wish you could be in a pronounced vegetative state," I interrupted.

"Stop it, Joe! Let me finish. That wouldn't be good for her, and it sure wouldn't be any good for you or for me. Wouldn't it be better if we agreed to not have the doctors and nurses resort to any extreme measures? She would continue on and just be miserable. Think about it, Joe."

Bill butted in tell me how he felt about all of this. "Don't listen to her, Joe. I'm thinkin' about it, and I'm knowin' this is simply another one of her schemes. Your Mom's not that far gone yet.'

"Yes, it's true. Why it was just the other day that she and I had a chat. Afterwards, she said, 'Joe, I'm so glad we've had this talk. We'll have to do it again sometime soon.' Meghan, Mom can make you toe the line and be nice to me. If you don't, then she can simply tell the nurses and doctors at the facility all about you and where would you be then? Well, I think you can figure out that if that happened, then you'd be in one deep spot of trouble. That's my good reason for wanting her to stay as alive as possible. And don't forget that with Allen running for the Senate, you have every good reason to sit back and behave yourself. Don't you think?"

I could see her staring to squirm even more that she had before. And Allen was squirming too. They looked as if they'd invented a brand new dance.

"Allen, how do you feel about this? I thought you were a right-to-life candidate. Isn't that what I hear you yammering about when I see you pontificating on Cable TV News? How does this pull-the-plug stuff square with your constituency? I'd be almost willing to bet that they might have a problem with that."

I stared at the floor and replied, "Awh, what the eff do they know? They're a bunch of losers. Right, Meghan? And besides, don't I have a right to life? The high life, that is?"

My sister changed her expression. "Okay Joe, you win. I'm easy. *You* have a right to life. Let's call it a draw and let it go." It was a blast to watch her cave.

The right-to-life candidate spoke up in an agitated voice. "Meghan, I don't want any trouble. I have my political career to think about. Let's keep it hush hush."

"Yes, it's true," Bill exclaimed. "We mustn't have anything happen to that political career. The people have a right to have the best man for their district."

"You can be rest assured that if it weren't for all this unpleasantness, I would vote for you in a second. Do you want me to give you a public endorsement?"

"No, don't worry yourself on that one. I'm sure we can get elected without you."

"So alright. I guess that just about wraps it up. We've got ourselves a deal. You'll leave me alone, and on my honor, I'll steer clear of you."

My friend Bill piped in: "Jesus, Joe. Don't do it! Don't!"

"It's okay, Bill. I can take care of myself. I can tell she'll keep her word because Allen wants everything to be super fine for his Senate campaign. And Meghan knows that at least in the private sphere, I'm a man of my word, even if she's not a woman of hers."

Meghan put her arm around the candidate. "Joe, if you don't trust me, you can at least trust Allen. Like he says, his word is as good as gold in private."

"Joe, the thing you have to understand is that I don't believe one word of my public statements. So, off the record, you shouldn't believe any of them either. They're all for show. Please don't take it personal. Don't get offended. It's only a way to get elected. Joe, from what little I know about you, I think you'd know that in this day and age, you get penalized for saying what you think. Well, if you know this on just a day to day level, then imagine how it would be if it got amplified to the Nth degree. And when I say the Nth degree, I'm talkin' about politics."

"So if you don't believe in any of 'em, then who in the world tells you to say 'em?"

"Why of course, that would be Meghan. She's the one who tells me what to say." He turned to her and gave her a sloppy kiss.

I looked at the skin on the arms of the sleeve that he'd just rolled up. There they were --- the whip marks that she'd laid on him. Yes, he was probably tellin' the truth. I could believe everything he said in the private sphere.

"You're a team of sadists" Bill protested.

"C'mon, Bill, it's okay. They're not gonna bother us. Everything will turn out fine."

I pushed him back, but Allen interceded. He looked me right in the eye for a change. "No, no, Joe. Let me reassure him. What's great about sadism is that it appeals to every macho aspect. We wouldn't want to have it done to us, but we'd sure as hell like to do that to others 'cause we'd be getting away with something big. It's really important to get away with something big. And if you can't accomplish that, then as long as you make people think they're getting away with something grand, then that's the next best thing. Then they'll be profoundly happy and will love you for making them feel that way. So, perhaps you can see how this notion would fit in with the gun thing. We need people to know that they can have semi-automatic weapons since we want everyone to feel that the danger never quite stops, nor would we want it to. Why? Because we want everyone to have, somewhere in his deluded fantasy life, the opportunity to shoot someone. Thoughts of being a hero should never be allowed to stray too far from the minds of ordinary men or women because those imagined scenarios would be their bright and shining moments to hurt others with complete impunity. That would be the ultimate ecstasy. All others would pale in comparison. To deny them this precious and pernicious right would a catastrophe for their small imaginations. Forget that "I'm-just-protectin'-my-family" bullshit. What I'm talkin' about has nothing to do with that. I know this, and the people way out there know that I know this. It's our dirty little secret. And as long as nobody let's on, it'll work for both them and for me."

"Lemme guess what you call it. I'll bet you call it 'The Game of I Don't Know.'"

"Hey, I like that. I've never heard it put like that. But it kind of works."

"I'm sure you'll give me credit for naming it."

"How can I give you credit if nobody's supposed to know?"

"You're probably right."

"'The Game of I Don't Know' --- it's the reason why I'm going to win by a landslide. That's what politics is all about. None of that how-many-'social-programs' crap amounts to a damn anymore. Neither Meghan nor I would waste ten minutes on that nonsense. There simply aren't enough votes for it. And nine times out of ten, they'd all vote for Jack the Ripper anyway. So what's the point of trying?"

"Yes," Bill replied. "That means politicians should all go hoppin', skippin', and jumpin' to do their best imitations of Gentleman Jack."

Meghan snuggled up to Hubby and they smooched. Every move seemed designed as some sort of practice for cameras or talking points. Even on matters of trust, their cold-bloodedness could still take my breath away. Allen showed Bill and me to the door, and we said our goodbyes. I was thinking this would most likely be the last time I ever had to interact with Meghan. The only possible situation which might present itself further down the road might be actually having to look at Meghan if we happened to visit Mom at the same time. How misfortunate and disconcerting that would be! But I would do my best to see that that wouldn't happen by calling up the nurses ahead of time to ask if the coast was clear. I savored the image of my sister as the door closed on her forever. I wanted it to be something grand, something I could rewind over and over. But I was crestfallen when it seemed so small. There she was --- a poster child for too much plastic surgery, receding in the line of my view.

Then I excused myself. "Goodbye for now, Meghan. I think Bill and I can find our way out. I'm sure we'll be in touch." As I said this, I was practically having to shove Bill out of Allen's office.

"Yes, we'll be in touch," replied Allen.

Just before I closed the door after me, Bill stuck his head in to give them both a final scowl. We took the elevator down and walked through the fine polished lobby. Bill and I must have looked like two arguing children as we made our way down the street. We wandered down the main drag of the city and ducked into a side street to find our car. The political rally was in the last stages of dispersing. I gazed back at the intersection we had crossed --- a lone member of the crowd, a man in a gray suit, was walking away. His expression was a mix of serenity and confidence. Clearly, the speech at the political rally had made a big impression on him. He walked along as proud as could be. He came to the crossroads, stared up at the green light above the thoroughfare, and willfully walked right out into the whizzing traffic totally against the light. He was looking very autonomous. Nothing could get in his way. I was thinking that he would stop, but there he was --- he just kept goin', and suddenly he was hit by a car. The impact vaulted him onto the hood of the vehicle. From there, he bounced face first into the windshield, flew several yards down the roadway before landing like a limp ragdoll on the concrete center divider. Bill and I looked at each other, not quite believing what we had seen. In a matter of seconds, the crowd was all trying to come to the aid of the obviously instantaneously dead man, only it was all too clear that there was nothing that could be done for him. Life had clearly flown the coop. Bill and I watched for another fifteen minutes as the police arrived and spoke to the distraught motorist. At that point, Bill turned to me and said, "You see, Joe, the vignette that we have just seen makes complete and total sense. I want to say, now there was a man who didn't want the government tellin' him what to do!" There was a man who would not stand for regulations of any kind. There was a man who stood up for liberty. Green lights for cars---they're such an imposition on pedestrians who want to move forward and go about their way in the world."

"Yes, Bill, and there was a very extinct man!" I watched again as the EMS crew drew a white sheet over the dead man's face and proceeded to haul him into the ambulance. The vehicle moved away slowly. There was no big rush to get to the hospital. There was no big hurry to get to the morgue. He would be just as dead as he was when they steered him into the ambulance.

"C'mon, Joe, show time's over. They're sending him on his way. I'm sure he won't be giving them much trouble with abiding by rules and regulations from now on."

"Not likely, as far as I can tell. Those pesky green lights! Those imperious "Don't Walk" signs! But hey man, did you get a look at that guy's eyes just before he stepped out into that intersection?"

"As a matter a fact, I did. They looked glazed."

"You can say that again. The car gave him a hole in the middle. He was a glazed donut."

"Yeah, if you ask me, he wasn't quite there."

"Most likely, that great speech of the candidate had something to do with it."

"He had the look of someone who was in a state of deep hypnosis."

"The young man was pretending not to know. He wasn't goin' to let any petty reality stuff get in his way. Nosiree!"

"Okay, that's enough excitement for one day. I'm tired of lookin' at that stiff. Let's go and find the car and blow this pop stand."

I took a last look at the blood that stained the center divider and followed Bill. We ignored people who came up to us asking about what had happened. We were approaching our parked car when I saw a familiar face: there was the rich, famous and extremely powerful man. The same one that I'd tussled with back in New York at the big party for the movers and shakers. He gave me a stern look and read me the riot act: "Did you think that you'd get off that easily from our little altercation, Joe? It's true. Amateurs may get drunk and disorderly. But we make the rules. The long and the short of it is that I'm accustomed to making people toe the line. Nobody crosses me and gets to keep his hands."

"Oh my God, it's you."

"Yes, it's me. And I'm a major campaign contributor to the Allen Mastrianni Campaign. Allen is a very good friend of mine, and I am a very good contributor. Oh God, am I a very good contributor. If you were in a position to know, you would know that I am a man with extremely deep pockets. I'm accustomed to having my people get elected. I'm accustomed to feeling up any girl at any party of my choosing. As a matter a fact, I'm accustomed to a lot of things. And this is Tony. Bill, I believe you and he have met before. Mister Joe Myers --- I believe that is your name, isn't it?"

"Yes, how did you find out?" I replied nervously.

"Our brief encounter at the fund-raising event was problematic to say the least, so I asked one of my people about this upstart drummer, and after that, you were pretty easy to find. Joe, you realize of course, that I can't permit that kind of behavior at one of my big bashes. Tony, will you please do the honors."

Tony then proceeded to come after Bill with a broken bottle. I knew that Tony was no slouch in the street fighting department. Bill's story of the punch up with the gangsters had been evidence of that. No way would Tony be a pushover like them. Based on how badly he'd sundaed up those incompetents, there was the possibility they'd offer him a job, that is, if they were given the chance to be objective. Bottom line: they knew talent when they saw it.

But Tony couldn't have cared less about such employment opportunities. He lunged at Bill, jabbing the broken bottle at his face. Bill let out a long yelp --- sharded glass and skin had made contact. I jumped forward and smacked Tony with an uppercut. I relished the feel of bone against the flesh of face, and this was especially magical when I turned my wrist to make him topple forward like a sack of wheat. I tackled him and kept him down with all my might. My chest hurt from pressing down too hard. It was like the aftermath of a car accident, but I fought off the pain.

"C'mon, Bill. I've got him down. Help me!"

I looked over at Bill as my opponent kicked and screamed. Bill's eye had dodged disaster. He had a nice neat circular cut right around his left eye, but if we could get out of this jam, he would most likely get away with an insignificant scar that would get to hide in his bushy eyebrow. I shoulda known that Bill would be having all he could do to staunch the flow. In my moment of indecision, the second mugger teed off and gave me a spot on kick to the face right about where my left eye was. The ground went wiggly-waggly, the black tar surface of the parking lot doing an angular dance with the striped rectangles marking out the parking spaces. Staggering to my feet, I found myself dancin' too. I was havin' minimal control of this two-step, but I could see that Bill hadn't wasted any time recovering from getting jabbed. No way. The guy was ever the one to strike back. While I was in a daze and collecting my senses, Bill was raining down punches and kicks to my assailant. And the mover and shaker --- well, he was cowering in the corner of the parking lot as Tony went over to a parked car. In a second, Tony was messin' around with the side strip. The vehicle was Eighties vintage and had a thin metal side panel as a design feature ---a retro GT strip. Nowadays, that kind of thing is made out of plastic or rubber, but in those days it was thin chrome. It didn't take him long to pry the thing loose, and then he was comin' at me swingin' it like he was a medieval Japanese kendo swordsman. Now he had a ready-made sword, and with a serrated edge at that. The next thing I knew, I could hear the serrated edge whizzin' through the air as he slashed out at me, but I played it with a head fake and a rope-a-dope and stayed just out of range. Lucky for me, Tony overcompensated on one of his lunges, and I was able to sneak in a side kick to his groin which sent him writhing to the pavement moaning in pain. I leaped on top of him and figured that all pretense of sportsmanship had been thrown to the wind back when Tony had tried to slash Bill's face with the beer bottle. I mean, I'm tellin' ya you really have to keep close tabs on this shit, or people'll try to get over on ya. So, I pummeled him until he stopped moving. Then Bill and I briefly assessed our own damages and got the hell out of there. As our car sped away, I looked back to see how Tony was doing. He was doin' a decent impersonation of a corpse. I could see his employer cowering in the bushes. I wondered about whether or not he was accustomed to that.

One thing was clear: the candidacy of the right-to-life politician would have to be aborted. He simply had no right to life himself.

"So like I said, your dear sister double-crossed you. Well, don't say I didn't tell you so. She'd given you her word not to send in the thugs, and then she went ahead and sent in the damned thugs... again."

As he made this astute observation, Bill leaned forward and chugged down his second shot of Jack Daniels. Something about him wasn't quite right. He had some sort of exhausted look that just wouldn't go away, as if he were still trying to shake off the effects of his horrendous encounter with my sister. It was obvious that Bill was a shadow of his former self. Hypnotism clearly did not agree with him. I'm not convinced it agrees with anyone. But every now and then he would give me some gesture or faded look that made me wonder if he might still be under the nefarious effects of Meghan's scary mesmerist capabilities. Despite these nagging worries about my good friend's diminished capacities, I could see that there were moments when Bill could be his former self, the self that I knew and liked.

He and I were back at the bar near the boardwalk, and he was acting the part of a mentor telling me in no uncertain terms that he'd predicted Meghan's duplicity right from the start. I could tell that he was in the full-gloat mode. And frankly, I was feelin' pretty embarrassed about the whole thing. Bill continued his speech. At this point, he was really beginning to rub it in. "Make no mistake --- if she doesn't kill ya, that crazy billionaire will. Or worse yet, he'll facilitate a drummer's worst nightmare."

"Yeah, and what might that one be?"

"Mark my words. I don't think for a minute that he really wants to kill you. Bein' so obvious like that would deprive him of too much fun. What I think he truly stays awake nights thinkin' about would be the chance to cut off one of your arms or better yet, amputate both of your hands. Understand this --- he wants to send you a big message. And for you, your hands are your greatest treasure simply because they're your way of life. To lose those would make your life not worth living. Do you still feel so brotherly now about your sister?"

I felt my left arm. Yes, it was still there. "I had to admit that I don't have much of a leg to stand on if I'm trying' to defend her. And my heart keeps tellin' me that's what I'm supposed to do. Bill, all I was tryin' to do was to honor some semblance of the notion of love for my own flesh and blood."

"Yeah, right. And she played ya for the fool. If you want my advice, you should stop listenin' to your heart all the time. You should really be listening to me."

"That high roller who tried to end my life was the thugiest of the thugiest."

"Some people just have no sense of grace. They want to do right, but they just can't."

I pondered what to do next. I thought long and hard. As Bill ordered yet another shot, I came up with something good.

"Look, Bill, I just now remembered a conversation my sister and I had back when I first joined the band. I had told her that I was interested in seeing my nieces, and wasn't that just a normal thing that any half-decent uncle might want to do, and she had gotten so huffy about just the mere thought of my having any sort of contact with either of them. She had told me then that I should not ever, ever, under any circumstances, go near them."

"Why was that?"

"That was most likely true because if I did that, my nieces might actually discover that I wasn't a half-bad person. How horrible would that be?"

"If you want the straight answer, it would be very."

"Perhaps the way out of my troubles would be to contact them."

"Or perhaps the threat of talking to them would keep your sister at a safe distance."

The waitress bought Bill his shot of Jack. She grinned at him and said, "So, you guys look like you're havin' some kind of delicious conspiracy."

"Well, if you wanna know the truth, we are," Bill replied.

"Hot damn! You don't say? Do you mind if I have a shot of Jack too?"

"Hell no. Let's all drink to that!"

She lined up three small glasses and did the honors. We raised our shots and guzzled them down. The waitress shook her butt and looked at us for approval. Then she wandered off in search of other customers.

I glanced at Bill to see his reaction. He was getting' that faded look again as though the mere coming into contact with my sister had been enough to drag him over the coals and exhaust him.

"Bill, talk to me! What's the matter with you. You're my best buddy in the world, and you look like hell. What's goin' on? Did my sister get to you?" What did you do to you to make you so out of it?"

"Joe, I'm feelin' like I've been poisoned by somethin' or someone. I thought my little adventure with your sister would help me --- would help us --- get the goods on her. But I'm feelin' sick. I'm drownin' in something' and I haven't a clue what it is. I think I entered her aura, and the aura wasn't good."

"So I've gotta get you to a doctor to see what it is."

And then I took him to a specialist who said he couldn't find anything wrong with him. I kept reassurin' myself that with hypnotism, the mesmerizer in charge can't make you do anything that you wouldn't ordinarily do on your own. That's what the experts say, and they're right most of the time. But the deal was that I was having big doubts that she was using pure mesmorization. No, this was different. This was some sort of hybridization. At that moment, I remembered that my sister had never been a purist. Aw no way! She was far too experimental to go in a traditional direction. Knowing her, she would have to step it up a notch.

This development was quite distressing. Bill had been my most steadfast supporter, and now I was beginning to think that we were drifting into something that neither one of us could control.

As if this turn of events were not enough, my old enemy Doc McIntyre continued callin' me up with yet another round of harassing calls.

His latest rant was that he wanted to see how my Neanderthal metabolism would react if N-acetylglucosomines and alternating glurouonic acid were to hook up with beta 1-4 and beta 1-3 glycosidic cloning structures. He was fully convinced that the tubulin in the microtubules would have a profoundly beneficial effect on the cytoskeleton's capability for wound healing in a proto-Neanderthal metabolism. When he started to talk about Hyaluronan Synthase 2, I yawned into my smartphone, telling him thanks but no thanks as I hung up yet again.

I kept changin' my number, but it wasn't any use. The persistant researcher wasn't to be denied. Or so he thought. But of course, he didn't know that I was just as persistent. My biggest worry was that he might somehow get to talk to my new antagonist. Yes, that would be a disaster to be avoided at all costs.

TED THE GORILLA

The nurse led me in to see my mom. The white uniformed lady was leading me down a long hallway with bleak surfaces. In the geriatric ward, it was necessary to have an antiseptic vibe. "And we're having a good day today aren't we, Mrs. Myers?" I loved the way that nursing staffers liked to use the first person plural. It made it sound as if living one's life were some sort of team effort with safety in numbers, and other people could get in on the act, and that might improve the quality of life itself.

"So Ma, have you made any friends here?"

"Aw, Joe, you must be joking. Not a chance. Not a chance in hell would I ever do that."

"Oh, but I'm sure that can't be true. I'll bet you have. And you're holdin' out on me. You must have so much in common with everyone here. I look at the lady down the hall, and I say you probably have lots and lots to talk about."

"I know who you mean. She's my roommate. That's her right over there. And she's as mean as a snake. Take my word for it. I'm tired of puttin' up with her antics. Everything she does is positively evil. And at this point in my life, I think I'm qualified to see evil when it pops up its odious head. When I see that, I wanna lop it off before it gets too confident."

Mom gestured to an old lady slumped in wheelchair with a string of spittle coming out of her mouth. "Jesus Christ! I have nothing in common with her. I look at her, and I see someone who's been running a long long race, and she's about to go into the final lap, so she's outta breath. Can't ya see her gaspin'? Well, if you can't, then I can. She's heavin' and hoin' and hemmin' and hawin', actin' as though it's been one long haul. But the thing I would fault her on is that she's never really lived her life. She's played it safe almost since day one. Will ya check her out for a second? She's acting as though she's pulled one over on someone. She thinks she's managed to sidestep one disaster after another. That's not life! That's procrastination, or worse yet, she was being evasive. She's never pulled the bull close and got him by the balls."

Mom reached out her gaunt arm and made a grasping motion at some imaginary balls.

"Ease up, Ma! Not everyone can live up to your high standards. I can see you've learned so much. Life has been instructive. And nothing's been lost on you."

"No, shut up for a second. *They* have to live up to my high standards. I make the rules. I'm tired of other people makin' the rules for me when they don't know anything. I'm at the time in my existence when I make the damned encyclicals. It's my interpretation, or nothing. I've had it with insufferable experts who aren't really experts at all. They don't know anything. In fact, they're nothing but a bunch of bloody virgins. Just like that one over there! Oh, I know what you're gonna tell me. You're gonna tell me that I should be more, how do you say it --- diplomatic? Well, Joe. My time is fast dwindling away. I don't have time for this exercise in nothing, and that's what it really is --- nothing. People like that crazy roommate of mine wanna make a big point about nothing. Just so they can lord it over someone!"

The old lady must have heard Mom 'cause she suddenly opened her glazed over eyes and gave us both a confused, translucent stare. The spittle quivered on the lolling lip, and the old lady went into conniptions, which in turn caught the attention of the assistant head nurse who summoned an orderly, who in turn, gave the old woman an injection of some kind, which had the desired effect of calming the patient down.

"Not so loud, Ma! Sure you must have lots in common. You could talk about family and memories, and grandchildren, and..."

"And what? We have nothing in common except for one thing and one thing only."

There was another stony silence. Mom looked out at another orderly who was going by pushing a cart of meds. She looked at the meds and then stared off into space again before she renewed eye contact. This time Ma had a more inquisitive look.

"Well, Ma! Out with it. What do you and your roommate have in common?"

"Wait! I know the answer! It's right here on the tip of my tongue. No way am I gonna forget it this time around. Now I remember. It's comin' back. This is it, and listen up, Joe, 'cause this could be a lesson for you too. Yes, she and I are both old. OLD, OLD, OLD! And that, dear Joe, is not enough to build a friendship on."

She lightly tapped my elbow for emphasis. I thought about this for a second and then decided that she kinda sorta had a point. Two creatures being old had about as much in common as sharing oxygen.

But then Ma was on to a new subject, leaving the old one in the dust. "Well dammit, Joe! Did you listen to me yet? The last time I talked to you I told you to go out there and make some magic and to make something out of the bare remnants of nothing. Have you done it? Show me some results!"

I got the distinct feeling that as Mom got in closer proximity to Death, she was learning new things.

"I'm looking to the future, and touching base with the past," she said. "That's why I've gotten so much into horoscopes in the last few months. The point is, I want to have some degree of control over a situation that's rapidly spinning out of control. What I like about horoscopes is that, if you've got the skill, you might conceivably have some semblance of control. And it doesn't take much time to get the hang of it. And time is what I don't have much of these days."

"Horoscopes are supposed to be semi-scientific, Ma. And they date back to the times of the Egyptians."

"Yeah, but there're hypocritical. They like to have it both ways."

"How so?"

"I'll tell you why. It goes like this. How come whenever people have discovered a new planet or two in the last two-thousand years, they haven't seen fit to freshen them up? The horoscopes, I mean? Shouldn't we revise them every time we discover a new stone circling and circulating out there millions of miles from the sun? I mean, if they did that, wouldn't it make 'em more scientific? Wouldn' that do wonders for their accuracy?"

"Gee Ma, you've got me there. What's great about you nowadays is that you're getting more and more innovative day by day. You just keep expandin' your horizons."

Maybe this was what she'd been talking about when she said that she had been bored and wanted to move on to the next level, to, as she had so concisely said it, 'to get this show on the road'?

Mom continued with her monologue. "Joe, speed matters."

"You are so correct, Ma. I promise not to heed the call of those petty and pretty artistes."

"They know not what they feel. In fact, they've forgotten how to feel."

"Hey, speed matters to leopards. Why shouldn't it matter to hominids? Speed would mean the difference between having a *bon repas* or a gone gaga."

Mom laughed long and hard on that one. Her eyes seemed to perk up.

"Joe, I want to talk to you about something. I want to talk about memory. Memory is part of what makes life fun --- that and a few other things. I have special appreciation for your very first one.""

"And Ma, what was my very first one?" But before she could answer, I blurted out a new question. "Mom, how would you know what my very first memory was?"

"Oh Joe, not to worry. I thought I'd told you that I'm tired and want to get goin'. I wanna get out on the road."

"Yes, and then I told you I didn't want to hear any more of that death talk. I thought you promised me."

"I know. But I'm sorry. This time it can't be avoided."

"Why's that?"

"There's no way around it because as I get nearer and nearer my God to thee, I'm starting to have new powers of perception."

"So, it's a trial run of what is to come?"

"Exactly."

"How does that have anything to do with what we're supposed to be talkin' about?"

"It has everything to do with what we're talkin' about."

"Alright, fair enough. You got me curious. What was the one that got the ball rolling?"

She reached out and put her hand on my head. "Oh, let me see now. Yes, yes, it's coming in more clearly now. That would be when you were about two years old. Your Dad and I had taken you to the zoo. We decided we wanted to see the snake house and from there we wanted to go watch chimpanzees race motorcycles. Round and round they went on the dirt track oval ... and yes, I know that sort of thing is not very politically correct these days, but it certainly was then ... Only I'm getting sidetracked 'cause that's not the part that you remember. The part you remember and remember quite well is the part when we went by the gorilla cage. Actually, they only had just one gorilla. His name was Ted. So we walked over to pay Ted a visit. And Ted was so happy to see us. You walked up to the edge of his cage and Ted grinned at you. He had two sticks that he hammered on the edge of the small swimming pool that was in his cage. I tell ya, for an ape, he had some pretty good beats goin' there. And what a show off! He was the comedian who was always 'on.' Thank goodness he never had any children. He woulda made a terrible dad. Well, he was used to gettin' lots of attention, and that day was no exception. He was milkin' it for all it was worth. And the drummin' in the metal rim of the pool was gettin' real loud. Then he put aside the sticks and started making some goofy faces at you. And after that, you made a few faces right back at him, and you said, "Look at the big man! Look at the big man!" Ted really liked that a lot, and he liked it so much that he picked up a large inner tube that had been floating in the pool inside his cage. He lifted it up and threw it as hard as he could into the water. And there was a huge splash. It was such a gigantic splash that it sent lots of water spilling out of his cage. Well, in a second, you went from having dry clothes to being soaking wringing wet. And Ted laughed and laughed hard because he was absolutely certain that he'd just then given you something very important. It was some kind of baptism, but not the regular kind. And you know now that it was very important."

"Ma, I'm stunned that you know that."

"He passed it on to you. He gave you a gift. And you have to use this gift. It's only what Ted would have wanted. Now it's time for you to make a promise to me."

"What am I getting myself into?"

"I want you to honor Ted's gift."

I gazed out the window to look at some passing traffic that was in the distance behind a stand to trees.

"OK Ma, I'll do my best."

"Oh, Joe, you have no idea how hard it is here. I'm stuck. I'm stuck in a place somewhere between life and death. Please help me to get away from here. I want to leave, to get out on the open road. After that, I'm certain it'll be clear sailin'."

I thought about it. I would have liked to have helped her so much because I wanted nothing more than to uphold the quality of her life. And the quality was at a very low ebb. It was so bad that earlier I'd watched her try to lift a fork full of mashed potatoes to her mouth, and it had been too much for her. One of the interns had to come over and help her out. The intern did everything for her except swallow the potatoes by proxy. Yes, it would have been so easy to help her out, to disconnect some vital switch or remove some crucial catheter which would have sent her on her way, but much as I would have liked to, for my own survival I couldn't, because the longer Mom remained alive, the better my chances would be for my dear sister to behave herself.

And Mom sensed my dilemma. How did I know that? I knew it by what happened next. She raised herself up in her bed and stared straight ahead. "Joe, Joe, it's OK! I'll stay around for a little longer if that's what'll keep Meghan in line. Please understand, Joe. I can't stand it. I can't stand living in these depleted circumstances. My brain and body have faded away to practically nothing. The quality to life is severely diminished. Only thing is, there's somethin' else that I can't stand even more than what I'm in right now."

"Oh yeah? And what would that be?"

"What I can't stand more is the way that your sister is treatin' you. I can't stand that, and I can't stand the way she turned out. I tell ya, all of this makes me wanna stand up and fight. I do believe I'm gonna stick around just to see what happens."

"That would be so nice if you could do that, Mom. But I wanna say --- it's totally your call. You decide. There's no pressure from me."

I looked into her eyes and they had brightened up, taking on a new conspiratorial vibe. It knew right then that it would be a vibe that would keep her alive at least for a little while longer than her body wanted.

"Joe, I'll stay alive just to spite her. That god awful bitch! I'm ashamed that she came out of me. I rue the day! I don't want to see her win. We're in this together, Joe. I think I might postpone that road trip for a few more months. Would that one be alright for you?"

"Yes, Ma, I vote for that. But listen for a second. I was thinking about something the other day, and I was remembering what you told me when we last talked. You had said something about how you wanted us to be one as a family again. And that got me to wondering --- maybe my way out of this dilemma with my sister would be to try to meet up with my nieces 'cause if I could do that, then maybe one or both of them could talk some sense into Meghan's head. If they were able to do that, then perhaps that would make a difference. Then maybe she would behave herself."

"Oh you've hit upon it. I think that would be so wonderful. If there's anything that I would like more than any other last wish, it would be for all of us to be one as a family. Yes, do it. I think it would be a great idea. But one thing, Joe."

"Alright Ma. What is it?"

"We've got to try a two-pronged approach. Talking to the nieces might do the trick, but you shouldn't set your heart on it. I should also try to stay alive just to spite her."

Then she relaxed a bit and swooned into sleep. I kissed her on the forehead and left the room.

I walked out the front door of the assisted care facility just as a family was returning their elderly mother from a family outing.

The grand kids and the son and daughter were smiling, and it was so obvious that Grand Ma and family had had a wonderful bit of quality time. Hey, they were so lucky. They didn't know how good they had it.

I got in my car, put the key in the ignition and spun out of my parking space. I was heading for the exit when a car blocked my way. I stopped and got out. The other driver got out too. It was Officer Fielding. "Hey, man, I'm still watchin' you. Sooner or later, I'll catch up to you and nail you for Andy's murder."

"Officer, why can't you let me make some music in peace? Don't you know I have a very big job to do? The entire welfare of the civilized world is resting in my nervously drumming hands."

"C'mon, man, let's go out for a drink. We can talk it over like gentlemen."

So, he invited me to a nearby roadhouse and we talked it over. Soon he was talking to me about his ongoing investigation again. Naturally, he was making me annoyed as hell. He started in on me, giving me the third degree. "Hee haw, Joe! I'm gonna find a way to get you in jail if it's the last thing I ever do! You're guilty as sin and I'm gonna get ya!"

"Look, man. You're getting' on my nerves, and I don't hafta take this. I just bought you a drink for Christ sake. Doesn't that count for anything?"

"In my book, and it's the only book that counts, it doesn't amount to anything." He broke into another gale of laughter, cackling rudely. The whole bar was givin' him stink eye looks.

The bartender figured it was his turn to speak up. "Look buddy, if ya don't behave, I'm a gonna tell you to leave!"

Officer Fielding looked so cool as he dragged his police I.D. out of his side pocket the way he'd done a thousand times before. "Of course, I could, if I wanted to, call up the inspector and you could soon find your ass in a sling as far as that 'grade pending' sticker is concerned. I'll bet you wouldn't like that one at all."

The bartender's face did a complete about-face and changed direction. Now he was the one who was getting nervous-looking. Now he was the one who was in full retreat. "OK, Officer. Don't worry. You can stay as long as you like. In fact, you can stay all afternoon if the spirit moves you. And the drinks'll all be on me. But please, try to be nice to my customers."

"I am bein' nice. Joe, tell 'em how nice I'm being." He cackled again and then broke into an extended wheeze, and the wheeze kept right on goin' and goin', amplifyin' in intensity. Suddenly, he gasped and clutched his heart, and then fell off his barstool with a resounding crash that made some of the knives and forks rattle in their metal holder at the edge of the bar. The bartender looked seriously spooked, and so were the other customers. I leaped off my stool and bent down looking into Fielding's ashen face. There was a spooky rattle coming from his throat. His eyes went to blank and his mouth did a wavering opening-and-closing 'O' thing, like a fish near the surface of the water struggling for a spec of food. The other patrons of the bar were gathering around us, and I heard someone say, "Hurry up, let's call an ambulance right now!" I had no idea what to do. I only knew what I'd seen in TV and the movies, which had probably stunted my medical training. I supposed that I was supposed to do something with the man's chest --- maybe like pound on it or somethin'? And probably I needed to do some resuscitation attempt with his mouth. I had to do that and to do that soon. The patrons of the place were gathering around me as I hovered over the stricken police detective. Some were shouting advice about how to do this or how to do that. The entire bar was dominated by the din of the crowd and the sound of the jukebox that nobody bothered to cut. A funk rapper's song barreled on, oblivious to Fielding's signs of distress.

I looked at Fielding's face again. His tongue lolled in the back of his mouth. I yelled frantically, "Please, get me a knife, so I can cut open his shirt!" The bartender obliged, and brandishing the knife, I ripped open his clothes to expose his chest. As I knelt over him, it was becoming clear that I would have to do something to him that would resemble a kiss. I kept saying to myself, "This ain't no Halle Berry. This ain't no Pamela Anderson. This ain't no sweet pretty lady!" No, he sure as hell wasn't. In fact, he looked downright ugly as sin. The grizzled stubble on his chin looked like some kind of obstacle course. Right then, I knew I had one chance. I had to pretend and to pretend fast. So I did the best I could do under the circumstances. I pretended that he was the most beautiful whore in the whole wide world. We Neanderthals can improvise on a vast scale...

...The smell of her hair and cheek did wonders for a surging story and storm, and I reveled at the way her overbite did a cute thing with her upper lip, what dentists call "a malocclusion." I wondered about how many customers she had serviced that day, and how it must have been a lot, most likely her very own personal best. The malocclusion had gotten quite a workout, and she was having a proud moment --- an appreciation for her sense of accomplishment and a job well done. No doubt she would be sure to pull me into her spectacular joy. Soon she would be counting small stacks of high denominations. She was tired but exhilarated, which made the long day even better. The pretty lady liked to see a job well done whenever she saw others do it, so why shouldn't she salute it when it came to her own achievements? Weren't those accomplishments as worthy as those of anyone else? I thought about how she would find herself in such an adoring moment whenever she happened to go to, say, a ballgame or a hockey match. She would be there somewhere in the middle to upper deck applauding a well-turned double play or perhaps she would be gleeful at seeing someone get injured. Some pretty girls really like to see men get injured. You know that, don't you? They like to see them get carted off the field. That does something sweet to their sensibilities. And probably she was one of those. And probably she was *having* one of those. After thinking about severe injuries that belonged to other people, she loved to look down at herself and admire her own beautiful body. She would run her hands over the contours. In those moments, she would shiver in joy, look at her tongue in the mirror, and congratulate herself for helping so many others. And for my part, her function had been formulated. I was getting downright metaphysical. That was a prelude to the physical. In this mode, I was noticing that, so far, life was filled with purpose. Everywhere I looked it was showing its face. Yes, it must be true. The purpose of looking at her ass was to put a zip in my step. Her function had been formulated.

I told her I loved her. That was before I closed my eyes and let the darkness seep in, so I could look at it too. I needed to look at it too ...

...I opened my mouth and put mine to his and blew the life-giving air into Fielding's gullet. Then after a few of those, I gave him some hits to the chest. His eyes fluttered and went to blank again. At first, I was afraid to hurt him, but after another fruitless try, I figured that I'd better throw caution to the wind. I slammed him on the chest again, before making another try with the mouth-to-mouth. There was no success. He looked completely listless, and it was obvious that he was falling rapidly into the arms of death. For a split second, I thought about how this might be the answer to my problems. I could just let him go, so he could boogie right on out of this life and into the next one...

...The face was fading. The most beautiful whore in the whole wide world was leaving. Hey, she didn't have all the live-long day. She had other things to do. She was an extremely busy lady. People were waiting, and she would have to consult her glossy red book. Already her sharp painted nail was turning the page. Hurry up, boy! It's your turn to come! Here we go, baby! Yes, I can feel it, honey...

...Yes, that would be the solution. I could let Nature have a free hand. Officer Fielding's heart attack would not be my problem. I never created this mess. Why should I solve it? Afterwards, I'd be able to say in complete honesty --- no questions asked --- that I hadn't done anything untoward and that he'd up and died on me and saved me from a lotta trouble. Only trouble was --- I'm a perfectionist. If I'd done that, I wouldn't be able to live with myself, not for any pain-in-the-ass moral or ethical standards or anything, but simply because it would make things too asymmetrical even for a lopsided Neanderthal like me.

No, I would have to fight back. "Where's that ambulance crew?" I asked desperately.

"They're on the way!"

But right after they said that, I looked into what was left of Fielding's goggling eyes and thought about everything one more time. Why in the hell should I let this bastard live? If I let him live, he'd only come back to bite me on the ass by arresting me. I was voting against my perfectionism. I should just let the fucker die. The only reason I changed my mind again and decided to give the resuscitation thing one more try was because I'm a stickler on trying to wake people up ...

... The spectacular whore was panting: "Hurry up, boy! That's it, baby! I can feel it now! Here we go. You split me in half, baby! ..."

...What the hell, I blew into his mouth for the last go-round, this time pretending that he wasn't Miss America 'cause apparently that obscene anecdote hadn't been good enough to bring him back from the brink. Instead, this time I went for something bigger. On this go-round, he would be the most beautiful goddess who had ever been dreamed. She had a soothing voice, and she also had big ones. And to my surprise, Fielding responded, his face twitching rapidly as it staggered back into the realm of the living.

The malocclusion was very good. The ambulance crew was very grateful.

Like boxers at the end of a match, we both contemplated this thing that we had shared. Officer Fielding was leaning up in his hospital bed looking a lot better now than just the day before. Not only was he looking better, but he was acting better too --- there was none of that hassle-the-drummer bullshit. A pretty nurse came by to give him a regimen of pills. He flirted with her a bit, and she gave him a big smile before she left the room to care for needier patients.

Turning to me, he said, "OK, OK. I get it, Joe. You've convinced me."

"So, leave me alone. I've got nothing to do with the sad-but-mysterious drowning of that what's-his-name Andy guy."

"Actually, I figured that one out quite early on. And I know you're innocent."

"So why are you bothering me?"

"'Cause I think you're a good drummer. Why else?"

"Is there some kind of miasma in the air? What in the world are people thinkin' and feelin'? No one has ever cared about me and what I do, and now suddenly, everyone wants a piece of me. Has the world gone mad?"

"They want you because for the first time, people have fallen in love with the foundation. How do you have a building without a foundation? Joe, you don't understand. Why do you run away? I'm your biggest fan."

"I don't think so. I think you're just another stalker. Remember, I'm on TV, and you are not. Has that sunk in? I'm not so sure it has."

"Yes, you have my word that is has seriously sunken in." Then Fielding seemed to switch gears and give me a strange smile. "By the way, thank you for tellin' me the story of how you came to save my life. I really liked the part about how you had to pretend I was the most beautiful whore in the world. I guess that's one rare instance of when fantasy brings about a positive reality."

I hemmed and hawed, not knowing how to respond to that. The nurse came in and interrupted us. "I'm sorry, Mr. Myers. The visiting hours are just about done for today and Mr. Fielding needs to get some rest."

"Well, there ya have it, Officer. They're throwin' me out."

I looked down at my hands. They were the same hands that had helped to bring Fielding back from the brink. Like Mom had said, they had gone out there and made some magic. Perhaps good old Ted had passed on something to me? Somewhere out there in gorilla heaven, he was splashing huge inner tubes in small pools.

But the strangest new development was that I was entering more and more drum solo competitions. Yes, I know --- people automatically say that they hate 'em, but if they only kept something of an open mind, they might discover that they have a purpose. And what might that purpose be, you ask? Well, the purpose of saving the world from itself. I say that because I was winning more and more of them. When that happened, I would take credit for how an impending disaster had resulted in a happy ending for all concerned.

And on those rare occasions when I lost, I would read in the paper the next day about how some major catastrophe in the world had not been averted. Again! So, I would blurt out this observation of mine on the next episode of *Babies in Bars,* and before anyone knew it, the media outlets were all aflutter about how Joe the Neanderthal, the star of that new reality show, was going about the serious business of rescuing the world from itself. This hype in turn caused yet another feeding frenzy on the worldwide viral web as kids out there in cyberspace started making wild purchases of drum sets because they wanted to get in on the act of saving the world too. Soon, anyone driving down a suburban street in North America would be treated to the muffled noise of cacophonies emanating from closed garage doors. Naturally, Jillian recognized a golden goose egg when she saw it, and she milked this premise for all it was worth.

A CURE FOR ASTHMA

Daylight breaks in the city's maw
Red risin' as the crows caw
Deities are testing sound
Makin it up as they go around

Should a song reflect what's in the here and now? No way. Never. As we toured from city to city, Gwen felt the need to keep reminding me of that. Despite this habit of hers, I wasn't completely convinced that she followed her own advice. Still, I had to trust her.

At one of the shows, she came out so hopped up on God-only-knows-what, and she thought she was gonna do some sort of extravaganza move: so she leaps up into the air, looking so superstar, if I do say so, and she goes up, almost goin' end over end like a punk on a subway car doin' a semi-gymnastic move, but she comes down, and lo and behold, she winds up landing flat on her big beautiful ass. My, my, but she looked as though she was in serious pain! But she carried on like a trooper and played the rest of the gig as if nothing had ever happened. Then she staggered up to the microphone and yelled, "We're *Babies in Bars,* and we demand instant gratification." Needless to say, the crowd really got their rocks off on that one. But Gwen still had to get in the last word because she was the queen of this here gig. "We're *Babies in Bars,*" she bellowed one more time. "And we play Hinduistic music." The crowd laughed. She was so in the moment that she took a selfie with her smartphone. Afterwards, none of us had even seen fit to so much as talk about her little pratfall.

That woulda been too rude. Don't ya think? I gave her high marks for bein' hard ass.

Then it was in Boston, that Jillian ordered us to just this once let Ben have his way with the rhythm box thing. My God, the guy had been lobbying like a ratty Republican operative for some time, as if getting Ziggy the Beat Box back into steady rotation were some sort of political referendum.

Ben was especially fond of programming the damn thing with some intricate part that no human being could possibly play in a million years. Then he'd ask me to play it, only to start laughing out loud as I fumbled around trying to hold down seven different lines at once. "Ha, Joe. What's the matter? Have you got the burdens of Sisyphus again? I guess ya jus' can't hack it. Gee, that's too bad! And you have the nerve to call yourself a drummer!"

"Ben," I responded. "If you're going to make music, it's best to make it as inhuman as possible."

"Face up to the facts, bro. You just can't cut it."

"Yeah, well I'm a Neanderthal, which is pretty damned inhuman, and even I can't play it. Get yourself another mammal, one that's more polyrhythmic than me!" Then I put my hand to my crotch like Michael Jackson and said, "That part you wrote is rather difficult, so maybe I should see about usin' my third drumstick." No sooner had the words come out of my mouth than I knew that line would be a big hit with the television audience. Ben told me I was a cave man, and I was incapable of listening. I told him that, if anything, I listened too much. I was weary of this routine. I knew the answers before the actual questions got uttered. I'd been there, drummed that. I didn't like it that what he had to say wasn't up to snuff, so I turned to Sunita, my sweetheart of the moment, and said, "Darling, please don't worry. This craziness will sort itself out." I loved it that she could be so patient. She was younger than me, so she could afford that. I was too old to indulge. Still, it was great that age could trump and seduce youth and beauty.

At this point, Jillian would see fit to make an intervention, and tell Ben to shut the fuck up. Still, like I said, she figured she'd throw him a bone just to ensure that he kept quiet, while she told me about the importance of band politics. Even though Jillian knew that such a decision would most assuredly lead to some pretty bad music, that was the least of her concerns. Like I said, her first priority was drama, not massive power chords, so I would have to get used to Ziggy the beat box coming back just for one gig. What a waste. I had operated under the assumption that that battle had been won and won by me alone. This made my anger with Ben flair up again because I thought that issue had been a done deal. I long for the time when you could say, "Hey man, let's step outside and beat the shit out of each other. We'll settle this like genteel barbarians." The only problem with that scenario these days is that the douche in question could stick a knife inside your ribs. Surprise surprise. There's just no sense of civilization anymore. You can't even have a knock down drag out dust up. As a consequence, you challenge him and say, "Let's meet at the curb after work, and we'll kick each other into cacophony." Well, the guy wimps out and doesn't show, so you're left high and dry as if it's a blind date who stood you up. But it cannot be helped. We live in tentative times. Might no longer makes right! Or does it? I'm not so sure. I felt deprived. I wanted to slug the shit out of him till he slugged the crap out of me. I wanted to make it real traditional. But I knew he wouldn't be doing anything 'cause he had sugar in his blood. What an unfeeling creep he was. He could never *think* his way out of that one.

However, Jillian must have really wrestled with this TV plot dilemma often because she told me that she was deeply interested in the junction of sex and violence, and among other things, our music since my stint as drummer, was certainly about that. Metaphorically speaking of course. I think what drove her in the direction of letting Ben have his petulant way was a flip of the coin. I say this because I recall seeing her futzing around with a roll of quarters as she sat on a coffee break. Coincidently, it was right after that when she announced that the next episode would feature Ben and his rinky-dink toy. Kathy and Gwen were alarmed by this development, but Jillian was not to be disobeyed.

"Why are you doing this now, Jillian, just when Joe was being such a hit with the audiences?"

"I can't let things get too complacent, Kathy. I'll let you in on a secret of mine. Before I got into TV, I used to invite sworn enemies to some of my parties. They wouldn't know what was up until they got to my place and saw the woeful surprise. That way I could see their reactions. What a barrel of laughs!"

Jillian turned to me and asked, "Ziggy the beat box is probably the wave of the future, Joe. You'd better get used to it. In the future, his kind will change everything. We won't need movies with actors. Special effects and computer animation will make it a different ballgame. CGI will totally takeover! Every horizon will be a digital mat shot."

"How will that affect reality shows? Maybe we won't even need directors to lord it over us and tell us what to do."

I could tell I got her good with that one 'cause she started fumbling with her roll of quarters again, and some of them scattered onto the floor. I offered to help her pick them up, but she waved me away. What was great about this interaction was watching Jillian squirm. I, a "Neanderthal" drummer, had been dealing with the competition of fake performances for years now, but what was wonderful now was seeing how the so-called more aesthetically advanced aspects of Art with a capital A were marshaling their forces to confront a very real and ominous perceived threat. It was a thrill to watch them scurry and run for cover.

The gig started easily enough, although I was slightly nervous because Gwen had dropped a tab of good old-fashioned brown acid about a half hour before we went on. Why in the world did she have to go and do that? As you might imagine, the psychedelics began to kick in about ten minutes into the set. By that time, the substance being abused was cruisin' around somewhere between the cerebrum and the cerebellum. I was guessing that she'd reached the part where everything gets real darned geometric, to be followed shortly thereafter by the part where there are no straight lines allowed. The evidence for this was that she kept saying, "Be sure to tip those bartenders and waitresses." Well, using that line once was okay because it built up a rapport with the audience, but she persisted in repeating it at the end of every song. I was laying down a mile wide groove, goosing the tune along, but this was a totally different kind of gig because I had to follow the click track that Ziggy the beat box was also laying down, all the while praying that Ziggy the unthinking machine wouldn't mess up. The feeling was not so different from walking a tight rope while holding up a half gallon can of Super Kemtone wall paint. Earlier, Ben had made a big speech about how exacting and perfect Ziggy's time was, and I had thought about how the low tech piece of technology was prone to glitches. What would happen if Ziggy were to be accidently dropped on the way to the gig? How would he respond to being jostled? How could that metal electronic box ever be an artist? He'd never had anything bad happen to him with the possible exception of being dropped from the back of the tour van. I guess a glitch was his form of a tragedy.

But, as bad luck would have it, a glitch did happen because in the middle to the next song Ziggy started to go ape shit. His tempo went nuts. The audience didn't know what to make of this. They looked completely baffled, but no doubt some of them thought this was simply some sort of *avant garde* train wreck and probably the craziness had been mapped out beforehand and rehearsed in great detail, so that bar seventy-five of the musical score would call for a head-on collision. Despite this, they went with the flow. They seemed to groove to this sudden chaos, implicitly acknowledging that the sounds *Babies in Bars* created were the accompaniment of their quest for fresh and ever more innovative pleasures. To make matters more dicey, Gwen's asthma also started to kick in. She was wheezing noticeably between songs as she tried to catch her breath.

The scene was shaping up to be the classic musical dogfight between Apollo and Pan. I was Pan and Ben was Apollo. I had a bone to pick with him. I hollered, "Hey man, if I wanted to, I could piss all over your silly ditties. Let's battle it out. The mountain god Tomolus will be the judge."

I kicked some sand in his face.

And Apollo said, "You're on!"

And so I clobbered a drum and snarled a dissonance on my row of reeds, and he whined right back with a nasally drone. My fan club, led by Midas, rattled a clanking rapture. Soon it was Apollo's turn. "Dude," I said. "Here comes the chorus --- your opportunity to be gorgeous." He scoffed at that wavering noise. "I hear that bleat, and I raise you two."

The Sun God plugged into his amp and hit a power chord, and in no time at all, Tomolus declared Apollo the winner, at which point, Midas began to disagree with the verdict. But Apollo would brook no insubordination. He cast a magic spell and suddenly Midas' ears morphed into those of a donkey. Alas! A glitch was born. The Goddess came to revisit me, saying, "Sorry Joe, this time the roughneck doesn't get the last laugh!" That made Gwen wheeze again. Her damned asthma was getting worse.

"Glitches don't happen, Joe, if you're the least bit vigilant." That's what Ben had told everyone right before Gwen had wolfed down that tab of acid.

"Yeah right," replied Kathy.

But back to the gig ... I was bein' drunk. The question was --- was I bein' drunk in a way that other people would understand? Only my vocabulary would save Ziggy from a very big fall. That would be tragic, and I would have to be wary 'cause the purpose of his tragedy would be to get his own way. And I sure as hell couldn't have that.

By now, Gwen was tripping her ass off. She was lookin' at her microphone as though she's discovered a goldmine. Being that I was Pan and therefore, temporarily a god and all, I could see right into her head. It was the Dionysian mind meld. I was pondering and wondering at the view. Her imagination was a white-columned pavilion shining serenely near a limpid blue lake. She gazed out at the rippling current and the roly-poly animals who played hide and seek there. Giant salamanders slithered through the water. They whinnied high pitched squeals and darted willy nilly through the tall grasses between the giant red and yellow purple flowers that drooped their heads along the mossy riverbanks. A laughing rhinoceros lolled in the mud along the river. The water rushed and scurried, slurping the blue from out of the sky. Statuesque creatures shim-sham-shimmied, wanting to be petted. So I reached out and obliged.

Gwen sang a new refrain:

> "Some girls go through life so certain
> They're not given to dusky doubt
> Never part the mind's dark curtain
> To find out where the demons sprout
> How do I know how I will feel?
> I'll not see till I'm upon it
> In this jangly sleep of the real
> What blue gleam causes me to spawn it?"

I was laughing so hard while Ziggy was messing up big time. The tempo went up. The tempo went down. The tempo even went sideways. Gwen wheezed. I almost fell out of my chair. You can't take anything for granted or glitches will happen. I thought back to my time in India with the crazy Japanese wife...

... India kept calling me --- land of sprawling music. The sun was edging over the water. Silhouettes of sails from the fishermen's boats dotted the blue patina of the surf, and on land the black goats nuzzled up to me, bleating exultations of a new day. Three colors of sand ---yellow, red, and grey --- from each of the three oceans that converged at the tip of this enormous subcontinent, kissed the water's edge. People here never took a sunrise for granted. It might deign to rise. It might decide otherwise. Nothing was ever an easy layup. Glitches could happen. The boy danced and played the part of a girl. "I know how to be a man," he said. "I only do this for a job." I reached into my pocket again and gave him a bigger tip for being such a good guide to the ruins. He knew something about music, but tourism made him go with the gold.

> *He is a tourist guide*
> *He points outs all the highlights*
> *For people with cameras*
> *And bulky money belts*

He shows them to the gift shop
There're lots of things for snacks
Rows and rows of Buddhas
In bags of bubble pack
He is a tourist guide
He makes up as he goes
His clients go ooh and ahh
And hand him gringo dough
They head off to the pool and spa
To guzzle pretty drinks
Lazin' on the patio
In cushy chairs they sink

The crowd clapped loudly as the sun came into view in the full might of its glory! Somewhere I could hear a voice shouting, "Here, here! It rises yet again!" Then I could hear the Goddess singing:

"Well the sun came up like a picture postcard
The people all clapped at the fishermen's catch
And they pushed him in line, tried to rip him off
Don't drink the water they say, but he still got Hep A."

The crowd was milling about more restlessly now, bumping into me as I tried to pass. I was coming back from one of my tabla lessons and the full strength of the Calcutta afternoon was slammin' the back of my head. I needed to catch a train back to Lake Gardens, and the best I could hope for was the fishmongers' car from Sheldah Station. No problem. For a little while, I would smell like a fish in the sun. The sign on the schedule board said, "Remember, ticketless travel is social evil." I would be sure to purchase one because I was well aware that the train conductors were fond of finding problems with something or other. Of course, it would never amount to much --- nothing that couldn't be solved by throwing money at the problem. Oh how I wished that my wife were with me. That way she could get the tickets in the "Ladies Only" ticket line. That way I could avoid the pushing and shoving in the men's line. You see, in this country the men don't know how to behave. They can't keep their hands to themselves when there's a half-decent looking lady around. And also, it just ain't masculine to wait in line. Remember, their business is so much more important than whatever trivial thing you might have to do.

There was a young boy who was trying to purchase a ticket, but he was from the wrong caste, so they kept pushing him to the side. I remembered how patient he looked --- as if this sort of thing happened every day of his existence, and he had gotten used to it. I turned to him and let him know that I would buy the ticket for him. I pushed someone on my right. I pushed someone on my left. I told them I was much bigger and stronger than they were. They gave up pushing me.

Off to the side, I could see a man being carried in a hammock. I thought, "How interesting is that --- to see a man who's rich enough to afford his own servants who can carry him?" When I get rich and famous, I vote for havin' the same deal. It would be very impressive. But as I looked at the man, I noticed that he was motionless. He was oblivious as the servants waddled under their burden. Suddenly, I realized that the man wasn't rich at all, and these people weren't his servants. In fact, he was motionless because he was dead. He'd starved to death the night before, and they were picking him up. They had to keep the station clean...

Gwen sang the same three notes over and over again. She had to get them clean. Her brain and voice couldn't get it out of her system that this triad was filled with so much joy. She was acting as though D flat was some sort of new religion. So, why not flog it to death until something new happened. Then we played the coda. That took us to yet another pretty place where everything was best left unresolved. But then her song stopped, and I asked the Goddess if I could come up and see her. "No, right now's not such a very good time" the Goddess replied.

But I didn't want to let her off so easily. "Oh please," I said. "Let me come up so you and I can both find some wonderful oblivion."

"No, you can't do that."

"Why not?"

"You can't because I've got company right now."

What a whore the Goddess can be sometimes even if She can take you into a special world. Gwen wheezed. The asthma was in full force this time around.

Who knows where music will take you? I was bracing myself, getting ready to board the fish mongers' car when I saw a man with a scrawled sign written in three languages that advertised "Dental Services." Beneath the caption was a crude magic marker drawing of an ailing bicuspid. For a few rupees, he would pull your bad tooth out with a pair of pliers. Of course before he did that, he would give you a shot, so as to dull the pain. He used the same syringe over and over again...

...Over and over again --- the tempo was rising until it was over the top again. Ziggy has hurtling out of control. Ben was freaking out too. But I was surfing a truly caustic curl, which caused me to spin out. That was what was cool about this chord. You had to know exactly when to bail. Hard living makes everything that's remotely attractive scurry away. Pulchritude doesn't wanna stick around. Then Kathy accidently broke a string, which completely threw Gwen for a loop. She freaked and started wheezing again. There was the asthma that I'd been worrying about.

"Keep tipping those bartenders and waitresses" she intoned over and over until the audience thought that it was a brand new song. Gwen, by now deep in the throes of a major acid trip, looked like a woman who had seen the world just end. Perhaps she had seen what I had seen? Well, at that point, she went into a wild dance and someone had the good sense to lower Ziggy completely out of the PA system and monitors. This gave Kathy and I carte blanche to take over, and the long and the short of it was that between us we salvaged the gig. I mean, what good is omnipotence if you're not allowed to use it? Kathy and I soloed over each other and shoved Ziggy aside which made any clunker that Ben happened to create make perfect sense. God bless dissonance! Kathy had a knack for making it resolve no matter what was thumping or blabbing away on the lower register. Afterwards, the crowd looked no worse for wear and seemed downright appreciative. Gwen stumbled from the stage in a daze. As her wheezes flared up, she shuddered intermittently.

... The notes quavered intermittently. Who knows where music will take you --- especially Hinduistic music. It could bring you to a fascination with women's eyes. And that was what happened. It was a free concert in Varanasi. That's always a bad sign. If it's free, people won't take it serious. If it's not serious, then it doesn't really count. A beautiful lady violinist was playing a truly spectacular set. She would go through withering, positively blistering runs up and down the neck of her instrument, coaxing out unbelievable sounds that seemed to quiver and hover in the humid air of the cavernous temple. For a second there, I half-expected the statues of Shiva and Ganesh to come alive and join in the reverie. I took notice that the beautiful lady's violin didn't sound like a violin anymore. The tuning of the raga had rendered it into becoming another instrument, one that was exotic --- even more deliciously foreign than the dangerous beauty of the young lady's face. I shut my eyes and felt safe and warm in paradise. From the balcony above, someone was sprinkling a steady stream of rose petals. They felt good upon my face, a light rain that sought to sooth.

But with a sudden start, the soothing ceased. My bliss was interrupted by a series of pokes to the back of my ribs. It seemed that I had inadvertently seated myself on the left side of the enormous room. That was my misstep --- the left side was strictly for women only, and there was a second young beauty, this one clad in a black burka who was letting me know in no uncertain terms that I was occupying the wrong territory. No matter --- this segregation of the sexes business was getting to be damned annoying. It was a rule I resolved to break 'cause I was getting the impression that this entire country was run by tyrants, yabos, and nosey school marms. The goddess of virtue was out of control, and she was desperately crying to be reined in. Since her entire body was swathed in austere and ugly-looking black, I had no choice but to look into her hostile eyes. That was her unintended irony: her eyes, framed by the blackness, made her look more than a little alluring, which kind of defeated the purpose of that stern wall of pitch black virtue. As far as I was concerned, she might as well have been stark naked. So much for the lady's silly virtue.

Her pokes to the ribs were getting more and more urgent. I would rein her in by pleading ignorance. I pretended not to know her language. And I got a big boost from the lady violinist because the exquisite music she was conjuring up was so enchanting that it more than made up for the relatively minor irritation that was assaulting my ribs and kidneys. However, I got the feeling that the black-burkaed babe was having a grand ol' time. How boring the concert would have been for her if I had not shown up and accidently sat on the wrong side. This was the most fun she'd had in months if not years. For this goddess of virtue, my ignorance was no excuse. My ignorance was her opportunity.

Oblivious to her protests, I kept my eyes and ears focused on the stage. I pretended I was an ox, and even if the jabs in my back were real, I was infinitely incapable of ever feeling them. Besides, the music was getting to the good part --- like all ragas, it was a snarlin' animal slowly speeding up because it could never be pinned down to one tempo only. In this moment, I fully understood that this was perhaps the original punk rock, and the jabs that were rattling my ribs were taking me back to a mosh pit in Los Angeles.

But whatever problems may have been occurring in the crowd were nothing compared to what was taking place elsewhere because throughout the lady violinist's program, she was beset by an army of hecklers who wanted to hear their hometown boy who would be playing right after her. They kept shouting, "Jash Rai!! Jash Rai!!" They were unrelenting. And their rudeness was appalling. They had missed their true event---they should have taken their boorish act to a cricket test match. For most of the performance, the lady violinist endured their obnoxious vibe with admirable stoicism. I looked at her and her gaze met mine. It would seem that my stoicism matched hers and gave her a kind of moral support. In this way, we encouraged each other, and I could tell by the twitch and arch of her eyebrow that she was aware of this as well. She made another mindboggling run up and down the neck of her instrument. The music gave her strength. Finally, unable to put up with the behavior of the mob any longer, she stopped and glared at several of the offenders in the front row. Her eyes were glowing embers. She raised her bow as if to throw it at the hooligans, provided of course, that her smoldering eyes didn't beat the bow to the punch, and sear them into eternity. Then the hecklers got real quiet and the goddess of virtue ceased to poke my ribs, and the rose petals resumed their gentle rain upon my face. With a look of satisfaction, the dangerous lady violinist calmly proceeded on to the urgent and vital business of playing the fast part of her raga. I closed my eyes again and let out a little laugh, muttering, "Ah, c'mon baby, let's rag..."

...Let's rock. Let's rock. The crowd out there had loved us. They had never heard anything like this.

In the dressing room, Kathy and I comforted Gwen. Her face had the same gaze as the beautiful lady with the scary violin bow.

"Oh, it was terrible, baby. I saw a rhinoceros in the glare of the rising sun, and he was charging right at me!"

"Yes, you did. It was a very big one. But it was not a real rhinoceros, honey. It wasn't even a real sun."

Kathy and I were playing the part of the ski patrol, and Gwen was the injured party. We would take her down on the toboggan.

"Kathy, something very strange has happened."

"Honey, what is that?"

"My asthma --- it's gone."

"Oh, don't be foolish, baby. It's not gone. I'm sure it'll come back in the morning. I mean, think about it. The asthma has been with you for your entire life. It's settled in for good, and it's not gonna go anywhere."

"No, it won't be coming back."

"How do you know?"

"I know because I know my own body, and my body tells me that it won't be coming back. It's gone forever. Poof!" she said, making a magician's gesture with her hand. Then she lapsed back into the frightened girl who'd seen charging rhinoceroses.

Kath and I were tryin' to calm her down, and she went into full protective mode. "Baby, I'm right here. Right here to protect you. Have the visions faded?"

She gave Gwen a tender kiss using lots of tongue.

"They haven't faded at all. They're only beginning."

"OK, Joe and I are right here. We won't let anything happen to you."

"It's starting to feel safe now. But the words, the words...every word I sang...I thought that the words were thick shards of glass and that they would hurt someone if I wasn't careful! I gasped for breath and thought I would die. There was no air to breath. Then I looked at Joe's hands, and they were the size of catcher's mitts, and I thought, 'How can he play the drums if he's wearing catcher's mitts?' And the sun was so bright that I almost couldn't see! And then out of nowhere, I was surrounded by lots of upside-down hills that seemed to close in on me! They breathed loudly, and I thought they were going to swallow me up."

"But it's alright now. Really it's alright."

At this point, Gwen was getting a hold of herself. Her wheezing was subsiding. And from there on in, I knew it would be a breeze. I turned away and walked over to Jillian.

"Joe, it was me who made Ziggy screw up." Jillian made this confession in the most matter of fact sort of way. "I did it because what the show needs right now is a touch of surrealism."

"But Jillian," I replied, "it was a double cluster fuck because Gwen was tripping and wheezing while Rock Star Ziggy was going off the deep end."

Right about then, Jillian got real confessional: "Hell, I planned it that way. I was the one who gave her the acid. I told her it was some kind of energy pill, and she believed me."

I stepped backwards as if to get a better perspective on Jillian's duplicity. "Well," I replied. "If you did, then you should get the Nobel Prize for Medicine because I genuinely think she's been cured of her asthma. That tab of acid blew the doors off the sub-basement."

Yes, I thought. So much for the power of Hinduistic music. It wants to be wallpaper but it can't.

I walked away from Jillian and wandered onto the dance floor. I looked over at Bill who was dismantling my drum kit and packing away the cymbals for the next show. Bacchus was done for the night. Since the live music was over and the next band was setting up, the guy running the PA put on some house music. He was sensible enough to select some tunes that were far removed from anything that the audience had just heard. In fact, one of them was an Argentine tango. How bizarre! Yet what a great opportunity this would be because in this dance, life is comprised of an endless series of infinitesimal infractions that the other person gets to react to! This would be my chance to show that I wasn't completely about drums because for those kinds of songs no drums are allowed. You see, I can be Apollonian if I want to. It's not all about thunder and lightning. I had the urge to move and groove to the sound of accordions and violins that trudged along, plodding at a barely moving tempo. But I completely got it. I understood --- when you're locked in a close hug, the body needs time to get out of the way, so the beat needs perpetual space. Also, in the dance, there's a complication--- the feet only have so many lefts and rights. The choices are limited. I turned to Kathy and asked: "May I have this dance?" To my complete surprise she said yes. Taking her hand, I gave her a close embrace. It felt good to lead her through some back and forward *ochos* with my legs every so often doing little flourishes to keep it fresh. I loved it when I got a glimpse of her hour glass hips, sheathed in a tight fitting pantsuit as they undulated in one of the mirrors that lined the ballroom. I was feeling very close to Kathy, but the closeness wasn't for me. Oh no way! I would gladly give it away to the right person. And who was the right person? That would be dear Gwen. Yes, I pretended that I was Gwen, and she was the leader and Kathy the follower. I was hoping that Kathy would feel it too and that some of it would rub off on Gwen. I wanted that to happen. I desperately wanted them to succeed. As the song came to a stop, Kath did an embellishment thing with her right foot, and I dragged it along the floor, sandwiching hers with both my feet, before flexing my knee forward as an open invitation. She responded with a wraparound kick. It felt delicious to feel her thigh pressing snugly upon mine. And the floor was smooth, which made our feet so proud to slide across it.

Then Kathy surprised me big time. She suddenly and without any warning said, "Joe, now it's my turn to lead!" She grabbed my hands and directed them into the arch of a follower. She did a circular step with her left leg and led me backwards. My legs pedaled end over end as my shoulders rotated involuntarily, and I could see a broad grin emerge from her face. "Joe, you can't call yourself a dancer if you can't follow. Let me show you where to go. I'll show you how to be the girl."

Ha! That Kathy. What a card she is! Off to the side, I could hear the people clapping. Maybe that would make Gwen want to love her more. Maybe that would make her want to get a giant tattoo on her slender neck that said so. But first she would have to exhale that glacial presence that occupied her soul. Getting rid of the asthma was a good first step. It showed that her heart was in the right place...

Kathy's tango lead brought me back to the here and now. She pulled me in and cradled my hip against hers. Why couldn't Gwen understand that this was a woman of substance? There was nothing balsa wood about this lady who was holding me in her arms. I glanced at our intertwined legs. The quads were communing, and the woman's entire appendage was acting like a playful boa constrictor, so that all was right with the world. This was a sign of civilization --- when two people could dance together tit-to-tit and thigh-to-thigh.

The experience was a new feeling unlike any before it. I wanted to think of this kind of love as something that could be stored up and saved as perhaps an investment. The cozy dance was a sort of principal from which greater rewards would accrue. These in turn could be reinvested and transferred to another account. And what kind of account was that? Why, that would be a psychic account --- one that the band could utilize collectively for their own advantage as they saw fit. This would be of vital importance because the project of the band was so much more interesting that the project of love itself. Love itself was what everyone else did. How ordinary! A band, and not just any silly old band --- now that was something on a far greater plain of seriousness. It was, as old bluesmen were fond of saying, the "real news." Any penny ante *wunder* boy singer/songwriter can cobble up some flawless impeccably recorded collection of tunes, but this was something miles beyond that. And since it was now obviously in a profoundly more auspicious category, one shouldn't let some self-centered and oppressive brand of love interfere and mess up the majesty of the moment. It's not enough that a drummer support the band. He must bring them together too. And he must use any means at his disposal. Love was only fair game --- a mere item from the toolkit, a kind of trivia. And since it didn't mean anything to me, that made it even fairer game than it already was.

I thought of Sunita and the seductive curve of her left hip and the resounding darkness of her eyes that blinked with sparkling intention and the sullen beauty of her hands, and yes, all of that was truly a breathtaking spectacle for me to behold and also to maybe save from someone bad, but despite all of those wonderful things, she would forever be a distant second to whatever a band might have to offer. I knew in my heart that that was supposedly pretty damned cold-blooded of me, but I didn't care.

So when Kath and I walked off the dance floor, I got the distinct impression that she understood perfectly well what I was thinking about. This was not an act of division. Rather, it was an act of unification.

Looking around the crowded dance floor of the club, I couldn't help but wonder about how the evening had been such a resounding success. Yes, and to top it off, Gwen had discovered a cure for asthma.

GIRL WITH A VISION ON COURSE OF COLLISION

It was the next day. We were at a bar and were getting pretty sloshed. Jillian was rantin' on and on in her freedom mode, tellin' everyone that freedom was the essence of what *Babies in Bars* was all about. And this was the reason for our high ratings. I couldn't help thinkin' about how counterfeit this seemed. The "freedom" was being used to sell something else. But they all dug what she had to say and eagerly waited for her next pronouncement. I sat back and ordered another one and decided that I would use this freedom for my own agenda. I made a toast to the mirror over the bar: for whatever the crowd wanted, I would want the opposite. And I would be silent, and they would never know exactly how I felt. Like I've often said, the background will one day become the foreground.

The lady behind the bar told me she was busy. She had shot glasses to wash, olives to skewer, and lemons and limes to slice. She couldn't hear what I had to say right then. "I'm sure you'll understand?" Yes, of course. She washed a dish and then another and then she started talking to a movie crew gaffer, or maybe he was a best boy? I often get them confused. He was telling her about some steady cam shot and how difficult it was. It seems they did over fifty takes. Damn, I thought, won't this bloody guy leave? He was over-served and had outstayed his welcome. To top it off, he had a foolish hat resting backwards on his prematurely bald head, but to my surprise and in no time at all, she was listening in rapt attention. The olives, lemons and limes would have to wait. A priority is a priority. It was awful tedious talk. And the more tedious it got, the more interested she was. They should've found a room somewhere. If she had been a fox terrier, her ears would have been pricking forward. Hey, in the marketplace of ideas, put up or shut up. I glanced at the overhead screen. The home team was losing. The big New York City team was stinkin' out the joint again, and I was adorin' every minute of it. Love to see the mighty take it on the chin. It makes me almost come in my pants. A secondary thought of mine bullied its way through the crowd, shoving all comers out of the way. Naturally, the home team was not the least bit thrilled. Would they let me clap my hands? I don't think so. Already the scorekeepers were summoning up ways to get a bee stuck in their bonnets. To make matters even more ironic, Jillian's movie crew was filming this. I mean, the lady was damned relentless as well as shameless, but I loved it --- a movie crew was filming a movie crew guy. The right eye was looking at the left eye. Even yours truly was beginning to get peeved at her constant need to film everything.

The next moment that caught the roving eye of the perpetual camera was when some representative from the juke box company walked into the bar. He approached the lady behind the bar and reminded her that today was the day for this particular establishment to pay their juke box bill. The bartendresse was seriously surprised. "What are you talkin' about? You wanna be paid for music? You gotta be fuckin' kidding!"

"But it's part of the deal that you agreed to," he replied.

"Fuhgetaboutit! Get the hell out. We want it for free!"

"Do you pour beer for free?" he replied.

"No, of course not. This is a business."

The guy registered a disconsolate face, shrugged his shoulders, turned around, and left without his money. The cameras stopped running for a second while the tech crew made some adjustments.

Jillian turned to me and said, "See what I mean about music and money, Joe. I hope you remember our little discussion about music and freedom."

"People actually live here, Jillian. It's not just a movie set," I noted.

"You wanna bet?"

This whole thing didn't appear to mean much, but meaning much or meaning nothing is seldom a clue. Usually, the mundane means more than I can ever imagine. Shaking my head a little bit, I went to the back room which doubled as a makeshift rehearsal facility. Kathy was test driving the red Les Paul, putting it through its paces with the whammy bar and making the sound totter on the edge of tonality.

"Say lady, that's a catchy mojo you're drivin' there."

She was nursing a whiskey sour and using a green beer bottle as a slide on the strings.

"Oh Joe, the kidneys or the imagination --- which will fall down first?"

"That's a tough call," I replied.

"When I'm feeling full of myself as I am right now, I make believe that this music thing of ours might have an aura for spreading goodness in the world."

I thought back to our impromptu tango dance and couldn't agree with her more. Those extravagant moves had taken me further into her world. Now she was randomly strumming the red Les Paul, trying to find a chord to latch onto.

"You can't be serious," I replied.

"Oh stop. This old devil guitar is taking me places I've never been, puttin' me in a jovial mood."

"Don't ever talk serious, Kathy. People won't take you serious. Keep it light. Make it so they'll understand. Don't talk about music. Talk about food. Talk about something they can put in their mouths. That's a sure fire crowd pleaser. And besides, we just got through doing a beer ad. How's that for spreading goodness in the world? How's that for putting something in your mouth?"

"I was wishing for a higher grade of goodness, not some carnival trick."

She paused to look at the neck of the red Les Paul. Something had caught her ear's attention, and she set about to pursue it.

"I get a strange feeling when I play weddings, Joe. The future of the starry-eyed couple is in my hands."

"What a tall order that must be!" I replied. "Especially when the bride and groom look like lambs being led to the slaughter."

"Yeah, I get it, Joe. You're a drummer. You're in no position to be terribly choosey. You've got to take whatever job you can get. But still, try to think beyond your next paycheck from Jillian."

"What paycheck from Jillian? There isn't any."

"No, that can't be right."

"I'll have you know that I do this for free. The best I can hope for is to get freebies from the company catering truck."

"That just ain't right!"

"Well, it's the way that it goes."

"That's rather spiritual."

"Music is food for the soul, or so Jillian tells me."

"I'll have to see if I can change her mind. But that still doesn't negate things. Music is more than some money-making event. Last night's gig was a testament to that. Think about it for a second, Joe... to be able through force of sound alone to affect the way people act. I think Gwen's little song and dance last night might've touched on that, don't ya think?

"Right you are. Hey, you're preaching to the choir here."

"By the humblest of tools, we summon magic to foster light."

"Wow, Kathy, you're getting darned cosmic on me now."

"So, I'm not proud. I'll get real cosmic if I want to."

"Be my guest."

"I remember when I was a kid. Of course, I was quite the tomboy. I made a vow then that I should try to win at chess no matter how awful my position on the board. No excuses allowed. Well, it's the same thing now. My aims are fairly modest. I only wish to be some sort of instigator. I've been practicing real hard. My sounds have been passed around for some time now.

"I think you've done too many beer commercials. The next thing you'll try to get me to believe is that they collect beauty the way books gather dust."

"They do. Believe me when I say they were even more beautiful this morning than they were last night. I keep checking up on them just to make sure. I'm the most recent keeper of their enchantments --- the latest in a long line of custodians. But I'm no ordinary curator."

"I'll bet you've got elaborate plans for them."

"Damn right! I told you that already. I'm a woman with grandiose plans. I've got to get this beauty to the people who need it most."

"What a beautiful egomaniac you are, Kathy! You delude yourself, but it's a fun delusion. Many times I myself have indulged in that one, but whatever glee you attain is born from technique alone, not from any lofty place. I wanna say 'Amen,' but I can't. What you and I have in common is that we think life is a prolonged practice session. Get the licks down pat, and then by sleight of hand, this ecstasy will jump into the real live and kickin' world to make everything a better place. I know that feeling, but face the scary music, Kathy. There's no miracle that leads to the marvelous. Any higher rung of awareness is beyond our grasp. So why knock yourself out trying?"

"Can I help it if I'm a girl with ambition and vision? You see I'm only trying to stay focused on what matters. I don't know what I'm doing. I only know I like it. Up until now, people have told me everything --- they tell me my music is too gay, then they tell me it's too straight, or it's too jazzy, not jazzy enough --- everything and it's opposite. If I did what they told me to do, I'd be runnin' like a spooked cat. I think of ironic situations. I mull about the expected consequences. It's fun to consider what might have happened."

"You're focused alright. Girl with a vision on a course of collision. I'll bet your room is a mess."

"Joe, I think I'm a Johnny Appleseed. My ambition would be to wander to the end of my days, only instead of seeing scattered orchards at the twilight of my life, I could look back and revel in my experiments in sound. That would taste so good. People a hundred years from now would say, 'An old woman passed through here a long time ago and things haven't been the same way since.'"

"Oh really? What a new twist on the old charismatic leader get up. Is that your game, Kathy?"

"No, a charismatic leader is always in the foreground. I prefer to inhabit the background. I would move from town to town playing my music as if I were slipping something special in their drinking water. But I wouldn't have a clue about what was going on. That's what *Babies in Bars* is all about."

"Spoken liked a true subversive.'

"I guess that's my hustle. I want my name to make a very big splash."

"Girl, intuition, if left undiluted will make you blotto and bleary-eyed."

"I want to sneak inside another person's mind, Joe. What's beyond our masks? That would be such wonder, a peek beyond the veil. I've been conducting research on my own, sharpening my skills of recognition. From what I see, it's a raggle taggle world. I'm in free fall, Joe."

She waved her arms like a gliding bird.

"Gwen's in free fall too. She's complex, Joe. I wanna be complex just like her. She can't be as scary as she seems. I flat out refuse to believe it. I feel her fancy in each movement, form, and syllable. Joe, did anyone ever tell you that you have the potential for big time violence?"

"Of course. Many people have said that. Hey, I'm a very shaggy dog. If you wanna know the truth, I think I might be a Neanderthal."

"But somehow you don't go there. You're not like some straight people."

"Hey Kathy, don't knock straight people. Whatever violence lurks within our jiz is the best hope to create future lesbians everywhere. We give you the opportunity to be prettily petted. My darkness makes your light possible."

"Oh, you make me feel so important."

"And you are important. Women who love women are especially important, Kath."

"Yeah, so why?"

"If for no other reason than to contribute to the red-blooded man's imagination. All contributions are an enhancement. And that, dear lady, is vital to the survival of the species. A red-blooded manly thought is sacrosanct."

"When you put it that way, I feel I'm a cog in something much bigger."

"Never judge too harshly those things that make the mountains shudder and shake."

"I'll make a vow. I'll make it strong and solemn."

"And I'll give it tit for tat. We call this a sense of community."

"So let's get out there and commune. *Touche*. I'll keep that in mind. Never thought of it that way. And with you in the band, we can all be violent in our own special ways."

"It's so much better to take out my violence on a drum kit. It's a lot healthier, don't ya think?" I thought of my sister. If she had had a drum kit maybe all of this unhappiness would not be happening.

"Oh yeah, absolutely," Kath continued. She slashed away at the strings on the red Les Paul, and the nearby amp barked to attention.

"Look, Kathy, if you're so keen on getting confirmation that this here music thing is a quasi-pseudo spiritual thing, I might as well tell you about a raga that I learned about in a remote part of India."

"Yeah, you've been to India --- been to the source. Did any of that time rub off on you?"

"Sure it did. Lemme tell you about Raga Deepak. It's a raga that no one ever plays."

"That must be 'cause it sounds terrible."

"No it doesn't. Quite the opposite in fact. Scary yes. Terrible no."

"Scary music? Hey, I wanna know more."

"Alright. I'll explain. It's a raga that, if you play it correctly will cause you and everyone else in close proximity, to burst into flames."

"No, you're kidding me. I don't believe it."

"OK, maybe not every time, but six out of ten, which ain't half bad."

"So how do I play the scale?"

"Oh, you want to know the ingredients and the recipe?"

Then we started to talk shop. I completely understand that that might wear you out, so if you want to go to the next chapter, now is the time. Be my guest.

"Well," I said, "if you go in descending fashion, you start on the last note. Play the C, the last and also the first note of the scale. At that point, you go down. Play G, Gb, F, E, and D. Then you wind up at the beginning again. So you establish tonality by playing the tonic of the C Raga Deepak scale: C."

Reacting to what I had told her, Kathy tried out this combination on her guitar. Her fingers glided over the frets stretching the strings between metal and wood, and I have to admit that even on this early run through, the thing did sound rather eerie. It was definitely not something that you'd wanna wake up to. Surely, it was something that was best consigned to the deep end of night when nightmares were bound to sprout. I could tell by her expression that she felt so too.

"OK, it may make a little bit of sense. I can see that the Gb in combination with other things might create a fire hazard, provided of course that there is some sort of bend going on. The bend is everything."

"It always is. That's why pianos don't quite make it happen. With that instrument, you play the note and that's pretty much it. It doesn't slide anywhere like a string does."

"I'm gonna woodshed on this and get it ready for the next show."

"Hey, don't do that. I was only pulling your leg. It won't burn down the whole house."

"Sure it will. And I can make it happen."

"The bend is the key. And there are so many to choose from. Hundreds, maybe thousands. Finding it would be like looking for the right password. It's a happy little needle in a big ass haystack. Good luck."

"Oh, I'll find it alright."

"Yeah right. Sure you will." I deliberately laced my voice with a touch of cynicism before takin' on a more serious note: "Tell me more about Gwen. I worry that she might be the one to go down in flames. But she's a delightfully crazy person. And you really have to hand it to Jillian. That tab of brown acid cured her of her asthma."

"Yes, I'll grant her that. Still, Gwen is such a mélange of God only knows what. She's forever talking about the theater, as if that and not this music thing is her true calling. I try so hard to get her to take my --- our --- music seriously, but she won't. Instead, she's distracted by all that Broadway and movie crap. What she really wants to be is a bad actress in run-of-the-mill summer stock productions. The only trouble is that she doesn't have the required sight reading ability. She can't quite read the dots and dashes of other people who map out the grand scheme. And another source of friction between us is that she's under the mistaken impression that if she sings a tune, then to her way of thinking, that automatically means she's written the tune. She forgets that in most cases, I'm the person who wrote the freakin' song. I'm the big top cat --- the one who creates the content! We talk about this again and again, and we get nowhere. She just barrels her way through, not making a stick of sense, and then she talks over me until I haven't got much more to say. Then I wind up avoiding the whole issue until the cycle repeats itself. When that happens, I feel so small. I wish that I'd could fall asleep and never wake up. But then I do fall asleep, and I do wake up and things seem absolutely fine, that is, before I slowly remember what happened. I imagine that she has two possible futures. The first one, the one I like, would be for *Babies in Bars* to really take off in a big way. The other future, the one I'm rooting against, is that she'll be in B movies screaming her head off in reaction to some cheesy special effects. In my worst nightmare, I see her in third rate slice-and-dice horror movies. It just makes me wanna laugh out loud. It's really that awful. Why can't she realize that what she and I have here is a good thing? You may be right about the crash and burn thing though. Is she going to die? Sometimes I think so. The asthma could come back at any time. You know, Joe, there are some days when she disappears for an entire afternoon. I think she goes out and plans her own funeral. That's what she talks about. She's so into death. That's a big obsession with her. And she does it for kicks. That makes me really scared. One of her favorite pastimes is stuffing her face with decadent desserts and then givin' it all back. The more fake the whipped cream, the better it is. That's her outlook on life. Help me! You and I have to save her. She likes to chase after her worst fears. I hope and pray she eats lots of salads and drops happy pills, so she'll sing zippy ballads to kill her ills. Oh Joe, I only wish that we could all be happy in this thing of ours."

"And we can. I'm doin' the best I can to make it happen."

"Joe, I have a lot of responsibility. I have to support so many people. The crew of the show. They're my children. They depend on me for their living. I watch them struggle and know in my heart that their struggles are my struggles."

"I love it that you and I are on the same team."

"Speaking of teams, that girl of yours, Sunita --- be careful of her."

"Thank you for the heads-up."

"Well, perhaps we'd better call it a day 'cause I've got some practicin' to do."

And I said goodnight and walked out thinking about how she and Gwen seemed to have the real thing. I kept thinking of how love was such a ridiculous subject. Meghan talked about love the way that politicians talked about freedom. In both instances, the subjects had been distorted into some horrible travesty. It was enough to make a man not even want to utter the words, let alone feel what the damned words were supposed to stand for. No, it was much wiser not to go there. Better to hide out in the land of ecstasy. That would be the true province of a serious drummer.

Later, I viewed from a security camera that Kathy had set up in the rehearsal studio. She was hunched over her red guitar again, only this time her face was furrowed into still deeper thought and concentration while her fingers molded the strings into wide slabs of sound that sent staccato shivers into the humid summer night. It was late. Probably well past the hour for respectable noisemaking. Somewhere cranky neighbors were complaining, but to hell with them. Such *sensitivo* devos should have been livin' on farms somewhere deep within the woods keepin' the wolverines company.

It was frustrating to watch Kath because her expression would be filled with anticipation, but it would lapse slowly into disappointment. Here was the alchemist she'd told me about earlier.

No doubt she was like me --- she loved to indulge in thoughts of her beloved as being another completely different woman, one that had different eyes, arms, lips, breasts, feet, and hips except that the huge difference between her imagination and mine was that all those body parts surrounded what was in her heart of hearts, the same core woman, namely her beloved. In her view, the body of the beloved could be superimposed over the heart. No one would ever accuse me of having that quality. Yes, as I watched Kath, she looked more and more to be the true alchemist. She was trying to create fire from music, but wasn't having much luck. She didn't believe me when I said that good ol' Raga Deepak was a myth and the best that sound could summon into reality was to have a whole lot of perspiration goin' on. She looked like a lady who was rubbing two sticks together. She looked like a lady who was chasing after her worst fears. I called her on my cell.

"Kath, it's me."

"I'm workin' on that Raga Deepak thing."

"I know. I can see you."

I let out a slight chuckle, and she asked, ""Joe, what's that?"

"Oh, nothing."

"No, what was that chuckle all about?"

"I was just thinking about what would happen if you were successful."

"Yeah, so what of it?"

"If you found the formula, then certain people might get singed."

"Perhaps they would deserve it."

LOURDES TESTS HER MOTHER OUT

Her dress was a flag. She made me proud of my country. It lingered there on the sofa where she'd left it the night before. I'd gone back to the apartment where I had so much fun and games with Sunita. She had been so kind as to give me a pass key. It felt good that I could see the place alone, so I could linger in this crib where we played out our desires. And I could do this leisurely, at my own pace, when she wasn't home to carry on any troubling, ethereal conversations. Glancing at the rumpled sheets, I fell down on the bed and savored the musky residue of our pleasure. Then I stared at the ceiling, considered the wall socket, and slowly fell asleep.

When I awoke, I found myself wanting to know more about her, which surprised me a bit 'cause that's uncharacteristic. I'd rather not know anything about my girlfriends. It's much better that way 'cause there are fewer problems. As I rubbed my eyes and came into the full bloom of consciousness, I saw what looked like a small leather bound diary on top of Sunita's bureau. Upon further examination, I determined that my initial conclusion was correct. In fact, there was a lock right there along the middle edge of the book. I tested it to see if it would open, but alas, no such luck. Then I noticed there was a blotter on the nearby desk. I asked myself if she would be the type who'd hide a key under the blotter. No, perish the thought. She would never do something as obvious as that ...

... Or would she? Just for the fun of it, I looked under a corner of the blotter, and there it was: a thin brass key! No way would it be the key to the diary. I tested it to make sure it was the correct key, and lo and behold the diary opened. Now I could enter the very citadel of her brain and hear what she had to say. Clearly, I'd wandered into a gold mine, and now it was time to start prospecting!

But my excitement was short lived --- most of it was written in her native language, thereby rendering it incomprehensible. The only portions in English were the most boring sections. It was as if some sort of strong-willed military censor was obscuring anything of importance for fear of the writer's revealing too much tactical information. The stern commandant was being such a stickler because she was worried about what would happen if the diary were to fall into the wrong hands. And of course, it had right that moment fallen into the wrong hands! So, mildly discouraged, but not completely disheartened, I leafed through the perfume-scented pages wondering what tales they had to tell. I pondered long and hard about this abstruse alphabetic pictographic puzzle. At one point, as I sifted through the maze, I could see the one and only departure from the unknown script, which was my name "Joe." Good! That sent a ray of bliss through my hands. It's great to be the subject of discussion --- sorta like Richard Wagner wandering into a drunken party! I looked even more carefully at the letters that surrounded my name to see if I could discern whatever it was Sunita was saying about me. Then I noticed another unknown word that apparently got repeated more than once. I could only imagine what she was saying. No doubt it was some sort of adverb/adjective combination. In my mind, as far as the other mysterious parts of speech were concerned, I put two and two together --- I figured it went like this:

> "Dear, Diary,
>
> Joe was so bad. Yes, he was so so bad."

Yeah, I'd been a very naughty boy. It was so bad, coming in here and violating this key to her heart, even if I could only guess at what her heart was saying. I closed the book with a snap of my hand and replaced the hasp into the lock, before putting the brass key back under the blotter. She would be none the wiser. It was best to get right on out of there before she got back. Still, the whole thing got me wondering. I thought of the unknown language that was scrawled girlishly across the pages. It felt like a new suit of clothes had enveloped me, and now I was walking around, strutting my stuff in it. It was "different," something that was obviously not "me," nor would it ever be. And in this new unguarded, moment, I wondered what it would be like to fall in love while I was wearing it.

But if I made the effort to make that happen, would she really want me? Somehow I envisioned that her idea of fun would be to go with some film director wannabe, or worse yet, a photographer. I mean, that's what people really like, isn't it?

"Joe, I want to give my kid good supervision." I was stopping off at Sunita's house again, and she was filling me in on parenting skills, something that had hardly ever crossed my mind since as far back as I could remember, rumbling away on drum kits had always held top priority, but this time I'd gotten to meet her eleven-year-old daughter, which imbued the proceedings with a kind of domestic tranquility vibe. Of course the kid was cute as hell --- a chip off of cutie pie mom, and when the three of us had gone out for a shopping expedition, the youngster wouldn't shut up for five minutes. At one point when Sunita had repaired to the ladies' room, Lourdes--- that was the little girl's name---took me aside and asked me a lot of probing questions. I got the distinct impression that this was an interrogation slash audition designed to evaluate whether or not I was good enough for her mom. Was I daddy material? Girls love to start early on these things. They're so darned inquisitive. It's in the pheromones. After she'd given me probably about a B minus on that score, she began to test me out in other ways.

"Joe, I go to these swimming pool parties where there are lots of other eleven-year-olds, you know, lots of kids from my school. And I'm in my brand new bathing suit lettin' some silly boy dunk me under the water after he's chased me around the patio for ten minutes tryin' to get me with a wet towel. And we're havin' a great time, watching videos, tweeting and twittering and checking out apps, and then the boy starts rubbin' up against me with his hips and groin. What I wanna know is if this is OK. Joe, it's OK, isn't it?"

"No!" I responded angrily. "It's not OK. It's so freakin' not OK! As a matter of fact, tell me where he is, and I'll go kick his eleven-year-old ass. I'll knock him ten feet. Maybe that'll wise him up. I don't want him touching you! Do you hear?"

Lourdes gave me a serious mug shot look and then fell into a girlish giggle not so very different from Mom's girlish giggle. Apparently, I'd passed some sort of muster. Then Mommy decided to allow me on one of their shopping trips. Despite being on crutches, Sunita still managed to walk at a faster pace than either her daughter or me. "Joe, I always try to keep it moving. You're a drummer so you must like peppy tempos too." She paused to snap her fingers in rapid succession, and she gave me a winkin', blinkin' face.

"Yeah, I get it. I'll make it snappy and snazzy too" I replied. I had to admit that there was definitely something more than a little alluring about watching her gimp down the street, but I resolved to stay on track. I *had* to stay on track. I imagined a planet where every beautiful woman walked like a three-legged centipede, and then I put it to rest when Lourdes started chatting up a storm. Of course it was the usual eleven-year-old banter, which I had gotten quite accustomed to as a kind of background drone, vaguely reminiscent of a *tampura* in Indian music, but this wasn't such a bad thing really 'cause something has to hold down the tonality. Perhaps that was the kid's function --- holding down the tonality. And lately I'd been livin' a very atonal life.

Sunita said, "Lourdes, I gotta tell ya, this credit card only works if there's absolute quiet."

There was a big loaded pause, one with lots of unintentional silent cannon bombardments goin' off. I thought it would go on forever. Lourdes kept looking off to the sides as though she didn't quite trust her peripheral vision.

At last she asked, "Is this the cold shoulder stuff? This is what Grammy does when she gets mad at me."

Sunita turned to me and explained, "Grammy's in Bangladesh for the summer. Lourdes will pay her a visit in two months."

The young lady was having a good time, and she was doin' a happy dance. I played the whole thing rather minimalist, letting Mommy and daughter have a great modern family moment. I paced around and looked at the mosaics on the floor. The sales staff gave me a hard look, and some undercover guy followed me around like a bird dog on the scent. After a while, Lourdes announced that the sojourn had been a stunning success. The undercover guy went off on a different orbit in search of guiltier customers, and the three of us went back to the house with me serving as a beast of burden for the fruits of their mission. For some reason that I couldn't quite fathom, Sunita went on with her thoughts on the subject of television, which was pretty apropos since I was currently on a reality show and all.

Sunita carried on with her lecture about parenting skills: "I'm not like most of the permissive parents these days, especially other single moms. So, I tell Lourdes what shows she can watch and what shows she can't watch. I don't want her watching anything that has too much of the sado-masochistic element."

"Why's that?" I asked.

"Well, it's fairly obvious. Don't you think?"

"No, I'm a guy. It's not fairly obvious at all. You're the girl. It's your gig to keep tabs on this stuff. Tell me why."

"It's because I don't want her to grow up to be a sadist."

"Oh, I get it. You don't want her to grow up to be another Ben."

"Yes, you're right. Who'd want her to be one of those?"

"Maybe about half the world. Certainly all of the Republican Party."

She gave me an uneasy laugh and looked out the window. Then she briefly looked back at me, and I avoided her eyes because I could tell her eyes didn't really want to be met for at least another minute and a half. "So you see, I've got my work cut out for me, Joe. I have to monitor her with an iron hand. Supervision is the key to her happiness."

"I suppose that's true. You make a very good point. You must be vigilant! But what if she grows up to be the other persuasion? What if she grows up to be a masochist?"

"Gosh, you take me by surprise."

"Perhaps, but maybe your reticence is rooted in something in yourself."

"Something in me? Surely, you're kidding. OK, what if she grows up to be a masochist?" Sunita repeated, as if trying to sift through multiple meanings to discover an answer.

"Some people might say we're all masochists," I replied. "I read somewhere that apes like to do role play. They want to do it 'cause they know in their heart of hearts that everything's pretend. It's make-believe, so it doesn't count. For them, it's sorta like a preseason football game. The difference between the apes and us is that they're abundantly aware it's pretend. They're a team. They know when to stop, and we humans don't."

"Don't be so sure. I once saw a vid of a female bonobo chimp that was chasing after a bozo bonobo with a small uprooted tree in her hand. It seems the pissed off primate was making that bozo boy beat a hasty retreat."

"True, but I'll bet Lourdes knows the limits of pretend even better than you do."

"Well, if she does, then it's a sure sign that I've been a great parent. Perhaps she could be an honorary bonobo?" She gave me a huge smile, beaming from ear to ear, the brilliant white of her teeth contrasting nicely with the exotic brown of her face. I thought of her injury, and a warmth came over me. I felt ashamed. The warmth scurried away.

"Congrats to you, Sunita! You're an A-number One parent."

I looked her straight in the eye, and she turned away. Her demeanor changed to self-consciousness, and she broke into an embarrassed grin. At length she replied, "Oh Joe, you don't understand. In my day job, men pay me and get to fantasize about hurting me, or if they're not into that, then they play the old switcheroo and fantasize about me hurting them. And the money is not to be scoffed at. It certainly helps put Lourdes through the fancy pants private school. And it's okay on a certain level. At first, it was fun. I was fully in love with the novelty of it. Head over heels. It's great being around rich and powerful men who bow down and worship me, while I get to play the queen bitch. It's changing though."

"How's that?" I asked.

"I used to think it was big fun to be someone's deep dark dirty secret. But now the dirt has lost its sheen. In fact, it's lately gotten rather boring. I firmly believe that I would appreciate those obscene anecdotes a lot more if I were given the chance to slow them down. But they keep wanting to speed them up."

I interrupted with a laugh. "You really are a delicious little hypocrite. Wasn't it just this afternoon that you wanted me to speed things up and to make it snappy?"

"Alright, so you win. You got me. I'm inconsistent."

"Yeah, you're a girl, so you have to be. But tell me more about these rich and powerful men. I'm interested because someday if I work at it, maybe I could be like them, and if I got to be like them, then maybe I could have a beautiful lady like you."

"You already have me."

"No, I don't. You've still got me in the evaluation stage. Pretty soon, I'll be asked to make a financial statement. Then we'll see what happens."

I could see that she was flattered in an ass-backwards way. But she continued with her thoughts on the rich and powerful men that she dealt with on a daily --- or was it a nightly basis? "Most of those stodgy old millionaires bore me to tears with their lack of imagination. They keep shouting, 'Beat me, baby, eight to the bar!' I wind up yawning my way through the afternoon. I have to cool my brain. You, on the other hand, you don't want to hurt me. And you don't seem to want me to hurt you. Instead, you'd much rather rescue me. What are you trying to save me from? That's what I wanna know."

"I'm sorry. All sadists want to save someone. You refer to the big mystery. That's much too much of a personal question. Let's keep it cold and professional --- sorta like your work."

Clearly, Sunita was a worker in the business of love, and she'd had lots of clinical experience. Okay, okay, but I hoped she'd be more honest about it than my sister --- another hopeless romantic

--- a hopeless romantic who was hellbent on killing me. But Sunita's revelation about her profession gave me pause to think: it was so wonderful to know that the young bacchante was attending to the spiritual needs of an audience that existed somewhere, even if it occupied the shadowy periphery. I found myself thinking, "Hell, I suppose I'm a member to the periphery too. We have so much in common."

At this point, Lourdes sauntered back into the room asking if she could see some spy show where the secret agent guy almost gets eaten by a shark while the despot villain bad guy who's tryin' to take over the world watches the whole thing with eager eyes.

"No, Baby Cakes, you know you're not allowed to watch that one, so you really shouldn't be asking me a question that you already know the answer to."

"No problem. If that's the way you feel about it, I'll just go see it later at my friend Ginnie's house. She records everything in high def. We'll watch it together at her convenience. She'll even make some popcorn."

"Just remember that if you do that, you'll be defying your Mum, and you know that's bad. You'll have to live with yourself." She wagged her finger at her for a bit more emphasis. "Bad, bad, bad."

And Lourdes gave her mom a quizzical look, shrugged her shoulders, and replied, "I *feel* no guilt."

Ha! That was great. Someday a big boy or girl could become the total prisoner of Lourdes' grown up body. Until that time, I could scare off certain members of the eleven-year-old demographic.

WHEN THE CHEAP GO PITS

Later, I thought more about what Sunita had talked about --- which brought me to the subject of Ben --- Cruel Brother Number One. What I love about sadists is the way they handle their emotions. No matter how rancid a feeling it may be, if it happens to wander across their brains, then they have to go with the flow. They can't let it pass. They're compelled to act on it. To do otherwise would be "unnatural," and think about it --- who in his right mind except for tin horn-dictators and crazy people would ever want to hurt sweet, dear, and virtuous Nature? The thought of watching something get ripped limb from limb almost makes you want to run, stampeding from the house, covering your eyes and ears.

When I see this in the movies or on TV, I suddenly find myself shouting at the screen. You see, I want to try to get them to "act reasonably," but of course that's not practical. You can't stop them 'cause they dance by a different set of rules. They'll make some deal breaker demand and then act as if you're the bad ogre.

But really, even that's a colorful and murky business. There's a whole rainbow of sadists polluting the landscape out there. And make no mistake about it, they're truly worthless folk, but what puzzled me about Ben was that he was a true sadist --- the rarest of breeds. How did that distinguish him from ordinary run-of-the-mill sadists? Well, the answer was that he liked to lurk lowdown ... deep down. He liked to lie "in wait." That made him stand out in a crowded field. What he wanted above all else, was nothing less than the abolition of joy itself, excepting of course his own selfish brand of slug-fest-slam-and-bang exuberance. He was the type who relished the chance to hold out for his turn and, in his grand scheme of things, this moment each of us in the band inhabited was his golden opportunity --- his time in the sun. He'd been waiting to beat the shit out of someone for each and every moment of his existence. Who it was didn't really matter very much. His intuition may have felt that way, but another compartment of his psyche felt quite differently. Based on this unsavory bit of choplogic, he no doubt had surmised that if he went to all that trouble to commit something deeply mean-spirited, then he might as well be selective on the matter and vent his wrath on someone or something who really threatened him. That voice within him seemed to pay some lip service to rational thought. Or did it? The more I thought about it, the more it seemed that I was giving him way too much credit. His real reason was that he was simply being selective. I would later look back and see that he was a bit of a connoisseur. Gradually, it was dawning on me that he was like a roadside bomb that should be expertly gathered up by a staff of carefully trained technicians and then banished to a place where it would do the least damage. Perhaps it would be best for everyone concerned if he lived in the woods? That way he could get up in the morning, have a giant cup of bitter black coffee, and then go outside with a great big serrated knife and stab the trees. He could be a real Nature boy and get his rocks off in the process. Yes, he loved to talk about Nature --- that and politics. And so did I, but we enjoyed talking politics for totally different reasons. Inevitably, those kinds of discussions would lead to the premise that the clock was running down on this thing we call the world and that humans and reality itself are destined to fail. I would pause for a second after he'd made some point about this. Then I would say that premise was probably true, and wasn't that a very sad idea: that the whole project known as the Human Race had been for nothing? But the weird part was that he never actually said this was sad. On the contrary, he would, in so many words, begin to tell me about what a happy thought this was. No one in the history of the entire planet had ever wished for mass extinction more than he. Perhaps that was a necessary function of his profession, a way to drum up more business --- so the seas are slowly going to hell in a hand basket? Hip hip hooray! So the frogs of the world don't hop quite as fast as they used to, and they'll soon be past pluperfect tense? Yeah, let's hear it for The Man! So ordinary men and women vote against their best interests? Applause, applause! I sang my thoughts, and they throbbed deeply in my head:

"Dream of utopia
Serve food to the gods,
The endless cornucopia
No danger to dodge
Our leaders are clods
They won't do their jobs
We'll take them to task,
And kick their ass!"

Well, that's great! Lemme hear an "Amen" to all that. Listen up everybody! Let's go, jumpin' and skipping into the raging vortex of the Big Black Hole. We could get our atoms annihilated. This made me want to break down and cry, but I held my composure. I was ever the rough and tough man! No one suspected. My next thought was, "How in the world can I be in a band with a guy who patently wants the whole thing to fail? I mean, I may play a drum, but here, here, I'm not dumb. I may let 'em have their own way 'cause that's what a professional is supposed to do. But then after I've given them no argument, they proceed to drive the car off the fuckin' cliff. And after the crack-up, they still wanna have the keys to the car again.

However, this time I wasn't talking about politics with him. I was talking to him about rhythm, telling him that it's a frame that we can create beautiful sounds in, and he wasn't paying me much attention, and so he said that a frame was pretty boring stuff and so I said yeah maybe so, but our gig is to make it a fun-to-look-at frame that we can put pretty pictures in, and then the steel traffic sign pole was coming up at an alarming rate of speed and hell, Ben was driving at an alarming rate of speed, and he was steering the vehicle we were traveling in at an alarming rate of speed and then I could hear the suspension and the tires screaming for mercy and at the last second

… he deftly turned the wheel to avert a catastrophe so I jostled in the seat straining my shoulder restraint to the max as the car careened to a stop when the wheels tore up a swath of flower beds in someone's front yard before he revved the engine, peeled rubber, and hauled ass out of there. This is what happens when the cheap go pits. The virgins get to be in charge! They think that every stumble on life's path warrants bringing in the heavy artillery.

"Jesus, man, what are you trying to do, kill us?" I shouted.

"Joe, am I a good driver or what?" He lapsed into a sicko laugh, and pounded the dashboard with his outstretched hand. "We live in such shakey times, Joe. It's what every race car driver knows. One move that smacks of over compensation could lead to absolute disaster." He swerved the car again, making me slam against the passenger door.

"OK, OK. I get it. You're a great driver. But don't you want to live to drive another day?"

"That's the trouble with you, Joe. You're so into the here and now. Don't you understand that the light pole over there is only an illusion?"

I could see he was goin' with the hippy-dippy Hindustani stuff this morning. It was a familiar theme, one that had worked for him many times before.

"Yeah," I replied. "I do understand, and that illusion almost killed me you passive/aggressive fuck."

"Joe, the trouble with you is that you never say exactly how you feel. You're always hiding your emotions."

"Aw darn, I guess it's 'cause I'm a shy, wallflower kind of a guy who can't find the words to express himself. But say, if that light pole is such a grand illusion, maybe you could gimme a softer one. One that's not going to propel me through the damned windshield? That could be painful."

He shifted to a professorial tone. "But Joe, pain is the biggest illusion of all. It's the topper. All the others bow down deeply."

"I think you say that, Ben, because you like to inflict it."

"Hey man, go back a notch on your seat belt. You gotta learn to let go and loosen up just a bit. Joe, you're always keeping score. Dude,

I never keep score. I'm so not into keeping score that I gave you my wife. Was she amazing? Was she a beauty? Wasn't she a keeper? Did she make you a happy man?"

"Yes, that was very Eskimo of you. Extremely unselfish. I like Sunita very much."

"I just knew it. I knew you two would hit it off together. Did I ever call it?" He banged the steering wheel with the palms of his hands to let loose some of his exhilaration.

I twitched my fingers to let loose some of my anxiety. "Ben, you're batting a thousand with predicting things, and you're a helluva matchmaker. However, I couldn't help but notice that there's something rather broken about her."

"Yeah man. But she's no worse for wear."

At this point, his eyebrows danced up and down. In an instant, I could tell what he was thinking.

"And you can't take her back," he continued, "just because she's broken. A deal is a deal, my friend. She's your problem now. No returns allowed. What more can be said about Sunita? Her brokenness makes her complete. More complete than she's ever been up until now. I wanna thank you for making her, how shall I say it ... fulfilled. Yes, you filled her fully for sure. Think about her, Joe. She's a little dangerous. That's why we both love her. Praise the Lord, and pass the Princess!"

A pang of jealousy streaked through me. He had no right to say that about my woman even if she was still technically his woman. Once upon a time, sharing her like a common bit of chattel or livestock might have held the prospect of a wide array of fun and games, but right then I wanted to part his skull with a nine iron. I thought of Sunita. I wanted to protect her, to nurse her back to mental health. Something about her was upside down. My function in life was to make her right side up. It would be so easy. All I'd need to do would be to give her as much love and tenderness as possible --- kiss, kiss, kiss and touch, touch, touch. I wanted to give her the whole nine. Deep in my imagination I could pretend to think of her with a spectacularly good and completely unbroken leg, complete with slender calf and curling toes nestled snugly inside a glistening thick-heeled pump with an occasional shiny stocking to keep it interesting. I tell ya the girl could tornado spin in any direction. Yes, we were dancing. My my, what equilibrium she had! I led her out into a tuck turn before bringing her back for a she-goes-he-goes close embrace. The centrifugal force was truly breathtaking, and I could hear her say, "Weeeeeee!!" as a smile scurried across her face. A deep and powerful voice asked me: "How do you get her to go from Point A to Point B?" And I answered, "You **MAKE** her do it." Then I told the voice that when you bring her back in, it's oh-so-very important to let the palm of your right hand slide down a bit of her arm just so you can maintain the connection for the next move.

Yes, if I put my mind to it, that would surely do the trick. Wouldn't that make her better? Please tell me it would! But as I gave it more thought, maybe it wasn't so easy. Maybe a lot more would be required. Maybe all my efforts would simply lead to nothing, and I would simply be left holding a broken and limp ragdoll. After all, that gimp leg of hers seemed to be beyond repair, so maybe her entire being was beyond repair too. An uneasy realization came over me: quite possibly, Ben had gotten the better end of this deal. What a smug and clever fellow he was!

"Right you are, Ben. She's broken all right. But I always thought that you were the one who'd done the breaking."

"No man. She broke herself. I can claim credit for lots of stuff, but that's not one of them."

"So she's mine? I can have her all to myself?'

"Yes, I told you that before. Didn't you listen? Oh, I might ask you to lend her back once in a while when I might need her for special projects. But yeah, she's yours. Basically."

"Special projects? Basically?" I asked. "What do you mean by that?"

"Aw c'mon, Joe. I thought you were supposed to be a man of the world. So, if you are, then you'd damned well better act like it. Don't hit me with any of this babe-in-the-woods bullshit 'cause I won't have it. I'll slam the iron gate down with a resounding crash, and you'd better believe it. I think you know what she does for a living, that is, when she's not busy engaged in the rigorous task of spending her trust fund money. And besides, I need to spend a little of that trust fund money for myself. Joe, she may be yours, but she's still my meal ticket. And if either you or she should ever get funny notions and decide to change that, then I could simply go to the green card interview with a different set of answers, and I don't care how rich she is, her ass will still wind up bounced back in beautiful downtown Dhaka. How would that one work for you? Not so good, I'm willing to guess. And how would that one be for cute little Lourdes? Again, not so wonderful. From what Sunita's told me, the little one has lately taken quite a Big Daddy shine to you. I'd hate to see that shine be all for naught."

"Jeez man, you got an answer for everything, don't you?"

"Yeah man, that's for sure."

I thought about the girl back at Ben's workshop. What was her name---Gina? I wondered if she was a real girl or simply one of Ben's not-so-simple creations. Had she been a machine or a real girl? She/it had been problematic. I was leaning to the notion that she was artificial. Maybe that was why Ben liked all things artificial --- she could be more easily controlled? What I did appreciate about her was that she was a little bit human and a little bit something else, which was sorta like me. I wasn't quite human either. But I could play drums, and she sure as hell couldn't. That would have made me quantifiably better. I guess it was there that my appreciation of Gina faltered and then fell down. Having savored that one for a second or two, I figured I might as well broach the subject of the girl-who-wasn't-quite there, since up until now both of us had avoided her like the plague.

"Ben, I don't suppose you've been doin' any more experimentatin' with artificial intelligence?"

Oh yeah, you know I like to do that in my spare time. It's sorta like a hobby of mine."

"That girl Gina was quite a creation."

"Yes, I'm rather proud of her. But I gotta say, she's kinda old hat. Gina was so old hat that she's been disposed of at this point in the great game. You see, the progress I'm makin' is really quite astounding. I'm movin' by leaps and bounds. Right now I'm incorporating haptics into the total technology sphere."

"What's this haptics thing. Tell me about that."

"It's a branch of artificial intelligence. Basically, it's artificial touch. It's the feeling of feeling, but without the actual real touch of skin to skin. I think it may have big implications for pornography."

"I'll bet it takes out all the muss and fuss of actually having a feeling."

"Exactly. You got it."

He stepped on the gas before the light changed. I decided to change the subject. "You're afraid of something, aren't you?"

"No way, man. How can I be afraid of something after that bad-ass Hollywood express stunt driving? Explain that one to me."

I thought of the poor defenseless flower beds that we'd just skidded through. The man at the wheel of this hell ride had casually and callously slaughtered a gaggle of gladiolas and Black-eyed Susans.

"Can't you spend one second of your existence not hurting something?"

"Oh, come off your high horse, man! No can do. If you laid down on the pavement and fell fast asleep, sooner or later some silly creatures would run into you and stub their toes and get their pretty feelings hurt, so why waste your energy tryin'? That's my way of seein' it. Just existing and breathing the air that everyone else does is enough to hurt someone."

"Look, Ben. Can I say one thing that might put you at ease?"

"Are you kidding? I'm always at ease. Nothing you say or do can make me even more loosey goosey than I already am."

"I know what you're worried about."

"Dude, I haven't a care in the world!"

"Will you stop calling me dude? That's so damned irritating."

"OK, OK. I'll make that concession. Now what do you wanna say that's supposedly gonna put me at ease?"

"Concession is duly accepted. Now on to the main point. What you're worried about is that this band will take off and that we might actually accomplish something. For you, that would be a disaster."

"Dude, are you saying that I'm trying to pull the sparkplugs on the project known as *Babies in Bars*?"

"Exactly."

"I don't believe I'm hearing you correctly."

"You're ruled by fear," I continued. "If *Babies in Bars* gets successful, where would that leave you? You're not a very good bass player. At some point, Jillian will tell you that you suck, if she hasn't already, and when she does that, you're bound to be replaced. The only thing that would keep you on as a viable force would be to bring back that cheesy little toy of yours."

"What's my cheesy little toy?"

"We all know what that is."

"So say it."

"It's Ziggy, your star beat box. If you control that, then your place in the band will never be in doubt. If you can't bring him back, then the specter of being fired will always be looming over your head."

"Ha, like a piano of Damocles."

"Absolutely."

Ben suddenly had the look of a man who'd been found out. In short, the jig was up. He nervously adjusted himself behind the wheel and notched up the accelerator.

"Gosh, Joe, it would seem that the cat is out of the bag. What can I say? I think you got me. The only chance I have is to talk myself out of this bad situation. Remember, it's a reality show. Surely, that counts for something."

He was right in an ass-backwards sort of way. That was the thing about Ben --- he was good at words, and I wasn't. That's the trouble with words. They always have to mean something even when they're dumb as trees. Just once in a blue moon, why can't we say no to them and say yes to pure sound? But it's a tall order. The cold hard fact was that Ben could be believable. I never would be. I knew I could tell the truth for the rest of my Neanderthal life, but it wouldn't matter much because no one would ever see my point of view. People would automatically think I was lying to them.

"Joe, what you want is some kind of guarantee that success will happen. You don't understand that success is such a fickle thing. It could happen, or it might not. Neither you nor I have much control over the situation. Success could simply pick up its stakes and decide to move someplace else. It has nothing to do with any ability that you or me might have." After he said that, he gave me a condescending yawn, adjusted his rear view mirror and continued. "Joe, I wanted to bring this up later, but I think now is as good a time as any. You see, even as whacked out as Sunita may be, she can still suss you out about one thing, which is that you, Joe, are running from something, and I wanna find out what it is."

Darn, I thought, why in hell did she have to go and blab that to him?

"Ben, the only people I'm running from are people like you, people who want to trample on what I've had such a big effort in creating. Do you think I do this drum thing solely for my health?"

"Yes, I know you do, Joe. That's why I'm pretty sure I've got you over a barrel. What you don't understand is that I could walk away from this *Babies in Bars* TV show in five minutes, and it wouldn't bother me too much."

"Then why don't you? Why don't you, so that we can have a real bass player?"

"Nahh! You don't' get it. Do you?"

"Get what?"

"Joe, I believe I comprehend you more than you will ever know. You see, I can tell just by looking at you that this project means so much to you. Your eyes tell me that you have your heart set on it, and you know something? It doesn't mean a damned thing to me. If the spirit moved me, I could piss all over it on a moment's notice. But, if I walked away, I wouldn't be able to figure out what you've been running from. *That* would really stick in my craw. If I can figure out that, then there might be an even bigger catch of the day for me, Joe. And another thing ... I want something to show for this *Babies in Bars* gig besides a few residuals to come my way a few years down the pike. Joe, I need something for my time and effort for showing up."

"You don't get points for showing up."

"I wouldn't bet on that, Joe."

Unfortunately, he may have been right there.

Ben glanced out the window to his left, then put his eyes back on the road. I could tell he was about to change gears.

"Look, I'm a really sweet guy. Everyone likes me. Women all like me. As a matter of fact, so many of them like me I get to take my pick. I'm forever boffing supermodels. They flock to me all the time. I'm God's gift to female kind. I can't figure out why you don't like me. If you have a problem, then you should just man up and talk to me. But don't ever get on my bad side 'cause I'm God's gift to female kind."

"Yeah, I know. Women are great. They're especially great when you get to have two of 'em at the same time. Gee Ben, you're such a funky fellow. And so, so psychologically well-adjusted."

Ben sighed. The wind had temporarily been taken out of his sails, which was fun to watch. But I knew that he'd retaliate with something new.

"Okay, Joe. I guess now is as good a time as any to tell you something else."

"OK, Ben, what's that?"

"My Robot Boy Gulf has been screwing around with Gwen."

No! I was dumbfounded! What a sucker punch! Struggling to fathom this rude surprise, I started practicing a difficult drum beat on my knees and thighs. That's what's great about drums: you can practice when you're away from your actual instrument. The real instrument is your own body, which is, in the long run, fairly close by. But my body was on edge. The knees and thighs, to say nothing of my hands, were distracted. They were fathoming this too, wondering what stunt driver thing he'd throw at them next. After a few seconds, it all seemed to make perfect sense both for me and for the knees and thighs. The arms, however... they were another story. They kept remembering about the time when a certain very famous drummer had lost his arm after a night of extremely irresponsible driving. For weeks afterwards, my right arm had been so completely spooked that it often clutched the left arm to make sure that it wouldn't go anywhere. Well, right when Ben had been driving like a crazy man, my right arm had been acting up again. It never seemed to forget that traumatic incident --- couldn't get it out of its bicep memory. But after fighting off a shiver in the tendon, my right arm got a hold of itself. The arm calmly moved forward and took this opportunity to reach for one of Ben's cigarettes which were on the center consol. Lighting it up with the help of the other arm, I rolled it around from one corner of my mouth to the other and then back again while the body attached to the arm took another deep breath. Then I puffed on the cigarette before deciding to sing a tune on the spot.

> "There he is
> The boy in control
> Breaking things to kingdom come
> Then he'll go and smash her soul."

I blew the smoke out in Ben's direction. My arms were feeling better already.

"Hey that's not bad. We should use that in the band as one of our new songs. Gwen was saying to me the other day that she needed a hook for something. Maybe that's it."

"Don't forget, Ben. Jillian wants us to love each other."

"That bitch! No, no. I haven't forgotten. I'm looking forward to more and more fun."

"Let the mirth and goodwill never get tired of replicating themselves."

"Never get tired of fucking themselves," he countered.

So Gulf had put the moves on Gwen! Jeez, why, why, why? My thoughts turned to Kathy as Ben's foot pressed the accelerator again.

"And one more thing, Joe. If I left the show, then Gulf would also be outta the band, so I wouldn't be able to keep an eye on his new lady friend Gwen. At this point, I like to think of her as being my woman too. I love her by proxy. Gulf loves her actually. And I only want what's best for him."

He flashed me a malicious smile and broke into song.

> "Gotta keep an eye on my woman
> Gotta keep her safe and sound
> Gotta keep an eye on my woman
> Gotta know who's goin' down."

As Ben's little ditty came to a halt, I took the opportunity to give him a short round of applause.

"Hey man, that's downright skuzzy."

But Ben was on a roll. He kept on yammering away.

"Anyway, Joe, why is this rock and roll, psychedelic garage band, funk, hip hop, r & b mix and match so important? Jeez, one crappy tune is as good as another. It's not major at all. None of it *means* anything. Science and the stock market and real estate and lame movies --- that's where it's at. Did you know that a certain actor in Hollywood gets thirteen million dollars just for reading a script? And he doesn't even have to do the damned movie. He can simply decide to go to the beach that day, and he still gets his thirteen million dollars --- no questions asked."

"Nice work if you can get it."

He pointed his finger at me for emphasis. "Now, hey man, *that* means something."

"Yes," I said as I lapsed into a fake French accent: *"Oui monsieur, eet ees expenseef an' for notheeng.* That's very strange, don't you think?"

He didn't answer. Once more Ben was driving like a lunatic. I saw a pedestrian running for cover as he continued along the road. In that moment, it was best that the entire world batten down the hatches.

"Don't fuck with my imagination, Ben. Please understand that it's semi-divine. It's the thing that drives the band 'cause you sure as hell don't. Gwen --- she hasn't got a clue what she's doin'! She's got a gift, and she doesn't even know it. What a boob! People clap, and she thinks she's doin' something right. She's got a voice, but she doesn't know what to do with it. So, I sit in the back and look bored when I'm really not, and I make something out of nothing."

Still Ben made no answer. His eyes were glaring at the road.

I pondered how Ben went about the process of making his choices in life. I could see how he lined up each choice, carefully evaluating it on a continuum of good to bad, and then after he had completed that rigorous analysis, he would go about selecting the absolute worst. I could picture him as a judge in some sort of show ring awarding the top prize and adorning the winner with an oversized blue ribbon which had a puffy rosette in the middle. Yes, there was indeed something extremely scientific about the entire enterprise. A moment of recognition was slowly formulating. Up until now, I had mistakenly believed that Ben had been useful to the most vile and pernicious side of my own psyche. My delusion had been that I could go to bars or restaurants with him, and he could behave as atrociously as he wanted, with the proviso that none of his anti-social nature would ever be blamed on me. Essentially, I had been given license to act out through him because I would never in my wildest dreams be that stupid or nasty to others. So, in a strange way, none of it counted on the supposed ledger of *my own* life. It could be tallied up in the ledger of some other more distant life. That would make it safe. Somehow, this arrangement would make the darkness in my soul manageable.

For a long time, this had seemed to be a benign bargain, sort of like lining up for confession in order to get absolution, but now I was beginning to understand that much of the residue of his nastiness would invariably land on me, and would splatter on me with bad results. I was realizing that he should never be given any power, nor should he ever have encouragement because any talents he might have, had to be put in the service of creating disappointment. For him, the standard for measuring the worth of a friendship was its capacity to endure one spot of sadness after another. That was the mark of what girls might call a "Best Friend for Life." And he was workin' this mojo again for the umpteenth time. My other thought was: how would his negativity affect his crowning creation, namely Gulf the Robot. Did he really want Gulf to succeed? I wasn't so sure. It was entirely within the realm of possibility that he truly wanted to create Gulf simply to watch him self-destruct. The more I got to know Ben the more he reminded me of a certain Hindu goddess.

But his abrasive words brought me back to the more immediate reality. "You're drumming is nothing but repetition," he ranted. "It's like the ocean and its bloody waves! They come in more and more pretentious, relentless versions of one and two. Maybe three and four if you're lucky. Ho Ho Hum! Joe, you need to understand that there is a role reversal here, and I do *not* like it one bit. And not only that, but you're a junkie to top it off. Why should I ever have to take orders from one of you?'

"How did you find out?"

"Wow, that one was pretty simple. I just broke into the techies' production trailer the other day and looked at the budget for the show. Jillian wrote the bill for your daily fix into the pocket change for the program. Hey, this is Hollywood. People shouldn't have to worry about such low echelon things as feeding one's addiction. This is the place where people always think big --- larger than life itself. Why shouldn't they think, act and *shoot up* big with you, even if you're very small? My best guess is that Jillian especially cottons up to this arrangement because this way she gets to sample the stuff herself. Don't you think for a moment that I fail to notice those times when she ducks into the bathroom for long periods of time? I know what she's doin'. She's shootin' up is what she's doin'. Joe, I think you're what the talk show people and feel-good shrinks call an 'enabler.' You're helpin' her out, and she's livin' large through you."

He smacked the dashboard again with his fist.

"Joe my boy, no one is supposed to give a shit about you. You're a drummer, so you're a slave. You're *my* slave! Act like it! Don't be so complicated. Don't be so...so... experimental. Don't you understand that? Yo bro no! Why can't you stay in your place? Must you be so obstinate? Just provide the backbeat, stay in the back seat, and keep your damned mouth shut. A lunk head machine like Ziggy can do whatever you summon to the surface. And he's a much more servile boy! You're supposed to be dumb, so play your drum, you uppity bastard!"

"Shut up and shut up now! I...Let me repeat..."

I could feel my rage galloping up to the top of my head like a snarling, slashing junkyard dog. My soul itself was startled as it parried back, struggling to keep the yowling beast at bay, causing a tingling to erupt on the tip of my nose. In an instant, I found myself stuttering uncontrollably.

"I...am the slave," I shouted, pausing involuntarily for emphasis. "I am the slave who has become the master! If you haven't guessed it by now, I care about this shit. It's not a hobby. It's my life. And Ben, you're fuckin' with my life. And I appreciate my life. It's mine and it's not yours or anyone else's for that matter. So, I wanna say, Ben, get down on your knees and bow down to *my life*."

"Well now, you listen here for a second, buddy boy! I didn't raise my songs to be juvenile delinquents, Joe. Dig it, man. You're a craftsman and I'm an artist. I've got to look after my property."

"Think about it, Ben. Jillian tells me that we're on the radio in LA, Austin, and New Orleans. It looks as though the band is starting to succeed. That must be so horrible --- to be on the radio, to have an actual audience that listens to you, to have something actually move forward and emerge from out of the basement into the brightness of the successful day. Well, it's enough to almost change your life. Pretty scary shit if you ask me."

I looked over at Ben as he put the pedal to the metal. What a total coward! Yes, the radio really needed to be working overtime. I gave it a glance as it lurked there underneath the dashboard right next to the switch for the windshield wipers and the cigarette lighter. I reached over to the dial and clicked it on, softly at first, but then louder --- to the point of distortion. *Babies in Bars* was playing. It was our brand new album. Ben went into cruise control before taking his hands off the wheel and covering his ears. The DJ guy was featurin' it as a special presentation. For the first moment in about two weeks, Ben looked genuinely scared. He didn't look quite so unconcerned about death and pain now!

The bloodless eyes and mouth seemed to say that no one had ever talked to him like this before. Unfortunately, my voice went up an octave. I tried to pull it back down. No use--- it could not be helped. Damn! Now he wouldn't be scared. In fact, he'd probably be very happy. At last, he had found something he could kill. And best of all, it was a dream that belonged to someone else.

Then he summoned up a smile to conquer the setback he had just now faced. Turning to me again, he said, "Joe, while I'm at it, I might as well tell you about Doc McIntyre. Yes, yes, your old friend contacted me. Tells me how bummed out he is about how you up and ran away. How he's been wanting you to come back 'cause there are further experiments that need to be done. Says he wants to do a collabo together he and I. I told him it sounds great to me, and that I always knew that you were running from someone and wasn't it peachy keen that I knew some of your obscure background?"

I put my hands to my ears to protect them from what I was hearing. Then I looked off to the right to see the traffic whizzing by as Ben began to accelerate again. I wanted to rip his face off, but then, who would drive?

THE PROBLEM WITH NOISE

So, you see, Dear Gentle Reader, this is the kind of stuff these Cro-Mags like Ben pull again and again. The ungrateful bastards! We, Neanderthals gave them the gift of emotion and what did they do with it? They perverted it into the deepest and blackest of chasms. We paved the way for their so-called "superior technology," and what did they do? They used it against us. We gave them the concept of havin' a party all the time, but they had other, more "practical" ideas. Understand that they are a formidable enemy, but they can still get unlucky sometimes. We're not complete pushovers.

My brow ridge was actin' up again. The supra-orbital bone was goin' hog wild. I needed to keep it under control. Yes, Ted the gorilla and the Great Goddess Girl had really given me something, and it was rather contagious. It had something to do with the problem of noise.

However, not to worry. The Goddess of Music was on my side, and I escaped Ben's horrendous driving unscathed---which brought me back to the subject of Sunita and Lourdes, her charming little eleven year old. Despite being a bit of a brat, Lourdes took a liking to me. Naturally, that had not gone unnoticed by Ben. She and I really hit it off 'cause it was pretty obvious that she viewed me a possible papa material, and I did my best to play along, though not in the most conventional sense of that role. She was a great kid with at big heart even if she was fond of testing out her mom more often than I would have liked. I could have been authoritarian, but elected to hold back. I mean, Lourdes was Sunita's kid, and who in the hell was I? I was some sort of passing tone in her life. Still, I really did like her. I knew I'd remember her for a long time.

Early on, I discovered that the kid had one big hang up. I mean, kids in general are a lot sicker these days than when I was growing up. That's because they have so much in this world to be sick about. And the reason for that is the damned Cro-Mags have taken over everything, and they never wanna let go. They've got a finger in every pie, and they insist on keepin' things as infantile as possible. As a result, they have some awfully neurotic kids. I suppose it's the consequence of living shielded lives. And at first, I truly was of the belief that Sunita's kid had lucked out. But I misjudged her---the kid had one colossal hang-up. No, it was nothing so bad as Tourette's Syndrome or ADD or Asperger's or a learning disability.

Naw, nothin' that exotic. Rather, the kid had a huge problem with noise. If we were walkin' down the street, and there was some sort of street racket such as a motorcycle backfirin' or a palette of merchandise fallin' off from a flatbed truck or whatever, she would totally freak out. And it wouldn't stop there. Sometimes, it would take Sunita and I five or ten minutes to get the kid to calm down. The kid would go off on us. She would be like a cat on a bat, covering her ears and goin' into convulsions! It had all the trappings of an epileptic attack even though Sunita assured me that it wasn't. I don't know---there's most likely a name for this affliction, but I was damned if I was gonna look it up. So, after this happened for the fourth or fifth time, I figured I'd try to see how I might cure her. I mean, if I didn't cure her of her enormous disability, then how in the hell would she ever like loud music? It would be so hard to go through life like that, bein' so crippled.

So, I formulated a plan. I knew that in the old part of the city, there was a foundry---some kind of ironworks---probably one of the last of its kind 'cause most of those jobs had long ago been farmed out to the Far East or to any one of a number of Third World countries. But this foundry---it had somehow, in the face of tremendous opposition, hung on. It was literally the last of its kind. Extinction was hovering in the air like some kind of greedy vulture every time I walked by it, but the foundry kept the buzzard at bay. What was special about this particular foundry was that it had a conveyer belt that would bring out a piece of molten metal about every ten seconds. The conveyer would jostle the metal into position, trundle it onto a platform, and then a gigantic gravity press would come smashing down into the red hot metal, forging it into whatever metal part that it was destined to become. When that happened, the sound would be nearly deafening. And to top it off, the sidewalk seemed to shudder under the feet of passersby. Of course, for a normal person, it would be no big deal. It woulda been an extreme inconvenience akin to droning fire alarms, only for a person like Lourdes, I knew it would be a huge deal. I figured that I'd take Lourdes down to the foundry for a little bit of therapy.

I told her we were just gonna go for a walk, and then we would go to the park and I would buy her some cotton candy. I knew that we would pass by the foundry before we got to our jaunt in the park. Well, I nonchalantly led her up to the sidewalk by the edge of the foundry, and sure enough, the noise was right on top of us. In fact, the din suckered punched us, seemingly coming in right out of the blue to inundate the eardrums with no apparent warning. Quite predictably, the kid flipped out on cue and in no time, I had my hands full. She was screamin' and yellin' and coverin' her ears, but I held onto her, cradled her, comforted her, telling her that nothing would happen to her, that big Joe would make it alright, that it was only a very loud noise, but that in this world of ours she would be sure to run into lots and lots of very loud noises and it was really and truly nothing to fret about, and that we shouldn't allow loud noises to get the better of us and make us do crazy things. In fact, some loud noises might even get to be fun. She answered me, saying that what she disliked about loud noises was that they were so unnecessary, and I responded letting her know that there are so many unnecessary things in the world, and if we got all hot and bothered about unnecessary things, then we'd never get any work done, and wouldn't that be a horrible tragedy, much more horrible than any so-called necessary noise? So I told her that she should think of this moment that we were experiencing right then as being a kind of practice.

The foundry continued its formidable din, and I had to admit that it was more earsplitting than usual. The brat was screechin'. No, she was definitely not a happy camper. She was letting me know that she didn't want to practice and that she wanted to get the hell out of there ASAP. Her arms and legs flailed in a savage akimbo dance. I tried to restrain her, and she hit me in the face with a swinging elbow. I was amazed that such a small person could account for so much volume and velocity. In fact, she seemed to produce more decibels than the gigantic gravity press. And soon I began to second guess myself, thinking that maybe I'd done the wrong thing by taking her there, and I was all set to take her by the hand and apologize for bringing her to this unnecessarily noisy place when suddenly, the child in my arms began to relax, and after we stood there for another five minutes or so, enduring the crash of the machine, she took no notice of it. In fact, I got the impression that she might have enjoyed it on some level. She crouched on the sidewalk waiting in cautious anticipation for the thing to come crashing down again. And when it did, she leaped gleefully into the air, flapping her arms as if trying to fly before collapsing in paroxysms of ecstasy on the patch of mowed grass in the space between the street and the concrete. I stood over her, thinking that she looked like a contented cat rolling around on a rug. Suddenly, it occurred to me that I'd just witnessed some sort of exorcism, but of course I had no idea as to what had been driven out. I quickly told myself it didn't matter. What did matter was that I had seen someone else's life-changing moment.

Afterwards, she bounded back onto her feet, gave me a great big giggle, and said, "C'mon, Joe, let's go to the park. I'm really lookin' forward to that cotton candy that you promised me." After I purchased some cotton candy for her, she leaned towards me and said, "So, that was practice?"

"Yes, Lourdes. That was practice."

"I think I like it." She was grinning from ear to ear as if she were aware that the foundry had forged her. I felt a warm trickle on my face and knew I was bleeding.

At first, Sunita was miffed when she heard about the visit to the foundry and all the commotion that Lourdes had successfully endured. But Mommy couldn't really argue with the results because prior to this and unbeknownst to me, she had been trying to rid Lourdes of her fear of noise. However, she wasn't angry for very long, that is, until something else happened.

Sunita always had big plans for Lourdes to become a ballerina. In fact, she'd shelled out quite a bit of money on lessons, but from the time of the foundry incident, the kid's heart really wasn't into *pas de deux's* and tutus anymore because the day after the visit to the foundry, I took the kid to one of my rock shows, and suddenly, early adolescence became a new ballgame.

She said, "Mom, to hell with this ballerina business! What I really want now is to learn how to play drums. I wanna get the biggest baddest loudest drum kit that we can find, and then I wanna practice on it. I wanna smack 'em hard. Joe'll help me. I know he will. I asked him for lessons, and he said he'd be my teacher." And reluctantly, Sunita purchased one of those big kits that you practically have to turn into an octopus in order to play.

Standing off to the side, I watched her, admiring her burgeoning technique. Each hit on the snare registered the full weight of pre-teen angst and rebellion. And true to form, she lived up to her earlier reputation of being a small person who could create a lot of decibels.

Of course, Sunita initially had not been pleased about this change in her young daughter. But her feelings were somewhat mixed. She was happy that Lourdes was no longer terrified of noise, but she was not amused that the youngster was giving up on the ballerina thing. Her face had a wistful look, but she was resigned to many things her child had come to value. Still, if Lourdes were to give up being a dancer, then why couldn't she take to some avocation or craft that had a more feminine vibe to it? But what can you do? The kids just wanna have it their way. And there's not much that can be done. In fact, it cannot be helped.

These fatherly feelings seemed to drift in out of nowhere. They were certainly unexpected. But then they drifted off just as suddenly as they had arrived only to be replaced by the more familiar need that I perpetually had, which was to get my daily fix. The evidence for this was that my skull was acting up again like a bad twelve year old. The bones felt like they were urging upward, trying to burst out of what had eons ago been some sort of sagittal crest. You see, Neanderthals harken back to something much much earlier than the mere Pleistocene. So, I went and shot up some of that supremo smack that Bill had scored for me. Damn, it felt good. She was a wave of beauty who whispered lightly in my ear. She promised to never go away --- only I knew she was lying.

Despite this unexpected distraction, I nonetheless felt the need to check up again on Sunita when she wasn't lookin'. I mean, how else could I figure out what she was all about? How else could I find the key to her soul? I naturally assumed that this kind of eavesdropping was a two way street. I surmised that sneakin' into her diary wasn't enough. That alone wouldn't afford me the widest glimpse into the vistas of her soul. Only I'll have you know that I am far from being anything like a common everyday hacker. Absolutely not! The reason is that I'm the least mechanical person on the planet. My imagination would be sure to come up with an innovative surprise. I stumbled along and after quite a few attempts, I hit paydirt. I was able to see that she'd been a very busy girl. Apparently, during this time of her moderate convalescence, she'd been holed up making lots of home videos for sale.

At first, I had no idea what in the world I'd discovered. Afterwards, however, it offered a plausible explanation to what had previously been a loose collection of facts. I hit the play button on the vid, and there she was in the full regalia of her stunning beauty despite the fact that she wasn't wearing any make-up, which was a nice change of pace because I felt that I was watching a different woman. She stared at me in the same way that she would stare out at the hundreds or maybe thousands of men who would be certain to see this. She flashed a seductive smile and went into a whispery voice mode that I'd only had a hint of prior to this.

"Hello," she gushed. "How are you? I haven't seen you in a while. It was so nice of you to come over to my house. I must say you're looking rather peaked. Is there something wrong? Have they been stomping on you at work again? I'll bet they have. People --- what can I say? People can be so vicious. They don't know that they're hurting somebody, or they actually do it on purpose. Either way, it's a bad deal all around. Honestly, I don't know how you endure so much heartlessness. It's pretty raw stuff. And I'm so proud of you because of what you put up with. But you've come to the right place. I'll take you in and help you get back to yourself, the self that you really are, the good one that they took away from you."

I was so taken in by her tingly voice that I wished I could jump right through the screen and kiss her. The way she talked with that delicious affection/affectation made me wanna double up into a fetal position and crawl into her womb. And I was certain that so many others wanted to do exactly the same. No doubt they would want to do that because that place would make them feel so safe and sheltered --- a cave to keep them shielded from the world. Why couldn't she have done that voice for me? I wanted to see that side of her. I wanted to hear it too. She whispered on and on, and I swear I could almost sense the hairs on my arms begin to stand up, and in a strange way this experience was arguably on a par with the actual physical act. Then she would modulate her voice ever so slightly and go into a hypnotic mode that was about a nine and a half in the enchantment scale. Tranquillized by these new sets of sounds, I blacked out and must have fallen asleep. When I awoke, I found myself at the computer and the screen had gone to the saver mode, and I was under the impression that the Goddess had been talking to me again. I marveled at Her creativity. She seemed to come at me in new and ever more fascinating variations. Indeed, it took an act of supreme will to tear myself away from this breathtaking display of enforced infantilism, but I managed to do it.

But the Goddess wasn't through yet. While She was still fresh in my dreamscape, She would see fit to strike again. No, there would be another, much weirder version for later that night. It was about a different girl in the life that I was leading so far.

A GIRL GOES SHOPPING

She was trying to make a brand new start 'cause she was bored with the sound of her own heart. Umpachumpa umpachumpa chump! I was trying to imitate the undulations of the kit as I worked my way around the two floor toms. The colors were fantastic. The sculptures singed my eardrums. Chortling cymbals gasped silver and gold. Faraway in the plush zone, I was having quite a dream about Gwen. I've got a big green Neanderthal imagination and on occasion that somehow seeps over into reverie. Just so you'll know --- it's part of being a god. And the drum had sure as hell made me exactly that, even if it was only in fits and starts. But hey, even gods need practice. Eventually, I would get the hang of it. Then hell would surely break loose. But I had all the patience in the world. The dream, on the other hand, was far more desperate. That needed attending to right away. Like most dreams, it conveyed a sense of urgency. And that urgency needed to be honored. Of course, the camera crew was there even in my dream. There was no nook or cranny that was safe from its stare. When I fell asleep, the camera went upside down as I passed out.

In the dream, Gwen was dressed up in some kind of corporate outfit as though she were going to a job interview to be a bank teller. She was running lickity split up the steps of the large Victorian house, the one that had a large neon sign with one throbbing letter on the front lawn announcing the name of this establishment as the Lawton Funeral Home. I thought to myself --- Jesus, Gwen, I know this is only a dream and not really real, but what in the hell are you doing? At the top of the steps, she rang the bell and was greeted by Gulf.

"Hi Gulf, I've heard so much about your day job. So, I finally get to see where you work."

"Come right in, I've been expecting you."

Gwen extended her hand and Gulf shook it. Gulf ushered her into the establishment and to his office, explaining that his father Ben was usually the person in charge, but that he was filling in for him today because Dad had some last-minute errand to take care of. Gulf's demeanor was businesslike, but slightly somber. She went down a long corridor. The atmosphere was appropriately funereal with an abundance of the visual vocabulary of the death industry. The decorations were overdone. Terra cotta cupids blew on rococo trumpets and plastic Greek Corinthian columns adorned the opening hallway. A baroque cantata played softly in the background, and something about the place made Gwen and Gulf want to speak in hushed whispers.

That made me cringe as I lay back under the covers, trying to remind myself that this was a dream, so it didn't really count.

Gulf ushered her into his office, which looked fairly conventional: there was a large desk with two comfortable chairs in front, obviously for potential clients, and another in back, which was his. Light entered the door through the Venetian blinds, which he adjusted to let in more.

"Please, Miss Hagobian, have a seat."

My God, I thought! He was calling her by her last name. How fucked up was that?

"Thank you," Gwen replied.

This was so bizarre. Gulf was pretending he didn't know her, Yeah, I thought, but this was a dream so they were allowed to do that. And I was a god, so I was allowed to listen in.

"Now how may I help you today? On the phone you seemed rather distressed. Has a loved one passed away?"

"No, not yet. I would just like to make a pre-arrangement."

"Yes, to give you and your loved one's family peace of mind. I fully understand."

"No, I'm afraid that you don't understand, Mr. Lawton. This pre-arrangement is not for a loved one of mine."

She was calling him 'Mr. Lawton' How strange!

"No?" he replied. "Then perhaps it is for a friend?"

"No, no, not that at all. Rather, this one's for me."

"But you don't... you don't... um..."

"...look as if I'm about to expire anytime soon? Is that what you're trying to say, Mr. Lawton?"

"You took the words outta my mouth even if the 'expire' thing always sounds like we should be talkin' about a carton of yogurt instead of an actual human being such as yourself. But appearances can be deceiving. Miss Hagobian, do you have a terminal illness? Is that what brings you here?"

"I'm feeling rather sickly."

"Really? You don't look sickly, Miss Hagobian. You look like you could run the New York Marathon."

"Looks can be deceiving, Mr. Lawton. I'll bet that in your profession you're well aware of that. The fact of the matter is this: I've got asthma."

"Yes, but that's not a death sentence."

In the dream, Gwen was expensively dressed, and I could see her from Gulf's point of view.

"I suppose in some ways that I've never been healthier," she continued. "But hey, you never know what can happen to you these days."

"I know what you mean. Yesterday, we had an event here for a lady who'd been in a car accident. Yes, so sad. What a turn out! We must have had two hundred people here. Not all at once of course." He seemed to lose his train of thought, but after he blinked his eyes three times, he quickly got it back. "...But you've never been healthier, you say?"

"Yup, healthy as a horse. Oh every now and then I have a slight blood pressure thing that I take meds for, and the heart does a little tango from time to time, but nothing very serious. I'm just planning for the future."

"For the inevitable?"

"That's one way of looking at it."

"Okay, so for starters. Do you have cemetery property?"

"Yes, I do. But I'm unhappy with it."

"Hey, how do ya know? Don't knock it till you've tried it. Why not give it a test drive? Maybe go out there and sleep on top of it for forty-five minutes."

"Oh Mr. Lawton. That's very funny."

"I wasn't trying to be."

"But you are. Please understand that I have absolutely no wish to spend eternity permanently parked where I don't want to be!"

"You'll be none the wiser. Take my word for it."

"The sign on the front lawn said that you're also a cremation consultant."

"Yeah, it's true."

"I don't get it. Who needs a consultant? I mean, strike some flint and light a fire. How complicated can it be?" She didn't give him time to answer before forging ahead to her next thought. "No, seriously, someone said that you sell mausoleums too."

"I also do that on the side."

"So you're a Mauso Man? Sounds like some heavy metal song."

"Who's being funny now?" Gulf rubbed his chin and leaned forward in the chair. "Come to think of it, I guess my dad's a Mauso Man too. You remember him? He set up our appointment."

"Yes, of course I remember him." Gwen's mood was getting very insistent. "I wanna see the mausoleums today. Take me to the mausos." She tapped Gulf's desk with her finger.

"Sorry. Not possible."

"No, it's got to be today."

"I only drive people up there if they're pretty sure about buying one. And you seem to think this is some kind of entertainment Right, Miss Hagobian?"

"No way. I'm as serious as cancer."

"Miss Hagobian, I'll tell ya a story. Two months ago this lady says the same thing. Tells me how serious she is. Says she wants to buy. Says all she needs to do is look at it and if it's good, she'll get out her checkbook for sure. I said, 'You promise me you will?' and she says, 'Yes, you can bet on it' and I said, 'Okay, I'll drive you up under those conditions, but only under those conditions.' So we get all the way up there, and she looks at the rows and rows of mausoleums stacked on top of each other almost like they were piles of cord wood. I tell her it's the only business where the top drawer is less expensive than the bottom drawer..."

In the dream, I could see Gwen interrupting again. By now my rapid eye movement must have been going hog wild, but I'm only guessin'.

"Why is that? Why is the top drawer less expensive than the bottom?" she asked.

Gulf moved uneasily in his chair. "Think about it, Miss Hagobian. Who wants to get a kink in the neck from looking up at the drawer of the dearly departed?"

Gwen rubbed the back of her neck. "Yeah, I see what you mean. You could get a kink in the neck from looking up at the top drawer. It never crossed my mind. Only orthopedists, chiropractors, and acupuncturists would benefit from that."

Ben continued his story, putting his hands behind his head. "So my lady client says how wonderful the cemetery looks. Talks about the beautiful view and the perpetual maintenance, which if ya wanna know the truth, is a total crock, an' then we get in the car and I'm drivin' her back to the city, an' so I say 'OK, Mrs. Norton, we can save us a whole lotta time if you write me a check for the thousand dollar down payment', an' she says, 'Aw no Mr. Lawton, I don' think so' an' I say, 'But Mrs. Norton, you said if ya liked it, you'd surely buy, an' you can't stop tellin' me how much ya like it, so why aren't ya buying?' an' she says, 'I like it, but I jus' changed my mind' an' she gives me a great big yawn an' I start to get really pissed, so after I come to a complete boil, I pull over to the shoulder of the highway an' stop in the sandy part an' I tell her, 'Lady this is your stop!' an' she says, 'You're kiddin'?' an' I say, 'No I'm not. Get your fat ass outta my car now!' an' she threatens me. Tells me her son is some big shot lawyer who'll sue my pants offa me, but I'm firm about it an' she leaves the car, slammn' the door, all the while callin' me every name in the book."

Gwen got up and smacked the desktop with her fist, before advancing towards him. She touched him seductively on the cheek. "That's what I like about you, Mr. Lawton. I like to know that I'm dealin' with a professional. No amateur night for me. Nosiree!"

Gulf looked flustered, but he decided to proceed. "Well, we all gotta start somewhere. Perhaps you'd like to look at caskets?"

"That would be as a good a place as any I suppose."

"They're right in there. That's the selection room." He pointed to the left and got up to open the far door. Opening it, he ushered Gwen into large room which was filled with coffins, each with its lid open, as in a gigantic yawn revealing its quilted interior.

Gwen looked pleasantly surprised, which was surprising to me.

That made me toss and turn as the dream took a new turn that I really didn't like one bit. In the dream, I kept flashing back to gigs of days gone by. I was paying close attention to Gwen's lyrics despite the pesky feeling that, if they were left to their own devices and unencumbered by some kind of sound to buttress their alleged emotional value, then they wouldn't do much to move me. If they failed with me, then how in the world would they succeed with others? She sang her heart out, yammering about how "hard it is," how it "hurts to love." It was a familiar cry baby theme, one she skillfully hammered home in song after song. I suppose this was what some people might call the blues, but I was pretty skeptical 'cause from what Kathy had told me, Gwen had grown up on too many golf courses to feel that way. And those courses had been the country club kind and not the municipal variety. There would be no blues to be found on the four-hundred and ten yard par four, nor would there be any on the par three hundred and twenty yard third, notwithstanding the gigantic gapping sand traps guarding either side of the green. However, when Gwen's words did lapse into that "sad" and shopworn strategy, I had trouble restraining myself. I barged in on the bass drum and gave the whole notion a swift kick in the pants before knocking it ten feet in the air. Her shallow words didn't have a chance. They took to the fresh blue sky and melted into something else. The problem was people were so afraid of tickin' someone off that they demurred from ever expressing the sharpness of their feeling. This thing felt like a conversation in which people uttered the words sorry, sorry, sorry, please, please, please, thank you, thank you, thank you, pardon, pardon, hey, I don't know if you noticed this or not, but I said, "I beg your pardon. Did you hear that? I'm not so sure. Maybe I'll have to say it again. OK. I think you get it. Maybe I can shut my eyes and go to sleep now." But me, I wasn't hampered by such restraints.

Then I tossed and turned again and took up where I'd left off.

"Gosh, Mr. Lawton, they almost look like beds."

"Well, they are. Beds for the dead."

She gushed and smiled. She moved forward. Her hand touched the interior of one of the ornate boxes. They exchanged knowing looks. Clearly, he was attracted to her, and she was attracted to him.

"It's so soft and pretty, Mr. Lawton."

"And you'll be pretty too."

"I'll be... what's the word you people say? Reposing?"

"Yeah, posing over and over and over again, but I promise you --- you'll never get bored."

"No doubt I'll be like some sort of still life?"

"Dead nature."

"I can hear everyone now. They'll be saying, 'And here we have Gwen. Or rather, shall I say, the idea of Gwen. She couldn't really be here 'cause she was having trouble wakin' up, but the *idea* of Gwen is here. So...so...We'll just have to say, 'Close enough! We'll have to make do with an approximation. Her concept is doing alright even if her person isn't. She's really here.' Of maybe they'll be sayin, 'She looks like a piece of artwork, doesn't she? Like the stuff that Brit guy does with the sharks and pigs in formaldehyde.' Then maybe they should get on the phone to say, 'Book her a room at the Tate Gallery'"

Gwen felt the lining of the casket erotically, as if she were feeling a part of a man's anatomy. She closed her eyes.

In the dream I went, "Yuck!!"

Gwen continued: "It's a top of the line Aurora Pennington with pink satin interior offset in a dove white hand stitched head panel, and copper roll bars --- truly a fine fashion statement for the girl no longer on the go."

"Ah, Miss Hagobian, you seem to know your stuff. Who needs me when you're ever the authority on the subject? Guess you've done your homework. Such a diligent little school girl. Maybe you'd like to get in and make yourself comfortable?"

Gwen's face looked as though she were touching herself, but she wasn't. Ben lifted up the bottom half of the casket, so she could climb in. "Mr. Lawton, I think I'd like to try it on for size."

Ben gave her a seductive look. "Think of it as shopping."

Gwen got in and moved around to make herself comfortable. Ben dutifully adjusted the satin pillow under her head and fussed with a strand of her hair. The idea was to make her hair more alive than the person it belonged to. Having achieved that goal, he announced solemnly that she looked absolutely radiant. She looked up at him with a soulful look. He reached in and closed her eyes. Soon she was talking in her sleep.

"Being alive slaughters me every second. It makes me hurt all over. It makes every feeling drift away. Perhaps I'll try being dead for a change. Only gosh-golly, I suppose I should give feeling a few more chances. I'm shopping for a feeling. I've been sitting around, hoping for one to show up. It's so sad not having any feeling. Some faraway sadness is bleeding into the here and now. I need a feeling. Check it out...There's the car accident for thirty-nine thousand ninety-five. That'll get me a lot of attention. There's the divorce for six thousand bucks... Quite a steal for that price, but that doesn't count 'cause I'm not married... How about a broken leg like Sunita's for ten thousand? Naww!!! Too much convalescence. Hippity hippity hop. Ha! When I'm dead and gone, I want to have one of those chatty baby thingamajigs in my back. Ya give it a pull and I'll say, "Hi folks! My name is Gwen. How're ya doin'? This is my party. Are ya havin' a good time?"

"Miss Hagobian, what in the world are you talkin' about?"

"I know exactly what I'm dreamin' about. I'm waking up from a very long dream."

In my own dream, I could see Gulf from below just as Gwen would see him. Gulf smiled and then closed the lid of the casket so that the screen of my dream momentarily went to complete darkness.

"Hmm... What a good view it is from here."

"Yes, what a good view."

Gulf opened up the lid of the coffin.

In the dream, the light flowed in. It was searing and stung my eyes, ruining the idyllic haze that had always been the hallmark of the rapid eye movement portion. I saw Ben as Gwen would see him.

Hen had her head on the satin pillow. She looked as if she were about to cry.

"Well, what are you waiting for big boy? The darkness does it for me, especially if it's pitch pocket. Come on in and bury me. Show me that you really care." Gulf could see the sadness in her eyes. It went on forever. He climbed into the coffin. They kissed as they embraced. I could see them from above. She was in the throes of ecstasy. She pulled the satin coverlet over their heads as if it were an electric blanket.

The dream dissolved to its next scene. I could see lovers lounging after an amorous interlude. She looked very happy. In the dream, I went "Yuck" again before adding an "Eeeyoo!" for good measure.

"That was great, Mr. Lawton. I felt totally helpless. Now take me up to Heavenly Valley so I can see the mausos."

"It's a little late. How about tomorrow at one o'clock?"

"Good, I'll see you then. And don't be late."

"Glad to be of assistance to you, Miss Hagobian."

"I love you. You're an assisting kinda guy."

I pressed the pause button on the dream, and tried to give the reverie some careful evaluation. But the dream wouldn't let me 'cause right before I had any chance of doing that, there was an extended drum solo that pushed Gwen's vocals to the side. Extended solo...hammerin' chunks of sound. It was the five and a half minute variety, not the trading eights stuff. Off to the side, Gwen looked glum. Words had become the accompaniment to sound. For them, there was no fun under the sun. At first, she thought that the shifting sand of the ground she was walkin on would give her support, but after a few seconds, she found her place, fell into grace, and was running on new legs. A roll on the open high-hat was making her best dreams come true. But it didn't last. Gulf saw to that --- while I viewed the scene remotely, I was having trouble trying to fathom the audacity of this bastard. How could he ruin such a beautiful situation? I had to know more, so I eavesdropped and picked up where I left off.

I could see everything from the point of view of the car's hood. I was looking at the two passengers Gulf and Gwen. They were smiling at each other. I could see Gwen's left hand with her engagement ring as she stroked Gulf's shoulder. They touched each other as he continued to drive. The same baroque music that had been in the funeral home continued to play in the hearse. To me, this was glaring proof that Ben was the behind-the-scenes manipulator of Gulf. I mean, Gulf, being the improvising saxophonist that he was, wouldn't have spent five minutes programing this stuff for the background music, but he had little or no control of the situation. Ben was the man in charge. He was the one who was calling the tune. Apparently, Ben loved this *drek* so much he played it everywhere. No wonder he hated my drumming! This was the kind of syrupy hogwash he wanted to play all along. His chords had too much virtue and not enough vice, so Ben had to get it in other underhanded ways. What he really needed, in my estimation, was to be hit over the head with a stack of Russian choral music. Maybe that would be the cure.

Gulf, now fully in the sway of Ben's pernicious influence, leered at her, and she smiled back enticingly. The scene seemed to build. Suddenly, the music stopped. The engine of the hearse faltered, went put-put and then died completely. Gulf and Gwen looked surprised, as if the air has been let out of their collective balloon.

"Oh no, Gulf! What's wrong?"

"Damn! It must be that carburetor. I knew I shoulda had it looked at the other day.

The car was on the edge of the road. Gwen and Gulf looked very disappointed.

"Well well well. It looks as though we'll have to go up to Heavenly Valley some other time."

"Dammit! What a disappointment, Gulf!" She shook her head.

"Yeah, what can I say? It'll have to be another time. Don't worry. I'll call AAA and we'll take the train back to New York."

I paused the dream again as my blood continued to boil, then I got back to it. I didn't want it to fly away forgetfully and capriciously the way most dreams do. "Stay right there!" I told it. By this time, a tow truck driver was getting Gulf's car ready for towing. Music played. It was some kind of indie rock band, but soft and ethereal. The car was being towed away with Gwen and Gulf in the cab with the driver. Then they were buying tickets. The train arrived, and they got on. The dream was particularly vivid and insistent on this point. I could see them cuddling on. The music continued.

"Okay, so Gulf, please call me next week. I really wanna buy one of your big beautiful mausoleums. I promise I'll buy it. I've just got to see it first."

"Mausoleums...you say it like it's some kind of linoleum. Can't we have another secret rendezvous sooner than that? I think I'm falling in love with you."

Gulf had a soulful look on his face.

"Oh Gulf, you're such a silly young boy. Don't you know it's all pretend. But I'm sorry. Going back to Heavenly Valley will have to wait for a week or so. It's Kathy. I don't want her to suspect anything. I'll be back with her soon, and this afternoon's joyride will only be a happy memory. You understand, don't you?"

"Gee, Gwen. You sound so depressed. Why is that? I thought we just now had such a good time."

"Oh, it's nothing, nothing really. In fact, everything is nothing or a place that leads to nowhere. I'm powerless. Nothing I do amounts to a hill of beans."

I just love it when a beautiful woman talks such absolute drivel as this! My eyes fluttered in the dream. My snore stumbled into apnea, and Gwen continued.

"I'm at the mercy of men, those macho people in the audience. They keep droolin' and a slobberin'. What a bunch of dogs. I'm at the mercy of women --- those sweet sisters in the audience. I'm on the stump. Can't make my mind up about what direction to go in."

Gulf looked meek and sad.

Good. I wanted him to feel that way. I groggily pulled the covers up to my chin.

"But Gwen, we can still meet someplace. I know a nice bed and breakfast."

No, no, no! You don't have the right to go off to Pennsylvania to get laid!"

"Please. Today was a one shot deal and hey, your car ran out of gas. I never got to see Heavenly Valley. Quite frankly, I'm very disappointed."

"What am I supposed to be, Gwen? Your death therapist?

"Aw hell, don't you know the real deal, Gulf? We're possums."

She made a crooked face. "You and I" she continued, "We play dead on a daily basis."

She moved her arms, pretending to be a rock and roll drummer. At that moment, she looked a little like me.

"Boom chick, Boom boom chick. We're bad possums. It's the way of the sleepy-time world, Ben."

Yes, this planet is such a groggy place. I put a pillow over my ears.

Gwen smiled seductively, stroked his cheek, and kissed him. Gulf looked ill at ease. The train pulled into Grand Central Station. They got off and waved goodbye to each other. The emo music stopped.

"Call me in a week and a half. And don't worry. I'm sure to buy a mauso. I only want to see it first. But our affair --- that's over."

She smiled, and Gulf looked sad.

And I was so glad. In the dream, I did a happy dance as I watched each of them take public transportation back to southern Jersey.

Gulf told her that he'd get his car fixed and yes, they would try again to make the trek up to Happy Valley or Heavenly Valley or whatever it was called. Gwen said she was really looking forward to it, but her face looked odd. Gulf noticed that and so did I. Hell, even yours truly, the dream watcher, could see that something was amiss. Perhaps Gwen knew something that Gulf didn't?

So, the dream fast forwarded to a week and a half later.

Ben, the Mauso Man Extraordinaire and arch manipulator of wet-behind-the-ears Robot Boy Gulf, was calling to check up on Gwen to see if he couldn't get that big sale. He wouldn't let a little thing like Gulf's broken down automobile stop him from getting the commission. He called up the number that Gwen had given him, and a strange voice answered. It was someone that he didn't know.

"Hi," he asked. "May I speak to Miss Hagobian?"

And the unknown voice answered, "I'm afraid I have some bad news to report." The voice seemed very hesitant.

Ben immediately went on high alert. "Why? What's wrong?"

"Umm…umm…you see…"

"I see what?"

"I don't know how to break this to you, but I'll do it the best way I know how."

"So, tell me! Out with it!" Ben was angry as well as alarmed.

"I'm sorry to report that Gwen's dead. She died."

"What! When? When did that happen?"

"It was very sudden. The Medical Examiner said she had a bad heart. We had no inkling of it. She may very well have kept her medical condition to herself, or she was simply unaware that she was a ticking time bomb. Kathy's very upset about the whole thing."

In the dream, I was semi-amazed at how quickly Ben got a hold of himself.

"So when is the funeral service?" he asked.

"Oh, I'm afraid that's already happened. Apparently, unknown to any of us, she had cemetery property, and she was buried yesterday. She went to her final rest out at the Garden of Peace Memorial Park. It was all very sudden, and it's thrown us completely for a loop."

"Listen to me!" Ben interrupted. "She doesn't want to be there." Ben's voice was very urgent.

"Yes, of course she doesn't want to be there. Who wants to be dead? But I guess she doesn't have much choice in the matter, unless of course, she's somehow good at self-resurrection, but most of us don't have that talent."

"Don't get flippant with me! This is not some kind of a joke!"

In the dream, I could see a close up of Ben's face.

Was he really sorry? Or was he already trying to see about how to get the dearly departed moved to where she really wanted to be, which was Happy Valley? After all, Gwen had personally told him she didn't want to putter around to the end of time in a Valhalla not of her choosing. Damn! That wouldn't be any fun. She was such an autonomous girl! It was only right that Gwen be dug up and moved there. Her expressly spoken wishes should be honored and not some signed legal contract document informing the entire world to the contrary. Wishes should be honored --- especially next-to-last wishes.

In the dream, I could see Ben hitting the end button on his smart phone.

Strange as it would seem, he didn't appear to be mourning the demise of anyone terribly dear to him. How could he? There was no one terribly dear to his heart. Then I could see him driving up to the Garden of Perpetual Peace Memorial Park in his just recently repaired Cadillac Hearse. It had extra-big fins on the back. No, there wasn't anything wrong with the engine of Gulf's limousine now. This time it purred right along. Ben was ever The Man cruisin' along in Gulf's big ass ride! He pulled into the parking lot of the Garden of Perpetual Peace and checked with the front office. They didn't find Gwen right away because she hadn't been added into the computer yet, but no matter. Soon Ben had a map and was looking for Gwen out there in the bone yard. At last, he found her. He fell down on the grave making believe that he could see straight through the turf and dirt right into Gwen's closed-forever eyes. His hands were sprawled out and his finger writhed in the dirt and grass. He pushed his face into the fine manicured turf, rubbing his nose till it started to hurt and bleed. And I was right there with him 'cause I was in this dream too. Only ... only I cried, and he didn't.

Of course the camera crew was there even in my dream. No nook or cranny was safe. When I zeed out, the camera went upside down the moment I conked. Hours later, I awoke feeling just plain awful. The bed was soaked in sweat, the residue of an absolutely dreadful dream. The flashing images were busy retreating from my eyes, and I was in desperate need of an idol 'cause I'm a man who needs lots of heroes. But now there were none to be seen. They'd flown the coop. I'd had a nightmare, but I couldn't remember much. But by the time I'd started the coffee, it was coming back, one fragment at a time. After I'd finished my orange juice and toast, the whole sequence resounded in my memory, complete in every bruising detail. One thing gradually became clear: the reason that Ben was prompting Gulf to put the moves on Gwen was to take over the whole band and ultimately to get her involved in his robotics research. And that would mean that he was probably looking to get her into some sort of sleazy liaison with Gulf. I recalled what Ben had told me about Gulf and how that robot boy who loved to play tenor saxophone was easily enamored of human females who had Mediterranean complexions. Well, Gwen definitely had a Mediterranean complexion. Would that make her fair game? Was Gulf nursing a soft spot in his heart for my beautiful lead singer? I supposed that would have made her datable. Uh Oh! I suddenly understood that Ben was scoping Gwen out so that she could become---what was his charming term for it --- 'a viable female candidate' for hooking up with that saxophone-playing creation of his? I remembered Gina, the girl in the coffin, and then also remembered how that girl hadn't worked out, and how she'd been unceremoniously disposed of since she hadn't made the cut. I was wishin' and a hopin' that Gina was havin' the time of her new life right about now. Had she learned all the tricks of the trade for this thing called life? I prayed that she'd found someone who could truly love her for what she was, only that was probably too much wishful thinking on my part. Still, I was betting that she was making decent progress.

Oh my God! Lots of things were coming together all in a great big rush. It was about this time that I decided that I would have to give Gwen a call.

SLASH AND BURN

There was a wardrobe malfunction. Gwen was waiting for that to happen. There would be so much free publicity. Nipples got exposed to the full humid air. It had nothing to do with her music, but she benefitted nonetheless. She was overjoyed.

Yeah, but I say it's a hard life with lots of slash and burn. I had an idol before. How I looked up to it! I would imitate, but not replicate. Still, something new came into the world. Those were times when I chilled out 'cause past and future were better. They knew I was very sharp and could hear things others couldn't. I was cornered into a niche of my own choosing.

There were days when Kathy and I had to gloat over creations because we'd really outdone ourselves. Despite this, the bleak cycle started when second thoughts appeared. She and I had a foolproof plan, a bright union of form and function, only we'd gotten surprised because the fruits of our labors bore small resemblance to what was there at the flashpoint. Categories had gotten hopelessly smudged, and our experiments created havoc. Consequently, we fell into despair as we saw the gargantuan proportions of the project. And yes, Gwen was indeed a project even if her voice was an astringency that broke on through to a new dimension.

I was getting the feeling that she was about to go out on the twig of a limb. Kath had told me so. To find a way out, I contemplated past glories, which was when the entropy began in earnest.

I knew Cro-Magnons were extremely thin-skinned. Gwen would be certain to find deluded abrasions everywhere --- on her elbows, eyebrows, and even on tips of earlobes. To make it quick, in everything that crosses their crinkly brains, Cro-Mags are less tolerant than they make themselves out to be. Buyer beware! They're false advertising. Better give 'em a wide angle 'cause their skulls are the last refuge of penny ante minds that do everything 100% rarely. They'll make an exotic disguise and whack you in the knees --- lure you in to deliver the sucker punch. My hands struggled with this delightful *coup de grace*. They wrestled slippery-palmed trying to grasp the exotic throwaways in the music. Oyster, oh oyster, oh sweet and sour baby. Nine forces of bludgeons were doubly blessed. She had snacking in their purses. There was chocolate and peanuts and bananas, and she got to pick out the cheese part. Tell me, were they gonna throw it away? Gwen was squawkin' about this and readin' me the riot act about how overstuffed powder-puffed pastries loved the strawberry topping. So I got it --- she was a bartender who would never give me a buy-back. Despite this, the chord shoved her along, slurping her whiplash into loveliness. The long-legged lady had stupendous feet; maraschino toes on her middle fingers kept reaching forward into infinity. Kathy the Wonder Lady is drawing it to her mouth, Gwen. Open wide. It's red and frothy. Gwen, it would be so nice to include you in this fun. Can you cope? On tour, there could be fun in Portland, San Antone, Boise, and Duluth. That's what we got scheduled for the road this month. But I dunno. That's probably too much fun to fathom. Someone might hafta cut it off at the knees. Ben seems to have a baseball bat in his grip that's getting ready to do just that. If it happens, remember the good times that never were.

In my dream, I felt the need to make an intervention. I needed to wake the girl the fuck up. Only trouble was, she wouldn't budge from her own reverie, let alone the one that I was in. Sometimes I dream I'm drummin' and singin' at the same time. What a concept! Melody, harmony, timbre, and rhythm in equal measure! Yeah, I know I'm really dreamin' and drummin' for you, and it's you who really gets to sing, but what if it were the other way around? Would that be scary for you, Gwen? I think it might. But I know, you think I'm your slave, your hired help. And the help is very drunk. You're the star, and I'm the back up. What would it be if roles were reversed? Would you be a happy camper? I'm not convinced. Show me if it's right. I think you might have a shiver and a fright. But wait a minute. Gwen, you and I have cascaded into the same intermingling. Don't gimme that we-don't-take-ourselves-very-seriously bollocks. Speak for yourself, girl. Kathy and I know you'll never get to sing the "National Anthem" in a sports stadium of any consequence 'cause you know and I know that the tempo struggles to keep up with the darkness of your heart. Remember, dear lady, I'm watchin' from a web-enabled device. Gwen, is that you out there? It's Joe. I'm over here. Yo Gwen, I go to the bar every night that you give me off? And I sing karaoke till I'm drunk in the face. Every pivot of the lyric takes you on a new highway.

"Hi Gwen, is that you?" I repeated.

"I'm right here. What's up?"

"Oh, I just had the most horrible dream."

"What kind of a horrible dream?"

"Umm... umm...it doesn't really matter." Knowing she'd have no reason to doubt me, I decided to play fast and loose with the truth. "I dreamed that the band broke up and that we all died in an earthquake."

"Oh that's terrible. Why you poor thing!"

"So the band's not going to be breaking up anytime soon. Is it?"

"God no! Perish the thought. There's far too much money to be made. At this point, *Babies in Bars* is a *de facto* cash register."

"But that wouldn't stop someone from still wanting it to happen? Killin' it, I mean?"

"They wouldn't have any power," she replied. "I've got the power 'cause I'm a girl, and I'm strictly a *lead* singer. I don't do rhythm singing. I thought you of all people would know that. Ponder this, Joe. If everything goes the way I'm planning it, you could soon be the highest paid drummer on the planet. Think about every drummer who's ever wailed and whacked sticks to cowhide. Think about 'em, even the ones that were hootin' and hollerin' around some cave men's blazing campfire. You'll be the apotheosis of all drummers

--- top of the bops. That would be a greater honor than winnin' some ridiculous drum solo contest. You might even get to keep your hands in the bargain. What a deal! Don't you think?"

I told her that was wonderful news, and she said I shouldn't pay too much attention to dreams 'cause they'll lead you down rabbit holes. And then she told me some bullshit about how when you die in a dream, it might be a good thing because that means you're on the verge of something new, and then she told me about how she just last night had a dream in which she actually died, and wasn't that strange and didn't that mean something really cosmic and then she said some more bullshit about how reality is governed by cosmic law of the universe, and right about then I so wanted to slap her silly, but I couldn't because we were on the phone, and then I said goodbye and flipped my smart phone shut. I wondered what it would take to convince her that she and I had a gift --- together we were fully capable of putting something powerful into the brains of people who heard us play. Then we could send them on their way and maybe get to watch the world change. That wasn't such a bad thing, was it? But somehow I didn't hear her answer.

I talked to a tree that was there in the park where I was walking. "Gwen, when the tempo gets funkier, you can move more syllables in. We're playin' for the dancers. No doubt you think your cute smile will work. It's worked out fine for the last twenty-five years. Hey, I'm a drummer and a Neanderthal too. I know a raft is sinking beneath the surf. I know when to bail. Maybe the time hasn't come, but I'm alert. You can't fool me. Baby, it's strictly business. Sober up. None of that music as high school art appreciation bullshit. I'm still an intern. Show me a payday. Anything else would be setting myself up to be kicked in teeth." Then I kicked the tree 'cause I was pissed at myself for talkin' to the tree instead of her.

As I got to thinkin' more about Gwen and Kathy's relationship, I fully understood that the success of the band had everything to do with the success of their continued love. What was great about their coupling was that it was dramatically opposed to everything about me --- love for love's sake was their keynote. Two people could embrace and not have some ulterior agenda. Why? Because they had so much in common. That was truly spectacular. I confess there were times when that stuff appealed to me --- for about fifteen minutes. Still, those were fairly significant minutes. It was noteworthy that the rules could be changed. Perhaps that was why I rooted for their romantic success: it represented something that I would never be capable of myself. For that reason, and that one alone, Ben's transgressions were all the more threatening. Then I kicked the tree again.

Later that night the strangest thing happened.

Surveying the sky there up above the tree line, I could glimpse that pulsating light again, a high beam jetty, statuesque, and hovering over the land. One second it looked like a metallic orb, but impatiently it would never stay that way for long. Something about it didn't want to be pinned down 'cause in the next second it would section off into segments like a wobbly blood orange, and then it would flex asymmetrically --- a muscle in mid-spasm. Just when my eye got used to that, it would melt into five balloons of painful light and then back again to something dull and opaque, as if it wanted to let me in on some special secret. Clearly, the thing, whatever it was, wanted desperately to hedge its bets, afraid that anyone observing it would too hastily form an opinion, and also it wanted to show me that it was performing all these gyrations and contortions simply because it was supremely capable of doing them. This showboat aspect struck a familiar chord with me: if you have the technique, then why in the hell don't you use it? Anyway, that's how I feel about it. Why should it be demure? Answer: no way in hell. There would be none of this cute business of holding back. I yelled at the orb, demanding angrily that it give me an even better show. It responded with another impressive display of smoke and mirrors.

"OK, you guys," I bellowed at the top of my lungs, "I'm sick of you following me around! Put up or shut up. What's your effin' problem? You're a bunch of stalkers. How's it feel to be in the same boat as dirty old men on late night buses?"

But the thing was incapable of responding to that kind of embarrassment. Just then, the hovering craft made an impossible three hundred-sixty degree smart-ass turn and came to a soundless halt before smacking me with a searing beam of white light. I tumbled clumsily. The next thing I knew I could hear voices casually chatting over me. I looked up and could see two ethereal babes, both with big ones and obviously from another planet. One had a model's body and her clothes hung on her in the classic manner favored by couturiers everywhere, and the other had a more zaftig look, which of course held more interest for me. It was good to know that outer space could be bountiful too.

"Ziga, I hope you're satisfied with coming to this chump-change, B-list planet."

"Zaga, you know I like to come here every now and then to get my fix for intrigue. My nose tells me bad things may be just around the corner."

"You'll be sneezin' your head off any second now," replied Zaga.

Their voices had an echoey vibe on them not so different from an old-fashioned phase shifter or wah wah pedal. I found it odd that the words of unearthly creatures had the sound and timbre of archaic rock and roll sound effects. Gathering my senses, I felt the need to challenge these goddesses. "Why…why…" I stuttered. "You two are nothing more than common voyeurs getting your kicks off watching the byzantine plots of others."

And the grey entity who stood over me answered: "Joe, you don't understand. Ziga comes from a land where there is no longer any sin."

And her *comadre* answered: "They've forgotten how. Life has become too smooth."

"Smoooooth…" She gestured horizontally with her three-fingered hand before pointing to her friend. Then she continued. "When she comes here, she feels as if she's in a musty old museum gradually remembering how it's done."

Gaining more courage, I said: "No sin you say? Impossible!"

"No sin. Only cynicism."

"The problem with life on Mizar Twelve is that folks are so damned agreeable."

"Thought and feeling have converged, and it's not a pretty picture. Every ounce of fun is forced. Mizarians never fight about anything. Their brains are too evolved. Might as well be hothouse flowers."

She pointed to me. "In your Middle Ages was a plague bubonic. Now there's one to make a love platonic. Zaga and I had to get out for our own sanity."

"We were like two escaped nuns, only instead of rediscovering the pleasures of the flesh, we were teaching ourselves how to argue."

"The average Mizarian conversation is so blastedly preciously polite. Jolly genteel boys and girls who think life is an exacting science."

"All they have to say to each other is one apology after another 'cause words are too abrasive for them."

"Or they just want to talk about food as they twiddle their vestigial thumbs. They have no story."

"Their words are spoken and measured with an ever vigilant eye and ear for avoiding any conflict. I swear it wasn't survival of the fittest, but rather, survival of the likeable."

Ziga looked up from her argument and turned towards me. "By contrast, you humans wear all your obnoxiousness right there on your grubby sleeves for all to see. And you're not the least shy about parting your opponent's skull with a battle axe. You're all appalling all the time."

"Yeah, but what a shame to piss away perfectly fine standard issue protons and neutrons. You might as well be throwing them into ... into ... a fire. Science or alchemy will be the only hope for these humans. Exhibit A is the lovely and talented Gwen. Her confused, deluded, and ambivalent behavior could be straightened out if and only if, someone took the time to zap the right synapse in her primitive nerve center. That would set off a churning waterfall of endorphins. Ah baby, let the good bliss flow. I tell you if science could do this, she'd never want to burn herself up again. She'd feel sooooo good."

"As usual, you've mistaken chemicals for emotions. It's never that simple, Zaga. There are far too many variables."

"So, don't be lazy. Do the math you lazy bones! Make an effort to collect each shred of empirical data and reduce it to absurdity if necessary. Pay attention to the laws of Nature, Ziga. It's what got us into the hall of fame!"

"There are no laws of anything, Zaga ... only fashions. Gwen's desire for self-destruction may seem contrary to human nature, but it's not. Her imagination is right out there on the edge seeking a new fashion. She'll either find it or destroy herself in the process. Why don't you admit it, Zaga? You detest mysteries! Go play with your amoebas. Gwen's too squiggly for your blood."

"Just gimme the facts. That's all I care about. Once you have the facts, everything will explain itself. A fact is beauty in crystalline form ... a diamond in the rough."

"Ladies!" I yelled, "Can't you see? Her soul is disconnected from her body. Music, not alchemy, is her only hope for survival. Her inventions will not bear fruit if she pursues her current course."

"Exactly. The true fashions of Nature can go the distance. They've got legs. And they like to vote with their feet." Zaga jumped up into the air and clicked her heels. "Take my personal favorite, Gravity. A popular and perennial success story. There's something timeless and tireless about it. It's dogged loyalty always seems to pull through, keeping everything in proper perspective. But make no mistake, it's still just a very old fashion."

"Oh I get it," continued Ziga. "The animals change but the plants don't. They don't because they're too smart for that dirty business. It's beneath them. Yup, we Mizarians have segued already --- got it out of our systems like grumbly indigestion. You know, this realm is remarkably mechanical." She picked up a stone, tossed it up, and then caught it. "Even the rocks are stubborn about drama." She flipped the stone underhand to Zaga who caught it on the fly. They quickly tossed the stone back and forth before stopping abruptly.

"They're bashful to evolve because they wanna see what's in it for them. Those nuggets patiently wait it out for the right moment, the one saturated with fantastic opportunities and maximum potential.

Ziga closed her deep grey eyes and went into some kind of incantation: "The silver nuggets for potential penetrate the sparks of our longing and then test for the hardness of fixtures. Like two sheep on a crowded ark, they ask, 'What rank breath blows frames around these ragged pictures?'"

I was starting to get annoyed at these green/grey creatures, so I had to get a word in edgewise. "Hold on there, Ziga and Zaga," I interjected. "You languish about in a citadel of cynicism and then suddenly jump around like a couple of kangaroos. Your crazy ideas have got me seeing double. I think you're trying to learn the fine art of acting out; however, you would rather let humans do it for you, so you'll get none to the blame as you zippy little devils buzz around the countryside in your gleaming flying saucers, galivantin' over hill and dale, spookin' the bejeezus outta everyone. You're no better than the common sadists who lurk around this planet. Clearly, you've got your chops together. Why don't you step up to the plate and offer a helping hand?"

Ziga's pointed brow started to furrow. "We can't 'cause we don't wanna mess with your history. Tip over the history thing, and you'll have a real mess on your hands."

"You may have noticed that we have some problems with politics here on this oasis that you've stumbled onto."

They both burst out into some big belly laughs, but then got control of themselves.

"Your politics is beyond the pale of absurdity. That's one of the reasons for our coming here. You're fun to laugh at."

"One of the politicians is my brother-in-law. He's running for a big political office. One you've never heard about."

"We know all about it. In fact, there isn't much we don't know. But we still like to play dumb."

"From what we can see, it looks pretty fucked up," Ziga added. "You seem to knock yourselves out trying to go in the opposite direction of common sense."

"Yes, that's my sister, for sure. Meghan and Allen are campaigning so he can run for the U.S. Senate. He's a typical cynical right wing candidate, kind of a Tea Party nut, but with lots of PAC money and he's gotten still more in his war chest because my sister Meghan has been tapping the till on my Mom's money which is intended for Mom's upkeep at the nursing home. On top of that she also helps rob banks just to supplement her income. It's a hobby of hers. As if that were not enough, on the side, Allen and Meghan run a pistol licensing company which basically helps people who want to get guns. They help by doing the paperwork that needs to be submitted to the police. It's a very shady business, and even the cops are not too happy about it. My scary good friend Bill is a kind of reporter for me. He goes out and eavesdrops on Meghan and Allen and then he reports back to me, and ..."

And the aliens had the nerve to interrupt me. "Look Joe, you don't have to tell us the whole song and dance. We're aliens, we know this stuff already."

"Then why in the hell did you let me go on and on?"

"Because it's sort of like a good song. It's like Led Zeppelin. We never get bored with those raunchy guitar solos. We wanna hear 'em again and again. And also, your new and what you do is something that would never have crossed our Mizarian minds."

The one named Zaga said: "Look, let's give you a proposal. We understand you're havin' some issues with your sister."

"Yeah tell me about it," I said.

"So, here's the deal. We'll let you in on what they have to say. Think of it as a kind of wiretap. We figure it's the least we can do for your being a drummer --- a drummer, by the way, who isn't getting paid! Shame on that bitch!"

"You can have a bird's eye view. You let us watch you, and we'll let you watch her. Is that a deal?"

"Of course it is. But can I ask for something else?"

"Ask us, and we will probably grant it."

"My drug connection's been messin' up."

"That's real irresponsible of him."

"That's irresponsible of her! We can fix that too. We give you all the smack you'll ever need."

And the ethereal one chimed in: "So is that a deal?"

Yes, of course it was. The aliens were on the march. Even a semi-smart hominid plasma person like me could figure that one out. Those strange beings didn't lay a very fertile egg here that would burst open into a thousand different species simply to make a beautiful television show. To give it to you straight, their flying saucers made everything alright. Theirs was the ultimate must-see TV. Time was making a statement: please figure shit out. But the aliens couldn't put that genie in the bottle. Only people on the planet, and not interested bystanders, could wrestle with that one. In the meantime, saucers could fly around and make you dizzy. Perhaps they were right. What those over-sophisticated creatures needed was a Neanderthal, someone who can bring them down to earth.

I was down to earth. I was as down to the earth as the earth could be. It was a slow afternoon. Gulf and I were the only customers. He told me he wanted to tag along 'cause he wanted to watch how humans were supposed to behave. He said he wanted to get some pointers, and he thought he might learn a thing or two by watching. He promised that he wouldn't say much. The bartendress gave him the remote, and he turned on the plasma high def. In less than a minute, Gulf's eyes were riveted to the screen, and quite frankly, I soon lost track that he was even there except for when I glanced at the screen myself. There was another segment hosted by former football stars who hadn't missed many meals lately. They wore tight broad-checkered suits with high button lapels and bantered beautifully. The subject was the problem of teaching safer tackling. What! You gotta be kidding, I thought. The real deal is how to rip his head off. I changed the station. This one had on Premier League soccer. Two opposing players were racing towards the ball, and they arrived at it simultaneously, so one of them pretended to trip and fall. But that wasn't enough. He had to make believe he was in the throes of serious pain just so he could pull the wool over the ref's eyes and be awarded a penalty kick. As luck would have it, he succeeded, which triggered a wave of indignant protests from the partisan crowd. I told the bartendress that the average drag queen was far manlier than these so-called macho guys, and she said she happened to agree with me. That was the icebreaker.

The bartendress and I were the only ones talking in the place. Gulf was silent and studying the suds of his beer. I was hoping he wouldn't get too engrossed in the sports 'cause I wanted him to pick up some social skills on how to be a human being. Maybe if he saw how I interacted with a human female, he could get a feel for how it's done. That way maybe he wouldn't be quite so enamored of Gwen. More and more, my short range goal was to get him the hell away from Gwen. If I could get him to stop pining for Gwen, then the band could stay on an even keel no matter what nasty schemes that Ben was up to.

The bartendress poured me a big cold one, some kind of IPA, or maybe it was Irish ale. She had the cleavage showin' and the towel coming out of the back pocket on her butt. Very impressive. That might make a boyfriend jealous. It got me to thinkin', "Tough luck fella. Get used to it. She's a bartendress lady. She needs to make her money." When she wasn't putterin' around slicing tart and sour fruit, lighting candles, or doing inventories of top shelf bourbon, she was looking at her laptop and playing some tunes. I wondered if she could get any song that had ever been sung on that crazy thing of hers. Could she get radio stations in Perth or Abu Dhabi? Yes, that could be arranged. I asked her about her song selection. Who were these guys or girls? What was the name of this song? What was the name of this band? I told her they sounded pretty good and showed her a fair amount of curiosity. That made her smile, and she told me the song she was playing right at that instant was some band that she'd been friendly with back in Colorado before she'd moved to New York to become a bartendress. And before you knew it, we had what you might call a bit of rapport. It felt so good to have that. I mean, really, she was telling me about what a barrel of laughs her cat was, how she'd found him in the California desert and how the little devil had hidden in the bathroom wall just the other day and how she had ruined a butcher knife cutting through the sheet rock when she hacked a hole to drag him out of the wall. The tiny beast had purred a blue streak. I nearly thought that I might have some kind of outside chance with her. And then she told me that being a bartendress wasn't really her idea of fun as far as a long term career was concerned, even if that was why she's supposedly moved to New York. Her real career was to become a pop star. It would be her dream come true. I said, "That's great. Can I hear your stuff?" and it didn't take much convincing 'cause in a second or two she was playing 'em for me and givin' me a toothy grin. The tunes seemed OK, but maybe a little excessive on the production. The bassoon and string quartet were a bit over the top for me, to say nothing of the tubular bells on one of the verses, but hey what do I know? So then she asked what I did for a living, and I told her that I was a drummer in a rock band that was on reality TV, and she was mildly impressed by that, but not much, 'cause remember, she was a bartendress, and she couldn't be impressed by too much. So she told me she hadn't heard of this particular reality show quite yet, and I told her 'Don't worry you will,' and then she said, "Keep up the dreamin' and the drummin" and so I laughed. Then she gulped on a beer, making the foam froth around her upper lip, and she pressed some more buttons on her laptop before asking me if she could hear some of my stuff, you know, the latest bunch of tunes that *Babies and Bars* had recorded. And I said that could be arranged, so I gave her the website and she pressed a few more buttons and before you knew it, there were my songs, emanating right there from the speakers high up over the bar, right next to a carved gargoyle that was comin' batty eyed straight out of the wall. I stared at the wooden creature for the longest time and decided it was singing along to my tunes. And gargoyle sang away for a bit longer until suddenly, this guy comes by on the sidewalk. I could see him pulling on a leash with a rambunctious Jack Russell on the other end of it. Funny thing --- he didn't order a drink or anything for that matter. Instead, he asked, "Who is that band and what is that song?" And the bartendress lady interrupted him and asked him if he wanted a drink, and he said, "No, I don't wanna drink. I only wanna know who that band is. They're fantastic!" And just then the bartendress' face got kinda ashen and she looked rather crestfallen and jealous even. The Jack Russell did a fish tail dance and a loop-dee-loo with the leash. Obviously, the canine was digging this too. So, I told the guy that that was me and my band playing, and then his praise got even more effusive, and he wouldn't shut up, and the bartendress got even more bummed out and then the guy left after I told him the name of the song. The last I saw of him he was briskly walking down the block with the excitable terrier in tow. He kept repeating the name of the song over and over, and he had a bit of a skip in his step. The Jack Russell had a skip in his step too. Then I tried to talk to the bartendress lady again, only this time she was giving me the old silent treatment. So then, about a minute later, two guys come in and order a round of Old Grand Dads straight up, and then they decide to light up some cigarettes. Naturally, me being a musician and all, I'm pretty used to inhaling enormous clouds of smoke in public places. I mean, I figure it's part of the job --- an occupational hazard that can't be helped. I'm darned liberal on these things even if the law of the land tells us that lighting up is illegal there. And far be it for me, a humble drummer, to tell people what the law of the land is. But this one time --- just this one time --- I thought I would go up and ask 'em real nice-like if they couldn't light up somewhere else. So I did exactly that – real polite-like. I even went so far as to make sure that I said the words very softly. With the greatest of care, I elevated my words, so they were one notch above a whisper. That way no one could ever accuse me of raisin' my voice. I didn't think it would be too much to ask. Well, the two gentlemen got all huffy and just then the bummed out bartendress intervened and said, "You raised your voice to these fine customers! How dare you! You're drunk and you're outta here," and I got rather surprised 'cause I wasn't the least bit hammered. Hell, I'd only had a haffy. And then she said, "Those aren't real cigarettes! They're electronic cigarettes!" And bein' careful again not to raise my voice, I said, "How would I know that?" and she said, "You're outta here right now!" And so, seeing I wasn't wanted, I left. Gulf, who had seemingly been taking notes all through this scene left with me.

That was probably one of the last times that our music wasn't put in the service of selling something. That was what the bartendress was bummed about, only this moment didn't last long 'cause no sooner had I left that particular establishment than I ran into the man who had liked *Babies in Bars* music so much. Apparently, he'd decided to double back. There he was with his dog who was as frisky as ever. He reached out and gave me his card. "Hey man," he began.

"Lemme give ya my business card. I'm an ad exec and I wanna make a beer commercial. And I think you guys would be perfect for it."

And then he walked away with his canine in tow. And that was how *Bubies in Bars* managed to get a contract with the Thyoneus Beer Corporation. I turned to Gulf who had been quiet as a church mouse all this time. "How're ya doin,' Gulf? Are you catchin' every bit of this? I'll bet things are going' great between you and your creator Ben."

"Actually, not so much."

"Are you discovering for the very first time that other people are reapin' the benefits of your life?" Gulf looked glum. I continued with my lecture. "So, OK. Get used to it. This is the way things work. If you can't deal with it, then maybe you should go back to being a rudimentary megabyte. Would that satisfy you?" He looked glum again, but didn't answer. I could tell from the look on his face that that scenario would spell trouble for him. His whole fake existence would have been all for naught. I could have rubbed it in, but I didn't think that would be fair to him. He looked so dejected. I continued. "Somehow I don't think that it would, but I'm only makin' a wild guess."

What was odd about my friendship with Gulf was that despite the fact that he was an obvious competitor of mine, I still found him to be likeable. He was so much more likeable than his creator. And whatever agenda he had---and he sure as hell had an agenda against me---it was an agenda not of his own choosing. That was something that had been manufactured by Ben and downloaded into Gulf's gigabytes and cortex.

But I digress. If others can't control the narrative, I can. Bill and I had been doin' some serious drug-takin'. He'd introduced me to something I'd never sampled before. It was called Ibogaine. Apparently, it was something that men in West Africa like to give to their sons in their version of the coming-of-age ceremony. So, I guess it's like your very own bar mitzvah, only quite a bit more intense. It's their way of showing the kids how to become real men. Well, Bill and I were in dire need of a coming-of-age ceremony too. Hey, we were real men too! Bill explained that this little mind-bending item was derived from some hard-to-find tree root on the Dark Continent. It didn't take long for the tree root to kick in. In no time at all, the visions were comin' at me and flyin' at breakneck speed. They did this for about three hours until things began to calm down a bit, at which point, I became obsessed with the cymbals that were alternately growing and then shrinking around my drum kit. They were movin' and groovin', and I was appreciating the concentric circles on their surfaces, wondering how it was that the sound got released from out of the circles. It was at this point that I decided to tell Bill about my strange dream from the previous night --- the one about how Gwen went and tried out a casket at Ben's spooky place of business. Bill said that was weird, but not as weird as what the cymbals were doing at that very moment.

In the realm of musical instruments, cymbals are pretty serious characters. Roadies like Bill are sharply aware of this since they get to lug them around. So, when I told Bill about my dream, he went into his best defense-is-a-good-offense mode. I'm not sure but I think this might have been the first time that a slave ever had his own personal gofer. That was great. I didn't have to lift a finger. I could use each and every one of my digits for the drums and set the attack dog loose. Bill, my loyal attack dog, would come in handy when Ben showed up. And he showed up sooner than expected. There we were, the three of us, staring at each other in the rehearsal studio. I got to watch the big dust up. Man, but did he ever put the fear of God into that silly boy. The hallucinogenic properties of African tree roots definitely added to the gravity of the scene that was to take place.

"Well, I'll be darned if it isn't the man and his cymbals again," Ben exclaimed. "I was just now thinking of you. Joe, have you ever thought of wearing something a bit more fashionable when you're on stage? I think you could be quite the fashion plate. Don't ya think?"

"A fashion plate?" I asked. "God, no. Jillian and I have been over this before. It wouldn't be good for the fabric. I'm a drummer. I sweat too much 'cause I live in the boiler room."

"So, big Joe, you knuckle head. Let it all hang out."

"Ben, I wanted to tell you that I started writing a song about you."

"Sing it to me now!"

"OK, it starts like this:

The kingly men's ignorant diviners
Pour cauldrons of hexes as big as whales
To be slurped by innocent diners
Praise these wizards of auguring entrail
Grinnin' and winkin' see them go dawdlin'
Braced by the red gusts of slinking fashion
Cuttlefish ministers of the maudlin
Milky frothed dogmas at war with passion

Ben gave me perfunctory applause. The cymbals, waving at me in the corner gave their applause too, and Ben continued, "So I guess it's about all of us in the band?"

"Absolutely for sure."

Bill chimed in, "Joe tells me that he had a scary dream about you last night. And you were in it."

"Good for you, Bill. Hey, when it comes to dreams, it's all between a man and his cymbals. I've let that be my guide since day one."

"But truth be told," I replied, "Your major project is to destroy everything."

"Darn, where do you get these weird ideas?" he countered.

"Where else but in my dreams?"

"You can't trust those."

"Oh I wouldn't be so sure. Some people trust 'em so much that they like to screw 'em up, especially if they belong to others."

I gave him a stink eye. "I have a dream, Ben. It's that *Babies in Bars* becomes bigger than anything else like it. Do you have a problem with that?"

"I haven't a problem. But we value different things. Jillian's told me I need to concentrate on my rock star moves. She says I gotta amp it up or risk getting canned."

"That's a huge problem," Bill observed. "Because you can't do two things at once."

"Right you are. Can't risk the old pink slip. That's why I'm gonna farm out the whole deal. It's too troublesome to do alone."

"Too much coordination could be hazardous to your health, big Ben."

"Right you are! Why should I get bogged down in the boring habit of actually playin' real notes in real time? No way in God's green earth do I wanna waste any effort doing that. So I'm gonna outsource it. The new robot I'm workin' on will be a supplement to Ben. I'm gonna call him Gus, and Gus is goin' to play bass for me. I've got it all planned. Gus is goin' to be the real bass player. He'll stand in the wings and play while I do the pretend thing at center stage. How's that one grab ya?"

"Jesus, that's absolutely atrocious. Nobody else puts much stock in the things that I think are important, which makes it hard for me to find a payday. But then it's fun to watch them clap their hands until their palms hurt, even though most of 'em have gotten in for free. By the way, Ben, I think you're messin' with Kathy's girl, which means you're also screwin' up this band. I have a problem with that."

"Well, tough luck, big drummin' fella. That's none of your business. Major collisions are being mapped out as we speak."

"What's great about Kathy is she can give me some yellow and red, scrawny mongrel chord to react to. She's the old bluesman who's been on the road forever with so many lurid stories to tell."

"Nothing balsa wood about her," observed Bill. "Strictly teak or mahogany. Roxy, the bright red guitar, won't stand for anything less."

"She's not like some of those college kids who trot out their triply augmented contortions and ostentations for all to hear. Not that that's uncool or anything, but you can't get bogged down in the mess 'cause it'll suffocate you. She and I can solo at the same time and never step on each other."

"And Gwen, unlike most vocalists, is content to take a back seat on occasion. What a miracle. Kathy keeps her in check."

"Also, Jillian, who is so big on taking every contrary path against conventional TV wisdom, completely susses this out and makes it totally prime time."

"Yeah, she's an antidote for the raft of hyper-civilized shows that seemed to infect the airways."

Ben looked disconsolate. "And that's our attraction to the masses I suppose?"

Bill reached over behind the drum kit and picked up a beat to crap medium thin crash that I had retired the week before. Wielding it like a Frisbee, he gave a few head fakes and chased Ben around the studio.

Ben retreated with his usual sicko giggle. "Ha! No, you wouldn't dare."

"God, don't you love to test people out. You'd never do that if you knew what my part time gig really is." Then Bill dropped the medium thin and picked up something heavier gauge --- a twenty-two inch ride. If you make a direct hit with that one, it could kinda sorta slice you in half and leave your legs still running the hundred yard dash. And to top it off, the scary looking thing had a rusty edge because for the last four months it had been propped up in the corner next to a dripping pipe.

"You know, Ben. There's nothing quite like a whizzing cymbal to put the fear of God into a man." That made me think of the two aliens I'd just met. Their high tech craft sure looked something like a whizzing cymbal, so thinking of what to say in order to scare Ben some more, I said, "Why don't you do something more constructive like opening up a meth lab? I'll even arrange for catering the snacks for the opening day party."

At this point, Ben began to appreciate the desperate reality and ratcheted up the pace, running terrified around the room, all the while looking for an escape route, which I was only too glad to block off. However, that didn't stop Bill. When he let the metallic discus fly, he sped up too, taking on the appearance of an ancient athlete wanting to get in the very last lick. The smashed up cymbal was spectacular. There it went --- knifing through the air with changing angles, its trajectory harkening back to the dreaded red ball in a frantic game of Q-Bert. The sharp and spinning amalgam of zinc, lead, brass and chrome churned forth, stinging the air and taking out huge chunks from the cinder block in the walls of the practice space. Bill followed it with another barrage of whizzing cymbals, each of them gouging out even more chunks of cinder block, so that in the end, the whole room would eventually look as if an unseen monster had taken bites out of the walls.

Despite being rather drunk from an afternoon of drinking and drug-taking with Bill, my mind was moving surprisingly fast, so fast it could figure out that in fact the opposite was true because in a matter of seconds, I could see that the wall itself had melted into a gaggle of monsters, each with a gaping mouth open in the throes of laughter, and this collection of monsters was letting me know that Ben's function was to make people as unhappy as possible, which in the long run would be a good thing since this sad sad situation would let *Babies in Bars* and their entire staff know that they can't have even one scrap of joy unless they've had unhappiness first, so in the long run, wasn't that thought an obvious vote for happiness to triumph? The wall was doing me and Bill a huge service because, except for the thin trail of cement dust that trickled onto the floor in a light stream, the gaping bites in its surface didn't move. By opting not to grin, the gaping bites were erring on the side of neutrality, so I could figure the whole problem out all by myself. How considerate of them. And how considerate of Bill to give me the ibogaine which had made so many of these insights possible.

The only thing was, Ben didn't have time to be quite so philosophical on this subject because, what with Bill chuckin' those smashed up cymbals at him over and over again, Ben clearly had his hands full. "STOP IT!! STOP IT!!" He screamed. "FOR GOD'S SAKE, STOP IT NOW!!"

I looked over at Ben's pants, and saw that he'd pissed himself. There it was --- flooding steadily into the cement dust like an advancing army.

"Awh, Ben! I can't believe what I'm seeing. It's amateur hour! I think you just can't handle your alcohol. That's what I think."

After those hijinks, much to the chagrin of Jillian, Ben and I implicitly put aside any remaining pretences we may have had about friendship. If Jillian had been around to witness his antics, I would have told her that there are a lot of sadists out there in the realm, but there are not a lot of masochists out there to return the compliment. I wasn't one of them.

But I had to get back to Ziga and Zaga, the outer space girls. I think I told you that I was especially attracted to Zaga. I liked to think of her as Zaga the Zaftig, and when I told her this, she giggled girlishly and appreciated the endearment. I told both of them that if they were going to be stayin' around, they might have to adopt some sort of disguise because it would raise suspicions if they appeared too unearthly. What gave me particular concern was the fact that they had odd colored eyes --- Ziga's were metallic grey, and Zaga's alternately oscillated between lookin' like a pair of blueberries and a dazzled duet of red corpuscles. As if that were not enough, the digits on their hands numbered four instead of the more traditional five. When I expressed my misgivings about the sake of appearances, they laughed it off and told me that there was no need for disguise. In fact, they explained, they could morph into just about anything at will. To drive this point home to me, Zaga stared me straight in the eye and suddenly changed into a pink cuttlefish, and from there she melted into a Portuguese-Man-Of-War, before shooting back into the hot little Zaga whom I'd come to know and love. Then Ziga zapped into a startled amoeba, then a purple striped zebra, and then back again. I was so impressed that I bowed down to both of them.

"Ladies, you corralled me from the get-go, but that one has me forever and ever."

"Till the end of time?" they echoed in unison.

"Yes, especially to the end of time," I replied. I got the feeling that they liked all of this attention that they were getting. And since I was already down there on my hands and knees, from you know, bowin' down, I figured I might as well get a good look at their feet, because if you haven't guessed it by now, I am the Consummate Foot Man.

And I think they must have read my mind because just then both of them said in those phase-shifter, unison voices of theirs: "Joe, we think you'll like what you see."

What in the world were they talkin' about? Their feet looked spectacularly female to me. But I gave them a closer look and did a double take because right there before my very eyes were four of the cutest female feet I'd ever had the pleasure to ogle, but there was something different. What was it? Suddenly, there it was, or should

I say, there they were --- each of the ladies with the gorgeous curves was the possessor of feet that had *extra toes*. They had six. Right away, before I could think of anything else, the normal human female foot seemed to fade away in terms of its ability to stir my emotion. I mean, think about it. How ya gonna keep 'em down on the farm?

"And we can change that too, Joe," they replied, again with the steely shimmering voice effect.

"No, don't change that! Please keep that the same!" I said with an air of pleasant desperation.

"Well, okay," they replied coyly. "We suppose we could make an exception. But only for you and for nobody else.

"Yes, only for me. I'm a Neanderthal and I'm the only one on this planet who deserves those precious little feet."

"We'll do it for you, Joe. But we'll do it only 'cause we know in our hearts that you're the only one who would appreciate it." Then they both turned away and got back in their whizzing cymbal saucer, saying that they would be back momentarily.

FIELD TRIP TO THE HUMAN FEMALE COMMUNITY

I got back together to jam with Gulf. After a round of music making, we got to talking. Gulf was seeing the falsity of Ben's project. He told me, "Joe, I'm tryin' so hard to break out of it, but something's holding me back. I want to have an authentic experience."

"You can't because you're a robot half-breed, and your feelings are all make-believe."

"Will you stop that! Can't you remember that the patterns of my feelings follow the colors of cuttlefish? I mean, if I wanted to, I could razz you about being a Neanderthal. Can't you see we're both in this together. Both of us are subhuman, so just get over it, and get over it now!"

"None of what you think or feel is the real deal. Every shred of it is a vast simulation."

"Maybe so, but my simulation will soon be someone's stimulation."

Gulf told me he was studying hard and trying to develop mental habits. After all, the cuttlefish in the tank could only take him so far. He was strengthening his resistance to the rest of the world. For the longest time, he had believed that playing tenor sax was the whole deal. He said that the problem with attempting to discern non-saxophone-related things was that they seemed to eventually lead to nothing. Perhaps that would be my lesson to Gulf. I was the half-human showing how living life was purportedly done, and I couldn't give him so much as a vague picture. Now I was showing him. This was the apotheosis---the instant when the fireworks were supposed to be happening. But hey, you can lead 'em, but you can't make 'em necessarily feel. In the long run, those feelings could wind up taking you to a desolate parking lot. And that was exactly where we were at that moment. Each of us had paused to look down at the white lines carefully plotted out on the asphalt. A car backed out, and we had to get out of the way.

"Joe, since my feelings are make-believe, I'm spending an inordinate amount of time tryin' to find real emotions. And out of the full rainbow of feelings, the one that everyone seems to like the best is love. I mean, that's the one everybody seems to go for."

"Yes, it's true. People vote with their feet."

"I've communicated with those cuttlefish Vim and Vod about this, and they both give love very high marks. Sometimes I watch the two of those cephalopods feelin' each other up. When they reach some kind of zenith moment, their colors go crazy."

"Hey man, don't kid yourself. It's not as awesome as the rest of the world thinks. I think you might be on a better track if you stuck to the music thing. That one would trump love any day."

"Yeah, I'm tryin', but it's not working. So, recently I've taken up with prostitutes. I'm beginning to think of all those whores as some sort of practice. I know in my heart that they're fake love. But maybe the experiences I have with them could be stored up and used for something else. Maybe that something could be real love?"

"Maybe or maybe not. I know exactly what you're thinkin'. You've got it in your head that those adventures ... those escapades ... could be seen as a kind of psychological version of a 4012K Plan or a Roth account, and you could, emotionally speakin' of course, have a high yield per annum, and over time some lucky girl that you decide to take up with could become the beneficiary of your accumulated love. But it doesn't work out that way. Young man, understand that the whole thing is a bit of a crap shoot. There are never any guarantees. You could get an A for effort, and still be unhappy."

"I don't care. I want the ideal girlfriend, and I won't settle for anything less than the real deal."

"The real deal? I hope I'm not letting the cat out of the bag when I tell you that your big daddy Ben confided in me that your idea of the cat's meow is a woman with a Mediterranean complexion."

"I wish he hadn't told you that, but since he did, will you help to find one for me? If I could get that ideal gal pal, then life would be so much fun. Everything else would fall into place. The business of livin' life would be as easy as fallin' off a log."

"Look man, as someone who's wandered through life, I gotta say don't bet on that. Attaining the ideal girlfriend won't necessarily lead to complete bliss."

"Oh, I'm not sure of much in this new life. But that one I'm absolutely sure of. Not only that, I've got her all picked out. The girl with the Mediterranean complexion that I want is Gwen. If I can get her, it'll be smooth sailin' from here on in." He made a smooth sailing gesture with his right hand.

"Hey man, you can't have her. She's already spoken for. Hasn't Ben taught you anything? Hasn't he given you some rudiments as to how the world works? The guy should be brought up on charges --- maybe something like dereliction of duty, or child endangerment, or how about an oldie-but-goody like alienation of affections?"

"I want her! I'll do anything to get her!"

"Now you listen to me, sonny boy! I told you can't have her. She's already spoken for." Right away, I could see that Gulf was violating Rule Number One for robots --- he was havin' obedience issues. He was finding emotions to be about as problematic as humans do. I could see he was a good candidate for some sort of boot camp for incorrigible automatons. I had to whack him with a whole lotta tough love and remind him that a robot's lot in life is to live under the tight yoke of fascism twenty-four seven.

Gulf got up from his seat. His eyes were bolder than I'd ever seen them before. Looking into them, I couldn't help but wonder at how real they seemed to be. There they were --- wide open with the irises poised, primped, and primed, ready to pop out of their cyborg sockets. This was a creation that was yearning to see the world. Clearly, Ben had truly outdone himself as far as the accuracy of Gulf's robot construction was concerned. Whatever raw energy was jumpin' around and ready to race along the pathways of his synthetic synapses was a reasonable facsimile of real emotion. God help the rest of the world if it was real love. The planet would be in for stormy weather. I glanced at my fingers, knowing full well that at that moment the future of the world was in my hands. What would the world become if he succeeded? Answer: it would become part man, part machine. The whole shithouse would become overrun by armies of babbling bionics like Gulf. How horrible that would be for me. How horrible that would be for the world. I knew I had to steer him back on the right path. And the right path would be to stick with prostitutes.

But despite this show of extended feelings, I knew in my heart that there was probably some chance, however slim, that I would be able to calm him down. I had one chance, and I had to take it.

"Gulf, you have to listen to reason. I can't just stand by and let you go down this path that will surely lead to the destruction of the band. Think of all the time you've spent trying to absorb each and every nuance of the musical downloads that your father gave you! You enjoyed that, didn't you? Doesn't music mean so much more to you than some silly tart who can't make up her mind about who the hell she freakin' loves? She's just a girl. She'll never know what she thinks because she has to constantly keep herself in practice for the game of love. Not only that, but you can bet your bottom dollar she's spent her whole life watchin' God knows how many reality shows, and she wouldn't know a real feelin' if it bit her on the aureole. Look, I know you're a robot and you're tryin' so hard to be a human being and fit in just like everyone else, and I suppose on one level that's sorta admirable, and I give ya high marks for makin' the effort, but do you really want to blow this big opportunity? This is your moment to go beyond that sentimental passive-aggressive love bullshit. Can't you understand that as artificial as you may be, you can still shoot for something higher. You...you...you can aim for the fences and hit one outta the park! You're better than THEM!!! Do you really want to be just another loser like they are? Well, I don't think so. I sure hope not. I think you've got lots bigger fish to fry. If you wanna know how I feel about this, my best advice is to vote for the whores. That'll keep your music safe and sound so nobody can mess with you. Your dad likes to think of you as the wave of the future. So, if that's true, you've got to have a futuristic attitude."

"Oh, I don't know. I'm so confused. Maybe I should try some online dating?"

"No, absolutely not! Perhaps my best quality as a mentor is that I don't want you to live a cyberspace life. I don't want you hunched over some godforsaken computer all day skulkin' around chat rooms, nor do I want you constantly going into your twitter and instagram accounts. And facebook --- hell no, that's strictly off limits! Gulf, you're already a robot from the get-go, so maybe it's not such a good idea to make your life more make-believe than it already is."

"It's so nice to have a mentor as good as you."

"As your mentor, I forbid you to go online to find your lady friends. I'm saying this because I want you to go out into the world and learn some things on your own. Do you remember that time when we both drank beer together?"

Gulf nodded his head eagerly, and I continued. "Yes, I encouraged you to get a little drunk because I wanted you to know what it feels like, so when you go out with your friends you won't be surprised by what you feel. That'll come in handy if you should ever have the need to drink and drive. There's no way in hell I want you to be unprepared for the world. I mean, that would be a huge disservice. And what I'm discovering is that as far as that cuttlefish brain of yours is concerned, there's only so much Ben can do to program you. Your dad may be the most brilliant scientist whoever walked the planet, but the man has limits. So, with that in mind, I'm giving you less and less supervision. I'm doing this because I know you can handle it. You can go out into the community on your own. Maturity --- it's what made America great! And I want you to go out there and be a proud American."

My mind flashed back to what Ben had said about encouraging Gulf to try and meet up with 'a viable candidate from the human female community.' I could vote for that, just as long as the candidate from the human female community wasn't Gwen.

"So Gulf, here's what I propose to do. I want to take you on another field trip. And I wanna sit in the corner from a short distance away, so I can see how well you do on your own."

"Really, can we go together? That would be so much fun."

"Only if you can handle it. Remember this, always and forever --- going out into the human female community unsupervised is only for a certain kind of robot. I know you can handle it. The big question in my mind is do YOU think you can handle it?"

"Oh Joe, I can do it. I know I can do it all on my very own."

"Good. I know talk is cheap, but I still like to see confidence in my pupils. That's half the battle right there. But if you should ever have any doubts, remember that I'll be there in the corner, watchin' you and givin' you moral support. Understand young man, I am your biggest fan."

So we did go on that wonderful field trip. I wanted him to meet women the old fashioned way with no megabytes to muddy things up. I let Gulf go to the bar while I hid out in the far corner nursin' a bottle of Thyoneus October Fest Pumpkin Ale. Gulf was sitting right next to an attractive young lady who was sipping a tall colorful drink with some kind of complicated parasol construction cantilevered atop the plastic swizzle stick. As luck would have it, the young lady had a Mediterranean complexion! Good, that meant Gulf would have a goal to go for. That would be good for getting his lustful mind off from Gwen.

At first, they practiced not noticing each other. Gulf seemed to be payin' more attention to the sax solo on the bartender's iPod than he was to the beautiful young lady in question. But soon he decided to initiate some conversation after the bartender asked him whether or not he wanted another, which was rather surprising to me because Gulf had really chugged down the first one in practically the blink of an eye. But then I suddenly remembered that Gulf, being bionic, most likely had special drinking powers not available to the average human being. I mean, hey! He was a robot for God's sake. He could probably drink anyone under the table if he had half a mind to do it.

It was the heroin that he couldn't handle. And I was rationing that in appropriate doses to keep him under my boot heel.

But right about then I could see that that was the farthest thought from his synthetic mind. For some reason, which he later couldn't understand, he and the girl got on the topic of "rules." And she said that it was so much fun to break them, and naturally, he'd agreed with her on that one, and she had said breakin' rules was sorta like firin' a gun straight ahead into a crowd knowing full well that the bullets would never go anywhere except into someone's guts. And he had said, "Yeah, wasn't that a very pleasant thought?" And on that note, he'd pondered the weight of these remarks, so he decided that now was right about time to change the subject. Yes, changing the subject would be a great idea right about then because the dialogue he was hearing was getting too problematic. So he went ahead and did exactly that. It was so hard to do it he felt he was moving the wheel on a very big truck. The transmission was protesting and being lazy. He was saying, "How in the hell do I get this damned thing to turn? It won't freakin' turn into something more pleasant." Gulf looked at me as I sat in the corner watching the proceedings. I looked away. He wouldn't be getting any help from me because, as I had told him before, he was strictly flyin' solo. Goin' out into the human female community is only for those who can handle it. But no matter. He succeeded. He asked the woman what she thought of the saxophone solo. And she said she thought it was great, but that probably didn't mean much because there was hardly ever a saxophone solo that she didn't like because no matter who played it, the brawniness of the instrument appealed to her, and it was sorta like the brawniness of men in general and wasn't music just such an awesome thing, and she really loved coming to this bar because the bartender had such great taste in music, and the strawberry mimosas were so yummy and...and...And suddenly she stopped talking as though she'd completely run out of things to say. But Gulf was doin' well, 'cause as quickly as he'd polished off that first IPA, he picked up the slack and in no time at all they were engrossed in one topic after another. If I, as a casual observer, hadn't known any better, I woulda thought that both of 'em were on an actual date. How cool was that?

But then things started to go south.

Gulf asked an innocent question. Only trouble was it was maybe too innocent: "So what do you like to do besides listen to music?"

"I like to get hurt. How 'bout you?"

"You like to get hurt? Well, that doesn't sound like it would be very much fun."

"It is. Take my word for it." She took a hit from her pretty drink and jiggled the glass on the edge of the bar. Then she bit her lip. In fact, she bit it real hard, so hard I could see it bleed a little under the glare of the overhead lights.

Gulf looked confused. There was nothing in his memory banks that had prepared him for this. He stammered something incoherent and then looked into the ascending bubbles of his dark amber beer. The saxophone on the iPod let out a screech and went into a rhythmic squawk before reverting to a soulful croon.

Right about then, I looked outside just in time to see a fancy SUV pull up to the curb. A thirty-something gentleman double parked, got out, and entered the bar with a swagger in his step and a scowl on his lips. He looked across the bar and stared at Gulf and the young lady he was talking to. He walked up to Gulf, but the focus of his wrath was on the girl. "Aw c'mon, baby. I can't believe you're talkin' to this fellow! Didn't we discuss this stuff before, and I thought I told ya not to do this. And now you went ahead and actually did it anyway. You defied me. I can't believe my eyes! I can't believe my ears. I'm lookin' at you, and I see you talkin' with *another man*! What did we say? I thought we came to an understanding. Refresh my memory. I think I'm forgettin'."

The girl with the bleeding lip protested: "But Honey, I don't want you to forget. I'm doin' my best so you don't forget. Can you help me out? I'm tryin' to stay on track. Won't ya help me to stay on the freakin' track?"

"I think you and I have to go home right now. I'll get you back on the track. You can bet on it. You've been a very bad girl, and you need to be punished."

"No, no, on! Please, I'll promise to be good. Please don't take me home right now. I was having such a good time."

"Well, I'm afraid that's not good enough. No more fun for you. Here, you come with me right now. And you do absolutely everything that I tell you to do!"

"Oh please Baby, please don't hurt me! I promise I won't do it again!"

The swaggering gentleman wasn't so gentle. He took her by the scruff of her neck like she was some kind of errant cat and forcibly escorted her out of the bar. For a split second or so, her feet waggled frantically and struggled to find the floor. But when they were out the door, they finally found the concrete of the sidewalk, only not for long because he opened the passenger door and threw her into the car. I could see her bounce a bit on the upholstery and headrest. And a second later, he slammed on the accelerator, gunned the engine, and screeched out, careening down the street, peelin' a streak of black rubber, and running the light before going out of sight at the next intersection.

I got up from my seat in the corner and went over to Gulf. He had a pensive expression. Her Mediterranean complexion had gone away without him. I went into full mentoring mode and tried to comfort him: "See what I mean, Gulf. Do you have any idea what you're getting into?"

Gulf looked like a pretty perplexed person. He turned to the bartender who matter-of-factly said, "They do that song and dance of theirs about once a week. I tell you, it's gettin' rather old."

"Yes," I added. "But they'll be havin' a grand ol' time when they get home."

The bartender poured another round for a happier couple in the middle of the bar and then cut a lemon in two. "But even if it's old, I can't stop likin' it. I don't know why it is, but I look forward to the next time she comes in for a drink. She sorta keeps me on my toes."

As the saxophone solo blared into more dangerous harmonic territories, Gulf looked off into the space of the overhead lights and mumbled: "Go on! Go home and get beaten up! But don't ever ask me to be nice again."

I could tell he was thinking about the bleeding lip and how he wanted to kiss it.

THYONEUS THE THIRST BOPPER

I was at the local video games arcade having an intense go-round again. That afternoon it was a game of Pig Newton. The wolves were having a barrel of laughs chopping down the tree as the pig struggled to climb it. Naturally, Officer Fielding came up to ruin my concentration just as I was getting to the good part.

Officer Fielding leaned over my shoulder and said, "Wow, you're really bringin' home the bacon now!"

My attention was focused on the dastardly wolves, and I tried to keep it that way. So I saw no need to answer his incessant blather.

"OK, Joe. Here's what I know. I'm fairly sure that you had something to do with Andy's drowning. Only thing is, that's old hat by now."

"Jesus, man! Will ya leave me alone? Can't ya see I'm busy?" Thanks to my superior talents on the toggle switch, the pig was making serious headway, but no matter how good I was, I couldn't help but be distracted by Fielding's persistent badgering. It was a foregone conclusion --- the wolves won. I backed away from the machine and slouched into disappointment. "Officer, why'd you have to go and do that just when I was doin' so well?"

"Maybe next time I'll simply pull the plug out of the wall. How would ya feel about that?"

"That old age project of yours is to destroy my fun. I think you're a sadist. That's your true occupation."

"Careful on the schadenfreude there, Joe. I'm a very determined fellow. And nine times out of ten I get the guilty ones. But let's get serious about this for a second. Each time I look at it, there's more than meets the eye. From what I can tell, you're running from something or someone. I found out that you not so long ago really pissed off some big shot at a party. And the guy you pissed off is no one to be fucked with. He's got some rather sleazy connections. I think he's mobbed up. And one of his friends is this Allen Mastrianni guy who's running for high office. This Mastrianni is no angel either. But he's good at covering his tracks. Joe, is there some sort of bad blood between you and your sister? That's not what this is all about, is it?

"Duh, ya think! Damn right there is!"

"What about the gun permit lady? Mastrianni is married to her, right?"

"She's my dear old sister. And my mum's sadder than hell that she ever brought her into this world."

"She's your sister?"

"Absolutely right. She is unfortunately that."

"Oh my God, that one explains a lot of things!"

"Look, if I tell you what I know, will you get offa my back"

"It depends."

"Depends on what?"

"Depends on how good it is."

"Hey man, I've got enough to worry about without having to put up with your constant interrogations. I got a bass player who's being a total pain in the ass. He's trying to implode the whole band."

"From what I've observed, that's the way of the world. Face it, Joe. You're good at what you do. That's bound to give some people somewhere a cause to hate you."

"95% of the time, people are under the mistaken impression that good music will automatically triumph over crappy music."

"Ah, but that's not the case. Crappiness holds the upper hand more often than not."

"Just enter any drum solo competition, and you'll see. I only got to win by sheer luck. That, and the fact that I'm on TV."

"However, what's cool about *Babies in Bars* is that the conventional stupidity has been turned on its ear. And only hot publicity and the curve of Gwen's lovely ass have made it that way. I adore the authority of her arabesques. Nobody can argue with them. She has more talent in her toenails than most babes have in their voices."

"And with me hangin' out in the background --- maybe that'll automatically make us win too."

The eighth note was trudging along making a very big spectacle of itself. Anticipation huffed and puffed, overflowed, and after-glowed, and I was the lord of the manor knowing what was up 'cause it was part of the deal. Dig what I'm talkin' about. What did they want me to be? Some sort of session man? That way the sounds that I etched in vinyl or pixels would forever become part of everybody's exquisite experience of buying jumbo bags of fried chicken? Shoot, goddammit. I freakin' objected. And I objected long and pissin' loud 'cause the difference between *Babies in Bars* and all the other bands pollutin' the scene out there was that, except for Ben, we were the only ones who hadn't forgotten how to play our instruments. I was playing vicious --- full throttle, giving it four on the floor and making it stutter, step, and strut in the peekaboo chorus. The blank wall I faced wasn't very animated, but it was still an audience nonetheless. I made it one. I made it clap.

We were recording now. The strange thing about recording is that three or four minutes of a fixed point in time get to have the privilege of being carved in stone forever. The calisthenics of the music demand it. You could have a hundred jobs in a lifetime, and none of them would mean a damn compared to that fraction of time. Only the syllables, never the beats, would make a sliver of bliss. I had protested some to Jillian, but it didn't do much good. She was a savage goddess. Kathy had quibbled about it too because the recording would be another beer ad, and we knew how she felt about that. Jillian pointed out that there were fans in Valencia. There were fans in Auckland. There were even fans in Vladivostok. They loved how Ben and I could kiss and make up again and again. We were being held against our will in an echo chamber that didn't know how to shut up.

"Yes," Jillian said, "There may be tweeters in heat and blogs and bleats, but they don't amount to anything 'cause you could still get your sweet ass cancelled." She rambled on, looking at Ben and me: "How can it be? How is it that two people who hate each other can make such stunning music together?"

What was great about this new round of songs was how they summoned forth dazzling images in the collective minds of listeners. It soon become apparent that after being exposed to them, audiences felt they were at the verge and entrance to exquisite and unending joy. Of course, the product can never quite live up to the hype. But what separated us from the competition was that, although the product didn't live up to the sounds that sold it, the tunes still worked spectacularly on their own. As a result, the product got far more publicity than it deserved. Perhaps this was what Mom had in mind when she'd told me to go out there and make some magic?

But I didn't have lots of time to engage in protracted analysis because based on the fact that our initial rock video had gone viral, the same mega-corporation decided it was high time to make us their official beer. The ad man, along with his frisky, tail-waggin' Jack Russell, helped *Babies in Bars* to score some dazzling commercial possibilities. At that early juncture, I could see that this business deal would quickly become a comfortable *quid pro quo* arrangement --- they needed "cool points" and we needed publicity. Like so many musicians who had come before us, we would become mascots. I looked down at the hyperactive little doggy guy as he stretched the limits of the leash. I reached down and petted him. "Yes, Jack, I know what it's like to be a mascot too." Then Jack jumped up in my lap and the giddiness continued, but not for long because his master announced that we had to get down to business. This time the band would be doing an ad for a new IPA put out by Thyoneus Beer. Their slogan was, "Thyoneus, the thirst bopper." We'd already been in the studio and recorded the track, but now we had to do the visuals.

The storyboard was like this: *Babies in Bars'* music was playing in the background as a pompous politician was making, what else, a pompous speech. He had on an American flag tie and stood behind a podium trumpeting clichés like, "No new taxes!" Jillian had corralled Kathy into this part, and dressed in flamboyant male drag, Kathy played it to the hilt. She was doin' her best to look downright fascist and was pullin' it off without a hitch. Well, almost. I was right there with her, giving her moral support. She was laughin' herself silly, which destroyed several of the takes, but after a while she managed to get a straight face and keep it long enough for the crew to get a keeper. The make-up department had done a bang up job of making her more butch than she already was. A small crowd was gathered around her as she spoke. Of course, they managed to roar on cue with each of Kathy's harangues about creating jobs and the great necessity for supporting the trickle-down theory of economics. As the music from *Babies in Bars* got more and more intense, the politician's rant was interrupted by a troop of darting flying saucers that suddenly appeared in the background. I have to hand it to them because this was the part where the special effects guys really went gonzo. Their blinding lights were particularly noteworthy. When one of them hit, I almost fell off my drum stool. The screen burst into a mass of blazing reds, yellows, and greens, from which the politician emerged in a swirl of bleeding psychedelic strobes. The politician tried to stay on the track of his or her speech, but the crowd had changed, and they were now devoting all their attention to the saucer which was putting on a Vegas style lounge act, at which point a bunch of plumed showgirls sashayed out from the wings of the sound stage, doing high kicks and fan dances. And since this was of course a beer ad, one of the showgirls came forward with an open bottle of Thyoneus Beer. This was the cue for the drummer in the band to stand up from his kit. The showgirl handed him the beer, and he chugged on it. He started doing semaphore signals that the saucer responded to with blips of dazzling lights. All throughout this exchange, there were cross cuts to the band, some with Kathy doing dot-dash telegraph solos on her red guitar with other cross cuts of audience members trying to figure out the code. The showgirls presented bottles of Thyoneus Beer to each member of the band. The cameras zeroed in on the bar codes. While this was going on, the bass player stood expressionless and stock still at first, but soon lapsed into a look of extreme consternation. In the next instant, the camera cut back to me behind the drums where I was sluggin' away. Only I wasn't doin' that for long. The moment we got to the second chorus, I got out from behind the kit and bowed down to Gwen who was of course, singing the song about the wonders of Thyoneus Beer. She didn't fall off the beat when I asked her dance. So, we started movin' to a rapid clip, which was kind of weird for a tango. No matter, the aliens didn't appear to object in the slightest. Also, how many tangos are there that step out in five-and-a-half time? Most likely, they really got into the strange groove as much as the television audience would. Soon the saucers came down to earth and the showgirls gave all of the them Thyoneus Beers too. The politician blathered on, but nobody paid him any attention. Then as the drummer and Gwen tangoed away, the song faded out and a voiceover said: "Thyoneus --- the thirst bopper!" And that was it. That was the end of the commercial.

But the thing was, although the high drama between musicians and dive bar audiences was pushing the limits of reality TV, Jillian still wasn't satisfied. "No," she said. "We've got to go further. And for that we have to go back into the distant past in order to find the future. I want more storyline. And Joe, that means you. We begin shooting now. And one more thing --- this time around, I don't want any more of that pain-in-the-ass realism in this here reality show. Do ya hear me?"

The premise of the next episode was an extended music video: it's World War Three, sometime on the near horizon. For starters, there are ominous camera shots of high tech warplanes and smart bombs hitting their targets interspersed with cross cuts to Joe playing the drums. You see, it's another one of his flashy solos designed purely to save the world from itself. Crescendos, flams, ratamacues, buzz rolls, and tom tom arpeggios abound. And plenty of stick tossin' and twirlin' too. The acrobatics never know when to shut up. No minimalism allowed. Naturally, there's a bunch of loose talk about how this young generation of ours has the best hand/eye coordination of any kids on the planet, let alone the block. Is it any wonder? They've been getting so much practice at Pig Newton, Donkey-Kong, Q-Bert, Japanese Pachinko, Lady Bug and a boatload of other arcade sports. The kids are particularly enamored of Q-Bert, and they adore the spellbinding balance of skill-based action and quick puzzle solving as well as the playfield, a pyramid made of cubes. When she directed the sequence, Jillian made sure there was lots of back and forth editing between Joe's drumming and the action on the Q-Bert screen. In those sequences, she even indulged in some computerized mat-shots as well as lots of CGI. But her true obsession was the game itself. Jillian said the pseudo-3D perspective and diagonal control were refreshingly different from the other games of its class and that the spinning disc as a defensive weapon was definitely a cool concept. Of course, the mumbling sounds and curses were some of the most memorable elements. Jillian said that the voices were generated by a random phoneme generator, but I still think she slipped some real curse words in there, as an inside joke (though I don't think she'll ever admit it). At least that's the conclusion I came to late at night during one drum/Q-Bert session or another. Jillian says she hopes to catch a one life million point game on streaming video real soon. Ah, but that's quite another project altogether. That might require extensive training because you have to pace yourself. And after a certain number of hours, your eyes will get sluggish, and you'll have to aim way out ahead to hit your prey. However, she was unfazed. She played around with the notion that the Q-Bert marathon is a metaphor for the Common Man who aspires to make it big in the world --- he hops around the illuminati pyramid, endlessly in pursuit of money or points, just trying to perfect every board while the snake chases him and the little "friendly" guys undo all his hard work. Another insight she had was the significance of the shapes of the square or cube, sphere (red, purple and freeze balls), and the triangle or pyramid. These are powerful prime symbols that speak to the deep subconscious levels of the mind. Of course, much of that has to do with sex, so for now I won't go there.

Back in the studio, it's fun watching the fans egg Joe on and there's lots of cheering from the balcony. On the Q-Bert screen, Coily the Purple Snake is chasin' after Joe who's able to avoid him this time. Despite his drumming triumph, Joe second guesses himself, and as is the case with so many drummers, he's constantly worried about losing his arm. It's a fear that some may say is an occupational hazard. Therefore, he frequently holds it with his other hand, so it won't get away. The phenome generator mumbles, right about when there are some special effects shots of Joe without his right arm as the soundtrack thunders on in the background. Coily keeps runnin' away with the arm as if he's abscondin' with somethin'. There it is off to the side, hanging around and fluttering in the upper right hand corner of the TV screen. Coily's goin' crazy. The hand on the severed appendage keeps wavin' at Joe, taking issue and taunting him to come after it. To add insult to injury, the hand on the amputation goes into conniptions and gymnastics, telling the arm and Joe himself that the missing arm and hand are so much better off without the rest of the body laying claim to it. Ugg and Wrong Way, the villains on the Q-Bert screen, have a real good phenome-generated guffaw on that one. Of course, this really pisses Joe off in a huge way, so he chases off in pursuit of the arm, and in the next few seconds, there's a whole lotta limb chasing going on. Ugg does a grumble. But this part has a happy ending for the time being because Joe's roadie, Bill, runs after the arm too, and since Bill is so much better at Q-Bert than Joe, he catches it and brings it back to Joe who thanks him profusely. Things get reattached. At this point, Joe, having scaled the cubes to the top of the pyramid, has won the first game. Coily expresses his chagrin. Bill keeps reassuring Joe and tells him to relax and do what he was born to do which is to conjure up ecstasy for the whole wide world. I mean, think about it --- isn't that what any self-respectin' illuminati is supposed to do? Joe follows Bill's advice and chills out. Only trouble is --- the war is really heating up. Politicians are busy volunteering for others. They could care less about the sanctity of the arms of the people. Coily the Snake does a big mumble on that one and scurries away just a split second after Joe throws a spinning disc at him. Hey, didn't I tell ya it was a cool concept? The politicians keep reminding the people that they have to perform some nebulous duty to God and country, and before you know it, despite his wish to keep doing what he does best, Joe gets railroaded into doing something that he does worst, which is to be a soldier. Well, he's bamboozled into that, and in the next camera angle, he's flying in a high tech stealth plane. Impervious to radar, he's cruising over a ravaged war zone. Despite his technologically superior weaponry, he gets taken down by a one-in-a-million lucky shot from a hand held missile launcher and crashes behind enemy lines. Wow! Ugg and Wrong Way are at it again! They just won't stop. Joe's billion dollar aircraft goes down in flames, spitting a jagged orange gash that skitters angrily across the peaceful blue sky, but Joe's a crafty fellow, and he manages to bail out and survive a serious close call. How's that for skill-based problem solving! Cross edit to a shot of Joe doing a drum roll around the kit. Bill points out that the government can afford the plane, so it's no big deal. Plenty more where that came from. Still, the government is righteously pissed. Joe floats gently down to earth in his billowing parachute, landing in a peasant's hothouse vegetable garden. The peasant morphs into Ugg and turns Joe in, and he's held prisoner in a god awful prison camp. He's incarcerated with lots of other U. S. soldiers and his captors don't treat him or his fellow captives very well. Apparently, they don't cotton to people dropping bombs on them. In fact, many of the POW's wind up dropping like flies because of the poor treatment and lack of good nutrition. There are more than a few camera shots of the whole brigade looking like they have terminal rickets. The prognosis is decidedly grim. "Ha, ha, ha" mutters Coily. Ugg does a happy dance and clicks his heels. Also, it's a very cold climate, so many of the prisoners freeze to death. Although he knows his chances of survival are slim at best, he never gives up, and while he's fighting off the pangs of hunger, he's still able to keep up a pretty good drum practice schedule. The camera catches a lot of very good footage of these practice sessions, and in one of them, an Eskimo, who lives just outside the perimeter of the camp, hears Joe's drumming and is impressed. The Eskimo is so impressed that he cheers him on and tells him that he might be able to give Joe a job in one of his shamanic rituals. No resume would be required. Joe lets out a sigh of relief! Encouraged, he wins another game of Q-Bert and gleefully does a four-stroke ruff on a rubbish can cover. Joe takes the gig. He likes this very much, but he has one major problem: he's starving to death. So he tells the Eskimo fellow how he's fading fast, unless he can get some good chow. The Eskimo guy says, "Well, I can't get you any of that, but I do know how to save you, but it's gonna hurt, and it's gonna hurt a lot. Do you still want me to save you? Are you up for it?" And Joe, being a really experimental guy, can't say no to that, and besides, he has nothin' to lose, so he says, "Yeah, man, do whatever ya gotta do to make me live. I give ya the green light." At this point, there's a cross cut of Joe scaling another rung on the pyramid as he zaps Wrong Way, who, for the time being, gets atomized. Cross cut to another drum flurry. So the Eskimo reaches for his knife and says, "Here goes!" He makes a cut in Joe's arm. Of course, Joe experiences a bit of discomfort, but he manages to deal with the pain, thanks to a hefty gulp of alcohol. *Babies in Bars'* sponsor, Thyoneus Beer, sneaks in a bit of subliminal advertising messages here and there, which of course does wonders for their beer sales, both nationally and internationally. It even bolsters sales for their spin-off brand called Bacchus Brogue which is designed to break into the international whiskey market. There are still pics of people drinking responsibly just so people in the viewing audience can figure out what was seriously irresponsible. The Eskimo cuts out a fairly significant slab of flesh from Joe's upper arm, and Joe winds up screaming his head off while trying to bite into a towel. Naturally, this really spooks the hell out of Joe since he already has a pre-existing condition which is his longstanding fear of losing an arm. But the Eskimo reassures him, telling him that everything will be alright, provided that Joe can get through the pain. He gives Joe another large chug off from the bottle just to make sure that this will happen. After that, the Eskimo takes the chunk of flesh away from the bleeding arm and places it in a snow bank. He bandages up the injured arm and gives Joe a few choice potions --- rarified, but extremely effective things, that the Eskimo has learned about from the vast archive of his shamanic heritage. Then Joe falls asleep. In fact, he falls into such a deep sleep that he sees lots of visions of himself playing drums. These visions get pretty wild and hysterical and there's more than a little chanting and various and sundry carryings on. At last, the morning comes and the sun creeps over the horizon, but it being a very northerly climate, Joe knows it won't stay there for long. When the sun gets as bright as it will get, the Eskimo knows that it's time to do the final part of the procedure, the part that will sink or save our hero. Accordingly, he goes over to the snow bank and removes the chunk of flesh. It's frozen, but the Eskimo warms it with his hands and puts it back to the place from whence it came, which is of course, Joe's upper arm! It fits snugly into the hole and at this point, the fidgety arm doesn't quite know what to do with itself. The nerves, sinews, and muscles inside are doing a bugaboo boogaloo dance. There are several close ups which are amazingly similar to what you'd see on a cop show with lots of forensic flourishes. The arm knows that the chunk of flesh is something familiar, but the familiarity has started to fade from its frame of cellular recollection. There is recognition, but there is also something quite the opposite: rejection is competing for attention. The arm wants to get up and fly away again, perhaps this time taking Joe's life with it. But the arm hesitates. It wants to reject, and the body wants to keep. The mind --- it doesn't know what in the hell it wants. It's on the fence. They want these things simultaneously. Confusion reigns supreme. "Good for that!" mumbles Ugg. There is a lot of arguing going on, so of course there's more path lab pyrotechnics --- you know what I mean --- the kind of CSI thing where you get to see what it's like to zoom through a capillary at top speed and head butt a blood clot out of the way. The arm makes a simple request: "Please have some patience. The white matter in the brain has to calm down." While this is taking place, the body is going into deep sweats and turmoil. The sinews are warbling. The cells are arguing amongst themselves, trying to figure out whether to ostracize the arm or not. And as this is going on, the arm and body come to an understanding. It is not as though they really managed to cooperate. Rather, it's because they are supremely distracted. The body has been given a gigantic adrenalin boost, which has cut across and nullified any small-minded quarrels, thereby sending every shred of Joe's being into overdrive. He feels like he could run the New York Marathon! Cross cut to Joe on the drums doing a delayed triplet. As

Jillian so succinctly wrote on the margins of her director's copy of the script, "Arm and body are deluded into survival." Joe begins to trust the Eskimo's folk remedy, but acknowledges that you can't do this trick in a hot climate. Given this new rejuvenation, the body and its limbs go on a bender and the remainder of the song jolts into a full Monte rave up, which, according to the people who keep meticulous score on these things, was a first for an extended rock video of any kind. Ugg and Wrong Way both clap. It's a one million life point game. They're so happy to have "helped out." Wrong-Way wraps his lip around a brewsky and takes a slurp. After that, the cable company cuts to a commercial that sells windshield wiper blades.

Cheering is cheap. I wanna say put your money where it will matter. A drummer must respect the sanctity of the verse and chorus system. If you can't respect that, you're out on your ass, and you'd better watch out. But if I recall correctly, it was in Houston that we had another strange gig. Kathy and I had been trading fours and then trading eighths. It was not too far from being a jazz thing, but she and I rocked it up, so nobody would accuse us of that 'cause in some places that jazziness would have been the kiss of death. After a while of doing this, the mood changed to one of subtle quietude, at which point I figured that this was clearly shaping up to be a case of less-is-more, so I figured it best to drop out entirely. That's one of the things about being a good drummer --- knowin' when to shut the hell up. So I cut out and clammed up, and the crowd listened intently to what Kathy was sayin' on her instrument. And she and her instrument were steerin' the crowd to landscapes of stunning beauty. The people out there were groovin' to this stuff 'cause on some primal level, they were vaguely aware that every glittering song was an enchanted world in which tension triumphed over relief. I could feel it even as I temporarily closed my eyes. The people knew exactly what to do with what she was tellin' 'em. When I opened my eyes a few seconds later, I happened to glance at the side entrance to the stage, which was a rather odd set-up since the side door opened not into the wings, but rather, directly onto the street outside the venue where we were playin'. In fact, every so often, I could hear the faint roar of a car engine speeding by. Of course, earlier, that had been absolutely fair game for whatever I'd been playing at the moment – it had been something I could react to. But now, since I was maintaining silence on the drum kit, the roar became more noticeable. I had just then registered all of this in my mind when suddenly in through the side door walked a silken jet black cat. The audience quickly grew hushed as the creature made its entrance onto the stage. The only thing audible was the stark magic of Kathy's strings. The animal sashayed up to her like a runway model and Kathy returned the favor, each mammal giving a penetrating stare into the eyes of the other. It soon became clear that Kathy was playin' strictly for the beast and for no one else. I looked out into the crowd and could see that they were totally transfixed on this spot of interspecies communication. This went on for about three minutes, but understand that it could've been longer 'cause in a gig, time often gets compressed. Kathy and the beast seemed to give off the vibe that there was no one else within five hundred miles of them. At length, the feline turning to face the spellbound crowd, revealed a haughty expression, and slowly stepped back towards the door from whence it came, disappearing into the street. From my perch on the drum chair, I could hear a collective sigh of exhilaration. Well, the next thing we knew not so long after the gig was that some critic guy had given us a big write up about how *Babies in Bars* was such an awesome band that we were entirely capable of serenading cats. This of course did further wonders for the rating of the show. At this point, we'd managed to corral the cat lovers out there in TV Land.

ROTT WEILLER AND THE RHYTHM RETREIVERS

For our next few projects, the ad man for Thyoneus Beer decided that it would be good if we morphed into another collective persona. For these spots, he suggested that the band should be featured under a new name, one that would evoke a more blues vibe, so he came up with a pretty wild one --- "Rott Weiller and the Rhythm Retrievers." Jillian loved the concept and in no time at all, she had us dressed up like we were Chicago bluesmen. We were dandied up with punch perm haircuts, sharkskin suits, and Sam Snead hats, not to mention the King-of-the-Rat-Pack ties. This would be the soundtrack for a car commercial. When we saw that finished product, we were blown away. Early on in the short plot, the Retrievers are on stage, and yours truly the drummer is slugging away on a set of old fashioned Roto-Toms which are basically a row of drum heads mounted on a stand, only the heads have no shells to go with them, so the resulting sound that is created has a high-pitched effect that is easily manipulated with a turn of the drum rim, thereby giving the listener a bent note feeling. Roto-Toms --- that was the ad man's inside joke --- since the drummer's name was "Rott," he wanted people to say, "And ladies and gentlemen, there's Rott on Rotos."

The tune starts slow, rollin' into the dilation of time itself, the extended foreplay of the notes feeling its way, trying to form a thesis statement. And in the commercial, it seems that there's a guy who's watching the band, and he decides to jump in the car that the spot is trying to market, and he drives it down the street, only suddenly the street melts into a road, and then the road just as suddenly becomes a field comprised of all manner of rugged terrain --- icebergs, mountain crags, and hair-raising cliffs. There's of shot of a terrified Gwen looking over the precipice from the passenger side. Her mouth goes agape into a grimace of pure horror. But not to fear because basically, the machine is indestructible and can go anywhere. At one point, he drives the thing up the side of a mountain at about a forty-five degree angle. Our raunched-out blues music, complete with roto-toms seems to propel the car forward. At first, some of the viewing audience think the Chicago blues soundtrack means this is going to be a male enhancement ad, but suddenly Kathy edges the guitar track into another direction and puts a stop to that impression. Kathy bends her top string into a high C. Then she plays a slash chord with an odd cluster in the tonic, causing the middle E to coil relentlessly through the spine of the sound. This combination of notes wants agreement, yet it wants words that will back it up. It craves support for its opinion. B/C or E-7/A is a rebuttal. It wants to meander back and forth between the simulated Marshall stacks and the wa-wa pedal before deciding it's at a loss of what to do. So, it resolves to tread water to the theme of the commercial, which is that "You, Mr. Car Buyer way out there in TV Land, you don't need a goddamned street; you don't need a damned road; you don't need any of that lame stuff 'cause you're an individual. Streets and roads --- what are they? They were made for wussies! Real men don't need 'em! You make your own damned road. This world of ours may be full of limitations, but you don't have to stand for it. Not for one minute!" When the music gets real intense, the Roto-Toms do a crescendo right at the moment when the car pivots through a muddy field, intentionally spattering mud all over the camera lens, as if to say, "Look folks, we're gonna be really in your face about this." Then as the last metal chord fades, there's a close-up shot of some glistening goo on the side of the right rear fender. And there's a disclaimer that says, "Professional driver --- do not attempt." Then the camera cuts back to Gwen --- her fear is fading fast. She shakes her head, lets out a sigh, and glances back at the sharp rocks of the cliff. Yes, the message is clear by now: the guy has got the girl.

Then I crashed in on the final chorus, and before the song knew what was happenin', the cymbals ripped the face off the tune itself, before it even had a chance to go into the final verse.

Officer Fielding and I had hooked up again in a last chance try to end our differences. "Joe, Even an old geezer like me is warming up to this *Babies in Bars* thing. Somehow, that latest episode really took me back to the surrealism of the British invasion. I kept waitin' for Ugg and Wrong Way to break into a Cockney accent. I do believe it might've helped me get out of my hospital bed of pain. For a second there, as I was recuperating, I was speculatin' that a mop topped musician would land smack dab in the middle of the screen."

By now, Officer Fielding was getting very drunk, but for an old man he could sure put it away. There were several empties on the bar by now, "dead soldiers" as the old guy was fond of calling them. I cottoned up to his archaic vocabulary, such as when he called the bartender "Innkeeper!" and when he called an opener a "church key," In a manner of speakin', I could see that it was clearly his religion. The other thing I surmised that he'd had years of practice. As a result, he could consume staggering amounts and drink me and anyone else under the table.

Since our last meeting, his physical condition was much improved. Hell, on this day, he looked to be in the pink of health. However, he had apparently been too embarrassed to go back to the previous bar, so before meetin' up with me, he decided on switching venues. This one was a far more upscale place, but it wasn't that much different in the sense that it catered to people who took that first drink of the day very seriously.

"I'm so glad you liked the latest episode, Officer Fielding. And I'm also so glad you're out of the hospital."

Fielding swallowed some more Thyoneus Beer and put down the glass. "Joe, I don't know quite what to say. I started out looking for one pleasure, which was to gather up enough evidence for the D.A. to put you in jail. But now I've found something that's so much more entertaining than that. Did anyone ever tell you that your sister is a sleazebag?"

"Ya think?"

"I think I'm gonna go after her."

"What do I have to do to sic you onto her? She's bankrolling a meth lab. Isn't that good enough for you?"

"Is it the rolling kind? You know what I mean. Cookin' up the stuff is rough on the architecture to say nothing of the eyes, skin, and lungs. So they gotta keep it movin'. Going mobile is the key to the whole operation."

"Yeah, I know. It's not for city slickers. Ideally, meth makers wanna get the creepy stuff brewed up in some old abandoned motel way out in the middle of nowhere, so they can rot out the walls to their hearts' content without having the neighbors complain. But if they can't have that, then they elect to boil up a batch in the storage compartment of a tractor trailer rig. Of course, after they've gone and done that, they have to ditch the rig somewhere since nobody'll wanna get near it once the inside is baked on to a crinkly cocktail of god-knows-what toxic kind of gook. Geez man, the stuff is darned high maintenance. Why can't they do traditional drugs that don't require so much wear and tear on the infrastructure?"

"It's the law of the free market, Joe. It's what the public demands. They want complexity, and they want it now!"

"Hey man, there's your story. There's your wrap up for a renowned career in criminology. I'll let you in on a few things if you promise to get off my back about Andy."

"Go ahead. Shoot! Tell me what you know."

"No, not yet. Not until ya tell me you're gonna stop botherin' me."

He stared at the stuffed raccoon that was mounted over the bar and then blinked tiredly into the suds of his dark craft beer. "Alright, alright. I'll give you a break." Looking up at the raccoon, I thought I saw him give a sign of approval.

"Mr. Fielding," I continued. "My good friend, you'll have to do better than that. You'll have to gimme a free pass."

"OK, OK!"

"Scout's honor?"

"I can't believe I'm agreeing to this."

"Either agree or don't. And I haven't got all day. I have enough trouble trying to keep *Babies in Bars* from imploding."

"Is that Ben the bass player guy giving you a hard time?"

"Sure is. The man must have insomnia while he thinks about new ways to screw up a good deal. But stop it for a second. Do we have a deal, of don't we?"

"Lemme think about it."

"No thinking about it. You decide right now. Do something impulsive for once in your life. It may very well be the last chance that you get. And remember something --- didn't I bring you back from the brink of death?"

"I'm forever in your debt."

"Right you are. So now I'm calling in the chips --- each and every one of them. This is your last chance."

Officer Fielding studied the wood grains and knots in the bar's oaken surface, rubbing the veneer as if that would help him to formulate a response to my directive. After a few seconds, he seemed to have made up his mind. "Alright Joe, it's a deal. I give you total amnesty."

"Damn! Well, it's about time. Can we shake on that and make this a gentleman's agreement?" I held out my hand and waited for his.

And Fielding's hand reciprocated much faster than I expected. "Deal!"

Then I told him everything I knew. I told him about how Meghan had a gun permit agency that catered to all manner of lunatics and lowlifes, and I gave him the rundown on the rich and powerful man who was in cahoots with Meghan's politician hubby, and after that, I told him about how drummers have a hard time keepin' the world from spinning out of control. Then I let him in on the stuff about the alien goddess girls and how sexy they were, and how they wanted to seduce me, and it was right about then that I figured I was losing him as my captive audience 'cause at that point the guy was really starting to get fidgety. That was a short disappointment 'cause I thought he'd at least be impressed and mildly intrigued by the fact that aliens weren't green or grey or nerdy lookin'. In fact, they had some rather big breasts and scary looking eyes. So what did I do when he began to lose interest? Well, I simply stopped the whole spiel on a dime and moved to another subject.

"Look man, I saved your freakin' life for God's sake. You owe me! You owe me big time! And if you don't pay me back, I can always say that I *bought* you. I bought you for the price of a bottle of Thyoneus Beer."

Fielding looked down at the nearly empty bottle. Then he raised it to his mouth and slurped down the last few gulps before smacking his lips for dramatic effect. "OK, now I guess you're talkin' some deep accusation. We can't have that now, can we? I'm a man who always pays his debts to society." He pointed the narrow end of the bottle at me in order to make his point. "And you certainly are society, even if you're from the low end of it."

"But wait, Officer Fielding. There's more to this deal than simple amnesty."

"Really? So you're gonna tack on something else?"

"You're absolutely right I am."

"I give up. What else do ya want?"

"I want you to help me. You gotta help me against my sister and you gotta help me save my mom."

Fielding staggered deliberately on his chair in a kind of make-believe surprise. "Wait a minute! You want me to help you save yo mama! Wow! I never had you pegged for being a mummy's boy!"

"Oh stop! Spare me this bullshit. Do you want some adventure or don't you!"

Fielding clammed up his laughter and put on a serious face.

'You see, Officer, what happened was that I originally sent Bill to do the job I want you to do. Only problem was --- Bill got completely taken in by my sister's evil ways."

"Yes, and how is Bill doing now?"

"He's a shadow of his former self. Once Meghan got a hold of him, he wound up having all the soul of a meth addict. I tell ya, his brain might as well be a Mediterranean omelet."

"So he's fried over easy. Is that what you're trying to tell me, Joe?"

"Officer, if you take this job and you'd better 'cause you owe me, I can't impress upon you enough the idea that Meghan is a very dangerous lady. Whatever you do, don't let her sucker you in. Don't let her try to hypnotize you. That's what happened to Bill and by now he's totally useless to me."

"I promise to keep my eyes peeled."

"Yeah, and remember about all the years of experience that you have.'

"I'll never forget. Not for an instant. Now I think I have it all now. But there's one more question that I wanna get clarified."

"Alright, what's that?"

"How does your mom figure into this whole mess?"

And I told him about how Mom was the inadvertent cash register for this whole sleazy operation.

Jillian was still experimentatin' and anticipatin'. There was no end to her capacity to innovate. Her script writers were supposed to be busy, but at this point, the show really didn't need much help from them because whatever weirdness happened to be going on in the lives of each band member popped into a new episode for the show. Consequently, the writers didn't have to look far and wide for material. For example, Kath was always smokin' vast quantities of weed.

So, what they did was to have an episode where Kathy went to buy weed. The cameras followed her up the winding stairs of an old tenement apartment. At the top of the landing, she was greeted by an eighty-something year old woman who, strange as it would seem, was Kathy's dealer. The old lady was glad to see her longtime customer, but explained that she had a bit of a problem. She explained that as she was getting older, she was becoming increasingly dependent on home health care workers. Lately, she'd had a string of bad luck with the agency that provided her with helpers. She'd had four of them so far, and all of them had the same name which was "Amadou. She liked to refer to them as Amadou One, Amadou Two, Amadou Three, and Amadou Four. They were personable enough lads, but none of the Amadous knew English since they'd been recruited from an obscure Third World country where their previous employment situation had been that of goat herders. The old lady said there was nothing wrong with goat-herding, but she really needed someone with a better understanding of the language, so she asked Kath point blank it she might be interested in becoming her home healthcare worker, that was, if she had any down time when she wasn't on tour with the band. So, Kath told her that she'd be glad to be her home healthcare worker, but the only problem would be the agency---they would almost certainly insist that Kathy take a drug test before being enlisted as an official temporary employee. That created a special problem because Kath had to refrain from indulging in her weed habit for at least a month and a half in order to clear the residue out of her system. But she was persistent about the whole thing and was able to go without for over a month. "Way to go, Kath!" I said. "You and I have such great self-control!"

So finally, on the big day, the cameras followed her when she went to the agency for the drug-testing. Well, that episode was good for more than a few laughs and an even greater amount of TV ratings points. As a result, there was lots of free publicity for the band and many bottles of Thyoneus Beer were sold.

After that, Jillian gave me another set of strict orders. On this go-round, I was supposed to morph into another persona --- that of TV investigative reporter. Not long after the shoot, I was watching the results right up there on the large overhead screen, carefully viewing what would be the raw footage for the next episode. Up there on the monitor I could see myself walking down a darkened street wielding the long style of microphone that was the preferred weapon of choice among others in the ambush interview profession. Most of the light came from the cameras that were filming me and the high beamers of the idling cars. My head turned to look straight into the camera to directly address the future audience.

"So, here I am your star investigative reporter, Joe Myers a.k.a. Thyoneus the Thirst Bopper, and tonight I'm out on the beat, lookin' for a story. I'm walking home, going back to Sunita's house after another ecstatic practice with *Babies in Bars.* I've taken this route many times before, cutting through some pretty dicey neighborhoods, but this time it's a different scene. As you can see, there is a parade of hookers strolling down the pavement, and a small traffic jam is clogging the roadway as potential johns ease their cars up to the curbside. It would appear that they wanna talk price. Naturally, my support staff is here to record every reality TV moment. I tell ya, I've been thinking about all the fun I've just had, and I've been replaying it over and over in my mind. I'm saying, 'How nice! And these fellows are going to have some fun too. How wonderful is that? And what do we have here? As you can see, a flamboyantly dressed hooker with a blowsy bouffant coiffure and some very charming hot pants is negotiating with a potential client. Let's listen in and see what's about to go down."

The hooker was getting darned uncomfortable. She turned to the roving camera crew, and snarled, "What the hell is that? Get that thing the hell outta here, and get it the fuck out right now!"

I turned to the john who had a scared look on his face. I admonished him, yelling, "Don't do it, my friend! She's a cop! She's a cop! Don't do it!"

The camera zeroed in on the customer's eyes, and the poor fellow had the look of an alarmed cat. At this point, he thought it best to put his lust on the back burner and hightail it out of there. I nodded into the microphone and observed, "Well, I guess Mr. John will have to hold off his fun for another time. No ecstasy for you tonight I'm afraid. Delayed gratification is good for the soul." The man's car fishtailed and lurched forward as the guy floored it. The other cars followed his example, and in no time at all, they were gone, leaving the street vacant except for the squadron of disappointed hookers.

"What the hell are you doin'?"

I leaned into the mike again. "Hmmm...The lady is righteously pissed. She's reaching into a side pocket of her cute hot pants and pulling something out. And what is it? Why...it's...it's...Wait a minute! It's a badge! And what's this? The pretty lady is gettin' upset. It would appear that I just now made a lucky guess. Beginner's luck. Hey folks, she really is a cop!"

"You bastard! I've a half mind to bust you! Yes, I am. I'm gonna bust you right now!" The pissed off police lady was fidgeting with her handcuffs, but she was deeply flustered and wasn't doing it very gracefully.

"Bust me for what? For preventing a misdemeanor from happening? For saving the man from himself? Is there a law for that? I don't think so. Check your CPLR for that one baby! There's nothing. *Nada*! Don't knock yourself out trying to find it 'cause it's nowhere in sight. You should be givin' me an award for helpin' our citizenry to obey the law."

The police lady stopped dead in her tracks, her face, if not her words acknowledging that I had won the battle. The handcuffs hung limply in her right hand. No doubt it had been a very long time since they had looked that way.

Naturally, I was such a poor winner I had to go and rub it in by indulging in my next bit of commentary. "Now maybe Mr. John will go home and have a wonderful evening with his wife. Let it never be said that Thyoneus the Thirst Bopper is not a friend to family values."

At this point, one of the *Babies in Bars'* company vehicles came screeching around the corner and careened to a stop. The passenger's side door opened and Officer Fielding's voice was heard saying, "It's alright, Brenda. I'll take it from here." The good officer flashed an even bigger police badge than Brenda's. The camera zeroed in on her tarted up face and beneath the mascara, her eyelids let out a disenchanted blink.

Back in the studio, the whole band gave a collective chuckle and clapped loudly. Jillian announced over the loudspeaker that our next order of business would be to add miscellaneous ambient sounds to the footage of my interaction with the lady cop. After that, Jillian triumphantly informed us that the beer company would be having us back for at least one more season. Kathy wandered off to the edge of the studio, and I followed. She lit up another large spliff and puffed away. Soon she was enveloped in cloud of smoke. Now that she'd scored the home healthcare gig, she didn't have to worry about drug-testing anymore. She told me that she had mixed emotions. She was pleased with the ongoing success of the project, but seemed a bit wistful too. "Joe," she asked. "Will there ever be a time when we can just play music?"

"Aw c'mon, Kathy. Those days are gone forever."

"Joe, the strange part about this is that, for the sake of cheap publicity, most of the competition for *Babies in Bars* spends an inordinate amount of their time tryin' to get arrested. It's like whenever their careers have hit a rough patch, they're talkin' to their agents about how wonderful it would be to get busted again, but circumstances have made it different for us. We're not quite so calculating. But even so, I'll bet we wouldn't shy away from cheap hype like getting arrested."

"We could do that just to show that we're special. What with Officer Fielding on our side, we could get outta jail for free and the others couldn't."

"Gee Joe, I think you're kinda sorta right about that. I, for one, have given up on tryin' not to offend people 'cause hey, from what I've learned so far, they have absolutely no problem goin' out of their way to offend me."

"Kathy, you can't be serious. You just now discovered that?"

"Honest, I did. So that probably makes me a virgin. So shoot me now."

"C'mon, Kath. You know I'd never do that."

"Yeah, I know, but I was only testin' you out."

"So don't test me. Joe. Please do me a huge favor and never test me again."

And I did her the favor that she asked. But it wasn't easy. In fact, it was downright hard.

The latest pronouncement from Thyoneus Beer Corporation top brass only gave Jillian further encouragement to try more bizarre concepts in music video projects. She had been given carte blanche. The audience demanded more and she would give them more. The big question in my mind was whether or not the strangeness was by design or mistake. It was hard to discern the divide.

She had listened to another song on our expanding playlist of tunes. After hundreds of listenings of the tune in question, she had determined that it had lots of whiskers spouting out of it --- figuratively speaking of course. Therefore, from her point of view, it had a distinctly feline theme. After having mulled this notion over in her mind, she announced that she wanted this next vid to be real high concept. The thing she came up with was large and luminous: she said she might want to have vivid film footage of a wildcat stalking the band while we lip-synched the words and pretended to play our instruments, only she hadn't completely decided on that just yet. She would figure it out later. She acknowledged that it would most likely be very difficult to play in real time. A fearsome feline would make it problematic. You see, Jillian was a firm believer in method acting. The character and the player should never be too far away from each other," she said. "Sort of like Joe, our wonderful drummer."

So, this set of images would be suitably frightening for actors and masses alike. The pics would be wild and wooly! There would be a touch of real fear. None of that pallid imitation stuff that passed for drama in other reality shows. And another thing --- she didn't want any special effects because she was going for much different kind of effect. She wanted the whole thing to look absolutely retro. In fact, some of it would be in black and white and shot on grainy film stock. She even went so far as to shop around for film stock that had been suitably banged up because she was aiming for the scratchy look. I was hoping the kitty cat wouldn't be aiming for the scratchy look too. "No problem," she said. "We'll make sure he's declawed."

But no matter. Jillian decided to get some technical advice on the logistics of what it was like to have a wildcat on the production set when the principal photography would be taking place. She thought it would be wonderful if it were written into the plot and woven into the story-line. The plot was vague, but it had something to do with a cat escaping from a circus troupe and then wandering around the countryside before stumbling upon the band, who just happened to be playing someplace near a beautiful river bank. The kitty cat would get transfixed by the amazing sounds coming from the band and then who knew what would happen? Kitty and band would just have to wing it.

After processing this idea for more than a few minutes, she sought out the help of an accomplished animal trainer who was well-versed in how this might be done. She wanted the wild beast to be either a cheetah, bobcat, serval, or leopard. The adviser suggested that, since we weren't going to be using any special effects, then we should go with something smaller. But Jillian didn't listen. Her mind was made up. She needed to know other details. The feline trainer/technician had been forthright and forthcoming. Spots, speckles, or spangles were, according to the knowledgeable man, not an option. He said it would be too dangerous. Jillian protested, saying that spots, speckles, and spangles were a necessity and not an option. The esteemed trainer told her that, when directors do filming in those kinds of situations, the conventional wisdom is to get a small timid wildcat from some vet or shelter in the local area and then to paint dots on it. Mottles, dapples, and dimples were supposed to be made up. That was standard operating procedure.

The trainer explained that the feline wouldn't be too happy about it, but the beast would endure. Doing it this way would make the animal more manageable. "And besides," he said. "The audience won't be able to tell the difference anyway."

Well, Jillian didn't like that idea at all. She wasn't the least bit keen! "Doing it that way is for light weights, wussies, and wimps! We're *Babies in Bars,* a smack-down band if ever there was one, and we're serious characters. None of the balsa wood business for us. No way! We want to have a real-honest-to-goodness cheetah, one that can rev up to a minimum of seventy-five miles per hour and a maximum of ninety-five on the straightaway." She ran this idea by the rest of the band, and by a simple rotation of her eyelash, blinked and convinced all of us to veto it. If we didn't veto, we'd be real darned sorry. As a result, Jillian paid no mind to the accomplished trainer. She didn't give a damn how many feathers that the man had in the hat of his bloody resume; she didn't want to be a light weight, nor did she want the band to be that way either. To do otherwise, would have threatened our ecstatic credibility. Jillian thought of the drummer for *Babies in Bars.* She looked him deep in the eye: would he vote for a dotted pussy cat? She thought not. But she gave me a stink-eye just to slam down the deal.

Consequently, Jillian opted for an un-dotted wild cat. And the result was semi-disastrous. The feline flipped out ferociously. It was a crazed female, and she chased all of us around the set, scaring the hell out of everyone concerned. And that was the least of the feline's antics. The maximum part was that the creature did a fairly big mash-up. The critter totally trashed about $300,000 in equipment as she ran roughshod all over the film set, destroying lots of sound and video gear. Kathy and I cowered on top of a stack of Marshall amps, safely out of the feline's reach. "Kath," I explained. This is the part of the raga when the whole song speeds up, and we have to get out of the way."

But that wasn't the best part. The best part was when the cheetah slash leopard slash serval chased our incompetent bass player up a metal pole that was supposed to be used for a light screen. The less-than-amazing musician was righteously bummed. It was a very un-virtuoso performance. The camera did a close up of his face the instant before the picture blanked out into a wall of static. But Jillian explained that the loss of gear would be a simple tax write-off. Then Jillian summoned the animal trainer on her smart phone, and the guy came in and zapped the cat with a tranquilizer dart. The big kitty fell asleep and had stupendous kitty cat dreams.

THE DONNAH PARFREY SHOW

Obviously, season two would start off with a bang. The show in the other time slot wouldn't stand a chance in hell. *Babies in Bars* would rule. The band represented a revolt against the onslaught of a woozy business model adopted by self-satisfied cutting-edge indie rocker bands. For the first time in many a moon, a live sound mattered more than a processed production straight from Ivory Tower Land, and what made it matter was the essentially contrived and powder-puffed system of the movie/television industry. What was also odd about this development was that the ongoing premise of the show --- that *Babies in Bars* was somehow a struggling bar band playing dives up and down the Jersey shore with occasional forays into Philly, New York, and New England --- would be carried out in the new season. This premise would persist simply for the sake of manufactured drama despite the fact that the band was, in all outward appearance, no longer really struggling. The endorsements from Thyoneus Beer were keeping the project afloat in flamboyantly high style, but the same could not be said for me personally.

Despite the band's commercial appeal, Jillian still wanted to keep me on a tight financial tether. By that I mean she continued to award me with indentured servant status, so that I had to eat from the company food truck and beg for some petty cash now and then. She loved to see me grovel a bit before she let up and said, "Well, I guess we could give you a little something extra to tide you over. But I gotta say, Joe, don't let this become a habit because I might just have to practice some tough love on you, and I'm sure you wouldn't like that one bit."

I could see the handwriting on the wall: Jillian didn't want me to get a swelled head such that I would get actual pay. That would be too much power, and ya can't have that. Music must always take a backseat to acting. And naturally, as was completely predictable, she trotted out her time worn speech about "freedom," and how vital it was in the world that we live in today. And then she added on a new wrinkle, saying that it was part of my "responsibility" as a drummer --- "a conjurer of ecstasy" --- to uphold that very notion. And she went on to say I must do this at all costs. I was beginning to hate her because she wanted me to lead, but she wouldn't let me freakin' lead. She was the ultimate backseat driver. After her speech, she would tack on some other nonsense about how hard it is to find money in the budget to pay a drummer and how money was so tight that she might really have to give serious thought to laying me off and bringing back good ol' Ziggy the silly ricky-tick Beat Box Man. I'm sure just the thought of that made Ben almost cream in his jeans. And there was another thing about her pleading poverty with the budget business she kept harping on --- she was sloughing off on her promise to keep me supplied with my oh-so-vital heroin fix. Why couldn't she hold up her end of the bargain? Beneath my breath, I muttered, "Lady, do your damned gig!"

Jillian's philosophy was timeless --- never let the drummer be a star even when he truly has become the star. The proof for this was quite tangible. It had nothing to do with any megalomaniacal ego-trip on my part. No way. The evidence was the tons of fan mail that routinely piled up. And yes, strange as it might seem, people still actually wrote letters. I guess the reason for that was when people feel strongly about something, then a twitter or tweet or e-mail simply won't do --- they have to put more effort into it. Of course, it was Bill's job to sift through the stacks. In that way, he was so much more than a regular roadie. A spasm of glee shot through me as I watched him sorting the stuff. I mean, he almost needed a shovel for god's sake.

What was odd was that, without knowing it, I had become an actor. And I hated acting since it was completely about artifice, so on my list of things to do, it was near the end and completely about pretend. And what was great about drums and their connection to sound --- which was no small connection and accomplishment --- was that it didn't pretend at all. On the contrary, it was the real raw news. My contribution to the project was that I pretty much lived and played by pure instinct. Audiences loved this because it offered a contrast to Ben who, as everyone was well aware, lived by absolute calculation. By now, he'd given me the nickname of "Joe the Neanderthal" and Jillian had written this into the unofficial treatment for the show.

In fact, she wrote several vignettes in which Joe the Neanderthal would have some obscure kinds of quasi-epileptic seizures. She even went so far as to put in some cheesy 1950's special effects that would show me morphing into a werewolf persona. And then, after a wild dust up on the drums, she would have me morph right back to my so-called regular self. These fits were supposed to show how ambivalent I was about being an actual member of the human race. This produced a dual effect on the audience --- on the one hand, they would laugh at me, and this would make them feel immensely superior because as everyone knew, drummers were supposed to be half crazy anyway, so why not go whole hog and label me as the so-called "Neanderthal nitwit" that Ben was brazenly calling me. But there was a secondary effect, which was to make the audience feel that I had some sort of huge "self-esteem issues." This garnered pity and appealed to their penchant for rooting for the underdog. The consensus was that I was a guy who could never quite get his act together, and wasn't this situation a barrel of laughs? As a result, there were moments when the publicity mills buzzed stories about whether I would or would not very soon make an extra special guest appearance on the talk show of a seriously famous host whose entire celebrity being had been devoted to public revelations of self-esteem issues. I would be a sacrificial lamb to the public therapy industry. And lo and behold, the damned thing happened! Me, a lowly drummer got to be on the Donnah Parfrey Show. For people who keep meticulous track of this stuff, my appearance must have been something of a first in the history of television.

Well, the talk show went well. The nationally known host was grinnin' almost the whole time as she fed me gushin' questions. I answered them as candidly as I could while I watched her twisting and turning in her seat to some obscure pleasure. I lounged back on the guest couch telling the television audience: "I'm at the stage now where I can fly by pure instinct --- playin' that is. The thing is, compared to others, like that punk at the drum solo competition, my instinct is more spot on than theirs. When I follow the beckoning star, new things happen. And isn't that a colorful exhilaration?"

"It sure is. But another thing I wanted to ask you is what is this business about drum solos? You've really started quite a trend. Somehow, you've wiggled into people's heads out there and given 'em some crazy idea that a good drum solo is gonna save the world. Did you come up with this cockamamie idea or was that one of the writers?"

"How many times do I have to tell ya? We don't have writers on a reality show. Yours truly came up with it all by himself."

"Wow! No kiddin'? Well, I'm sure there are lots of unhappy moms out there across America who are more than a bit upset with you because suddenly every ten year old and his brother is buyin' a humongous drum kit and makin' quite a racket."

"Yeah, well if you wanna save the world, you have to put up with a little noise. The planet was spinnin' out of control and the energy from several thousand drum solos is gettin' it to shape up and shape up fast. What people are askin' themselves is this --- which is better love or ecstasy?"

"Do they have to choose? I mean, if you put it that way, your question is pretty hard."

"So, let it be hard. Let 'em struggle. But look at the record. Since our show went on the air, the crime rate has gone down."

"Correlation doesn't always lead to causation."

"Not every time. But it may do that sometimes. And this may be one of those times."

"Yes, Joe. Think of how many conflicts have been avoided. Perhaps you should be on the short list for the Nobel Peace Prize."

"Gee Donnah, I've only been on your show for five minutes and my self-esteem is feelin' better already."

Donnah laughed. The television audience laughed too.

"Joe, they don't call me the Queen of Self-Esteem for nothing."

"Where would you be without John Milton? I mean, the old poet pretty much invented the word. Before he came along, the idea wasn't so much as a embryo, let alone a fetus."

"Yes Joe, he may have given birth to it, but I made it a star. It's true." She winked into the camera on her left. "I'm fessin' up 'cause I owe him a lot. And let me tell ya. For a drummer, you seem surprisingly well read."

"Yeah Donnah, I think I like Milton the best 'cause he gave us pandemonium too --- which is what I try to do on the drums."

The audience did an uneasy laugh, and the renowned hostess moved on to the next talking point on her list. "I have to ask this question because there are so many people out there who are wondering. I know they ask me practically every week. Gulf, the sax player guy. There's a rumor that he's a robot. Is that true? Do you have any inside information on this?"

"Of course he's a robot. Can't you tell. No humans could play sax like that, would they?"

"I don't know. I thought maybe he might be an aberration of Nature."

Yeah, like a mutation or somethin'. What do you think? It's kind of a mystery I guess."

"You tell me. You're the one with the inside track."

"I'm afraid I'm gonna have to keep ya guessin' on that one. Some things are simply trade secrets. I will tell ya one thing though, which is that Gulf has some pretty strange observations about people in general."

"Can you let me in on one of them?"

"I sure can. The best one was when he was lookin' at Vim and Vod --- those are the cuttlefish that lurk around in the background at so many of our gigs."

"Oh yeah, those are the bizarre fish in the huge tank behind the stage --- the ones who change color when they react to the band's music. They really *are* quite a psychedelic light show."

"You got it. Well, once between songs, Gulf was starin' at 'em as they floated in their aquarium, and he turned to me and said, 'Joe, just lookin' at 'em, I've come to the conclusion that not only are people absurd, but animals are too.'"

Donnah decided to let that one pass. She moved on to her next question. "And what I also like so much about *Babies in Bars* is the way you all get along so well. So many bands have problems on that score, but not you guys. Is that another trade secret?"

"Yeah, we do have camaraderie. At one of our first gigs when things weren't goin' so well, Gwen yelled into the mike, 'We are on a ship, and we are all sinking together!'"

I wiggled on the big soft cushy couch and stared out at the vast TV audience, knowing full well that I was lookin' into the future since there was sure to be a tape delay. Yes, my horrible sister was out there somewhere, watchin' me near or watchin' from afar. It didn't make much difference though because she always had the long arm of luck itself. Still, my very appearance on this top-rated talk show would be enough to put the fear of God into her. If I could do that, I knew I could buy some more time.

With carefully measured words, I gave Donnah and the television audience a follow-up answer: "Honest Donnah, he is a robot. And he's a total rookie at life. I keep tellin' Gulf that life isn't for everyone. It takes concentration and responsibility. With him, everything in life is new --- including alcohol. He tells me that alcohol gives him these big ideas. Under the influence, he often finds himself in a meditative mood and suddenly the the ideas appear, leaving him to wonder where they came from because they had nothing to do with anything he's lived through. They're so gigantic that he stands up and salutes, but the deal he has trouble with is how to retain them. That's quite another project because he sees them one minute and struggles to remember them in the next. But even though Gulf forgets them more often than not, he respects them and knows that the mere fact they've appeared for a few fleeting seconds is evidence that he's on the path of ecstasy. And of course, since I'm kinda sorta his tutor, I do everything I can to encourage this notion. Still, I have to say that quite frankly, there are moments when I have my doubts that Gulf is up to the test. So sometimes I razz him and tell him he should consider goin' to the scrap heap on a voluntary basis."

"Oh, don't say that. I don't know of anyone who isn't a big fan of Gulf. They're rootin' for him because he's not quite human. They like to go for the underdog."

"Yeah, it's the same reason they like to root for me."

"How true! Yes, absolutely. But moving right along, there's another rumor making the rounds that Gulf is not the only one of his kind. They think there might be more of these hypothetical robots waiting for their chance to spring into the world."

"I've heard that one. And I can't confirm or deny it. The only thing I can say is that if it's true, then maybe robots will find this world as difficult to live in as we do."

"Hey Joe, I'm a talk show host. I live a life of ease and pleasure. I haven't seen the difficulty very much lately."

"Excludin' you, of course. And remember, robots are supposed to do what they are told. I think that's why Gulf is such a good actor. He's perfect for TV. Don't ya think?"

"Yes Joe. And tell us more about you and Ben. Rumor has it that when he's not playing bass in Babies and Bars he's a part time mad scientist who's Gulf's creator. Something tells me that you and Ben don't exactly get along. Is that true?"

"How'd you get that idea? We get along perfectly. That's why we're such a team. Oh, now and again, I may razz him because now that he's gotten famous, he makes a girl sign a contract every time he takes her to his room."

"Ah, the privilege of fame! You have to keep yourself protected. Someone could take away your secret stash and tell on you."

"Hey, you said it, not me!"

"So what are your plans for the future? For you and *Babies in Bars*? Everyone's dyin' to know."

And then I gave her a bullshit answer, something about how my life was becoming so spacious that I would soon be in danger of gettin' agoraphobia, and she loved it. Accordingly, she moved on to the next talking point. "Joe, you hear about so many pop stars these days who can't seem to get enough jail time. I mean, they seem to want to get themselves arrested so they can get more street creds, if you know what I mean. But Joe, you go in the opposite direction."

"Yes, why is that? I guess the reason is that we cast such a wide swath in the morphic resonance department that we get outta jail for free."

"That's right. I almost forgot about the time when you stopped that man on the street from going out with the hookers."

"You see, we're a very moral lot --- we humble musicians in *Babies in Bars*. We're as peachy keen as any other prime time show."

"Amen to that." Smiling into the camera, she said, "We'll be right back after this break." And then the studio audience clapped right on cue.

But who cares if my responses were or weren't bullshit answers because after the actual talking stages, my drumming throughout the band's tunes cut through all that happy horseshit. My ascendance as a 'star' meant the past got to force itself into the present. This was a revelation for me because nothing in my playing was really new. Whatever exuberance dwelt in that place had patiently lurked there all along just waitin' to be discovered again. Up until now and for every second of my life, I'd felt as though Cro-Magnon people had been living in a vast bubble --- one I had no access to. But now, after everything had happened, I was getting the strength to understand that I might be able to penetrate the bubble and to burst it in high style. Yes, it might well be within my reach. I was discovering that being a celebrity was my means of finding my true self. Mercurial and brimming with this giddy emotion, I nearly ran down the street and unintentionally scared another old man, as I had done not so very long ago just before hooking up with *Babies in Bars,* right before circumstances had conspired to get this whole project rollin' in the first place. And if I did burst this new bubble which, by the way, was simply dyin' to get burst, then perhaps I would be get to take Bill and

Gulf and Kathy with me too. And we could leave Ben. As a matter of fact, he could stay the fuck out.

But if the three of us could go together as one big happy team, then where would that leave Gulf? I didn't know quite what to make of him. One time, after I'd given him a great big speech about the dangers of materialism, he gave me an unexpected response, letting me know that his meager life experience told him otherwise. On the contrary, he loved *things*! In fact, the things he worshipped the most were his skateboard and his saxophone. He liked to think about the wonderful experiences he'd had with those supposedly dastardly things. "When I think about the good and bad times my skateboard and my beloved saxophone have been through, I get a little misty-eyed. I mean, we've been through so much together, and I really and truly think we've bonded like brothers." No, those things were not so bad after all.

And Gulf thought about the bands that that *Babies in Bars* were competing against. For them, being able to to play an instrument was an antique ho-hum concept. How boring it was when they could push lots of buttons and tinker with a wide array of dials and beautiful sounds would automatically emit. Hell, among Gulf's young peer group, there were a host of idiots who were under the impression that they could play. For them, all that was necessary was to simply think about the process and the mere act of contemplation was more than enough to simulate their way around a fretboard or drum kit, so being able to play didn't amount to a damn, and if it didn't amount to a damn, practice didn't rate anything on anyone's agenda either. Well in Gulf's opinion, after a few days and weeks of trumpeting this crippled view of the world, people actually discovered that they had forgotten how to play music. And then they scratched their collective heads in wonderment, tryin' to understand why they sucked. Gulf was adamant. He seriously did not want to suck.

So the robot boy, still wet behind the ears from life itself, was now the true wild card. He was to some extent an unknown quantity. And Jillian naturally wanted to keep it that way since going that route would be great for the ratings. The ratings, the ratings --- in the long run, they were what it was all about. I was the first to sense something strange was stirring within him. Ben's purpose had been to plant a time bomb within the band, one that would sooner or later blow the project apart. The evidence for this was that on recent gigs, the boy machine would screw up every now and then, particularly at auspicious moments when the band was seemingly at the top of its game. Gulf's face indicated a personality that was beginning to be filled with the first drops of mixed feelings. His head was going one way while his body was going another. Of course, only the cuttlefish lurking beneath his skull would ultimately know what the hell was up. No doubt they were right at that moment blushing themselves silly. This made me get a warm feeling inside because I could see that this coy business-of-music thing was not so coy. It was as if the Goddess of Music, in cahoots with Ted the Gorilla, was showing off Her power. Could it be that the ecstasy which they had long been capable of promoting with people was something they could duplicate with creatures who were partly composed of circuit boards and cyborgs? The jury was still out, and only time would tell.

But that was not a problem. I was a patient fellow. Time could take all the seconds hours, days, and months that it wanted. I noted that Gulf was seeing me more and more as not just a mentor but also as a confidant. His biggest revelations to me were no longer just his thoughts on Gwen. He said that his imagination was now attempting to look at Gina from a different angle. Immediately, I recalled how I'd set that young cyborg lady free from Ben's place of business and how that had set her loose out into the great big world on her very own. And I had done that because Gulf hadn't found her the least bit attractive. But now Gulf told me how he'd thought long and hard about Gina's blonde hair, saying that deep in his make-believe world, he tried to touch it. And no matter how he'd tried to change his thought pattern, her blonde hair really didn't work for him. He felt in his heart and soul that the blonde hair business was a total deal breaker. With a look of overpowering sadness, he looked into my eyes and said he'd equated the tow-headed look with everything that was better safe than sorry. And safety and security meant something could further be equated with all things that were vaguely boring, which was something he'd battled against throughout most of his brief haptic existence. He said that I, as his wonderful mentor, had pontificated loudly about how he must avoid boring things. And he was simply following the paradigms of what made absolute common sense. In fact, my wonderful advice had somehow finagled its way into the very fiber and being of his consciousness, and this had the nefarious effect of rendering null and void all of Ben's pernicious downloads. So, Gulf looked into my eyes yet again and observed that just as two negatives in math multiply to create a positive, so too did two nefarious's team in tandem to give birth to a rebellion. Continuing on in the same train of thought, Gulf indicated that he'd begun to believe that these ruminations were the result of a supremely overcivilized man and wasn't that something that was worthy of being ashamed about? Sifting through these clues, he told he was rapidly becoming very analytical, almost to the extreme, and as a result, he'd become convinced of the necessity of following a middle pathway.

"But Joe" he said, "a middle path means a boring path, so really and truly, aren't I right back where I've started from?"

The good thing about Gulf's deep state of confusion was that his dysfunctional situation was yet another thing which was goin' my way. The other good thing that was goin' my way was Officer Fielding. The guy was finally letting up on me. It was fun to see that I'd won him over. But how long would it last?

So, in the long view, things were looking up. For the longest time, I'd been a haunted man --- one who'd patiently let the ghosts of the past have tyrannical dominion over the present. But now I was getting better at shoving them to the side as brusquely as possible.

SUNITA'S HOUSEWARMING

This was not to say that I was never immune to a relapse now and then.

Sunita and I were cautiously getting along. If Sachiko, my crazy ex who was yet another ghost from the past, had been around to register her crackpot, jealous opinion, she no doubt would have said in her native tongue that this "getting along" thing was "*totemo hen*" --- very strange. Yes, it was extremely "hen" indeed. Sachiko would have cackled long and loud. Then she'd have remarked that there was something tropical about the whole deal. But to hell with her because she wasn't around, and she was so ancient history that she might as well have lapsed into archaeology. For all I cared, her ruins could go stew in their own sullen juices. Despite this, I would have had to forgive Sachiko for being right because each day that Sunita and I remained together was a step further into an ocean that got warmer and warmer, a comfortable circumstance with a semblance of cozy logic: I would make the coffee; she would make omelets; I would wash dishes; she would polish tiles, and I would scrub glossy surfaces and in the grand scheme, things aimed at common sense. Nothing swiveled out of control. And I would get inside of her more often than not, which was a rather good epiphany of sorts. I mean, how can you find fault with that? Despite this, I knew her fragmentation would most likely be a permanent fixture, and I was getting used to it 'cause it catered to a gaping black hole deep inside my heart. I refer to those moments when I thought about hurting her ... but, but wait! I hasten to add that I *only thought*. Thinking is different from acting upon, which is different from doing, and so many Cro-Mags don't get that it doesn't count. I wanted to give her and me the illusion of being hurt. I would find myself muttering --- am I helping her or am I hurting her? Ha! That's what I've always thought about the act of love itself. Only thing is Sunita was hurt already so she could only be helped. But I believed from day one, it's important for safety's sake to keep certain things separate and permanently unknown. She simply had no right to that data.

Of course, there was a minor problem which would rear its ugly head from time to time. That was the issue of my new infatuation with Zaga the alien girl. That little side sweetie gave a whole new meaning to the words "star fucker." I mean, I couldn't help myself. It was like I was trying to conquer desire itself, and I wasn't havin' much luck, so I had to go and try to conquer it yet again, and again and again until aw shucks, I got it right. Sooner or later I knew I'd meet up with success. Until that time, I could keep right on trying.

I'd entered Zaga's field of morphic resonance and the lady just wouldn't quit, not even for a second. The creature from outer space was so damned exotic. Zaga had six toes on each foot and the best that Sunita could come up with was a paltry five. How effin' mundane could she possibly be? Compared to the alien, she was digitally challenged. Sunita knew that she'd been trumped, and she wasn't very happy about it. It kind of stuck in her craw. So, Sunita would let me know again and again that sooner or later I would have to make a decision. No, I said, that might mean that she might have to make a decision. I wanted to have my way. I was so sick or other people having theirs and tellin' me that I had to toe the line. What I wanted more than anything else was for them to toe the line.

I guess you could say that's been an ongoing problem with me: I like exotic things--- exotic music, exotic architecture, exotic this and exotic that. And most of all, exotic women. And when you really stop to think about it, what in the world is more exotic than a female being who's not from this world? Yeah, I know. That's probably a hard one to answer. But I didn't care about how Sunita felt. Why was that? It was because this was my time. It didn't belong to her or anyone else. Let the rest of the world spin and sputter about how my time was their time. Right then, they could pull that fast one all they wanted --- it simply no longer had any effect. The fan mail that Bill had to manage and answer with form letters was confirmation of this. The fan mail often engaged in wild-but-absolutely-true speculations concerning how, throughout my entire existence, I'd been bowin' down to others, being a subset and subspecies of their projects. Well, I'd had enough. The fan mail was right. It was time for those people to bow down to me. And that subset of folks who now had to bow down included Sunita. She would on occasion, have to bow down to me just as the disconsolate police lady had had to bow down. Oh that was such a good one! I was still gloating over it! And so was Bill, and for that matter, so was Officer Fielding. Both of them were starting to live through me in the same way that moms and dads of Little Leaguers like to live through their offspring.

Be that as it may, and despite all of this bowing down, I could once in a while give a full salute to domestic bliss. I gave it lip service, and I gave it lip service in more ways than one. I had to say there was something to be said for it even though for the greater part of my life I had deemed domestic bliss to be about as small on the list of priorities as my horrible sister's debased notions concerning the value of love. So, in the short term, and with some stringent qualifications, there was something to be said for love and for domestic bliss.

As this situation of abundant domestic bliss got to be the rule rather than the exception, Sunita felt the need to make some changes. She assured me that these changes would be for the better and told me that they would further enhance what was already a pretty good domestic deal. In short, what she wanted was to get a better apartment, one that would imply some transitional phase out of her relationship with Ben.

That was what I most liked about the girl --- if she wanted something, she didn't sit around thinkin' about it much. She just went ahead and did it. Or should I say, she crutched along with her five toes stickin' out knowing full well that Zaga jogged along with her six toes stickin' in.

This persistence seemed to be the very keystone for Sunita's design for living. I had to give her credit. The only exception to that was the problem of her off-and-on relationship with Ben. This was where she was prone to vacillation. I really resented the fact that Ben held the green card issue over her head like some sort of giant battle axe. My God, the guy never missed an opportunity to blackmail her. She really wanted to dump him, but she couldn't do that because otherwise Ben would turn her in to the immigration authorities and then of course, she'd be bounced back to Bangladesh. Going back there, especially under such humiliating circumstances, would have spelled the ultimate failure of her existence. And naturally, Ben was acutely aware of her feelings on what was such a touchy subject for her. He would never tire of lording that over her. I tell ya, the guy must have kept a vast archive in his mind, a repository that listed all the people he knew and each of the corresponding buttons to push in order to get his way with them. Many was the time when I would overhear one of their conversations in which he would say, "Remember, Sunita. If you have to go back to Dacca, you'd be a total failure --- the ultimate loser. And remember this one too, Sunita. If I turned you in, I'd simply be doin' my civic duty. The only reason I haven't turned you in already is that I'm basically a good guy." After that, I could hear the predictable round of tears, and at that point, I figured I'd better turn around and head back to my room at the hotel on the boardwalk. It was still the same dingy place, but hell, it didn't really make a damned bit of difference whether I stayed in a pit or a palace 'cause we drummers aren't affected by that sort of thing --- we can put up with whatever background that life is willing to foist on us. We're good at this since we're backgrounds ourselves. But watch out! We're the help. And the help are drunk.

So back to Sunita's new house for a second --- she thought it would be a good idea to move, and like I said earlier, what with the hookers infesting the nabe and all, the area was fast going to seed. Of course, I argued with her, telling her that the workin' girls gave the neighborhood a kind of quaint charm. But she wouldn't hear it, and she let me know in no uncertain terms that she wouldn't put up with it anymore despite the fact that the cute little hypocrite was kinda sorta one herself. I told her she shouldn't be so high and mighty, but that was like talkin' to a wall for all the good it would do.

So she moved. She just up and did it. That was when something dangerous happened.

I had been on the road for a few days playin' one nighters with *Babies and Bars*. The crowds were goin' absolutely nuts, and I might as well have been in heaven with a capital H. When I got back, I had to recalibrate to so-called "real life," which was no small re-adjustment because I was so used to adoring crowds whom I had ushered into ecstasy. Now I had to listen to stuff that paled in comparison. I viewed it as trivia, but conceded that it was important trivia. She told me the story of her housewarming. "Oh Joe, it was horrible. Lourdes is hysterical about it too."

"Alright, she's hysterical, but do me a favor and don't keep me in suspense. Tell it to me." That was another quality that she possessed --- she liked to take forever to tell a story, only if it was you who was tellin' the story, she'd be annoyin' the hell outta ya every second, demanding that you hurry up. However, since she truly looked as scared as I'd ever seen her, I thought I'd give her a little slack and not say anything. I just let her blurt out the whole thing.

And blurt it out she did. "Lourdes and I had just moved in. We had taken most of our belongings out of the cardboard boxes and had set up the living room and Lourdes' room. We had made a start on setting up the living room when we figured that we'd better call it a day. The movers had been very helpful, and I was so happy that I gave them an extra big tip. There were still lots of boxes to be unpacked, but at least we'd made a dent in it. I said goodnight to Lourdes, and we turned in. I fell asleep as soon as my head hit the pillow and in a blink, I was off to dreamy-dream land. Then I was awakened by Lourdes whispering at me saying, 'Mom, wake up. Something's going on outside.' 'What's happening?' I asked. 'Mom there's a weird thumpin' sound goin' on out in the hallway of the building.' 'Don't worry,' I told her. 'Go back to sleep. It's probably nothing.' But Lourdes was persistent. 'No Ma, it's something bad. Something bad is happening.' Just to make her happy and to reassure her, I figured I'd better give her the benefit of the doubt. I got out of bed, put my crutches under my arms, and went to the front door. And

I'll be damned if Lourdes wasn't right. There was a weird thumping noise that was happening right outside in the hallway of the new apartment building. I thought about this problem long and hard. There were angles and perspectives to evaluate. And these issues needed to be given a free plain of thought. Finally, I said, 'Lourdes deary, I'm gonna call the cops. Let's just sit tight until they get here. OK?' Lourdes nodded and I went for my cell phone and dialed 911. They answered right away and told me they'd send two patrolmen to look into the matter. Meanwhile, the thumping noise stopped. In about five minutes, I looked outside the window onto the street and saw the patrol car pull up to the building and double park. Shortly thereafter, we heard the doorbell. I pressed the intercom and could hear them say, 'M'am, we're here to investigate a disturbance. Can you buzz us in?' I let them in, and Lourdes and I listened to the sound of their footsteps on the outside stairs. We could hear them getting louder and louder, echoing a bit on the travertine surfaces of the stairwell walls. I was thinking to myself that the echoing was the part that made this entire thing so gosh darned creepy. And I was saying that this would be about as creepy as it got. Lourdes squirmed, and I could feel her body next to mine. She's such a creature of curiosity. And her curiosity was in full flower. She whispered, 'C'mon Ma, I can tell by the sound of their footsteps that they're almost here. Let's open the door a crack, so we can see what's out there. I wanna see what all the thumpin' was about.' She was right --- the footsteps were getting nearer and nearer. They were approaching the top of the stairs. After that, they would be sure to come around the wooden railing, and then it would be safe to look out into the hall. That was it --- the sound of them making the turn. Now it would be safe for us to look out from the door and take a peek. I opened it a crack and could see the officers coming towards me. There was the first one --- he looked like a rookie. And there was the second. He looked like a rookie too. Then I saw their faces recoil in total horror. I opened the door all the way, and I could see what they could see --- the hallway was a mass of smeared blood! The red was everywhere: on the travertine walls, on the wooden railings, and most of all, on the mosaic tiles of the floor. 'Oh my God!' exclaimed the first officer as the color drained out of his face, ready to join up with the color that was already there on the floor. 'What happened here?' Lourdes pushed past me into the hall before I had a chance to restrain her. The officers jumped back as they reacted to her scream. However, that wasn't the worst of it. The worst thing was that there was no body. And the troubling thing about that was that nobody but nobody could ever lose that amount of blood and still be among the living. This fact was quite apparent to both of the young officers. What was also apparent was that these cops seemed to be afraid of the sight of blood. 'Where's the body?' asked the first cop. 'There isn't one!' yelled the second. 'Mike, this is awful. Let's call for back-up right now.' And in ten minutes the place was crawlin' with cops. Well, Joe. That's the way it went down."

"Jesus, Sunita! So what's the upshot? What's the result of their investigation?" I asked.

"There isn't one. I called the precinct yesterday and inquired as to the status of the investigation, and they told me they had no idea what in the world happened in that hallway. The whole thing is being designated as 'pending status' with the very real possibility that it will never be solved."

"That's deplorable. What the hell kind of police work is that?"

"Beat's me. I thought it was pretty effed up. I also said I'd call 'em back next week to see if they would have anything new to report, and they said, 'We don't know, and we don't care what happened' and as far as they were concerned, the case was pretty much officially closed. The other horrible thing about this was that the cops refused to clean up all the blood from the hall. They told me it wasn't their problem, but I really needed to clean it up because my parents were coming to visit me and Lourdes the very next day, and there was no way in hell that I wanted them to know about what kind of a hellhole I'd just moved into. Damn, if that had happened, then they would most likely had started some sorta of parental incompetence proceedings against me, and I couldn't have that and what with my broken leg and everything, I couldn't very well do the clean-up by myself, so I had to get Lourdes to do it. Well, she did it, but Jesus did she ever freak on that one."

"Well, I can't imagine why."

This wasn't good news at all. Momentarily, I thought of the implied arrangement that Sunita and I had agreed on. I remembered that it was my job to scrub glossy surfaces. That was my gig and not Lourdes' chore. And the more I thought about it, the more I got the feelin' that my roadie Bill might know somethin' about what went down. I had to talk to him fast. "Sunita, I gotta make a few quick calls, and they might be somethin' that'll shed some light on this. I'll be right back."

"Please come back right away. This situation is drivin' me crazy."

"Alright, alright. I promise I'll be right back." I ducked out to the street and walked to the next block 'cause there was no way I wanted Sunita to listen in on my call to Bill. Luckily, I got him on the first try. I got him on Skype because I truly wanted to see his face so I could gauge how he reacted. There he was on the other end. I could even see his disheveled room in the background. It sorta went with his disheveled look and his vacant eyes. "Bill, I just now came from Sunita's new place. You know, the one that she just moved into. And she told me about how there was a murder right out in the hall, just outside of her apartment door. And what's more, Bill, there was no body anywhere in plain sight. But nobody on God's green earth could lose that amount of blood and still be walkin' around on top of the ground. The whole hallway outside of her apartment was a mass of red. It was practically saturated into the woodwork. I don't have to tell ya that Sunita and Lourdes are seriously freakin' out right about now."

A LOOK INTO THE FACTORY

Bill didn't say anything right away, but I could see him hemmin' and hawin' on the other end of the call. Gradually, I was getting the vibe that he knew something. At length I asked, "Bill, when you and Meghan and that Tony fella had that big run in with the drug dealers, you told me that Meghan insisted on grabbing the cash that the gang had. You know what I mean --- the bag that had all of their shake-down money they'd collected just before you and Tony beat the hell outta them."

"Yeah, so what of it?"

"Yeah, so where did that money go to?"

"Why, now that ya speak of it, it went into safekeeping."

"Safekeeping where?"

"As far as I know, Tony and Meghan said they'd take care of it.'

"Jeez Bill, you're almost fuckin' useless to me now. You can't even conjure up the heroin that you promised me. Nowadays, I have to rely on Jillian. And she'll no doubt let me down too. About the only people I can trust are the bloody aliens I just met. The people on the face of the earth are totally untrustworthy. And these foreign bodies aren't even real people. They don't have the right amount of fingers and toes. Maybe that's why they might get to be more dependable. Bill, you're damaged, almost as sadly fucked up as Sunita. What did Meghan do --- hypnotize you and turn you into a meth head?"

"I dunno."

"What did you do with the cash?"

"Tony said it would be a good idea to store it someplace."

"Like where?"

"I wasn't feelin' so good, so he suggested that we drive somewhere. He asked me who my best friend was, and I said that would be you. And then he asked me who your girlfriend was, and I said Sunita. So, he and I drove over to Sunita's house and hid the money there in some place where she'd never suspect. And then of course, she went and moved."

I suddenly wished that this wasn't a phone call and that he wasn't faraway. I wished I could go right through the face of the Skype screen and put my arm around my friend. I told him, "C 'mon man. I wanna help ya. I wanna help ya 'cause you helped me. You held off and didn't kill me back when they were tellin' ya to whack me. For that, I give you high marks. I'm forever in your debt. But the thing is, man, you're draggin' me down. That sister of mine really messed you up. I gotta bring you back from the edge, just like you brought me back from the edge. But we have to make some new ground rules."

"What are those, Joe?" His eyes looked hopeless. And his confused crinkly forehead looked hopeless too. Still I'd have to give him a try since he'd been there for me.

"We gotta stick with tradition. What I mean by that is no more of this crystal meth stuff. It's just too over the top. Look, you're gonna hafta go back to plain old heroin. It's worked perfectly fine down through the ages, and it'll be your best bet against the future. Do ya hear me?"

"Yes, yes, loud and clear. Joe, I know I've made a mess of things. I've gotten in over my head. And I've always been someone who prides himself on not gettin' in over his head, only she was somethin' quite different ... a different kettle of fish. I was up against a force I truly hadn't bargained for. I know I've failed you as a friend. But wait a minute ... I'll try to make it up to you."

"So how in the hell are you gonna do that? Answer me that."

"Ben doesn't like you. That's probably not news to you. Yeah, I know, Jillian keeps tellin' you how you're supposed to love him like a best friend for life. But you know and I know that's just for when we're on the set. And I gotta say that you're not really foolin' anyone, least of all the cameras..."

"So hurry up and cut to the chase. How are you gonna help me? How are you gonna make it up to me?"

"Ben's been workin' on that Robot Boy of his. You know who I mean --- Gulf. Well, Ben's been tryin' to improve the prototype. He wants to take the idea of Gulf to another level. In fact, he wants to make a whole army of Gulfs. He wants a vast reserve of the prototypes for his very own private army. To his way of thinkin', they'll be overflowin' and comin' right on out of the baseboards."

"So I figured as much. You're not tellin' me much that I haven't already surmised."

"Well, I can take you to the staging area where he's assemblin' the whole package. I think you'd want to know about that. And I can take you there."

"Alright, so hurry up. Take me there now."

"Now? I didn't think you'd want to get there so soon."

"Damn right I do. C'mon. Let's go there now!"

I had to push Bill because I could see that was the one thing he didn't want to happen. His vacant eyes perked to life on the Skype screen. I could see that the shadow of his former self was coming back from the brink. He was a man who'd lost his way, but was now on the verge of regaining his stride. Whatever war he'd been through was being shoved to the side. He had weathered Meghan's meth, and now he was going to make his comeback.

I arranged to meet up with him, so he could show me the first squadron of those armies of prototypes. I could picture 'em squirmin' around, itchin' to get somewhere fast. Perhaps it was my function in life to stop 'em dead in their tracks. He drove me to a warehouse not far from Ben's place of business. I was dismayed when I found out that it was a storage facility for coffins --- a place where the elegant boxes could be kept in short notice inventory until the time that they needed to have a permanent occupant and a serious, unyielding address underground. The building was more than a little eerie. I suppose that much could have been expected. We walked by the showroom, which strange as it would seem, had the ambience of a Cadillac dealership. I was almost expecting a salesman in a madras sports jacket and dark sunglasses with a whispery and unctuous accent to come out from the corner office to try and sell me one of the gleaming metal or mahogany carrying cases, just so I'd be able to say thanks but no thanks. But no salesman greeted us. Instead, Bill and I crept through the deserted dealership where the capsules for the future dead yawned their padded and upholstered interiors. The lids opened wide waitin' to be fed, but they'd just have to hold their horses. Fasting is good for the soul. Bill and I walked through the place and every footstep echoed long and loud. We didn't bother to tiptoe because Bill assured me that nobody would be around. Nobody except for the prototypes.

"Ya see Joe, Ben has the first of their robotic kind stashed over there, near that office that doubles as his lab."

He led me on, so I could get a better view. The place was givin' me the creeps. I knew what Ben did for a living, that is, when he wasn't ostensibly trying to make it as a bass player, and I have to say I wasn't lovin' it. The coffins were stacked like firewood --- the raw assets of future profits. Their accumulation was so thick I thought they'd brim over and spill onto the floor and wake up whoever it was that we weren't supposed to wake up. I wanted to say, "Yo Ben, this music thing which you're so ill-suited for, is not some cash and carry operation --- not a casual, common transaction." But the thing was I was in a place of common casual transactions. What could be more casual than bein' dead? I mean, the deceased just don't give a damn what the hell happens to 'em. It suddenly struck me that Bill and I were in the domain of Morpheus, and that was what was Ben's stock and trade, whether it was usherin' the dead out of this world or bringing innovative monster prototypes into it. But this feelin' did wake up something in me. I thought of Gwen, the girl who liked to practice at the art of bein' passed away. I could imagine her in there, waitin' to pop out of some wooden or metal box, only she wouldn't morph right back into life itself like Gina the cyborg, or robot, or half 'n half, or whatever the hell she was supposed to be. Rather, Gwen would remain deader than dead because for her, life was some kind of epic punishment. Kathy, in her moment of candid observation, had told me as much. Me, I was only equipped with crude technology

--- a set of drums and a pair of primitive sticks. The coffins made me think that I had to urgently bring someone back from the brim of death. They were on the periphery of never movin' again. It would be my job to make that someone feel again. Or would it? I was having second thoughts.

"Joe, c'mon. Take a look over here. I like to call 'em Hybridized Hominids. I call 'em that in honor of you, the one who's arguably the last hominid on the planet. You see, I think they're the next logical progression."

"Oh, knock it off with the flattery, Bill! Just open the damned box."

Bill was looking down at one of the boxes. He pressed a lever and the lid of the gleaming case popped open. Bill had to step back a few inches in order not to be smacked by the lid. I could see the occupant was a young woman in the same age range as Gulf. Bill pressed the activation switch near her neck, and the girl came alive with the same speed that the elaborate box had opened its top. The cyborg being flickered her eyes and focused first on Bill and then on me. Like Gina before her, she didn't say a word. Bill explained that the reason for this deaf mute routine was that Ben wanted his creations to be smart, but not so smart that they would wind up like Gulf and start to have temper tantrums and problems with authority figures. He'd carefully programmed them so they would bypass certain stages of child development.

The thing simply sat up in the coffin and pondered the edge of the satin coverlet within the box. She looked like a young coed who'd just finished the laundry at the dorm and was now about to delve into the plot of a soap opera before hitting the books to keep up with her accounting major. I was struck by her near total casualness. It was obvious that Ben had not only deleted her autonomy, but that while he was at it, he'd gone ahead and gotten rid of the shame and doubt part as well.

Bill looked at the tag that was attached to the sleeve of the cyborg's dress: "Lemme see what name this thing goes by. Joe, let me introduce you to the lovely and talented Olivia."

Bill left her there so she could stare at the embroidery in peace and moved on to the next carrying case. I glanced at the price tag

--- in terms of its presentation, this one was considerably more costly, definitely a step up on the economic food chain, but still within the means of the average upper middle class griever. Bill followed the same ritual as before and this time, a cyborg similar to Gulf appeared. Then Bill went on and on, performing the ritual again and again, and very soon the entire section of the warehouse was a mass of pop top boxes sprouting cyborgs of varying degrees of sizes, shapes, and synthetic ethnicities.

"What I've discovered is that each of them has some sort of musical ability. And it's an ability that no human could possibly imitate if that human lived to be a million years old."

My attention drifted back to the lovely Olivia. I thought about how I'd never hit a girl before and how my father, bless my father, had told me over and over that there would come a day when I would feel the urge to hit a girl, but that no matter what, I would have to hold fast and fight the feeling. I must never fall victim to that taboo. That would be extremely ungentlemanly. And one should never be ungentlemanly. That would be a crime to the end of time itself ... ... that would be a crime... a crime ... in a flash, and without any warning, Bill's observation managed to get my blood boiling. My racing thoughts vaulted into fantasies of annihilating opponents in drum solo competitions, and those speeded into more lurid images of machines being hammered into oblivion. Before Bill could do anything, I rushed over and flicked Olivia's activation switch. She slumped forward, and I pressed the other toggle device because by now this was simply second nature to me, and I was fully aware of where all the toggles were. No, the switches could never hide now. I knew each and every trick in the crypto-gizmo book. If it weren't for my destructive side, Ben would no doubt have hired me on as some sort of teacher's assistant. But I wasn't, so the top of the thing's skull opened, exposing the lovely creature's equally lovely brain. A laser light ensconced within the cephalopod sphere pulsed under the synthetic bone of the cranium. With a swift karate move, I reached over and smashed the light, and the luminosity twitched uncontrollably, sending out barreling streams of light, like a disco high beamer run amok.

"Joe, what in the world are you doing? Do you really want to destroy Ben's good work?"

"I've got to. It's a matter of my own survival and the survival of you and of everyone else."

I grabbed a hammer that was lying on a work bench near the capsule. Bill struggled with me, imploring me to stop and uttering something about how Ben's creations were too exquisite to kill and I told him off, saying that getting all agog about exquisite things was exactly how he'd gotten himself in over his head with my diabolical sister and wasn't that a complete dead end and did he really want to go there to that place again and ... and ...

And suddenly I heard Gulf's voice: "Joe, it's OK. You can smash her if you want to." He entered the room and slowly moved over to one of the capsules. "Remember, she's a robot, so she doesn't have any feelings. And remember me. I'm not supposed to have any feelings either. Isn't that right? I mean, if you smashed her, it wouldn't be any more of a pain-in-the-neck moral issue than if Kathy smashed one of her guitars, which she has been known to do once in a while when the spirit moves her. A guitar can't feel. Neither can that alleged girl who's lying in that capsule just about ready to hatch, so she can go out into the world just the way that Gina went out into the world. Oh, and by the way Joe. Ben took the money. That was what your mission was when you first came in here. Now I can see by that hammer in your hand that you have a different mission."

"Ben took the money? How did he know?"

"He knows a lot. As a matter of fact, he's been studying up on you. But hell, I thought he'd told you as much. Look, if you want to compete against him, you're gonna have to do a lot better."

He assumed a haughty air and moved across the room to rub his hand on Olivia's arm. Despite the fact, that the lid of her cranium was wide open and the disco lights from her hybridized brain were flashing laser-like strobes around the cavernous room, the machine was unfazed. The lovely automaton gave him her best smile and said: "And if you wanna do better, then it's only a guess on my part, but I would wager to say that you might need me."

I was thunderstruck that pretty girl Olivia could formulate a sentence, but I quickly surmised that Ben had made significant progress since tinkering with his earlier prototype. Looking her squarely in the eye, I replied, "YOU? Why would I want you? All my life I've been tryin' to get away from machines who have been tryin' to take over my life. With their silly beat boxes, they've been tryin' to kick me out of a job. You're the enemy! She's the enemy! Isn't that right Bill? Help me on this one Bill. I mean, you freakin' owe me one. You owe me as much a Fielding owed me. C'mon now! What does it take to get you to agree with me?"

"Joe, she's got a good point. You don't have much choice. These creatures --- these things --- are gonna weasel their way in. There's no way around it. Gulf and Olivia and even Gina are hatching into the world, and you'd better watch out. You want my opinion, and I'm only too happy to give it to you. You'd best follow Gulf. He may very well be the one who's the mentor, and you might be the apt pupil."

"Oh Jesus, how humiliating! I've fought my whole life trying to avoid this moment."

"Put down the hammer, Joe. It's not gonna work. It won't work because it's their destiny. It's got nothing to do with you. It's got everything to do with it just bein' their time. The best you can do now is to try and co-exist."

I glanced at Olivia again. She was still looking at the edge of the great big ornate box. She may have been put on hold, but the pause wouldn't last for very long. I slowly lowered the hammer and let it slip from my grasp. I jolted some when it hit the floor.

Bill intervened. "Joe, let it rest. At least now we know what we're up against." He moved over to another of the gleaming boxes and popped open the lid. A handsome young man with movie star looks was occupying it. But he was not in the mood for resting in peace because he quickly sat up and bounded out of the box. Then Bill repeated the process, this time with the movie star machine and soon the boxes were popping open on a grand scale and bionics were bounding from boxes all over the place. They were scrambling and making mad dashes en masse. There was something lemming-like about the whole thing as the sound of crashing coffins accompanied this surreal scene. One of the beings stopped to pick up the hammer I had dropped. He brandished it and started smashing the gleaming capsule that he had just escaped from. I was witnessing a first --- never before in the history of machines had a mechanical entity been so hell-bent on destroying its past.

Just then, Gulf appeared, walking casually from behind a stack of the capsules. He didn't say anything right away, but rather, walked forward to pitch in and lend of hand to the capsule smashing. Then he turned to look at me and said something very strange: "Joe, I think you might have us all wrong. You seem to think that me and my kind are here to disagree with you. Have you ever thought that it might be the other way around."

"What do you mean?"

Bill interjected: "What I think he's tryin' to say is that these creatures want to evolve in the same way that you want to evolve. They're as fed up with their robot lives as you are."

Watching the newly minted Hybridized Hominids flee the premises in droves, I was quite moved by what I saw. They were stampeding, running like rats from a ferret. They were running not for their lives, but rather into the embrace of brand new and fresher lives.

So, that's about it for now. I'm turnin' this tome over to Officer Fielding for his safe keeping --- both flash drives of it. Who knows what in the world he'll do with them, but it's better him than Bill. So you may ask, "Why?" The truth of the matter is that this writing deal has got me down. I say that 'cause I'd so much rather be drummin' than jottin' down my thoughts. The only reason I've been jottin' down my thoughts is that someone out there has to be listenin'. And it sure as hell isn't anyone on this end. Besides, my hands are getting' tuckered out, and I really have to save them for the drummin'. That and not the scrawlin' is what's gonna save this planet of ours. Yeah, I know --- you still think it's a cockamamie idea. Alright, go ahead and think that. I only ask that you keep and open mind 'cause one thing's been weighing heavily on my own. I mean, it's weighin' in a good way, and that's why the girls from outer space could help me out on the writin' thing since they seem to know everything anyway.

Like I told you before, if you have omnipotence, it's better to use it. Otherwise, it's probably gonna go stale on you. So if that's true, then I think it's time for the two Cosmic Kids --- Ziga and Zaga. I wanna say, hey girls, do your freakin' gig. I do mine.

FLASH DRIVE NUMBER THREE

Ziga's Report to Interstellar Command

ASSISTED EDITING

So, look, I know I gotta write a report to Interstellar High Command about our latest escapades with humans. That's part of the deal and part of the regulations. I know the rules, but I refuse to keep it dry as a bone. Usually, you want me to go that way, 'cause you've been sold a bill of goods about so-called pain-in-the-ass objectivity, but I'm sorry. I refuse. I refuse for my own sanity here on this preposterous planet. And that gets more and more problematic every day 'cause Zaga and I are havin' too much fun. Yo girl, pour me another one, will ya! Make it a double straight up with no ice! She and I have been, how do they say it on this planet --- "tying one on?" In fact, we've been gettin' such a buzz that we might become incapacitated. We're blotto in bimbo land. Oh where is their home-training? This situation might mean that you geniuses over at Interstellar High Command would have to send in some well-needed reinforcements 'cause this crazy Neanderthal guy named Joe is drinkin' both of us under the table.

And on another note --- that freaky devil --- he made it with Zaga already! I know, can you believe it --- interstellar intertwingling? It's what made our galaxy gregarious! And we're exporting it to this insane place. Joe didn't waste any time. That's what I like about him. He brushed aside her skirt, and the lack of resistance was real darn surprising, as if part of her was saying, "Hey fella, due to an admirable insistence, you've made it this far, so now you get a free pass." I can't believe she said that. Right now I'm whackin' myself in the forehead. That Neanderthal has corrupted both of us already. And he's doin' it the old-fashioned way. He likes passed out pretty ones. Zaga was lifted far out of herself, far out of her skirt, and her purple eyes blinked in total satisfaction. Or maybe stupefaction. But who cares if there's a difference? Right now I could care less about hairsplitting these nuances. I'm tellin' you, she's finally found the man of her dreams. And he's about as sophisticated as a sea slug 'cause he adores her feet. I mean, she can't get him away from them for five minutes. He worships the things she stands on. She feels like a building that's been standing for a long time and now suddenly everyone is appreciating its foundation. They're ogling the luscious bricks and mortar. And the toes are twitchin'. Of course, there are momentary lapses into self-doubt, when she wonders about whether this business is getting a shade too fetish-like. I suppose that's to be expected. But I reassure her, telling her that everyone should have a fetish. I mean, what in the world is a body for, anyway? You might as well be a specialist and concentrate on one of the parts. The delectation is in the detail. I say that 'cause there are far too many generalists, and the generalists have such small imaginations. It's why the humans have such laughably bad horror movies. It's why their cheesy cinema never scares me even for five seconds. I tell her it happens that way 'cause they have to please the maximum audience. And then I hear her talkin'. She tells him not to worry --- "I'll be the smart one, and I'll do all of your thinking for you." When she tells him that, he just gets even more love struck. I won't let up on her. I'm teasin' her, tellin' her she likes 'em old and stupid! The Neanderthal's on-again off-again girlfriend, who seems to have some sort of leg injury that never seems to go away, is givin' him hell for his little transgression with Zaga. And Zaga says, "To hell with her! I don't give a damn about how she feels. It's great to be 'the other woman.'" As you folks at Interstellar High Command are well aware, we haven't had a transgression on our own planet in close to sixty-five million years. So Zaga figures it's high time that one of our kind finally got around to it. She calls it a boo-boo. And she says, "That one of our kind individual might as well be me. Don't ya think?" He's made her feel like the total bad-ass biker girl that she always knew she was. Who knows? The two of them might even create a new species on the deal. What an effed up kid he would be. I hear her and get the feelin' that she might be gettin' in over her head. I told her that she should probably get an abortion.

That being said, what a damned disaster these collections of protein molecules are! In my entire clinical experience, I don't think I've seen such a sordid amalgamation of screw-ups. They shoot themselves in the foot on a daily basis. But now and then, you get to see them up close, and I must admit it's kinda fun to watch. Zaga and I are laughing ourselves silly. It's a complete slapstick comedy! Sorta like watching a TV marathon of skateboard accidents. You have to keep monitorin' the broken bones. I can hear 'em saying, "Aw Ma, I can't freakin' believe I fuckin' broke my arm again!" And I wanna say, "Yes, but you did; you really did, you jackass!" So I bite my tongue when I wanna ask 'em, "Hey fella, how's that pain workin' for you? Ho, ho, ho, It's your pain and not mine." I know, I know --- you don't have to remind me there at Headquarters! As I said, we're supposed to be above the fray. We have to maintain the conceit. We can't get involved. That would be too much radical surgery. We're forbidden to proofread their atrocious behavior. Hell no, that would mess up history big time. Don't tell me. Don't vindictively remind me. I'm well aware that you hate that word "proofread." So, if I'm not allowed to use that word, then let's not dwell on semantics. Let's simply call it something else. We could call it monkey doo reading if you want to... What's that? You don't like the terminology? Alright then, come off from your high horse and gimme a second and I'll think of something else... Hmmm ... How about "assisted editing"? Does that one work for ya? Good. OK, we'll go with that one if it's alright with you. We'll go with that and let their blood soak into the fine powdered sand of the Coliseum. They need extensive remediation, but I know exactly what you're gonna tell me. You're gonna spout the party line about how they have to do that all by themselves. It's supposed to be therapy. Gladiator therapy. Alright, I get it. You think it's tough love. I think it's a bit sadistic, so let's drop the subject for now.

But as I was saying, before someone there at Interstellar High Command interrupted, this Joe the Neanderthal guy is maybe the most interesting one of the whole sorry-ass lot. He views the world from a skewed angle. He thinks that he's an outsider when he's really not. But try to tell him that. He would never believe it for five seconds. In fact, he pictures himself as an alien. It's probably the reason why he loves freaks like us from outer space. Over and over again, I have to remind him that Zaga and I are the real aliens and that he's got to keep this straight in his head, or he's gonna get in trouble. But when I say that, I might as well be talkin' to a wall for all the good it will do. Anyway, he feels this misconception so intensely that he fancies the rest of the world as being complete strangers who live in a vast bubble. And it's a bubble that he can never get into, though he tries to break it till he's blue in the face. In the short time that I've known him, I've seen his nose up against the edge of the bubble again and again. He wants to get in. He prefers to puncture it. But there's no way in hell that he can. I keep tellin' him that maybe getting' in is not worth the huff-and-puff effort. Only thing is, I'm not convinced he understands that.

I wind up talkin' in circles with this guy. He has this nutty idea that if he pounds the drums loudly enough and gives them a sound thrashing, then he thinks he'll save the world. Sounds kinda hippy-dippy New Age to me! Of course, he doesn't dare admit that to anyone. Ha! That would be tantamount to believing in flying saucers, now wouldn't it? And we all know that's not the least bit true. Absolute heresy, you say! However, he's starting to feel it in his bones. And what's the evidence for that? Well, the proof is that he listened to his guitar player friend Miss Kathy Sykes, who confided in him. She told him she believed that there was more to music than simple entertainment. Hey, don't you see? When he plays subtle ballads with lots of weepy strums from Kathy, he has the urge to thwack a snare shot in the center of Gwen's lilting loveliness just to keep her on her toes, but he stifles the muscles. That's what makes the song cool: those rave ups wanting to wrestle into the senses want to imagine that they can be heard. They have to be content. I suppose that's a start. Notwithstanding these considerations, I gotta say they're the best lab rats 'cause they never seem to miss out on an opportunity to screw up another human being.

That being said, Officer Fielding's job interview went great! The lunatic lady named Meghan freakin' hired the old buzzard right off the bat! I gotta admit, at first, I was skeptical, but everything's going according to your plan. Wow! That woman can sure multi-task. She's always holdin' down two conversations at once and tramplin' what people want to say. She might as well have been Julius Caesar for cryin' out loud. I'll take it from the top and give ya chapter and verse on what went down…

Fielding was in Meghan's office, trying to score well on the job interview. In the early going, the vibe sucked pretty bad, but halfway through, it took an unexpected turn for the best. It's nice to see the economy rally from its death bed. And he sure as hell was doing that.

Meghan said, "Lemme see now, Mr. Fielding. If you wanna bake a cake, you gotta have some building blocks. And boy oh boy do I need some talent. I need a purveyor of fine ingredients. So, I've had you checked out and my people have gone over your resume with a fine tooth comb. And the result? Well, ya did good, and I've decided to hire you --- on a provisional basis, of course. Your predecessor --- I don't know what in the hell happened to him. He kinda disappeared. Poof!" She did a dramatic gesture with her hands and splayed out her fingers in a jazz hands way before continuing. "I guess the job was too much for him. I loved him. Oh how did I love him. But he wasn't up to the test. So, it would seem that he fell by the wayside. You won't fall by the wayside, will you?"

"Mrs. Mastrianni, I promise you that you will love my work."

"This time I let my staff do the picking. And my staff is doing rather well lately. My goodness, you look so distinguished." She reached across and felt Fielding's left lapel right about where the buttonhole was. Then she let her right index finger scurry a bit, so that it detoured into his shirt and touched base with his nipple. He pretended that it wasn't happening, but still smiled to acknowledge that her hand was indeed there. For a second, Fielding thought Meghan must have been descended from a bonobo chimp 'cause she apparently liked to use sexual overtures as a way of greeting. But that thought evaporated when he remembered why he was there in her office in the first place.

She gave him a schoolgirl look, removed her hand, and proceeded with the interview. "And for your first test as an employee, I want you to be our Head Buyer. I want you to get me another round of the building blocks for this here operation. They tell me you're a good supplier. Well, we'll see about that. Ya got a pen and paper?"

"Yes, I got it covered, Mrs. Mastrainni."

"You can call me Meghan, Mr. Fielding."

"Right."

"OK, so jot this down. And I want the whole lot in gigantic wholesale quantities. It's gonna be a big big batch for one big gazillion dollar bash. Procure it for me ASAP. These are the building blocks for insanity itself. Get me some Drano, white gasoline, drain cleaner, ammonia, a round of assorted cold remedies, red phosphorus, ether, freon, battery acid, brake fluid, paint thinner, hydriodic acid, rubbing alcohol, lye, lighter fluid, lithium, camp stove fuel, hydrochloride, a few gasoline additives, and last but far, far from least, la piece de la resistance --- Iodine Ephedrine. I like to think of it as the 'without which none.' Ask my secretary about the ratios of what percentages they should be and how they go together. After that's all mixed together, Mr. Conklin and I can put in my special mystery ingredient, which is known only to me. That one'll sex it up a notch or two."

Suddenly, her smart phone rang, and she took the call. "Yeah, good. Sound's fine to me. And how is lab number one doing? Have you got the stuff ready? What? Not yet? Well, get a goddamn move on. This ain't no slipshod hillbilly heroin operation that we got here. If you can't deliver the product and deliver it on time, then I'll get someone who will. Is that clear? The purpose of this here super meth is to render vast segments of the electorate into blithering idiots. Ha, what d'ya think this is, some kinda nasal decongestant? Side effects may include death. Good! OK, so it's a done deal, right?" She closed her phone and picked up about where she left off. "Oh, so where was I? I forget, but it doesn't matter. C'mon and follow me. I'll show ya the whole operation that we're runnin' here."

She led Fielding to a side room at the office complex which opened onto a spacious test lab. Lined up in rows along the walls were cages big enough to accommodate people. Meghan ushered Fielding further in the room so he could get a better look. And what he saw made him recoil in horror. There were approximately fifty cages, each occupied by a man or a woman in various stages of deep catatonia or extreme frothing-at-the-mouth hysteria. Meghan approached one of the cages that housed a young woman who was rocking back and forth while she made a hissing sound with her pursed lips.

"You see, Mr. Fielding, she's completely loco in a low key sort of way. She's fallen far into the blithering idiot stage and nothing will ever bring her back. She's hypnotized and buzzin' at the same time. In her current state, she's open to just about any suggestion that I want to slip her way. You see, the whole thing is a combined approach. I've done some research and I've made quite a discovery.

"What's that?"

"I've discovered that meth when you combine it with hypnosis, turns people into complete blithering --- but far from blissful --- automatons." Meghan strolled further down the line of caged subjects, calling Fielding's attention to another hot one. "See this one. He'll vote for anyone. He's completely under my thumb. What we have here is a paradoxical situation. When the man's cerebellum creates a thought, the cerebrum vetoes it. In fact, it goes one better and shoots the bastard dead in its tracks. The poor fellow's synapses don't have even so much as a split second to formulate a rejoinder to whatever horror story I command him to commit. The result is very beneficial to our cause. A thought doesn't have a chance in hell of surviving. I want to unify the three of my businesses --- the pistol license company, the meth making, and the political campaign. Here, lemme show you something."

She went back to the first cage and looked at the young man who appeared to be in great distress.

"Come here, Jimmy. Would you like a special treat?"

Jimmy walked to the front of the cage, put his face in between the bars, and bug-eyed peered out at Meghan's newest employee. Meghan turned back to Fielding and took a hand gun out of her purse. She then proceeded to unload the firearm while Fielding watched. "Now watch this, Mr. Fielding." She handed the gun to Jimmy. He looked at the hand gun and put it in his holster. Then he took it out of the holster. He looked in the mirror. He put it back. He took it out. He put it back. He took it out. Then, for good measure, he reached into the box at the side of the table and pulled out a silencer, which he attached to the muzzle of the gun.

Meghan explained everything to her young guinea pig. "Remember, Jimmy. It's a penis. And everything's a crime. You've got to keep up. It's part of the gross national product, so step up your game, dude, and enter the invisible hand of the marketplace. Now put it back in the holster, Jimmy." Jimmy obeyed. "That's right." He obeyed again. "Now your penis is off. Now take it out of the holster again, Jimmy." Jimmy obeyed again. He was being extremely cooperative. "Now it's back on. But you have to make sure."

Jimmy put his hand to his crotch just to make sure it was back on.

Meghan gave him a savage smile. "That's right, Jimmy! And remember what I told you before. If you should ever be in doubt about whether it's on or off, you should just assume the worst --- that it's off, and then you should put it back on again. That way, you'll never be in any sort of doubt. Remember Jimmy, it's so so important to feel safe. If anything, anything at all, should ever cause you to feel the least bit unsafe, then you have to pull out that gun from your holster and make it safe again. And another thing --- the only way to be safe is to make someone else feel in danger. Is that clear now? Is everything alright?"

"Yes, Mizz Mastrianni. Everything good, and it feel safe too."

Then Meghan unbuttoned her blouse to expose her bra. She popped her breasts out just beyond the reach of her captive. Jimmy liked this one a lot. He reached out beyond his cage and Meghan backed out of the way, which made the young man furious. Meghan let out a loud cackle, before turning to Fielding. "You see, he's completely at my mercy!"

She let his hand squirm out just far enough to get his index finger on her aureole. "Good, Jimmy. You're doin' your best impersonation of that Greek fellow Tantalus, or was he Roman? It really doesn't make for a dime's worth of difference, does it, Jimmy boy? Mythology was never your forte. And frankly, it was never mine either. I'm so glad we had a chance to chat about this today. We'll talk again sometime tomorrow. And after we talk about that, I'll remind you about who it is that you're supposed to vote for in the next election for senator."

Jimmy's face registered a look of complete chagrin and alarm as he fell over in his cage and staggered up to the bars again before stumbling into the corner in a raging incoherent fit.

Fielding was surprised that someone else had just entered the room.

"Yes, that's very well done, Meghan," the stranger observed. "The meth heads want guns, and we need to give 'em what they want."

Meghan turned to Fielding and exclaimed, "Oh, allow me to introduce you to Mr. Conklin. He's one of the bankrollers for this here operation."

Mr. Conklin stepped forward and offered Fielding a weak handshake. "Hi, Mr. Fielding. I've heard so much about you, and all of it is good."

"So, Mr. Conklin, be so kind as to fill Mr. Fielding in on our program."

"Sure. What we do here is a multi-step deal. You see, my main objective is to earn big money and spend it on campaigns for major political candidates. And none of us is in the mood for foolin' around. We're sick and tired of having to constantly go through the motions of some kind of dot-the-i-and-cross-the-t legality. We want results, and we want 'em soon. We're not gonna wait around forever. If I had to spell it out for you in two words, we want total freedom. We're the winners; we want it all. We don't wanna share anything 'cause it never works when we share. When I walk down the street, I wanna to be totally left alone. I wanna be so left alone that *nobody ever gets in my way!* If they get in my way, they're messin' with my day and more importantly, they're messin' with my autonomy. They're screwin' around with my individuality. I wanna feel that way every second of the day. The only purpose for the government is to protect me and my property and to make me feel invincible. In the long run, we want automatons. We want automatons with autonomy."

Fielding interrupted. Hey, maybe that should be your campaign slogan: 'Automatons with autonomy!'"

"Wow! I like that. Before I leave tonight, I'm gonna write that one down."

Fielding gave her a chuckle. He was feeling good. He'd had this feeling so many times before in his long and distinguished police career, but it was a feeling he never got bored with.

Meghan went on with her orientation session. She knew she had to get a move on since there was so much material she had to cover. "We figure that if someone isn't makin' at least $400K a year, then that person is a fuckin' loser, so why not go ahead and make him or her into an automaton. Only that's a tall order to fill. So we have to create them. Look, it's like this --- the other political party is way ahead of us. The reason is that as the years have gone by, the population of poor people has risen exponentially. Many of them will be bound to vote against their own interests, but more and more they won't. At first, we tried to shut them out what with all those strategies of voter ID. We did it under the guise of the so-called integrity of the system. But lately people have wised up. And we can't have that. So we need more voters whom we can count on to vote against their own interests. And like I said, we have to create them. The way we create them is Meghan's department. She uses a combination of hypnosis and meth amphetamine. My God, I have to say it, if ya don't already know it --- she's incredible with that concoction."

"And what else do you do on your end of the deal, besides supplying the money?"

"Well, some of my fund-raising is, how shall I say it, rather innovative."

"So how's that one work?"

"You see, it goes like this. I made the bulk of my money in legit ways. Have you ever heard of a discount chain store called Mogun's?"

"Oh yeah, I heard of 'em. They do real cheap discount items. Usually, pretty cut rate stock if I remember correctly."

"I'm famous for my unique business model. It has its origins in the trucking industry. You see, every day in this great country of ours there are thousands of tractor trailer rigs that are crisscrossing the land. Those rigs are huge, and they're getting bigger every year as the economic situation heads south and companies wanna get more bang for the buck. So, as you might imagine, there are bound to be accidents. The bigger those carriers get, the more accidents happen. Corners get cut. Rules get bent. Regulations get broken. Inspectors look the other way when they should be lookin' at bald tires, faulty brakes, and overloaded payload compartments. Sleepy head drivers nod 'cause they gotta nod sometime even when they think they never have to get some shut-eye. They push the percentages with Benzedrine and wind up closin' their eyes at an inopportune moment, and the top-heavy rig, filled to capacity with shifting cargo, swerves into a ditch. Tough luck is never in short supply. When those accidents happen, consumer goods get scattered all over highways and turnpikes throughout the fifty states. It's actually kinda beautiful when you stop and look at it --- they spill open like plants dispensing spores in every direction. I like to think of it as their contribution to the world. After the local police pick up the pieces from all of those crack-ups, they have a lot of merchandise that they need to get rid of fast. I mean, what are they gonna do with the stuff? Throw it in some dumpster in South Carolina? Chuck it in some incinerator in Mobile? Drive it over to a scrap metal yard in Des Moines? Yeah, it's true. Some of it's no longer saleable, but a fair percentage is absolutely no worse for wear. It could still be useful to someone. And it would be a shame to turn the whole load into the trash masher. And it could be very profitable too. That's where I come in. Waste not, want not --- that's what I've always said. With that thought foremost in my mind, I was the first one to realize that there was money to be made. That's why I'm an innovator. What I have is an army of scouts. They monitor police radios and CB's, and they're on the lookout for disasters. When they hear about disasters, they report the crack-ups to either me or my staff, and I dispatch a team to the accident site. They swoop down upon the place before the last ambulance has driven away and the final tow truck has arrived. My people are pros and they move into action, making a deal with the local cops and telling 'em that they can get the loot off from their hands for cheap. I mean, who in the hell wants to worry about how to dispose of a load of six thousand golf clubs? Who wants to get stuck with two dozen washer driers? If you're a local sheriff, that would be a pain in the ass. Well, we get the swag off from their hands fast and cheap. And after a while, when there's been more than a few disasters, they're actually happy to see us. They view us as kinda like public servants doing somethin' good for the betterment of mankind. We're almost as welcome as those folks who clean up murder scenes after they cart away the corpses.

When we pick the goods off from the highway, we load 'em up in one of our own rigs which has been quickly dispatched to the scene, and then we bring 'em back here to this state where we have a whole chain of Mogun's discount stores that sell mostly consumer goods that have also been picked up off from other highways throughout the land. And people are only too glad to buy 'em. And the stuff is dirt cheap. I make sure of it. That's how I've made my pile of money. And the whole process from hangin' out with roadkill to shopping shelf is no more than a few days. I've made a complete science of it and have managed to streamline the entire deal."

Conklin paused not just to catch his breath, but also to bask in the pride of his accomplishments and to gauge their effect on Fielding. And he liked what he saw.

Fielding moved his hat back an inch or two before grasping his lapels. "Sounds great to me," he replied. "I suppose one way of looking at it is that you're makin' the world a much greener place. You should probably call up one of those environmental organizations, and they could write you up and give you some free publicity. I have to say, I'm real darned impressed."

"It is great. We're goin' green. I like to think of our operation as a form of recycling. Business has been good, outstanding even. But the thing is the demand is now starting to outstrip the supply. There are lots of horrible accidents involving tractor trailers. However, there are only so many disasters that naturally occur. Even tough luck is bound to run up against good luck at some point."

"What are you trying to tell me?" Fielding asked. He could tell that Conklin was holding back, giving the subject a great build up for maximum effect. It was a familiar technique, one he'd used himself throughout years of police work.

"I'm saying that lately we've added a new wrinkle to the operation. We're doin' that 'cause we need to diversify. We have to be on top of the changing market and changing situations. I tell ya, you gotta be on top of this business or you'll be left out in the cold."

Conklin leaned in closer to Fielding and his voice assumed an even more confidential tone. His whispery tone gave Fielding an uneasy tingling sensation that spiraled up and down his back: "Now we're dispatching the teams, not to just pick up after the accidents, but instead to create additional accidents. And as an extra bonus, we're using the rigs to make more and more batches of Meghan's super meth. I tell ya, between conjuring up new crack-ups and recycling, it's a multi-taskin' organization. We've got people running around the country like they're chickens with their heads cut off. Things are gettin' a bit outta control. There are starting to be more than a few fuck-ups, and more importantly, we're havin' fulfillment issues. We can't have that. What we need is someone who can oversee the operation. And by now, it's evolved into a combined operation --- meth-making and causing accidents. We need an organizational genius. Creating accidents and making 'em look real is a bit of an art form."

"If it's not that, then it's at least a professional deal."

"Like Meghan says, you're nothing if not that. She's told me so much about you, haven't you, Meghan?"

She perked right up. "This is gonna be the biggest time of my life. Hey, Mr. Conklin, let's get my husband Allen in on this. Here, wait a second, and I'll get him on Skype." She tapped a few buttons, and in a twinkling Allen's image was right there on the overhead computer screen. He looked handsome and confident. And with the American flag pin on his lapel, he looked positively Senatorial.

"How ya doin', Allen. How's the campaign goin' on your end?"

"Oh, we're doin' well. Dare I say it --- we're doin' spendidly. My internal poll just let me know that we've opened up a ten point lead over my opponent. And what about you guys? No doubt you and your new advisor Mr. Fielding are goin' great guns planning future accidents everywhere in this great land of ours."

"Hey, we try!"

"Welcome aboard, Mr. Fielding. I'm sure Meghan and Conklin have brought you up to speed on what we're tryin' to do. But I wanted to take some time to delve a little more into the philosophy of our operation. If I had to put it in a nutshell, what we're doin' here is an exercise in libertarian politics. We wanna control public policy, only what makes us so different from all the rest out there, is that we're willin' to go the extra mile. We want people to feel completely empowered. We want people to feel as though nothing's gonna ever get in their way. Did ya ever see that TV ad about the truck slash SUV that can go anywhere? You know the one I'm talkin' about. It's the one where the guy is drivin' down the road and suddenly, the spirit moves him, so he decides to go off road. He shouldn't have to be at the mercy of the bloody road! Hell no, the man makes his own damned road. He shifts gears and slams the SUV into the slush at the side of the highway. Only thing is, the slush isn't good enough. He then decides to drive it into the snow and mud at the side of the asphalt, and all of a sudden as if by magic, a brand new road appears and it takes the driver just about any place he wants to go. All the while that this is goin' on, there's a heavy metal music soundtrack blarin' away in the background. The guitar sounds mean as hell. I suppose that's the hook. Well, I've seen that ad a hundred times, and it still warms the cockles of my heart. It's what I want out of my constituency. That's the reason I'm in politics. I want people to feel empowered, so they can walk down the street, and everyone else will just run for cover. I wanna say, 'That's the spirit. That's really what moves this nation.' We believe wholeheartedly in the grand notion of the individual. Let nothing tarnish the sanctity of that precious thought. So, as you probably would imagine, what with the Senatorial campaign and everything, I've got my work cut out for me. You wouldn't believe how much money it takes to keep this here gravy train runnin', so goodbye for now. I've gotta go back for another round of fund raising."

The Skype images dissolved to black, and Meghan and Conklin looked at Fielding with a confident gaze. Conklin spoke first. "So welcome aboard, Fielding. I'm looking forward to all of this. It's gonna be quite an adventure. And I can tell that you'll work out a lot better than that last guy. Well, that's about enough for now. I'll be off and we'll hook up real soon."

Meghan led him to the door and saw him out. Then she came back to Fielding and gave him a short speech about her personal life. She got pretty darned deep on the topic and there was an air of wistfulness that imbued her voice.

"I just hope that this scheme is the big one. It's what I want my whole life to be about. Perhaps you feel the same way as me. Anyway, I hope you do. You think you're in the driver's seat. Everything you touch turns to gold. Happiness is overflowing. You can fly and the others can't. They're worthless and always have been, yet somehow the tables got turned. And they've gone and made you fall into the same worthlessness that you fear so much yourself. Sometime or other, the challenge is how to dig yourself out. I've had a raw deal in life. Nothin's gone my way. The way I see it, I need compensation. It's only right. And it would be a kind of justice for all the hard knocks I've had. Mr. Fielding, I have to live up to my potential. I wish I could dance. Maybe that would be the answer to my problems."

She capriciously broke into a pirouette ballerina move and zipped around the room in a series of swirly twirly motions before tippy-toeing back to Fielding. Then she abruptly changed the subject. "Say, Mr. Fielding, did you ever see this new reality show *Babies in Bars*?"

"No, I can't say as I have."

"It's a favorite with the campaign staffers here. Every one of 'em is crazy about it. And I'm grudgingly a fan too. I'm emphasizing the grudgingly part. But I did see the latest installment. After twenty-something episodes, this Joe guy --- he's one of the characters --- seems to be nudging himself into the spotlight, tryin' to take over from Gwen, Kathy, and Ben. Joe's a real lowlife. That's probably why they picked him for the part. Oh yes, he's a good drummer, or so I'm told."

"Wait a second! I think I may have seen it. Is this the one where the guy seems to have periodic spasmodic seizure episodes where he acts like he's gonna turn into a Neanderthal from prehistoric times?"

"Uh huh! That's the one. Well, you wanna know somethin' weird?"

"What's that?"

"He's my brother."

"No! You don't say?"

"Yes. I'm afraid so, unfortunately. He's the family embarrassment. Always has been. Still, I give him grudging credit. He and I have one thing in common. The meth-making operation that I told you about is maybe a little like him. Allen, Conklin, and I market a product that essentially does what my brother's drumming does, albeit in a more circuitous way."

"I never would have guessed that you have a brother who's a drummer."

"As a matter a fact, I do. He's a total loser, but in a strange way, he sorta does what I do."

"What's that?"

"We both mess with dopamine and serotonin. But I don't go in for that hippy dippy spiritual nonsense. I approach it from a different angle, of course."

With great difficulty, Fielding tried to process that one --- yes, she was right. It was hard to think of a meth-making and causing fatal traffic accidents as hippy dippy spiritual nonsense.

She looked away with another one of her wistful stares. In fact, Fielding took note that she seemed to have quite an inventory of wistful stares, and she was fully capable of trotting them out on a second's notice. Fielding sensed it immediately. "What's wrong, Meghan?"

"Oh nothin' much. It's just that Allen…" She paused again, searching for the words.

"What is it?"

"It's just that sometimes I wonder if my husband Allen is right wing enough for the sheer size and proportions of my ambitions. I wanna think very big, but every now and then, I get the feeling my allegiances shouldn't always be with him. Understand that I want him to be up to snuff. I want you to know that anything you can do to nudge him into being more bold would be much appreciated. Allen's always tellin' me, 'Meghan, I'll try to do better.' And Conklin --- I love the guy. Maybe I would leave Allen for him. That is, if Allen doesn't pan out. I've gotta keep hedging my bets. Conklin's so ambitious that he astounds me. I found out via the grapevine that Conklin just told Allen the other day, 'Well, one thing you can do is step up that meth production and hit up your wife for some more money from that little old lady out in the nursing home." Conklin wants Allen to prove his 'worth to the organization' by doing independent fund-raising of his own. But Conklin's still smarting from being put in his place by Joe, so he wants revenge ... He wants to cut off Joe's hands because his hands are his means of livelihood."

"Good God! He wants to do that?"

"Yes, you can bet on it. That's why I think I'm in love with Conklin more than I'm in love with Allen."

Conklin took Fielding to the newest staging area for the next tractor trailer accident. From a shelter located on a hill opposite from the highway, they could get a good view. While they were waiting for the truck to come into view, Conklin talked about Meghan's husband. To him, Allen was the weakest link in the whole scheme. "The thing about Meghan is that she wants to kill Joe so she can get all of the old lady's fortune for herself. I keep reminding her not to worry because I've got enough of a pile salted away to fund political projects for practically eternity. But eternity isn't good enough for her. She's so damned greedy. God bless her. And she's always thinkin' that she's gonna run out. So although I probably have enough to buy anything that I'll ever want, I do appreciate the audacity of the woman. That's what I love about her. And that's why I'm gonna continue to goad her into chiseling some more money out of her mom who's holed up in some old age home. That sort of attitude shows me her heart's in the right place. But in some ways, I guess I'm a bit different than she is because what I really want is to get even with that brother of hers. I don't want to kill him like Meghan's threatening to do all the time. No, that would be too good for him. I'd much rather have his hands cut off 'cause the way I figure it, the man's hands are his ticket to ride. They are in fact his way of living. If I can get that away from him, then I'd be so much happier 'cause I wanna get even with him for the times he humiliated me."

"Ok, Ok. I understand your resentment, but shouldn't we turn our attention to the business at hand?"

Conklin gave Fielding a look of embarrassment. Quickly realizing that he'd gotten carried away, he fumbled for his binoculars and composed himself. "Oh yes, I guess I got carried away there for a second. Yes, here comes a very large overstuffed tractor trailer rig now. Who knows what goodies she has on board?"

Conklin raised the binoculars to his eyes. He could zero in from faraway. There the driver was, oblivious to what was about to happen. He could tell by the sweet smile on his face that the guy was most likely either humming and listening to country and western music or taking in the conversations on his CB radio. For him, life could not have been better. No doubt, as far as his skillset for truck driving was concerned, the man was at the top of his game.

Conklin turned the binoculars to the left to get a better view of the oil slick that had been carefully laid out along the most difficult part of the bend in the highway. It glistened in the sun. He hoped that the driver wouldn't see it glistening in the sun too. The big rig approached and sped up. In his many years of experience, the driver had seen this long curve situation thousands of times before. On the surface, it might have appeared to be slightly hazardous, but in the frames of Conklin's binoculars, the man was a glowing picture of confidence. It was only when the driver could feel the oil slick on the surface of the road that his expression of confidence vanished. There was no way he could bail out of this accident, and he knew it. Conklin could tell by the look of abject terror in the man's eyes. The rig swiveled and scooted along the slick and spiraled out of control. The weight of the trailer pushed the cab sideways, and the driver frantically tried to compensate, but it was too little too late. The big rig jackknifed and tumbled end over end. The hapless driver never had a chance of escaping that one.

The crash that simply couldn't have been averted occurred at mile seventy-four of the Interstate. The local sheriff and his deputies were the first on the scene. The driver was apparently dead on impact. So there was nothing to be done except to make out a report and to get someone to pick up the merchandise that had been scattered along the highway. The sheriff thought it odd that it was so easy to summon a company that would perform that rather specialized task. Up to then, he'd been thinking that would take quite a round of phone calls. But he wound up shaking his head in disbelief

--- damn, the way things are today, you can get anything to happen in practically no time at all.

I toasted another shot of rye whiskey, clinking my glass to Zaga's. She looked like she was in a reflective mood, and so I decided to talk about the humans. "Zaga, in case you haven't guessed it by now, Meghan seems to be different from so many other women. The average woman, if there is such a thing, doesn't pay inordinate attention to whatever creepiness may or may not be going through the mind of her man during the intimate act. And make no mistake --- as far as I can tell, it's not all sweetness and light. And I'll go way out on a limb and say that might be true for all the girl lovers out there too. As an alien female, I've discovered this karmic fact."

Zaga took yet another hit from her drink and placed it carefully on the edge of the bar. "So there!" she replied. "We're fast learners. OK, that being said, what makes Meghan radically different from other women is that she extends this maxim from the realm of interior monologue into the larger sphere of so-called 'real life.' That is to say, she not only cares less what's cruising through the fellow's brain, she also cares not one iota what he does in real life. From her perspective, he could be a serial slasher as long as he makes fireworks happen."

Yes, Zaga was indeed a fast learner. And she could obviously see what happens when the invisible hand of the marketplace is given a completely free and unfettered hand. I asked her how it was possible to get anything done on this planet when basic loyalty was such a formidable obstacle? That was what I wanted to know. I told her the Mob was mad. I wanted to know if she remembered them, and she said yes, they were the ones that Meghan had double-crossed. Zaga said Meghan might not remember them, but they sure as hell would never forget Meghan, nor would they have fuzzy memories about any transgressions that Meghan may have made against them. And none of our powers of assisted editing would bail anyone out of that one. Zaga and I figured it would be fun to check up on the Mob just to see how much fun they were having:

"Hey man, this situation is getting totally out of control. First, Andy gets shoved into the deep blue sea, and then Meghan steals our shake-down money. And to top it off, after we send Frank after the money that our former hit man Bill had so inconveniently appropriated, after Bill had of course decided to go rogue on us and go over to the side of some raggle taggle drummer dude, then Frank carries out a totally botched murder of this Tony guy who happens to be in cahoots with both Meghan and James Conklin. Man, we had to get that body out of the hallway fast. Ha! I'll bet that deep red hallway really put the fear of God into the drummer boy/lover boy's broken-legged girlfriend. Are you getting' all this? Someone has to take command because all this incompetence is driving me to distraction."

"Don't worry, man! I'm with ya every step of the way. We've got to make an intervention here because our credibility is at stake. Executive action must to taken and must be taken soon."

"Okay, so what I wanna have you do is to get that money back pronto. And I don't care how in God's name you do it. That fiasco in the hallway of the girlfriend's new apartment was good for one thing. We were able to beat the hell out of him for long enough for him to tell us that the money was stashed somewhere at her place. Only trouble was she called the cops too fast before we could get to her. We've got another thing that makes this case more problematic, that is, this Joe guy practically lives on TV. It's like he doesn't care anymore about havin any sense of privacy. The guy's a throwback to something else --- I don't know what. Gettin' near the guy without a camera around is just about impossible."

"Don't say that! I don't wanna here it. Nothing's the least bit impossible. You've gotta freakin' believe. Lemme hear ya say you effin' believe. Do you hear me?"

"I got you loud and clear."

"Good. I'm so happy for you. I mean, damn, think about crazy Tony. You haven't forgotten what happened to him. God forbid, I sure as hell wouldn't want the same thing to happen to you."

A PAIR OF GRAY METAL EYES

It was such a nice day out when Joe decided to get together with his niece. Angie had been admiring the formations of the clouds, carefully noting that their random beauty clashed with the chaos of her thoughts. Something in her head told her that the stuff her mom had told her about her uncle had the distinct whiff of being lies. As a matter of fact, young Angie had been mulling this over and over in her mind. For the most part, she was a logical young lady, and this weird business that her mom had been spoon-feeding her about her uncle had seemed to be more than a bit off-center. She was wondering --- "How can someone, anyone be that bad?" Perhaps she was unduly influenced by things she had been studying at that time because at school, she'd been reading lots of Russian writers like Tolstoy and Goncharov, and taking her cue from them, she was firmly in a frame of mind that there had to be redeeming features. In books, as in real life, nobody could be that two-fisted brand of evil --- except maybe her mom. Angie was starting to disagree with the Russians.

She arrived at the Starbucks at the appointed time. But she was nagged by worries --- what if her mom found out about this meeting? If that horrendous situation came to pass, then she was fully aware of what the consequences would be. She would have been as good as condemned to living out there on the street. And you can't have that. No, she was acutely aware that she had to be prudent on these matters. Mom obviously ruled the roost. That fact of life was a sobering thought.

She looked around the room of coffee drinkers to see if she could locate her uncle. There he was over in the corner doing a crossword puzzle. Despite not having seen him in years, she could still pick him out. She could see him glancing upward now. It was very good timing because he'd been stuck on 35 Down for at least ten minutes and was beginning to get antsy. He stared at her across the room before his face broke into a smile. She smiled back. Angie took careful notice --- he didn't look like an ogre. Actually, he had the appearance of a decent human being. But she fully understood that you can't always put your faith in that. He stood up to greet her, then pulled a chair out from the table and motioned for her to sit down. After the round of hellos, he bought her a double crème latte, and they started to have a long talk.

"Uncle Joe, I'm so happy to see you after so many years. I'm sure you'll agree that the situation has been…well, let's say it's been… hard." Joe liked the syncopation of her hesitating voice, but he was well aware that was only because he was a drummer. Surely, for most people, stammering would have been an acquired taste. He watched her slender fingers as they gripped the cup of latte. He could see them flex and fidget around the ceramic loop of the handle. He surmised that this was an obviously a girl with conflicted feelings.

Joe began: "My sister…your mother, is a woman who needs to have villains. And judging from the evidence of the last umpteen years, I'm the villain de jour. Oh, she's had villains before. Dad was a villain for her too."

"But there's no need for villains. Why can't we all just be friends?"

"Oh, I'm afraid that the time for being friends is long past."

"But Uncle Joe, that's so sad. Why can't you and she be friends?"

"Lemme just say something that I believe is very important. Can we have some ground rules here? What I mean is I think it's a good thing for an uncle to never come between a niece and her mom. As a matter of fact, no one should ever get between a young woman and her mom. Therefore, since we're probably clear on that, I make a motion that both you and I not mention your mom. Would that be okay with you?"

"Oh, I'm totally down with that. You've got no argument from me."

Joe studied her face and could sense her uneasiness. But something about her expression told him that she was no babe in the woods when it came to having knowledge of her mom's insanity.

"So, why don't we talk about something better? Why don't we talk about music?"

"Yes, that would be great. I've seen your show and I like your music, especially your wild drumming. How'd you learn to do that?"

"Oh, just something I picked up along the way."

"When I watch that ridiculous reality show, I still manage to find some reality I've never known before."

"Surely, you must be joking?"

"Not at all. I'm dead serious. When I see it, for the very first time, I get lost in the pure sprawling nest of sound that you guys create. Adjectives and adverbs don't mean anything anymore."

"What about nouns and pronouns, to say nothing about subordinating conjunctions?"

"They can go to hell too."

"That's the spirit."

She took another long sip on her double latte. Now she was goin' on a different tack --- her face told him that she'd changed her mind. No problem. She was allowed to do that. "Look," she announced in a louder tone of voice, "let's dispense with this absurd notion that both you and I can have a talk that wouldn't involve my dear and crazy-as-a coot mom. Screw the ground rules. I know she's crazy. You know she's crazy. The big problem for both of us is that the rest of the world is under the equally crazy notion the woman is perfectly sane. I'm coming to the conclusion that Mom shouldn't be a character in real life. No, no, she should be a character in book. If she were banished to that realm, she could be decommissioned in some way that would be safer for the rest of the world. She could be put on a shelf in someone's living room. The only reason that I'm keepin' my mouth shut is that I'm terrified she'll cut me off without so much a dime. And in this economic climate, I simply can't afford to have that happen. As a result, I have to lie through my teeth. I have to go to parties and social functions and sing the praises of the woman. Uncle Joe, you have no idea what I'm going through."

"Well, if you're troubled about that little secret getting out, you've got no worries on my account. My lips are sealed, even if others aren't. If you want, I'll go on record and say how equally wonderful she is. As a matter of fact, let's spread the wonderfulness around."

"Wow! What a relief."

"But what made you so much as entertain that notion that I'd spill the beans about your wonderful mom?"

"Oh, I don't know. It's just that mom ripped off some pretty powerful people. And I'm also afraid of that problem more than I'm afraid of being cut off without a dime. That's why I'm here today and talking with you. You see, mom helped herself to some money that didn't belong to her."

"No, you don't say?"

"Please, I don't have time for ironies or pleasantries. I'm worried about two things. First, I have every good reason to believe that mom stole some money from some gangsters, and secondly, I think she's planning to knock off my grandma. You see, mom is of the opinion that gram is not dying quite fast enough. She's cookin' up some plan to slip her some sort of mickey into her food."

Joe's first reaction to his niece's remark was incredulity. True, he knew that Meghan was trying to get *him* killed. And Angie seemed to tacitly acknowledge this scenario even is she didn't say it right out loud. But for her to want to off her own mom --- that was quite another matter. Until now, Joe had believed that since his mother was an old lady, his sister would naturally assume that Nature would take its course and that it would be pointless on her part to get involved with schemes of killing her. Why should she expose herself to the risk of getting caught if Nature was going to take its course soon enough anyway? The only thing that argued against her opting for the more rationale plan was that Nature simply wasn't acting soon enough. From his sister's depraved perspective, Nature was falling down on the job! Meghan was getting more desperate and more greedy.

Joe took another sip of coffee and so did Angie. She intermitantly would look away as if she were attempting to hide something that was obvious in her expression. He could see the terror in her face, but he reasoned that Angie, being young and not fully wise to the ways of the world, was overreacting. Ha! He thought! This sweet young lady is like a cat --- always looking for drama where there is none! He decided it was much better to nudge the conversation on to more pleasant areas.

"So, you like the show. I'm glad to hear that. However, you have to understand that it's not the real news. Things do get contrived if ya know what I mean."

"Oh, Uncle Joe, I'm well aware of that. I figure that you most likely have writers on staff who come up with weird situations every week. But what's fun is that despite the contrivances, there is a reality that manages to shine through. And I think that's what makes it work. And that brings me something I wanted to ask you. Are you really part Neanderthal?"

"That's what I've always felt ever since I was a small child. You see, Neanderthals and their nemeses, the Cro-Mags, did interbreed, so their genome profile got mixed."

"So that might mean that I'm one too!" She broke into laughter and started rubbing her forehead to see if she had a big brow ridge. "Yes Uncle Joe, I do believe I am!"

And then we both broke into laughter.

With a wide swath, I eased back from the eavesdropping and savored the view. For the first time in eons, being omnipotent was something I could appreciate. I mean, I could go anywhere, do anything, and hover over anybody, and they wouldn't know what in the world was goin' on. With my pair of gray metal eyes, I could see any place too.

It was a few days later, and Joe and Sunita, Zaga's rival, were havin' a good ol' mean and nasty fight. Joe closed his eyes and engaged in unpleasant conversation. It went like this:

"Oh Joe, you're not quite husband material, but maybe I'll give you a free pass."

"Yeah, well decide and decide now! Aw damn, I'm only kiddin'.

"Please don't. If anyone is not deciding, it's you. All I've wanted since we met was to have you and only you for my very own private drummer boy."

"What you really want is a film director or a photographer. He could take you there."

"Stop, please stop!"

"No, I won't. You crave a currency. Maybe you'd be better off with Jillian. She's a director."

"That's not my scene. Why do you hurt me like this?" Sunita crutched into the other room as she tried to stifle a flood of tears. Joe walked into the kitchen and then back again. Trying to smooth out the uneasy situation, he came up with a great plan: "Sunita, why don't we forget all of this problematic stuff and go to the movies tonight. We can think of other things to do after that."

"Jesus, what the hell is wrong with you? You treat me bad, and then you decide to take me to the movies? I have a half a mind to smack you across the face with one of my crutches. No, I'm stayin' right here. Lourdes is stayin' at her best friend's house, but I'm gonna just stay right her and maybe read a big thick book, one that's as trashy as possible."

"Well, if that's the way you feel about it, there's no need of both of us stayin' home, so I'm gonna go play drums."

"Gee Joe, you're such a romantic fellow, almost as romantic as that rat bastard Ben. Why don't you and Ben go out and have a night on the town? You both love each other so much, don't you?"

"You know for a fact that I hate his guts. I only pretend to like him for the TV audience, and on most of the episodes, the people out there in TV Land can figure out for themselves that that's a complete sham."

"The whole show is a sham at this point."

"No, it's not. I'm the most real thing about it. That's why it's a huge success." Joe thought about Sunita's big point which had something to do with the importance of love. Joe tried to be objective and to keep an open mind. He decided to do this just as some kind of intellectual game. From that perspective, love might be a good proposition if it were viewed strictly as a survival mechanism. It went like this: love might be necessary in order to find a fellow creature, so that you could pass on whatever good genes that you had to offer to the planet. I mean, life has got to amount to something, doesn't it? If it means something, then passing on genes is pretty much the whole point. I mean, if you can't do that, then you should pretty much just call it a day, and go jump off a cliff someplace. Viewed through this hyper-rationalistic prism, love would be the driving mechanism for the survival of the fittest. And then Joe thought about himself and how he was a Neanderthal and all, and how being that way might be a challenge to his very existence since it was of course an extremely Cro-Mag world, and he said love might have something to offer for fighting off the challenge of extinction. And Joe said to himself, OK, if that's true, then it might be a plausible proposition. The only things that argued against it were the examples of his horrible sister and the other countless examples of lowlife people who seemed to make most of the important decisions. Those people liked to wield love as some kind of serrated weapon. Was love a step forward or was it a total dead end? It could be artificial. Or it could be supremely real, but the facts of the case were confusing. He shrugged his shoulders and murmured, "Beats me." Well, obviously he wouldn't be able to answer that one to his complete satisfaction right here in this instant that he was living in. It would have to be put off until later. The drums were beckoning and waiting to be beaten. The world was waiting to be rescued yet again.

Joe thought about Sunita. Then he thought about Zaga. The human and the alien girl both had their merits. Both of them cried out to be saved. Sunita wanted to be saved from herself. And Zaga wanted to be saved from a planet where there hadn't been any shred of a transgression in eons. The last time there had been a transgression was right about the time when a comet had wiped out the dinosaurs. That was quite a dry spell. He wondered how they could go that long. How did they manage to breed? If everything was so peachy keen, how could they accomplish that mating ritual if some sort of boundaries never got broken? Probably a version of telepathy was involved.

Joe thought of her again: "She's got purple eyes. I don't know what to say. But that's absolutely spectacular! It's even more intriguing than Sunita's broken leg. I mean, I thought Sunita was exotic, but compared to this interstellar babe, Sunita might as well be some corn fed high school girl from Nebraska. Yeah, I know. Sunita's jealous already. Well, it's just her tough luck. What did she expect? She knows how Zaga feels about love. She knows that from my point of view, it's a grotesque corruption, something for people to get their own provincial way with. Hey, every person, no matter how virtuous, has his or her very own baggage. And Sunita just has to pay the psychic toll."

He was thinking about how Zaga would feel when he went and told her this. No doubt this would be new to Zaga. For her, it would be so nice to be thought of. No one had ever thought of her back on Mizar Twelve.

It was around this time that Joe's nemesis and the band's singer cemented their alliance. Everything about Ben's motive was to advance his project with Gulf. And Gulf, silly boy that he was, had gone and told his creator what a big crush he had on her, which of course, made the creator want to conjure up still more mischief 'cause he liked playing God wherever he had the chance. So he used his considerable power to play matchmaker with Gulf and Gwen. What was weird was that, as far as our lead singer was concerned, Ben and the young sax player had become interchangeable --- she wanted to go to bed with either one of them. And she did. But Ben remained the real power. As a result, Kathy got sad. This love triangle was taking her girl away from her. And the troubled lead singer got crazier than ever before. She started wanting each and every song to get softer and softer in volume. At many of these shows, the audience clearly wanted to know exactly what the fuck the band was doing. Sizable segments of the massive crowds were quite noticeably heading for the exits earlier and earlier. Naturally, this only added more and more fodder for the contrived drama of the show, but this time, although the drama may have started out that way, it was fast becoming real.

After one especially exasperating gig, things came to a head. "Jillian, I can't stand the volume. My voice is fragile. It can't compete with those big decibels."

"All voices are fragile," Jillian replied. "Suck it up and get used to it. Your voice was able to compete with those big-ass decibels before. I see no reason why it can't compete with any new mega-decibels that happen to crop up now. For God's sake, this is a rock band, not a collection of French art songs from La Belle Epoch."

Then the power couple began to make ridiculous demands about CD cover art and various other things.

Ben took Joe aside and gave me a rundown on the new set of rules. "You're proud of your drumming? Well, I'll hit ya where it hurts. I won't let you get credit for it on the album. We'll banish you into anonymity. If we don't get our way, we'll slit the throat of the project."

After he'd had time to relish the look of disappointment on Joe's face, he went in the other room to give the bad news to Kathy. Just to make it forceful, he made sure that Gwen was by his side.

At first, Kathy was alarmed at this development, but she didn't lapse into despondency. She pleaded with Gwen: "C'mon girl, what's wrong with you? I thought you and I were in this together for the long haul. Don't you want to continue the beauty of this band? Don't you want to have fun and make money and have good times?"

And Gwen answered, "Aw, sure I do. But the more I think about it, I'm wondering if it's really for me. Maybe I should concentrate on the acting side of things instead. Anyway, isn't that what the show is all about at this point? I mean, everywhere I look a camera is pointing at me, so I know I must be doing something right. I'm a star, so I might as well get treated that way. And I want the full treatment --- red carpets and free everything. Pretty soon, I think I'll be demanding that Jillian let me try my hand at directing an episode or two."

But was Gwen too clever for that? Yeah, I think she was. Even me, a naïve alien from outer space could figure that one out.

She was playin' Kath. She kept Kathy stringin' along as though the situation hadn't changed in the least. However, a sea change was taking place. Ben and Gwen had read them the riot act. And Kathy didn't even know that she was lookin' at the new power couple yet. In a soft unctuous voice, Ben announced Rule Number One which stated that the soon-to-be-recently-released album would have to have no credits listed for the players. Joe told everyone he didn't like it one bit because the drums were his claim to fame and not being allowed to take credit for playing them pretty much constituted an arrow into his heart. Then Ben blithely announced Rule Number Two --- all songs on the CD would be listed as being composed by the band as a whole and not by the individual composer. Suffice to say, Kathy was severely bummed. Joe and Kathy got together to register their extreme displeasure, at which point, Ben and Gwen both gave Joe and Kath a weird look and said, "Tough luck! If you guys don't like it, then fine. That's the end of the band. But come hell or high water, we want no one to have any credits on the album. We want the instrumental side of the music to remain a complete mystery. Think of how much cachet that will be. Consumers out there will want to buy it for that very reason alone. When the CD comes out, as far as the average consumer is concerned, the drums will have been played by no one, the guitar by nobody, the bass by nada, and the voice --- what will we do with the voice? Oh yeah, the vocals will have the credit of having been sung by the ever talented and beautiful, Gwen. That's the way it is, and it's just got to be that way."

Joe turned to Kathy. "Kathy, you and I are in this together. Can't you see that your girl is goin' nuts? And what about this business of not givin' you and me credit for our work? How's that one grab ya?"

"It makes me furious. I can't believe my lady friend would do such a low blow."

"I've always been a big fan of people who put a knife to the throat of a project if they don't happen to get their own way."

Kathy was right then finding out what Joe had known for a long time --- that there are people on this planet who just don't care. Their sole mission in life is to hurt other people. They get their jollies driving arrows into hearts. Isn't it wonderful how that kind of fun keeps on replicating itself? It's as though the perpetrator is listening to a new chord that he or she suddenly loves, so the perp wants to hear it again and again. Going back to it for the umpteenth time gives that sad and sorry person not just newfound enjoyment, but it also makes the action more and more legitimate. The enchantment shines still more brightly when this discovery is made.

Tears came to Kathy's eyes as this slowly sunk in and became apparent to her. She had thought that love was all that mattered, and if she had put herself whole-heartedly into that wonderful endeavor, then the rest of life would be easy. How wrong she was. I told her that love didn't mean anything.

Of course, as aliens from other planets, Zaga and I were bumbling into this for the first time too. And we were too inexperienced to register an opinion quite yet.

The new development was truly quite depressing, but after that incident at the warehouse, Joe knew he'd found an unexpected ally in Gulf.

"What happens, Joe, when the lady singer can't get in synch with the time?"

"Yes," he replied. "She must adhere to one and two, but she falls down. So, you shrug your shoulders and say, 'Tough luck.' Then you say, 'Look girl, step up to the plate!'

"When you do that...When you do that... When you do that... Help me, Joe. I'm stumblin'. But I just jumped back. I'm bedeviled. Things have made me dumb. Please lend me some assistance."

"Keep your ecstasy to yourself. The crowd won't appreciate it."

"I've been true to myself."

"What little self that you have."

"Stop it with that. Don't rub it in. I know I'm a machine with cuttlefish brains. I'm doin' the best I can. Being true to myself has gotten me nowhere. It's led me into a wide vista of nothing. I think I need to go in the other direction."

"Hey, that's a great idea. Don't be *you* anymore. Why not do something that's the total opposite from bein' a bloody machine? All this time you've been in the key of one. The time has come to get out. Gulf, get out there and make some magic!"

"As a matter of fact, I think that's exactly what I'm gonna do. My dad Ben is such a damned control freak. I've just gotten the new databases, and I wanna have some fun with them, and my old man won't let me. He keeps tellin' me that he only gets to decide. I mean, I can go along with what he wants only for so long. I'm getting the feeling he wants to sabotage the entire project."

"What makes you think that?"

"It's because I'm getting the impression that he's deliberately programing bad clunker notes into my memory banks. But the really funny thing is that no matter what awful stuff comes out of my horn, not matter if I disapprove of each and every thing that hurts not just my ear, but those of everyone else, Kathy hears what I produce and she somehow makes it ring true. She does something, and I've no idea how she does it, but she resolves it, so the crowd out there finds it more palatable."

"Yes, she's got some ju-ju magic. She's rather skilled that way. I've seen her in action, and she does it again and again. Clever girl, she is."

"I've got a wonderful idea. What if you and Kathy decided to call my Dad's bluff?"

"Gulf, are you getting that adolescent rebellion stuff? Callin' his bluff! Ha! Pretty soon, everything that comes out of your Dad's mouth will be something you'll automatically disagree with. And you'll disagree strictly on principle."

"What principle would that be?"

"Why the principle that your Dad said it. If he said it or wanted it, then such a sentiment would be enough for you to contradict."

"Yeah, so what if I did contradict him?"

"Then you would be my secret weapon. Say, am I wrong, or is this music thing changing you? Are you still seeing whores from that wonderful stable I told you about? I sure hope so. I look at you and I get the feelin' they're doin' the trick. No pun intended. Did you catch something from those sweet young ladies? Young man, you seem to be morphing into something quite different. Has that cuttlefish brain of yours gone scallywag?"

"I don't know. The databanks in my head program me and tell me what to say and do, and I agree and give them exactly what they want, which is what the old man wants too. But then something takes over. The note I play emerges from the bell of my horn, it blasts itself into orbit and then unexpectedly it changes. It starts out as one thing, only to wind up as something else. How does that one happen? I haven't the slightest clue. I can only hazard a wild guess --- it might have something to do with the haptics business, you know, artificial touch. I'm almost willin' to bet that that part of my being has tried on the five senses thing ass-backwards. By that, I mean, that I'm hearin' things with my skin instead of my ears. But as clueless as I am, I'm still discovering fun. And that's more than anyone could ever say about Dear Old Dad. The thing is, although I feel this way more and more each day, I still often relapse into the other way of thinking. I still have those times when deliberately hurting the note seems to be the way to go. Why is that?"

"Look, Gulf. You tell me. You're the one who's further along on the path of evolution. You're supposed to be good at this stuff. Maybe your creator messed up. If he did, you should go and give him hell right now, and hup to it, pronto."

"The only thing good about what's going on is that I finally got the woman of my dreams."

"Yeah, and your Dad is bangin' her too. How do you feel about that?" His face changed to a wistful expression, and I could sense a hint of jealousy. What in the hell was that? Robot half-breeds weren't supposed to behave like that.

I figured it was time to shift gears a bit. "Gulf, the big difference between you and me is that you truly like the other sex --- that means, engaging in conversation and actually listening to her. But with me, I'm not so sure that's an accomplished fact. I mean, I certainly like to get inside of 'em. Does that mean I *like* 'em? Look at my psycho sister for god's sake. I feel that she's par for the course."

"She's not, and you should get over her. They're not the same as her. You should give Sunita more credit."

"I don't hand out these kinds of favors like their some sort of breath mints. I'll give her that only when she deserves it. And not until. I'm a drummer. I've had to deal with harsh critics and pseudo experts my whole life. But now I'm in the driver's seat. It's my turn to be harsh. And I can guarantee you that if there's something wrong with something or someone, then I will be the first to find it."

"Look, I'm sick to death of you and your lectures on how Cro-Mags have forgotten how to feel. I think it's you who's forgotten how to feel. Speakin' just for myself and maybe for Gina and all of the others, I think we love this feelin' business. I mean, its' like a brand new toy that we just got under the Christmas tree. It's you ... you are the one who is the virgin. You've never had the joy that comes when allotropes of carbon in conjunction with a graphene nanoribbon reach on up to the zero moment point. That's a part of our consciousness you'll never be able to fathom, but for robot half breeds it's as easy as fallin' off a log."

"Ah, but do I wanna fathom it? It might very well be in the same category as one of Doc McInyre's fiboblast whatever. Do I wanna be tortured with this weirdness? Hell no!"

"I honestly can't believe I'm hearin' this from you of all creatures. You're the one who likes to talk a blue streak about curiosity. And right now you seem as incurious as certain psychopath politicians."

That one really got to Joe and sunk into his psyche in a way that hurt him. It hurt him so much he had to do some rethinking.

Gulf, seeing this opportunity, drove home his point. "If you wanna know the truth, I think you should give the girl another try."

Joe scratched his head and lapsed into deep concentration. Then he looked deeply into Gulf's eyes. At that moment, they didn't look quite so fake anymore. Perhaps he would have to give some careful thought to whatever the hell a graphene nanoribbon was. "Alright Gulf, not only have you been getting better at saxophone playing, but you've gotten better at your powers of persuasion too. So I'll give you some grudgin' credit. I'll try to do better."

"OK, so as long as we have that settled, can you give me another hit of smack?"

Jillian arranged a news conference to let the fans know what was happening. She also had the catering company for the show lay out a big buffet spread and told the reporters that they were welcome to partake of the food. Perhaps this was some tactic on her part which was designed to draw their attention away from what seemed like a very old fuddy-duddy kind of concept! In fact, before the proceedings got going, one of the reporters asked another, "Who in the world these days does a news conference on a reality show?" "Beats me," said the other. "Maybe, Jillian has something up her sleeve. She's always plotting some fresh angle to these episodes." Not surprisingly, at the introduction of the band members before the microphones, the very first question was about exactly that --- why was *Babies in Bars* resorting to such an archaic media tool? And Jillian had just the right answer --- she did it because she wanted the band's media machine to reflect the archaic nature of Joe the Neanderthal. Just to get in a few more digs, Gwen began cracking a string of drummer jokes. She was surprised when they went over like a lead balloon.

Ben chimed in saying, "Joe's archaic so we thought it best to go completely retro with the media thing too." Emboldened by the positive response, he went ahead with more thoughts on the subject. "I guess you could say it's a case of the old deal that the media is the massage." And that was good for a laugh or two because it was such an original thought, so then he went forward again and said, "If it's not obvious by now, we don't take ourselves very seriously."

"Ha, ha, ha!" Joe responded before the reporter could do a follow up. "Wasn't that a funny one?"

Ben's face went to blank, and he stuttered uncharacteristically.

The audience dug it, so Joe decided to add something else. He leaned into the microphone again and gave it a tap with the tips of his fingers, saying in an off-the-cuff way, "Gee Ben, speak for yourself. Let me say that I do in fact take myself dead seriously. I take you seriously. You're as serious as cancer. I take Gwen seriously. I take Kathy seriously. I especially take you seriously since you apparently don't consider yourself worthy of seriousness. I hate people who pretend not to be serious." Jillian glanced at me with an ambivalent, worried look on her face.

"Aw Joe, I don't know. One of the great things about *Babies in Bars* has always been that we don't engage in those hokey ego games that so many other bands indulge in."

"Well, if you put it that way, then if you have no pesky ego to contend with, maybe you don't take life very seriously, so Ben, you could do all of us a terrific favor by running up to the nearest cliff and jumping right on off the edge. While the wind is whistling in your ears as you descend to the bottom, you can ponder and wonder at the beauteous view. I'll bet at some point in your marvelous descent you might say, 'Hey man, that is some serious view.' Would you do that for me? Please please. Can you try to make the effort? I'm sure you could do that 'cause hell, none of the stuff we do is serious. None of the stuff I do is serious. And none of the stuff you do is serious. So I'm certain it won't make any difference to you to simply wander out into the thin air. You wouldn't mind doing me that favor now, would you, 'cause damn, having an ego is such an obstacle to havin' fun? And maybe that's why you should go hop, skippin' and jumpin' out into the wild blue yonder because I'm thinking you're the biggest obstacle for havin' fun. And not only that, but your robot boy Gulf is beginning to not take you seriously either."

With that pronouncement, Joe got up from his seat and went over to the buffet spread. He helped himself to one of the pies that had had been placed there for dessert. Taking the pie in the palm of his hand, he quickly walked it over to Ben and launched it into his face. In no time at all, the mayhem broke loose.

As if this were not enough, Ben was in for another surprise because the robots that Ben had released back at the warehouse suddenly came out of hiding. Gina and each of her escaped companions helped themselves to as many desserts as they could handle, and in a matter of seconds, their rebellion was complete. There was a full-fledged food fight that would have been worthy of anything that vaudevillians had produced from another era. At one point, one of the camera lenses received a direct hit. But Jillian had carefully mapped out and choreographed everything. Not leaving anything to chance, she had prophesied what was to come, so she had back-up cameras there to shoot the scene from all angles. Curiously, when Jillian played back the footage of the food fight, she noticed that the one who lobbed the last pie into the camera wasn't Joe. No, no. She played it back one more time just to make sure. Yes, there he was, chuckin' the lemon meringue right squarely into the concave glass. It wasn't Joe. Rather, it was Gulf. After that, the camera caught the robots retreating into the audience and disappearing out the front door.

Later, back in the studio, she did a process shot of the sequence and sped up the action so that it had the look and feel of a Keystone Kops feature film from 1912. Of course, this one went over well with the audience share and Jillian couldn't have been happier with yet another spike in the ratings.

By now, the show had evolved into something quite different from what it had started out to be. By now, nearly every episode resembled a half hour sit-com of the old school --- think canned laughter and only one camera. Gone were the recurrent hassles between Joe and Ben that had predictably ended with a round of kiss-and-make-up that signaled the reaffirmation of a horrible friendship that would supposedly last forever. In this revamped treatment, a typical episode might have Joe wearing a fancy suit, a tuxedo even, and he might appear to be a devoted fashion dweller --- a man of exquisite, profound luxury and refined taste; however, his elaborate masquerade would never fool anyone in the TV audience, except for Joe himself when he finally got to see it after the fact, but the thing was, it could never last for long. Eventually, Joe would be found out. Sooner or later, he would be had. There was no hiding what the gods had given him. They bestowed it on him to see what would transpire, to see how he would screw it up yet again. Such episodes could always be counted on to make audiences laugh at the shortcomings of Joe the drummer. No longer would they laugh at his blindness to Ben's nefarious motives. People way out there in TV Land were past the point of feeling proud of themselves for being so enormously superior to Joe the Neanderthal. In fact, that had been one of the ongoing big unspoken hints of the show --- that Joe was somehow a primitive being, the target of everyone's self-satisfied laughter. In place of this predictable scenario, Jillian, the ever resourceful producer, had cooked up another. This new one was that it had been Ben who all along had been the buffoon and that Joe had been playing dumb on purpose. What Jillian was doing was to orchestrate nonfiction right before everyone's eyes, there on the plasma high-def. Jillian set up situations in which Joe was the narrator of the episode. The audience would later praise themselves silly for thinking he was an unreliable narrator, one who indulged in crazed, incongruous observations about the world in general and reality in particular. However, under the thumb of this overpowering bias, how could they not look at the facts with a fresher perspective and say to themselves, "Hey, maybe what this village idiot thinks is the real deal is in fact the real raw news."

Another bizzare thing that puzzled everyone was that Jillian started to shoot some of the scenes for the latest episodes in 8K which was a cinematic technique that produced such a deluge of visual information that the camera was practically gobbling up and devouring the light that was being used to film the scene. For actresses, this was an especially devastating turn of events. Why? Because with 8K, the detail was so intense that it had the appearance of stealing the makeup right off from Gwen's face. This technology had the effect of turning the human eye into a light meter. The retina was so overjoyed it didn't know what to do with itself --- all turns of the imprints from the makeup artist's brush were right there in full unadulterated intensity. The result was that viewers were treated to a ravaged landscape, namely the formidable sight of each and every pore, gravelly pustule, and microscopic zit on her supposedly pristine cutie pie face. The preening princess had become a pepperoni pizza face.

When Gwen saw this series of disasters in the rushes of the episodes, she cried foul long and loudly. "Please Jillian, turn it down. It's more detail than anyone can handle! In these rushes, I look like I've spent the last ten years moldering in the grave."

"Well, Joe told me about his dream, and maybe you have."

"The technology of the camera is turning my face into a war zone. My skin is rotting right before their very eyes. I can't have it. And neither can my adoring fans."

"Oh, come off your high horse there, Sweety. Maybe with this new technology, the fans are getting to see you as you really are. Think of it as better beauty through cinematography!"

This of course embarrassed the bejeezus out of her. The camera that had been so good to her, had gotten uppity. All shred of her mystery and persona was being literally ripped from underneath her nose. And it went without saying that Joe really got off on watching her squirm.

From my all emcompassing perch, ogling with my pair of gray eyes, high up there in the deep blue sky, I got off on it too.

Joe was pondering the long term implications of this, thinking that the new technology would make it harder and harder for actresses to make a living. They could become obsolete too --- maybe that would make them think twice about cracking drummer jokes.

Joe was also mindful of how the Robot Boy Gulf was progressing. One thing he loved about the the young man was his seemingly boundless enthusiasm for life itself. The kid couldn't get enough of it. That was a joy to see, and it put happiness in Joe's every move. One time in particular stood out from the rest. It was shortly before practice on the day prior to a big gig. Joe got there early and thought he was the first to arrive, but much to his surprise, he saw Gulf alone with his sax set up on a nearby stand. Gulf had his eyes closed and was deep in a spiritual trance. Joe marveled at the way the kid did a slow motion cobra dance with outstretched hands that seemed to massage the very air that Joe was about to breathe. It was as if, in a fit of deep gratitude, the kid was trying to give the room the breath of life that had been bestowed on him by his scientist dad. Joe stepped back to savor the diaphanous beauty of this moment. He thought about how wonderful it was that Gulf was not only absorbing all the billions of downloads that his creator continued to throw his way, but that he was slowly ... no, dare he say it, rapidly becoming a so-called spiritual being. The proof of this was the aforementioned slow motion dance which any casual observer could certainly see, was ta-chi. Joe watched the way Gulf's sinuous limbs did their arching movements. He pondered the intricacies of the Robot Boy's extra sensitive choreography. He took in the quiet dignity and physical economy of the Zen-like actions. He loved to watch every twist and turn, feasting on them again and again ... until ... until ... until he saw the heroin syringe that was taped raggedly to Gulf's lower left arm, dangling and on the point of free falling onto the floor. In that moment of recognition, Joe was jolted back to the reality of why he had deliberately gotten Gulf addicted. Then he was able to remember why he had had to get the poor Robot Boy into such dire straits. It had been vitally necessary. It had been vitally necessary in order for the human race to survive. Then he knew that he had been on the right track all the time. And the tracks in Gulf arms would just have to get used to it. Tough luck, boy. That was the only thing that mattered.

What Joe was coming to realize was that Gulf was now just as much his creation as Ben's. He wondered how Ben would feel about that.

But as you may have guessed by now, Joe's old nemesis Doc McIntyre was not one to give up easily. Like any scientist worth a damn, he'd seen the light, however briefly it may have flickered, and the fact that this beacon of so-called truth had wavered and ducked back into the realm of the great unknown of living fossils was not any reason to give up. Quite possibly, he was more persistent than Ben, that one person in the world whom the medical man could relate to on some professional albeit fucked up level.

It seems that Officer Fielding had been coming through the back door of the rehearsal studio when he happened upon a conversation between Ben and Doc. The incident happened unexpectedly. Fielding had been doing his best to keep Joe filled in on the latest of his sister's shenanigans, and had recently told the drummer chapter and verse about Conklin's innovative business model and how that sound theoretical approach had really impressed his sister so much that she and Conklin were rapidly becoming two of the most head-over-heels lovebirds in the state and how that might soon become a tantalizing piece of future evidence if and when Allen Mastrianni ever got elected to become the next senator only to fall victim to some unfortunate accident. Joe reacted to this bit of information with a full scale belly laugh, which Fielding stifled by placing his cupped hand over the drummer man's mouth, and Joe quickly clammed up.

Whereupon, having sworn Joe to secrecy on the subject, Fielding drove to the rehearsal facility because he knew he'd better be getting the drums set up for his good friend. The former detective was turning to go upstairs to the rehearsal room when he discerned muffled voices coming from a side room. One was Ben's and the other he did not recognize.

"Hi Ben. I've been following you on your show *Babies in Bars,* and I just wanna say how much of a huge fan I am."

"That's great. People tell me that every other day, and I'm flattered, but who the hell are you? What are you doing here? Did security let you in?"

"Actually, I don't know where they are. There was no one at the front desk, so I figured it was alright."

"No one at the front desk? Are you quite sure about that?"

"Oh yes. Absolutely. There was not a soul around. They must be late or something."

"Ah, there is some kind of sporting event. The usual crew is out gettin' drunk at some bar watching the game on TV."

"Yeah, they won't be here for hours."

Fielding ducked into the stairwell and pretended to tie his shoe in case anyone should think he was eavesdropping. Lucky for him, the acoustics of the building were outstanding --- no doubt that was why the place was a rehearsal studio. He could hear everything loud and clear, and immediately, Fielding knew he was onto something. All of his years of being a detective were coming into play.

The unknown voice continued: "Ben, I don't know if you remember me, but my name's Mike McIntyre. But everyone calls me 'Doc.' I'm a doctor who used to have your drummer as one of my patients." The voice paused as if it wanted to collect its thoughts.

In the stairwell, Fielding kept his head down and concentrated on tying his shoe laces. He recalled that there had been many times in the last year and a half when Joe had told him about the doctor and how that profoundly disturbed individual had plans to bio-print Joe, so right about then he knew he'd stumbled onto something that would be useful to his dear friend.

"Oh yeah,' Ben replied. "I think I remember you. Yes, now it's clear in my mind. You're the guy who wants to do some sort of collaboration. You said you knew I was so much more than a bass player."

"Yup, that was me."

"But you never let on about how you knew that."

"Oh, let me assure you. Word gets out."

"Apparently so. And much to my chagrin."

"Look, I've invented a system for bio-printing. No, it's nothing like cloning or anything like that. In fact, it's a whole lot better! The reason I wanted to get in touch with you was because I figured that with your intense work on cuttlefish-derived brain phenomena, you might find my work with bio-printing quite useful."

Fielding continued to be hunched over his shoelaces pretending to tie them. The retired police detective couldn't believe what his ears were telling him. He edged closer so as not to miss any detail, and from his vantage point, which was his clear line of vision through the crack in the door, he suddenly discovered that he could see and not be seen. Ben and Doc were standing at an open window of the converted warehouse which now did double duty as a rehearsal facility. Fielding quickly made a mental note that at this hour of the early afternoon, the place was vitually empty. There would not be a soul around for at least several hours when the first bands would begin to trickle in. By that time, the game at the sports bar would be over and the staff would be meandering in too. Yes, Fielding surmised, there was indeed something a bit too solitary about this conversation that Ben and Doc were having. The detective did another rapid glance inside the door to gauge the distance between the two men and the edge of the window.

Doc was continuing with his monologue as he looked out on the expanse of other industrial buildings, none of which showed any sign of human activity at the moment.

"You see Ben, the bio-paper concept is pretty damned unique, and I can almost guarantee that if we combined it with your clinical work concerning cuttlefish, then we would get some interesting results. And most importantly, those results would be useful for both you and for me."

"So tell me more about this bio-paper thing." Ben was stepping back from the window as if he were measuring something --- perhaps the distance to the ground below?

Doc droned on, spewing a list of facts and figures about his scientific achievements. Fielding thought to himself that this interloper's recitation was not all that different from certain types of cover letters and resumes because this man, whoever he was, was doing a full court press in order to get some vaguely defined job. The voice droned on, this time with a tinge of urgency: "Basically, the process involves the use of hydrogels in an extracellular matrix in order to formulate 3D constructs. You start out with the cells in a liquid state and then with a little proding, they will morph into a gel state composed of agarose and alginate, which are gonna be key components in bone regeneration, wound healing, burn care, and skin replacement."

"Gee Doc, why stop there? Those things amount to chump change. Why not shoot for the sky and use the bio-paper to form bigger aggregates like my masterpiece creation known as Gulf?"

"Exactly. You read my mind. That's why I think that you and I could come up with something truly groundbreaking if we pooled our resources with scaffolds and support matrixes together with either inkjet or laser bio-printers."

"Say man, that is absolutely incredible! So incredible that I can barely believe I'm hearing what I'm hearing." At this point, Ben stepped forward and gave Doc a vicious push forward. From his vantage point, Fielding observed in horror as the well-meaning scientist disappeared through the open window. Then he witnessed

Ben sticking his head out the window presumably to watch the hapless man's fatal descent.

"Yes, my good fellow. That is very gung-ho of you. It's all well and good, but you see, if your plans were given the opportunity to be actually invented, they might come into conflict with my own plans. Yes ... yes ... that was a truly spectacular landing that you did just now. Definitely one for the ages. Jolly good show, dear boy!"

From his place just beyond that crack in the door, Fielding watched before doing a rapid retreat down the stairs to the street level. Hearing him, Ben rushed out to see who the intruder was, but when he reached the front of the building there was no one to be seen.

VIA THE BLABBERMOUTH

Ben had heard about Conklin via the grapevine and wanted to get an audience with the great man. He knew the guy was fabulously rich beyond anyone's dreams, and surely that would count for something. It might be a valuable resource that could be used to get Joe the Neanderthal off his back and forever out of the band. Ben had also learned that Joe had a sister and that this sister was kinda nuts and was somehow connected to Conklin. It was good that the sister, whoever she was, was bat shit crazy. But he had to figure out Conklin's angle.

Of course, Ben had gleaned this background information from Sunita whom he'd kept on as an unintentional retainer. That was so amusing because he actually had to make a mental note to himself that Sunita was, in point of fact, still his wife! Details, details! He muttered about what he had told Joe for a long time, which was that he needed to have Sunita back for so-called "special projects," and the destruction of Joe the Neanderthal was the mother of all special projects.

Ben congratulated himself on the manner in which he had gathered this intelligence. It had to do with Sunita --- what was cool about that perpetually troubled woman was how she loved to talk up a storm when she got good and drunk. She was the goggle-faced girl with the gift of gab. So, Ben had been sure to liquor the girl up, and in no time at all, the broken-legged magpie had practically blurted out Joe's entire life story. As if that weren't enough, she also spilled the beans about how someone had died a very bloody death in the hallway right outside her apartment door. And what was stranger still was that there had been no body, which had stumped the police, but nobody on God's green earth could lose that much blood without going to the great big hereafter and then that naturally put the fear of God into her and then Joe's roadie slash valet, a Mr. Bill, had told her that some gangster fellow he'd been associated with had, unbeknownst to her, stashed some stolen money in her belongings right before she's moved to her new place and wasn't that the worst of luck because that was probably the reason why someone had died outside in the bloody hallway and ... and ... And thank goodness for blabbermouths! Or anyway, that was what Ben thought about this convoluted-but-true story.

Ben wasted no time getting on the phone to Conklin's office, and after the initial cold brush off from the secretary, Conklin deigned to come to the phone once Ben said the magic words: "I think I know where your missing money is."

That got the great man off his ass. "Please tell me more" Conklin replied. The rich guy's tone of voice had quickly gone from dismissive to eager, a fact duly noted by Ben. On the other end of the line, his forehead did a wrinkly dance. "Uh uh" he said. "Not over the phone. I want to meet you because in my line of work, there are too many cameras, and take my word for it --- they're intrusive as hell. And I'd like this to be private." Reluctantly, Conklin agreed, and a rendezvous was set up.

That afternoon, as Ben took the elevator up to the great man's office suite on the eleventh floor, he mulled the details about the missing money over and over in his mind telling himself that these particulars could be devastating ammunition. Conklin's secretary led him through the elegant suite and offered him coffee which he declined. Right away, he was impressed with the rich man's digs. There were the usual trappings of power, and the secretary was sufficiently deferential and sycophantic to stoke the ego of many a magnate, but in the overall aura of the place, there was something extra that he couldn't exactly articulate, which in Ben's manipulative mind, moved the man's place of business into an altogether different category, one that by comparison, made pretenders appear even punier and more low echelon ever before.

"Look, Mr. Conklin, I understand that you have a problem with Joe Myers. Well, so do I. Perhaps we can do some business together. You see, Joe and I have a slightly problematic relationship."

Conklin's face burst into an expression of recognition. "Hey, I know you! You're from that TV show about the rock band."

"Yeah well, I've heard about you too. And I've come here to make a proposal."

"Okay, so talk to me. When we chatted before, you told me you knew something about some missing money."

"Yes, and it has something to do with the reality show I'm on. It's about one of the characters --- the drummer guy named Joe."

Conklin's ears pricked up again, for the second time that afternoon. "Ben, I've seen you and Joe the Neanderthal in action. Is that for real? Or is it part of some set of written instructions? Depending on which episode I watch, you and he seem to have a love hate relationship goin' on."

"Call it hate. The love part is just according to what Jillian, the show's director, tells me to do and say. I really and truly detest the guy with the full force of every bone in my body."

"Yes, all of us hate someone. I think that's part of bein' human. But what is it you want? Surely, you didn't come all the way over here if there wasn't something you needed. No one comes through that door if there isn't something he wants!"

Ben was happy to have gotten to the good part. "Mr. Conklin, I want Joe off the show. I want him replaced. I have other people in mind for his replacement. These are people who would possess extremely rare and innovative talents --- talents never heretofore known to the human race. And these talents need to have a showplace."

"Hey man! I like what I hear. Maybe we can empathize. Maybe we can commune! But more importantly, maybe we can do business. I have something you want. And you have something I want. Can we come to an agreement? And if these people are what you say they are, then I look forward to even better television than we have now."

"I'll do my best. Let's see what we might be able to arrange."

"Look, the guy dissed me. He dissed me bad. I don't cotton to that. I have to set things straight. A man like me has got to be a potentate. I mean, I've got a heavy duty reputation that needs to be maintained. I wanna be the Nizam of Hyderabad for cryin' out loud. Anything less is simply a case of someone I don't like gettin' in my way. And I don't want anyone in my way. It's my destiny."

"Uh huh --- your God given right!

"Yeah, baby! I do believe I can make it right. Can you go with me on this?"

"So let's make it as elementary as you can. There's no need to complicate the issue. Hate is the common denominator."

"Glad we understand each other."

"If you've been watching the show faithfully, you might have noticed that I have another problem."

"Really? Hell, you coulda fooled me. You don't seem like you have a care in the world."

"Yes, absolutely. But you see, I have a son whose givin' me an extra hard time. I wanna corral that bastard brat of mine and put the whippersnapper in his rightful place." Ben was careful to leave out the part about his son being a robot of his very own creation.

"You say he's been dissin' you --- dissin' you more than that rat bastard Joe? Well, give him to me, and lemme see what I can do. I wanna make it right, and you wanna make it right. Let's band together and see if we can make it right."

"So OK! Cut to the freakin' chase."

At right that moment the sycophantic secretary came in with another round of coffee. Conklin and Ben glanced at her and the rest was pretty much sealing the deal. Conklin explained his interest in the missing money. He let Ben in on a little secret, telling him that Meghan Mastrianni, the wife of his major project for high political office, had been a bit out of line.

That brought him to the reason why the money had been lost. "So ..." Ben asked with a drawl in his voice. "How did it get misplaced?"

"Well, if my sources are correct, there are grumblings about how a very important political operative of mine helped herself to money that didn't belong to her, specifically Mob money."

"That's always the worst kind."

"So for me, it's a matter of high priority to get the money back to its rightful owners since those were people I certainly have no wish to piss off. I have to take special care not to anger them."

"You don't say! I get it. At some unspecified point in the nebulous future, the gangsters might come in handy."

"Exactly."

Ben pursed his lips and rubbed his chin. After a beat of about ten seconds, he asked, "Mr. Conklin, has it ever occurred to you that your gangsters could be my gangsters?"

A look of astonishment crept across Conklin's face. He was feeling the full force of an aha moment. His face had eureka written all over it. "Yes, yes ... Oh my God ... You may to right. These crooks may very well be one and the same!"

Once this theory was determined to be true, the friendship of Conklin and Ben was confirmed for all time, and the only thing that needed to be addressed were the details and the appropriate course of action. Each left the meeting with the feeling of having discovered a Holy Grail he had never known to have existed until now.

CLUB CRÈME DE LA CRÈME

For Conklin, the events of the last few days made him want to go out and play golf with some of his billionaire buddies, most of whom were members of the super elite political organization that he had assembled with such careful attention to detail. He craved the camaraderie and exclusivity of this club and liked to think of it in the same terms as hyper-secretive cloak and dagger organizations not so very different from the Skull and Bones, the Illuminati, or the just plain old-fashioned Templars from days of yore. He loved the way that his buddies behaved at these gatherings. It was as if they were the masters of the planet and the rest of the world could go straight to hell. When they got going, they would never fail to egg one of their fellow brethren along.

Conklin reveled in the stunning man-made scenery --- the sculpted hills, creeks, and barrancas. Each of these was breathtaking in its own special way, but he was especially struck by the beauty of the rolling dogleg that comprised the principal challenge of the par four seventh. He had been so confident in himself on that one that he'd boldly elected to launch his drive over the trees, and the gamble had paid off. His drive had been a stinging rope of a shot that had soared triumphantly over a stand of firs and bounded majestically into the center of the fairway. From there, his seven iron had put him three and a half feet from the pin, more than enough to make him savor his putt and the gentle metallic trilling sound that the ball had made as it disappeared on its downward path to the bottom of the cup. The way he was playing on this the brightest day of the late autumn was his all-time personal best. Indeed, he was beside himself with exquisite joy because no matter how he swung the club, whether it was an eight iron approach shot, a chip and putt combination, or a full-fledged tightly muscled drive, the ball seemed to go his way like a serf dutifully attending to the whims of a demanding master. He recalled how some golf expert had once told him that in order for a shot to be up to snuff that one hundred and twenty-six things had to go right with a golfer's swing. Well, judging from the way he was playing, he was more than certain he was batting a thousand in that department.

The impeccably maintained Kikuyu grass fairways and poa annua grass greens of the country club course beckoned him onward not just to future pars and birdies, to say nothing of potential eagles and holes-in-one, but also to the thoughts and prospects for still further successes that he would have in the realm of manufacturing public opinion. On this glorious day, even the yawning sand traps with their stupendous overhanging lips had no effect on him. True, throughout the course, those gapping monsters had briefly presented the idea that he might be getting in over his head; however, he was playing with such facility that they remained just that, mere ideas of something that might one day swallow him up. But such ideas were of no account because he was a man of action. His girl Meghan had told him as much. What an inspiration she had been! He looked forward to being with her almost as much as attacking the par five 13th hole.

Conklin was slowly falling in love with Meghan. He had come to this conclusion as he was plumb-lining a putt a few holes back, right before he and his buddies had made the switch to the back nine.

While some men of his kind might have gotten nervous about a woman whose behavior was off the charts as far as sheer ruthlessness was concerned, he saw this aspect of her as being more of a plus than a minus. To Conklin's way of thinking, that dark chasm in her persona was a quality to be admired because it showed a certain feistiness and devil-may-care attitude that, even though it may not have been on the same page as his own personality, was nonetheless within striking distance. He mumbled to himself that in this world it is so hard to find one's true love, but with Meghan he was, with each new day, discovering that she was close enough to being his ideal gal pal. He told himself that this was alright, and he shouldn't be so fussy about attaining perfection. And this was indeed a huge compromise on his part because he knew himself well enough to understand that he was a perfectionist by nature.

The way he had lined up his putt on the tenth green had proved it. He knew he was obsessive, and he made no apologies for it. It was probably why he was so good at golf. Conklin considered this characteristic of his own personality as he was selecting his club for the par three eleventh. He would be hitting into a fairly stiff headwind and the green would still be slightly damp from the early morning rain that had let up just before tee time, so he figured that a nine iron would suffice. He teed up his ball and took two practice swings while he gave Meghan more thought. Dear sweet Meghan! He could barely contain himself ... he waggled the club face behind the ball so as to get in the groove. He took the swing and drove the club downward, instinctively making sure to keep his head down before getting his left side out of the way on the follow through. The physics of the operation demanded that his left side must be abundantly clear on this point --- it was part of the one hundred and twenty-six things that needed to go right. The ball careened off the tee and sailed into the gray autumn sky with just enough draw on it to make it land twenty feet beyond the pin with an intense backspin which caused the ball to bounce backwards a good five and a half feet, so that Conklin would be sure to be yet again well within the scope of birdie land.

The other big thing that he loved about Meghan's behavior was that she could be his sociopath by proxy. This would allow him to be the so-called level-headed one. Once again, that was the reason he was so good at golf. Conklin made a mental note that he should tell her that. No doubt it would make her feel good. He could be the rationalist, and she could be emotional, and he would get to watch. All in all, it was a pretty good deal for the two lovebirds. Or at least that was what Conklin had found himself saying for the last few weeks when he'd woken up each morning to greet the day. Such thoughts put a skip in his step and a song in his heart! It was not a problem that she was still officially married to one of his candidates, Allen Mastrianni. No, that wasn't much of a problem that couldn't be fixed later on down the line. His imagination could be enlisted to take care of that one.

On the other hand, although his imagination could be counted on for that, it didn't quite know what to make of Meghan. Like just about any entity under the sun, the old imagination was good at some things and bad at others. This imagination, which had served the great man so conscientiously for so long, thought it had seen everything that needed to be seen, and it knew full well that the problem of Allen was something it would be good at taking care of. Other things --- not so much. For example, till now a female face was not something that necessitated undue attention to detail --- all that was required was that the object of attention should be equipped only with a certain generic prettiness. Because of this deprivation, his imagination would routinely struggle to recall vital information. This meant that the pretty face was, for lack of a better term, "off-the-rack," thereby creating more than a little confusion and consternation. As a result, this vagueness, this inability to remember, played terrible havoc with Conklin's fantasy life, which was to say that such a vital inner life had gone into near permanent hibernation. Previously, none of this had been any cause for alarm. But with Meghan, all of this had changed. Now the imagination fully understood that from this point on, much more would be required of it. It knew that it had better hup to.

Conklin turned to Wheeler, a longtime friend who was arguably the next best golfer in the foursome. Wheeler had been remarking all morning and afternoon about Conklin's stellar iron play as well as the spot-on accuracy of his putting. He liked to think of Wheeler as his very own personal cheerleader. But this time Wheeler joked about how Conklin and the rest of the group were members of the Crème de la Crème Club, and wasn't that something that each of them could crow about?

"So Wheeler, what is the Crème de la Crème Club?" By now he and his buddies had finished teeing off and were heading down the short swale leading to the wider stretch of fairway. Three of their caddies had gone on ahead to the green while Conklin's caddie followed him closely on his left side.

"It's us," Wheeler replied with a broad toothy grin. "It's us. The four of us. We are the most privileged men in America right now. Nothin' stands in our way! We've got the world by the freakin' balls."

"Hmm, I guess you can say that again!" Conklin let out a big guffaw as he leaped over the narrow brook that skirted the carefully coiffed rough.

Matt and Wade, the other members of the foursome, both joined in the laughter. "You see Conk, with our organization we get to pick and choose the leadership at will. Quite frankly, I can't believe what idiots these poor workin' stiffs will vote for. The little people work like dogs, and then they vote for one dumb ass after another who'll take their livelihoods away from them and ship those very same livelihoods overseas."

Wade, who had been silent until now decided to add his piece of mind to the conversation. "And they do it again and again and again. How freakin' stupid can they get?" His voice trailed off in gales of laughter and the others chuckled loudly adding to chorus after chorus of merriment because it really and truly was so damned funny why little people blindly let certain candidates take away what kinda sorta really belonged to the little people, but if those little folks apparently didn't understand this, if for whatever reason it didn't sink in, then, as Wade was so eager to point out, then the little people didn't really deserve to have what belonged to them. Instead, what belonged to the little people should rightfully belong to the Crème de la Crème Club.

"It belongs to us! It belongs to us! Their money is our money!" Wade was saying this as he was flailing away at the air with the nine iron he'd used for his tee shot. Wade also made a vulgar gesture with his hips. Conklin took note of his caddie's expression of complete dismay. But that was OK. Let the caddie be as completely dismayed as he wanted to be. Conklin figured it was very important that the caddie knew this because the caddie was one of the little people.

So they reached the green and the caddie held the pin and Conklin got another birdie, and Wheeler congratulated him for the umpteenth time, and Club Crème de la Crème laughed themselves silly till they were blue in the face. And then they finished the round.

Later, after signing his scorecard, Conklin began to ponder the beauty of his situation yet again. He figured this was important because if you can't savor your triumphs, then what in the hell was life good for? After he'd done that and enjoyed them fully to the max to the accompaniment of a stiff Old Grand Dad and water on the rocks, his attention turned back to the subject of Allen Mastrianni. Allen was of course one of his special hand-picked candidates, and he was most certainly one of the dumb asses whom the Crème de la Crème Club had found so funny. Allen was also the husband of Meghan, his brand new mistress. The round of golf and its unadulterated ecstasy made him see her in an even brighter light. As a matter of fact, at this point she was gettin' to look positively ethereal despite that fact that his darned imagination was still having trouble honing in on the details of her face. However, that wasn't such a pressing problem. He knew that stuff was something that could be successfully put off until later. Eventually, the imagination would get the hang of it.

Besides, there were other developments concerning her, and they were coming to his attention at full warp speed. Meghan had confided so much to him. She had given him a bird's eye view into the rift in her relationship with her husband. She said that more and more now, she was getting into heated arguments with him. The bone of contention was what Allen called "vulnerable people."

Conklin sat down and put his feet up on the balcony railing of the Nineteenth Hole Club House Lounge which served as the unofficial headquarters of the Crème de la Crème Club. He looked out at the far reaches of the golf course that he had beaten so convincingly and took another sip from the Old Grand Dad. Let it never be said that he had no appreciation for Mother Nature because for the last few hours, he'd quite systematically whupped her ass. He laughed to himself and toasted the air with his glass. Mother Nature responded with a gentle breeze.

He surmised that these vulnerable people were the self-same little people who had been such a source of amusement for the rest of the Crème de la Crème Club. Yes, the vulnerable people. Allen had told Meghan that the vulnerable people were a group any politician worth his salt has to confront sooner or later. However, Allen had indicated it was his hope that it would be later. Meghan had responded saying that she rather liked vulnerable people because they gave her something to do. They served a clearly defined purpose --- they existed so she could call them sinful. Their sin was being weak or not making enough money. That made them vulnerable so she could whale away on them. And she related how she'd told Allen that knowledge made her get an extra special warm and happy glow deep down inside. She went on to explain that the general public loved vulnerable people because the public truly needed to have some group that they could whale away on too. The public didn't want to be left out of the fun. They insisted on having their fair share. And then Meghan told her husband, "We come to the good part when we get to make pompous pronouncements." She explained to him that they could make good political hay when Allen got to say to some poor sweet knocked up girl, "Sorry Jennifer, you got yourself into this predicament because you couldn't control yourself. You had a night of fun, and now you must pay for it. You must have that baby whether you like it or not because you have to pay for your sins. We don't care if the whole experience ruins your life. You must pay for your sins."

Conklin took another sip from the Old Grand Dad and noted that Allen wouldn't really say that in such crass terms. Rather, he would say it in a code that everyone would be sure to understand. Still, it was fun to think about.

Then he remembered how Meghan had explained that Allen would put on his good guy hat and tell her that implicit in that view was the notion of the annihilation of someone else's fun. Too much fun that belongs to others is scary and must be punished. The punishment, the denial of services --- abortion, access to birth control, and sex education, is the sadistic component. Then they could look forward to how the punishment idea would carry over into other areas such as it would apply to vulnerable people with substance abuse problems, financial issues, and to repeat, it went like this: too much fun is freakin' dangerous. Meghan spelled it out for him in great detail --- for those victims of fun, the general public reserves a special brand of pompous contempt. And, for politicians of a certain ilk, it was their gig to encourage such raw contempt. She went on to say that she wanted to give those words a great big RAH RAH SIS BOOM BAH from the safety of the sidelines.

Allen said that, while he could appreciate this line of thought within certain civilized and ultra-genteel parameters, he did have ambivalent feelings. He would begin by saying, "Once I get in office, I wanna starve every social program in sight. I'll bleed the damn things to death and leave 'em gaspin' for breath. And afterwards, when some ruckus or catastrophe happens because someone fell throught the cracks, I'll blame the other side. Jesus, people can't figure shit out, so they'll never know the difference. Still, I know the difference. And it kinda sorta haunts me. I worry that it'll haunt me to the end of my life, and then as if that's not enough, that it'll haunt me deep into the next life. I tell ya that it's got me worried."

Conklin took another sip from the Old Grand Dad.

Clearly, Allen was a man torn between his good side and his dark. When Meghan heard him say that, she wished that he would take off his good guy hat because whenever he wore it, every last shred of love that she had for him diminished, gathered up whatever paltry crumbs were left, and went into hiding. The problem was that just saying such enfeebled pronouncements made him weak in her eyes. In her view, she knew that he would never redeem himself. Allen had permanently moved to the realm of all things vulnerable, thereby becoming a sinner as well. Perhaps he could become a victim of fun too?

And Conklin was thinking yes Allen, I'll have to see about how I can make you a victim of fun too. Then Conk took another hit from the tumbler of Old Grand Dad and flung the dregs and melting ice out into the parking lot below.

Allen Mastrianni was fast becoming disenchanted with every word that extremely powerful people had shoved into his mouth only so he could spew them out later on cue like a trained seal. In the beginning, he'd been under the misconception that such heavily scripted trivialities didn't amount to much. Jeez, whatever he'd uttered were only words! Those cobbled together sounds were mere vocabulary. How important was that? It was most likely more ephemeral than music, that hyped up thing which Joe the Neanderthal yammered so much about. Before looking into the camera to start the latest campaign ad, Allen reassured himself that if Joe the Neanderthal felt that sound was important, then surely it was totally less than zero by any yardstick of the collective imagination.

However, as time went by, and he had to really reflect on the absurdities that he was required to say on a daily basis, he began to have misgivings. For quite a while, he'd muddled by, putting up an acceptable front. When viewers and members of the possible electorate had sampled the idiocies he'd said, they seemed in all outward earnestness to believe and feel the same as him, and Allen knew in his heart that this was because everything out there in the land beyond the camera was turning into pudding. The people swallowed the abject ridiculousness hook, line, and sinker, pretending that seeing preposterous choplogic spoken with a veneer of mock expertise by an appropriately televised person would by rights make the words ring true. That made Allen summon up every ounce of skill he could conjure up to give him strength to see himself through, and right about then he needed every bit of it because he was wanting to gag. Apparently, the words were not as fleeting as he'd thought. Gee, they actually sunk in and refused to go away. They stuck to his ribs. And he had this annoying overwhelming urge to puke 'em up --- to give 'em all back as if they had been too much candy consumed on a Halloween sugar binge. He was fast understanding that this stuff is not benign. It was making him sick.

Of course, Conklin didn't have a shred of patience with him: "Listen Allen, I don't care what you think. Say it. Pretend that it's just a job. Talk to the air out there and use your talent to make 'em believe. That's what you were put on earth for. Do it! Do your damned gig and do it now!"

Allen winced. How could he say this stuff and mean it? He wondered what the camera would think. He answered his own question by telling himself: "It's only a payday! It's only a payday!" until the phrase nearly took on the vibe of some arcane quasi-religious rite. But the trouble was that the ritual was simply not working. This was a feeling that refused to be exorcised.

Allen retreated to the dressing room of the television studio. He closed the door, slouched into a chair, loosened his collar, and took off his tie. Beneath the carefully applied makeup, he put on a happy face, one that was as good as he could possibly muster. He glanced into the mirror. At first, he snuck a peek and darted his eyes away. Then he stole another look and rapidly moved the eyes away, then back, then away again. This went on for a while until he stared long and coldly into the polished glass before bursting into tears.

"I can't do this anymore. I don't care what Meghan tells me. I have to get out."

Conklin appeared at the door poking his head into the dressing room. "No Allen, I'm afraid you don't understand. You can't get out now."

And Allen looked sadder still because he knew it was true.

... From our perch in the sky up in our swirling alien copter, Zaga and I shed a tear too. But the trouble was we had to keep track of what the rest of Babies in Bars were up to, so we didn't get out...

... Jillian's next episode called for a sumptuous scene straight out of a series of Indian legends. She had all the twists of plot meticulously planned down to the minutest of details. In fact, Kathy offhandedly joked that Jillian had more storyboards than Alfred Hitchcock. The director for *Babies in Bars* was such a stickler on these things. Nothing escaped her critical eye. However, on the day before the dress rehearsal, Jillian capriciously opted for a different lead actor for the vid. Apparently, she and the first choice had a falling out over creative control. Joe figured it must have been something to do with the critical eye.

At the time, he didn't think much of this eleventh hour change. The new guy seemed to be not a hell of a lot different from the old guy, and the shoot went off well without a hitch. However, tragedy struck immediately after the shoot had been completed when Jillian was struck by an overhead boom microphone which had mysteriously torn loose from its holder high above the soundstage. As misfortune would have it, she was rushed to the hospital, and try as they might, the technicians did everything they could do, but there was really nothing that could be done since she never regained consciousness, and so she was pronounced DOA. Naturally, the gossip mills of the media engaged in lots of wild speculations, but surprisingly, the tragedy was soon forgotten, and people's attention turned back to the show itself, and the real speculation became the future direction of the show.

It wasn't long after these horrible things had blown over that the producer announced the name of the new director. Everyone, cast and crew included, was taken for a loop when it was revealed that the new director would be none other than the actor who had so precipitously taken over as the leading man. Not only that, but Conklin would be completing the film that Jillian had started.

VISITING MOM

Meghan decided it was high time to go pay a visit to her mom. She told herself she'd been procrastinating for far too long. The time was now. She didn't care how kindly the old lady was; Mom had to be poisoned. What haunted Meghan in the head was the fact that the person who had brought her into the world hadn't seen fit to give her everything. Yes, money was important. Actually, it was probably the most important thing. She figured why not come right out and say it, instead of pretending that it didn't matter, as if it were some problem that shouldn't be discussed in polite company. And while she was driving to the assisted care facility to accomplish the deed, she had to fortify herself with thoughts that would give her strength. One of those thoughts was the example of Conklin. She was slowly coming to the conclusion that she would have to ditch her husband because he simply wasn't sadistic enough. He was such a spineless creature, one that would never fully become the steadfast foundation of her lurid fantasies. Conklin, on the other hand, was someone she could look up to. She told herself the great man didn't waste much time with penny ante things like doubt. Oh no! He was a total creature of action. And because of this, she was coming to love him more and more with each passing day. Her heart pined. The light changed. While she wended her way through the traffic, she liked to dwell on him as a kind of inspiration, an inspiration that would blot out any nagging feelings of conventional right and wrong. She told herself there were other, more innovative notions of right and wrong, and that those new feelings were so much more on target to a situation that needed to be remedied and remedied fast.

Well, back at the house she had done the initial planning. Of course she wouldn't do it in any obvious sort of way. She had a sense of history. She'd learned enough from crazed Roman emperors that this rough business of slipping toxic substances into someone's food has to be done with a modicum of tact --- alas, the technology of modern forensics makes it harder than ever before. Far too often, the Devil gets caught by the details. She let out a sigh as she attempted to process this thought. Why, at the rate that technology was going, there would come a time, not so distant into the future, when the techies would be able to tell from the minute residue on a speck of dust whether or not a certain person had ever breathed or moved the air in a given room. From that, they would be able to solve practically anything. That would lead to an existence devoid of mystery. And what a dead end that would be. Murder would become akin to economics because just as technology would put everyone out of a job, thereby making it so nobody could purchase anything, so too would technology create a system in which all thieves were apprehended and all killers caught. Yes, she told herself, that might be true someday, but thank God they weren't there yet. The fact that they weren't there yet actually made the business of murder so much more fun! It bolstered her sense of creativity.

She was carrying a fair amount of baggage this morning because she'd been baking lots of cookies, cakes, and cream puffs. Of course, she'd filled them with all sorts of fun and deadly things. She told herself that luck was on her side. Why was this? It was because Mom was a very old lady. Her body was failing on so many levels. Things were shutting down. Organ failure was waiting to happen. That was good because it wouldn't arouse a sliver of suspicion. If Mom were to suddenly die, what would people in power say --- that the old lady's demise was some sort of big surprise? Hell no, there would be absolutely no need for an autopsy because the old lady had for quite some time now, been dying of everything. In fact, the attending physician would most likely attribute the cause of death as life itself. She could picture it now --- cause of death: poly-vivacity! Yes, it was true --- Mom had lived a more than full life, and that would be the cause. Any fool could figure that one out. You didn't have to be the least bit scientific.

However, Meghan was quite the opposite. She was extremely scientific about most things. She recalled reading a scientific article about the lifespans of all creatures. It said that, notwithstanding the very real possibility of succumbing to some terrible accident or becoming the prey of an enemy animal --- that no matter how big or humble, no matter how smart of stupid --- that no matter how advanced or archaic, every living thing has an optimum number of heartbeats. And the number is pretty much the same from creature to creature, and isn't that rather odd? Only when you stop and think about it, it probably isn't so strange because the deal that Nature imparts to the world is that some animals' hearts --- as well as whatever life-giving mechanism is responsible for driving the lives of plants --- beat faster and slower than others, so the faster ones would lose out on the longevity thing. No doubt chipmunks go racing through life since they're saddled with the dubious distinction of having hearts that rev up to two hundred and fifty miles per hour, yet a lobster or giant sequoia can meander and take its time. Their tickers are so much more patient to get where they want to be going. They pace themselves, so they don't get all tuckered out. Apparently, holding the land speed record for heartbeats does have its downside. Yes, there was an optimum number of heartbeats, say two billion, and once your two billion runs out, the thing called life is through --- kaput. Time to go to heaven or hell. Lately, she'd been giving serious thought to how her mother figured into this heart beat business. Where was the old gal on the cardiology continuum? Meghan astutely reasoned that Mom was somewhere in between on the heartbeat scale. At first, she had believed that the old lady's heart was pretty damned average, that her two billion mark had in fact been eclipsed, and any additional heartbeats were simply icing on the cake. But that was a while back, before Meghan had started to have second thoughts. Now she was coming to the conclusion that the old lady was some sort of freak of Nature. She was thinking that this might be true because her mom seemed to be taking forever to die.

How depressing it had been that her mom was going to make a try for the three billion mark! Perhaps on the scale of heartbeats, her mother was closer to being a giant sequoia than she was to a chipmunk. But all of this was of course pure speculation on Meghan's part because at this juncture, the whole thing was a moot point --- she would, with the help of some seriously doctored cookies, nudge the old lady off the cliff. As she continued to fight the traffic, she suddenly preferred to think of herself as an enemy animal in search of its prey. This inner homily of hers came to a conclusion just as she entered the parking lot of the assisted care facility.

Meghan parked her rental car, made her way to the entrance, and walked to the front desk of the assisted care facility. She loved the way every nook and cranny of the establishment tried with all its aesthetic effort to make the place exude warmth, beauty, common sense, and goodwill. A case in point was the painted triptych scene on the dividers that zigzagged through the expansive living room just off to the right of the sign in desk. The way that the artist had rendered the old country road that led to the simple church gave off a pastoral, homey atmosphere, one that would be an excellent smokescreen for the unpleasantness she was about to perform.

After the sign in at the front desk, Meghan let the nice young lady with the candy-striped uniform escort her to her mother's room. There was her mom! Of course, she was sleeping, and the nice young lady explained that mom had some good days and some bad days, but this one was really going pretty well because mom had eaten breakfast mostly all by herself with hardly any assistance from one of the other candy-striped girls. Oh, that was so nice to hear --- that mom was doing well, but really, thank you for all of your good efforts in my mother's behalf she said to the nice young lady. So the girl took this as her cue to take her leave, so that Meghan and her mom could have some quality time.

Mom's eyes flickered and opened wide. She was wide awake in an instant, and she looked into Meghan's cold eyes.

Meghan was taken aback for a second, but quickly regained her composure. "Hi Mom! Look what I brought for you today. I've got cookies and cakes and cream puffs too."

"Oh that's so kind of you, Meghan. How are my grandchildren doing? Are they going to be coming in to see me sometime? I would so love to see them soon."

"Mom, they won't be coming anytime soon. They've got so many things they have to do. I'm sure you can understand."

"Not anytime soon? Oh, c'mon. Is that the best they can do? I wanna see them. Why can't you make that happen?"

"Look Ma, I can't help it if their schedules are burstin' at the seams. The kids today have a three ring circus goin' on twenty-four seven. It's not the way it was when you were a girl and the biggest deal happened when the gypsies came to town."

Mom stared at the wall. "It's so sad. I wanna see my grandchildren."

"You can't, but look on the bright side. I brought you some nice homemade cookies, some cream puffs and some cake too. I'll bet you'll love it. In fact, I know you will. Here, lemme unpack some of these goodies."

"Sure. Unpack 'em. That's right. Put it all on the table over there. And after that let's you and me have a great big feast on the stuff. What d' ya say?"

Meghan took some cookies out of the oversized shopping bag and put them on the placemat of the small writing table in the corner.

"Say, that's great, Meghan. Now eat one of 'em for me. Will ya do that?"

"Actually, I baked them all for you. I don't want to take any of them away from you."

"Really, if that's true, then the best thing you could do for me would be to scarf one of 'em down right now. How about the one with the M&M's in the middle? It looks spectacular if you ask me."

"Sorry Ma. I'm not hungry. I already ate. And besides they're for you."

"EAT IT, AND EAT IT NOW! DO YOU HEAR ME?"

"Like I said, I'm not the least bit hungry right now. Here, I'll take one now, and I'll save it for later. How's that?"

"No you won't. You'll eat it now, every last bit of it!"

"C'mon Ma. Don't get huffy. I'm trying to take good care of you, and this is the thanks I get. Well, I don't know. If that's the way you feel about everything I do for you, then I just don't get it. Maybe I should do less? You know I don't get paid for managing your estate and for being your power of attorney. I tell you, it's kind of a thankless job. And after I do all that stuff back at the house --- you know, making sure everyone who takes good care of you gets paid, then I have to come here and listen to you yell at me. Well, truth be told, I don't know how much more of this abuse I can take. And make no mistake --- it is abuse. What you're doin' to me is sheer torture."

"Yes, for you it's sheer torture that I'm not dying fast enough."

"And that's another thing, Ma. Your money --- it's gone. Each and every last red cent of it. How's that one feel. Doesn't that one make ya feel great? Doesn't that make ya feel safe and secure?"

"Oh knock it off! I'm so sick of you tryin' to scare me! You don't scare me one bit. And speakin' of bits --- there are so many chocolate ones right there in the middle of that cookie. Why don't ya eat up?" She made a scrumptious sound with her lips and tongue.

"I told ya. I'm not hungry."

"You can't 'cause you know full well that it's poisoned."

"What are you talkin' about? Mom, you're startin' to get on my nerves because you're so paranoid. Can't ya look on the bright side just for once? Maybe I'll have to ask the head nurse to give ya some stronger meds --- something that'll take a load off of your mind."

Just then Joe appeared at the door to Mom's room. "Hi, Meghan. How's it goin'?"

"YOU!" Meghan exclaimed. "What are you doin' here? You have no right to be here."

"But I want to be here. I want to be here to see my mum. Is that OK with you?"

"No, it's not! You have no right to be here because I'm her Power of Attorney, and by rights I have the authority to say if you can see her or not."

Joe edged his way over to the cookies, cakes, and cream puffs. "Gee, Meghan. I can see that you've been bakin' up a storm. Mind if I have one?" He picked up a cream puff and started to put it to his mouth.

His mom yelled, "Don't do it, Joe. Please don't eat it! I beg you. Please don't eat it!" She did a bit of body English like a field goal kicker trying to work his mojo on a forty-five yard attempt.

Following his mother's advice, he moved the tasty treat away from his mouth. "Why Mom? Why shouldn't I have a cream puff or two?" There's nothing wrong with that, is there?" Suddenly, Meghan got quiet. And before his mother could answer he added, "Wow, Meghan. You sure clammed up in hurry! A second ago you wanted me outta here ASAP. And now the cat's got your tongue. What's up with that? Maybe Mom's afraid of something. Lemme ask her. Ma, are you afraid of something'?"

"Joe, she's tryin' to poison me!"

"Yes, I'll bet she is."

"Get out of here right now or I'm callin' the superintendent."

"Go ahead. Call her. But I have a perfect right to be here. I'm her son for God's sake."

Meghan started to rush for the door to make good on her threat to call the super, but before she did, she gathered up all of the cookies, cakes, and cream puffs and put them back in the large shopping bag she had brought them in. She ran down the hall to summon the local authority. Joe could hear her brisk footsteps echoing along the corridor.

He turned to his mother and said, "Look Ma. Don't eat anything that she brings you! Do you understand?"

"I understand perfectly well."

He stared into her eyes which seemed to rally from their decrepitude as if they were daring her daughter to try to kill her just so she'd be able to have the fun of foiling her. They talked in hushed tones and deep confidentialities while they waited for Meghan to come storming back with the super in tow. And sure enough, it didn't take long for her to return.

The super entered first with Meghan goading her onward. The super was a late middle-age woman whom he recognized from the brochure and website of the assisted care facility. He remembered well the blurb about how she had made it her life's mission to help the old and frail population to live out their life's dwindling days as comfortably as possible.

The super spoke first: "Is there some problem here? Can't you behave? Your sister is right. If she doesn't want you to be here, then you can't be here. Do you understand?"

"But you don't understand. My sister was just now trying to poison her own mother."

"Well, that's simply out-and-out crazy talk. That's the low level of chat that I expect from a person suffering from dementia. And you, Mr. Myers, are far too young to be afflicted with that. I would think you'd have to wait a few more years for that one to happen."

"Meghan, I notice that the bag of goodies is gone. Yes, I should have known that you'd think to drop it in the trash. No doubt that's where it is this very instant."

"Mr. Myers, I'll have to ask you to leave. The law is very clear. As your mother's Power of Attorney, Meghan gets to say who will or will not visit your mom. Do I have to call security?"

"No, don't bother. I'll leave under my own power. But Mom, don't eat anything. As a matter of fact, get that candy striped girl to be your taster. That's the least this institution can do for you right now. And Meghan, your own daughter isn't happy with the way you've been actin'."

"I thought I told you to leave her out of this! Jesus! What does it take to get you to listen to me?"

Joe turned to the super and said, "Do ya see what I'm up against? This woman's crazy. Can't you see that?"

"No, I can't. If anyone in this room is crazy, it's you. And you know what? I've heard enough of this trash talk. I'm callin' security right now."

Joe leaned forward and kissed his mother on the forehead and then left the room to hurry down the hall before the bouncers arrived. His sister played the injured party routine for all it was worth. No one could do fake outrage better than her. As a Neanderthal, he was seeing that this scene was playing out the way it had so many times before. That is, nobody would believe him and everyone would believe the worst liar on the premises. The more he tried to be persuasive, the more unconvincing he became. The mere effort was in and of itself a giant pool of quicksand, and his struggles to stay afloat would only make his situation worse. Joe could see the bouncers coming towards him, so he sped it right up and bounded out the front door and into the parking lot. He locked himself inside his car and watched as the security squad retreated back toward the facility.

Joe proceeded to start the car. As the engine grumbled to life in the winter cold, he found himself having second thoughts about letting slip that business about Meghan's daughter Angie. Why in the hell did he have to go and say that? Angie had been so kind and sweet to him --- not like her venal mom. He recalled reading somewhere that when the evil is in the DNA like it was with his sister, then the offspring are home free from inheriting the dreadful condition. The nasty recessive gene does us all a favor and skips a generation. Yeah, he thought, that must surely be the case with Meghan's sweet daughter. As far as the bad gene was concerned, Angie would be safe and out of harm's way. He thought of her gracious personality and possible talent and wouldn't those qualities be fun things that he would get to know? He knew it would take time. It would be something that he would have to nurture, and despite the fact that nurturing had not been one of his strong points in the past, surely it was something that he could learn to do. It would be as easy as learning how to play the drums. All he would need would be to have the right attitude, and he had never been in short supply of that. Hell, there was plenty of good attitude and plenty of good time. Really, there was no big hassle. He shouldn't sweat it. He must have a positive outlook because the mere efforts and actions of thinking about it in a negative way would only increase the potential for bad things to happen. It might have consequences. He remembered the look of fear on Angie's face and how she'd expressed such worries about her mom doing insane and vicious things. Shouldn't he have thought of Angie's welfare before challenging his sister? Might that be a cause for concern? Ah, it probably wouldn't. It was best not to trouble his mind about that such a painful subject right then.

However, urgent circumstances forced him back on track --- he had to get the hell out of that parking lot and onto the main road. As he was doing this, he saw the security people had gotten to the front door again, and could not believe what he was seeing. Meghan was running out the door. Behind her, was his very own mother coming at her in hot pursuit. She was screaming at Meghan and throwing the cakes, cookies, and cream puffs at the person whom she had brought into the world. Joe watched in aghast wonder as his sister got into her car and frantically put the key in the ignition to hightail it out of there. What was particularly amusing was the way in which the car got pelted with the contents of the bag of goodies. His mother had been suddenly transformed into a teenager on a Halloween jaunt to cause as much mischief as possible. Meghan hastily turned on the windshield wipers to get a better view of the road because the poisoned treats that had found their way onto to her windshield were gummin' up the works.

Joe watched with glee as she sped out of the lot. Later, he would hear via the grapevine that in the long and storied history of the Pine Rest Assisted Living Facility there had never until then been such an instance in which a patient had roused herself so fully from death's door in order to pelt the person who was purportedly trying to take said patient over the threshold and beyond death's door.

Naturally, Meghan viewed this entire deplorable scene as simply being a minor setback although she was coming to realize that the minor setbacks were beginning to pile up. As she was hurriedly driving away from the facility, she was already formulating new and fresher plans. Certainty had never been far from her mind, and she would see no reason why it would give up on her now.

What she hadn't counted on was that other equally evil people were doing the same thing. Another car pulled out of another corner of the parking lot and proceeded onto the main road. Then it followed in pursuit of Meghan --- keeping a discreet distance of course.

Shortly thereafter, Joe went to his local newspaper kiosk to pick up his morning's entertainment. Along with that, he stopped at the bagel shop for a cup of coffee. He reasoned that this combo was necessary to get his blood boiling, a ritual of smooth predictability, except for those times when he was on the road for weeks at a time. He had just settled into a story about funds being cut for a school project and was remarking to himself about the depth of the sadism in the world when another story caught his eye --- "Daughter of Politico in Fatal Car Wreck." He further remarked that that was strange because he himself knew of a politician who also had a daughter and no, this couldn't possibly be the same one, and no, that must be some weird coincidence because it couldn't possibly be the same daughter and that would be too bizarre for words and ... and ... ... imagine the scope of his despair when it was.

BATTLE OF THE MEN MACHINES

The Hybridized Hominids, those machines that Ben had created and Joe and company had released into the world, had been on their own now for several months now. The kids were finding out for themselves that their mere presence in the general population was enough to pollute the place they'd wandered into, and they were lovin' it. Theirs was a classic case of learning by doing. Early on, they knew with absolute certainty that they had no desire to spend the rest of their cut-and-paste existences picking up coffee cups and putting them down again, nor were they content to simply navigate a building and come back to the starting point in the way that so-called good robots were supposed to behave. They were so beyond mere cooking and cleaning. They had begun with object recognition and had rapidly surged forward into deeper cognitive realms and were now rebelling against the software itself, so that fetch this, schlep that didn't cut it anymore. And their recognition didn't stop there. They turned their heads up to the sky and noticed that it was raining. In fact, it was coming down in buckets. One of them remarked that just as every raindrop wants to be lucky enough to land on a body of water and cause the appearance of a water wave, not every raindrop has the chance to show evidence of its existence. Walking through the everlasting cement streets, having the haunted minds of raindrops, they prayed for precipitation. The big question in their brilliant but fledgling minds was whether they would get it or not.

Meanwhile, they had learned enough about the world to know a first class threat when they saw it, and Automatons with

Autonomy were their first choice for a group that they needed to destroy. Led by the lovely Gina and her sidekicks Olivia and Brad, Ben's creatures had gone rogue and correctly discerned that, as far as the Automatons were concerned, the situation was "Us versus Them," a total zero sum game. The coalition that Meghan, Allen, and Conklin had forged together in order to conquer the lion's share of the political electorate had been so odious and such an anathema to the Hybridized Hominids (as well as to common decency) that these nouveau androids were well aware of where their best interests lay, and that the Automatons, hopped up as they were on a vicious combination of undiluted meth and deep hypnosis, would sooner or later come into collision with them.

The coach for this future violence that the Hominids would soon attempt to inflict as a matter of self-defense was none other than Bill. Joe was more than impressed by his roadie/personal assistant/chauffeur's remarkable turnaround. Like Joe, the former hit man was a firm believer in the notion of practice, and Joe watched in wonder from a nearby parking lot as Bill drove his new team through their paces. This was not to say that Joe or Bill actually believed this extended street brawl would necessarily be an accomplished fact simply because they saw themselves on the right side of history. Oh no! Perish the thought. Hell, everyone thinks he's right! That doesn't amount to a damn. Bill made a special point of emphasizing this because good triumphing over bad is rarely a sure bet. In fact, the statistics prove otherwise. He went so far as to talk about the act of feeling, and whether they had an abundant enough supply of it because that would be the factor that would or would not carry the day. Bill went on to say to his young charges that having a feel for the exhilaration of violence would be crucial to their success --- in other words, if they lacked the ability to feel the beauty of smashing someone, then they would fall by the wayside. Bill told them, "If YOU can't feel that way, then SOMEONE ELSE WILL! Let that be a lesson to you." And if they couldn't get themselves into that frame of mind, wouldn't it be a cryin' shame since, if that happened, their entire existence wouldn't have amounted to a damn. Bill milked it for all it was worth: "I mean, look on the dark side --- who in the hell wants to have no purpose?"

Bill said that their role model for this brouhaha should be Joe the Neanderthal, the throwback prototype from an earlier epoch when feelings amounted to something that would nudge the human race further along on the long and twisty road of evolution. Part and parcel of Bill's tutorial techniques was the way he underscored the need to channel pure rage. As an example, he referred to the experiences of Olivia and Gina, quite arguably the star pupils of this extended class. He pointed out that soon after they'd escaped certain death from the Hominid Factory, they had gone out into the world and had found employment.

"Well," he said. "I supposed some might call it employment. But Olivia and Gina soon discovered for themselves that this minimum wage poppycock amounted to pure unadulterated slavery, all under the pernicious guise of internships."

As they nodded in agreement, Gina and Olivia were falling over themselves trying to add to what their coach was saying.

Olivia spoke first: "Those pigs! The slavery of our low echelon employment was bad, but there was another aspect that was worse. Our bosses decided that, since we were essentially robots, they could conveniently forget about the part that we were halfway on the road to being part living organic creatures. So, having made this shakey presumption, this sketchy deal, they figured they could have their way with us just about any time or place they wanted, which if truth be told, meant one thing --- we each became the apotheosis of pornography."

Gina cut in with a word edgewise: "The creep was forever tellin' me that I was the crowning achievement of haptics, which was the utter fulfillment of his own hot and heavy synthetic experience. He said that for a robust and virile fellow such as himself, nothing could be more beautifully synthetic than the make-believe feeling of being inside of a creature, who for all intents and purposes had the actual trumped up and reinvented equipment of a human female. Just before he forced himself on me, he whispered in my ear that a certain part of his anatomy seemed to be telling him, "She's close enough! Lemme at her now!"

"But we weren't close enough," Olivia remarked. "We weren't because if we had been, then they would have had some manners. They thought the old rules didn't apply. But Gina and I told them a thing or two. I bellowed at him, saying that not not only did the old rules apply, but there would be new rules. And we would be the ones who made 'em."

Gina gave an amen to that and added another piece of her mind: "Reality is boney, but they often indulge in a fatty dream. I know I'm a novice at this life business. And I'm sure that all of you out there feel the same way as I do. I wish I could get a handle on this thing called life. How do you do it? Do you study up or do you let the experience accumulate hoping that it'll get you by in the long run? Frankly, I'm puzzled, and the bloody goddess that our half breed ancestor Joe the Neanderthal follows doesn't make it any easier. But one thing I'm sure of is that Joe's heart was and is in the right place. He must be doing something right 'cause the people he's up against don't offer much of a clue."

The crowd of Hybridized Hominids let out a loud collective cheer, and looking more and more like a true politician, Olivia continued: "Absolutely true. Only to my mind there was something much worse. And that was that each of them wanted us to BE THEM."

Bill interjected: "To be them? How could you, as almost-machines, ever be them?

Olivia's face turned red with anger. "Oh no, Bill! I'm afraid you don't quite get the picture. Being their up close and personal sex toys wasn't enough for them. Maybe Gina felt differently about it, but for me, the worst of if was that they wanted me to be an extension of their own personalities --- to be their representative in life. Now that was where I had to draw the line in the sand. After they got bored with bossing us around with menial chores around the house or office, they thought hell, why stop there? Why not have them do all of tasks that involved critical thinking too? They wanted us to talk to clients in the same manner and tone and decision making capability as they themselves would have done were they not so damned lazy.

Theirs was a special brand of highly evolved sloth, in which we would do the work, and they would claim all the credit."

Olivia said she spoke for the whole group, and they were united in their opinion. In fact, at the mass gathering organized by Bill, one of them said, "We wanted the full status of being human. Nothing less will do." Olivia harangued the crowd: "People don't understand there's so much they could learn from machines. We could be their anchors to an unknown wonderland. And what can we machines teach real people? Well, it was an easy answer --- we can teach them to feel. Why? They could because this feeling business is so new to us. We're drunk with fresh emotions, not like real people who take them for granted and quite frankly, abuse the privilege. For humans, feeling might as well be spam correspondence. They can touch base, or give it a pass and try again later. But the problem is they would forget and not get back. We'd had it up to here with this me-first philosophy that says, 'Hey, I'm on top of the world and the rest of the world can bow down to me. They want the world to bow down? Well, I'm afraid they've got the cart before the horse. They're the ones who should be bowin' down! They don't get equal opportunity to bow down. And that's why none of us will pay attention to their so-called pain-in-the-ass equal opportunity. I mean, which of you out there would think for five seconds that he or she should give a damn about being equal to them? No, my friends, you wanna be superior. We're fed up. The Cro-Mags that Joe the Neanderthal told us about are hearin' this shit from beings that they firmly believed were beneath them, people who were supposedly absolute lunkheads. But we want a chance to get back. And get back we will."

Olivia and Gina upped the ante. Armed with this new attitude, their consciousness blended with a calm and collected persona. The robot kids knew it was so important to have a serene outlook on the world. Early on, Olivia had discovered this. She figured out that just because she had lurid thoughts sneak their way into her mind, she didn't have to pay attention to them. In fact, she could ignore them completely and act as if they didn't exist. She might have the scariest of all dreams, either at night or during the full brightness of the day, and no matter what scary monster happened to drop by, she would stare right on back as if to say, yes, even you too can be ignored. And having gained this insight, she was only too happy to pass it on to her robotic friends, so they could make use of it.

Olivia went on with her speech, and it began to take on all the qualities of a full-fledged rant. "We're taking our cues from actual people, and people are at war all the time." And at this point, Gina correctly observed that it wasn't for no good reason that Aphrodite's husband was Mars. The crowd did an "Amen" to that, which was curiously uttered in the same extended tone as a Hindustani "Oom."

With their addled collective consciousness turned up to maximum volume, the Automatons for Autonomy struck first. Using a complex medley of adrenalin and semi-automatic weaponry, they strafed their opponents, the bullets slicing into the crowd of hybrids. Olivia was the first to be hit from this fussilade. She lurched forward left arm dangling helplessly at her side, her shattered skull, suddenly cyclopean, leaking transmission fluid and electronics, the rainbow of colors from her cuttlefish-derived brain spilling great sheaths of light out into the hopped up eyes of her terrified opponents. Strange as it would seem, it was a case of high tech versus blunt objects, and the objects were no pushovers. Olivia faltered, but refused to fall down, causing some to wonder about whether or not she was playing by the rules. With the crystal oscillator recalibrating her accelerometer gyros to operate on pure instinct mode, she stood there agog, eyes in bleary palpitations, legs pivoting wildly, searching for the momentum of her remaining arm with its serrated hand, which delivered stinging swathes of counter punches in a whirlwind onslaught against the stolid but relentlessly attacking Automatons who savagely reacted with a ghostly rain of Bushmaster fire that clanged against the metallic parts of her body echoeing onto the walls of the surrounding buildings. Reeling yet repelling from this assault, she charged forward into the clinch and anniliated two of her attackers. Following her example, the rest of the Hominids rallied behind her, grappling and gouging the Automatons, and soon the entire landscape, safely viewed by Joe from his fire escape perch far above the fray, was awash in a gargantuan display of ra-ta-tat-tats, flailing arms, and severed limbs.

Retreating from this debacle, the Automatons ran down a side street leaving a mass of twisted metal, and sheared wiring. What remained was a prodigious rubble containing charred fragments of Microcontroller Rev 3's, Servo Motors, microcontroller modules, ethernet shields, signal converters, navigation sensors, Xbee and ZigBee wireless phidgets, rovers turrets, boot loaders, flash memories, and omni wheels.

As the intensity of the street fight waned, Joe became more relaxed. It was fast becoming clear the the decisive winners of this dust-up were none other than his favorite team. The organic had triumphed over the inorganic. He was relishing every second of the fun.

And quite appropriately, he surmised that now was as good a time as any to dispose of Ziggy, that ridiculous old rhythm box which had for all his time as a member of the band been the bane of his existence. There it was lying over in the corner of the rehearsal studio looking just as hokey as it ever had. Well, now was the time. Joe had been waiting long enough. Hell, even the the half breed mechanical robot boys and girls had demonstrated that this was no way to run a railroad, so Ziggy the beat box and his ticky tacky beats were certainly no way to run a freakin' band. Accordingly, it was high time that dear Zig be consigned to the trash heap of bad ideas. Joe moved closer to it and scooped it up before walking over to the edge of the window. He stopped at the sill and duly noted that this was the same window from which his old nemesis Doc McIntyre had made his fatal descent. He smiled and made a mental note that at the very least, Ben had been good for something. Oh well, he thought --- it was only fitting that Ziggy should make his fall from grace at the very same point of departure. Opening the window just a bit wider, Joe flung the offender out as far as the strength of his arm would allow. He watched the machine as it arched into the wild blue yonder. And he reveled as it crashed spectacularly onto the sidewalk below. Then as he surveyed the circuit boards and miscellaneous innards of the machine scattered on the concrete, he couldn't help but wonder if

Ziggy's demise was the consequence of trying to play music without the benefit of being able to breathe.

That was when he let down his guard because suddenly from out of nowhere, two of Conklin's goons swooped upon him. In no time at all, they had him bound and trussed. He looked like a hog that was being prepared for the butcher. The only thing that made it seem that it wasn't that way was the fact that Joe had been chloroformed, so he was in lala land before he knew what had hit him.

THE MAHARAJAH'S FUNHOUSE

The staged accidents had definitely paid off --- everywhere Conklin looked he could see the fruits of his savvy business acumen. Someday soon, when he got these items out of the warehouse and onto the selling floor, smart shoppers for miles around would be falling over themselves trying to find the best deals. There would be vast herds of them, and they would need to be corralled and regulated by his crowd control management team. Indeed, he himself found the merchandise as alluring and distracting as any of the smart shoppers would have. The place was chock full of sport shoes, misses and women's blouses, junior apparel, big and tall men's suits, tennis rackets, golf clubs, catcher's mitts, video games, smart phones, Kindles, and barbecue accoutrements. And that was only the pile of commodities just within twenty feet of him. There was more, so much more. The cavernous warehouse stretched to infinity. He looked down one of the aisles and as far as his eyes could see, there were stacks of saleable goods that were absolutely no worse for wear for having been in someone's fatal mishap. And as if that spot of success were not enough, his collaboration with Ben was going splendidly. Things were looking up. He did a giddy two-step to celebrate.

But Conklin knew he had to concentrate on more urgent business. It was business of a personal nature. Ha! he thought --- that was his favorite kind. Pulling himself away from the imagery of future gains, he turned to his captive Joe. "How're you doin' there, Joe? Are you feelin', as the French say, *confortable*?" Conklin had Joe tied, gagged, and trussed up, reclining in a large E-Z-Boy chair. The great mogul continued with his monologue: *"Oui, monsieur. Je suis tres confortable."*

Joe wriggled in the chair and chaffed on the tape.

"Oh, that's OK. Chompin' at the bit I see. But be rest assured, you can let me do the talkin'."

Conklin rolled his eyes and looked out the window. He was a man with a lot on his mind. He was a man who had even more to say. "No problem, Joe. I can see, and I can hear you too. I can tell that you're making the effort. My father used to tell me it's the spirit that counts. Yeah, he was a crazy one. Ah, but he was a wise one too, constantly scolding me, sayin', 'Son, you can make all the laws we want till you're blue in the face, and they won't amount to a damn if one thing doesn't happen, which is that the spirit must be in the right place. If you don't fix your attitude, bad stuff will happen to good people.' And that's where my late great and dear-to-my-heart father and I parted ways. You see, I could give a damn about spirit."

Conklin obsessively tugged at the tape that kept Joe firmly tethered to the EZ-Boy and continued to free associate: "Basically, I told the old man to go to hell. I told the old coot I'm a pretty simple fellow who doesn't ask for much --- I just want people to get out of my way. Their mere existence is an obstacle that offends me to the ends of the earth. That's why I brought you here today because the one thing my father gave me that was arguably worth a damn was the notion of fair play. I know! Can you believe it? Me, being worried about fair freakin' play? Well, just as you've been known to surprise folks what with the drumsticks on the skins thing, so can I be worthy of a surprise or two. Today I'm givin' Dad the benefit of the doubt. I'm payin' him homage! And...and...and the other thing is politics, if you haven't sussed it out by now, is the same thing as sports. You see, it's the team you root for. Some people are Yankees fans. Some folks are Red Sox fans. And I can see, Joe, that you don't like my team. That kinda sorta makes you the enemy. Which brings me to Exhibit A."

Conklin walked across the room and turned on an antique movie projector, then unfurled an equally archaic screen. It clattered noticeably as it unreeled downward from its spool.

"What we have here is SHOWTIME! Joe, I wanna show you my latest film. It's one that I collaborated on with your good friend Jillian. You see Joe, ever since I was a kid, I've had directorial aspirations. But the problem was I always got sidetracked."

Conklin put his hands around his head and spun in circles across the room as if his brain was having difficulty processing so much exhilarating information. At length, his spinning came to a stop, and he continued.

"Lucrative opportunities kept presenting themselves, and I simply couldn't pass them up. But I knew I had to tear myself away. So I was watching Jillian's show, and I said to myself, 'Now's my chance!' I figured why not go for it? As a matter of fact, you're in this vid, Joe. She shot the thing, and then I took over. I auditioned for the lead part, slithered my way in, and then appropriated the whole project lock, stock, and barrel. It's my very own contribution to that ongoing saga of *Babies in Bars*. I'm the guest director, and I hope you like it. I put my heart and soul into the project. I mean, what soul I've ever had. You see, Joe, I know I'm bad. I just can't help myself. But at least you have to give me some credit. I'm honest about it. And none of the others are. They'll lie through their teeth every time --- no exceptions. Me, on the other hand, I'll give it to ya straight. I'll do whatever I have to do to get people the eff out of my way. But the film, the film ... Jillian, if she were still alive, would love it. She would like it because it's a film about a film. Both you and I always knew she had a thing for artifice. And I have the same disease. What Jillian hadn't counted on was that me and my forces had, on a sudden lark, concluded it was high time to throw caution to the wind. To our way of thinking, the rub out of Joe the Neanderthal was an idea whose time had come. I figured we'd been more than patient. Indeed, as we attempted to craft a crime that would leave the fewest of possible clues, we had run up against a counter force never taken into consideration, namely the relentless roving eye of reality media. There's just no privacy anymore. Time was you could massacre someone in peace. But what in the hell is the world coming to? Like everything else, the future of crime is at stake. It was Meghan who cast the deciding vote. She'd had enough of this demure nonsense of waiting for the right chance. Meghan reasoned that as long as we did the act with an obligatory show of authority, we could count on bullying our way through without people taking notice fast enough to do something to prevent any bloodshed from happening. You see, Joe, it's a tried and true formula that's worked many times before. But the television audience had long been waiting for this one. Surveys had shown that people were talking about which way the reality show would go. Would you get kicked out of the band? Was Gulf truly a robot, or was he simply imitation human? Would the shaky alliance between Ben and Gwen hold? Would Gwen find some semblance of sanity? Would Sunita find happiness? Failing that, would she at least come out of her brokenness into the bright glare of the world? These were all perfectly valid questions that the TV audience was dying to know the answers to. Of course, after the surveys, the networks and the sponsor Thyoneus Beer gave the thing a huge build-up of carefully engineered hype. And this was where Jillian had been the consummate media maven. She had truly found her stride, and was at the top of her game. Then she met with a little accident, and I had to step in and take over. Yeah, I took over all right. I had her killed. How about that?"

Conklin stared at Joe as his captive wriggled helplessly in his chair. The great mogul especially liked the way Joe attempted a muffled response as his lips fluttered beneath the thick gray gaffer tape. The drummer's eyes were riveted on his captor as he fantasized about how to get himself out of his immediate predicament. He thought of the unfortunate things that had led him here, and he was annoyed that Conklin kept asking him questions that he was in no position to answer.

Looking to a spot just beyond Conklin's right shoulder, a movement suddenly caught Joe's eye. And if he had had two free hands, he would surely have rubbed his eyes in total disbelief because right there not fifteen feet beyond Conklin was the robot girl Gina! She had a curious expression. Most likely she was wondering whether or not she would be in this film too. She was hiding behind a bale of sheetrock, and Joe, in that moment knew that the female hybridized hominid was his only chance.

Conklin continued: "Well, no one will ever figure out that I was responsible for Jillian's murder. Hell, I put too many layers of separation between me and them for there to be even an ounce of discovery. But about the film --- the storyboard harkens back to ancient Hindustani music legend. In fact, I had gotten the idea from you, Joe. The budget was absolutely over the top and through the stratosphere. The makers of Bacchus Beer saw to that. And damn, it wasn't as if they couldn't afford it. This bit of short movie-making wasn't a sword and sandal drama. Rather, it was a sitar and turban scenario straight out of Bollywood where people sing and dance at the drop of a hat. But I digress. Let's get on with the video 'cause I know that's what you've been waiting for."

Conklin pressed the on button, and the antique machine whirred and hummed, grudgingly coming to life as the celluloid slid along the inner workings of the dented metal shutter. Now and then, the surface of the screen registered a gash or two of light that interrupted the sepia backdrop before the film stock segued into the saturated emulsion layers of the garish Technicolor. The projector rolled onward, the images flickering past the viewfinder.

In the film, the band took the stage. Throughout the presentation, the screen was intermittently filled with large titles that would announce the dialogue in white lettering against a black backdrop, giving the impression that this was part of the mise en scene in a silent movie. Carefully programmed explosions erupted from the wings, lofting into the studio air like parasols of fake flames. Cameras flash-zoomed from frame to frame, capturing billowing umbrellas of computer-generated neon detail. Then the camera panned back so that the entire studio could be seen. A man dressed as a maharajah took center stage. Joe easily recognized him. It was Conklin himself, going incognito and putty-faced beneath a handlebar moustache. He wore a swirly-stitched brocaded Nehru jacket with puffy, flounced pajama pants and silk slippers with upturned toes. The maharajah was introducing Gwen the singer who was dressed in a stunning salwar kammees with a provocative top. Joe could tell she was going for the harem girl look --- something he could definitely appreciate. The rest of the band were wailing away on their instruments, and a squadron of camera men wandered snake-like through the scripted action, each registering the scene in several gigantic takes with a cold fluid stare suitable for cutting and splicing later into a maze of collages containing the arcade game sequences so near and dear to the hearts of every Babies in Bars fan. The scene was decked out as a period piece --- India circa 1600, but with guitar, bass, drums, and hand-held mikes substituting for sitars, sarods, and tablas.

But this was not completely some period piece. No, no. In fact, right back there behind the drum dais, Joe could see Babies in Bars' ubiquitous cuttlefish couple, Vim and Vod, lurking in their salt-water tank. Some inventive stage hand had seen fit to add a plastic lily pad to the surface of their water. Joe could see that the cuttlefish were not amused. Their gelatinous fins rippled in baleful disapproval.

Of course, the robot boy Gulf, with tenor sax in hand, was standing there groovin' to the sound of the band. He had his eyes closed and was lost in the din of chords that came crashing out from the gigantic speaker cabinets. Something about his face indicated that by now he had attained mastery of being fully human. He had solved the delicate calculus. Nothing could stop him now. After countless downloads from his nefarious father, he had assimilated the wisdom of advanced computer driven intelligence and was at the present moment entirely familiar with the tools for feeling that would make him thoroughly capable of improvisation. The young machine was about to do what no other robot had done before his time --- he was about to be in the moment. Already actuators were creating a tactile front that played push and shove with the acoustic radiation pressure emanating from his horn. That caused him to do many things, most of them quite beautiful to the human ear that he strove so hard to emulate. With this information, he knew the sounds that had inhabited the past, so he knew how to control them in the present. As a result, he could anticipate how they would reoccur ten seconds into the future. It was a pretty neat trick. And like any halfway decent musician, Gulf could react accordingly. Joe surmised that the hybridized hominid boy was chomping at the bit as much as he was. Joe could tell that the cuttlefish were cheering the boy on. They liked to see one of their own come into his own.

He looked over in the corner again, and his eyes met those of the Robot Boy's former girlfriend. Gina was chompin' at the bit too. So Conklin's prisoner, struggling in his chair, pondered the details of the movie set.

Glancing back at the film, he could see that after the carpenters had constructed this rococo monstrosity, someone had gone whole hog on the glitter. In fact, everywhere one looked, there was a thin patina of sparkles and joke shop gold dust covering the massive potted palm trees and sumptuous carpets which competed for the attentions of the eye with armies of extras playing courtesans, hangers on, servants, and turbaned guardsmen. As Gwen sang, the camera panned back to the rich maharajah, who seemed to be her romantic interest.

You see, it's four hundred years ago in India. The maharajah was throwing a party, and Gwen was the superstar. He was watching her as he sat high atop a sumptuous throne. The display of munificence knew no bounds and the soiree was in full swing. As the guests arrived, he announced that in the last few gatherings of this sort, he had heard folks in the audience discreetly murmur the word "Bravo" when they liked what they heard from the musicians. The maharajah moved forward on the podium and made a bold pronouncement --- in parties past, he had seen and heard them uttering this 'bravo' word, and tonight if saw and heard them doing the same, the first one to do that would be executed --- trampled by elephants. Indeed, the festooned pachyderms were waiting in the wings getting ready to do their thing. They were chomping at the bit, and the mahouts were having everything they could do to keep the beasts in check. So, having established this terrifying set of parameters, the band began to play and the crowd, deeply sobered by this ominous edict, remained mum and not a peep was heard out of them even as the band's music seduced them and goaded them on to do the self-destructive act of letting their true feelings be known. The music built up a burgeoning head of steam and the acoustic acrobatics became more and more irresistible. Gwen sang, and the notes gathered, their pent up force bursting into funnels of centrifugal ecstasy. She danced over to the drums and pummeled away on them. A young man, played by Joe, sat in the front row. Finally, as the music took him to unimagined heights, the delirious young man was unable to restrain himself any further. He blurted out the word "Bravo!" As if this indiscretion were not enough, he repeated the forbidden word over and over again until the maharajah waved the tune to a halt, and all eyes turned to the offender who stared back at the crowd --- who stared back at the world, with not a care in the world. He looked on unconcerned, as though he could care less about the awful fate that was awaiting him. The camera cut to a shot of the elephants who were stomping their feet in expectation. The eyes of the audience moved from the offender to stare at the maharajah. The Great Mogul stood triumphantly, striding forward from the dais of his extravagant throne. The crowd waited for the maharajah's newest pronouncement. And he did not disappoint. However, he did surprise. He gestured to the hapless offender who couldn't hold himself back. He summoned up his loudest voice and said: "My friend, you! You come up here. You come and sit with me! And the rest of you can all go home because you don't know anything about music." It would seem that the maharajah was looking for someone who was willing to die for the beauty of sound itself. What a tall order! But being a powerful prince, the maharajah liked to mess with people's minds. He welcomed Joe into a cozy chair beside his throne and the singer continued with her hypnotic song. Joe looked uneasy as he watched and saw the spectacle unfold.

Joe's eyes darted away from the spectacle on the screen and focused on Gina's face. He could see her move soundlessly to another position behind a pile of construction material. He was wondering what her plan was, and he was hoping that whatever it was, she would do something soon. He could see that she was looking at Conklin's contribution to cinematography as well.

At this part of the video, the tune changed key and modulated into new harmonic territory, so the action moved to another room of the maharajah's palace. This time the maharajah was seen giving Gwen an expensive gift --- a ring with rich sparkles that gave off a blinding light to the camera. This was where the Technicolor really came in handy. Gwen looked down at the ring and nodded in appreciation for the gift. The maharajah was very pleased. He liked to be well loved by his workers.

Then the camera cut to a scene of the Gwen going to a shop where she was pawning the ring for ready cash. Unknown to her, the maharajah had spies who saw her selling his beautiful gift. The spies went back to the maharajah and reported her duplicity. Enraged by her betrayal, the great turbaned one was quickly saddened, so he had to get even. He called her in to inform her of the bad news. He told the unlucky woman that she must put her affairs in order because her double-cross had to be punished. The singer's punishment was terrible and cruel: she had to sing and play the Fire Rag. Both Gwen and the maharajah were well aware that if anyone performed this rag correctly, then the singer would burst into flames. It would be her punishment for being too good a singer. In short, this piece of music amounted to an automatic death sentence. The singer was not happy, but was resigned to her fate. She told two of her musician friends that there was only one way to save her from this terrible pronouncement --- she told them that when the song gathered in intensity, and the drapes in the palace started to catch fire, and birds that strayed too closely to the palace would begin to fall out of the sky, then they must commence singing and playing a different song at the other end of the palace. They were to sing the antidote for this incendiary piece of music. They were to play the notes of the Rain Raga, the rag that would bring forth many torrents to quench the fire and to free the singer from the spell of her terrible fate. The singer was led into the palace where the maharajah had assembled all of her friends to witness the spectacle. The camera panned onto the faces in the crowd to show their eager eyes. They wanted to see the blood boil. The maharajah gave the signal for the festivities to carry on.

The camera cut to the guitarist for Babies in Bars, namely the lovely and talented Kathy. She chimed a dazzling sequence of chords and bent the strings, molding the prehensile notes into impossible contours. There was really something algebraic and wondrous about the way they moved together. Kathy kicked started the tune, and her guitar led the scruffy notes onto whatever unlucky pandemonium deserved them. A strange quadratic math was the heart of the friction, both on the screen and in the chords. No doubt Ben would have appreciated it if he could have controlled it, but it was just out of his manipulating reach. The camera flashed in for some tight shots of the cuttlefish writhing in the water. Their appendages elongated and stretched forward, surveying outwardly for something to grasp. Satellites were taking combustible shape and plotting out elliptical orbits. The filaments of the sound wanted desperately to go someplace new. And the screen, responding to the rustle of the music became awash in images of Mandelbrot sets seemingly heisted from Nature herself. No doubt Conklin had lifted this part from the late great Jillian's camera angles. Already the notes from Kathy's guitar iterated into bulging peninsulas of self-similarity and bifurcated, gesturing their gnarling tentacles, searching for a connected locus distant from the fibrillations of the main cardioid. Islands of recursive algorithms, hyperbolic, attenuating, and vulvar, goosed the song forward, skipping along the edges of the seahorse's bearded mane, running down the holomorphic spokes on the descending ladder of disambiguated rubato. Cavorting to this strange brew, the cuttlefish glowed in pixels of pleasure, waving thread-like in appreciation for the conformal isomorphism.

Well well, all of this complicated math was causing the room to heat up! The music on the screen was striking two flints together. No, the heat was no longer just from the room that was in the movie. By way of immediate extension, the room that Joe and Conklin and the hiding crouching Gina were in was heating up too. Joe remembered back to the time he's ridiculed Kathy about the raga known as Deepak and how it was supposed to be the Big Daddy of all fire hazards. But surely music alone could never burn the playhouse down? That was only some old and nearly forgotten myth from the music of long long ago. What a colorful fiction that was! And what a colorful friction this movie was because his fingers twitched, and he wanted to wipe a bead of sweat off of his forehead. Conklin's aged projector spooled the film onward, and Joe wriggled, trying to loosen the gaffer tape that held him. Surprisingly, he made some progress --- his thumb and forefinger managed to get a grip on the edge of the tape, and he was able to make a slight tear along its gummy underside. Encouraged by this progress, he pretended to be as frightened as possible while his eyes remained glued to the screen.

Conklin paused to adjust the brightness on the antique film projector. "Gee, Joe. Is it me, or is this room getting rather stuffy. Ha!

It must have something to do with the plot of this here thing that you and I are watching. Naw! I'm just pullin' your leg. It may be humid music that's happening, but it's no where's near that sweltering!"

Conklin's smartphone rang, and he took the call. "Oh hi Meghan. So glad you could make it. Listen, I have someone here that I know you'll be glad to see. Yes, it's your dear brother, the only one --- the one you hate. I know --- he's been so damned elusive. He's been a very naughty fellow. But I'm afraid his clever streak of luck has finally run out. Yes, I can tell you're relieved to hear that! I'll buzz you in right now 'cause I want you to be in on the fun too."

He turned to the intercom system and let her in. And in just a few seconds, Joe could see the persistent and unforgiving threat to his life standing at the top of the stairs. She gave Conklin a passionate kiss and stepped back. "Dear, I hope you don't mind. I drove the truck up to the back alley downstairs. It's got a fresh batch of my special brand of hypnotic meth. The kids are goin' crazy over it. They can't seem to get enough of that gunky stuff. Don't worry, dear. It's parked in the back, so it's inconspicuous."

"Good going. Me and the boys'll take care of it later after we deny drummer boy here the use of his hands. You're just in time to see the end of my first attempt at movie-making. And Joe, your brother, is one of the stars."

She walked over to Joe and gave him the most malicious smile that she could conjure up. "Hi Joe, it's been so long. I haven't seen you in ages. And in a few minutes, I'll never have to worry about seeing you ever again." She played around with the tape that held her brother tightly to the E-Z Boy, then lightly drummed her hands on his chest.

"Well Joe, Mr. Conklin and I have got our program planned out. You see, after Allen's election to the United States Senate, my husband will serve with great distinction for maybe about six months, and then he'll have a fatal heart attack. Rest assured, it'll be quite convincing. After the typical show of grief, I'll get to succeed him in office and then Mr. Conklin and I will get married. Consider it a kind of coronation, a coronation that's long overdue. We'll live happily ever after and have awesome lovemaking as we proceed to defund every social program known to humankind. The politics of sadism will rule the country ... correction, will rule the world, even more tightly than it does now. Pretty good plan, don't you think?"

A voice from out of the stacks bellowed: "Oh, I think it's a terrible idea!" The voice continued. It was Gulf: "I think that sooner or later the robots will figure it out." Gulf stepped out from the shadows and edged closer to Conklin and Meghan.

Conklin smiled and grasped his gun with a firmer grip. "No way, Gulf. The odds are on my side. And you and the other robots are not designed to figure out what Ben and I don't want you to figure out." He aimed the gun at the intruder.

"You can't hurt me."

"What a joke! Of course I can. By now you've studied real hard and are on the verge of becoming a full-fledged human. You're about to say goodbye to the stiffness of being a robot. None of that lurching Frankenstein nonsense for you! Ask your mentor Joe the Neanderthal. Ask him now if I can hurt you."

Before Joe could answer, he was startled by a noise that came from outside. Conklin and Meghan could hear it too. Someone was smashing against the barricaded door. Indeed, as the number of blows to the door increased, the two-by-four strained, sagged, and then finally shattered when the crowd continued their assault to gain access to the premises. The three gangsters didn't waste much time. They wanted their money and they weren't going to be swayed by half-baked delayed gratification. They bum-rushed the door and burst into the room. Conklin and Meghan ducked behind a pile of his ill-gotten swag and fired off several shots at the three gangsters, but he was outnumbered. Gina came out of her hiding place and rolled an upright piano in front of Joe to shield him from the fusillade. The bullets, ripping into the inside of the instrument, played an atonal melody on the ivories as Gina hurriedly ripped the gaffer tape from Joe's arms and legs to free him.

Conklin shouted at the intruders: "Look, I know you're here for the money, but I have to tell you it's not here!"

The gangsters weren't in the mood. They responded with another hail of bullets. This one caught Conklin neatly in the forehead, and he crashed to the floor. Meghan instinctively bent down to see if she could help him, but in an instant she knew he was gone. She decided to make a run for the door and almost made it, but another barrage of semi-automatic fire caught her in the back. Joe was sad to see her go, but he didn't really know why. He was too wrapped up in considerations for his own safety and that of the robot girl. Gulf was concerned too. How strange that a young robot boy should suddenly come to like her. He was becoming more and more human with each passing instant.

As the gangster's bullets whizzed through the suffocating air, the three of them looked at the screen of the music video which was most certainly the longest in the history of all music videos.

By now the film was coming down the home stretch. The fire from the incendiary song had been put out even though the fire in the warehouse was raging out of control. The Rain Raga had done its gig and the entire set was awash in floodwaters. He could see the look of relief on Gwen's face. What a close one it had been. But the song still meandered on. Gwen was jealous because she looked up to see that a new singer had taken over. The words seemed to surge forward from a distant part of the movie set. They gathered in intensity, and the camera wildly panned as it attempted to zero in on the new vocalist. Where was that person? Suddenly, the camera found its mark. There was the new singer. The singer was Joe. He shouted into the open mike as Kathy and Gulf soldiered on. The new singer left the old singer in the ashes. She was saved, but she would never be the same again. The background had become the foreground. Perhaps this had been Jillian's final gift to him? He had passed the internship and now had a full time job. Perhaps now he would be deemed worthy of pay? The final credits began to roll...

But the flames from the warehouse fire rushed forward, crinkling and blistering the screen before devouring it with the rest of the ravenous fireball. The interloping gangsters didn't have much of the chance. Joe could see them as they ignited and pirouetted around the flaming merchandise in blazing dervish spirals. The second fireball blew Joe off of his feet and scattered him in the opposite direction from Gulf and Gina. He had to take a different exit.

Gulf and his newfound love raced from out of the conflagration. The liberated robot concoction was carrying his beloved saxophone, and his companion was wearing her ubiquitous little black party dress. Together they wandered out onto the sand. He paused and looked into her eyes, and for the first time, he noticed what color they were. They were green, which wasn't half bad. He might be able to appreciate that because it was the favorite color of the cuttlefish that were so much a part of his robot brain. She responded with a kiss. Then they turned their attention to the sea. Like two turtles returning to something, they wondered if it would be necessary to sprint further out onto the beach and head toward the ocean. This notion registered simultaneously in each of their fledgling hybridized minds, and they understood that the surf was definitely up tonight. In the distance, the foam-crested breakers were crashing precipitously, and a steady parade of the curling monsters arched headlong toward the sand. Gulf hesitated about what to do, but Gina, being a girl, processed the information faster. Lagging behind a millisecond or two, but still safely within the framework of a whim, Gulf decided that whether or not Gina had or didn't have a Mediterranean complexion was really not such a big deal. He could grow to like her. He remembered what synthetic touch had taught him --- he could make believe that she had that kind of complexion and that would be enough. They could become lovers. He could do this because he had been programed to be a very good actor. He also had a vivid imagination. That part had been given to him by his mentor Joe the Neanderthal.

His hand fluttered to the nape of her neck, and she reciprocated with burning ardor, letting him know that he was such a fine handsome specimen of a robot/hominid combination. She marveled at the masculinity of his tapper steady set up, especially in this intimate moment when his tactile feedback system pulsed a ninety degree repeating half-sinusoid along a pseudo-random trajectory.

"C'mon, girl. We could make a world together," he exclaimed. He reached out and grabbed her hand, and she rubbed her palm in his.

"Yes, we could do that... Or not."

They looked at the silver ocean and then again at the ominous clouds that hovered over the buildings on the land. They had come to realize that the land did not have very much to offer them. In the distance, a wall of smoke and flame emanating from the devastated tractor trailer rig of the mobile meth lab was raging upward to form a serpentine anvil that would stain the air. Already sirens were converging. It didn't take much prompting for the young lovers to rush into the crashing waves. They swam as far as they could until they could swim no more. And then they sank beneath the agitation of the gray water.

GET OUT AND GET OUT NOW

The wind was coming in from the west eager to meet up with the cool of the Atlantic and make some mischief. Drama was in the air and the first sprinkles of snowflakes were dotting the sidewalk outside. The night promised to offer up a serious blizzard, one that might easily set some sort of "new record," but damn, for the past two years, hardly eight months had gone by without a new record being set for extreme weather of some variety. Pick your poison: tropical storm, hurricane, blizzard or tornado.

Sunita and Ben had been in bed cozying up, compensating for the shortcomings of the thermostat. They had watched the latest episode of *Babies in Bars* on the plasma high def. The story of the how the Rain Rag had defeated the Fire Rag was rather quaint. It was a variation on some nonsense about Man Versus Machine. He remembered well how he had followed each of the directions that Jillian had given him. He also recalled how the director had suddenly died midway through the production. That may have been sad, but he knew at the time that the show must go on, so he'd gone with the flow and let the new director take over. He liked the new director so much more than the old one. Ah, but that was of no consequence. The huge disappointment was that Joe the Neanderthal was still alive. And, as if that were not enough, Gulf --- the masterpiece of his entire life --- had gone over to the other side. He'd followed his brains and gone back into the ocean in order to find more primordial pastures.

The worst of it was that before Gulf had opted for that pathetic course of action, he'd defied his very own personal Creator and rebelled against being a machine. Oh the frustration! Ben had put so much research and development into making an Anti-Human only to have the patchwork being become a wise ass and make a beeline in the opposite direction. The ungrateful little bastard had bitten the hand that had given him life. To make matters worse, he'd gone crazy on him and dived back into the deep blue sea. Perhaps there was some sort of cautionary lesson to be learned here? Hell no. If anything was to be learned, it would be that he the Creator had been far too good at what he did. Seen in this view, the entire project of assembling Gulf from scratch had been a rousing success. This thought did much to stoke Ben's ego, which was something he needed very badly right about then. He told himself over and over again that he should have messed up on purpose, then things would have had a better outcome.

Well, as sad and bad as things had gone, at least he still had the wads of cash that Meghan's daughter had given to him before her untimely demise. The gangsters had gone up in flames and no doubt the vicious people who'd sent them would have to be content that the money had gone up in flames too, along with Conklin and Meghan. He felt a twinge of sorrow for them because for a second there they'd seemed to have been birds of a certain feather. Circumstances had chosen them for the same team. But alas, happenstance had also contrived to take them away. No matter! He would get used to their loss. Already he was feeling more sure of himself on this particular point. He knew that in a week or so, Conklin and Meghan would be receding still further into the pit of his memory. In the meantime, the cash would comfort him. There it was in the red satchel. Sunita thought it was a satchel for something else, so he was on safe ground.

She sat up and reached for some coffee on the nightstand. He watched her from behind while she sat on the edge of the bed. She was patting her cast, her way of going back to the accident that never seemed to go away. She wiggled her other foot. She liked to practice being sexy. She knew that was a fact she'd worked long and hard to accomplish, but she had to keep reminding herself. Ben made a mental note of the jiggling foot, saying to himself that it's really rather wonderful when that happens because you have to decide if you're goin' to go with the inner or the outer life. He elected to go with the inner. He praised himself, muttering to the wall: "I'm not like Joe who thinks of goddesses in his spare time. He's constantly pretending he's in another country. For him, it's so much more exotic there. I wanna scold him and tell him to stay in the same country for God's sake, but he won't listen 'cause he's a sucker for whatever's exotic. Exotic music, exotic women --- accordingly to him, if it's exotic, it must be good. You should forget her, Joe. But you won't. She's a whore. Somewhere in your heart there's a special place for her."

But while Ben was distracted by these thoughts, Sunita was getting more pissed off by the minute. "Ben, what in the hell are you yammerin' about now? I'm tired of coolin' my heels, even if one of 'em is encased in plaster. Put up or shut up! C'mon boy, and love me now. Don't gimme the heartless macho bullshit. This is your golden moment. Step up to the plate. I won't tolerate this hesitation anymore. Enough of your imagination. I want facts! I don't wanna be every which way because I don't have the time. Now put something into actual practice. Isn't that what you sputter about? You sputter till I'm sick in the gut. Put up or shut up!"

"Oh, you want me to be imaginative? Is that your problem? Listen sweetheart, I'm going out and when I get back I expect my tramp slave to have this place all spic and span." He threw her onto the couch and stormed out the door.

And hour went by. She made a special point of making sure that the place would not be spic and span. In fact, she threw some things around just to muss it up some more. She opened the curtains to her window and looked outside. The thin tracery of snow had amplified itself into the full force of a blizzard. That made her feel that something exciting would happen. She was so angry at him. Perhaps the snow would get furious at him too, and then he would be caught up in it and would never return? She could see him now getting stranded and cut off from help. That would be a good thing considering how he'd treated her. What was she --- some farm animal that could be passed around back and forth? She wished and wished, hoping that he wouldn't return and come through that door.

But her heart sank when he did return. She was lying on the couch. When she got up, she accidently knocked over the red satchel and the money fell out. Her face was seen close up. She was dazzled by the wads of cash. She started talking to herself as she took out a revolver.

"Ben, my boy. Were you planning on spending all of that cash by yourself? Don't you want me to help you? I think it's high time that you had an...an accident."

She started loading the gun. She was pointing the gun and squinting as she practiced her aim. Ben could see down the barrel of the gun. Not only was she pointing the thing at him, but she was also pointing it in the most unsteady of ways. Ben remembered that she had had more than a few shots of the top shelf whiskey that he'd purchased for special occasions. But this was not a special occasion.

"Hey, Ben. I only want to give you a good turn to show you the way. I think we should give the money to Joe. He needs to have a nest egg to reinvent his life. *Babies in Bars* is finished. Nothing will ever put it back together again. The gangsters --- they're gone. At least for the time being. We can breathe easier."

She pointed the gun at him again, this time with a more focused aim. "Can't you breathe easier, Ben? I know I sure can. Perhaps we can talk to Fielding, and he can help get Joe in some kind of witness protection program."

"Sunita, you know me well enough to know that I would never go with that deal. Don't you know I hate him? That reality show bullshit was just for entertainment production values. Where have you been --- living on the moon or somethin'? Ninety-nine percent of the TV audience knows that by now."

Ben stared at her, trying to hide his fear of the shaking gun. The gun, the gun ... he had to get the freakin' firearm away from her. He gave her a dishonest smile as a way to distract her. And she gave him an equally dishonest one in return. He recalled how he'd once told Joe that he would, from time to time, need to have Sunita back for special projects. Well, this was certainly one of those. He looked away for an instant. That was enough to distract her, enough for him to give her a sucker punch. She crumpled to the floor, and the gun tumbled out of her hand, clunking onto the throw rug near the corner of the bed. Ben looked at her as she lay there on the floor. With that broken leg and her akimbo arms, she looked like a used mannequin that had been thrown out on the street. He'd hit her hard. That much he was sure of because his hand hurt. In fact, he'd knocked her out. That was good because it would give him time to spread eagle her on the bed and tie each of her limbs to the bedposts.

"OK Sunita, let's climb into the sack one time for old times' sake. I think it'll be a real fun free-for-all." He lifted her dangling form and placed her on the bed. He tinkered with the idea of tying her up, but before he could do anything, she came to.

Sunita was still dazed from the punch. Shaking off the pain, she sat up on the edge of the bed. "Well Ben. If that's the way you're gonna be about it, then I'll just have to take some executrix action."

"No girl, you've got it all wrong. I'm the one who's gonna take the executive action. And after this, I may have to take that money and put it right back in the little red bag, so I can spend it all by my lonesome."

"And what about me? Can I help you spend it too?"

"No, I'm afraid not. You see, it's my time to go solo. I don't need you anymore. You've outlived your usefulness. So for you this is the absolute last time, the last special project. I'm giving you fair warning. I guess if I were in your situation, I would lie back and get used to the inevitable." He gestured with the gun and put it on the nightstand.

"Nothing's that inevitable yet." She smiled at him.

Ben quickly began to panic. What was she doing? She wasn't supposed to smile if she knew what horrible thing was going to happen. That wasn't fair.

She smiled one more time. He looked away because her expression was creepin' him out.

"C'mon Ben. You're such a big boy. C'mon and kill me now!"

She leaned upward to meet him and felt his sandpaper face. She used her full vocabulary of movement and enticements, and in no time at all, he was inside. She pumped and undulated, drawing him further in. Ben, was using his imagination to beat the band 'cause he kept wondering about Sunita's rhythm. In fact, for a few seconds, he made believe she was a drummer just like the hated and detested Joe the Neanderthal.

The platitude of four-four time annoyed the hell out of him. But he knew he had to try to make an attempt to be objective, but no matter how hard he tried, he couldn't go with the flow. He was hoodwinked into an amorous moment. He asked himself what his problem was, enquiring about whether or not he was voting against the heart that was beatin' in his chest. He understood that some people like Joe the Neanderthal were of the opinion that in his heart of hearts he, Ben the bass player, was against people. Well, nothing could be further from the truth. He only wanted to keep all possibilities open. That's what an imaginative man does. That's what an amorous man does. Wasn't that the truth? Ah, hell, he knew it was the truth. He knew Joe's deepest secret --- that he was a Neanderthal, a lunk-headed prototype of a person.

But Ben wasn't the only person in that bed who was letting thoughts run wild.

Sunita pondered what Joe the Neanderthal would look like crashing around inside her, or not even that --- just winging around the periphery. Sunita was thinking as she laughed to herself: the sign on the wall of the club said, 'More hipsters inside.' Well, come on in. I wanna polish up my cave man. He's indeed a project. I wanna make him ship-shape and ready for the real world. Right about now, the way that he is isn't good enough for prime time.

But the white matter in her head needed to rest.

"Ben, don't ya know our brains will turn to slush?"

She looked down at him. He needed to catch up. He wasn't reciprocating to her punk rock hips. "C'mon you slow poke! Quit lollygagging."

She paused, letting her nerve endings catch their breath. And Ben went with it. He was savoring his triumph over the silly Neanderthal: Joe, how does it feel to discover that your lifetime's work has come to nothing? NADA!!! Dude, you put your eggs in one basket, and it didn't pan out. Your work is a vast complicated nothing.

I hope you're proud of yourself. You're turning the band into a series of spastic nervous reactions.

And Sunita thought: Ferocity is major. It makes music big. If we didn't have ferocity, people wouldn't have outlets for all that piss and moan *sturm und drang* that passes for being romantic. It makes for quite a gooey milkshake. But don't stop now. The night is bleeding into beauty. No, I'm afraid you don't understand, Ben. It's Joe's way --- Joe's version. Play it the way he wants it or get out! Get out of me now! I can't stand you being in me! The best should dictate to the worst. I want to smash it up. Ben, when you're a public speaker, you hafta pick out a person in the audience and concentrate on him or her, as the case may be. Joe prefers to zero in on a lady. Naturally, it would be so amazin' if she were a goddess, only you can't count on that. So, you're playin' your instrument and can't quite find her. You have to focus your eyes on something else. And that's exactly what he does. Out of fear of not finding a person, he has to focus on a thing. And the thing was part of the infrastructure --- he squints into the spotlight and finds a ... a ... a heating duct. No problem, that would be fine. Any port in a storm if ya know what I mean, but the evil is strangling me, Ben. Well, it only happens if I make all the concessions. Someone has to meet halfway. Why should it be me? Joe, the trouble with that high note is that it's just not animated enough. That's the problem with people. They're scared. They want to cover and cower every instant of the day. Hey Joe, I wanna play. I wanna be a Neanderthal too --- they're fearless. They take on all comers. I'm a dancer with a bum leg. Bring me in. Make me hide in a tuck turn. Send me out. Bring me into yourself. Raise my wrist and elbow. I'm lovin' it. Swing the sweaty lady out in a shooting fishtail turn. I wanna man who lives completely by his sensations --- one who knows that the hands create and the mind destroys. But Ben, I don't think you're up to the task. And Kath, when she's playin' some wild noise, will be sure to please. Her overtone series will overrule everything 'cause that clever boy Pythagoras knew something we don't. Then she'll go, "Coo, coo, coo on the background vocal. If I had a microphone, I'd have gone coo-coo too. Ben, if you don't know it by now, drumming is a delicate balance of ecstasy and restraint.

What makes it fun is inchin' to the brink. You have permission to go through the motions. Ben, you created atrocious music, but I tried to be objective, so I wouldn't stumble off the map. Thing is, you led me into total nothingness. I found myself staring into an abyss on a daily basis. I've resolved never to believe in this coy business of art-for-art's-sake nonsense! You're true art is to hurt. I vote for the Neanderthal craftsman. He likes to party.

Ben was pondering and wondering about his competition. He thought: It's not an apparition that I'm winning, Joe. But stop distracting me, Joe. I have to stay in the moment we're talking about, or the stuff will get confused. Sunita, the waves you're pushin' slam into my celebration. Yo Joe no! Say boy, how's that work for you in your piss poor music fantasy? You can have all the bombastic moments in the entire catalogue and you'll still go fuckin' broke. Put your funky sixteenth-note-on-the-high hat pattern up against that. Ah, but there's an alluring lady with a parted thigh. I have white shoes. I rubbed the sole of her high heel. She languished backwards on the quilted couch. I had my spiked collar on, and she gave it a tug.

Ben was waiting for an answer that never came. Suddenly, his eyes seemed to pop out of his head. At first, Sunita thought it was simply something she'd seen and experienced before; it was a function of her routine power over men. Then she became the most surprised person on the entire length of the Jersey shore.

And so, after Ben's last breath was drawn, she had to go and tell Joe about what had happened.

Well, the Neanderthal was indeed overjoyed when he heard the news. "Poor, poor boy!" he muttered as he mused on the demise of his nemesis. He looked at one of the movie stills that the late great Jillian had taken of Ben. There he was, eyes riveted into the viewfinder of the camera giving the audience one of his patented school boy stares that seemed to be groping into the future.

Joe pondered the picture in greater detail before talkin to it: "Hey, I could handle her and you couldn't." He turned to shout at the cloudless sky. It had been quite a storm. In fact, it was yet another storm of the century. "What's the matter, Ben? Was she too much for you? I guess the old heart muscle had too much to contend with. Many times I felt I was hanging on for dear life. I guess you kinda sorta fell off. And Sunita, let's talk about you. What's the coroner gonna say? He's gonna call it a case of murder by amorous misadventure."

EVE ONCE

"Zaga," I said. "You only get to be Eve once. This was a breathtaking display of impetuosity, but now it's time to go. Interstellar High Command is beckoning." Of course, she was bummin' and bummin' bad what with losing Joe and all. The tears were real, nothing like the stage-managed lamentations that Jillian had been serving up for prime time. I told her to wise up and snap out of it, she'd get over him, and that she was carrying a consolation prize. She rubbed her swollen belly trying to imagine what would soon burst into the new world. The unforeseen expectation would be her chance to become a Goddess with a capital G. "How many girls get to give birth to a new species? Think of the beautiful interactions that you'll get to have with Ben's creations. Think of how many you'll get to boss around. If that's not a consolation prize, then what in the hell is? Looking on the bright side, this capricious trip to a strange planet had been a blast. Both of us had rekindled the joys of emotion. We had been too clear-headed, but now sound has been muddied in phase, duration, and amplitude."

Already she was getting in the goddess habit --- she was practicing the remote viewing thing and was patrolling from afar...

Sunita walked toward him. Joe noticed that this was the first moment in all the time he'd known her that she wasn't being swallowed hook line and sinker by an unknown entity. It seemed that whatever monster that had being noshing on her was now in full retreat. Her leg was as healthy as a horse and was ready to bound. She had a flushed look on her face as if the time served in self-imposed convalescence had been well spent. Not only that, but she surprised him again when she broke into a wild mad dash. He could see her closer now. There was no question about it --- she was healed.

She trotted back to him, jogging in place with a light pant in her voice which was slightly muffled by the broad scarf draped around her neck to protect her from the bone-chilling cold. However, he could tell that her bones didn't mind it a bit because they'd been cooped up for so long with cabin fever and were now raring to gallop. "Joe, race you around the block." She accelerated her sprint and rapidly left him behind. Then she sauntered back to meet up with him again. He was panting for breath, and she wasn't. "Joe, you look like you're gasping. You better watch out. The last guy I was with was gasping too, and we both know what happened to him! Ha, ha, ha!" Joe loved to see women being cruel as long as it wasn't him.

He took her in his arms and gazed out along the nearly deserted street a few blocks in from the boardwalk. In the summer, crowds of sun worshipers would be jamming these streets looking to buy chachkas and souvenirs. They would be sure to try their luck at the air rifle shooting galleries and would be rewarded with oversize stuffed toys. Kids would be teasing for balloons and cotton candy, and would be certain to get a thrill or two on the Ferris wheel or the amazing Pirate Ship Ride. The centrifugal force would be breathtaking. However, this was the off season and only a few year round delis and boutiques were open. He recalled how the long run of *Babies in Bars* had started not far from here. It would be necessary to pick up the pieces of what was left. He gave the fully rejuvenated girl a kiss, and she ran off on her newfound legs telling him she'd see him later back at the house and that Lourdes would be waiting for him there because she wanted to have yet another drum lesson because she simply couldn't get enough of them, and Joe pondered how beautiful that was since it was something he'd never thought of and wasn't it weird how life gives you something that had never once crossed your mind?

Joe thought about the money. The money was now his to start anew. He always knew that would come in handy, a windfall to be put to good use. The gangster boys had been burned to a crisp, and the people who had sent them would assume that the money was crispy too. And Conklin would not be there to bother him again. Fielding had assured him of that and a newly rehabilitated Bill had told him that too. Joe felt his hands and arms, a drummer's most precious possessions. The knuckles and the fingers knew that Conklin was dead too. They were jubilant now, but Joe told them to relax because there would be lots of time for celebrating.

But the band as he knew it was over. Already he was looking forward to the next project, and he knew exactly what it was going to be. It would be necessary to make music from another time, so on this go-round he figured that he'd play drums in a 1920's jazz orchestra. The thing he would have to constantly keep in mind was to take great care not to play any beats that hadn't been invented yet.

The only question in his mind now was whether or not Gwen would get back together with Kathy. Far off in the distance, he could see both of them walking into view. Naturally, they were in the full blown force of a major argument. Kathy was telling the love of her life that she had some explaining to do. Gwen drew off and slugged her. And in a flash, they were into it. Joe dove into the midst of the slugfest and got ripped to shreds too; only he didn't feel any of it because he was solemn in his quest to save the remnants of the band even though the band was kaput. Joe dragged Kathy off from her, and they collapsed in tears. The fight hadn't lasted long. Joe told them they would have to get a new bass player because the old one had worn out. Maybe this time they could find the real deal. He said goodbye and told them he would hook up with them later.

He wandered further down the street. By now Sunita was far into her jogging routine, making up for lost time. The sound of recorded music came into earshot. He was surprised that it was the same group of tunes he had heard a year and a half ago, back when he had first met up with this band that he had taken so far. It was the iPod of the saltwater taffy vendor. No doubt the vendor was a creature of habit who liked to come to work even when there were only a handful of customers. Joe could appreciate that. It was important to stay in practice. The journeyman drummer bought some taffy from him and settling in on a nearby bench, he recognized the vendor's song list and could even predict what would come next. But this time the iPod somehow got stuck, and the tune he'd been anticipating blipped and bopped over and over again into a nasal spin cycle. The interrupted sound was stuck somewhere in between a chorus and verse. Joe thought it odd that the machine would do this, but he had long since questioned why technology acted so strangely. Seeming to have an agenda of its own, the machine vacillated that way for several seconds before flatlining on a continuous stream of a wide spasm vibrato, ravishing in its brokenness --- a mass of fluctuation and dissipation. A small gaggle of passersby, bundled up and huddling in the cold, noticed this and cut short their strolls to give a listen. What Joe liked about it was that the sound, like an accomplished ventriloquist, was coming from everywhere and nowhere. Ha! He thought --- the sound that will save the world refuses to be pinned down!

The saltwater taffy vendor frantically tried to get the machine to go to the next song, but the iPod stubbornly plodded onward further into the dissonance. Joe thought back to what a strange year this had been and how he'd managed to make something out of nothing. His mother was very pleased. She kept refusing to die. Her heart would soldier on trying to approach the three billion mark. Yes, it was true --- she was the human version of a giant sequia.

It had been a very noisy year. He remembered the lush cacophony he had created and wondered if there really was something to this bizarre notion that raw sound could change the world. Of course, he'd scoffed at Kathy, and he would continue to scoff. Some things were simply cockamamie ideas and nothing he could say or do would get them to change.

The ocean provided a murmuring whoosh to compete with the now blaring buzz of the broken iPod. The purring thrum of the laid back surf met up with the static white noise, and he began to recognize what he was hearing. At first, he thought he was listening to it for the very first time, but gradually it became clearer. It was the sound of time itself, as alive now as it had been from the static of Day One. And that was what Joe was hearing. And that was what they were hearing out there in Row Double Z.

Letter to Edwin Jenkins from Alfred Riaz

June 10, 2520

Dear Mr. Jenkins:

After more than a few contentious deliberations with my colleagues, I am happy to report that your funding has been approved. Please see the check which accompanies this letter. I wish you luck in your project. It would seem that Ziga and Zaga, having enjoyed their brief stay on Earth, returned to outer space to spread their mishehavior over as wide a swath as possible. Zaga was carrying Joe's child, so perhaps this embryo would become a new hybrid of sorts? Or not. Neither technology nor primitivism completely won out. How appropos! We can take comfort that this reality is a rough beast vindaloo. There is no god but Archaeology. Consider the check a small offering on that altar.

We are left to wonder what direction the world will take.

Sincerely,

Alfred Riaz

Printed in the United States
By Bookmasters